THE COLLECTOR'S EDITION OF
Victorian Erotic Discipline

Brooke Stern, editor

The Collector's Edition of Victorian Erotic Discipline

Copyright ©2006 by Magic Carpet Books, Inc.

First Magic Carpet Books, Inc. edition November 2006

Published in 2006

Manufactured in the United States of America
Published by Magic Carpet Books, Inc.

Magic Carpet Books, Inc.
PO Box 473
New Milford, CT 06776

Library of Congress Cataloging in Publication Date

The Collector's Edition of Victorian Erotic Discipline
Edited By Brooke Stern
$17.95 /Canada $24.95

ISBN# 0-9766510-9-2

Book Design: P. Ruggieri

Introduction

It shouldn't surprise the knowledgeable reader that Victorian erotica is replete with all manner of discipline. Indeed, it would be hard to find an erotic act as connected with a historical era as discipline is with the reign of Queen Victoria. So accurate is this stereotype that a competition for best ever discipline erotica would certainly include seven Victorian works in its top ten slots (the only non-Victorians in the top ten would likely be the Marquis de Sade, Leopold von Sacher-Masoch, and Pauline Réage). Given the wide variety of punishments in this collection, it can safely be said that not a single form of erotic discipline has been invented since the Victorian era. While some methods are patently impossible and a few others hopelessly outdated, many of the disciplinary encounters represented in this collection would be right at home in even the most daring collection of contemporary erotica.

One might even say that all erotic punishment, no matter the era, is Victorian erotic punishment. The language of erotic discipline, with its sir's and madam's, its stilted syntax and its ritualized roles, sounds Victorian even when it's used in contemporary pop culture. Is it any wonder that the film *The Secretary* was set in a most outdated office, where the typewriter and hand-corrected manuscripts were more reminiscent of Victorian clerical practices than of an era of email and spell-check?

Erotic discipline requires that a mannered propriety be intact so that dignity can be deprived as an element of the punishment. True discipline requires that innocence and naughtiness be poles along an unbroken continuum. What can innocence really mean in an era as contaminated as ours, when grown women wear t-shirts with "Brat" emblazoned on them and thongs extend above the waistline of the average teenager? The essence of Victorian discipline is the shock of the naughty, the righteous indignation of the punisher and the shame of the punished. Today's literature of erotic discipline can only play at Victorian dynamics, and all subsequent writings will only be pretenders to a crown of the era whose reign will never end.

Lest there be any doubt, this collection is submitted as exhibit A in the case for the legitimacy of the Victorian era's dominion over all discipline erotica. In this collection, all manner of discipline is represented. Men and women are both dominant and submissive. There are school punishments, judicial punishments, punishments between lovers, well-deserved punishments, punishments for a fee, and cross-cultural punishments. These stories are set around the world and at all levels of society. The authority figures in these stories include schoolmasters, gamekeepers, colonial administrators, captains of ships, third-world potentates, tutors, governesses, priests, nuns, judges and policemen. The victims are punished with bare hands, whips, paddles, straps, canes, martinets and even stinging nettles. They are punished in every form of undress and restrained in a wide variety of ways. There are pony-girl scenarios, enemas and other edgy content that is rarely found today. Finally, there are the imaginative forms of sexual humiliation that accompany the punishments.

This variety in subject matter is combined in Victorian erotica with varieties of genre, ranging from the travelogue to the epistolary novel, from the *Bildungsroman* to the memoir. There are comedies of the absurd, cross-cultural explorations, genuine self-reflection, and classic Victorian novels of land and marriage. Taken as a whole, the oeuvre of erotic punishment prose offered by the Victorian era is second to none.

Critics of Victorian erotica claim that it offers nothing more than an endless monotony of sex act after sex act, punishment after punishment, or a mixture of the two. These critics claim that it is without variety or variation, with no regard for the lives of its characters and with no purpose other than the arousal of the prurient interests of its readers. Yet in these qualities, Victorian eroti-ca most resembles the erotic imagination. Indeed, when an individual's mind is struck by erotic reverie, the fantasies typically run roughshod over all other of life's concerns, spinning scenario after scenario for the gratification of the rich inner life of the libido. The Victorians understood this and wrote their erotic literature to accommodate the way the human mind worked. The current gen-eration of erotic writers might do well to learn a lesson from these masters of the art.

Brooke Stern

TABLE OF CONTENTS

MISS BIRCH

t is only proper that I should commence my book with a short story of my own experience, when a college girl.

I was an orphan, and after having a nursery governess for some years, my guardian placed me as a boarder with Mrs. Birch, who kept a high-class college for young ladies at Acacia House, near Hounslow.

There were only twenty young lady boarders, ranging from about eighteen to twenty years of age; so between ourselves, when free from Madame and the governesses, we lived happily enough.

Our English governess, Miss Birch, the daughter of the proprietress, was awfully hard on us; nothing seemed to give her greater pleasure than to birch and punish us on any slight pretext, and the youngest pupil Missy Bruce, who slept with her, was her spy and telltale.

We longed for a chance to pay it all back with interest. The holidays were near, and as four of us had finished our education, we should not return.

Miss Birch was in the habit of rising very early, leaving Missy in bed; of course we were curious to know why, but could only elicit from her, "that she was fond of study, and reading, in the early morning;" but, she never invited any of us to join in her studies. The old garden was full of trees and shady shrubs, so it was easy for one or two of us to spy out, and we found she always went direct to a large bower, at the end of the grounds, and which abutted on a lovely country lane.

Our espionage had no result for two or three days; but, one very fine morning, we caught a glimpse of a fine handsome fellow, who joined her in the bower. There were six of us, and we speedily crept up close, till by looking through the dense foliage of creeping plants, which covered the bower, we could see and hear everything: It was a large bower, with a rough strong oak table in the centre. They were too engrossed with each other, to notice any thing else.

She was a handsome brunette of twenty-two, dark hair, and almost black eyes, in fact, it was difficult to say their exact color, especially when flashing with excitement. They were standing up by the table, facing the sunlight, which made them a remarkably handsome couple, as he was fair in exact contrast to her style; each one had an arm round the other's waist, their lips were billing and drinking in luscious kisses; but, her right hand was mysteriously feeling and caressing a certain very improper part, in fact she was proceeding slowly button by button, to let out his engine of love.

Their faces flushed more and more; she had taken it out, and there, we girls, beheld the fearful male penis, in the full glare of sunlight. "Oh, the darling love", she sighed, in a low voice; "I must give it just one little kiss".

She stooped for an instant to imprint that kiss, on the fiery, ruby, uncovered head; then he gently pushed her back over the table, lifted her skirts, and exposed a fine, black-haired fanny; the pouting lips were just visible, as he opened her legs widely, then dropping his trousers almost to his knees, he stood between her legs, seemed to push into her; her hands pulled up his shirt, and patted his fine white fleshed buttocks, as she exclaimed; "Oh, Darling, let me have it!"

His reply was "Have I put it in right? Do I please you my love?"

No more words were spoken, their lips were glued together, in one long ravishing kiss, and their bodies oscillated violently.

Having seen so much, I was destined to spoil the fun; just at our feet lay several sticks, which the gardeners used to support heavy plants; seizing the biggest I could see, and the others doing the same; I was upon the lovers in a moment, raining desperate blows on his beautiful white bum, but my stick was too old and broke almost immediately, the others did the same, and before he could get away, we could see long red marks, as the result of our attack. He fled in disorder, without studying the order of his going, vaulting over a small gate, into the lane, disappeared, thoroughly routed. But, who can describe Birch's confusion, she lay stupefied, on the table, covering her eyes with her hands, forgetting even to put her clothes down, with her legs still wide apart; the black hairy fanny gaping for its lost tenant, who had evidently paid his due in a hurry; the lips looked creamy and slimy, as the frothy ooze trickled out.

"Fie, for shame, Miss Birch! What will Mama say, when she knows about this? Was ever any thing so disgustingly indecent? Why, we were punished for looking at each other in our bedroom; whilst you do a dirty thing, expose yourself to a man in broad daylight; what shall we do girls? Shall we fetch Madam at once? Ah, there's the man's handkerchief!" I said picking it up; "Finest cambric, and marked S."

"Oh! No, no, pray do not tell my mother; I will be kind and do anything for you all in future"; she pleaded, jumping up, her face crimson with shame, and tears running down her cheeks. "Oh, do have some pity; what can I do?"

"Why, Miss Indecency, you must submit to a good birching, at once, and Missy too, the nasty little spy; run, and fetch her, two of you girls, and bring some good swinging rods out of the study", I said, acting as mistress of the ceremonies.

"No, no, not this morning, do let me recover myself, Mama will be away this evening, then, I will bring Missy to your room, and we will submit to any whipping, you like to give us," she pleaded.

"Certainly, but if you fail in any way, Madam shall know at once". This settled the affair for the moment; and during the day, we elder girls, made great preparations for a real birching séance, at Mademoiselle's expense. As soon as Mrs. Birch had started out for her evening visit, we were, all ready in our large dormitory, and every pupil was present, except the two culprits, who presently appeared, dressed as they had been ordered, in evening costume; little Missy, with quivering lips, and eyes full of tears; Miss Birch looked almost defiant, although a close observer, could see she was very nervous.

"Young ladies", she said, "we are at your disposal for punishment, and I hope it will have such an effect, that we may be quite altered in future; but, Oh! Miss Gay, don't be too hard on poor Missy, however you serve me out for the past".

"For shame, Miss Birch, how dare you impute that to us, after your lewd conduct this morning in broad daylight; you ought to thank me and these young ladies, for consenting to punish you ourselves, instead of denouncing you to your Mama".

Several good birch rods were now laid upon the table, and two of the girls began to prepare Missy.

"First of all", I said, "Anna, you are the strongest, just lay her across your lap, as you sit on the bed-side, open her drawers, and give the little tell-tale hussy's wicked bottom a good preliminary slapping."

Anna was my chum, a devil-may-care, pretty blonde of eighteen; her face flushed a little at the thoughts, of what she was going to do, but she took. Missy across her lap, having first turned up her own skirts and petticoats, till she showed her pretty lace trimmed drawers, with her legs so far apart that had any one stooped in front of her, their curiosity might have been rewarded, by glimpses of the road to pleasure.

Jenny Prior, another nice girl then proceeded to open Miss Missy's drawers, and we presently saw, the two half-moons of her plump little buttocks, fully exposed.

"What a nice little bum to slap! Stop a moment, for what I have to say to her; 'Missy Bruce, you have brought this whipping upon yourself, by a long course of spying and tale-bearing to our governess, the most despicable conduct of which any young lady could possibly be guilty, should you continue the same mean spirited ways in future, you will be hated and despised by all in the college"!

"Go, on, Anna and let her feel some real good spanking slaps."

Three good sounding smacks followed in rapid succession, each one making the pretty bottom more rosy. The victim tossed her legs about, but did not scream.

"Go on, let her have a good dozen, just to warm up her wicked bottom ready for the rod."

The other nine fell rapidly on the devoted buttocks, making Missy fairly moan as she squirms under each impact of Anna's heavy hand.

Without delay a good rod of birchen twigs was now handed to the flagellatrix whose eyes fairly beamed with excitement, whilst her face was flushed up to the roots of her hair.

"Now Miss," she said, "this is the real tickle toby, how do you like that?" Giving a good swish right across both of the glowing cheeks of her bottom: "there — there — there!" each word heralding a goodly cut; the flesh reddens more and more at each stroke, and dark red marks show the effect of the twigs on the delicate flesh. "I'll never do it again; Oh! Oh! Oh Lord! Oh! Do have mercy!" pleaded poor Missy as she flinched under each cut; but Anna getting more excited, cut away, making the bits of birch fly at each stroke.

"You bad girl, you used to smile and laugh at us; now, you know what it is like. Give her the coup de grace, Anna."

The last was a fearful cut, which fairly broke the skin, making small drops of blood spurt and trickle, down her legs.

She then had to kneel and kiss the almost worn out rod, as she tearfully promised never to spy or tell tales any more.

It was now Birch's turn, but we took five minutes breathing time to recover and refresh ourselves, with lemonade etc.

"She's too big to lay on anyone's lap," I said, "undress her to her chemise and drawers, then four of you girls tie these sash lines to each ankle and wrist; so you can stand off a little, and spread eagle her on the bed."

The culprit was soon ready, and voluntarily laid herself face downwards on the bed. I opened her drawers, and tucked up her chemise round the waist. "What a fine bum to birch," I said, giving her two or three smart slaps, with all the force I could.

"But, turn her over, we must first inspect that lewd place, she was prostituting to her lover this morning; we have now a fine chance to see the difference a man makes in a virgin."

They turned her over, and I at once pulled her lace-trimmed drawers down to her heels, so as to expose to full view, the gaping vermillion lipped slit at the bottom of her belly; the black-hairy *mons veneris* above, and as Solomon calls it, a belly like a heap of corn; but it had a lovely white skin, in contrast to the black hair on her fanny etc. By my directions, the girls now tied both ankles and wrists to the four corners of the bed, so she was quite helpless.

"Look here", I said, taking up my lecture; "This is what is usually known amongst us girls as a fanny, but men use the stronger, and more vulgar name 'Cunt': come, look into its recesses, how wide it gapes, the hymen has been broken through, and nothing is left, but a deep looking, red, glistening cleft, large enough to take in the cock of a giant. You know what the boys at college do very often, if there is an extra modest young rascal amongst them. They make him what they call a 'Free Man' by looking at his cock, and spitting on it. Miss Birch's cunt here has been free enough, so we will all spit on it, thus," suiting the action to the word, and they all followed my example.

It is impossible to describe the looks of shame and confusion on Birch's face, as she suffered these indignities.

"Oh, for shame, Miss Gay!" she exclaimed, bursting into tears. "Have some pity, don't use me in that nasty way!"

"Nasty, you call it, do you? Pray how would you describe what we saw this morning."

"Don't be too cruel Miss Gay, turn me over, and give me my whipping, but spare me such shameful degradation," she implored.

"That's not my idea; we've seen too many bottoms whipped before this; the wicked fanny is to be punished, humiliated, and cut up; it will be a novel application of the rod, for once."

They handed me a fine swishing rod, made of very long twigs, which had been well toughened, in vinegar pickle.

She clenched her teeth, and shut her eyes, so as not to observe our triumphant looks.

"Swish — Swish!" I made the birch sound, as I flourished it over my head; before bringing it down right across the tender skin of her belly; this was followed up by several deliberate strokes, so planted, that each made a separate mark, gradually crimsoning the broad expanse, exposed to my operations.

"Oh! Ah-r-r-re!" she screamed with agony; "I can't bear it; indeed, I can't, you'll kill me that way!" sobbing, but she was so tied she could not wriggle about much.

My heart seemed dead to pity, I gloated over her pain and shame, my blood tingled, and seemed to rush in tumultuous throbs, from my head to my feet. Gradually, my whacks were laid on lower and lower, till the tips of the twigs fairly scarified the fleshy lips of that vermillion gash, which her distended legs kept very open. She moaned, screamed, and sobbed praying for mercy, but found none, the blood was fairly trickling, but I was too spell bound by the intensity of my own feelings, to look round and watch the effect on the other girls. A melting sensation came over me, and I felt all wet between my thighs, my head swam, and I dropped the rod, as at last Birch had fairly swooned under the excruciating torture of my attack. That ended the seance, and. we carried her to her room, leaving Missy to soothe and comfort her as best she could.

Next day I left college for good, and even Miss Birch herself, took a most affectionate leave of me.

JULIETTE

Dear Juliette,

I have so long promised you some account of my life since we parted long ago, and particularly to tell you all about the rod, for the use of which, inconceivable as it may appear to you, I have acquired an almost frenzied passion. Listen then, and prepare to be both shocked and astonished.

I have always been of a very sensual disposition, with a highly-sensitive nervous system, and, as a governess, never missed an opportunity of gratifying my lascivious taste for flagellation.

I was young when my father died, and according to his will my stepmother had to bring me up and educate me. She took a small house in the country, and we lived there, attended by only one servant, an aged female and well nigh impotent.

The indifference with which I was treated hurt my feelings very much, as my stepmother, then only twenty-five years of age, was really a handsome woman, and with whom I should have been glad to have been on more friendly terms, but I was considered a child.

It being decided that in consequence of our small means I should ultimately become a governess, my stepmother engaged a good-looking young man, a student about her own age, as a tutor for me: I soon found out that he was at the same time her lover, and she seemed to be particularly fond of scolding and punishing me in presence of Mr. Jones, although the latter was done in a rather childish manner, for instance, by making me lie on the carpet face downwards, or stand in a corner. My tutor seemed to be greatly interested in seeing my humiliations, for he was always complaining of my idleness, and once even I was ordered by my stepmother to go on my hands and knees before him, and while she pulled my petticoats up behind, he opened my drawers and slapped my naked bottom several times. You may imagine, dear Juliette, how ashamed I was, when I felt Mr. Jones's hand inside my drawers! But I have still worse things to relate.

One day, when in the kitchen, I broke a beautiful tea pot. My stepmother was exceedingly angry. She took me by the arm and dragged me to the room when sat Mr. Jones, telling him that I had from pure malice spoilt her best china tea service. Growing more excited, she cried -

"For that, Mr. Jones, I must ask you to give the little minx a good flogging at once. Wait a moment, and I will bring you the rod!"

While my stepmother was out of the room, I fell on my knees, and begged the young man not to disgrace me in such a manner, but he answered that he must obey my mother's orders, and that he never yet knew a girl had died from a whipping. My stepmother then entered the room again, with a rod of thin birchen twigs in her hand, and presented it to Mr. Jones, telling him to use the greatest severity. He caught hold of me, carried me to the sofa, and laid me with the upper part of my body across it, and my legs hanging down. With his left hand he held me in this position, while with his right, which held the rod, he turned up my petticoats and was about to begin, when my mother exclaimed -

"Stop, Mr. Jones, that would be a nice sort of a whipping, over drawers and chemise!"

As she spoke, she untied my drawers and took them off, notwithstanding a most vigorous resistance on my part. She then tied my hands behind my back, and my tutor applied the rod most severely, the strokes falling like red-hot rain on my bottom and thighs. I cried and shrieked with shame and pain, but my groans were of no avail, as my stepmother would not allow Mr. Jones to cease flogging until she saw I was almost fainting, and my bottom and thighs were streaked with blood in many places. I was then allowed to get up and kiss Mr. Jones's hand and the rod I was whipped with, and as a further punishment for having resisted so much, I was stripped to my chemise and made to remain in that half-nude state for the rest of the day.

You can imagine, dear Juliette, the state of mind I was in after such a disgrace. From this time forward, I was punished nearly every day in the same way. But as the whippings were often inflicted in the absence of my stepmother, my sensual disposition began to feel a peculiar gratification in having my clothes turned up by so handsome a young man as my tutor. The rod excited me much, and the heat concentrated itself in that one spot that so much puzzles young girls, that I often touched myself with my fingers and relieved myself in a manner, that once tried, generally grows a bad habit with children of my age.

Thus things went on, and as to my tutor, although he whipped me with the rod every day, and sometimes more than once in the twenty-four hours, and in the most shameless attitudes, I looked upon him no longer as a stern taskmaster, but as a lover; with a love which had, however, grown in my heart beneath the magnetic influence of the rod.

One day, my stepmother went on a journey to visit a sister of hers who had been confined, and I was getting dressed before breakfast, when Mr. Jones suddenly entered my room, and asked me whether I had done my French exercises. I had nothing on but stockings, shoes, and chemise, and although I wished to finish dressing, he made me cease at once and begin to answer his questions. I had to stand between his legs, and he put his arm round my waist in such a manner that his fingers touched and pressed the chemise between my legs. The feeling thus caused was quite new to me, and I got so excited that I stammered through my lesson in a most confused manner.

"You have never looked at your task", he exclaimed: "I'll teach you to be more diligent!"

And laying me over his knee, he turned up my chemise and smacked my bottom for some time with the palm of his hand. Then he made me sit on his knee, and kissing me over and over again, asked me whether I was fond of him. In a complete ecstasy, and burning with desire, I threw my arms around his neck. He called me his darling, and while kissing me tenderly, I felt his soft hand gliding caressingly up between my thighs. I was almost out of my senses, and did not know what to do, till I heard him whisper -

"Just open your legs a little, dearest!"

After toying most deliciously with my eager fanny, he slowly introduced

Juliette

his finger, saying, in a still lower tone – "Do I please you, Annie, my darling?"

What more can I tell you, Juliette dear, but that I sank on his breast, happy beyond utterance.

According to his wish, I went to his room before he was up the next morning, and after kissing me impetuously and straining me to his breast, he put my right hand under the bed clothes, and pressed something into it. Something! Juliette, I was startled at first, but guiding my hand, he taught me how to make him happy. I lifted my petticoats to enable him to repeat his delicious caresses of the day before, and thus we daily delighted one another until my stepmother's return.

You see now plainly what became of me. The whipping I daily had to submit to, and the necessary exposure therefore, of certain parts of my body, had dulled my moral feelings completely. More than that, I found delight in the pain the birching produced, and lustful joy in turning and writhing my body under the rod, lewdly presenting every part in its full nakedness to the eyes of the young man.

SISTER CONSTANCE

When I reached the age of nineteen, my stepmother told me I was to enter a convent for three years, to complete my education as a governess.

At the monastery, after the formalities of entry were over, I was given into the charge of a nun, about twenty-two years old, Sister Constance by name. Our cells were close together, communicating by a door in the partition wall, and they were similarly furnished, except that on the *prie-dieu* of my instructress a rod was always to be found. She was really beautiful both in form and feature, and as the favorite of the Lady Superior, was feared by all, on account of her strictness, or rather cruelty.

One day I was called to the Chamber of Penitence, where several nuns were assembled, when the Superior entered, announcing that two scholars who had been exceedingly disobedient, were to be punished in our presence.

Soon all the girls were mustered, and the two distinguished ones were called up and reminded of their fault and the punishment they had incurred, which was a sound birching on the bare bottom, before all their college-fellows. The culprits were made to stand in the middle of the room and strip to their chemise, when one of them was laid on a form and held down by a nun while another sister inflicted a whipping – "a discretion" – as it was called. All cries for mercy on the part of the tortured girl had no influence upon the nun wielding the rod, who, with evident gusto, flogged her so severely that her victim's beautiful white bottom and thighs were soon crimsoned, and tiny drops of ruby blood streaked here and there upon the violet wheals. The second girl, who had been standing by in her chemise, waiting with quaking heart till her turn came, was now forced on to the bench and held down. Her whipping was inflicted by another elderly nun, who lashed her about the soft parts of the thighs without mercy, causing the culprit to shriek with pain.

The Lady Superior enjoyed these executions immensely, and would certainly have flogged the birching nuns themselves if they had dared to let the girls off without making them bleed, although, strictly speaking, it was not allowed to whip the pupils in this manner.

Such was the first time I had seen a naked girl of my own age whipped, and the stripping for punishment, the wriggling and writhing of the body during the whipping, the legs flung wildly about with pain, the bare bottom moving to and fro in all directions, combined with the cries and shrieks of the sufferers, put me almost out of my senses with excitement.

Sister Constance followed me to my cell, and after making me confess how the correction of the two girls had excited me, told me that I was allowing an unchaste carnal desire to take hold of me, which it was her duty to expel. In order to do so she must daily apply either the upper or the lower discipline but as I was young she would use the lower for the present, and ordered me to strip. I said I had not done anything wrong, and did not see why she should be so cruel as to flog me for nothing.

"I see you must be taught implicit obedience first," said Sister Constance, and going out of the room she called in another nun, and explained how the matter stood. They forced me down on the bed, and the nun held me while my monitor turned up my clothes, unbuttoned my drawers, and pulled them down. She then commenced to whip me most severely, and although I promised to obey her commands, did not cease until my bottom and thighs were covered with weals all over. I was now let up and told to strip. I sobbingly began to undress, but begged hard not to be beaten again. However, the two nuns were determined not to let me off, and having made me undress entirely, they tied my hands behind me, held me down on the bed, and flogged me again still more severely, until the blood showed itself in several places. Although I had been flogged for being so wantonly excited by the sight of the two girls being punished, I could see that my birching had Sister Constance and her companion in the same manner, and they retired together to the cell of the former, locking the door which communicated with mine. They also took all my clothes away to prevent me getting dressed, and left me alone, naked and smarting.

I could see nothing in the other cell, but could certainly hear the sounds of whipping, and could easily guess the rest. It was quite an hour before they came out and allowed me to put on my clothes, but before leaving the cell I was promised another flogging the next day, and warned against resistance, which would cause the dose to be doubled.

The next day Sister Constance came to my bedside before I was up, and asked me in a bantering tone if my naughty little bottom had quite recovered from yesterday's well-deserved discipline. Lifting the covering of the bed, she pulled up my night-gown, and gave me some smart switches with the rod across the front of the thigh, causing me to jump with pain. She made me kneel on the bed with my legs well apart, and whipped my bottom smartly, several times flicking the tender spot between the thighs, which from my position was entirely unprotected, and any attempt I made to close my legs or ward off a blow was punished with several extra unmerciful lashes.

At last, Sister Constance, unable to control her excitement, threw the rod aside, and kissed my crimsoned bottom. Her naughty hands wandered wantonly over my body, and as she touched my burning pussy I made a sudden convulsive movement, but giving some smart slaps, she threatened me with the rod again if I did not remain perfectly passive.

I did not so much fear the rod now, but curiosity and lasciviousness made me remain quite still, while Sister Constance, with her skilful fingers, so cleverly excited the little crimson palpitating clitoris, that I presently sank inert on the bed in a transport of voluptuous oblivion.

That night, as I was in bed, Sister Constance entered in her night dress, and kneeling down at the bed side, stretched out her hands with an imploring gesture, like a child that is going to be punished, and cried out -

"Oh, dear Miss Annie, I will never be disobedient again!"

I stared at her with astonishment, but as she grew more urgent in her entreaties, I understood what she meant, and I jumped out of bed and seized the rod.

"Oh, pray don't whip me! Don't whip me this time!" she cried again.

I took no notice of her cries, but with indescribable delight, pressed the head of the kneeling nun between my knees, turned up her night gown, and gave her a smart birching, causing the long twigs to go well in between her legs until I saw by her movements and exclamations that I had caused her to emit the delicious juice of love. After she had recovered, she got up, embraced me and as she kissed her thanks, whispered:

"You have whipped me most delightfully, dearest, but you ought to have played with my pussy a little, as I did with yours. Don't forget it next time."

The following day being Sunday, I accompanied Sister Constance to the dormitory of the girls, who were all still in bed.

"Out of bed, and every one of you a clean chemise on, quick!"

That was the order given, and in less than a minute they were all out of bed, and we had the pleasure of viewing the naked forms of forty girls, as they changed their shifts.

They then put their stockings and shoes on, which allowed me to see other parts of their bodies, for most of them did not seem to have much idea of modesty.

Then Sister Constance asked them if they had bathed and washed themselves well the night before, and all replied in the affirmative. Notwithstanding this declaration, she took a chair, placed it behind a screen, and sitting down, told me to stand behind her. She then called the girls one by one to the secluded nook, and examined them closely in a most shameless manner, under the pretence of seeing whether they were clean in every part. Each girl had to hold her chemise over her head, and turn and bend herself in all directions, so that I saw that every girl had made more or less acquaintance with the rod.

Altogether, the different forms of these young girls, just attaining the age of puberty, some of them with quite well-shaped breasts and full rounded posteriors, afforded an extremely pleasing and exciting picture.

It was particularly interesting to notice the hair on a certain spot, which with some was like the finest down, and with others already like slightly curling fine wool, whole some very young furrows were quite bare.

Having been appointed to the post of assistant teacher to Sister Constance, I was able to enjoy this sight often. It now and then occurred that a new comer made strenuous objections to being handled and exposed in such a disgraceful manner, but a few good whippings soon taught her to submit, and at last she would begin to feel the charm of the mysterious twigs, and become as docile beneath their influence as the rest.

THE GOVERNESS

My first situation was with a very strict lady to whom I had been recommended by the Superior of the convent. She had two rather old yet spoiled girls of eighteen and nineteen, and a boy of twenty years of age. I was only twenty-two myself, and the lady's first enquiry was as to my capability of governing the children when unruly, as she wished them to be treated with firmness and just severity. Though they were so old, it seemed she still had not tamed their childish natures. I asked her to give me full control and free permission to use a birch-rod if necessary. This was accorded without hesitation, as her custom was to have the children punished with the twigs for every fault.

In a few days, I had occasion to find fault with the elder girl, and telling her mamma I intended to whip her, I was directed to take a rod from a certain closet, where I found several, steeped in the water contained in a Japanese vase. Selecting a good one, I took the culprit to my room, locked the door, and telling the trembling delinquent I was going to give her a good flogging, ordered her to take off her drawers.

She refused, so laying her on the bed, I turned her clothes up, exposing her handsome lace-trimmed drawers, which, after some struggling, I succeeded in unfastening, and pulling down to the knees. Tying her hands together, I prepared to birch her, and made the rod whistle ominously in the air.

You should have heard how that pretty damsel of nineteen begged and entreated me to spare her, but the more she implored the more determined I was to whip her.

Holding her down on the bed with one hand, I began to use the rod, at first gently, but gradually increasing in violence till she screamed with pain. I grew excited, and whipped on, without paying the least attention to her cries, now giving a severe blow on her weal covered crimson bottom, and anon making her fairly shriek in agony, as I inflicted some smart lashes, followed by a sharp draw-back twist of the wrist, on her delicate thighs, which I marked beautifully as far as the top of her stockings. Thinking she had now had enough, I let her up, and made her beg my pardon on her knees, and thank me for the wholesome discipline I had been at the trouble of administering. Fastening her drawers, I led her, still weeping, to her mamma, who after examining the damage done, complimented me upon the efficient manner in which I had performed my disagreeable duty, and made the girl take her drawers off, and stand with her face to the wall with her frock and petticoats pinned up behind, as a warning to her brother and sister.

The whole affair had transported me with pleasure. You may depend upon it, birching a nicely dressed girl is very exciting, as the pink plump flesh shows off so much better under the snow-white chemise and pretty drawers than under coarse linen, such as I had hitherto seen at the convent. Then the fine white stockings with rich blue garters and lovely little high boots, adorned in front with a tassel, as was then the fashion – altogether it was an enchanting picture for me, and I thoroughly appreciated all its beauties.

I now felt a desire to have the boy in my power under the rod I wielded with daily increasing ardor, and soon found occasion to punish him. I had whipped plenty of girlish backsides, but never the posteriors of a boy, and I anticipated quite a new pleasure.

I took him to my room, and locking the door carefully, told him to divest himself of his jacket and waistcoat, and let his trousers down. He cried a little, and entreated me not to whip him, but he little knew that nothing in the world would have induced me to remit this punishment. He struggled hard when I got hold of him, but my nervous strength was too great for the lad, and I had soon undone his little breeches. Pressing him on to the bed with the left hand, I took the rod between my teeth, and with my right, I pulled his trousers down to his heels. Slowly lifting up his shirt, I now had the bare limbs of the boy before me, and gazed on them awhile with eager eyes. Then I began to whip the hard cheeks of this miniature bottom, while he started screaming and twisting violently. In order to hold him better, I put my left arm round his naked waist, and as he plunged and struggled, my fingers came in contact with his little limp cool toby. I started, and so did the boy, but I tried to hide my excitement by flogging him still harder, which only had the effect, as I intended it should, of bringing my fingers oftener on to the little thing.

Oh! if the boy had only been my age, how much more I should have enjoyed it. You should have seen how ashamed the little fellow was, and how he blushed every time I threatened him with the rod afterwards, but as that charmed me all the more, I whipped him pretty frequently.

The elder girl had the audacity to tell me shortly afterwards, with a merry laugh, that did not fear my whippings now at all, but that one from her mother was no joke.

"Then, Miss Pert," I said, "you shall feel the effect of a good whipping from me directly!"

Bidding her go and fetch a rod herself, I had her clothes up in a twinkling, opened her drawers and laid on gently. At first she laughed, wriggling and kicking jokingly, all the time exposing herself in a most wanton manner. I saw she was really enjoying the whipping and resolved to take advantage of her feelings, so I made her sit on my knees, and told her to give me a kiss. She threw her arms round my neck, and kissed me ardently, while I put my hands under her clothes, and inside the front of her drawers, gently stroking her plump soft belly, and the top of the little slit below.

As soon as she felt my fingers in the downy plumage, she at once opened her legs, and gently introduced my finger. I skillfully toyed and caressed her, till she was in a state of delirious excitement, and when the climax was approaching, pressed herself madly to me, ejaculating:

"Oh – how – delicious! I – can – bear – it – no longer! I'm going to faint!"

I was no longer mistress of myself, and kissed her madly, pressed my hot tongue into her willing mouth, while she sank down fainting in a transport of bliss.

The next day, no one being at home but our two selves, I put my arm round her waist, and led her to my room, telling her that I was going to give her a more delightful birching than she had experienced the day before, if she would only do exactly as I wanted.

She consented at once, and after stripping her quite naked, I laid her over my knee and birched her gently for at least a quarter of an hour, till she was thoroughly excited, and wanted me to tickle her little "birdie," as I had taught her to call the centre of bliss. But that was just what I wanted to avoid for the nonce, as I had not finished whipping her.

I made her stand up, fastened a book-strap round her waist, and tied her hands firmly to the strap behind her back.

I now gave her a severe cut across the bottom, which made her jump with pain, and run away to the other side of the room. I followed, and giving her another smart stinging blow, made her scream and start off again. And now commenced a race, the pace of which I regulated at will.

There was the hunted victim running and screaming with pain, while I followed, sometimes slowly and sometimes quickly, cutting her unmercifully wherever I could, but principally on the bottom and thighs. She tried to ward off the blows by getting behind the furniture, but always unsuccessfully; the panting tormentor making play with the dear instrument through the backs of chairs and behind curtains.

Once she stood with her back to the wall, begging me through her tears and breathless sobs not to be so cruel, and even tried a smile to disarm me. But the view of this pretty girl, naked, helpless, and bound, writhing and crying from the smart of the lashes, and drawing herself close to the wall to save her bottom, was too tempting. It made me tremble with suppressed desire and excitement, and I gave her half a dozen smart flicks on the front of the thighs and the lower part of the belly, just below the navel, making her shriek with pain and jump into the middle of the room, where she doubled herself up, and sank on to the floor in an almost fainting condition.

I laid her on the sofa, and soon brought her round again, but left her hands still fastened, as I was not yet done with my beloved rod. In a quarter of a hour the painful smart of the flogging had given place to a burning glow, and she began to show signs of erotic excitement, by trying to rub her mount against the sofa.

"Don't do that yet, dear," I said, "one thing more, and then you shall find how nicely I can attend to 'birdie'."

Seeing me take up the rod again, or rather what was left of it, she prayed me not to birch her any more, but I said that I was only going to give her three or four cuts, and would afterwards reward her for all the pain, but that if she did not submit quietly, I would lash her round the room again.

This threat made her promise obedience, and I caused her to kneel up on the sofa with legs wide apart, head well down, and the low countries in the air. This brought out her bottom into a splendid position, and perfectly exposed her little coral slit. I jumped up and got astride her, passing my hand gently down her bottom to her "birdie," and softly separated the lips, toying with them a few moments, to her great delight. Not suspecting what I was about to do, she tried to make her secret charms still more accessible to my hand, as she thought. But seizing this opportunity, I gave her three sharp flicks on the exposed and palpitating lips, not sparing the large ones, while I do believe the little ones must have been touched, she had opened herself so widely. She gave three heartrending shrieks and sank down senseless, all of a heap, upon the couch.

After bringing her round, I laid her on her back with her legs wide-apart, and watched with absorbing interest her wanton and lascivious movements, as she vainly tried to subdue the burning irritation, till bending down, I pressed a glowing kiss on her cruelly inflamed "birdie". She started as if electrified, but I had taken care to leave her hands in the bonds, and in a few minutes, by skillfully twisting the tip of my eager tongue round and round the point of attraction, rendered her almost delirious with lascivious excitement.

Although the climax had been reached, I would not remove my mouth from the sweet and luscious morsel, but continued kissing it, sucking up its lips alternately, pressing it closely with my whole mouth, and darting the tongue in and out, quickly or slowly, as my fancy prompted. I studiously avoided touching the sensitive bud, till my pains were reward[ed] by her asking me to do so.

Thrice I transported her, and countless were the times that I melted away myself. I required nothing from her to allay my feelings; the mere fact of doing what I did, sufficed to satisfy me entirely.

MIMI DUBOIS

got tired of the country, and left for London with a good written character, and promises of glowing praise if I should ever require references.

After I had exhausted the sights and shops of the metropolis, I got
several good situations, but left them all, as they were not what I wanted.

At last I was offered a situation by a lady who was housekeeper to a rich old
gentleman, who by chance had seen me in one of my former places, and as she
informed me after much guarded conversation, had taken a fancy to me.

This person, a Frenchwoman, Mimi Dubois, by name, told me that her
master was very eccentric. I pressed her for details, and at last she plainly
told me that I should have naught else to do but perform the part of a little
child, and she would be my governess, as she was that of the old gentleman
for several hours every day.

I must, of course, submit myself to be whipped or punished in any way
she thought fit, and as often and as severely as she liked.

The old gentleman was very fond of being whipped with a birch, and
found great amusement in seeing a young, healthy girl well brushed. I was
expected to "play school" with him and assist Madame Dubois in whipping
and exciting him, and to occasionally submit to all sorts of humiliations and

punishments to gratify the peculiar fancies of the aged maniac. If I agreed, my salary would be a most brilliant one.

I did not know at first what to say, but was soon persuaded by insinuating Mimi, and made an appointment with her to come to my lodging the next day to ascertain for herself if I was possessed of such charms as were particularly valued by her strange master. She came punctually, made herself at home, and began to examine my teeth, then my breasts, and lifting up my clothes made me strand as straight and erect as I could, looking at my calves, my thighs, belly, and downy pussy, which she found highly satisfactory.

"Now for the principal thing – the bottom!" And she told me to lie down on my face on the sofa, and let her examine it. She turned up my petticoats, and opening my drawers, exclaimed:

"Excellent, my dear, excellent! I never saw such a beautiful round bottom before; just what my master likes. Oh! if I had a rod here, wouldn't I make it dance and caper!"

And she could not resist giving me a good slapping, which I dare not resist, although she hurt me very much, especially with her rings. But she compensated me for the pain by putting her hand between my legs and tickling my excited pussy so deliciously that I sank down on the sofa, emitting most profusely over her caressing fingers and into my clean drawers, which I had put on in anticipation of her visit and examination.

All this was very wrong, but Juliette, dear, let me impress upon you how difficult it is to try and change one's nature. I could no longer prevent myself itching for birching joys and triumphant games afterwards, than the old gentleman who was going to engage me could escape himself from the empire his manias exercised over him. No one could behave more respectably than me; no one could exercise more restraint over themselves than I did, but there were certain diversions, innocent enough in their effects, that I secretly enjoyed. I liked the stage, first for the ballet, for I was a great lover of feminine beauty, and when the principal danseuse would advance to the footlights and bowing to the applause of the audience, bend down so that her bosom was fully exposed, my heart would beat as if I was a man.

This taste did not prevent me closely watching the male performers through my glass, and I would eagerly scrutinize that swelling on the left thigh that looks so tempting when they wear boots and breeches, or in their gaily colored hose.

A fellow-teacher coldly dispelled my illusions one night, when we were both seated in the front row of the Drury Lane pit, by informing me that actors usually put a couple of pocket handkerchiefs there, to purposely draw the attention of the female spectators.

The contact of men, I also liked, as they would press against me while waiting at theatre doors, or in omnibuses, and my greatest delight was when looking in a shop some man would come behind me, and whisper the greatest indecencies down my ear. I would move on indignantly, and even threaten the more tenacious with the usual policeman, but I enjoyed it all the same. Another pleasure was when returning from the theatre, to remark the tricks of the fallen women who throng the streets, and if I could only catch some of the conversation, and overhear from time to time an indecent proposal, or unblushing offer of their charms, I was happy.

Many a time I fell asleep, my hand between my thighs, murmuring what I had heard, such as -

"Do come, ducky, and see me home! I've got such nice bubbies. Charley, dear, I haven't had a man for a fortnight; I feel so lewd. I'll show you some pretty pictures. Come down the court, and you shall feel my pussy!"

Still you know, Juliette, I was what is called an honest woman, and, physically, a virgin; but in spite of my rigorous observance of all conventional morality, I was a downright rake at heart. And how many ladies are there who are like what I was at that time? It is the fault of our nerves, nothing more, and if I did not become like one of the painted women who walked the London thoroughfares at night, it was because my convent teaching enabled me to satisfy myself in so many different ways and last, but not least, because my early education was sound. Heaven help the poor girl who knows not how to read or write!

But, to return to Mimi Dubois. She came for me next day, and took me to the old gentleman's home – a palatial mansion in a central square. The ensuing three or four days were occupied in getting my costumes ready. During this period the French housekeeper birched me several times, making me lie in such a position that I could finger her at the same time, and she always flogged me until the desired end was attained, cutting me more and more severely as the climax approached.

On the fifth day my duties with my master, Mr. Hay, commenced. I was dressed in a short frock of white piqué, trimmed with embroidery. It was cut very low in the neck, and very short in front, with a long waist, that was encircled with a broad sash of coloured satin to match a ribbon in my flowing hair.

I had short socks and a pair of children's shoes. The underclothing was the handsomest I had ever seen up till then, consisting of two petticoats, one of cambric, with several flounces, and the other of satin, trimmed with real lace. My chemise was cut like a heart, front and back, and the two shoulder-straps were made with button and buttonhole, so that if unfastened the shift fell at once to the heels. Some of the chemises were of soft foulard of the finest quality, and others of the most delicate handmade batiste, and trimmed with old lace and Venice point, for Mr. Hay was a great collector of ancient lace, and merchants bought for him in all parts of the world. The drawers matched the different chemises, but always showed some six or eight inches below the frock and fitted very tightly.

Thus attired, Madame Dubois led me by the hand to a room, fitted up as a nursery, with toys, low chairs, and even a very high fender round the fireplace, to prevent the "children" falling into the fire! On the walls were pictures and colored engravings representing scenes recalling the games of childhood, boys at school, babies pretending to be "grandpapa," little girls frightened by big dogs, etc.

Mr. Hay, dressed like a little boy of ten, but in a costume recalling the grotesque fashion in which the rising generation went to church in the early part of the century, was seated in a high chair, pretending to read a spelling-book, while in one hand he held a large wooden soldier.

"Now, Charles," said the governess, "here is your little schoolmate, who I hope you will treat kindly. Have you learnt your lesson?"

"I've not got it quite by heart yet, please madam," said the old gentleman, dropping his toy.

"Not done yet!" cried the governess, pretending to be in a passion. "Wait, you little rascal, I'll teach you to be industrious."

She took a large rod, and seizing her pupil, laid him across her lap, and pulled his trousers down. Then she commenced to whip him most vigorously.

Although prepared to be surprised, Juliette I was quite astounded! He behaved just like a little boy, cried, entreated, and twisted his body about in all directions, occasionally showing his small mark of manhood; which, at first hardly to be seen, grew gradually bigger and bigger, and at last, under a skilful and well timed caress of the part of Dubois, discharged with a couple of feeble jerks a small quantity of thin milk and watery fluid.

After allowing him time to recover from the enervating effects of the emission, she pushed him off her knee, and told him to fasten his trousers up. Then, turning to me, she said:

"Mind what you are about, too, for I don't stand upon much ceremony with little girls. Those short petticoats are soon turned up and the little drawers opened. Now the lesson."

I was seated close to my companion, who left me no peace, squeezing my breasts, and putting his hand under my petticoats until, mindful of the part I was paid to perform, I slapped his face smartly. He pretended to cry, and told the governess that I had hit him for nothing.

"I'll teach you to be so free with your hands then, miss," said Madame, taking up the rod.

She made me get up, laid me across her knees, and turned my petticoats up.

Then with a fresh rod, which was rather thicker and heavier, than I had been used to – she was about to lay on, when Charles, his face beaming with delight, called out;

"Oh, Madame, you have not opened her drawers; allow me to do it for you."

"Very well, Charles; pull them wide apart, then stand with your face to the wall, for it is not proper for you to look at a young lady's bottom."

He did it well enough, taking care as he fumbled about my posteriors, to poke a couple of fingers up my cunt.

"Now, face about, Charles."

"Shan't, I mean to have a good look, even if I get punished for it."

"Then, stand off, sir, or you will get the twigs in your eye; I'll see you get your deserts, sir."

Madame Dubois had an awfully heavy hand; every cut of that big birch made me feel as if I was being cut to pieces – my screams and yells gained no pity, but after being under the hottest possible rain of blows, for about five minutes, which seemed quite an hour of torment, she let me down.

This done, she made an excuse, that she was quite ill and upset by our conduct, and begging us to be good, left the room, promising to return as soon as she felt better.

"Hurrah-hurrah"; shouted Charles.

"Now you shall be served out; I know you will enjoy seeing her whack me. Now I mean to have a good look at your bottom, and see if she's really beaten it properly: then after giving it a good slap or two, I shan't mind how she pickles me."

"Indeed you won't, Master Charles, touch me if you dare, sir;" I replied.

His only answer was to rush at me, and after an ineffectual struggle on my part, he got me face downwards, on the hearthrug; tearing at my clothes, ruining the beautiful lace, as I resisted his efforts to look at my poor bottom; but, he was too strong, my drawers were soon in tatters, and he had my well scored buttocks fully exposed.

Slap-slap-slap-slap; his hand fell four times, on the already sore flesh, which I knew was trickling with blood. The sight of the ruby, ensanguined weals, seemed to drive him into a frenzy of passion. "Oh, the lovely blood stains; I must taste them."

Then I felt his tongue licking my bottom all over; but; oh, horror, he was biting me making his teeth meet. I kicked and screamed frantically, his ferocious bites going on all the while. "Help! Murder! Help! My God Help!" – till at last Madame rushed into the room and pulled him off. This was my last séance in Mr. Hay's house; Madame did all she could to persuade me to stay, but in vain; no money would pay me for being bitten like that.

So after being in bed for a week, I left that mansion, with a big sum as compensation and certainly draw the line at having my bum masticated in future.

THE SULTAN'S VIRGIN

A pretty trick you have played me. By Mahomet's beard, it is abominable! to look at her, who would have credited it? such a meek-eyed, timid-looking thing! By Allah, Ali, merely for thrusting my hands into her breasts did she fly at me like a tiger, and my face was instantly furrowed by her cursed nails like unto a field new ploughed. But I wrong you to suppose you could have known what a termagant she was; if you had, you certainly would have communicated the character of your present. I may properly say she was a termagant for she is now tamed. When somewhat recovered from the surprise her sudden attack created, I summoned some of the eunuchs, into whose care I delivered her, determined to defer my revenge until the wounds of my face were healed—and you shall hear how then this vixen was subdued.

In a few days my face was well; my directions that she should be treated with every possible respect in the meantime had quite put her off her guard. One morning the eunuchs conveyed her to my experiment room, where, before she could tell what they were about, her hands were securely fastened together and drawn above her head, through a pulley fixed in the ceiling. I directed her to be pulled up so as not to lift her off the ground, but that she should not be able to throw herself down. When this was affected I entered the room and dismissed the eunuchs. There she stood trembling with rage, but unable to help herself. I now drew a couch towards her, and having seated myself close to her, placed one arm around her waist, and with the other was about to lift up her clothes.

It is impossible to describe the exertions she made to prevent my proceedings, she twisted herself about and writhed and kicked until I was obliged to abandon my attempt for a moment and call in the eunuchs, who quickly (in spite of her kicking) secured each of her feet to a ring placed in the floor, about two feet and a half from each other. This, of course, considerably extended her legs and thighs. She was then secure every way. After dismissing the eunuchs, I again drew the couch close to her, and without further ceremony lifted up her clothes. Oh, Ali, what delicious transport shot through my veins at the voluptuous charms exhibited to my ardent gaze! How lovely was her round mount of love, just above the temple of Venus, superbly covered with beautiful black hair, how soft and smooth as ivory her belly and her swelling, delicately formed thighs! The cygnet down instantly disclosed that she was a maid, for where the bodies have been properly joined in the fierce encounter, the hair (particularly of the female) loses that sleek downy appearance, and by the constant friction the smooth hair becomes rubbed into delightful little curls. But, to put the fact beyond dispute, I thrust my forefinger into the little hole below. Her loud cries, and the difficulty of entering which was found, set the fact beyond dispute. Immediately dropping on my knees, grasping in each hand one of her buttocks, I placed on her virgin toy a most delicious kiss. I then got up and began to undress her. She appeared nearly choked with passion; her tears flowed down her beautiful face in torrents. But her rage was of no use. Proceeding leisurely, first taking off one thing, then another, and with the help of scissors, I quickly rid her of every covering.

Holy Mahomet! What a glorious sight she exhibited: beautiful breasts—finely placed, sufficiently firm to support themselves—shoulders, belly, thighs, legs, everything was deliriously voluptuous! But what most struck my fancy was the beautiful whiteness, roundness and voluptuous swell of firm flesh of her lovely buttocks and thighs. 'Soon,' I said to myself, handling her delicious bum, 'soon shall this lovely whiteness be mixed with a crimson blush!' I placed burning kisses upon every part of her; wherever my lips traveled instantly the part was covered with scarlet blushes. Having directed two rods to be placed on the couch, also a leather whip with broad lashes, I took one of the rods and (shoving the couch out of the way) began gently to lay it on the beautiful posterior of my sobbing captive. At first I did it gently enough—it could have no other effect than just to tickle her; but shortly I began every now and then to lay on a smart lash, which made her wince and cry out. This tickling and cutting I kept up for some time—until the alabaster cheeks of her bum had become suffused with a slight blush—then suddenly I began to give the rod with all my might; then indeed was every lash followed by a cry, or an exclamation for pity, such as 'Oh! spare me, for God's sake! have pity on me! you cut me in pieces!'

'Ah, I cannot bear it! I shall die!' Her winces and the delicious wiggling of her backside increased in proportion to the increase of the force of my lashes and these continued, heedless of her cries, entreaties and complaints, until both the rods and myself were exhausted. To recover breath I drew the couch close to her and seated myself; the entire surface of her beautiful buttocks was covered with welts; every here and there, where the stem of the leaves had caught her, appeared a little spot of crimson blood, which went trickling down the lily thighs. Again and again did I slide my hand over her numerous beauties. Again and again did my forefinger intrude itself into her delicate little hole of pleasure. She could not avoid anything I thought fit to do. Her thighs were stretched wide enough for me to have enjoyed her if I had thought fit, but that was not my immediate intention. I had settled she was to receive the quantity of punishment allotted her before she was deflowered.

Having recovered my breath, I stripped myself, and, seizing the leather whip, began to flog her with such effect that the blood followed every lash. Vain were her cries and supplications—still lash followed lash in rapid succession. I was now in so princely a state of erection that I could have made a hole where there had been none before, let alone drive myself into a place which nature had been so bountiful as to form of stretching material. Quickly summoning the eunuchs, I directed them to lay her on her back on the couch, properly securing an arm on each side to one of the legs of the couch. It was accomplished as quickly as ordered. They retired, leaving me with my exhausted victim to complete the sacrifice. I was not long in rooting up her modesty, deprived as she was of the use of her arms and exhausted by her sufferings. A pillow having been placed under her sufficiently to raise her bottom so as to leave a fair mark for my engine, I threw her legs over my shoulders, and softly (as a tender mother playing with her infant) opened the lips of paradise and love to reveal its coral hue and mossy little grotto—and each fold closed upon the intruding finger, repelling the unwelcome guest. Inconceivable is the delight one feels in these transporting situations! There is nothing on earth so much enhances the joy with me as to know the object that affords me the pleasure detests me, but cannot help from satisfying my desires—her tears and looks of anguish are sources of unutterable joy to me! Being satisfied in every way, by sight, by touch, by every sense, that I was the first possessor, I placed the head of my instrument between the distended lips, grasping her thighs with her legs over my shoulders, then making a formidable thrust, lodged the head entirely in her; she turned her beautiful eyes up to heaven as if looking there for assistance—her exhaustion precluded any opposition; another fierce thrust deepened the insertion; tears in torrents followed my efforts, but she disdained to speak; still I thrust, but no complaint; but growing fiercer, one formidable plunge proved too mighty for her forbearance—she not only screamed, but struggled. However, I was safely in her. Another thrust finished the job; it was done, and nobly done, by Mahomet! After having cooled my burning passion by a copious discharge, I withdrew myself. Crimson tears followed my exit; with a handkerchief I wiped away the precious drops, and falling on my knees between her thighs, placed on the torn and wounded lips a delicious kiss— delicious beyond measure. Only consider, Ali, to know beyond dispute that no one but myself had divided these pouting, fresh, warm, clasping and gaping gates of pleasure! Indeed it was rapturous beyond description. I now thought it time to untie the silken cord that confined the arms of this young vixen. On feeling her arms released, her only motion was to cover her eyes with her hands; there she lay on her back immovable—but for her sobs I could not have told whether she existed. I left her, but ordered the eunuchs to convey her to her apartments, directing the greatest care to be taken of her until my return from an excursion I was about to make to Bona.

I was gone twelve days. During my journey, I had refrained from women, consequently on my return I felt myself in an extremely amorous mood. Not intending to give her modesty (if she had any left) an excuse for resistance, I directed her to be again secured, but this time I had her fastened face downwards to a curious couch made on purpose, at the end of which, by means of a handle, the positions may be elevated or lowered to any height convenient On lifting up her clothes, to my great joy I found there was not the least remains of the flagellation so liberally administered to her. Her swelling ivory thighs and voluptuous firm buttocks had perfectly recovered their beautiful freshness. I think it is utterly impossible for anyone to possess charms exceeding in beauty the rising plumpness of her lovely limbs! How delightful the touch and squeeze of her bum! After tucking her clothes securely up as high as the small of her back, so that her twisting could not unloosen them, I undressed myself, and arming myself with a magnificent rod, commenced giving her a second lesson in birch discipline. Not intending this bout to make her suffer much, having (as I said) completely broken her spirit when I deflowered her, all that I now intended was to enjoy the luxurious wriggling, plunging and kicking which usually attends a smart flagellation. From the tears that already filled her beautiful eyes, I plainly perceived she expected the same treatment she had before experienced; but she was deceived for this time I did not lay into her with more strength than was necessary to cover her posterior with a slight carnation blush. But still the delicious struggles and writhes, as the expected cat fell upon her round buttocks, threw me into so luxurious a frenzy that it caused me soon to abandon the rod. By means of the wheel and handle I raised her buttocks until her delicate little hole of pleasure was properly placed to receive me. I directed myself to the entrance. Having thoroughly stretched her on my first attack, three or four thrusts were enough to engulf my fullest length into her; in fact she sustained the insertion without making any great complaint, only a little cry or so. Nothing adds to the enjoyment so much as the active reciprocation of the female when she returns the transport; when that return is not willingly given, its place must be supplied in the best way available. It could hardly be expected that any return would be made by my captive, consequently I was obliged to make the best substitute I could; so, seizing her round the loins as I drove myself into her, grasping her close and drawing her towards me, I made her meet the coming thrusts, thus famously supplying the want of her own free will in the exertions of my pleasures. Master of the place, I gave way with all my energy to the voluptuous joys with which my senses were surrounded. At every fierce insertion my stones slapped against the soft lips of her delicate slit. Everything conspired to excite, to gratify my senses. Driving close into her, I for a moment stopped my furious thrusts to play with the soft silly hair which covered her mount of love; then slipping my hand over her ivory belly up to her breasts, I made her rosy nipples my next prey. Then, All, I again commenced my ravishing in-and-out strokes. Oh, how beautiful was the sight in the mirror by my side, as I drew myself out of her, of the rosy lips of her sheath protruding out clasping my instrument as if fearing to lose it! then again, as the column returned up to the quick, to see the crimson edging that surrounded me gradually retreating inwards, until it was entirely lost in the black circles of her mossy hair! In short, All, overcome with voluptuous sensations, the crisis seized me. I distilled, as it were, my very soul into her! Satisfied, I now withdrew myself, then releasing her hands, I stripped her of her clothes (all but her shift) and carried her to a more commodious couch, on which I threw her, and placed myself by her side. She had now nothing to lose. Fear, no doubt, prevented her making resistance to my proceedings. The view and touch of so many beauties again fired my blood. I seized her, threw myself upon her, divided her thighs, quickly buried myself in her, and again and again drowned myself in a sea of sensual delight, in which it must be confessed the sweet girl did not to appearances participate. But in my next I hope to give a better account of her.

ANGELA

I n college I was inattentive, I daydreamed, and took little joy in planned learning. However, because Angela's industriousness and irreproachable conduct in college exceeded all expectations, father looked proudly into the future of his true daughter. He began to teach her Latin and French, while I was allowed only to listen to the lessons and not to participate.

At that time I showed little interest in subjects that could not prove their usefulness through practical application. I liked much better to concern myself with the active life around me. I took a lively interest in my classmates, the members of their families, and their way of life. I never neglected to ask my school comrades about their parents and brothers and sisters, about the sternness or tenderness in the family, in order to ferret out whether they were punished for certain types of misbehavior and in which way this punishment was administered, whether they loved their father or mother more, or whether they themselves were favored or punished by the father or mother. These were the favorite questions that I asked of every student. And my thirst for such knowledge was always satisfied.

Angela found less sympathy among her classmates; she was not interesting enough and her exemplary goodness bored most of them. Moreover,

Angela

Ella spent little time with children, preferring adults. I was overtly "bad" but guileless, and sympathetic to the fate of others, hearts flew toward me although I was not especially charming. I was never evil and never malicious. The leitmotif of my behavior lay in the injunction – love thy neighbor as thyself. That was practical reason.

At home there was a lively traffic of families with whom my parents were friends and they often came to visit us with their children. But especially, the reciprocal invitations among college friends often gave me an opportunity to practice my inclinations. Angela felt best when she was near father. I, however, ran around with students of my own age, or younger, whom I directed at my pleasure and ruled over.

I always chose my favorite game in such a way that a dominating role fell to me. The mother-and-child game was very popular as a way for the curious college students to explore under the guise of a childish game. I was happy to play this game as long as I could be the mother and play this role even from the birth of a child onward. I padded my breasts and belly, got sick as the situation called for, and finally let the child be cut from my body. It was always a doll swathed in the cloth forming the padding on my belly and which was removed at birth. I let the newborn infant suckle at my breast. Suddenly the child was big, the doll was replaced by a playmate who thereafter was made to feel all my maternal sternness. This game ended with a quarrel and disagreement between "mother" and "child," and it met with scant approval from the rest of our playmates.

Even playing school was a source of pleasure for me as long as I could play the strict, pitiless woman teacher draconically swinging the cane over her pupils. But this game too never lasted long because the ill-treated "pupils" soon ran away from it in tears, even though they were nearly adults, declaring that they no longer wanted to join in the game because the "teacher" really and soundly whacked them.

After such failures I would immediately propose another game of which I was equally fond: doctor and patient! I always wanted to be the doctor, another girl played the mother who brought her sick child to me. My chief pleasure in my role as doctor lay in thoroughly examining the body of the "patient," where I always concerned myself—at length and thoroughly—with the most private parts of the body. In this way I acquired an extraordinary knowledge of the anatomy of female and male genitalia and satisfied my secret longing to see, to touch and, at times, also to pinch the stark-naked

bottoms of boys and girls. Everything transpired in full secrecy and no one
was allowed to betray anything of the examination. But this game likewise
ended with the refusal of the "patients" to accommodate the "doctor"
because "he" hurt them by subjecting them to small tortures.

From the age of eighteen I was often invited to the homes of my girl
friends. To be sure, we harmonized well hut quarrels were nevertheless
unavoidable. We disagreed, quarreled, and after scuffling in such a way that
it was no longer possible to determine who originally had been at fault, we
complained to the mother of the house. She would rush over to us and first
of all ask about the cause and the originator of the quarrel. As the guest I felt
secure against any insult and boldly complained about the quarrelsomeness
of the other children. I accused them of so many bad things the mother,
angered and excited by my charges, without further ado would belabor the
rudely bared bottom of her offspring with a birch rod, a cane, or the flat of
her hand before all those present.

The ear-piercing screams and the struggling of the girl or boy being punished, the stark-naked bottom, glowing red and flashing under the stern
mother's hissing birch, the fascinating power of the punisher, all this taken
together had a wholly irresistible effect on the children. They were, of
course, afraid of beatings but the spectacle of someone else receiving a
thrashing was a prickling stimulant and constant attraction to them.

I myself stood rigid, as though hypnotized by the suggestive event; I was
fascinated and incapable of moving, shaken and overcome by the tremendous
impact that the maternal punishment had exerted on me. I preserved the
image in my fantasy, my mind was in a tumult I could hardly understand
myself. Full of admiration, I glared at the stern mother; passionately I wished
that I were in the place of the child being punished! At the same time there
arose in my consciousness the remembrance of my own mother whose body
scent and warmth formerly had so intoxicated me.

And at night in bed I imagined again the event that had so shaken me during the day. In my fantasy I was the mother of the naughty girl who had been
birched because of her bad behavior. I relived the whole procedure of the
shameful punishment. I saw myself as a stern mother, I guided my hands
under the child's clothes, unbuttoned her drawers, pulled them down,
stretched the bitterly weeping girl across my lap, bared her whole bottom,
grabbed the birch and belabored the bottom with slanting blows until the
skin burned. The more the girl showed her fear and resisted, the more she

wailed and screamed, the more her naked bottom glowed and smarted, all the more sharply did the stinging blows of my birch fall, all the more did her shrill and piercing screams sound like lovely music in my ears. I became hotter and hotter with such fantasies, a wondrous thrill of voluptuary pleasure shot through my body. I understood that an inner relationship existed between the birching of a naked bottom and the prickling feeling of happiness that suffused my soul.

Toward a smaller friend I liked to feel like a mother to whom it is handed over against its will. I also wanted to have such unlimited control over a child. Sometimes it happened that a child was naughty; I immediately led it to its mother and complained about its naughtiness. Back then every angered mother would soundly thwack her tot's bottom without standing on ceremony. I wanted to bring about these thwackings, it gratified me when they happened, and the punished child broke into a wild scream— not so much, of course, because of the thwackings but out of shame that it had to submit its bare bottom for such punishment.

I would feel myself drawn to this mother admiringly. I would nestle against her, sensing what she experienced when she made her offspring feel the weight of her absolute maternal authority. How beautiful the mother-child relationship in which one, in childlike trust, felt secure and sheltered and looked up in reverential love to the person held in respect, embodied by the stern mother!

My mother died when I was young. She had been mentally deranged many months before her life was fully extinguished by a heart attack after years of invalidism. Her death was beyond my comprehension. I cried night and day without knowing why. The whole house seemed to me to be shrouded in sadness, useless and desolate. I did not want to remain in it any longer without mother.

Father and Angela coolly and rationally made all the necessary arrangements after mother's death. They did not weep but showed their everyday faces and it seemed to me as if they viewed the death of this poor invalid as a wished-for deliverance. Nevertheless, it was a hard blow to all of us.

My father's sister, Aunt Regina, the widow of a district judge who had died early, came over to the house after my mother died, as she had so often done before, in order to see that everything was all right. The household was greatly neglected, the wardrobe of the children was in a bad way, and our upbringing left much to be desired. This time Aunt Regina remained several months with us, more for her brother's sake than for that of her mother-less nieces. She found us not at all properly brought up and worthy of love as her own son Peter, who was already grown up. Auntie, however, could not cope with the task of running her brother's household permanently and she soon returned to the loneliness and peace of her widow's residence. This certainly was the reason why father decided to marry for the second time only one year after mother's death.

* * *

The stepmother was a lady of thirty-five. When father took her home she had just become the widow of a seventy-eight-year-old doctor, to whom she had been married four years. Formerly she had been the governess of many children of socially prominent families.

Outwardly she was pleasant without actually being pretty. Practical, materialistic, and clever as she was, she had married father only for reasons of security. She was a model of a good housewife, a good cook, a foe of dust, and of stockings with holes, and tyrannized the whole house with her inveterate love of order. She shook me out of my daydreaming and urged me to take up needlework. Angela had to help with the housework and knit stockings. We were no longer allowed to be idle and to play.

We sisters quickly discovered that the stepmother was a lady of great energy and sternness who always knew how to make her will prevail. She demanded prompt obedience, good behavior, and an iron industriousness from us. When she was angry, and bored through us with her looks, her cold, steel-green eyes could look at us with a sternness that made hot and cold shivers run down our spines. Our freedom was limited and now we had to come home punctually, on the minute.

Despite her zeal in child-rearing, the stepmother did not show the slightest affection for us children. I believe she regarded us to be too old to remain at home and wanted to be rid of us. But she was ostentatiously affectionate with father. He was happy at her side, wholly henpecked; he even handed over to her the education of his daughter, which up to now he alone had directed.

When our mentally ill mother was still alive the atmosphere at home had been oppressive and unhealthy, full of mysteries and horror. Fantastic shapes crept toward me from all corners, the disorder in the rooms was appealing

45

and uncanny at once: I avoided touching the objects in them, bewitched as in a fairy tale. A needlework begun would lie for weeks in one place, untouched and covered with dust, the cat would lie down on it and fall asleep. Our toys were strewn all over the floor and our school things lay dreaming in a corner. The stepmother brought order and purposefulness into the idyllic peace of these slumbering things. She discarded, and radically, all which stood in the way of her practical sense.

A few months after the entrance of the stepmother into our house it happened that Ella did not come home punctually at one o'clock for the midday meal. It was served and eaten as usual and when Angela finally came home, around one-thirty, she was served afterward and had to eat alone. The stepmother darted angry glances but did not utter a word as long as father was present. Angela excused herself to father, explaining that she was late because she had accompanied a school friend home and believed that this explanation had settled the matter. As she finished her lunch with good appetite, father and stepmother returned to their bedroom to rest as usual after meals.

After this rest, when father had left the house, the stepmother came into the room where Ella and I were busy with our homework. She went directly up to my sister and, flushing red, angrily asked her: "At what time are you supposed to be home?"

"At one o'clock," answered Angela calmly.

"Good! And at what time did you come home today?"

"At one-thirty, because I walked my girl friend home."

"Yes, indeed! But you know that I have insisted again and again that you be at home at one o'clock punctually. Now, come with me!"

The stepmother grabbed the resisting Angela by the arm and dragged her to the bedroom next to the living room in which we had been sitting. It was clear to both of us that now something terrible was about to happen. Angela, too, sensed that something frightful was in the offing for her. I stared into space, stiff, as if paralyzed in every joint. My heart was in my mouth, and the air was laden with an oppressive mystery that took my breath away. Ella began to cry, to plead, and to promise that she would certainly never do it again. But the stepmother did not listen and silently dragged Ella along with her. After she and Angela disappeared into the bedroom, she locked the door.

The surmise that a thrashing was in the offing became a certainty. An oppressive stillness prevailed all around me, so that I could hear every sound coming from the bedroom. I heard the sound of a chair being pulled out and then I heard how the stepmother was speaking to Angela.

"My patience is at an end! If you will not hear, you must be made to feel. Now you'll taste the birch on your naked bottom, maybe that will make you mind my words better!"

Immediately the bedroom resounded with urgent pleas and implorations for forgiveness. Angela's promises to mend her ways were heard, her weeping grew louder and louder, her screaming ever more heart-rendering. A convulsion went through my body, I trembled like an aspen leaf.

"Here!" called the stepmother in the bedroom, and Angela, in a mysteriously fear-ridden tone, whimpered and wailed: "No! No! You can't... unbutton my drawers! I'll be good and punctual as you want, mother! I won't ever do it again! But not the... drawers... no! No!"

A piercing shriek ensued, betraying that Angela's naked bottom had received the first blow with the birch, and indeed the first birching that had been given in our house by our stepmother. Indeed it was also the first time that Angela had received a taste of the rod – but not the last!

I listened in a state of frantic, tense excitement to the whistle of the birch as it came swishing down, blow after blow, on my sister's bared body. Swack! Swack! Swack! So many were the blows that descended on Angela's bottom that it seemed to me that the birching would never end. I will never forget that day – my soul enflamed and my blood raged as in a fever.

A wholly new epoch was ushered in by this event. From then onward the stepmother thought of no other punishment for us children than the birch and always on the fully bared bottom.

Since that day hardly a week went by without my sister or me being summoned into the bedroom by the stepmother. Angela, who was older, always had to unbutton her drawers by herself, whereas any stepmother pulled them down from me, the younger, as from a moppet. When I received the rod for the first time, I almost could not endure it. The blows that had the effect of molten lead on the naked bottom singed any flesh like an infernal fire.

We were never birched when father was at home, but we lived in constant fear of inviting a punishment. One day Ella complained about the stepmother to father because she, now a big girl of almost fourteen years, had been birched. She did not want to put up with this anymore. But father calmly answered, "You must have surely deserved it, my child." That day when father left, the stepmother summoned Ella to the bedroom and birched her again and so soundly that she never again complained about the stepmother to father. Thereafter she meekly submitted to her punishments.

I always waited for such events, which stirred my soul so deeply, with taut nerves. I observed the stepmother's features searchingly and tried to read in them the riddle of her inner being. Never did her eyes beam more brightly, never did the smile around the corners of her mouth play more conqueringly than when she could belabour her step-daughters' bare bottoms with smarting blows from the birch. Then she would beat with a slow deliberateness and the strange sensations she felt filled me with awe.

Later, when I recognized the nature of my own being, when my eyes and mind had been opened wide for this sweet enjoyment of the rod, the image of my stepmother often cropped up in my mind. Then I would see her glowing cheeks, her flashing eyes, and I understood the zeal with which she sought occasions for calling us, big girls of thirteen and fifteen, into the bedroom. No doubt that was the stepmother's greatest enjoyment. Later I also learned that as a teacher she had likewise used the rod to punish her unruly pupils.

Strange to say, in this moment my thoughts turn to the drawers which my sister and I wore at that time. We never wore the open flap drawers that were prescribed in the convent. Ours fit tightly around the thigh and bottom, bordered with pretty lace, tied with ribbons: the front flap folding under the back as customary, the rear flap folding under the belly. A seamstress came to the house periodically to sew our outer clothing and our underwear. This seamstress was summoned to the house shortly after the stepmother's arrival in order to make drawers and other undergarments for us. My sister had to hold her dress high and try on the drawers so that the stepmother, in the presence of the seamstress, could see how they fit.

After a close examination and testing the stepmother ordered the seamstress to cut the side-slits of the drawers lower by a hand's breadth so that— as she put it—the drawers would not split upon being pulled up or pulled down. We made wholly futile objections against having such large side-slits, but the stepmother was adamant. This episode comes to mind now along with a crystal-clear explanation of her design! Obviously the only reason for the large side-slits was that they would enable the stepmother to pull down the rear drawer flap even lower. So at that time the stepmother was already thinking with "love and solicitude" about our bottoms hidden in the drawers and about her birch rod! At that time none of us had been birched and it is probably for this reason that the underlying purpose of the deep side-slits had not occurred to me earlier.

After the introduction of these "practical drawers" one could pull down the rear flap to the middle of the thigh once the front slip-knot was loosened. And when dress and blouse were then raised up to the waist, the full bottom lay smooth and bare down to the middle of the thigh – invitingly ready for the rod.

Angela received her first punishment on a bottom that had been bared accordingly. Since Ella had refused to, the stepmother herself had grabbed her and untied the front knot of the drawers, pulled down the rear flap, after which she stretched Ella across a chair, dress and blouse raised high above her waist. Thus the field of action was laid bare. In the evening, of course, I was bent upon finding out whether traces of the birching were still discernible on my sister's bottom. At bedtime I made her lift her long nightgown and with horror I saw a number of clear, fine streaks, partly red, partly reddish-blue, and also some that were all blue. Especially and strongly noticeable, however, were the yellow-blue spots on her right buttock which was precisely where the points of the birch branches had lashed in.

It was understandable that such a sight should excite me and fill me with a quaking fear. Which one of us would be the next to have her naked bottom birched so soundly? Oh, numberless times, I too was stretched over the chair like Angela and received the birch on my bare buttocks! In the beginning both my sister and I found it puzzling when the stepmother mysteriously came into the room or even merely stuck her head in the door, motioned with her forefinger and called out, "Edith, come over here!" Little by little, however, we understood what it signified: the birch rod, the rear flap of the drawers pulled down in order to lay bare the bottom, always face downward, across her lap or, especially as we grew older, across a chair! And while she once more rebuked the culprit for her misbehavior, she bared the bottom with great care while deploring the necessity to birch such a big girl on her naked – yes, on her *naked* – bottom. She would lay such a special emphasis on "naked" that one simply felt like crawling into the earth for shame.

At that time it seemed to me that a complete transformation had taken place in my soul. Until then I had been but an innocent college girl. My thoughts were divided between homework, my playmates, my sister, and matters affecting our household. New conditions had developed since the introduction of birching by the stepmother; the strict upbringing imposed on us played the most prominent role. In the beginning, however, this circumstance was considered merely as an exciting intensification of our education, as something unavoidable to which we had to submit with resignation. My sister Ella never grasped this circumstance in any other way.

As the years went by only I was consumed by the erotic power of birching. Why? This question has often occupied my thoughts. Is it an accident or did I possess this tendency from birth? Or was it placed in my soul from the ovum onward and had it waited only for this impetus in order to break out with elemental force? I do not know.

At that time I had still another experience that shook me deeply. One day father and stepmother had retired to their room after the midday meal as usual. Someone then came to us in the room and asked to speak to father. I was eager to be of service so, unthinkingly, I entered the room, the door of which was not locked, and surprised my parents in the act of sexual intercourse. The bed in which this was happening faced the door. I caught sight of my father moving rhythmically up and down astride the body of the stepmother. Paralyzed by shock, I stood there rooted to the spot, rigid as though bewitched, unable to utter a sound, The act was well under way. I wanted to scream but had no voice. I wanted to run but my legs failed me...

Minutes – perhaps an eternity – went by when the stepmother seemed to notice the open door. She raised her head, caught sight of me in the door, troubled and staring at the repugnant scene, and roared angrily: "Get out! Astrid! What are you doing in here!"

Father leaped off the bed in a flash, rushed at me, grabbed me by the arm, shoved me out the door and then turned the key in the lock twice.

Shivering from head to toe, confused and torn apart in my innermost being, reeling, I ran into the garden, threw myself on the grass and wept... wept. . . wept...

After I had calmed down somewhat, I heard the stepmother calling my name from the house: once, twice, thrice! Mechanically I obeyed and went into the home, where she was waiting for me. Without saying a word I let myself be led to the bedroom because it was quite clear to me that I could expect a sound thrashing for this "disturbance." For all that, the punishment on this day became for me the fateful hour of my life! In this hour I found myself on the 'send de la conscience', and now I stepped beyond this threshold of consciousness.

I had never known the feeling with which I received my punishment that time. The words uttered by my stepmother appeared to me in a wholly different light than was otherwise the case. To this day I hear the words, those wicked words – quasi-wicked I suddenly felt! – uttered by the stepmother when the door was locked and I was alone with her:

"Aren't you ashamed that you violated my command not to come into the bedroom, Astrid? You can't deny that I forbade you time and time again to set foot in the room unless you were summoned! Or can you, Astrid? You're too big a girl not to obey instantly. Now you'll get your well-deserved punishment for it. Unbutton your knickers!"

In a state of frenzied excitement I tried my best to calm the stepmother. Instinctively, however, I felt that under no circumstances did she want to release her prey. Finally the stepmother shrilled into my face, "Are you going to unbutton your drawers, yes or no!" Her tone was so brutal that I suddenly started with shock. A ringing slap in the face accompanied her words.

The stepmother heard my sobs and urgent pleadings with visible pleasure; she sensed my quaking fear and understood that I was ashamed to deliver my naked bottom to her blows. Pitilessly, in the grip of a wild sensuous excitement she finally achieved her desired goal. In well-delivered blows she made her birch dance hissing across my bare buttocks – a thrill shot through me like a hot spring and I felt the excitement being experienced by the birch-wielding stepmother flow over me as well. To me it was a wholly incomprehensible experience. I floated in a state of imagined bliss and cried heartrendingly for sheer joy. The blows fell over and over again on my stark-naked bottom and every blow became a sweet pain for my own mounting and awakening voluptuary pleasure.

At the end of the punishment I ran reeling into my room, threw myself on the bed and did something with such a compulsive necessity that there was no way out. The ticklish feeling of happiness in my sex swelled into a driving force, the flogged bottom burned like fire – I pressed my legs closely against each other and did not understand at all what was happening to me. I had never known such a feeling before! I did not yet clearly know that it was voluptuousness increasingly urging itself on in order to release a flow of still greater enjoyment. I made frenzied efforts to bring on this feeling. I did not yet know the technique, and finally I wept bitterly in the throes of an unappeasable sexual excitement.

The tickling, the urging and throbbing in my sex rose to an ever greater and more powerful crescendo, my vulva was swollen, my clitoris stiffly erect. I rubbed my legs against each other, it felt good, but all it did was to heighten the tickling sensation and finally I could not stand it anymore! My hand had to reach for the tickling spot in order to ease the tension but even this action required ever greater pressure; I rubbed the vulva with the finger and the more I rubbed, the more frenziedly did my fingers go to work in the centre of my voluptuousness, the more beatific became the feeling of happiness, a moan escaped my lips and the images of my fantasy filled my senses with a never suspected ecstasy. My hand was under the compulsion to rub faster, ever faster, at the focal point... I was still fully a novice—until at last the orgasm convulsed my whole body in an avalanche of pleasure. Thereupon my senses faded away...

I had never before experienced such a wondrously blissful hour, and when I awoke from the dream, I ambled about like a drunk. Only then did I become aware of the heavenly voluptuary pleasure in birchings and by degrees this passion saturated my whole sensory life. And from this hour onward I began also to understand the stepmother, and spontaneously felt myself drawn to her. I began to love her—although I still received the blows of her birch rod on my bottom! It hurt as much as before, and yet I could not prevent myself from snuggling against her, from kissing and caressing her.

The stepmother seemed to perceive the change in my feeling. When she called me into the bedroom, she always held me close to her, called me her "darling," kissed me and deplored the fact that she was forced to bare my bottom. She caressed me tenderly, and in the midst of these caresses she would furtively slip her right hand under my dress in order to pull down my drawers. She furtively "caressed" my drawers down, as it were.

* * *

Mother (for that is what I came to call my stepmother after a time) turned the book around this way and that and examined it from all sides. It did not take her long to grasp the dimensions of the disaster.

"Casanova! Casanova!" she shrieked wrathfully to the rest of the family members present. Her horror before this state of affairs choked her breathing, her pale face had flushed crimson. Finally she regained her self-control and turning toward me, she asked:

"What kind of book is that, you depraved child, and where did you find it? Was this the so-called homework that worried you so much? Answer me, Now!"

So saying, she gingerly took the infamous book between her fingers and held it under my nose. Defiantly, I turned my back on her. The others just stood there as if rooted to the floor, gaping at the scene. If I had been alone with my mother, I would have found impudent excuses and answered her boldly and brazenly. But the shaming reprimand in the presence of my father and my smirking siblings, this public disgrace, totally disarmed me. Tears welled up in my eyes and I remained in my corner, burning with shame and in a state of utter confusion.

"Talk up! Answer! Where did you find it? I'll give you the birching you deserve in front of everybody here."

The threat of the rod on my naked backside was not the worse threat that loomed before me. Face to face with my mother alone I had humbly submitted to the most violent floggings. But now, as an older girl of eighteen, I defended myself against a flogging in the presence of my father and my sisters. Mother perceived the reason for my refusal to submit and observed me with an icy stare. Then her eyes glinted with fury and, in a sudden movement, she tore out a handful of pages from the disreputable book. She turned to my father and declared in a tone of great resolve, not without a touch of hypocrisy:

"This has to stop, once and for all. If you don't take energetic steps now, we'll have worse trouble later with our little hoydens. And this one here is m – and right here and now. But I shouldn't be the one to do it."

"Why not? After all, you are the father, aren't you?"

"Indeed, but I can't punish her because I'm not angry enough with her. You can punish her in my presence, that will shame her all the more and take some of the arrogance out of her. Whip her behind to shreds!"

The maid appeared on the threshold to announce that dinner was ready at the very moment my father pronounced the last word. The whole family left for the dining room on the floor below; only I remained in my corner, in defiance of them all. Mother was the last to leave; at the threshold she turned around to me once more and after taking cognizance of my stupid stubbornness, in a very severe and peremptory tone, she declared:

"As punishment you will not eat with us today. You will remain in your room until I come back. Is that clear? Don't drive me to extremes or I'll let you have here and now what you certainly can expect later."

Shame welled up in me. I felt my face glowing like a red-hot coal. I could only stammer contritely: "Oh, Mother, please forgive me just this once?"

She came up to me, and tried to bend me under her left arm. But she

Angela

quickly realized that my resistance blocked her from carrying out her obvious intention. When I broke free of her grip, she released me and slapped me resoundingly several times on both cheeks with all her might, temporarily deafening and blinding me. I reeled back under the blows, half dazed, sobbing, and inwardly seething. My mother took advantage of this moment to leave the room. Hastily. I hurled myself at the door in an attempt to hold her back, but she was already outside and had locked me in the room, turning the key in the lock twice. Full of anger and shame, my senses in a tumult, I threw myself on the bed. Through my brain raced the wildest thoughts of revenge against Dora who had forced the book on me. I imagined myself flogging her naked backside to shreds and this image suffused my whole being with pleasurable sensations.

Little by little, however, a deep depression came over me. I rose from my bed and went out to the balcony, where I sank into a wicker chair. The fresh air cooled my brain and cheeks. I could hear the loud conversation from the dining room, which lay directly under my room. I leaned over the side of the balcony and saw that the window was open. I heard my mother's voice saying:

"It's absolutely impossible to get on peacefully with Astrid. Who owns the book, who lent it to her?"

My father's voice followed hers through the open window. Instead of trying to answer her rhetorical question, he struck a warning note: "You mustn't hesitate for an instant to use the rod unsparingly, and sooner or later the children themselves will be thankful to you for it. Mere words, tossed out like bubbles in the air, have no effect on them . . . A good arse-warming helps them remember warnings better than anything else."

This exchange was followed by complete silence; the noonday stillness was broken only by the clink of the cutlery and the clatter of dishes. My anger reached a pitch of absolute fury. I was hungry, sleepy, and utterly exhausted.

I was suddenly awakened from my drowsiness by the rattle of the key in the door. Blinking, I recognized my mother's silhouette. She was standing in front of me, holding a long birch rod. The whole family followed behind her, like a pack of sensation-seekers, my father and my five sisters. Their faces mirrored that singular prudence which I myself felt at the prospect of witnessing a flogging.

My mother came up to me without uttering a word and grabbed me firmly by the wrist. With a jerk, she tore me away from the chair and boldly swung me to the centre of the room, whereupon she said in an icy command:

"Unbutton your bloomers and lay face down and straight across the bed. Out with your naked bottom. I'll give it the whipping it deserves because of your shameful deed!"

Her wicked words plunged me into an abyss of shame. I also realized that any resistance would be useless, since I deserved the thrashing and therefore had to submit to my mother's commands. Trembling, I stuck my hands under my clothes, fingering them confusedly as I tried to find the buttons of my bloomers. My mother waited in front of me impatiently, the birch rod poised in readiness to strike, accompanying the mute scene with utterances that deepened and intensified my shame.

My hands, hidden under the dress, finally found the buttons of my bloomers. I undid them, and my underclothes rolled down to my ankles. Then I bent over the edge of the bed and lifted my dress high above my arched bottom, exposing it fully to the view of all those present. Mother came to my side and after raising all encumbering pieces of clothing still higher, she began to swing the rod viciously.

Swish! Huit! Swish! Huit! Huit! Sighed the thin birch branches as they landed on my exposed buttocks. Each blow seared my flesh like a hot iron and the wild sensation of pain first elicited plaintive whimpering from me. Although I squirmed and twisted like a snake and kicked wildly in all directions, I could not ward off this hail of hissing blows as they fell mercilessly on my tender backside. I burst into a terrifying scream and rolled up into a ball in a desperate effort to defend myself.

Under the crackling blows I began to scream, to kick about again, and to defend myself with all my might. My screams were so loud that the cook came running upstairs and stuck her head through the chink of the door to find out what the uproar was all about. When she saw that I was being given a sound thrashing, she went back to her kitchen pleased with the sight.

I was released me only after it was all over. I slumped to the floor and rolled on the carpet. I rubbed my sore buttocks, without thinking of the indecent spectacle I was offering the onlookers in view of my wild despair and confusion. It was the most terrible birching I had ever received. Never in my life had I ever received a similar sound thrashing, in double portion to boot.

"Get up now and pull up your bloomers, Astrid. I hope you will take good note of this," said my mother in a soothing tone of voice.

I got up dizzily and felt my backside; it was heavy and swollen, like a red-hot ball. I pulled up my bloomers with a feeble motion and arranged my clothes properly. Father came up to me, and in a pacifying tone of voice he admonished me emphatically:

"This should teach you a lesson, child. You have been very severely punished, but eventually you will see that your parents have acted correctly. And now, try to mend your ways."

Overcome by tender family feelings, I took a few steps toward my mother, threw my arms around her neck, and hid my face in her bosom. I sobbed heartrendingly. She loosened herself from my embrace, kissed me fleetingly on the forehead, and left the room with the others.

Once I was alone I fell prey to an extraordinary sensual excitement. A tickling stimulus in my private parts threw me into a turmoil. I pulled down my bloomers, threw myself on the bed, lifted my clothes over my head, and spread my legs. I daydreamed wonderfully about Dora's stark-naked bottom being flogged as never before. Fancy conjured up the most voluptuous images of a birching. My fingers unconsciously played with my clitoris, the area around which was moist with sexual excitation for a long time; until my consciousness was buried under an avalanche of voluptuousness.

* * *

When I went to college the next day, the professor made it quite obvious that she was fully and exactly informed about the disagreeable story of the forbidden book. She pointed at Dora and branded her as an evil-doer before the whole class. Someone had taken the trouble to hand the book over to the teacher and to disclose the secret to her with all proper discretion.

She took the Casanova book from her desk and fastened it up on the wall.

At that time thrashings were not only administered in families, but also in schools. Dora, an eighteen-year-old girl, had not only lent the book to me but had secretly removed it from her father's library. When the teacher called her to account for it, Dora flatly denied it and named as the real culprit another girl who had nothing at all to do with the matter. After reaching the end of her patience, the teacher announced that Dora was to be punished before the whole class.

During this announcement all eyes in the classroom fell on Dora, whose pretty face reddened with shame. She bowed her head with a saintliness that was hypocritical sham, because I could notice that under her lengthy whimpers she was winking over to me and striving mightily to suppress an outburst of mocking laughter. She believed that I had betrayed her. I was in a state of wild excitement and trembled all over with a lustful craving for a look at her naked bottom.

At the close of the lesson the teacher pulled from her desk a fresh birch rod, obviously prepared in advance, summoned Dora to stand before her, adjusted a chair, and then ordered her to kneel on the seat. In a trice the poor girl's clothes were flung high above her back, her bloomers were pulled down and her rotund buttocks revealed to view. Dora remained in this position for several minutes, exposed to the scrutiny of all her classmates.

She had a white, well-formed bottom, voluptuous and beautiful in its lines, as I had envisioned it in my fantasies. Dora contracted the churning buttocks so close together that the dividing line almost disappeared, and she sobbed bitterly into her handkerchief.

As the teacher's rod swished on the smooth, white rotundities, Dora grew desperate and began to scream so loud that the nerves of all the onlookers quivered with excitement. Her screams ring in my ears to this very day:

"Forgive me – *Fräulein* teacher – please forgive me! Oh! Oh! I won't do it… again… Oh! Forgive me… OH!"

Her act of contrition, however, had come too late because the teacher now took no notice of her shrill screams. Unflinchingly, she landed spirited blows on the repentant sinner's scarlet red buttocks. Swish! Swish! Swish! Swish!

Her flogged bottom danced and hopped according to this beat time, now expanding and contracting, now spreading the hams apart, now protruding toward the class and pulling itself in, only to meet again with the pitiless birch.

As if in a frenzy, the teacher counted, loud and slow, the blows that she landed on Dora's bottom, so slow indeed that she always counted two blows for one. She lashed Dora's red-hot and welt-covered buttocks pitilessly and vigorously without pause and her frenzy seemed to know no bounds.

Finally the procedure was over.

The teacher looked as though she were drunk and she was breathing heavily. Dora rose to her feet with feeble movements, dried her tears, and rushed, unnoticed, out of the room. I, however, had enjoyed this punishment scene.

It had a terrific impact on me and sent me into raptures. Even long after

Angela

I fed upon the remembered voluptuousness of the scene. I clearly saw the glowing, welted, dancing, twitching buttocks. I distinctly heard Dora's mad moaning in my ears, and with this vision in mind I sexually excited myself.

At this moment, of course, it is not possible for me to report on each case in which our teacher's birch rod threatened the smooth bottoms of her charges of both sexes, and just as little on the many pretexts which our parents knew how to find when it was a question of administering the favorite arse-warmings to us. But the older I grew, the more intensely I felt that I was no longer able to separate my sensual excitements from the corporal punishment administered to stark-naked bottoms.

* * *

When I was nineteen years old, a cousin of the same age visited our house during vacation time. He was tall and very handsome, and in him I had a welcome playmate. My mother was very fond of him and kissed and fondled him frequently. I soon noticed that when she kissed him she stroked and pinched his butt at the same time, and that the boy on such occasions clung very closely to her.

In the evening, when my sisters and I went to bed at nine o'clock, she always accompanied him to his room. Hans, my cousin, later told me that his aunt remained in the room until he lay in bed wholly undressed. Then playfully she kissed his naked bottom and gently slapped it.

Yet this was not my mother's only aim. She earnestly wanted to birch her nephew. It goes without saying that she finally found a pretext, whereby I was also guilty. One day as we were playing Hans threw the ball through a window. I was his play partner and I had incited him to do it. Enraged, Mother called us into the room where she waited for our arrival with her cat-o'-nine-tails. On this day I witnessed my handsome cousin being flogged on his naked behind by my mother. This was my undoing. If I say this, it is also certainly true, even though my earlier experiences had already made their contribution. It was the first time that I became distinctly conscious of the sensations that swept over me when I saw this fourteen-year-old boy with his pants pulled down and buttocks exposed, confused with shame and fear, awaiting punishment.

My mother pulled Hans toward her and forced him to bend over her knee. Her severe words sounded almost like verbal caresses and my cousin's flattering pleas for forgiveness were exceedingly exciting, sensually. I floated on the surface of hitherto unknown oceans of bliss, and I did not understand what was happening to me.

When Mother began to flog his bottom, the buttocks surged like waves before my eyes, turning and twisting in enigmatic movements, expanding and contracting, dancing and leaping crazily under the cracking blows of the whip. Hans pressed his belly very close against Mother's knee in a backward and forward motion, and his plaintive cry sounded like a voluptuous moan… I felt the sensual stimulus powerfully in my private parts. I felt the pulse beat of my raging blood hammering in my vulva. I felt close to fainting and almost threatened to sink to the floor, overpowered by the excitement.

Finally the flogging of my cousin came to an end and Mother called me to her side. I took a few tottering steps in her direction and noticed a big wet spot on her clothing, which stemmed from Hans; crying with pleasure, I threw myself over her lap. I felt the abyss of my sensuality opening up and I surrendered myself as prey to my sensations.

Without pulling up his trousers, Hans came to my mother's assistance. He grabbed me firmly by the wrists and brutally shoved his knee against the nape of my neck in order to force my face toward the floor. My clothes were pulled up, but my mother's nervous hands did not find the buttons of my bloomers right away.

The preparations seemed endless. Mother, my cousin, and I lost consciousness of our surroundings. The frenzy of the flogging gripped the three of us and transported us to a state of rapturous bliss.

As though hypnotized, I remained breathless, without moving. All I could do was to tremble helplessly in frenzied excitement. Suddenly like a lightning flash, I felt the cool air blowing on my naked bottom. My smooth buttocks quivered with a pleasurable sensation and pressed convulsively against each other. The first blow smacked against the tightly drawn arches of my backside with an unheard-of force. Defenseless, I opened my mouth to scream, but Hans drowned my wail under his weight. The subsequent blows fell like hailstones on my squirming and twisting backside, which helplessly surrendered to its tormentors.

About twenty blows rained on my burning buttocks without letup, in a rising tempo. My head was clamped between my cousin's knees, my body rocked back and forth on the lap of my rod-wielding mother, without the possibility of finding a balance. The reciprocal engagement between the biting leather thong and my glowing buttocks seemed never to end.

At times, under an especially strong blow, I became limp, my muscular tension relaxed. I spread my legs far apart. My knees lost their stiffness and I pressed my vulva in wild excitement against Mother's knee. Moaning, I yielded myself completely to the pricking hail of blows. I rocked and raised my backside up and down until in a final thrust against her knee I stiffened my whole body anew and strained every nerve in order to receive the last blows in the wildest orgasm of pleasure.

My bottom burned like fire, but I no longer distinguished between pleasure and pain. I felt only the mad sexual excitement that grew from second to second into the incommensurable. I heard my mother breathe heavily, and my own heart was beating as if it would burst. Finally, in a moment of unendurable tension my mother left off flogging me and I reached the peak of sexual ecstasy in the clamp formed by my cousin's knee.

I sank into a state suffused by a feeling of absolute eternity. I don't know how long it was before I came to normal consciousness, I did not breathe, I lay there bathed in perspiration, everything reeling around me. Slowly the magic spell waned. I slid down from my mother's knees and left the room with a tottering step. I staggered forth and threw myself drunkenly on my bed. I remained in the same position all night, motionless, without taking a breath. My consciousness was in a state of total dissolution and thrills of delight rolled over me like huge, heaving waves.

In the middle of the night walking in my sleep, I crept into my cousin's room and wordlessly laid myself alongside him in bed. He, too, was lying sleepless and dreaming blissful dreams in a waking state. He clamped his arms around me and whispered the revelations and sensual experiences of his fourteen years into my ear. He told me undreamed-of things about love and voluptuousness as his hand played with my sex, producing the very pleasures of which he spoke. He also guided my hand to his stiffened member and taught me the caresses that gave him pleasure. His warm flow of semen spurted in fits and starts over my fingers and I remained rigid with excitement. I remembered the moist spot on my mother's clothing after Hans's punishment, the explanation of the occurrence was obvious. Pleasure racked both our bodies in the torrential flood of the orgasm.

We were bound together by secrecy after that experience. Hans had a hidden penchant for cruelty and he took a mystic joy in practicing physical tortures. He inflicted them on himself before my very eyes and described the pleasure that he experienced in so doing. In order to feel this painful pleasure continuously, he had dreamed up the idea of trimming his trousers with pins that would penetrate into his flesh with every movement that he made. He loved fanatically to be birched on his naked bottom by my mother or to watch corporal punishment being dealt out to others. Without indulging in ambiguous thoughts or reveries, he sought only the sensation of pain, which alone brought him to the thrill of pleasure.

When we were alone, he invented bizarre and dangerous exercises, during which he spilled his semen before my eyes. He subjected his body to the weirdest tests and at the same time he tried his best to hurt me by devising all possible tortures. He stuck pins in my bottom, or dug deeply into my flesh with his sharp fingernails, while he himself for hours endured the strange puzzling torture of feeling his penis and testicles tightly bound with string to his body. For him it was a pleasure to suffer and to make others suffer.

My heart was seized with a feeling of physical love for the boy who was of the same age as myself. I perceived that there was no contradiction between pleasure and cruelty, but that both were fused into one, like body and soul.

* * *

When, as a young woman, I made my most intimate acquaintance with the birch rod on my naked behind as well as through witnessing the frequent corporal punishments meted out to my five sisters, and when it gradually dawned on me that my parents derived a great, indeed the greatest, pleasure from such floggings, my thoughts began to dwell upon this singular fact.

While witnessing the floggings of my older sisters, for the first time I became aware of an excitement, which at that moment, was not wholly clear to me. After all, I was an innocent into my late teens and even until my twenties and hardly in a position to analyse my feelings. The first feeling, surely, was one of fear produced by surprise. As the fear subsided, a second feeling took its place, curiosity, or better, the question: "How is Helen or Bertha being punished?" The thought of Helen's or Bertha's naked bottom surely lay in the background of this question. For, customarily, one of several slaps in the face were administered on the spot as parental discipline. But this mysterious withdrawal with my parents into a mom apart guided my thoughts toward the extraordinary. For what could this other punishment be except a birching on the fully exposed smooth buttocks?

This thought, for the moment not wholly clear, but which, as I have said, surely lay in the unconscious, soon produced a vague tickling in my nerve centre which received its definite object when Mother voiced her intention of using the rod on one of her daughter's stark-naked bottoms.

My excitement received a sure direction through this utterance, and it became the point of departure for my whole emotional life. The thought of the punishment to be carried out after the "verdict," which I could watch in all details, instantly kindled my sensual excitement, which increased according to the progress of the preparations: Mother's stern commands, Helen's or Bertha's pleas, entreaties, and tears, the act of unbuttoning the bloomers, the exposure of the smooth buttocks, in the end transported me into a hitherto unknown but very pleasant sensual state, as the rod did its appointed work on the stark-naked bottoms of my siblings.

From this moment, the word "rod" acquired a new ring in my ears, which stimulated my sex through the image forcibly conjured up in my mind of the rod as a punitive instrument associated with unbuttoned bloomers and fully bared buttocks, and which in this circumstance, besides inflicting the most terrible pains on the flogged backsides, also instilled an almost indescribable feeling of shame in the culpable girls. I became conscious of all these painful factors in my own soul and on my own bared bottom. Now for the first time it all became crystal clear to me. From this moment, my thoughts revolved more and more around the rod and naked buttocks, and were projected onto my college mates and other girls of my acquaintance. Do Ida or Else or Rigmor get birched? At home must they also unbutton their bloomers with hands trembling from shame and fear in order to expose the sweet, smooth hillocks of their bottoms to the merciless rod? How do their naked bottoms look? I tried to imagine the configuration of their backsides. And to assist my fancy, I used every opportunity to touch their bottoms – alas, only through their skirts – in order to ascertain whether the globes of their behinds were small or large, narrow or wide, firm or soft, arched or flat.

And at night in bed, I would relive all these tactile experiences in my fancy. I would play the role of the stern mother who unbuttons Ida's bloomers and who pitilessly exposes her bottom to view, despite her despairing entreaties and tears. My hands still preserved the feel of the spheres of their bottoms, which I had touched in the morning, and this fed my fancy more.

Thus, from my childhood on, the rod entrenched itself deeply in my psychic life as the central point of my sweetest dreams, as the climax of all that I anticipated in the way of bliss, and for me it has remained the peerless and truest form of eroticism. Every other pleasure in the world pales in comparison to the sweet birching of the naked bottoms of girls. And I am convinced that, no matter how old I grow, this sweet passion will constantly fill me with voluptuous bliss, and that I will eternally find this path to the gratification of my lust!

* * *

I looked for and found a job as a teacher in a government-operated reform school for college-age girls where today I am the directress.

You should know that this is a large institution. It has three sections, each of which comprises two teachers, a nurse, and thirty to thirty-five girl students. Ordinarily, students are accepted when they reach their twentieth year, and in exceptional cases, eighteen-year-olds are also admitted. Most remain in the institution until the age of twenty-two.

Our girls receive a good education, the aim of which is to train them for practical, useful stations in life. We instruct all our pupils up to the time they leave the orphanage. Every section is like a self-contained home and school. The institution is headed by a directress who is the highest authority. The orphanage consists of four villas forming a quadrangle, in the middle of which stands a large playground. The whole complex, further, is bordered by a park-like garden. I was engaged as a teacher here and in addition to helping the nurse. I had to work with another teacher in the section. Regulations are very strict, inasmuch as a high degree of discipline is absolutely necessary among so many students. On the day after my entry I learned from my colleague that in the event of an infraction of the rules, the girls were individually hauled before the directress for a birching; for instance, when they were caught lying, stealing, or being disobedient and naughty, and so on. If girls exhibit signs of sloth or indolence, or do not keep their things in order or themselves clean, they are likewise brought before the directress for punishment.

I asked my colleague: does the directress always punish the girls with the birch rod on their naked bottoms or does she employ other forms of punishment as well, and does she ever let a girl go without punishment? She answered me as follows: the directress punishes exclusively with the rod; the

Angela

rod is her "perogative" and it follows therefrom that punishment always involves a wholly exposed backside. There is only once chance in a hundred, indeed one in a thousand, that a girl up for punishment will escape a birching. Hence the desperation of the girls when they are brought before the directress. She herself will give you all the necessary information about the place as soon as possible. It is her practice, as soon as a new teacher enters upon her duties, to invite her to an orientation evening in her quarters, during which the details of the job and other general problems are discussed.

I was invited to tea by the directress on the very same evening. She discussed my duties as a teacher and as a supervisor of the children; she was greatly interested in seeing to it that the pupils received the best possible instruction. After we had gone over all the details of the daily instruction program, we came to the question of discipline. Here I pricked up my ears. At first the directress merely repeated what I had already heard from my colleague, but then she went on to discuss the different punishments that teachers were allowed to administer. She also enumerated the infractions for which a student was to be marched into her presence.

"And now," she continued in a tone of great solemnity, "it is my painful duty to explain what happens when they come before me. Since the founding of our reform school in 1851, according to regulations, corporal punishments for serious infractions have been administered solely by the directress, and the instrument of punishment has always been the birch rod. A visit to the directress, therefore, is always viewed by the pupil as a sign of the greatest reward and likewise of the severest punishment. Therefore you must know that if you lead a girl into my office, she will inevitably receive a birching. This is administered to her exposed bottom, after she has been ordered to unbutton her bloomers. A birch rod soaked in salt water is used. I always administer the punishments alone, without an assistant.

"After the teacher had registered her complaint with me, she leaves the office and the culprit remains. And now I shall show you how and where the punishments take place. My office is on the second floor, and adjoining is a small room which in the beginning was set up as a punishment area. Please come with me."

You can imagine my turmoil during these explanations. My heart beat wildly and I felt a violent throbbing "elsewhere," my vulva felt swollen. I felt dizzy and I was quite overcome by the waves of sensuality. Now, now for the first time I was to see with my own eyes the place where in this house what was for me the sweetest sensations in the world took place daily.

We climbed the stairs and entered the office. It is a spacious room with a huge window overlooking the garden. The room is furnished with a desk in front of the window, a round table in the centre of the room, several chairs, a sofa and two bookcases, a rug on the floor, and pictures on the wall. From this office a small door leads to the punishment chamber. It is very small and cramped, partially slanting under the roof. A skylight with six panes occupies this slanting part of the roof. The floor is covered with a thick rug, and a felt curtain hangs over the door! Below the window there is a sofa-like piece of upholstered furniture which in our language we call a "pouffe". Approximately in the middle of this item of furniture two leather straps are attached, whose function is obvious. A chair and a low closet in the corner complete the room's appointments.

The directress opened the closet and showed me her rods: a few small willow soap-rods and many birch rods in different sizes, which were being softened in a tall jug of salt water, so as to be in constant readiness to belabour a tender behind.

Upon returning to my room after this visit and once I was in bed, sultry thoughts began a wild dance in my brain. In my mind's eye I saw all the girls in my section, passing before me in review: who would be the first that I would have to haul before the directress? I longed for the moment when I could say to a girl: "Now, child, you will come with me to pay a little visit to the directress!"

Oh, beloved, heart's companion, you will understand what wonderful dreams such thoughts and representations gave me! In my fancy I immediately picked Marie, the most beautiful among the older girls, and on the way to the directress' office I slapped her face resoundingly, which intensified my excitement. Oh, if I could unbutton her bloomers myself! She broke into a violent fit of weeping, and trembling with fear over the punishment in the offing, she tearfully and vainly implored me to spare her the birching. Oh, if she only knew that the more desperately she begged, the more she excited me into a state of pitiless severity, the more I craved to see her naked bottom under the rod for an unendurable quarter of an hour, the more I want to cite her for punishment to the directress, doing the best to achieve the desired goal.

Ah, these joy-drenched dreams – unfortunately they were still only dreams! – but gradually they became so living, so exciting, so corporeal that

Angela

finally I saw Marie in the punishment chamber lying on the pouffe, her skirts raised high, her bloomers unbuttoned, her chemise held fast between the leather straps and her smooth bottom with the arched, still snow-white swelling buttocks posed, enticingly and invitingly, for a severe birching.

What excitement raged in my private parts, what a tickling I felt in my cleft, how stiffly my clitoris erected – I could not help myself, my hand sought for the locus of this ecstasy.... Marie, you won't get away.... your naked behind.... I wouldn't exchange your smooth bottom, squirming and twisting under the birching, for a kingdom.... Oh, how good it feels, Marie, your naked bottom. And the sharp, pitiless blows of the rod. Yes, go ahead and scream! It won't help you.

HELEN

It was decided between Vanessa and myself that we would deal with the girls separately and not in visible concord with one another. Thus both Helen and Susan would each be left free to think what they wished of us, and I had no doubt that such would be the nature of their experiences that they would be unlikely to indulge in confessions to one another until much time had passed.

I recognized in Helen—as did Vanessa—a stubborn case. Being just above medium height and with long flowing hair, she had such a figure as would rival the statuary of any of the Italian master sculptors. Her legs were long and superbly tapered, her breasts like full-grown melons and her bottom a perfect peach of delight, being so deeply cleft that its springy cheeks could ensnare a stiff prick firmly between them, once she was taught and tutored.

I intended to stable her—knowing that there was no other way to deal with her—though it took some persuading on my part to inveigle her to the stable at dusk, which I judged the best time for her initiation. Some bribery in other directions was requisite in the manner and I finally settled upon a farm worker of good aspect and sturdy loins who for a couple of sovereigns (and all the delight he was to have) would do as he was told.

"What is to do in the stable, then?" Helen asked me as we proceeded hence.

"There is a young filly who is restive. I thought between us that we might calm her and settle her," I replied glibly.

"Oh, I know little enough about horses," she made to say and would have turned back had I not insisted that someone must accompany me. Making further demur about the matter, she was nevertheless persuaded to. The stable at that hour had either a cozy aspect or a slightly forbidding one, according to one's thoughts at the time. Helen evidently having no heart for such a jaunt would have again turned back even as we approached the doors, saying pettishly, "Oh, I can hear nothing."

"There will soon be much to be heard," I rejoined truthfully enough and, taking her by the elbow, guided her within where my enlisted accomplice lay already in waiting. I do not doubt that she apprehended instinctively some danger then, but the very moment that the threshold was passed, her ensnarement was complete. To a wild cry from her, I pinioned her arms while the laborer, George, springing from the wall against which he had flattened himself, blindfolded her swiftly and then secured her held wrists with a strong binding of cord.

"Oh! what are you at? My God, what IS this?" shrieked Helen, being bundled now to a bale of straw which had been placed in readiness for her.

"Close the doors!" I snapped to George while bending Helen well forward so that her mouth was buried in the straw and her bottom reared well for our endeavours. Pressing down upon her shoulders, I then saw to it that George upped her skirt and wreathed it securely about her waist—all this to the wildest of cries from Helen who clearly had not even been uncovered to her drawers in the presence of a male before.

"You shame me! Oh, my God you will pay for this, you beasts, you beasts!" screeched she while George attended to the ties of her white cotton drawers. At their falling I shared his gasp of admiration, for never was a more desirable bottom unveiled—to say naught of the bewitching columns of her stocking-clad legs which supported her glorious moon. "I will die!" screamed she—her voice but partly muffled by the straw, and brought to a horrified halt as I accorded her a very sharp SMACK indeed on her bared bottom.

"Die, is it, Helen?" I laughed, "Why, my girl, your bottom is in full bloom to be unveiled and for what it is about to be accorded. I have no help for it than to put you to it in this way and will not regret it for a moment. Your dear Mama would have you inducted, my sweet, for there is no other path for you to pleasure than this. George—hand me that schooling whip!"

"AH! I dare you! Oh, you beast, your horrid beast, who is this awful man looking at my shame? I shall see you in prison if you whip me! Pull up my drawers—release me! Oh, help me, someone!"

"I am about to help you, my pet—I! Keep her shoulders well down, George, for the bale is at a perfect height for it."

And indeed it was, for with the upper part of her body laid across its top, Helen's long shapely legs were kept at full stretch and so her naked bottom with its alluring cleft and a peeping of dark cunt hairs beneath, was orbed to perfection.

"No, no, no, *no*!" came her wild shriek as I stepped slowly back and measured my distance. It would not be the first time I had used the schooling whip which requires a much-practiced twist of the wrist to make it most effective. I intended only using the very tip of course—as Helen discovered in a matter of a second or two as the scorching of it made itself feel like a bee-sting on her bulbous right cheek.

"Neeow!" came her shrilling cry, but I gave her no time to recover from it than I- had accorded the same salute to her left hemisphere. George—standing so close by her—was afeared, I think, that the long uncoiling whip would somehow catch him for he wore an expression of mingled apprehension and pleasure, yet he was in no danger whatever as soon enough he learned. I had judged my distance to the inch, as one must in such exercises and had given Helen only her preliminary. By moving just six inches closer I could so snarl the leaping whip that some six to eight inches would sear across her glorious bottom.

"STO-HO-OP it this MOMENT! Oh, my God, NO! Let me UP!" screamed she, all unaware of my insidious approach as I viewed the two pink spots which the first strikes had left and which other and more practiced damsels would have received as a distinct pleasure for they produce a positively sparkling fire. Helen, however, was to receive more than that, as she now discovered at the first real laying of the plaited leather across her writhing orb which brought a shriek such as might have lifted the rafters.

"You BEE-EE-EAST!" she sobbed. "Oh, you will kill me!"

"No, my pet, I mean to enliven you," I replied, remarking with my searching eyes the distinct protuberance which had made itself visible in George's

Helen

rough trousers. I had already made it my business, of course, to examine his penis in a goodly and upright condition and knew him fair for his intended task.

CRA-AAAAACK! Ah, what a satisfying sound a well-placed whip does make across a yielded bottom! It is to be remembered, of course, that I was still but giving her a small measure of it as regards length, for to have used the schooling whip in all its majesty would have been undoubtedly cruel. It might be said, of course, that by so indulging myself I was being cruel, but having years past taken the whip myself in such a fashion I knew full well how the cushioning effect of the female bottom absorbs the sting. True, its effect is felt for a moment or two as a fierce burning, but that diminishes very rapidly provided the required wrist action is used, for this causes the leather to skim the ardent female globe rather as a skier mounting a crest.

The cries and moans that emanated from Helen now as I proceeded swishing the long-reaching leather this way and that would have indicated that she was suffering the pangs of hell whereas—had she but known it—I was heating her up for the divine moments that were shortly to follow. As hot-eyed as any lusty male might have been as he held Helen pinned and observed the wild and salacious wriggling of her hips, George had already managed to unveil his long thick pego in anticipation of its entry.

Within a further minute and to diminishing cries from the over-proud young lady, I observed that her nether orb was already sufficiently well-streaked and reddened to require such cooling as only the male organ can render. Her sobs and wailings were piteous indeed, for now and again I gave her a particularly sharp one, sweeping the coiling whip right under her bottom so that she was forced to reach up on to her toes while her cries rippled and spread all about the stable walls.

"I can stand no more—no MORE!" she shrieked, raising her head briefly while George's strong hands bore down upon her shoulders.

"Very well, my dear, then the moment of your salvation is nigh. You know not who holds you—only his name. He is, however, furnished with as big a cock as you are likely to encounter in the next few weeks, and you are about to take it, my girl."

"I will not—I will not! How dare you whip me and then dishonour me! Oh, Mama, Mama, MAMA!"

"Were your dear Mama here, Helen," I said coldly, "she would wish you to comport yourself rather better than you are doing." So saying I dropped the whip and, signalling to George to hold her down as firmly as ever, stood immediately behind her and cupped her hot, wriggling globe as best I could in my palms. How silky and firm she was and how the cheeks throbbed! A gritting howl of course came from her which was rapidly choked-off by a firm SMACK that I immediately accorded her.

"Be QUIET, Helen!" I snapped above her mewings while her nubile hips endeavoured to swing her scorched derriere away from my encroaching palms. Nothing would avail her now, however. Resting my left hand upon her haunches—for the magnificence of her curves made them no less than that— I glided my other down and cupped the downy bulge of her nest which I found to be as moist as I had expected. "Put your hand over her mouth, George," I instructed, for I wanted no high screams at this particular juncture. Rubbing the heel of my hand suavely under the rolled lips of her quim and feeling the impending ooziness there, I withdrew it after a long, amorous moment and—wetting my forefinger in my mouth—I inserted first the tip within her bottom hole and moved it about a little.

Helen's response was to buck wildly, but this suited her purpose little and mine all the better, for one slight rearward movement of her proud, hot cheeks sufficed to lodge my finger in her to the first knuckle, whereat her thinly-pitched squeals sounded even through George's clamping fingers. Allowing her no leeway whatever, I then pressed my left hand into the small of her back and so in the main prevented the attempted squirming of her hips while working my digit back and forth until she received in slow in-and-out motion its entire length. Tight indeed she was in that narrow, silky channel, but this mainly by compression of her muscles which she would learn soon enough to relax.

"Missus—can I have her that way?" whispered George hoarsely, for country folk as I well know are given to a good deal of buggery in the seclusion of their cottages. It provides pleasure without unnecessary fruitions, so to speak, and many a young wench's rosy complexion and bold bottom is owed to this ancient game of Venus.

"No, you may not, for it is reserved. Withdraw your hand slowly from her mouth now while I keep my finger up her, for if she howls again or protests she will know the whip's snapping twice over again."

"HOOOO-AAAAAR!" came then from Helen in one long bubbling moan as her mouth was freed and my finger remained inexorably tight up her delectable rear. "Helen!" I uttered warningly, and at that she clawed feverishly into the straw and moaned, but otherwise made no further outcry. I saw some future for her then and slowly withdrew my digit while giving George the nod for which he had now long waited. Before Helen could properly sense our movements, I had quickly stepped to one side and he was upon her, his cock finding immediately its intended haven between her rolled lovelips. Simultaneously I seized the nape of her neck and to a long, wailing cry of apparent despair, Helen received in one slow, upward lunge the entirety of his throbbing man-root until the hot bulb of her bottom rested into his belly and his big balls nudged her well-nested quim.

"Take it OW-OW-OUT! Oh my God, he cannot—cannot—ARG H!"

Doughty stallion as he proved to be, George kept it a-throbbing full up her for a full minute the while that I had her secured. I knew this gesture to be of signal importance in the conquering of a proud young female, for her own inner nature would now in a short while overcome her scruples. Sobs resounded from her as George then at last began to ream her. His cock emerged glistening with her hapless juices at every long, plunging stroke which brought her nether cheeks to smack forcibly against his belly. I had counseled him in this also beforehand, for as relentless as I had been in my treatment of Helen yet I needed her now—and indeed wanted her now—to receive the full pleasure of his piston.

"No-ho-ho!" Helen continued to sob and endeavored to jerk her hips all about, though I saw this as a disguise for the pleasure she was absorbing. With my free hand then I began to stroke her long soft hair, murmuring to her that this was but her initiation and that unbounded joys would follow. Perceiving that I was now being tender with her, she began to sob in quite another fashion.

"Still your hips a little and let him rod you—come, dear—take the pleasure—what a fine cock he has, has he not—your future Papa's is of equal merit, as you will discover. Ah, you are panting now! Does it not stir you? Are you not on the very brink of coming, my pet?" So on and on I talked all softly to her, bending my lips to her ear and even running my tongue within which in moments of amourous play can produce a delightful sensation.

Softer whimpers broke from her then and indeed she stilled the otherwise incessant rolling around of her hips and began to breath softly if fretfully as the most succulent sounds emanated from the conjunction of their parts, by which of course I mean the juicy, sibilant noises that produce those tiny squelches which are the very music beloved surely by all devotees of amorous combat.

Helen's shoulders then began to quiver and her face hid itself in the quick cupping of her hands, for though her wrists were bound she was free to move her arms. Sensing her thus at a peak of pleasure as George's pego rammed back and forth, I deftly untied her bonds while he, rasping out a grunt and a groan, worked his charger in her to the full and commenced pumping his sperm in her, jet upon jet, to which she wriggled wildly and freely until all was done and the sodden member—still proudly thick and long— was withdrawn and dribbled its tribute in a snail's trail down her thigh. In her turn, Helen quivered and was still.

At that, I thrust my hand within the pocket of an apron I had earlier donned, fished out the coins of his earnings and, thrusting them into his eager hand, motioned him to make a retreat. Perhaps fearing retribution from Helen whose blindfold I then began to undo, he fled, buttoning up his trousers as he went. She, hearing this, rolled over and would have slipped to the rough ground had I not caught her.

"Oh, who was that? Who was it?" she moaned.

"One of no account, my sweet, but one whose manly cock has served you well. Why, your lovely nest is pulpy with his sperm," I murmured, cupping it fondly and drawing her lips so swiftly under mine that she was taken quite by surprise.

"Oh, how you whipped me—I hate you," she sobbed to my lips, but I was not fooled.

"Young women such as you desire to be taken thus, however hidden may be your thoughts, Helen. Think on it and you will know that to be true. You wish to be made to do what you feel is exceedingly naughty to do. Had I not whipped you, you would never have surrendered, and certainly not to Mr. Maudsley's prick, as now you will."

"Oh, what? I could not! Poor Mama! No, never!" Standing up quickly though on the shakiest of lovely limbs, she managed to repair the fallen state of her drawers while gazing at me with a mixture of wonder and resentment such as I had well expected.

"You will do as you must and as the path of fate ordains. This your Mama knows as well as I. Should he come to you in your bed, you will raise your nightgown to him and be dutiful."

"I will not, I will not, and you shall not whip me for it either!" sobbed she, though I no longer heard any deep sorrow in her cry. From being totally stubborn and proud she had unwittingly become half willing and knew not in her mind whether to move forwards or turn back to her former state.

Taking her hair at the back in a sudden grip and so drawing her lovely face under mine so that she winced, stumbled and was forced to clutch me, I seized her chin with my free hand and breathed upon her lips such promises of libertine pleasures as she had never thought to hear. To each she endeavored to shake her head, her eyes full wild, but my grip upon her was inexorable. Finally, I released her so suddenly that she fell back, which gave me a moment to retrieve the fallen whip and bring it smartly around the tops of her thighs. With a maddened shriek she leapt back.

"Into the house with you, Miss!" I thundered and at that she appeared to quail—or else saw thankful refuge there—and ran to the door, rubbing her thighs and I quick in her wake. It was by now dark and her stumbling figure preceded me across the paddock to where the lights of the mansion gleamed their yellow invitation. I had not finished with her yet, nor her hypocrisies.

She little knew, in any event, what awaited her within, which I shall write of in the pages of subsequent titles.

EMILY

At Tremaine Park, then, we found ourselves with our three charming girls. Much that happened you will readily guess! Yet I must detain you, if I may, with an account of the most remarkable afternoon's sport I ever knew.

These events took place after a very congenial lunch with Jack and several of his acquaintances among the local squires. I was walking towards the library when Emily approached me.

"Would you like me to do my dance for you, Captain Cooper?" she asked softly.

I was uncertain what she meant at first. Then she explained that Susan Ann, her governess, had been instructed by Jack to give her dancing lessons. He wanted Emily taught to perform an alluring harem-girl dance for the amusement of himself and his guests. There was to be such a lesson in half an hour—in the games room. Both Sue and Miss Catherine would be there to instruct her.

To please her, I agreed to come, not imagining the half of what would happen. By that time the rest of the party had gone out into the gardens and the fine old house seemed sunlit and deserted. I made my way to the games room, which was a small gymnasium with polished boards, parallel bars, and a climbing rope hanging from a crossbeam.

Sue wore her usual very tight trousers and boots. Miss Catherine was dressed in the same fashion, though without the boots, for both had been out on horseback that morning. There was no sign of their pupil, who was changing into her costume behind a screen. Miss Catherine, with her golden-skinned beauty and almond-eyed perversity, was with the girl as she dressed, for I could hear Car' say: "Where's the one you wore last time, then?"

It was a high lilting voice with a rather singsong quality. Miss Catherine would draw out her monosyllables in a long "Noooo!" or "Aaaaah!"

At last young Emily appeared before us. And what a sight she was! I had never doubted the appeal of her fair-skinned face with its firm features, the brown shoulder-length hair with its narrow fringe. What held my eyes now was her figure. She wore an imitated harem diadem, which sat in a helmet curve upon her head. Her pert young breasts were tightly cupped in a halter of green silk, secured by a band round her neck and another behind her back. Her young belly, taut and flat as a child's even now, was delightfully bare. From the waist to the knees she was encased in green silk knickers, which were both skintight and translucent.

Would you not have been stirred by the prospect of having a lascivious dance performed before you by so alluring a pupil? My gaze was drawn to the tilt of her pert young nose, the almost coquettish upward angle of her firm chin. Her brown eyes watched me tauntingly, her fine young teeth resting lightly on her lower lip in a teasing manner. Her neat fair-skinned young breasts were just visible through the taut silk of her halter, their nipples prettily outlined. Her arms were bare, of course, and so was her flat pale belly and the small of her back. Her graceful young legs were uncovered to the knee, above which the tight pale green silk of her translucent pants sheathed her to the waist. Her slim thighs had begun to assume their womanly shape. Indeed, from the front it was also possible to see through the tight silk of her pants the soft pubic moss in the triangle of her loins. It was a lighter brown than the head of her hair. As she turned, showing the rear of the tight silk pants, a childish tautness and a feminine allure were mingled in the shape of Emily's agile young seat.

The dancing lesson took the form of a game with rewards and penalties. Like any harem girl, Emily was to writhe her hips and belly to the music while her arms twined above her head. She was to squirm like a snake without moving her feet, standing on a mat about eighteen niches square.

Miss Catherine had conceived an original device to train the girl in lascivious writhing of her hips. From the beam overhead hung two cords, one just in front of Emily and the other just behind her, so close that they almost touched her. At the end of each cord—the front one level with the opening of her legs, the rear one touching the fullest curve of her behind—a china ball had been threaded. They appeared to be balls used for pool or billiards, drilled through for this purpose.

Emily must first squirm her thighs and hips to the time of Miss Catherine's tambourine, endeavoring to catch and hold the china ball in front of her between her legs—without using her hands, of course. Holding this pleasurable object between her thighs, she must then give all her attention to the ball behind her, rolling her young bottom in such a manner as to catch the second little globe between her cheeks. Her reward was to be a pretty Spanish fan which she had seen in a curio shop. She must continue her dance until both china balls were safely entrapped. Yet after quarter of an hour—if it took her so long—the penalties would begin. I had no idea what they might be, except that they were not severe enough to cause her any real alarm. As a final test, the two china balls were dipped into a bowl of soap solution, which Miss Catherine carried, in order to make them more elusive.

Emily stood upon the mat, her arms raised, twining and embracing each other above her head in the manner of a dancing girl. Miss Catherine began to beat on the tambourine, slow and hard at first. Emily jutted her hips side to side as she imagined a harem girl would do. There was hardly a crease on her flat pale belly as she did this, so firm and smooth it was. The cold china ball ran across her stomach and she gave a shivery little laugh at its chill.

Sue and I sat about six feet in front of her, watching, Emily shook the short slanting fringe of her brown hair clear, where it was tickling her. She opened her thighs a little and leant back slightly. The pretty little lips of her cunt and her neat clitoris were outlined by the tight silk of her pants. The china ball touched her there and she drew breath sharply. As she closed her thighs and the soapy china globe slipped out, she gave a little wail of disappointment.

"Five minutes gone, Emily," said Sue quietly.

I was glad to hear this for I was curious to see her incur whatever playful penalties were imposed. Emily arched her sweet little belly button out towards us and writhed her silk-sheathed thighs together as she tried to coax the ball between them. When she opened her legs, the ball oscillated against

Emily

her tight-clad vaginal lips. When she closed upon it, the soapy china surface slipped free again. As the ball dangled between and then escaped the tightening thighs, the girl writhed her legs together in a rhythm of touch-and-squeeze, touch-and-squeeze.

"Oh, I can't! I can't!" she wailed helplessly.

"Seven minutes gone, Emily," said Sue presently. At these words a devilish smile lit Miss Catherine's almond eyes and her sharp features. Perhaps it was this which spurred Emily on. The china ball swung between her legs and came to rest against her inner thigh. With a gasp she managed to close the other leg upon it and this time to hold it fast. She dared not of course open her legs again while catching the second ball. Yet half her task was now accomplished.

Sue and I moved round to watch her from the rear, Emily looking back over her shoulder. Her young bottom, visible through the tight green silk, was rounded out towards us with the most charming innocence. It was the cord of the first billiard ball which she held firmly between her thighs now, the ball itself peeping out of their rear opening.

So Emily's smooth adolescent backside arched and writhed in its turn. Soon she was warned that eleven, and then twelve minutes had gone. She squirmed her rump from side to side but the second china ball would simply roll over one rear cheek and off into the air.

The problem was that at her age Emily's adolescent bottom-cleft was not very deep, her buttocks not being as fully fleshed as they would be in her womanly maturity. She bent forward to open it wide, yet as she did so her stretched silk knickers presented a tight smooth surface and the ball ran off easily.

"Thirteen minutes gone, Emily!"

Miss Catherine picked up a canvas gymnastic shoe with a hard rubber heel. Emily was gasping from her efforts. A light sheen of perspiration gleamed on her belly and the small of her back. Suddenly the youngster took the little bowl of liquid soap. She looked down over her shoulder and slowly tipped the thick liquid over the seat of her pants, spreading it with her other hand. By doing this, Emily's wet knickers clung to her bottom and its crack like a second skin. The disadvantage was that they were now shining with a wet slipperiness to match the china ball itself!

Does not this little incident show her bewitching innocence? It was done with such naturalness that one wanted to hug and kiss her for it. Can you imagine a woman of twenty-five or even a proud beauty of eighteen soaping the seat of the knickers she wore to amuse her lover? Emily looked adorably naughty when she had done it, her teeth set teasingly on her lower lip as she glanced back at us. The slippery wet silk of her pants clung in silhouette to the cheek-swellings of her young behind.

Would you not like to catch her in such a state? To say with a smile, "You wicked, wicked girl, Emily!" Would you not take her to your room and, with gentle scolding, assist the changing of her knickers with your own hands?

Now she danced with redoubled energy but the ball slipped easily away on the soapy silk.

"Fourteen minutes gone, Emily!"

There was but one remedy. Emily took the waist band of her pants and pulled them down, jiggling her legs free one by one. She was allowed to remove and replace the first china ball already trapped between her thighs.

Prepared once more, she arched out her posterior in a lascivious yet wholly innocent tango. If I wax lyrical, I plead that this was my first sight of the firm pale resilience of pretty Emily's bare bottom. Her seat was no longer a child's though she lacked a woman's maturity and reserve. So there was a delicious and shame-free vulgarity in her arse movements. Emily rounded and rolled those hind-cheeks, which stern moralists would yearn to chastise and lechers would press apart for the tight entrance between them. The soapy ball rolled off her wet buttocks again.

"Fifteen minutes, Emily!"

Miss Catherine took her place. The first syllable of the gym-shoe heel spoke loudly on one cheek of Emily's backside. The penalty! This was the new rhythm of the dance. It was lightly done, though Emily gasped at the sting of it. Unlike a proud beauty of nineteen or twenty, she was a true sport who accepted the rules of the game.

I will confess that my prick stiffened at the sight of Emily's bottom-cheeks being tanned by the gym-shoe heel, wielded by a trim golden-skinned beauty. Car' went to the chastisement eagerly. The hard smack of rubber sounded about every five seconds. A minute passed. Longer. Emily, in a desperate surge of her bottom, caught and held the cord between its bare cheeks. This time she slid her arse down the cord until the china ball itself was safely trapped.

"Seventeen minutes!" said Sue.

They all laughed and both young women embraced Emily affectionately. Then Sue and Miss Catherine remembered some business in the stable block. They went out, leaving me sitting on my chair with Emily before me.

Emily

She now wore only her breast halter and diadem.

"Did you like my dance?" she asked breathlessly.

I assured her that I did. To my surprise, she put herself face down across my knee, trying at the same time to look down her back towards her seat.

"Am I in an awful state behind?" She giggled at the thought.

The cheeks of her young bottom were strawberry red from the tanning. Because they had been soapy wet, the gym-shoe heel had marked them with muddy prints. Wet soap glistened between her buttocks and on a single sweet hair near Emily's anus.

"Ouch!" she said suddenly. "What was that?"

"You have a hair growing in a place where young ladies ought not to have them."

I took my handkerchief and wiped her over until nothing remained but the perfume of the soap.

"Did you like seeing Car' tan me?" Emily asked with her usual direct innocence.

"Yes," I said, knowing that a lie would not deceive her.

"I was caned at college last year, when I was eighteen," she said. "The headmaster made me bend over his desk with my bottom bare. He gave me twelve strokes, with matron standing there and holding the smelling salts." She turned her young face to me, innocent and coquettish at the same time. "Would you have liked to see me caned then?"

I looked down at the taut pale cheeks of Emily's bottom with their first shape of womanhood appearing.

"Yes, I would, Emily," I said quietly, "very much."

"I cried like anything," she said, as if boasting, "and he left a stripe across my sit-upon with every stroke! Do men really like to watch that happening to a girl?"

"I'm afraid most of them do, Emily."

The answer seemed to satisfy her for a moment. Then the incorrigible little imp said, "If you'd been my headmaster, perhaps I shouldn't have minded it so much."

I folded my silk handkerchief and very tenderly mopped the lather of her exertions from between her thighs. She tolerated this for a while with growing impatience, then slid from my lap and knelt before me.

"You'd like to have seen me getting it at school," she said firmly. "So you can't mind if I look at you!"

I thought she was referring to my love with Susan Ann in the Albany. How wrong I was! Before I could protest she had unbuttoned me with great nimbleness and taken my member in her hand. She examined it curiously, then lightly kissed its knob. Small wonder that it grew stiff and sinewy in a trice! For a moment she played with it inexpertly—rather for her own satisfaction than for mine. Then, as if it were the most natural thing in the world, she slid her warm lips over it, enclosing it upon her moist and agile tongue.

With one part of my mind I was appalled at the outrageous act in which I was suddenly a partner. With the rest, I was aware of Emily's hands pulling me down to her. What you will think of me, I dare not ask, but presently I lay there on the floor with her. We were head to tail, she with the tool in her mouth, I with my head pillowed on her firm young thigh. With one of her legs drawn up a little, she presented me with a full-spread prospect of her thighs and backside.

I stroked her lightly for some moments. At length I could not resist my confession.

"I wish I'd been your headmaster, Emily," I murmured, caressing her. "You'd have spent a long time in the study, being spanked with your knickers down."

She drew her mouth free for a moment.

"I think that's mean!" she said with teasing reproach. "You'd have made me do this to you and then tanned me for it!"

"Perhaps I would have done, Emily."

Her lips and tongue drew harder upon me. I kissed her sweet virgin pouch and tickled its depths with my tongue. This exercise muffled my words of passion to sighs and murmurs. Emily gave a questioning little moan without ceasing to suck. She followed this with a timid, trembling little cry at the intensity of feeling which began to overwhelm her. My own excitement was burgeoning now and I lipped or tongued every inch of the private anatomy she offered me. Her own tongue worked hard and irresistibly upon the vent of my prick until the lust spurted from me. As if to prove what a sophisticated young lady she had now become, Emily swallowed as though it were the elixir of life.

We lay silent, except for our long-drawn breaths. The call of birds and the smell of mown grass came from the sunlit world outside. A warm scent of ancient timber and dressed stone filled the house. What was I to do.

"Emily," I said softly and at length, "you must forget what has happened.

Emily

I was wrong to permit it. The proper time will come for you in a year or two. Promise me to be a good girl till then."

There was a long pause. She sat up and looked at me frankly.

"I'll promise," she said gently, "but only if you promise me something in return."

"What's that, Emily?"

"That you won't love any other girl until I'm ready for you. You're my lover now, aren't you?"

Then, without waiting for a reply, she skipped up and away behind the screen beyond my reach. I smiled, watching her in amusement and admiration.

"We'll see, Emily," I thought to myself. "We shall see."

SARAH & HILLARY

When I reached home I tried to analyze my feelings and realize what had happened. I could barely believe it was true. It seemed like an impossible dream. Here was I just down from Oxford, aged twenty-three, submitting to be whipped like a naughty boy on my bare bottom by a woman whom I had only met once, and in the presence of another girl whom I had never seen before I called on her mistress. More than that, I had poked and "kissed" the mistress and had been "kissed" by both mistress and maid. Still more, neither woman was a whore in the usually accepted sense of the word. The one was accepted as chaperon for the cousin of my best pal and evidently mixed in quite good society. The maid to all appearance was eminently respectable. No. I couldn't believe my own experience. It was only when I sat down to think things out that my sore bottom brought the truth palpably home to me. I jumped up with a cry and rushed upstairs to my bedroom, locked the door, and in a twinkling had my trousers down and was investigating my bottom in the looking-glass. Gad I but I was marked. Long lines of purple and red crisscross all over both cheeks, with here and there a spot of bright red where the buds on the birch had broken the skin. I got some ointment which I used for soreness after rowing and gave myself a liberal dose. Then I washed John Thomas, who was looking thoroughly ashamed of himself, dressed myself and went downstairs.

My feelings were difficult to analyze. Shame, anger, and a wish for revenge fought with each other. At the same time Sarah's charms were ever before me, and at moments John Thomas made gallant attempts to persuade me that the afternoon was worth everything. Hillary's bottom also rose before my eyes white and plump and round, quivering under the blows of the birch, opening and shutting between the strokes and showing glimpses of the dark pouting lips of her pussy—that pussy which I had felt and found so responsive to my fingers.

What were her last words? "I should love you to whip me." By Gad, I thought, why not? Surely it was worth risking another whipping myself to get the chance of making those lovely cheeks flinch and squirm. And then Sarah! What a gorgeous poke. How her tongue had caressed my old man. How her pussy had drawn every bit of life from me I Yes, undoubtedly I must call again.

So I argued that night. But next morning doubt and nervousness came over me again, and eventually it was quite a week before I rang the bell again at the little house in South Molton Street.

Hillary opened the door and smiled when she saw me. "Madame was wondering why you had not called," she said. "She is rather angry with you, sir, in consequence, I fancy," she added with a meaning look. "She does not like to be neglected. But she is not at home now."

"Can I come in and wait?"

"Oh, yes, sir, if you like."

So I went in and shut the door. She led me into the little morning-room and for r. moment we looked at each other. Then without any delay or expla-nation, we seemed to fall into each other's arms, our tongues met, and our right hands dived straight between each other's legs. John Thomas rose at once and I found Hillary's soft little pussy already dribbling with expectation. I urged her gently back to an armchair and, kneeling before her, placed John Thomas in the haven where he would be. Her bottom lifted itself to meet him and we came together in a mutual flood of love.

"Tell me, Hillary," I said when we had finished, "does Sarah whip you often?"

"As often as she gets the chance," she said with a wry little smile.

"But why do you submit," I said, "and how did it begin? It isn't usual for maids to be whipped."

"I'll tell you someday," she answered. "It's too long a story for now. Besides, she's very good to me and I get more pleasure with her than I should anywhere else."

She cuddled close to me and fondled John Thomas, who evidently enjoyed it.

"You said something to me as I was going away last time that puzzled me," I said after a minute.

She blushed a little.

"Come," I said, "do you really like being whipped?"

"Don't you?"

"No, I'm damned if I do," I answered with a laugh.

"Oh, you will in time. I don't always. There are different sorts of whippings. I didn't like being whipped the other day by Sarah in front of you, for she was wicked and jealous. But you, when I whipped you, didn't you like it? Wasn't it different to the whipping Sarah had given you?"

"Yes," I said reflectively, "it certainly was different."

"Well," she went on, "if I like a person I *do* like him or her and want to do all and everything to please. With Sarah, for instance, when she's nice and wants me"—she blushed a little as she said this—"I'm willing to submit to anything. I know she wants to see my nakedness and watch my bottom wriggle, so I do all I can to gratify her, but when she's angry and only wants to punish me, I hate her and want to hurt her."

"Haven't *you* ever whipped her?"

"Good Lord no! That's not her game, she's no Masochist. I only wish she were and I had the chance. I'd pay her back. But she's much too strong for me, and besides, I'm different, I don't like giving pain and she does. It's only when I'm angry with her."

"Hmm," I said.

"What are you thinking of?"

"I was thinking, well, I don't know much about this matter, but I know this. I'd love to get my own back for my last call here. Now you and I together, eh? Couldn't we master her?"

Her eyes gleamed, then dropped. "She'd kill me," she said.

"Oh no. I'd see she did not do that. I'd make her promise to bear no malice and I don't think she would. If she did, I'd see you came out all right. The worst she could do would be to turn you out, and then you could come to me. I am looking for a flat to settle down in and should want a housekeeper, eh?"

"Oh, that would be lovely," she replied.

"But you haven't answered my question. Would you really like me to whip you?"

"Try," was all she answered. And before I knew what she was doing she had slipped off the chair and pulled up her skirt and petticoat above her waist behind, showing her dainty drawers.

"Sit down there," she said, pointing to the chair she had just left.

I obeyed her. She then laid herself across my knees, face downwards with her head towards my left arm, and pulled her drawers open behind, showing the beautiful curves of her bottom, the cheeks of which stood out like two lovely white moons, though still slightly marked from last week's whipping.

"Now smack me and see if I like it."

I gazed at the snowy globes with the shady valley between. Just at the meeting of her legs a few tendrils of dark hair showed themselves, promising other, more secret delights.

I smacked her lightly with my hand. It was more of a caress than a blow. She lay still.

Smack-smack-smack, and my fingers crept between her legs.

"No, not yet," she said, "I want you to smack me."

I humored her and I smacked both cheeks quickly till they began to grow pink.

"Harder, harder!"

I smacked more severely. Her bottom became appreciably warmer.

"Harder still," she said, "harder!"

I did as she said, and my own hand began to tingle. The joy and lust of domination began to grow in me.

After one or two really hard blows, she shifted slightly and heaved her bottom, opening her legs a little.

I gave her several harder smacks. She sighed and wriggled. I stopped.

"Go on," she said at once.

"But I'm hurting you."

"I want you to hurt me," she murmured fiercely. "I want you to hurt my bottom. Can't you see it growing red and hot? Hurt me, hurt me."

Her passion, though I didn't really understand it, fired me, and I took her at her word. Blow after blow fell on her plump cheeks and at length her sighs came quicker and quicker and became more like gasps. Her bottom heaved and opened and contracted, her legs parted and I could see the lips of her pussy parting and closing again as if eager for satisfaction.

Desire now took full possession of me and I smacked her as hard as I could, seizing every opportunity of making my hand reach the more hidden and secret retreats. It was a strange and maddening delight to me. After two or three blows on her firm bottom I felt my fingers strike the softer lips of her pussy. Once or twice I managed to reach that delightful spot with my finger tips while my palm just managed to get between the plump cheeks. This seemed to madden her as much as it did me. She flung her legs apart, pushing up her bottom, keeping it as wide open as possible. She muttered inarticulate cries, and at last after several blows which hit both marks full, she sank down heavily on my knees, imprisoning my hand between her thighs, which closed on my fingers like a vice. I felt her pussy throb and throb again and then a warm flood spread all over my hand.

I raised her up and held her close in my arms. "You darling," she murmured, "take me, I am yours utterly."

Her hands slid down and with feverish haste unbuttoned my trousers.

John Thomas, as was only to be expected, was rampant.

"Give him to me," she half-sobbed.

"How would you like him?" I asked with interest, for I had not forgotten how she had asked to be allowed to wash it in her own way.

"Any way, so long as he is in me… in front, behind, any way, I don't care. I'm yours, all of me. Take all of me, darling, my master I" and she threw herself at my feet, embracing my legs, half-sobbing and writhing with unappeased passion.

I lifted her up to her knees and she seized my affair with her lips and, flinging her arms round my bottom, began to lick and suck it with avidity. "Oh, so that's the way you entertain my guests in my absence, is it?" I turned hastily. There stood Sarah. She had evidently just come in. Her latch-key was still in her hand. She was holding the door open.

* * *

Hillary collapsed on the floor with a cry of terror. I stood stock-still like a fool.

Certainly I must have presented a ridiculous figure, trousers unbuttoned, a rampant engine well exposed. "Get up, you," said Sarah to Hillary, going to her and touching her with her foot. "You," turning to me, "can either go or stay, but if you stay…" She paused ominously.

"I'll stay," I said, for I had an idea.

"As you please. I see I have arrived in time," looking at my open trousers. "So you can… but… I rather think you will be sorry."

She led the way upstairs, and I found myself again in the boudoir.

Hillary was already there, shaking with nervousness. "Where are the cases?" thundered Sarah at her. "Did you think I had you up here to talk to you?" and she suddenly gave her two swinging boxes on the ears.

The poor girl hurried out of the room.

"Sarah," I urged, "don't be too cruel to her. It was my fault chiefly."

"Don't you fret yourself, my man, *you'll get all you want.*"

Hillary reappeared carrying the leather case which I recognized.

"Both cases, you fool," said her mistress.

Hillary gave an even more terrified cry than before, but did not dare to argue.

She went out and came back with another, similar case.

Sarah unlocked the first. "Undress yourself," she said; then to me: "And you tie her hands with this," giving me a long piece of webbing. "I must take my corsets off or I shan't have freedom enough for my arm."

Hillary tremblingly undid her skirt and let it fall, and waited.

"Everything," said her mistress, "didn't you hear? Everything, or it will be the worse for you." Hillary then undid her blouse and took it off. A dainty camisole appeared. That was removed. Then the petticoat. Then the little corsets were undone and she stood simply in chemise and drawers, the lace frills of the latter peeping alluringly below the hem of the chemise. Her trembling hands groped under the chemise, she pulled the string and the frilly little legs fell round her ankles. She stepped out of them and stood waiting.

"I thought I said everything!"

A crimson flood invaded the poor girl's cheeks and neck.

"You needn't pretend to such modesty," sneered Sarah. "A girl who will kneel down to kiss a man in a sitting-room needn't be shy of stripping naked before him in a boudoir, especially when there is another woman to protect her."

Hillary lifted the chemise and began to pull it over her head. I saw first her thighs appear, beautifully shaped and molded like towers of ivory, then the dainty little bush, still dewy with our mingled love; next a sweet rounded little belly, smooth and firm. I noticed the dainty waist line and, above, two perfect pear-shaped breasts with bright red nipples standing out firm and bold, though all support had been removed. As she raised her arms above her head, I saw the silky hair in her armpits, matching the thicker curls of her bush.

Then the chemise slipped off her wrists and she stood a slight timid figure, perfect, desirable and appealing.

I heard a sigh of appreciation from Sarah. "Now tie her wrists together," she said to me.

I had to obey. She watched me as I fumbled with the webbing.

"Now stretch her on the couch."

I bent her down as she had been bent down the other afternoon.

"No, not that way. She must be crucified."

"Madame," stammered Hillary.

"Silence," hissed Sarah as she placed some cushions across the middle of the couch, forming a ridge.

She then dragged Hillary to the couch and flung her face downwards so that the lower part of her belly and the top of her thighs rested right on the cushions. This naturally raised her bottom and thighs, making her body form a very broad inverted V.

"But what's the meaning of this?" she said as she saw the cheeks of the poor bottom still blushing slightly from my recent smacking. "Do you mean to say you've dared?" she went on, turning to me. "Oh, you, just wait."

She said no more but took hold of Hillary's right ankle and pulled the leg towards the edge of the couch. Then, stooping down, she caught hold of a silk cord that was fixed to the side of the couch, evidently for that purpose. It had a running loop at the end. This she slipped over the girl's foot and drew it tight. She then pulled the other leg as far apart as possible and fixed that in the same way.

Poor Hillary was now perfectly spread-eagled. Her arms were above her head tied at the wrists, her head was buried in the couch. Her bottom was raised, as I have said, by the ridge of cushions and seemed to invite the lash, and her wide-opened thighs revealed the mossy lips of her pussy, still slightly open. There she lay, a piteous little figure, all white.

The only contrast was her dark hair, slight silky tendrils in her armpits, the suggestive shadow between the cheeks of her bottom, the soft curls between her legs, and last of all, showing up vividly against the whiteness of her skin, her long black silk stockings, just a study in black and white, no touch of color anywhere, for she wore black garters. I feasted my eyes on the lovely vision. How could anyone, I wondered, hurt such a dainty graceful creature?

I looked at Sarah. Her eyes showed clearly that she was by no means insensible to the alluring picture. But there was a gleam of fierceness as well as admiration in her glance.

"Now," she said suddenly, "I must get rid of my corsets. I shan't be long. You can admire the dainty darling's white skin while I'm gone. There won't be much white left after I've finished with her," and she went quickly into her bedroom, leaving the door open.

Now, I had decided to stay in the hopes of carrying out my scheme of vengeance on Sarah, and I had no intention of assisting at the punishment of Hillary. But when I saw the preparations and how helpless Hillary was rendered by her bonds, I began to doubt the possibility of succeeding in my object. Though no doubt I could have mastered Sarah by brute strength, there would probably have been a struggle, and Hillary's help would have been of the greatest use. All the time Sarah was pinioning Hillary my mind was working quickly, but I hesitated to make any attempt to seize her, preferring to wait until the last moment.

Now, however, that she was out of the way I saw my chance. Quick as thought I sprang to Hillary's wrists and began to loosen the knots. She raised her head, gave a little cry of surprise and fear. I put one hand on her mouth and whispered, "Keep quiet and pretend to be still tied. Remember what I said downstairs. Now is our chance. Keep your hands just as they are, till I tell you. Then free your feet and help me."

I had only just time to loosen the knots and replace the webbing so that it still looked tight, and to get away from the couch, when Sarah appeared. She had put on the tea-gown again, with the loose sleeves. I was standing by the table when she came in, looking at the open case which contained the birches. There were four different sizes.

"Looking at my little ticklers?" she smiled. There are some more in here," and she opened the other case.

Then I understood Hillary's cry of alarm when Sarah told her that she wanted both cases.

There were no birches in this one. Two or three canes of varying thicknesses, a couple of old-fashioned ladies' riding whips—not the modern hunting crop, but whips of long flexible whalebone with lashes at the end—a whip of seven knotted cords, very fine, but looking very wicked, and last of all a sort of birch made of wire, the ends of which were bent at right angles.

"Pretty, aren't they?" said Sarah, laughing. "They'll come in later. We'll begin with this."

She turned to the other case and selected a long pliant birch, weighing it in her hand and swishing it in the air.

Now was my opportunity. As she turned from me to the couch and the prone girl waiting, I suddenly flung my arms around her, pinioning both arms tightly to her side.

* * *

She was completely taken by surprise. She had scarcely time to gasp out an exclamation of anger. "Hillary," I cried as she struggled violently in my arms.

Hillary quickly got her wrists free and, reaching down, got her ankles from the loops. Then she ran to me as I was holding the squirming, kicking Sarah.

The latter was like an eel. She kicked, she bit, or tried to, but my arms were tight round her middle, and as she had taken off her corsets, my grip crushed her ribs and gradually winded her.

Hillary, avoiding with difficulty the kicking legs, managed to get the band of webbing round first one wrist and then the other and draw it tight. My grip had not relaxed and in a comparatively short time Madame Sarah's wrists were bound together.

She still grasped the birch and all the time was pouring out indignant and angry expostulations. There was no trace of fear, however, as yet. Pride, rage, and hate showed in every glance and tone.

When Hillary had finally and satisfactorily tied her hands, I dragged Sarah to the couch and pushed her onto it. She sat and glared at me, out of breath and exhausted.

Her tea-gown had come unfastened at the waist and fell apart. Except for her stockings and shoes, she was absolutely naked. She evidently had intended to have a perfect field day. Well, she should not be disappointed.

I turned to Hillary with a smile: "Well, what shall we do to her? How shall we begin? You know more about these things than I do."

"Spank her first; the hand will prepare her bottom nicely for the birch," said she. "Shall I hold her down for you?"

"No," I said, "I'll hold her and you can begin. Come along, Sarah dear. This is a little different from what you intended, isn't it? It will be a new experience for you, eh? Will you turn over of your own accord or shall I help you?"

She made no answer, so I went to her and took her by the wrists. She dragged her hands away and suddenly, bending down, seized one of my hands with her teeth and bit it hard.

"You little devil," I shouted, "you shall pay for that," and I brought my other hand heavily down on her ear and cheek. The force of the blow knocked her head on one side and made her release my hand. With a quick twist I turned her over and held her face down on the couch, her legs hanging over the side. Hillary stood at one side of her and, dodging the kicking, plunging legs, proceeded to deliver a shower of smart smacks on the plump cheeks and thighs.

The blows fell at random, here, there, and everywhere, with no direction and without much real effect, as Sarah was dodging too much.

After a minute or so Hillary stopped and looked at her palm.

"It's hurting me more than her," she laughed, "we'd better begin seriously. Put her as she put me."

I pulled Sarah further onto the couch and managed to get her belly and thighs over the ridge of cushions, and then leant heavily on her back, while Hillary with great difficulty secured one leg in the silk loop.

All this time Sarah was struggling and shouting: "I won't be tied down, I won't be whipped. Don't you dare to touch me, or I'll pay you for this afterwards."

I took no notice, but when her legs were firmly secured, I pulled the tea-gown up over her shoulders as far as I could and said, "Yes, it's a little different to what you intended, isn't it? Instead of you feasting your eyes on our naked bodies and enjoying the sight of our bottoms reddening and writhing under your blows, it's your nakedness we are going to look at, it's *your* bottom and thighs that are going to blush and quiver. Are you looking forward to the treat? Come, answer me."

"I'll kill you," she hissed.

"Oh, no you won't, you're going to beg my pardon, to beg both our pardons, in fact, and thank us for showing you your proper place. Now Hillary, will you begin? I'll enjoy the scene for the moment."

I kept my left hand pressed on her back and with my right I stroked the beautiful loins and bottom and thighs, which lay bare to my touch. If Hillary had made an alluring picture with her dark hair and clear white skin, her mistress easily rivaled her. She was a little the plumper of the two and fairer, and whereas Hillary's coloring was pale, Sarah's skin was flushed slightly with pink. Their two bodies made a delightful contrast.

The idea struck me of comparing them, and when Hillary came back with a birch I asked her to lie beside her mistress for a moment so that I might see both their naked bodies together. She obeyed at once, and I reveled in the lovely vision. So lovely was it that I could not resist the temptation but took out my old man and was about to make good use of the favorable position of the two girls. But when Hillary saw what I was about, she stopped me.

"That will come later; business first," and she got up and stood by the couch, raising the birch in the air.

"Now madam," she said, "just a little gentle correction for your impudent bottom. How do you like it?" as the twigs fell right across the left cheek. "You are so generous with it to others, you ought to be grateful. Is it nice? nice, eh? Oh, you're sulky, are you, you won't speak, won't you, we'll see about that. Answer me at once, will you? at once—at once." The blows fell quicker and quicker, but Sarah made no sound. She lay practically motionless with her head buried in the couch. Her flesh flinched each time the blows fell across her bottom, but she made no cry or any sound.

"Still obstinate," said Hillary, "we won't allow that and must persevere." She came round to the other side and proceeded to visit the other cheek. Then she went lower and cut across the thighs, but though Sarah's contortions grew more convulsive, she still kept silent, until at last one blow of the birch curled right between her legs and a stifled cry of pain escaped her lips.

"Ah, I thought I should succeed before long," said Hillary, as she rested for a moment. "Will you begin now, sir?"

I took the birch, or what was left of it, for the twigs had broken off at every stroke.

What a change now in Sarah's bottom. No longer was the skin clear and pink and white. An angry red flush covered the centre of both cheeks, from which ran lines of red and violet which disappeared round the legs and cheeks towards the hips.

"Now Sarah," I said, "Hillary has finished for the moment. It is my turn now. I am going to give you a lesson in behavior towards your guests. How do you like that, and that," as the swift strokes fell. "Will you answer me?" I went on, as she still remained dumb, and the blows redoubled.

"There 1" said Hillary, pointing with her finger between the cheeks of Sarah's bottom and the legs stretched wide open. "That will make her speak."

I followed her advice and gave three crashing blows that cut and curled along the inside of her thighs and reached the hidden lips of her pussy.

It evidently proved effective. Shriek after shriek came from Sarah as she twisted and writhed.

"Not there, let me go," she cried. "Oh, oh, oh. No, don't, don't, no more," as the blows fell again.

Hysterical sobs shook her whole body. I stopped whipping her and said, "Ah, you've found your voice have you? Well, are you going to behave better in the future?"

"Oh, yes, yes!"

"And do you like being whipped," I went on, "and is it as nice as whipping others? Do you like showing your nakedness and your bottom to Hillary and me?"

She only sobbed in reply and I thought she was punished enough and was going to release her when Hillary noticed what I was doing and stopped me.

"No, no, not yet, she hasn't had nearly enough. Don't you remember, she said I was to be crucified? Well, I know what that means, I've had some." She went to the other case and brought out the two riding whips and a couple of canes and gave me one of each. I dropped the stump of the birch and waited.

"Now madam," she said, "you've shown me more than once what you call crucifixion. I hope I shan't forget your teaching. Let me see. This comes first, doesn't it?" and she brought the cane heavily across both cheeks of the quivering bottom.

A shriek of pain from Sarah. She raised herself up and twisted herself to one side to avoid the blow. I had left her when I had finished birching her, so that she could move freely, except that her hands and feet were tied.

"By Jove, that seems to touch the spot," I said, "how do you like that, dear? It seems a little more effective than the birch. What does it feel like? Come, tell me."

Sarah only groaned and writhed convulsively.

"Come, answer me, or can't you quite tell from one cut? Does that make it clearer to you?" and I brought the cane heavily down about half an inch below the livid weal left from Hillary's blow.

A positive howl of anguish came from Sarah.

She raised her body and twisted about as if she was on fire.

"You mustn't move about like that. Not only are you making a most indecent exhibition of yourself but you are doing no good. Come, what is it like? Is it nicer than the birch or do you miss the tingling twigs?"

Still no reply, but sobs and moans. I grew impatient. "*Will* you answer?" and I made the cane whistle through the air, but didn't touch her with it. Her bottom shuddered with apprehension.

"Oh, it's awful," she gasped, "it's like a bar of hot iron burning into my flesh."

"Ah, well, you're going to have quite a lot of those hot bars. In fact, your bottom will be quite a gridiron before we've finished with it."

"Yes, but she mustn't plunge about like that," said Hillary, "or we shan't be able to get a pretty pattern on her bottom and thighs. She likes pretty patterns, I know, for she has often shown me the designs she has traced on me after she has finished. There's nothing like neatness and finish for any work. If a thing is worth doing, it's worth doing well. That's what you often say, isn't it, madam?" she sneered.

Sarah didn't answer.

"Ah, she's lost her voice; we'll find it for her in a minute. Will you help me, sir?" She seized her mistress' wrists: "There should be a cord here. As you say, sir, there is no use in countenancing any more indecent exposure than is necessary."

She found a cord at the head of the couch similar to those that fastened Sarah's ankles. She fastened it to the webbing round the wrists and drew it tight. Then she took up the cane again and went back to her former position.

"Will you, please, stand opposite me, sir, and take your time from me? Don't hurry and be careful how you place your blows. There should be room for a dozen a side, I should think."

She measured carefully with her fingers the distance from the dimples just above the cheeks, where the plumpness began to swell, down along the thighs to just above the knees.

"Yes, she can take twelve easily, I fancy. Will you try to keep an accurate distance between each cut just as you have already?"

She pointed to the two livid blue marks, which contrasted with the untouched skin between them. "Now," she said, raising the cane and bringing it down just below the dimples at the top of the cheeks. An angry red line appeared and another shriek from Sarah.

I raised my cane. "Just there," said Hillary, pointing just below.

Crash fell the cane. Another yell. "What, more hot iron?" sneered Hillary. Crash fell her cane just below my mark and crash my cane followed hers.

"Don't hurry," she insisted. "We've only got a dozen each. It will do none of us any good; she won't be able to appreciate each separate cut and we shall be finished before we have begun. It would be a pity for her not to realize the care we are taking to do the thing properly."

"Shall we count the strokes out loud, then we shall be more deliberate," I said.

"Let her count them to us," said Hillary. "Let me see, that makes four. Four, do you hear, madam? Now please call the others."

I took hold of her hair and raised her head. "Do as you're told. That was four. Count the rest. What comes next?"

I pulled her head right back. "Five," she gasped in terror.

"Five it is," said Hillary, and again the cane fell.

"Oh, mercy, mercy," moaned the victim.

"Go on counting."

"Six."

I let go of her hair and, carefully directing the cane, brought it down just below Hillary's last mark.

We had just reached the summit of the rounded hillocks and the cane fell full on the firm flesh.

"Ah, God," said Sarah, "I shall die, you are killing me."

"I'm not dead," said Hillary, "and I've had more than this from you, and I haven't got so much fat to protect me as this," she added bitterly, rubbing her hand down over the wounded flesh. Sarah shrank under the touch. "Well, we are waiting, madam. Hadn't you better continue? The sooner it's over, the better for you."

"Seven," gasped Sarah, and the seventh blow fell.

"Eight." I followed. "Nine. Oh, finish, finish for pity's sake."

"Now, you're too impatient! Is it so nice that you can't wait? Well, there you are then, as you seem to want it."

"Ten, eleven, twelve." The blows had now reached the thighs, softer and more tender than the plumper cheeks. The cane gave quite a different sound and a still more piercing shriek came from Sarah. She tried with all her strength to drag her feet from the loops and bring her thighs together. But the cords held firm and she could only contract the muscles of her thighs, which rose and fell again on the ridge of pillows. Her hands clutched convulsively at the webbing and relaxed. Her head rolled from side to side. Her whole body heaved.

"Perhaps we may as well finish by ourselves," said Hillary, who seemed to be growing excited. I must admit that I myself felt a growing impatience. I wanted to strike and strike again at this helpless flesh, and my next three blows were rather at random.

"Steady," said Hillary, "don't spoil the gridiron."

"That's better, twenty-two, twenty-three, twenty-four."

"There, look, it could not be better, one could write music on those clefs."

She stood resting on the cane, panting slightly.

Sarah had stopped shrieking; only moans and hoarse choking sobs came, shaking her whole body.

I looked at Hillary. To tell the truth I was rather frightened lest we had done too much. I must have shown this in my face, for she laughed. "Oh, don't be afraid, we haven't half-finished yet, she can bear lots more. But we must shift her for the finale. Isn't it a lovely picture, though?" and she traced the straight lines with her fingers in a fierce joy.

"Ah, madam, do you remember the first time you crucified me? I haven't forgotten. How you laughed! It's my turn to laugh now, isn't it? You didn't think then that Hillary was to have the chance to write her name on your naked bottom, or you mightn't have been so keen on showing me how it was done."

She went to the loops which fastened the legs and took them off. "Now turn her over on her back," she said to me. "Perhaps she would rather display her breasts and belly than her hinder parts." I went to Sarah and pulled her towards me. She made no resistance. Her eyes were closed, her cheeks were wet with her tears, her whole body shook with gasping sobs. I rolled her over on her back and Hillary quickly refastened the legs. When she felt her bottom resting on the cushions, she started and screamed with the pain and tried to turn over again, but she was too late. Hillary had secured the ankles.

"Now, madam, for the real crucifixion." She pulled open the tea-gown at the neck and displayed all her mistress' charms.

There she lay outstretched for sacrifice, her breasts standing out firm, her belly raised by the ridge of cushions on which her bottom rested, while her legs, stretched as wide apart as possible, showed all her sex.

Scarcely a mark of her chastisement showed from our present point of view, only between her legs a few marks of the birch showed and the lips of her pussy seemed swollen slightly and flushed.

She presented altogether a maddening spectacle to my eyes, which wandered over all her body. Her position was ideal for any form of attack and I couldn't resist the temptation of putting my hand between her legs and investigating the gaping lips of her pussy.

Hillary watched me jealously. "Do you want to be in her? I should wait till to-morrow, but you can go on doing that if you like while I finish the crucifixion. It won't interfere with me. In fact, it will make it all the more amusing. She will have two different kinds of tickling at the same time."

My fingers began to probe the soft clinging lips of Sarah's pussy, while Hillary flicked the nipples of her breasts with the lash of one of the riding whips. She stood at the head of the couch and Sarah's white body lay stretched between us. Under the gentle persuasion of my fingers Sarah's sobs and groans gradually changed into sighs. Her thighs contracted, little twitchings and spasms ran over her smooth belly, evidently the pain of the whipping had not taken all sexual feeling from her.

"Tell me when she comes," said Hillary eagerly, as the little lash flicked here and there with a sort of wicked caress.

"Now," I said as I felt the lips of Sarah's pussy contract, and her bottom heaved with convulsive thrusts and her thighs contracted and imprisoned my hand.

I was not prepared for what followed. Without a word of warning, Hillary lifted the whip above her head and brought it heavily down on her mistress' body, straight up and down between her breasts, causing a long straight weal starting from the valley between her breasts, crossing the navel, and ending just above the dainty brown curls of the bush where the lash cut the skin and a few beads of blood appeared.

Sarah's sighs and moans of passion changed to a shriek of agony, but Hillary paid no heed. She stepped to one side and again brought the whip down on the unprotected body, but this time across from side to side, just across the breasts. Another weal appeared, making a perfect cross. I felt Sarah's body grow suddenly limp. I looked at her face; it was deadly pale. She had fainted. How beautiful she looked there, with her arms tied above her head, her eyes closed, her mouth partly open, her head drooping, the purple lines of the cross showing up on her deathly pale skin, her firm plump legs stretched this way and that, revealing the beautiful mossy curls and soft lips of her pussy, still dewy with the involuntary sacrifice to love. I looked to Hillary to see what she would do and went to unfasten the loops.

"Oh, she'll come round all right," said Hillary, "you needn't worry. I've had lots worse from her than that. Don't untie her yet."

"I won't have her whipped any more," I said. "We've given her quite enough. Get some water and bring her round."

Hillary went to the bedroom, and I chafed Sarah's hands and cheeks. Her eyes slowly opened and she looked at me. I was prepared for anger and resentment, but instead of that I only saw submission and appeal.

"Cruel, cruel," she murmured. "How could you be so cruel?"

I bent down and kissed her lips. "I'm sorry," I answered, "but you had to learn who was master. Have you learnt it?"

Her eyes said yes and I kissed her again.

Hillary came back with smelling-salts and cold water.

Her mistress' eyes glowered as she saw her approach. I saw the look. "Now there must be no resentment against Hillary," I said. "Let her help you to bed and take care of you, and I will call and see you to-morrow."

"No, don't let her come near me," said Sarah, I won't have her. *You* take care of me," turning to me, "I want *you*."

"You will do as you are told," I said firmly, for I realized it was the only way to keep my new found sovereignty. "Now Hillary, kiss your mistress and be friends."

"Let me help you, madam," said Hillary, "you know I have always let you help me when you have whipped me."

"We will both see to you," I said. "Hillary, get the bath ready."

I undid Sarah's bonds and gently raised her up. She could not bear to sit on her poor bottom, but hung round my neck and across my knees, the picture of abject submission.

"Oh, my lover, my king," she murmured, "you have won me, you have mastered me. I am your slave, I love, I worship you."

Hillary came back to say that the bath was ready, and between us we carried Sarah into the bathroom, which led off her bedroom, and laid her in it.

Hillary took the soap bowl and, making a lovely lather, prepared to cover her mistress with it. Some of the soap splashed on me.

"You'll get your clothes spoiled," she said, "you had better take them off."

I did as she suggested and in a minute or two was as naked as they were.

Sarah & Hillary

We soaped Sarah all over and then Hillary produced a flask of some sweet-scented oil which she gently applied to the poor scorched bottom and thighs. She dried her tenderly and laid her on the cool sheet.

Sarah gave a little sigh of fatigue and closed her eyes. I took a towel and began to dry myself. Hillary was putting things straight, going here and there quickly as she replaced bottles and soap and brushes.

It might have been Ancient Rome—Rome of the Empire. This marble bathroom, myself a young patrician, and Hillary a slave-girl attending on my wants.

I watched her slim form everywhere, my desire growing hotter and hotter, until at last she stooped down with her back to me to pick something up from the floor and in so doing showed me all her lovely bottom and the darling little pussy pouting out between her thighs.

I did not say a word, but silently came behind her, caught her round the hips and thrust John Thomas between the lips which were ready and eager to receive him.

She gave a little start of surprise, then a pleased laugh. "You silly impetuous boy. Why not wait until we can be comfortable?"

But I was far too eager to wait and began working in and out with vigor.

"Cecil," called Sarah, "where are you? I want you."

"I can't come for the moment, I'm busy. I'll be with you in a minute."

"But I want you now. What are you doing?"

Hillary chuckled. I made no answer, but went on working. I was just finished when I saw Sarah's reflection in the glass standing on the floor.

"I thought as much," she said.

I had finished my work and turned to face her. Hillary also turned coolly and faced her mistress.

I could not help comparing this interruption with the other, earlier one that afternoon.

"What are you doing here?" I said. "Go back to bed. Do you want another whipping?"

"I wanted *you*," she said humbly.

"Well, I was busy, as you see. I'll come to you in a minute, in fact, we will both come."

She darted a look of hatred at Hillary.

"None of that," I said, "I won't have it. You must be friends with Hillary. Go and kiss her at once."

She hesitated.

"Go and kiss her at once, or shall I fetch the whip?"

"Oh, no, no," she shuddered and went slowly towards Hillary.

An idea struck me. "Kneel down," I said, "and kiss those other lips of hers. You said you wanted me. Well, you'll find some of me there. Kiss her and thank her for whipping you."

It was lovely to see the conflict of pride and fear in Sarah. She gave Hillary and me a quick glance and then, sobbing, knelt down before her maid's naked body and pressed her lips on the thick curls.

"Say what I told you to say," I urged.

"Thank you, Hillary," she sobbed stammer-ingly, "for whipping me."

It was too much for her and she bowed her head and wept.

Hillary's pity was moved. "Oh, Sarah," she said, as she gently raised her mistress, "don't be angry with me, forgive me if I hurt you."

She raised her to her feet and the two women fell into each other's arms.

"That's right," I said, "now we will go to bed."

* * *

Looking back on my life, I date my conversion— as an evangelical person would express it—from that afternoon. Until I met Sarah I had really no knowledge or experience of the vagaries of vice. My life, till then, had been absolutely normal. Apart from the usual pseudo-sodomy of a public school—*Masturbatio intra Nates*, as Krafft-Ebing styles it—which practice I discarded and despised on going up to Oxford, I had simply sought women for straightforward fornication. Naturally certain subtleties of pleasure had been learnt, but until I had suffered at Sarah's hands and had been able to retaliate, I knew nothing of the intense, though recondite, delights of domination and humiliation. I realize on careful introspection that I had always a natural bias towards Sadism. Even as a small boy I played the game of "school" with my little sister, with the natural conse-quence of "whippings." I remember also, when on a holiday in Derbyshire at the age of fifteen, finding a book in the rooms where we were staying, in which there was a whipping chapter. The orphan daughter of a poor curate became a "town apprentice" to the wife of the local doctor. Her mistress ill-treated her and one day, finding her sweet-hearting with some man gave her what was called a "workhouse supper." The description of this thrashing with a strap at night on the bare bottom gave me, I remember, a terrific erection, and in spite of relieving myself in the usual way of a boy of fifteen, I had that night my first wet dream when the scene of the story was vividly re-enacted in my sleep.

Anyhow, whether naturally disposed that way or not, I went home that afternoon triumphant and elated. I had achieved my object of getting even with Sarah and had, at any rate for the time being, subdued and dominated her, and the joy of possession was far surpassed by the gloating satisfaction I felt at the thought that she was my slave, subdued and humiliated.

My desire towards her for the future was no longer sexual intercourse but domination, subjection.

In this spirit I hastened to see her the next day. Before leaving her I had given her strict instructions that she was on no account to retaliate either in deed or even attitude towards Hillary for the humiliation and crucifixion of that afternoon. I had also told Hillary that if Sarah attempted anything of the kind she was to tell me at once, and that for her own sake she was on no account to submit, or it might be the worse for her. "I am going to be your master," I said, "just as I am going to be hers, and I will have no one sharing my power."

Determined therefore to keep my new-won servants, I arrived at the house next day. Hillary as usual opened the door. She was rather pale and her eyes were slightly red. I asked her what was the matter.

"Sarah has been cruel to me," she said.

"But I thought I told you you were not to submit."

"I couldn't help it. She has been my tyrant too long, one cannot break one's bonds in a minute."

"What did she do? She couldn't have done much. She was too exhausted."

"Oh, she slept after you left, and during the evening she woke up and sent for me. I found her much recovered though still stiff and sore. She at once went for me for betraying her into your power and vowed that even though she might not be able to get even with you, I should pay for my treachery. I told her what you had said, and how you had ordered me not to submit, but she would not listen. I resisted all I knew, but she is very strong, much stronger than I, and you don't know, you can't know, what it means to have been in a woman's thrall for years as I have been. Luckily her experience of the afternoon had shaken her so much that she fainted before she had done much, but look!" She lifted her skirt behind, bent down, and pulled open her drawers. There were about a dozen livid weals right across her bottom.

"What did she do that with?" I asked.

"With the riding whip. She was going to use the wire birch, she threatened me, but the excitement and exertion of this was too much and she fainted."

"She shall pay for it," I said. "But you—I told you you were not to submit to her. How dared you disobey me?"

"I'm sorry, I couldn't help it."

"Sorry I Couldn't help it! Yes, you will be sorry and you'll learn to help it. Take me to her."

She looked frightened at my words, but led the way upstairs to Sarah's room.

Sarah was in bed, looking rather pale but very lovely. Her hair was loose about her shoulders. She looked up as I came in and smiled with pleasure.

"Oh, Cecil, I was hoping you would come. I am longing for you."

"Hmm," I said, "are you? What is this Hillary has been telling me? I thought I told you you were not to retaliate on her for your punishment of yesterday and now I find her with a bruised bottom and she says that but for fainting you would have done more."

"Surely I can punish my own property? I know I am your slave, but surely in my own house I am mistress."

"You may have been before yesterday, but now, I have learned what power means and—thanks always to you, you must remember—you are both my property, you obey me. If I give you permission you may perhaps be allowed to correct Hillary, but not without my permission, nor in my absence. Do you clearly understand that? Hillary, go and get the cases. I had better fix this new system in both your minds."

Hillary obeyed. Sarah turned white and began to sob. "You are not going to whip me again, surely. I'm sore all over still from yesterday, you could not be so cruel."

"Oh, there must be lots of places left. Let me see." And I pulled back the bed-clothes quickly before she had time to see what I was doing. Her night-dress had worked up and she was naked from the waist down. "Ah… well, the bottom and thighs certainly are fairly marked, but the back and calves are untouched. Turn over. Yes, I thought so. Why, there's lots of room."

Hillary returned at this moment, carrying the two cases. Sarah hastily tried to cover herself.

Sarah & Hillary

"Oh, modest, are you?" I laughed. "A little late, isn't it? Now Hillary, I have been telling Sarah what I think about her conduct to you, and she will have to pay for it. But you have been disobedient too and must be punished. You said you would love to be whipped by me. Well, your wishes shall be gratified. You had better undress, not altogether though, or you may shock Sarah's modesty. Stay a moment, I have an idea which will prevent any false shame on her part. Give me that webbing."

I took the webbing and tied Sarah's left ankle to her left wrist and her right ankle to her right wrist and then rolled her on her back.

She submitted as if in a stupor.

"There now, she can't see you, Hillary, and no matter how much she may gather you are exposed by the sound of my strokes, she must realize that she is far more indecently exposed herself. Besides, she will be in a most convenient position for punishment. Now go on undressing yourself."

Hillary looked a little frightened, but at the same time there was a look of expectancy in her eyes, which gloated over Sarah's nakedness. I took a birch and all the time Hillary was undressing, I was tickling Sarah's pussy, which was stretched open owing to her position, with the tips of the twigs.

When Hillary had taken everything but her chemise and drawers off, I stopped her. "That will do for the present. Turn the chemise up over your hips."

She obeyed. "Now bend down here," pointing to a spot at such a distance from the bed that her face would just reach Sarah's bottom and pussy as she lay spread-eagled on the side of the bed, "and put your hands on your knees. Now," said I, "I am first going to tan you as we did at school. Listen, Sarah, and think how you will like it when your turn comes. You can lie patiently there for the present."

I exchanged the birch for a cane, and swinging it back with a full sweep of my arm, I brought it down with full force across the half-open drawers. The force and surprise of the blow drew a cry from Hillary and impelled her forward, so that her face knocked against Sarah's bush. The latter uttered a cry of alarm.

"What's the matter?" I asked.

"I didn't know Hillary was so close. It startled me."

"Oh, she's quite close. She can see all you've got to show, can't you Hillary?"

"Yes, sir."

"Well, tell us what you can see. Listen, Sarah."

"I can see Sarah's bottom and her belly and her... her..." She stopped.

"Her what?" I insisted. "Her pussy?"

"Yes..."

"Well, tell her so."

"I don't like to."

"Oh, don't you. Does that make you want to?" and I gave her a vicious cut with the cane.

"Don't, oh, don't."

"Well, say it."

"Sarah, I can see your pussy..."

"Inside and out?" I asked.

"Yes, inside and out."

"There, Sarah, you hear that? What is the good of pretending to be so modest when you are showing your pussy, even the inside of it, to your maid and me. Why, we can see right inside you. We can see your clitoris there"—and I touched it with the tip of the cane—"we can nearly see your womb, I expect."

"Oh, untie me, and let me go. Whip me if you want to, but don't keep me tied up like this."

"Oh, you shall be whipped right enough, don't you worry. There's plenty of time. Still, if you're impatient we'll lay in now; move aside, Hillary. Now look out."

I lifted the cane, made it whistle in the air. I saw Sarah contract the muscles of her thighs and buttocks to meet the blow and, to tantalize her, brought the blow down about two inches from her body. She gave an involuntary cry.

"What's the matter?"

"I thought the cane was coming. I heard it whiz in the air."

"Oh, disappointed, are you? Well, things are always nicer when you get them when you don't expect them."

A vicious cut of the cane pointed the "expect" and Sarah shrieked with surprise.

I turned to Hillary, who was still bending down.

"Now, to go on with you. How many have I given you?"

"Two."

"Two. Ah, that leaves two more. We were only allowed to give four at school."

Sarah & Hillary

Whack, whack came the cane, and with each blow Hillary's face was buried in Sarah's mossy curls.

"Now take your drawers off. We will see what the cane has done. Now, lie on your back beside Sarah in a similar position to her."

There were four clear red lines across the white cheeks, in spite of the protecting drawers.

I looked at the two distended bottoms conspicuously displayed on the edge of the bed. They looked so quaint that an idea struck me.

I went to the dressing-table and found a pair of hairbrushes.

Then I sat on the bed between the two girls and began to play, as it were, the side drums on their bottoms. I kept time to a mad silly sort of rhyme, something like this:

Muriel, Muriel,
I will tan your bottom well
Juliette, Juliette,
I will see you don't forget

accentuating the alternate syllables with blows of the brushes, using alternately the backs and bristles of the brushes.

I varied the force of the blows also so that they never knew what the next blow was going to be like. I brushed the hair on their pussies, now softly so that they wiggled under the lascivious caress, now fiercely as if I was scrubbing a brick, which made them squirm with agony.

Getting tired of this I again addressed myself to Sarah.

"You asked me just now to untie you and whip you, didn't you? Well, I'm not so sure that I won't do as you ask. The position is a little tiring I expect."

"It's awful… My legs and arms are gone to sleep. Oh, please untie me."

"Hillary, you may untie her, if you like. Now go and stand in that corner with your face to the wall and wait until I am ready. Don't dare to look round. Hillary, take off her night-dress and your own chemise and drawers. That's right, now go and stand beside her."

I took a birch from the case and the whip of knotted cords.

"Now," I said, "I am going to whip you both for disobedience. I ordered you, Sarah, not to attempt to retaliate on Hillary for your whipping of yesterday, and I told you, Hillary, that you were not to submit to her if she tried it on. So both of you deserve and will get this," and I brought the birch heavily across both bottoms one after the other. Hillary only flinched, but Sarah's bottom was so sore that she involuntarily placed her hands on her burning cheeks.

"Take those hands away," I said, cutting them again and again. "If you don't I will tie you down… Now, will either of you disobey me again?" Whish—whish came the birch across Hillary's thighs.

"Oh, no—no—never," she sobbed.

"Will *you*," to Sarah as I stepped across and laid the birch across her loins and calves, which were comparatively untouched. She sobbed and shook her head. "Answer me."

"No, oh, don't whip me so low down," as the birch caught her on the back of her knees.

"Oh, don't you worry, you shall have enough higher up in a minute or two. Now, Hillary, I'll finish you off. Come here, kneel down facing me."

I got her head between my thighs and laid into her with the birch right up and down both thighs and cheeks of her bottom. Occasionally I directed a blow right between the cheeks, so that the tips of the twigs curled right into her pussy. She screamed and writhed and plunged, imploring mercy.

"Do you hear that, Sarah," I said. "That's nothing to what you will get in a minute. Perhaps you are getting impatient, eh? Well, there's something to go on with."

I could just reach her with the birch and let her have one cut and then came back to Hillary, whom I had kept tightly pressed between my knees. My blows had caused all her bottom and thighs to flush a dark red, on which the weals from Sarah's riding whip and my own tanning stood out across in darker colors. "There's quite a pretty lattice work across your behind, Hillary dear. I didn't know I was such an expert at designing. Have you had enough? Do you think you will be disobedient again? Well, we will just make sure." And I delivered a regular hail of blows everywhere as quickly as I could, until I was out of breath. Hillary's cries increased. She wriggled and twisted this way and that, but the relentless rod found her every time. Blood began to show here and there where the skin had been broken and even began to trickle down her legs. The birch twigs flew all over the room and at last I had only the mere stump left in my hand.

Then I relaxed the pressure of my thighs and she fell forward on the floor, twisting and groaning and her hands instinctively going to her lacerated bottom to protect it from further assaults.

All this time Sarah had been standing as I told her, with her face to the wall, a picture of apprehension. She knew she was within reach of my arm and so did not dare to move or look round.

I turned to her. "Now, Sarah, come here. It's your turn." She turned and came towards me with appealing looks. "Go down on your hands and knees," I ordered, "and pick up those broken twigs. We can't have the room in this state. The sooner you finish the job, the better for you." I threw away the birch and took up the knotted whip with the five lashes and to start her gave her a moderately hard blow on her flanks. She gasped and went down as I had told her, hastily picking up the bits of twigs here and there. It was a most fascinating sight in its shameless nakedness and humiliation. She crawled and groveled all over the floor, trying to avoid my blows and at the same time to pick up the twigs as quickly as possible. I pursued her everywhere, taking care at first to avoid the parts still sore from yesterday's whipping. All across her back and flanks the lashes fell. Now they curled over her shoulder or cut into her armpits. The tender flesh below her ribs received many, the knotted ends reaching round to her stomach. Livid weals began to appear and at last she flung herself at my feet, her hands full of twigs, imploring my pardon and protesting that she would never disobey me again. She even begged Hillary to plead for her to me. I allowed myself to be persuaded, and told them to see to each other's comforts, but warned both of them that if ever I found them disobedient again there would be worse punishment in store for them.

I then prepared to leave them, for though the whippings had excited me, I had no desire, as I had the day before, for any actual sexual enjoyment.

"You are not going, Cecil, are you?" pleaded Sarah. "Surely now you have punished both of us, you will be kind and give us what we want," and she came close to me and, like a suppliant, looked imploring into my eyes. Hillary also sent appealing glances at me.

I pretended to misunderstand her.

"Haven't you been whipped enough?" I asked.

"Oh, yes, but I want—I want—"

"What?"

"Well, if I must say it, I want you in me," she blushed and stammered.

"No," I said sternly, "you don't deserve it and I'm not going to satisfy your lusts. Still, you can both, as a favor, kneel down and kiss the God Priapus, whom you worship, but nothing more."

I undid my trousers and let loose the object of their adoration and let them both approach one after the other. To humiliate Sarah, I told Hillary to come first, which she did on her knees. I did not allow her to stay too long, but made her give place to Sarah. She knelt eagerly before me and, embracing me round the hips, kissed and licked the rampant head. Human nature was too strong, and I deluged her face and neck with spurting jets of my strength. But I had no pleasure from this, as compared with the delight I had experienced while flogging their subjugated bodies.

* * *

I f I date my "conversion" from the previous day, I may quite well look on this afternoon as my "confirmation." Until then I had been a man just with ordinary desires. Now physical union with a woman became quite a secondary consideration with me. The fascination of domination held me, and though, of course, I had both Sarah and Hillary as my mistresses, that was more for their pleasure than my own. For myself I was their *master*, they were my *slaves*.

1 quickly settled my kingdom, and as a first proof of my position, I demanded and obtained a latch-key. With this I was able to make surprise visits, but I will say this for Sarah, she gave me no cause for jealousy. She was quite content, for the time at any rate, with me, and although she admitted that it was quite a surprise to her to find herself submitting to any man, still she loved me for mastering her—or so she said.

With Hillary, however, she was quite different. She did not exactly bear malice, but she evidently meant to get her own back. She was, however, quite aware that I would not tolerate any sly vengeance; I had made that quite clear to her; but I could see that she meant, on the first opportunity, to pay Hillary out. Nor had she any intention of giving up the autocratic sway she had wielded for many years. She put this quite frankly to me one evening. "It's all very well for you, Cecil," she said, "you have mastered me— much to my surprise, I admit—still, you have mastered me, and I love you for it. But with Hillary, it's different. I've always had her as a subject; when we were at college together she fagged for me, and I used to whip her if I wasn't satisfied with her."

"At school together?" I repeated.

"Yes, didn't you know?"

"No, Hillary said she would tell me someday how your domination of her began—that was that afternoon you caught us in the morning-room and got caught yourself," I added maliciously. "But she said it was too long a story to tell then."

Sarah & Hillary

"Well, shall we have her in and tell you now?"

"If you like."

She rang the bell, and Hillary came in. "Hillary, Cecil says you promised to tell him how we got to know each other. Sit down and do so now." She was sitting on my knee with her arm round my neck.

Hillary hesitated. "Go on," said Sarah. "You haven't forgotten Clifton and South Parade? Let me see, it was Maude Jeffreys who began it, wasn't it?"

"Who was Maude Jeffreys?" I asked.

"She was a beast," said Hillary, and she stopped.

"Go on," I said.

"I was only a young woman of eighteen. I hated her and so did most of the girls. She was so strong, though, that they were afraid of her. All the bigger girls at school had little girl friends—mignons they used to call them—who used to fag for them and… do other things."

"Oh," I said.

Hillary blushed. "Well, Maude couldn't get anyone to be her mignon till I came, and no one took me up—you were away that term, Sarah, with scarlet fever—and all the other girls had their mignons, so she seized on me. I knew nothing at all then about things. I had come straight from home. Maude told me to fag for her, and as I saw the other girls of my own age fagging for the other big girls, I took it as a matter of course. They all seemed to like it, and got sweets and petted in return. Sometimes, too, the bigger girls called their mignons to them after the lights were out and I used to hear kisses and soft words of endearment. I thought nothing of that, I only wished someone would pet me… but not Maude, I never wanted her to pet me, she was such a beast… she didn't wash, ugh!

"One day, after I had been at school a week, one of the bigger girls had cause to complain about her mignon. Something or other had not been done to her liking, and when we went up to bed, I was surprised to be told not to undress at once. The other little girls evidently knew what was coming. The culprit was brought into my room—I slept in the biggest dormitory, with most of the little girls—and after a lecture from her senior, she was told to 'go down.' She was quite undressed and bent across a bed. Then her senior took a little cane out of her box and gave her about a dozen smart cuts on her little behind. The girl sobbed and got up and went back to her own room. I was stupefied, but the rest of the girls seemed to like it and to take it as a matter of course. I was told I could now undress, and did so, feeling very nervous and uncomfortable. When I was in bed and the lights were out, I heard Maude calling me. I went over to her bed. 'Get into bed with me,' she said, 'I want to talk to you.' I did so very shyly. 'You saw Elsie get whipped?' 'Yes.' 'Well, that's what happens to naughty girls here, so be careful. If little girls don't do as they are told, their seniors whip them. How would you like me to whip you?' 'Oh, Maude, please.' 'Well, mind you don't deserve it.'

"I didn't like the turn the conversation was taking and moved to get out of bed, but Maude put her arm round me.

"'No, you are not to go yet. You've never been in bed with any of the other girls, have you?' 'No.' 'Ah, well kiss me, kiddy.' I didn't much want to, but I did as she said. I was surprised to find not only her lips but her tongue meet my lips. I drew back, but couldn't get away. Her hand moved down and began to pull up my night-dress. I could feel my cheeks burning with hot blushes. 'You've got quite a nice little bottom for your age; it will be rather nice to smack.' 'Oh, Maude, don't... it's rude.' She laughed. 'Give me your hand.' She took it, and before I knew what she was doing, placed it between her legs. 'Don't take it away, but do as I do.' She pulled my night-dress right up and roughly put her hand between my legs to... oh, how ashamed and frightened I was. 'Oh, don't, please Maude, don't,' I said, and tried to take her hand away. 'Silly little fool, do as I tell you.' But I was too upset and burst out crying. 'Shut up, you idiot, or you'll be sorry. You shall pay for this to-morrow. Go back to your own bed.' I crept miserably back and sobbed myself to sleep.

"The next evening Maude told me not to get into bed until she told me. She then called the other seniors together and explained the case, while I stood in my night-dress. She was not popular, but the rule at South Parade was strict. A senior had an unquestioned right to punish her mignon, and though they didn't like her, the other seniors, for their own sakes, would not encourage insubordination in a mignon. Besides, as J learnt afterwards, they all used their mignons as Maude had tried to use me, and would not listen to any frightened protests on my part. So I had to bend over the bed, as I had seen the other little girl the night before. Maude borrowed a cane and, lifting my night-dress, gave me ten hard cuts on my poor little behind. Oh, the pain and shame of that first whipping. I shall never forget it. I sobbed and twisted and kicked, but Maude held me down with one hand quite easily. All the time she was whipping me she was jeering at me. 'Isn't it rude, eh, Miss Modesty? Fancy showing your nakedness to the whole dormitory.'

"When she had finished she said: 'Now go to bed and come to me when the lights are out.' I crept into bed, and, soon after, the lights were out. I did-n't move, but soon heard Maude calling me. As I didn't answer, she came across to my bed and roughly pulled down the clothes. She turned me over on my face and pulled up my night-dress and began whipping me again. I screamed but she kept my head pressed down into the pillow, which muffled the cries. She must have given me quite twenty or thirty before she stopped. 'Now, will you come to my bed?' I was too hurt and frightened to resist any more and followed her miserably, and did all she told me to do.

"Oh, how I hated doing it, and hated her for making me. I was too young to get any pleasure myself and, as I said, she didn't wash."

I laughed—I couldn't help it, and so did Sarah.

"It's all very well to laugh, but it was beastly."

"I expect so," I said. "But go on."

"Well, things went on like this. Maude was always getting into rows with her head-mistress, Mrs. Walter, and after getting punished herself used to get her own back on me. At last one day she was caught cheating in form and the whole school—there were about twenty of us—were summoned to the big schoolroom. I knew Mrs. Walter used to whip the girls, though up till then I had escaped, and the whippings were in private. This time, however, Mrs. Walter came in to us and read us all a lecture on dishonesty and then called Maude out before all of us, and, after lecturing her, sent her away with the French mistress to get ready for punishment. She then told us to go into the punishment room. I had never been in this room, known as the Vale of Tears among the girls, before. It was a large empty room right at the top of the house. The only furniture it contained was a cupboard, a long narrow table with broad straps on each side hanging down, a sort of vaulting horse, and a moveable scaling ladder fixed to one of the walls. There were forms round the side of the room, on which we girls sat and waited. After a minute or two, Mrs. Walter came in with the other mistresses. She rang a bell and the door at the other end of the room opened and in came mademoiselle leading Maude. The latter was a curious figure. She was naturally fat and lumpy, and her present costume did not improve her appearance. She wore a flannel dressing-gown, hind part in front, her face was blotched with fright, and she could barely walk. She looked such a ridiculous figure that in my astonish-ment and nervousness I giggled.

"'Who laughed,' said Mrs. Walter at once.

I stood up trembling.

"'Did you laugh?' 'Yes, madam,' I stammered, 'I didn't mean to… but Maude looks so funny.' 'Hmm, she won't look funny soon. Let me see, you're a new girl.' 'Yes, madam.' 'Oh, and you have not been present at a punishment before? Well, let it be a lesson to you. Come here, Miss Jeffreys.'

"Maude approached and stood trembling. 'You were detected trying to copy your French exercises from the girl next to you.' 'Yes, madam.' 'Very good, you know what to expect?'

"She signed to the French and Second mistresses, who took hold of Maude and led her to the table and laid her face downwards on it, so that her legs hung over at one end, buckling the straps which hung on each side tight across her back, one just below her shoulders, one across her waist, and one just across her hips. Mrs. Walter had gone to the cupboard and taken out a long cane. She came back to her victim and undid the dressing-gown. I realized now why it was backside front. As the buttons were undone, so it fell apart on either side, showing that Maude only had on a chemise. This was raised as high as possible and Maude's fat coarse behind fully exposed to view. Madam raised the cane to the full sweep of her arm and the first cut fell. I have never heard such a yell as came from Maude's lips. A second cut fell just in the same place, followed by another shriek. The elder girls smiled. Maude was notoriously a coward. But Mrs. Walter went on methodically with the whipping, taking no heed of the cries. Only when Maude began to kick, she said, 'Keep still, or you shall be tied.' But Maude's legs continued to fly about, making a most indecent exposure. At last when she had given ten cuts, each of which had left its mark, Mrs. Walter drew back and signed to the two mistresses and pointed to the horse. They wheeled that into the middle of the room, undid Maude, and led her to it. They bent her over it, and while one of them fastened her wrists to the two legs on one side, the other stretched her legs apart and tied her ankles to the other two legs. All that we girls could see was Maude's bottom wealed by the cane and her legs and what was usually hidden between. Mrs. Walter now put back the cane and armed herself with a long birch. If the cane had made Maude yell with pain, the birch made her scream. But Mrs. Walter took no notice. Down came the birch on the fat cheeks, until they were all crimson and purple. Quicker and quicker fell the blows, until at last most of the twigs had broken off and only a stump was left in her hands. Then she stopped and the mistresses undid Maude, who could scarcely stand, so shaken and weak with sobbing was she.

"'Will you cheat again?' 'No, madam,' she stammered, kneeling down.

'Very good, take her away.'

"That was the first whipping I saw at South Parade. We were dismissed and I noticed that most of the seniors retired to their studies with their mignons. I was congratulating myself that I should be free from Maude for some time; the whipping would, I thought, keep her mind busy. But I was disappointed.

"'Maude wants you, Hillary, in the dormitory,' said a small girl. I didn't dare not to go. I found Maude in bed sobbing. 'Oh there you are, you little beast, are you? So you laughed at me, did you? Well, I'll pay you out for that, my girl, when I'm fit again. Now I want you to put some cream on my legs; you'll find some on my dressing table.'

"I found some cold cream. Maude turned over on her face. 'Pull the clothes down, and put it on, and mind you be gentle.' I didn't relish the task of anointing her behind, you may be sure, but the sight of her behind and battered flesh pleased me much. She lay and moaned the whole time, muttering abuse of Mrs. Walter, until I had finished. That night she left me alone, she was too stiff and sore, though she had to show her behind to the whole dormitory (that was a custom of South Parade, and not even the biggest girls escaped doing it after a whipping). But the next night…. I had to pay for laughing at her and she made me do everything to her, ugh."

"Everything?"

"Yes, not only fingers… I had to… pah."

"Poor little girl, but it didn't last, did it?" said Sarah.

"No, thank goodness, you came back and won me from her."

"Won you?"

"Yes, that was a custom at South Parade. No senior could take a mignon from another senior unless she won her. Sometimes seniors exchanged mignons by agreement, but usually if a senior fancied a mignon she had to fight for her and win her. Oh, it was quite a formal affair. The Bedroom was cleared, a ring was formed, the mignon was perched naked on a chest of drawers, and the two combatants, also naked, fought with knotted towels which they flicked at each other. No wrestling or holding was allowed. I shall never forget that fight for me. There was that fat ugly Maude with her coarse skin and dark thick hair, while you, darling, looked so frail beside her. Oh, I did hope you would win."

"Well, what happened?"

"Oh, I won," laughed Sarah. "I'd had experience at home with my brother George. He'd learnt the game at school and used to practice on me in the holidays."

"Oh, did he?"

"With our night-gowns on, of course, you naughty boy. Well, I'd learnt the trick of wetting the end of the towel and I could aim much better than Maude. I was quicker on my feet too, and she was such an awful coward. She nearly gave in after I had touched her once or twice on the thighs, and at last when I got in a special cut of my brother's, right between her legs, she howled out: 'Oh, take the little beast, I don't want her,' and went to bed."

"Yes, and you have had me ever since, haven't you?" said Hillary, flinging her arms round Sarah. "I loved you then and I love you still, in spite of your cruelty to me sometimes."

"But how?… Why?…"

"You mean, how does Hillary come to be here?"

"Ye-es, and…"

"And what?"

"Well, she was at school with you… but…"

"Oh, you mean you thought she was my maid. Oh, that's your mistake. She told me when you called that she was sure from your manner that you took her for the maid, and we agreed to keep it up as long as we could. No, she's my companion really. Tell him how it came about, Hillary."

* * *

"Well," said Hillary, "my father died suddenly and we were left awfully poor."

"You must begin long before that," said Sarah. "It began with my leaving South Parade. You see, Maude never forgave me for winning Hillary from her and tried all she could to pay us out. There was no other little girl left without a senior, and no senior would share her mignon with her, as was sometimes done. She didn't tell about the games at night in the dormitory, for that would have brought down on her head the vengeance of all the seniors, for we were all tarred with the same brush, and she was an awful coward. But she hated us both; Hillary because she could never get her to make love to her gladly, and me because she saw Hillary was quite eager to do anything to, or for, me. So things went on for about a year, until one hot summer's day in the garden I couldn't wait till night, and Hillary and I were having quite a nice lit-

Sarah & Hillary

tle 'Flirtation' on the grass, which was rather long. Maude must have spotted us and told Mrs. Walter, for we were suddenly startled in each other's arms by her voice: 'What conduct is this?' There she stood looking down on us. 'Get up at once, Hillary, do up your drawers; go and wash your hands and then come to my room.' When we got there, she stormed at us, and talked about expelling us publicly. But I wasn't afraid of that."

"Two hundred pounds a year each," sniggered Hillary.

"Precisely. So she jawed a lot and at last said that in consideration for our parents, and the disgrace, etc., she would let us off with a flogging, but we must never do it again, would we promise? Oh, yes, of course, we would— and we never did—in the garden. She asked us if the other girls did the same sort of thing, and, of course, we said no, and then she asked me how I knew of such things. I said a servant at home. 'I expected as much,' she answered. Looking back now, I, of course, realize she was one of *us* herself, for she gloated over the details and her eyes glowed as she talked. Anyhow, we got our whipping—a private one, because she did not want to publish our disgrace and get the matter talked about, for fear of putting ideas into the girls' heads."

"Was the whipping severe?"

"Pretty well, I'd had plenty in my time; she loved whipping me, she told me later, after I left school."

"She spanked you, didn't she?"

"Yes, she always spanked us little girls. She used to put us across her knees, turn our clothes up, let down our drawers, and use her hand or the back of a hairbrush. My word, it hurt, too, I couldn't sit down for over a week with any comfort."

"But we paid Maude out, didn't we?"

"How was that?"

"Oh, that evening we held a court martial in the dormitory. We bribed the maid not to turn out the gas for half an hour, and we *tried* Miss Maude. Naturally all the seniors were eager to punish the sneak, and she was condemned to run the gauntlet and to be whipped by her two victims. It *was* fun. Picture this kid of twelve," pointing to Hillary, "laying into the fat behind of a girl of eighteen. 'I can't hit hard enough,' she nearly sobbed in her excitement, 'I can't hurt her enough.' I think, however, she managed pretty well, for Maude wriggled as we held her down. Then I had my turn; and at last she had to run naked three times up and down the dormitory between two lines of girls armed with canes. She was marked all over from her shoulders to her knees, both back and front, for she fell down more than once, and the blows never stopped. She didn't dare tell, however, and left at the end of the term, and so did I."

"Before the next term began, Hillary's father died, as she told you, and when I heard of it, I got my mother to have her to stay with us, and be taught by my sister's governess. When mother died, and I was married, I still kept her with me as my sweetheart and companion—my old fool of a husband suspected nothing—and here we still are."

"And she still lets you…"

"Whip her? Yes, habit is strong, and she never became a senior with a mignon of her own."

ANNA & TIM

A Word To The Reader

Y ou will readily believe that the letters you are about to read were never intended for publication. They were lately exchanged between a handsome, lusty young gentleman of some thirty summers and a mischievously pretty beauty who had just completed her nineteenth year. As the letters themselves will show, both these friends are persons of the finest breeding and the most amiable liveliness of mind.

I have known handsome Tim and pretty Anna for long enough to assure you that the events which this correspondence relates are utterly worthy of belief. After several months of my urging them, they have at last placed these papers in my hands with full permission to communicate them to the world. They make one stipulation, with which any sensible man or woman must concur: the full names and titles of my young friends are not revealed.

You may imagine how interesting their correspondence proved to be! Yet I have no wish to mislead the world. I strongly advise that these letters should not be read by the prudish or the narrow-minded. They will be shocked by the mere sight of a girl opening her legs for a succession of lovers; what will they say when a pretty pupil takes her master's passion in her mouth? Could they endure the sight of a young wife taking her lover's tool surreptitiously in her bottom? They will approve, perhaps, of the whipping of Tania and Vanessa. Yet with what horror will they then see the two naked girls make love together, lying head to tail, using fingers and tongues!

With that word of warning, I will detain you no longer. Tim and Anna shall speak to you now, telling their stories with the lively enthusiasm of youth.

* * *

Greystones, 23 April 1904

My dearest Anna,

Of course you'll say I've been neglecting you, my sweet. Or will you think me downright lazy? "Where is the letter he promised?" you wonder, and a frown wrinkles that beautiful brow of yours!

But that is nothing compared to the astonishment with which you will read the address from which I write. Greystones! What can your very own Timothy be doing as assistant in a reformatory for wayward young women? For, alas, I am only the assistant here. It is "Miss Martinet," as the girls call her, who rules the establishment.

It began when I inquired with the senile old Uncle Silas about my employment.

"Have no fear," answered the old swine softly, "your uncle was a benefactor of the Greystones charity. Arrangements are already made for you."

"The devil they are!" said I, quite taken aback.

"Very uncongenial to a shiftless young man of your habits, no doubt!" he murmured, "yet make no mistake, sir! Fail to fulfill the condition and I will see you cut from your uncle's will!"

He would too, I never doubted that! So I left his chambers, descended the steep wooden stairs of the old building, and turned away under the broad trees of Gray's Inn Walk, which were just then coming into early leaf.

All the way back to Jermyn Street in the cab I tried to puzzle out why a randy old uncle I had never seen should leave me all his spondoolicks, and on such conditions. What could it possibly matter to him if I spent a few months supervising the girls of Greystones, or working at some other profession, or doing nothing at all? Why not leave a chap the load of oof, as they say, and be done with it? Why blight his life by taking him away from the London season and sending him off to the seaside, where he might die of tedium?

Anna! Anna! How I wronged the frisky old fellow! Had I known what was to befall me at Grey-stones, I might almost have heard his laughter ringing out in the celestial spheres at my fury.

Fifty sovereigns was forwarded by old Silas Raven to see me safe to Pinebourne-on-Sea. Next morning, I received a letter from the Directress of Greystones, known to one and all as Miss Martinet. I was expected on the following Monday. The dogcart would be sent to the station to meet the three o'clock train.

Pinned to the letter was a list of useful clothing, including riding apparel for supervising the equestrian discipline of the girls. A further note, which made my brows rise slightly, referred to "instruments of correction." Such implements were provided by Miss Martinet for her colleagues. However, if I possessed a particular type of cane, birch, or whip, and if I preferred to use this, I might bring it with me. Naturally, the note added, it must be inspected and approved before I was authorized to use it on the bare bottom of any delinquent young woman.

I very nearly choked to death on my breakfast toast. With great care, I reread the sentence. The words were still there—"bare bottom"—I had not fallen victim to hallucinations after all.

That was Saturday morning. Already my regrets at being parted from the London season were diminishing, and it seemed to me that Monday could not come soon enough. Believe me, Anna, it was not the thought of tanning the bare backside of a schoolgirl of eighteen or a runaway young wife of twenty-five which thrilled me. I was possessed by thoughts of what else might happen once I was privileged to see them slip their knickers down and pose for me.

By noon on Monday my bags were packed and secured, all my possessions crammed into them, as I waited with impatience for the cab that was to take me to Victoria. The half-past-twelve train was prompt to the minute. Seated in the dining car, I watched the houses of Pimlico and Balharn speed past. Soon we were out in the countryside of Croydon and Purley, trees and hedges flashing by.

By breaking into old Silas Raven's fifty sovs, I sported a bottle of Chateau

Rothschild and a first-rate spread. I sniffed my post-prandial brandy and smoked a cigar as we pulled in towards Lewes under the graceful curve of the Sussex downs. By three o'clock I stood on the platform at Pinebourne, breathing in the clean sharp air of the sea, which lay just beyond the town.

I knew Miss Martinet at first glance. She was quite tall, and smartly dressed with a look which one calls "handsome." Nearer thirty-five than forty, she wore her brown hair in a somewhat old-fashioned coiffure. Her manner was well educated and pleasant. She might equally well have been a young widow or, as proved to be the case, a lively minded spinster with a predilection for bending wayward young women to her will.

We drove together in the dogcart, exchanging pleasantries. Pinebourne was an agreeable place, I supposed, with its tree-lined shopping streets and its elegant, broad-paved Marine Parade. The freshly painted pier, the bandstand, the ornamental gardens with their yellow blooms in flower, lay beside a quiescent sea.

Would you imagine Greystones as some grim fortress of vengeance, Anna? How wrong you would be! Though surrounded by a high wall, which the nimblest damsel would never scale, the house and grounds were delightful. The house itself accommodated thirty penitent magdalens, as old Silas Raven might call them, though their misdemeanors were more varied than the term implies. This extensive villa was light and airy, fronting onto ornamental grounds. Beyond the kitchen gardens at the rear stood the stable block with its little clock tower. To one side of the grounds rose the smooth turf of the downs, whose cliffs fell sheer to the tide. On the other side there was a gentle slope, where the resinous smells of warm pine led down to the rippling waters of the bay.

I took tea with Miss Martinet, who, because of my uncle's charitable interest in Greystones, treated me more as a guest than as an employee. Presently, however, she began upon one subject which had already crossed my own mind.

"You will find," said she, "that in such a place as this there are certain romantic passions which develop between some of the girls. A few of these are genuine affections, others are basely criminal. I cannot advise you whether to permit or punish such infatuations. It must be at your discretion. Whatever your decision, you may depend upon my support."

"I shall be grateful for that, ma'am," I said, swallowing my tea hard. The cup rattled nervously in the saucer, as I sat on the edge of the little chair in her drawing-room.

"Some girls," she continued, rather self-consciously, "are also liable to develop crushes or passions upon any man in the establishment. You, I am sure, will best know how to deal with that. They are also given to inventing stories about his activities. Have no fear, though, your word in such matters will always prevail with me."

"I shall strive to be worthy of such trust," I gasped weakly.

"As for the other matter," she murmured, "whatever course of action you feel to be necessary in matters of chastisement must be a decision for you alone."

As she spoke, Miss Martinet looked at me across the tea table with a new depth of meaning in her clear grey eyes. "I shall not interfere with your wishes in the matter," she went on, "except to assure you that the use of the rod is, paradoxically, the kindest form of correction in the end. A single severe punishment may save a wayward young woman from evil ways and repeated penalties later on."

'Tm obliged, ma'am," says I, awkwardly, "deuced obliged for that."

Miss Martinet smiled kindly at me. "Then we understand one another," she said quietly. "I knew that if your Uncle Brandon chose you as his heir he was certain that you would fit in with our way of doing things at Greystones."

Now, Anna, it may be that Miss Martinet understood, as she put it. I'll be damned if I did! Still I sensed, don't you see, some good sport ahead—just the kind that you and I love to hear of! Beyond the lace curtains of her upstairs drawing-room, the sun shone upon waves that were green as glass. Distantly, from the bandstand on the Marine Parade, came sounds of regimental brass.

"Tomorrow morning," said Miss Martinet, "you shall make your inspection. It was your uncle's wish that we should make you welcome here. I and the girls were, upon his instructions, to offer you every facility. Every facility." She looked at me, as she repeated those words, with that same depth of meaning which had made my heart beat faster a few moments before.

Ah, Anna! Tomorrow morning! What tales shall I have to tell you when I take up my pen tomorrow evening? For the present, as the lamp burns low, I bid you a loving goodnight and remain,

Your own adoring Timothy

* * *

Greystones, 24 April 1904
My dearest Anna,
How differently must we think of my Uncle Brandon after my adventures

today! You might easily believe he had *owned* Grey-stones—Miss Martinet and the girls included—and that it was a private seraglio with Miss M. as a duenna!

After breakfast my hostess led me across the sunlit lawns to the brick stable with its white cupola and clock. "We have two groups of girls at Greystones," she said proudly, "first, the more refined young ladies who are taught sewing or embroidery, and second, the young women trained to be stable-girls."

"Oh, aye," says I to myself, "buxom young trollops well made for vigorous riding and saddle work!"

"Before you proceed to deal with our young ladies," went on Miss M., "you must first prove yourself with these saucy Amazons. That was always your uncle's rule."

"Was it, by Jove!" I said. "Then I shall strive to be worthy of it!"

To speak well of Uncle Brandon is to win Miss M.'s heart. Do you suppose, my sweet, that she had such a letch for the old fellow as to supply him with young fillies to ride at Greystones?

"I shall put two young women in your charge at first—Katie and Noreen," said she. "They need nothing less than a man's absolute authority. For that reason, your dear departed uncle wished you to aid our good works."

I smiled at the old fellow's singular notion of good works. A moment more and we entered the main stable door, viewing a well-kept interior of red tiling, white-painted rails, and neatly piled straw. Miss Martinet pointed out Katie and Noreen to me, marking the beginning of my remarkable acquaintance with them.

I will not burden you with more than the briefest description of the two girls. Katie was to prove a casual and careless young slut compared with the staring insolence of Noreen. What shall I say of Katie? Her golden-blond hair hung straight and loose to her shoulders and was parted on her forehead in a long fringe. She was twenty-three years old, I learnt, the pale oval of her face marked by features which were firm and perhaps a little crude. Yet you would admire her blue-green eyes and the lashes which she darkens so skillfully. Katie is a bewitching combination of the brazen slut and the innocent child. She is firmly built, though not tall. Her lack of height gives her a coltish, almost stocky appearance. Yet her thighs are taut and her hips firmly covered without being fat. Her breasts are softly hung and Katie's bottom-cheeks have the trim maturity of womanhood. Though she wears no wedding ring, I'll wager that Katie's cunt has been well ridden.

Noreen, by contrast, has an impudent stare and a resentful manner. This pleases me, rather, for it will offer ample pretext for discipline! Noreen is a trollop of nineteen with no claim to refinement. Would you picture her to yourself? You may do so easily. Imagine quite a tall, firmly made girl, her dark-brown hair worn straight and lank to the level of her collar and cut in a level fringe on her forehead. Add to this a set of strong, fair-skinned features and brown eyes of lazy malevolence. Men who like a well-made filly to strap between the shafts of love's chariot would stiffen at the sight of Noreen in her tight working pants and singlet. Firm young breasts and straight back are damply outlined by clinging blue cotton. Now observe her from the waist down: her belly is quite flat, her pubic mound a gentle swell. Her thighs are taut and lightly muscled, as if from work or exercise. Noreen's bottom is certainly quite big-cheeked but without any surplus fat.

"Deal firmly with them, Mr. Timothy!" said Miss Martinet softly. "Be worthy of your Uncle Brandon! Remember, you are absolute master here. Not a word shall be heard against you from these girls!"

There were two grooms and several stable-boys to assist me in my task, which seemed to be no more than doing as I liked with the two girls! A room had been set apart for me at one end of the stable, and it was well appointed with a humidor of cigars and a decanter of fluid which looked, smelt, and tasted like the finest old malt! From this point of vantage, I settled down to watch Katie through the open door.

The young blonde was laying out the saddle harness for inspection by the grooms. In doing this she was also in the public view. On that side the stable wall is the boundary of the Greystones estates, the windows looking out onto the road, though securely set in stone and not to be opened. Men and women who stroll past can watch Katie at work.

Perhaps it was this which made Katie such an exhibitionist. First she found a black wig in a cupboard and fitted it over her own blond hair. It was not an improvement, though she paraded in it, her jaw slack and her tongue running on her lips. Taking it off at length, she ducked her head and shook it to and fro vigorously, her blond hair flying then settling at last into place.

The stable lads began to play with her. "Want a good gallop, Kate?" they called, as they seized her. "Take your pants right down, then!" She replied to them banteringly in a voice which was surprisingly soft and lilting. She tried to escape by climbing over the harness rail. Her legs were too short arid the boys caught her as she was astride it. One gripped her wrists and pulled her down so that she was lying forward along it as she straddled.

All this was done in play, Anna. Yet you may imagine the faces of the men who were passing by and who now pressed close to the windows to observe these proceedings. Because Katie lay forward, astride the rail, the men outside the window could stare at the weight of the soft young breasts hanging like delectable fruit in her tight, blue singlet. The wooden rail showed her pouched love-lips through the straining tightness of her denim trousers. Taut but maturely filled out, the firm cheeks of Katie's backside faced these spectators. There was such wrestling between her and the stable-lads! One of them stole a kiss from her lips, another smacked her arse playfully several times through the tight, thin denim.

In the end it was Katie who freed herself. Then, chewing insolently upon some sweetmeat in her mouth, she went to the stable-boy who was her favorite and took him by the hand. Now, it seemed, she was ready to pay any price for true love. She led the youth behind a screen which stood conveniently at one end of the stable. I heard the undoing of her waist and the whisper of Katie's knickers being pushed down to her knees and then to her ankles.

"Lie down and let me play with it first, you wicked boy," she said teasingly in her soft Celtic lilt. "None of the schoolgirls can do it as well as I, can they?"

"Head to tail, Kate!" he gasped, "please! Let us lie head to tail!"

"Ah!" whispered Katie, "you rascal! If I do that you will make me take it in my mouth!" '

"Do it, Kate!" gasped the lad again, "do it all the same!"

His long sigh of contentment suggested that the coltish young blonde, with her curtains of light golden hair, had obeyed him in this matter.

"I must kiss you between the thighs, Katie!" he murmured, "while my fingers stiffen those strawberry nipples on your white breasts. Was that nice when I kissed you there, Kate? Ah, how that makes you shudder—the tip of my tongue running in the love-slit between your thighs. Lie still, Katie, and let me do it again. What a soft little cry! Anyone would think I had put you to the torture!"

I listened in stupefaction, my dearest Anna. Was this the way in which our

English reformatories were run, I asked myself? Small wonder that such young whores as Katie took their sentence with equanimity.

"Now your backside, Katie!" sighed her adorer. "Did you see how the men admired you through the window each time they had a view from the rear as you bent over in your tight riding jeans? What would they like to do to you, Kate, if they had you as a slave girl? Suck softly, Katie! Run your tongue about the cherry top! Now let me press your pale seat-cheeks apart and admire what lies between. Ah, yes, Katie! If you were my slave girl, I should be pitiless in threading my shaft into that tight, dark hole as well. That frightens you a little? The thought of it makes you stiffen? To tell you the truth, Kate, the thought of it makes me stiffen too!"

So the lover's aria continued behind the stable screen. As I listened, I looked out across the green, ' sloping lawn towards the hedge which marked the steep fall of the cliff to the waves. It was the only side on which Greystones might seem unprotected. Yet no young damsel had ever been hardy enough to attempt a descent by that route. Nor, of course, had any randy swain ever managed to climb up by that way to woo his beloved in her reformatory bed! As I looked across the lawns and saw the pier and bandstand of Pinebourne glittering in the sun beyond, I could not help wondering what the respectable burghers of the town would feel if they knew the truth of the reformatory regime of which their lawmakers were so proud.

Just then the grooms returned. Katie, who had not nearly completed her chores, was sentenced to be chastised for her dilatoriness. When the first groom came to tell me that Katie was made ready to be caned for idleness, I could hardly find an answer! Imagine how eagerly the men who had watched at the window while she worked at the harness display would have taken this opportunity! I could scarcely believe that it was my own voice saying, "Ah… yes… indeed. To be sure. Perhaps, though, on this first occasion, you would be good enough to deal with her for me."

A broad smile crossed the groom's face. All the passion which he had pumped into Katie's mouth, the love with which he had spangled her thighs and backside, did not restrain his zeal for chastising her. We went into the main part of the tiled stable, where a padded leather bench stood at the cen-tre of the floor. Katie was stripped to her singlet, made to kneel at one end of the bench and lie forward along it. Her discarded pants and knickers (a pair of stretched cotton briefs) lay discarded on the table. They had tied her blond hair in a short pony-tail, and I was pleased at that. It enabled me to watch

Anna & Tim

more clearly her blue eyes and fair-skinned features. I nodded to the groom, who made the preparations required by the Greystones regulations. Katie's wrists were strapped to the far end of the bench, her waist buckled down, and her legs belted tightly together just above the knees.

All this will sound so severe, Anna, that you will scarcely credit how much pleasure there was for Katie in her punishment. Yet such was the truth, as I discovered when I made my inspection of her before she was bamboo'd.

I squatted down behind her and studied the area which offered itself as a target to the groom. Katie's buttocks, firmly and fully presented by her posture, were stretched hard apart. Both the rear pout of her vaginal purse and her anal cleft were in full view. I teased our blond shop girl gently. "You've been making love, haven't you, Katie?" I stroked her down the length of her cleavage, between the fair-skinned sturdiness of her buttocks, tickling the rear of her vaginal pouch and finding it moist. She was far away by now, her mouth open a little, and her blue-green eyes blank, as if she could not hear.

Can you guess the truth, Anna? Any of the other shop girls punished in this manner—Pat or Jennifer or the rest—would have trembled at the ordeal. Katie, however, was a lover of that delight known to us as "Birch in the Boudoir." Even a prison caning was the occasion for her pleasure. It is true, is it not, that certain girls, like the slave, Janina or the Grecian nymph, Sarita, have found pleasure under the rod of their Turkish masters? Katie was a worthy novice!

Already I could see that her pale, firm thighs, in all their stocky power, were squeezing rhythmically together. It was impossible to prevent, except by ordering her legs to be strapped apart. To tell you the truth, my curiosity was so great that I could not bear to do that.

"No wonder the men watched you as you set out the harness display, Katie," said the first groom, "if you were misbehaving like that!"

But the young shop girl had no shame, Anna! I vow she continued with the thigh-squeezing and the buttock-clenching as if she could not have stopped it for dear life.

The groom cut the air with a trial swish of his bamboo. Our young blonde masturbatrix stopped, frozen in a moment of apprehension, and then resumed her labors of self-love.

"Thirty strokes across your bare bottom, Katie," I said softly, and I nodded to the groom to begin the punishment with the long supple bamboo.

How the first stroke of the cane rang out across the firm, pale cheeks of Katie's bottom! She gasped, cried out, but never ceased to squeeze her love-lips hard between her thighs. Again the cane lashed across her seat, and again. She gave a soft cry but it was hard to say whether pain or pleasure drew it from her. The groom was quite pitiless with her. Believe me, any true disciplinarian who had watched Katie displaying herself at the window would have approved that. Six times the cane raised a weal across the cheeks of Katie's bottom—and twice across the backs of her thighs. She cried out with the hurt and with the pleasure of her own thigh-squeezing at the same time. In truth the vicious prison bamboo was a smarting agony across the bare cheeks of her backside. Only the swelling balloon of pleasure in her own lions enabled her to endure it with such insouciance.

After the first fifteen strokes, the groom handed the cane to his colleague for the rest.

"Almost at the summit of your climb, Katie?" asked the second man. "I shall let you get there before I cane. Then fifteen wicked strokes across your backside, with no distractions!"

Kate cried out again, begging him to bamboo her in her present state. But he waited until her thighs seemed to beat quickly in their squeezing, like soft white wings. He stood, undid her legs, and strapped them again with knees wide apart. Then he caned the impudent blonde shop girl without compunction.

I was conscious that the lads she had romped with earlier had their eyes pressed to every chink and keyhole in the place. Under the second groom's attentions, Katie screamed and her green eyes brimmed over. Unlike his predecessor, he was a moralist and no libertine. His righteous anger brought thin ruby trickles from the new weals across her bottom-cheeks.

At last Katie lay limp and gasping, her behind blushing and marked by swollen stripes. I stroked her blond hair, calming her. "Come to my room tomorrow morning, Katie," I said gently. "You'll be tanned now until the grooms are satisfied with you. Tomorrow, I'll treat you to some softer discipline of my own."

Was it pleading or was it gratitude she showed? Katie, the randy young bitch, brazenly licked my fingers in anticipation! Had she much to be grateful for? It depends which groom was the harder to satisfy. Was she given to the gentler of the two? He would surely allow her to ride the rubber dildo while his rod merely stimulated her passion. But Katie the young shop girl with her golden-blond hair touching her collar and fringed on her forehead, might well provoke a gentle, affectionate lechery.

Yet the other groom seemed more fiercely provoked. Was it by the rather hard, crude features in the pale oval of her face, or the blue-green eyes with their mascara'd lashes? Did her slight stockiness, the firm young thighs and buttocks, move him even more?

With the first lover, Katie might play out an amorous comedy. If the second was allowed to take her into the fateful room, a darker drama would ensue. It represents a more somber scene, shadows falling on a fixed block where Katie kneels strapped over it, securely gagged. Only her short, black singlet clothes her. I fear the tale must be one of Katie's wadded screams and flooding tears, her bottom bruised and swollen by weals which will not fade for a week. Even then, I suspect, this wielder of the pony-switch knows no pity.

I wonder which of my suppositions is correct? Perhaps neither. Perhaps, indeed, I malign the second fellow. Yet there was a certain look in his eye. Not that I think him alone in his inclinations towards such a young woman as Kate!

Now, my dearest Anna, I send this, my second letter, to you. As of this moment, you will not have received one. But, when you do, how sweet your replies will be to your own adoring,

Timothy

* * *

Ramallah, 4 May 1904

My dearest Tim,

Faithful to my promise, as ever, I write by the first post for England to tell you of the amusements which I have witnessed since our arrival in this place. Alas, my sweet, we must be separated for weeks—perhaps months—but I vow I shall entertain you with anything of a frisky nature which comes my way. Thus you may know that your adoring Anna still cares for you as fondly as ever, and longs only to keep your spirits up and your resolve stiff until our next dear embraces.

How shall I begin! A few hours after our ship docked, we were borne away in a regal carriage to the residence which my father enjoys here as Britannia's ambassador. Cool, white-paneled rooms awaited us behind a garden of palm trees and purple bougainvillea. All is gilt and embossed, fit for the king him-self. And yet what tedium would this have promised me—so much empty ceremonial and dull diplomacy—had it not been for the kindness of the Pasha of Ramallah.

The Pasha is a delightful companion, witty and courteous, always defer-ential to my rank and sensibilities as the daughter of a British envoy. He is a darkly handsome man of about forty, educated at the best schools in England and then at the Sorbonne. His house, overlooking the deep blue of the bay, is grand enough for a palace. Yet it is nothing to his country estate, some twenty miles away in a desert oasis, where he keeps his wealth and his harem.

Ah, you wicked boy! Do I sense that your ears prick up at the word "harem"?' Come, I will not scold you! To speak the truth, I was so intrigued by the notion, that my longing to see the beautiful slave girls in their silken and perfumed prison of love was quite as strong as is your own. However, my dearest, I, as a mere woman, might hope to be admitted there. You, alas, never could.

At first, indeed, it seemed to me that even I should never manage to prompt an invitation from the Pasha to visit that private place. We were, of course, given a general invitation to visit the fine country house. Tim, you never saw the like of it! The oasis is a green island in an ocean of brilliantly white desert sand. A high wall surrounds the place, and it is well guarded by his soldiers to keep marauders away. Inside are the most beautiful ornamen-tal gardens with little hills, lakes, temples of delight, and the bright, perfumed flowers of Arabia.

What shall I say of the house itself? It is a place of marble courtyards and ornate fountains, colonnades of Moorish arches, like the Alhambra itself. The rooms are sometimes open and sunny, sometimes deep and mysterious-ly dark, the scent of burnt spice rising from the braziers. England knows nothing as rich as the secret world of bright silks and dark tapestries, the stools and sofas which seem made to shape a woman's body to her lover's commands.

However great my curiosity, I was careful not to show undue interest in the harem at first. I talked of it casually to the Pasha. Tim! What do you think? He confessed to a taste for English and European girls as well as Arabian, Indian, and even Caribbean. I could not object to this, knowing that my father's power rendered me entirely safe. Yet my eagerness to see the beauties of his seraglio was now keener than ever. To my astonishment, he said casually, "If you are free to come on your own tomorrow, I shall order Nabyla to take you to the gallery from which you can view my treasures."

Can you doubt that I seized this opportunity at once? I was protected from harm by the position of my family and, even had this not been the case, my ravening curiosity would soon have conquered my misgivings. It is rare enough for a guest—man or woman—to see the beauties of the harem. What was still more provoking in this case was the knowledge that the Pasha of Ramallah had such a splendid collection of European odalisques as well as those of warmer climes.

Next afternoon, I was punctual to the minute. After the usual compliments had been exchanged, my host summoned a young Arabian beauty, Nabyla, who was to be my guide. She had a taut, swaggering voluptuousness of figure, skin like dark-gold satin, fiery eyes, and a sweep of silky black hair. In her company I was led to a gallery of white-and-black marble arches, rather like a cloister, which ran round one of the main rooms. Latticework filled the spaces of the archways so that we were able to spy upon the occupants without being seen ourselves.

Sunlight filtered through colored glass high overhead, illuminating one of the Pasha's favorites. My guide explained to me in English that this was Tania, a girl of twenty, from the Pasha's European collection. I was taken at once by the soft prettiness of her face and figure, her rather short crop of brown curls clustered on her forehead. Such a pert female cherub, I thought, the nose neat and straight, the chin nicely tucked in. Her sun-kissed face has, I imagine, a delightful tendency to dimple when she smiles. As with most girls from that eastern clime, her cheekbones are high and her blue eyes shadowed by them.

As we observed her, Tania was by no means fully dressed. She boasted only a snug-fitting, white singlet and a pair of light-blue denim drawers, which were tight as skin from her waist to her knees. We came upon her in this charming costume just as she was stooping over a table, resting on her elbows, reading a book. What a delightful picture she made!

Her soft young breasts hung tantalizingly in the tight cotton of the singlet. You would agree, I know, that her young hips are quite broad. Best of all, she has a charming tendency when bending like this to hollow the back of her waist downward so that the broad young cheeks of her bottom appear well separated in their tight denim. She has the easy, lewd pose of an *immoral-*

iste, however proper her upbringing. With her hips slack, one knee bent at a time, she offers each cheek of her rump alternately.

I could not tell you, Tim, what charming volume of curious literature she was reading. Yet its effect upon her was all too soon visible: her backside began to stir in a quiet rhythm as she bent over the table reading, and her thighs smoothed softly together in their tight knickers.

"You see how it is?" Nabyla said to me quietly. "There are so many harem slave girls. There are such numerous girls here that a night of excitement in the Pasha's bed is rare—unless they are one of his great favorites. Yet that occasional exquisite ordeal of her master's tool is enough to stimulate the itch of lust in such girls. Worse still, they live in the luxury of idleness with nothing else to think about. For the master's delight, books of amorous tales are provided as their only reading. The mistress appointed to supervise them will inspect them so intimately each morning with her fingers that love's demands will plague them the rest of the day. Tania would prefer another girl to console herself with at the moment. In default of that, she will take matters into her own hands."

Her words were true to the last syllable. As we watched, Tania slipped one hand down between her tightly clad thighs and began to finger her own love-pouch.

"Tell me," I asked. "Tania's body is surely her master's absolute property by the law of the harem? Every function of it, I imagine, is his to command or forbid as he chooses?"

"Indeed," said Nabyla, gently.

"Then, if Tania masturbates without his consent, will that not be a fault to be reprimanded?"

Nabyla's dark eyes had a gleam of amusement in them as she turned her proud Arabian face to me. "That will depend, madam. There will be times when the Pasha wishes to take Tania's knickers down and give her a sound whipping. What better pretext than such misbehavior as this? Yet at other times he will be delighted by her misconduct, either because it prepares her for his own pleasure or because he can then immediately oblige her to continue making love to herself as an amusement for his guests."

How intriguing this was, I thought! And what a new light it cast upon the amiable Pasha of Ramallah!

Tania looked about her, straightened up, and went across to the leather divan. No doubt she believed that she was quite undetected in her mischief.

Anna & Tim

I think she was still very timid over the matter of being caught in such misbehavior for, as yet, she did not even dare to take down her knickers. Instead, our young odalisque, with her crop of brown curls, lay on the divan, propped on her elbow. She turned slightly on her side away from us, crossing her legs very tightly and turning her broad young rump to our side with charming lasciviousness. Yet she had her shoulders turned so that we saw her face and the soft swell of breasts in her singlet.

I believe that Tania was looking over her shoulder because she feared that discovery might threaten on that side. At the same time, it was not possible for someone entering suddenly to see precisely what her hands were doing in front of her. For all that, there was never the least doubt in our minds what the young minx was up to!

Her thighs squeezed rhythmically together upon her busy finger. The broad young cheeks of Tania's arse pressed hard together and swelled out alternately. The blue eyes of the masturbatrix closed, fluttered open, then closed in a dream of bliss. Her luscious mouth opened softly to draw the deeper breaths which her rising excitement demanded. Her tongue ran repeatedly along her lips, moistening the dryness of love's fever.

Nabyla left me for a moment and I continued to watch Tania masturbate with the greatest interest. I vow to you, Tim, that I had never been privileged to see another girl do this to herself. Young ladies of my acquaintance were, of course," known to practice such dark rituals—either alone or in couples—but to see this done was an experience I had never hoped for.

In a trice, Nabyla was back. She was accompanied by a rather severe-looking young woman whose name I learnt was Judi. Unlike the others, Judi was the Pasha's mistress—in the English sense—rather than his slave. She was also the mistress—in the harem sense—of some of his slave girls. Judi was no more than twenty-five, her blond hair strained back into a short plait. Her fine-boned face with its sharp features matched the description of her as Tania's mistress. She was appropriately dressed in riding breeches and shirt, carrying a short leather switch.

Tania was allowed to make love to herself for a little while until Judi at last opened a door and walked into the room. What do you think Tania did? What could she do? Drawing her hands clear of her love nest, she lay down on the divan and pretended to be asleep. As Judi went across to her, she appeared to stir from a light afternoon doze!

There was no doubt of Judi's authority, or of Tania's state of arousal.

Tania's first act was to take Judi's free hand between her own, kissing its knuckles and gold rings as if these were the objects she loved most in the world. Then she held the blond woman's hand against her own face and nuzzled against it contentedly.

"Now," Judi said at last, "I fear we must satisfy the Pasha that you have been guilty of no act of wantonness, Tania!"

Tell me, Tim, how do you suppose that was done? I wager you would never guess.

Tania lifted her hips obediently so that Judi could slip her knickers down and off. As I suspected, Tania is one of those twenty-year-olds whose hips are broad and full without being flabby. Her thighs and bottom were what I would call fair-skinned, though perhaps a little muddy in their complexion. Presently she turned, holding and kissing Judi's hand again, showing the nice thatch of brown ringlets which adorns her pubis.

"Lie on your back, Tania!" said Judi sharply. "Bend your knees up to your breasts."

What was to happen now? Judi sat on the divan and looked down at Tania's vaginal pouch so conveniently presented by her new posture. Then, from a drawer, the blond mistress took a little tin and a badger-hair shaving-brush. Can you guess, even now, what was about to take place?

The tin contained a dry, white powder, a form of soap. In order to determine Tania's guilt or innocence of the act of masturbation, the dry powder was to be brushed into the suspected place by the soft teasing brush. If it lathered, then Tania was guilty. If, after several minutes, it did not, she was innocent.

One cannot quarrel with the ingenuity of such a procedure. Yet Judi had no intention of performing the ritual herself. She went to another door and called one of those slave girls who testify to the Pasha's universality of taste.

How shall I describe Shawn, eighteen years old? She is quite tall, a graceful Caribbean beauty with a high-boned facial beauty and tight-lidded slanted eyes. Her dark hair is strained back into a tight little bun or top-knot held in place by a tortoise-shell comb. This coiffure not only enables one to enjoy the fineness of her features more easily but gives an air of charming dignity to this tawny-skinned Venus.

Shawn was also in *deshabille*, in a bright-yellow cotton tunic, belted at the waist, and ending at mid-thigh. She was, I later heard, much given to dressing up in various costumes and admiring her reflection in the long mirrors of the harem *baignoire*.

Before leaving the two girls together, Judi positioned Tania's wrists above the young woman's head, by the ring at the end of the leather divan. Then the blond mistress joined us so that she might watch the results of her preparations.

Shawn was in no hurry, it seemed. She stood before a mirror, adjusting the yellow tunic dress. The firm, coffee-skinned elegance of her long legs, bare to mid-thigh, was admirable. The tight skirt of the short, yellow dress strained and creased easily across her lithe hips and the taut statuesque cheeks of her bottom.

At last she was ready, turning to her willing victim. You will easily imagine Shawn dipping the brush in the powdered soap and applying it to Tania's nether lips. But will you guess how she did it? She knelt astride Tania, almost sitting on the girl's breasts, facing her feet. Then she went forward on elbows and knees, her face above the open spread of Tania's crotch, as she tickled the powder-laden brush into Tania's cunt. Tania moaned and sobbed gently with the delicious torment of it. Our tall, agile Caribbean beauty smiled to herself at this, teasing the tip of the brush 'round and 'round Tania's clitoris. At the same time, the tormentress reached back and pulled her own tight, yellow dress up above her waist. What a view was now presented to Tania's eyes and lips!

Under so short a tunic, Shawn's knickers were a pair of white ballet briefs made of stretched cotton web. What a contrast they made with the smooth coffee color of her long, agile thighs. She has that natural Caribbean grace of the straight back and long trim legs, the instinctively upright carriage. Her hips are firm, though offering a slightly fuller appeal than the rest of her figure, her breasts being high and saucy. The tight, white cotton of the briefs perfectly shaped the triangle of her pubis and showed the charming little bulge of her love-pouch through their gusset. She had chosen a pair which were cut lasciviously high and tight at the seat, laying bare much of the soft, dusky-gold cheeks of her backside.

Inspecting Tania's furry pouch at very close range, Shawn tickled it pitilessly with the brush, touching and teasing, touching and teasing, until Tania's blue eyes widened and she cried out, her brown curls threshing from side to side on the divan. Shawn moved her knees back a little so that she was astride Tania's face. All the time she was manipulating the little brush with wicked skill, teasing and touching, teasing again and again.

To be masturbated in this fashion was almost more than Tania could bear without going into a delirium of screams and pleading. She kissed the in-sides of Shawn's nude thighs with an amorous, smacking passion. Then her tongue began to lick the soft, satiny inner surfaces of the thighs with long, infatuated swathes of moisture.

Shawn was smiling to herself as the brush continued its work on Tania's vagina. The result of the test was no longer in doubt for we could hear the first faint whisper of lather at Tania's own love-juice supplied the powder with ample moistening.

"Pull your pants down, Shawn," she whispered yearningly, "oh, please do, my dearest! Let me love you properly!"

I think the Caribbean beauty was perhaps more amused than flattered by the grand passion she had provoked. Yet Tania was now desperately kissing the tight, warm cotton where it cuddled the soft little bulge of Shawn's vaginal pouch. At this rate, I thought, she was soon going to taste Shawn through the pants in any case.

As it happened, the generous girl obliged her. Shawn reached back, took the waistband of her knickers and pulled them down so that they were drawn tight round the middle of her spread thighs. Now the two girls lay on their sides, head to tail, facing one another for a prolonged session of love-making.

Shawn began remorselessly working her finger in and out of Tania's love-hole, causing cries of gratitude and alarm from her soft-figured partner. It was Shawn who was the leader, quite shameless in her wanton use of the other girl. Her tongue now replaced her finger in Tania's little slit, trilling like that of an exotic bird in full song. Tania, for her part, was content to obey Shawn's instructions, kissing and tonguing according to order. Because her wrists had been placed out of harm's way by her mistress, she needed a little assistance from her partner. Shawn, ravaging Tania with her tongue, had to reach back and part her own buttocks so that Tania might more deeply explore her in that area.

Presently I saw that Tania's hips were moving in a hard, pumping kind of motion. She was about to have her "happy time," as they call it in French parlance. How she cried out, begging Shawn to love her, beat her, cherish her, enslave her—anything so long as they might spend the rest of their lives together on this divan in such a manner!

Anna & Tim

Tania's orgasm was accomplished with complete self-abandon. Shawn, to my surprise, was more controlled. There came a point when she thrust her hips out a little harder and when Tania had to use her tongue more energetically. Then with clenched teeth and a tense, quick palpitation of her brown thighs, our Caribbean beauty also came safe into the calm waters of love's haven.

Following this, they played with one another in the same posture. But there was a sense of calm now, as if they were merely a pair of schoolgirls curiously exploring one another's secret anatomies. This continued for about half an hour, until one sensed that excitement of a more adult kind was beginning to gather once more.

Judi spoke not a word. But, at this point, she returned suddenly through the door and caught the two culprits in the very act. The truth was that, though they must have heard her approach, this pair of lovers was now in a state where neither cared for the world or its reprimands.

"Undress at once!" said Judi sharply, "both of you! Tania has more than convicted herself of wanton behavior. In your case, Shawn, you have proved yourself a most shameless accomplice!"

Judi stood there, a severe young woman with her short, blond plait, her riding breeches and blouse, the leather switch flexed in the firm grip of her hands.

"Since you are so eager for illicit passion with One another," she went on, "we will make the punishment fit the crime. On this occasion, however, your ecstasies will be tempered by the sharp sauce of chastisement!"

I vow, Tim, I could scarcely believe my ears! In one afternoon I was to witness things which most men and women might wait a lifetime to see—and would often await in vain! There was no doubt in my mind that the scene about to be played out in that room was to be one of amorous punishment or of disciplined lasciviousness. It was that greatest of love's curiosities which you and I, in our familiar conversation, have often referred to jokingly as "Birch in the Boudoir." And yet, my sweet, often as we have talked about such things, it was not until this afternoon that I began to have some clear conception of the reality.

Alas, it grows late. I must save the remnant of my experiences for tomorrow's letter. You have no idea how the servants talk in such a place as this! Merely for the light to burn in the room of the envoy's daughter until 2 a.m. is sufficient to start all sorts of rumors. You know, my dear, that there can be no ground for them. Others might be less charitable. So I bid you a gentle and loving goodnight until tomorrow, when I will reveal the strange secret which I now share with Nabyla, Judi, Tania, and Shawn!

Your ever-loving Anna

* * *

Ramallah, 5 May 1904

My dearest Timothy,

Before I continue my account of yesterday's female debaucheries, I must tell you of the great joy I have had in receiving all your dear letters by this morning's post. They came in a single batch, for you know the post is weekly here rather than daily. Oh, how happy I am at the improvement in your prospects by the legacy of your dear Uncle Brandon! How sensibly this must affect dearest Mama and dearest Papa in their estimate of your worthiness as a husband! How strange, my dearest, that families care so greatly for a man's wealth and nothing for his abilities in the bedroom, where a woman's true happiness is made or marred!

I am delighted that your apprenticeship is served in so diverting an establishment as Greystones. What stories we shall have to tell one another by the time we meet again! I am true to my bargain, Tim. You may indulge in whatever indiscretions you please now, for it will make you a better and a steadier husband if that happy day should ever dawn. What a depraved young slut that Katie of yours is, however! And how richly you rewarded Katie and Noreen in their respective ways. I am surprised that you have not already whipped Noreen's bottom for her, as she richly deserves. Perhaps, though, by the time I have written this letter, you may have remedied that omission!

Let me tell you now of my own adventure, or rather of what passed when Judi returned to Tania and Shawn yesterday afternoon. Blond and severe in her riding costume, she flexed the switch between her hands and watched the two girls undress. She had, of course, released Tania from the divan, but, once the undressing was completed, she required each girl to wear a number of well-polished black straps. These adorned the waist, the wrists, the neck, the ankles, and the thighs just above the knees. You may be sure there was intense nervousness in Tania's blue eyes at what lay ahead, though Shawn's expression, darkly slanting and tight lidded, was enigmatic.

At first sight you might have thought Judi proposed to roast the two girls on a spit! I hasten to assure you that such was not the case. Yet she summoned two guards who brought in a strange apparatus, consisting of two supports with a long pole between them. The machinery showed clearly that this pole could be turned, if so desired, by the person operating it.

Tania and Shawn were attached tightly to the pole, pressed together and facing one another with the shaft running between them. Their ankles were strapped together at one end of it and then- wrists at full stretch above their heads to the far end. The pole, being metal, was thin though strong, so that their two bellies almost touched and their breasts kissed lightly under their own delectable weight. The two leather neck-collars were attached so that the girls' lips and tongues were in constant contact.

So these two delicious chickens were hoisted on their spit about three or four feet above the floor. Their lips and tongues mingled with promiscuous little meanings of desire. They smoothed their breasts firmly against one another's until four nipples stood hard as berries. At one end, the fingers of their cuffed hands entwined and tightened lovingly. Their legs and thighs were pressed tight to one another by the strapping. What a charming picture they made! Tania, with her cropped brown curls, her pretty little cherub face, firm, broad hips and muddy-white skin! Shawn with her Caribbean grace, high-boned elegance, long legs, and well-curved breasts and buttocks!

The pole turned, just as a roasting spit would. It might be turned by another person operating its handle, but the controlling wheel could also be urged forward by vigorous writhing of the girls attached to it.

Judi's face seemed sharp-eyed and expressionless as she took some hot-spiced paste on her finger, moistened it with saliva, and spread it on each of the girls' nipples. The hot irritant drove them into still more energetic writhing and mutual rubbing. Judi also smoothed the same erotic heat into each vaginal slit. Between each girl's legs, she attached to the pole a con-venient dildo so aimed that it would move within their love-holes by the surging of their hips but could not be dislodged entirely. Writhing passion-ately against one another, each cunt riding its rubber penis, the two girls faced each other, side by side or one above the other as their struggling turned the pole. Tania's mouth swam with Shawn's saliva, and then as they turned it was Shawn who was flooded with the tastes of Tania's mouth. With torsos thrust out, they rubbed their nipples hard against each other. The ingenious dildoes enabled each girl to be simultaneously the lover and mis-tress of the other.

Was this indeed the punishment they were to suffer? It seemed little enough like punishment to me! But Judi had not quite finished. She took two small rubber cushions, each very firm and about the size of a small plate. Each in turn, she forced one of these under the girls' lions so that then: two back-sides were thrust out quite hard.

Tania was writhing and squirming at the top of the pole, offering her rear view, while Shawn whimpered amorously from the lower position. Tania's pretty, sun-kissed face, with its clustering brown curls, was hidden as she applied her mouth to Shawn's. Her hips were working hard on the dildo, the cheeks of her bottom alternately arching out and contracting, parting widely and tensing together.

Judi raised the switch and brought it down across the broad weight of Tania's backside. I leave you to imagine the impact of a leather riding switch across Tania's bare arse-cheeks! Her cry was muffled by the pressure of Shawn's lips on her own and the busy wriggling of the Caribbean beauty's tongue in her mouth. Tania's backside squirmed desperately under the lin-gering smart but even this movement increased the exquisite sensations of the dildo, which was so snugly in her cunt. Judi touched the leather switch lightly upon Tania's bum and gave two more pistol-cracking strokes across the full whitish cheeks. Even at twenty years old, Tania had never tasted such anguish—nor such pleasure. Had her straps been undone, I wonder if she could have endured to part with the dildo and Shawn's loving even to save her behind from its punishment?

Judi printed a pair of swollen stripes across Tania's bottom-cheeks, enough to drive the girl into turning the pole by her writhing. As she swung into the lower position, sobbing with anguish and desire, so Shawn was turned arse-upwards for Judi's attention.

Imagine the target presented by our Caribbean beauty with her long, graceful brown legs and the dusty gold of her trim but softly luscious seat-cheeks! Even the top-knot of dark hair, with its pretty comb, and the tight-lidded almond eyes seemed to make her a more appealing subject for Judi's vengeance.

Shawn was trying to watch Judi from the corner of her eye. To her dismay, she saw the riding mistress lock the wheel into position so that the pole would not turn.

"Twelve extra strokes before the game begins, Shawn," said Judi quiet-ly, "your punishment for a betrayal of trust. Ah, you can't stop loving your-self on the dildo, can you? Give Tania your tongue properly at the same time—right into her mouth. How hot and swollen your nipples look! Still stinging a little from the spice? Keep rubbing them on Tania's tits, you young bitch."

So saying, Judi measured the riding switch across the dusty-gold cheeks of Shawn's bottom. Once, twice, and again the strokes rang out. The Caribbean girl's seat of beauty was soon striped by several swollen weals. Now the next strokes across Shawn's bottom must fall upon these. The anticipation of doing this was almost too much for Judi to endure. With an impetuosity belying her severity, she undid her riding breeches and laid them down round her knees.

A word of command was given somewhere beyond the latticework on the far side. Into the room came Connie, a beautiful Chinese girl of Judi's own age, naked except for the silver clips holding back the sheen of black hair which fell to her shoulder blades. Obediently, Connie knelt behind her mistress and applied lips and fingers to Judi's venereal anatomy. In this way, she was able to ensure the blond woman's pleasure without interfering in the chastisement. Muffled in her turn by Tania's mouth, Shawn received eight more strokes across her backside, two of them causing wet rubies to glimmer on warm-toned seat-cheeks.

When the wheel was unlocked, the pole turned again under the energetic riding and squirming of Shawn's hips. Tania contrived briefly to free her mouth from Shawn's and turn her face in a wild expression of anguish and ecstasy, pleasure and frenzy. Judi managed to give several strokes across the broad, young cheeks of Tania's bottom before the positions were reversed once more and it was Shawn whose rear-cheeks were turned upwards for discipline.

I swear, Tim, that, as the performance went on, I do not believe either Shawn or Tania felt anything like the so-called agony of the whipping. It acted merely as a stimulus to desire, in the same manner as the hot irritant paste, which had been applied remorselessly to the most sensitive buds and clefts of their anatomy.

Though Judi, with her severe-looking plait and her keen, blue eyes stood widely astride for Connie's attention, the strictness of her expression never faltered. 'Round and 'round went the spit with the two writhing, hip-pumping girls upon it. The leather switch sang out across each bare bottom in turn: Tania's, Shawn's, then Tania's again. The dildo shafts sank and rose again from their furry nests. In the heat of the room, Tania was sweltering. A gloss of perspiration appeared in the small of her back, under her arms, on the inner surfaces of her thighs, and between the cheeks of her bottom. Such energy she was putting into her loving and writhing! For the first time Judi's severe features softened in a smile.

"Your punishment has hardly begun yet, Tania!"

Punishment? It was not the word I would have chosen! Tania's broad, young hips rode up and down, up and down, on the rubber shaft as if her very life depended on it.

I believe that Judi's true excitement came from her sense of power over the two girls. Perhaps she thought of Tania before her abduction into slavery. How many men and women envied those clustering curls, the pretty dimpling of her face? How many were haunted by a glimpse of Tania bending, chin in hands, as she read a book, offering such a provokingly full rear view?

Judi locked the wheel into place as Tania lay arse-upwards.

"Twelve strokes for your wantonness, Tania!"

The blond mistress kept her waiting for several minutes. Even during this time, Tania never ceased to ride the dildo or to fill Shawn's mouth with her tonguing and kissing.

At last it came, an amorous whipping whose agonizing strokes served only to drive the "victim" into further and more desperate loving. However bruised or swollen Tania's bottom might be, however appalling the menace of further strokes, it was only what Judi called it: the sharp sauce of a greater pleasure.

You may imagine, Tim, that I sat there immobile and watched until Judi sank to her knees, conquered by Connie's busy tongue. The fulfillment of the mistress brought respite at last to the two miscreants.

It seemed that the curtain was about to be rang down on this first scene of a harem "comedy". Yet Nabyla had been sent on an errand and I was compelled to wait for her return before leaving my place. That being so, I was privileged not only to see the drama itself but also the epilogue.

Tania and Shawn were released. They left with their arms about one another, cooing or sobbing gently together like a pair of doves. Each bottom, Tania's broad and pale, Shawn's taut and brown, bore the prints of the leather switch. Judi followed them to the bedroom, where the three would pass a night of passion together.

What of poor Connie, I wondered? She dressed herself in a pair of tight, denim knickers from waist to knee—such as Tania wore—and a short, blue tunic opening at her waist. Her task was to put the room to rights. Sitting on her heels, she began to collect the debris from the floor. What a charming picture she made! Connie's rather flat features and slanting eyes are set in a face of heart-shaped delicacy. Like so many girls of her Asiatic beauty, she can assume a beautiful impassivity or a devil mask of laughter with equal ease. Her figure, like her face, has a slim, fine-boned appearance.

As Connie worked, I saw a tall, fair-whiskered English Milord of twenty-five pass the open door. I imagined him to be one of the Pasha's privileged guests. He stopped and surveyed Connie from her slim thighs and tautly rounded bum-cheeks to her slim shoulders, on which the black hair with its silver clips fell in a fine curtain. He watched her from this way and that, as if photographing upon his mind the images of her kneeling, stretching, bending. It was some time before Connie realized that she was under observation. When she did so, there was nothing for it but to continue her work while shooting a glance of sudden apprehension at the man from time to time. Presently he went away. Later he came back. I can scarcely describe the sudden shock in Connie's eyes when she saw him standing there once more, watching her. But this time he entered the spacious, well-appointed room, closing the door after him, and locking it.

"Your master has given you to me for a night of pleasure, Connie," he said, sitting on the divan. "Come to me naked and kneel down before me."

I truly believe that Nabyla left me there deliberately to witness what followed. Connie's knickers came down and her tunic off. This demure, submissive Asian beauty then knelt before her English lover. Without a word of command, she undid his trousers with her slim, quick fingers and drew out his penis. She touched her lips to it, ran her tongue 'round its knob, and, as it stiffened, took it in her mouth. The curtains of her black hair covered his thighs as she sucked. He made her suck for five or ten minutes, then restrained her briefly, then motioned her to start again.

Later she climbed meekly onto the divan, lay on her back with legs apart and feet raised, guiding him down and sheathing his quivering dart between her thighs. As he rode her, she softly taught him how to nip her with his teeth, to flick her breast buds with his tongue, to rake her flanks with his nails in the fury of desire. Later still, she turned over on her belly, offering the rear view of her trim, saffron-yellow figure, with the black, silken hair spread on the shoulder blades. Connie's bottom had those pale-yellow cheeks which are soft but neatly rounded. She had obviously been well trained in a slave girl's submission, for no word of command was needed even now. She reached back and pulled her buttocks apart, hiding her face bashfully in the pillow as she offered the tight dimple of her anus to the man's lust. He buggered Connie with such energy that she several times drew a sharp breath. He spent in her neat, young Chinese bottom and she thanked him charmingly.

Then she looked at him with great apprehension. She slid from the divan, walked across to the cupboard with a delicious little swagger of her bare hips, and produced a birch. Its three, yard-long switches were bound at the handle in the way that prison rods are. With eyes lowered, she took it back to him, presented it to him kneeling, and then bent herself forward over the back of a chair.

I could not guess what his response would be, for his tool now hung remarkably slack. First, he secured her wrists to the wooden legs. Then he took his place behind her and touched the long birch switches to the broad, well-separated cheeks of Connie's trim backside.

"If I were a judge, condemning you as a thieving shop girl, Connie," he said coolly, "I should order you eighteen strokes of the prison birch. I must not be too timid to carry out such acts for myself."

The birch made a soft, lashing sound as it cut across the pale-yellow cheeks of Connie's bottom, its fine tips curling 'round to catch her flanks. Even now there was a softness in her cries, as if she knew that a respite was impossible and that to scream for it would be a sign of defiance. The familiar raised scratches of the birching, long and curling, soon traversed her buttocks. Two or three times the birch just missed its target and caught her high on the legs. When it was over, her lover set her free, and led her back to the divan.

Now Connie had her reward. He placed her gently on her back and rode into her cunt with renewed lust so searchingly that Connie cried out with a greater intensity of joy than when she cried in distress during her tanning. They fell asleep together after the climax like a devoted bride and groom.

At two in the morning, her lover woke her gently, stroking her face. He required his Asian bride-of-a-night to turn onto her belly. He then made love to Connie's bottom. Little more than an hour passed before he woke her once more, this time spreading her legs and taking his way between them. In the pale, star-lit flush preceding dawn, their sleep was broken once more.

"Your bottom again, Connie," he murmured, as she stirred under his caresses. "Hold the cheeks well apart and rest your belly on the pillow. Arch your rump out even farther…."

I can scarcely describe the many sequels, as I am exhausted by my vigil. You may protest at a young lady writing of such things, but it is the very truth, as witnessed by

Your own adoring Anna

* * *

Greystones, 2 June 1904

Darling Anna,

With what relief did I receive your letters at last and learn that all is well with you at Ramallah! You may be sure that I read with great amusement the frisky doings of Tania and Shawn, as well as the amorous ordeal of Connie! I fear, my sweet, that you may find the news of Greystones dull by contrast, for there is much to be done in a harem which would be imprudent here!

Nonetheless, these past few days have produced one or two diverting little incidents among the stable-girls who are my chief concern even now. It is almost as if Miss Martinet believes I may find greater pleasure in their randy company than among the refined young ladies of eighteen in her sewing class. Who can say but that she may be right?

Since I last wrote to you, two more young women have come under my care, though they are ten years different in age. Jacqueline, the elder, is truly a self-regarding slut of twenty-five. She pretends to education and refinement but is, I feel sure, a young trollop who cannot get her pants off fast enough if it suits her purpose! She is not quite in her first youth, though she presents a challenge to any man. Her straight, blond hair has been cut in a short bell shape with a fringe, the style of the reformatory from which she came. Such dismissive blue eyes, Anna, so pert a nose and such heavy sulkiness in the mouth and jaw! In singlet and working trousers, her figure is not overblown, though I wager she may run to fat in a few years more—certainly if her belly swells with a brat! Her breasts are bouncy, her legs quite long and still trim. If you see her in tight, working trousers from the front there is an outward curve of her belly which suggests she may already have dropped a brat on the sly! On the inner edge of her thighs, either side of her cunt, a fleshy bulge swells out the cloth. Tell me, Anna, is this not one of the first signs of fat? If you see her turn and bend in fawn riding tights, Jackie's bottom is seductively fattish but not yet too much so for me. Under her disdainful manner, however, she is extremely wanton and eager.

My younger charge, Amanda Ticklepuss, known as Mandy, is eighteen years old. Yet she is quite tall and strongly built, with long, firm legs and sturdy hips which give her quite a broad and Amazonian arse. True to type, Mandy has a strong-featured face, softened by a pleasant, smiling manner and gentle waves of chestnut hair, which are combed loose to her shoulders—such a beautiful reddish tint.

After the randiness of many of the young bitches at Greystones, I was quite taken aback by Jackie's display of disdain and her pretence of injured virtue whenever one tipped her breast, stroked her thighs, or pinched her arse-cheeks lightly. I was almost deceived by this. Then, one morning, I was invited to attend Miss Martinet in order to discuss some manner of business. Silas Raven, the surly old brief, was coming down to Greystones—at our expense—to discuss some matter connected with my Uncle Brandon's will. I informed the grooms that I should not be visiting the stables that day, for I envisaged a prime lunch and a good blow-out.

As I waited with Miss M., a telegram arrived. There had been a most unfortunate incident in the gentlemen's lavatory at Victoria Station. The door of one of the cubicles had become wedged and two uniformed police constables had been summoned in the general alarm. When the door was freed by these two stalwarts, out tumbled Silas Raven and two young guardsmen in *deshabille*. The young soldiers were all for laying the constabulary senseless and making off. Silas Raven prevented the necessity. A few moments later, the entire party went its separate ways, the pockets of the two policemen chinking with sovereigns, and the zealous officers of the law saluting S. Raven, Esquire, as if he might be the Prince of Wales and Lord Rosebery all in one.

Yet after so disturbing an entree to the railway station, the respected counsel from Grays Inn was far too shaken to contemplate a journey that day. In consequence, Miss M. and I found ourselves at what is colloquially termed "a loose end."

It was a fine summer morning, the chestnut candles still upon the trees, and I thought it no hardship to stroll back to the stables and perhaps from there to the cliff walk and the sea. I made no great sign of my approach, walking slowly and in some depth of thought. Only as I approached did I realize that some kind of revelry was taking place in the stable block. This gave me pause. By good fortune, there was a side door which led directly into my own little office. The wall between the office and the main stable boasted one of those miniature internal windows which save folk the necessity of walking all the way 'round to the door when some paper or small object is to be handed through. Unobserved, I might yet discover the nature of the stable celebration.

I slipped in quietly and went across to the little window. Sure enough I had a fine view of all that was passing in my absence—or so everyone there believed. Jackie and Mandy were at the centre of the excitement, the two grooms were at one end of the room, and the stable boys at the other.

Twenty-five-year-old Jackie did not look as if she had been a volunteer for these japes. Under the bell shape of blond hair, her mouth was hard and sullen, her blue eyes frostily dismissive. She was twisting in the arms of the two men who held her, for they were trying to get her pants off.

The singlet parted company from her pants at the waist. She wriggled 'round. Now they had her bending, the tight, fawn riding trousers showing me her long, firm legs and the fattish cheeks of her arse as she stooped.

Fortunately the grooms soon undid the belt and pushed Jackie's pants down to her ankles. They threw her on the pile of straw, where she lay on her belly looking up at them over her shoulder. There was still hostility in her blue eyes as she shook the hair into place after the struggle. Her long legs were pressed tightly together as she lay there and the pale, fattish cheeks of her bottom were similarly tensed.

The first groom stood over her, muscular legs astride and the crotch of his tight breeches now swollen with the size of his erection. He unbuttoned himself and released the stout weapon. The sluttish young blonde defied him, continuing to lie facedown. Slowly, the groom drew the broad leather belt from his waist. Holding the two ends, he placed a foot gently on the young woman's neck to hold her, and brought down the strap half a dozen times across the white quivering cheeks of Jackie's broad, young arse.

With a cry she obeyed him as soon as her neck was released, turning on to her back, knees hugged up, and thighs open. He knelt at her, adjusting his penis to her love-hole.

"You'll enjoy it more for having had your arse strapped, Jackie!" he said humorously. Then he pressed home.

How Jackie loved it! Such sighs and soft crying, as her heels touched the small of her lover's back! When the penis accidentally slipped out of her cunt, she gave such a doleful cry at the loss of its comfort—and such a sob of contentment when it was replaced.

The groom pulled up the front of the blond girl's singlet and busied his mouth with her breasts. He kissed and flicked the nipples with his tongue. Then he gently and lovingly bit her shoulders and her neck. Jackie's own crisis came before his, in a series of short, rising cries. Yet the excitement of her fulfillment soon precipitated his own warm flooding of her cunt. The second groom ordered the young blonde to kneel on all fours, as he released his splendid tool from his pants.

What a sight was this! Our impudent young blonde now knelt like a bitch waiting to be mounted—and mounted she soon was! The second groom rode into her cunt with even more vigor than the first. Yet in his hand he also held a blob of saddle soap, well moistened by his saliva. Presently he used this to prepare the tight bud of Jackie's anus. Drawing from her cunt, he thrust hard and impaled her twenty-five-year-old bottom in the style of a champion. The young woman gave a cry of surprise rather than discomfort. Yet he entered so easily that I feel sure Jackie had been up to this sort of mischief with other men. She loves the penis, cannot get enough of it, and will take it in any way rather than be without it.

"You'll be getting a nice thick pressing of juice-up your arse, Jackie!" gasped the groom. "Lie still now and enjoy it!"

His words were proved right almost at once. Yet, while he was busy with the young blonde, the first groom had gone over to the stable-lads, who held Mandy between them. Perhaps she was not a girl to struggle with, for at eighteen years old she was tall, long-legged, and strongly made. The firmness of her pale features and chin was softened by the chestnut-red of the hair which was combed in gentle waves to her shoulders.

The stable-lads were rather young for the antics of the grooms with Jackie and none of them could rival Mandy's twenty years. Yet they had a natural curiosity and excitement about the way in which little girls—and big girls too—were made. Mandy's long legs and sturdy hips were tightly encased in riding jeans, which the groom now ordered her to take off. She looked at him with uncertain defiance.

"Want the strap across your bottom, Mandy?" he asked, "like Jackie had it! No? Take them off, then!"

Imagine, as she obeyed, how the lads clustered 'round! Some stroked her long, firm thighs, others were bold enough to fiddle with her love-pouch, a few preferred to slip their fingers between the strong, young cheeks of Mandy's arse.

"Lie over the pile of straw, Mandy!" said the groom. "Pull your singlet right up and show us those luscious young breasts!"

So our long-legged maiden tugged the singlet up under her armpits and lay back on the straw, looking up at the stable-lads with quiet amusement as they goggled at her.

"Want to be a dirty girl, Mandy?" said the groom, smiling at her. Mandy grinned back, as if they shared some secret, her strong chin and steady eyes challenging him. "Do it lying over the straw, Mandy!" he chuckled, handing her something closed in his fist.

It was Mandy's party trick, greatly admired by the lads. She took from the groom two china pullet eggs, each the size of a large plum. She popped them into her mouth and made a swallowing movement twice.

"Jackie!" called the groom, now that his colleague had finished with that luscious young blonde, "over here! Play at dirty girls with Mandy on the straw!"

Jackie obeyed, and we enjoyed the sight of the strapping, young Amazon of eighteen and the fat-arsed blonde of twenty-five writhing naked in each other's arms. Presently, Mandy sat up, with a look of feigned dismay. She parted her bare thighs and looked as the two pullet eggs popped out of her cunt! Her open mouth showed they truly had gone! The grooms turned, presenting the rear of her long legs, strong hips, her strapping young arse, and the auburn hair on her bare shoulders. The two china ovals were popped into Mandy's arse-hole. More writhing in Jackie's arms and then another look of dismay. Opening her lips like a magician, Mandy showed the little white eggs in her mouth once more.

It was easy, of course, but effective and rather charming. The stable-lads cheered and guffawed. Clearly there were several pairs of china eggs. Mandy transferred the two from her mouth into Jackie's as they kissed, then produced the two which had been lodged in her cunt before the show had begun. As they were thumbed into Mandy's arse, she took the first pair back from Jackie's mouth. Now Jackie's bottom produced another pair from between its fattish cheeks.

I was most diverted by the antics of the stable-lads—the manner in which these amiable young scamps amused themselves with Mandy and Jackie! Yet prudence dictated that I should not reveal my presence just then. I slipped out of the side door and crossed the sunlit lawns towards the main house. Perhaps I might entertain Miss Martinet at luncheon with stories of my past adventures.

Just then my attention was caught by the sight of one of Miss M.'s well-bred young pupils making her way to the music room. Vanessa was just short of her nineteenth birthday and in every way a contrast to a plump-bottomed slut like Jackie or even a strapping young wench of Mandy's type. Because she is rather short, Vanessa looks more pert than her years. She was dressed just then in her white blouse and striped tie, the dark-blue skirt, which came down to the middle of her calves, and a pair of white ankle socks. Is she seductive? Who can say? Her brown hair is cut straight, in a casqued shape which ends at her collar, her fringe parted on her forehead. Vanessa has a lightly sun-browned face, prettily heart-shaped with high cheekbones and light-blue eyes that have a narrow, crinkling mockery in them. She has the firm, clear-cut nose and chin of the well-bred college girl.

There is still a childish slovenliness about her which, in a grown woman, would be sluttish. The movements of her hips and thighs have a slow heaviness which lacks mature feminine grace. Left to herself, she would no doubt have grown up as a very self-centered young lady. How fortunate that she could be brought under discipline at Greystones. If Vanessa is to be chastised in any case, it may as well be by those who enjoy it!

I watched her enter the music room and I spied through the large picture window to see what she would do. To my surprise, Miss Martinet was already in there. I could not hear what passed between them, but the dumb-show itself was most eloquent.

Miss M. unbuttoned Vanessa's blouse and untied the school tie, baring the young pupil above her waist except for her breast halter. Her skirt was next removed. Vanessa's calves and thighs lack a mature woman's shape as yet, being midway between the lumpishness of an adolescent child and the grace of a young nymph. She now wore her white ankle socks and a pair of tight, stretched briefs made of white cotton web, the first sign that she was due for a dancing lesson.

Miss Martinet stood close, kissed Vanessa lightly on the lips, and began to work the briefs down over the youngster's hips and thighs. I stared with fascination, wondering if eighteen-year-old Vanessa would be compelled to have Lesbian sex with her mistress. Miss M. led her to a chair and sat down. She put Vanessa over her knee and stroked the bare back and hips for a moment. The taut, adolescent pallor of Vanessa's bottom-cheeks was so prominently presented that I thought she was due for a spanking from Miss Martinet, but that was not what happened.

The mistress slid a hand through the rear opening of the college girl's thighs and began to fondle Vanessa's vaginal pouch and clitoris. The pupil gasped and squirmed with the excitement of this delicious masturbation. She did not climax, but the lubrication began to flow in her young cunt and soon one could see its slipperiness on her inner thighs as well as on her love-purse itself.

What do you imagine Miss M. did next? She took some discs of red sticky paper, each the size of a small coin. One by one she wetted them with Vanessa's cunt juice and then stuck them here and there on the woman-child's body. The breast halter was removed and they were pasted to her blossoming tits. They were stuck to her belly, her thighs, and between her thighs. Yet more were glued lightly to Vanessa's taut, pale bottom-cheeks and some on her eighteen-year-old arse-hole. Then she was made to stand up.

Can you guess what was about to happen, Anna! I vow I could not. Never fear, my sweet. The mystery shall be revealed in tomorrow night's letter from your own adoring,

Timothy

* * *

Greystones, 3 June 1904

My darling Anna,

I now resume my account of the other day's adventures. Picture Vanessa, naked but for her white ankle socks, standing at the centre of the polished boards which form the floor of the music room. Her wrists are strapped together in front of her. A leather collar 'round her neck is attached to a slack cord which hangs from the beam above her, thus keeping her in one area of the floor.

I could not hear whether there was the music of a tambourine and flute, yet Vanessa now began the sinuous writhing of a harem dance. So clumsy she seemed for eighteen, though there was a knowing-ness in that light, olive-skinned face, with its mocking blue eyes and well-cut features, under the fringe of her brown hair.

She knelt open-legged before her mistress's chair and began to shake her pert young breasts eagerly. I could see Miss M.'s lips forming her words slowly.

"Have you been fondling and playing with your tits as I ordered, Vanessa, to fill them out? Good. Come to my room each evening at nine and show me how you do it."

The aim of the dance was to shake free the tiny discs of paper stuck to the youngster's body. At last they began to spiral like autumn leaves from Vanessa's sweet little breasts. Miss Martinet leant forward, took each nipple in turn, and erected it firmly with her skillful tongue. Vanessa rose and began arching and rolling her taut belly at Miss M., offering it to her kisses. By this means she contrived to make the mistress's lips brush her flat and taut abdomen, thus freeing more of the paper discs. Then, leaning far back, the pupil offered her splayed thighs, writhing them seductively to dislodge the red circles pasted between. Miss M.'s finger caressed Vanessa's love-slit until the schoolgirl thighs trembled from quite a different cause.

By squirming her thighs together, Vanessa managed to dislodge most of the discs on their inner surfaces, but those on her cunt itself proved so tenacious. Smiling, Miss Martinet intruded her fingers between Vanessa's squirming adolescent thighs so that her dancing pupil might smooth herself upon them and so free the little paper discs which clung there. With how many soft schoolgirl sighs and gasps were they dislodged!

Her mistress took a towel and rubbed it lightly between the girl's thighs, squeezing Vanessa's love-purse dry in such a manner as to bring her close to orgasm. Now the petite high-school charmer turned. The cheeks of Vanessa's bottom had the pale taut-ness and elasticity of childhood but also the first traces of a woman's more voluptuous fullness. She leant forward a little and writhed her seat-cheeks at Miss Martinet, as if trying to seduce the older woman by this performance.

Miss Martinet was not smiling now. She craned forward a little, lips pressed hard. Vanessa's arse-cheeks surged and parted so innocently. Miss Martinet chose a tawse, a broad lightweight strap, divided into three tails at its end. Vanessa's backside did a desperate jungle dance, but the obstinate red discs of paper still clung.

The mistress used the strap across the bare writhing cheeks of Vanessa's bottom. She caught the youngster on the backs of the thighs as well. Six tunes the leather exploded on the cheeks of Vanessa's eighteen-year-old backside. Twice more on her thighs. She tried to turn 'round, to shield her buttocks, but the strap kissed her flank savagely.

As the last paper disc fluttered down, Vanessa sank to the floor exhausted. Miss Martinet ceased to be the tyrant and became the lover once more. She knelt beside Vanessa, gently stroking her brown hair, comforting and caressing until her fingers slipped at last between the rather ungainly adolescent thighs. Vanessa's sobs became soft, questioning sighs of wonder. Miss Martinet kissed the tears from the eyes of her high-school pupil. With gentle skill, she brought Vanessa to a crescendo for ten or fifteen minutes.

Then I saw a curious thing: to one side of the room was a long curtain, reaching from the ceiling to within an inch or two of the floor. From under the curtain protruded a foot in a black, patent-leather shoe. In front of the concealed figure, whose excitement seemed to come from watching Vanessa, there knelt a young woman whose name was spoken as Julie. I recognized this as belonging to a nineteen-year-old girl in Miss Martinet's possession. Julie was one of those slender young women who make up their height by high heels, and whose thighs are no thicker than a man's upper arm.

Julie is a slut as surely as any girl in the establishment. Through a chink in the curtain I could make out her sulky, sour little face with its rather crude features and dark, hazel eyes. Her blond hair had been braided into a plait and was pinned up in a topknot, revealing her slender little neck. I can imagine how the men who were served by her in the shop where she worked must have coveted her. What would they have said now to see Julie rhythmically and expertly sucking the penis?

As she knelt at her task, her thighs were so slender, and yet the slight backward jut of her hips gave a certain rather childish fatness to the shape of her bottom-cheeks. There was a senile crowing from her lover and Julie was obliged to swallow down her repugnance. Two veined and gnarled old hands held her head close while the old man's sperm-spasm loaded her tongue and he made her gulp it down.

Your own adoring Tim

* * *

Ramallah, 12 July 1904

My dearest Tim,

I hope you will not be vexed, my precious, at what I have done. Never before, upon my maiden honor, have I shown one of your sweet letters to another living soul. Nor would I have done so now had I not been so intrigued by the manner in which Jackie and Mandy were set to work as "girl-ponies" at Greystones! Such a charming image was conjured up in my mind by your account that I could scarcely rid myself of it.

I know you will forgive me for showing that portion of your letter to our generous Pasha of Ramallah. As you shall hear, my action provoked the most amusing results.

To my surprise, he knew all about such games. Indeed, he said, the sultans and pashas of the East had long been accustomed to employ some of their favorite concubines between the shafts of their little garden carriages. He cited so many instances in history, from Sultan Ibrahim of the Sublime Porte to Mulay Ishmael himself, that I could scarcely hold any further doubts in the matter.

"Not twenty miles from here lives Pasha Ibrahim," said he, "a wealthy patriarch of sixty summers. His harem is extensive and, like myself, he is a great lover of English and European beauty. The use of harness, as he calls it, is indispensable to the management of his girls, especially if one of them should prove difficult."

I listened agog, Tim, for, though I could imagine that such things might happen behind harem walls, it was astonishing to be contorted so quickly with the proof of it.

"Then, sir," I said, "I suppose a great deal of privacy must surround these occasions. The good Pasha Ibrahim would guard such a secret closely."

The Pasha of Ramallah laughed. "Dear young lady! Why do you say so? All the world knows of the means he employs. In this country we think better of a man who is prepared to resort to such measures, provided he thinks them desirable. My brother Ibrahim opens his gardens on such an occasion to his intimate friends, just as he does on other days of hospitality."

Now, Tim, you may be sure that I questioned our friend so long and so ingeniously about Ibrahim's pony-girls that he soon saw my intention.

"I believe, dear young lady, that you would be ever grateful to me if I could contrive your presence at one of these afternoon outings. Am I not right?"

He was so amused at finding me out, as he thought, that I could only confirm his suspicion as demurely as I knew how. Pray, give me credit, Tim. You will remember well how I can counterfeit the faint maiden blush, the modest lowering of the gaze, the cloistered innocence of virtue upon these occasions.

"Very well," he said, "nothing could be easier than for you to accompany me in a day or two on my visit to the happy fellow. I happen to know that he has lately acquired a most rebellious young lass of eighteen, who is more than due for a lesson in obedience."

I need not say how I looked forward with the greatest curiosity to the day of that visit. It seemed best to say nothing of it to my dearest papa and mama, beyond telling them that I was to take tea with Ibrahim's ladies.

It was still morning when we arrived at Ibrahim's estate. Like our friend's, it is set in a green jewel of an oasis, remote from the city, its high surrounding walls well guarded to exclude intruders and immure the occupants. From the carriage window, as we passed along the drive, I was able to glimpse the ornamental pleasure gardens with their winding paths. A fine lake lay at the centre, quite half a mile long. Upon its shore stood replicas of small, pillared temples here and there, such as might have been built for Apollo or Jove, in the ancient world. Banks of mauve, silken-colored flowers rose on either side, others rising flame-red or fierce blue in the brilliant sun. Elsewhere the trees provided deep, shady retreats where marble fountains played.

Of the house itself I will say only that I was a perfect Alhambra of Moorish courtyards and colonnades, with dazzling sun on the marble and water, restful darkness in the tapestried rooms.

The tyrant Ibrahim, as I had imagined him, was a jovial gentleman with a twinkle in his eye. When the formal courtesies were over, he escorted us to a grassy knoll overlooking his splendid grounds. Here an excellent lunch was served: the most succulent fruits, the crispest roast, and the most savory dishes were moistened by fine vintages and champagne. Ibrahim's religion forbid him the use of wine, yet he is too generous a man ever to stint his guests.

It was here that I again saw Connie, the young woman of some twenty-five years, with her Asian or Chinese appearance. The black, silken sweep of her hair was once again held in place by a pair of silver slides so that it did not fall too far over her face. She was not entirely naked, though very nearly so: a pair of tiny cones, made of tight, black silk, covered her nipples, and were held in place by black silk cord over her two shoulders and 'round her back. Her other garment was a black silk cache-sex, a tiny triangle at her loins, held by black cord 'round her waist, its supports running down her belly to the silk adornment, and at the rear running back up to her waist between the cheeks of her bottom.

Several different girls acted as waitresses, Connie being given orders to minister to half a dozen of us. The rather snub features, slanted eyes, and pretty heart-shaped face she has are so very appealing! And what of her figure? No part of the world, I vow, can rival the Far East in that neat feminine charm; the slim, nimble forms, the tight rounds of buttocks, which never grow too fat even in a girl whose hips are broadened by her posture.

As she walked to and fro, the eyes of the men followed the light, graceful movements of her body. They contemplated her pale-yellow satiny skin, her tight little breasts, narrow thighs, and saffron bottom-cheeks. Even when she was on full view as a shop girl, I cannot believe she received as much admiration in six months as she now got in half an hour.

The meal ended. Now the men lit their cheroots and began to chaff one another. There was much daring of each fellow in turn to grasp a nettle from the hedgerow and find for himself if it had a sting. Wagers were laid and decided by the victim's silence or his sudden sharp intake of breath and muffled curse.

The English Milord was present, with a certain unsmiling coldness and he offered to prove the wagers another way. He beckoned Connie. The young Asian woman approached. I heard later that he had once encountered her before her life as a concubine began and that she had spurned his admiration. Perhaps that explained his conduct now.

"Put yourself over my knee, face down, Connie," he said quietly.

There was a look of apprehension in Connie's almond eyes as she obeyed him, the black silken hair hanging downward, her trim saffron-satin seat-cheeks facing upward. Now it was Connie who must make the wager, guessing the effect of each plucked nettle in turn. If she won, her reward was to be fed from the whisky flask. If she lost, she must endure the return of the last nettle to cause a gasp.

First she guessed it would not sting. The young man held the frond to her buttocks with no effect. One of his companions told the girl to turn her pretty face upwards, whereupon he held the whisky flask to her mouth. We saw her swallow once or twice, then make as if to turn her head away. He restrained this.

"A little more yet, Connie. We must fortify you for your ordeal!"

The man across whose knees she lay circled her waist with his left arm to hold her firmly. In his right hand he took another nettle, which Connie also pronounced harmless. This time she was wrong. As soon as he touched the spiked leaf to the demure saffron cheek of her bottom, the Asian girl cried out her mistake, her trim legs twisting to no avail. The young man continued to hold the leaf to the same place until the allotted time was up. A deep pinkness the size of a large coin appeared on Connie's left buttock, with two or three white sting points in it.

Then came the forfeit. Was it pure malice which made the young man touch the virulent sharpness to that same tender place, holding it there with lips so tight that the veins on his forehead stood out? That done, he looked down at the appealing innocence of Connie's charming Chinese bottom. With no hint of amusement, he chose another frond, identical to that just discarded. Connie made a submissive, imploring sound, for rebellion is not in her nature.

Just then we were invited to witness Ibrahim's garden outing. The young man who was engaged with Connie remained deaf to this invitation. We left him still holding the Asian girl over his knee, not guess-big what his eventual purpose might be. Looking back, I caught a glimpse of her face turning upward to him, its demure Oriental charm contorted into a devil mask of tears.

You will believe, Tim, that all this was done merely to avenge himself in one way upon Connie. I assure you that you are wrong. The cunning secret, they tell me, is that such applications of nettles add much to one's enthusiasm for love. Connie well knew that by enduring such a preliminary she might hope for a rich harvest!

We came down to the lakeside pathway where there stood the strangest little equipage. It was a light garden carriage with shafts. Across these shafts were two securely fastened crossbars, one at the very front and another midway. From the direction of the house, two of Ibrahim's valets were escorting a loud-mouthed, strident youngster whom I believe you may well recognize.

She walked with a contemptuous toss of the long, fair hair, which framed the broad oval of her face, combed from a central parting to lie loose on her shoulders. Certainly the narrow eyes and thin mouth completed a picture of snub-nosed insolence.

Can this be the young hoyden you once spoke of? While not particularly tall or plump, Elaine appeared a sturdy enough adolescent in her white blouse and tie, the pleated grey skirt worn scandalously short in a brazen display of robust young thighs.

There was no doubt of her rebellious nature, which was visible in her strident manner and the toss of her fan- hair, as well as audible in her vulgar speech. When she was given her orders at the carriage, she looked with contempt at the guests, undid her skirt and stepped out of it.

Because Ibrahim prefers such pupils to show their bare legs in brief dancing skirts, Elaine's schoolgirl knickers were no more than a pair of briefs in white stretched cotton. Her strong young hips and bottom-cheeks were thus admirably shaped for our observation.

She stood between the shafts, her back to the driver's seat of the little carriage. The harnessing began. Elaine had to bend forward over the first bar, which supported her young belly. A broad, stout strap was riveted to the bar and the valets now drew this tightly 'round Elaine's waist. Not only did it hold her down. By pressing her belly even more firmly on the bar, it caused her waist to arch downward and so increased the swell of Elaine's bottom in her tight knickers.

Her arms were at full stretch in front of her, each wrist securely held in a leather cuff to the front of the shaft. For the first time the impudence in the broad oval of her face and features seemed to falter. She saw one of the valets take a slim cane with a spring like a rapier. He laid it conveniently by the driver's seat, adding a birch and one or two other means of discipline.

Elaine tossed her fair hair clear, and craned 'round with desperate anxiety to watch these preparations. She was gnawing compulsively at her lower lip in apprehension. Her hands were clenched into tight fists and her bare legs shifted and tensed as the men kept her waiting.

A still heat pervaded the afternoon. In the deep shade where we stood only the drone of insects disturbed the silence. The velvet petals of the red flowers seemed to wilt and the lake lay bright as a burning mirror. With loving slowness, one of the valets took the waistband of Elaine's knickers and pulled the little pants down her legs until she could step free of them. There was another stir of interest at this. While the youngster still watched us over her shoulder, we moved a little closer to take advantage of this bare rear view. Though I can only speak from a feminine point of view, Tim, even I could see what it was that attracted the gentlemen of the party. Firmly broadened and rounded by her posture, the pale, sturdy cheeks of Elaine Cox's tomboy bottom had that robust, vulgar appeal which is perhaps at perfection in a girl of eighteen. The light-haired love-pouch peeped backward between her thighs; like her well-parted buttocks, it was within fondling distance of the driver.

One detail marred this charming cameo. The white tail of the school blouse still trailed slantwise across her bare seat. The valet now tucked it up, well clear of Elaine's young backside.

Anna & Tim

She appeared quite a big-bottomed girl in this posture, of course, and it was hard whether to think of her as pupil or woman. I imagine it is the fate of such a tomboy that her vigor and vulgarity lose her all consideration from the protective instincts of mankind. Certainly there was no suggestion on this occasion that she should be treated otherwise than a grown woman—nor any justification for that. Elaine was such a provoking mixture: the broad-hipped vulgarity of her backside in its present posture, the insolence of her manner, her schoolgirl tie and bare bottom, the impudence of a slut and the innocent awkwardness of adolescence.

Ibrahim appeared, applauded by the onlookers, who lined the lakeside path. He bowed to either side with gracious condescension. The greeting was returned. Then, turning in our direction, his eyes brightened at the sight of a bare-bottomed tomboy like Elaine harnessed bending between his carriage shafts. He took his place in the driver's seat. Elaine tossed her fair hair and craned 'round again, trying to watch him, with narrow-eyed anger.

Ibrahim leant forward a little. In his hands he seemed to weigh the full, pale schoolgirl bum-cheeks. Slowly his fingers moved.

"Such a warm little pouch," he murmured, "such sweltering lips! How many lucky young boys have been permitted a glimpse of it—and more. Back here, though, I sense a virginity. How tight! Even to the finger!"

Elaine twisted her hips as violently as the waist strap would allow. "You brute!" Hair tossing, face craning 'round, she vented her fury. "You dirty, filthy brute!"

Ibrahim sat back with a gentle sigh. "Such rebelliousness, Elaine? We must overcome that. Forward, if you please!"

As he spoke, Ibrahim took the slim cane in one hand and tapped it into the palm of the other. Elaine's defiance was tinged with panic now, knowing the caning would begin as she moved forward.

"No!" The dismay and the rebellion were plainly heard in her cry. "I won't! No! No!"

Ibrahim smiled at the outburst. His arm went back. Down flashed the bamboo with a whip-like report across the sturdy, bare cheeks of Elaine Cox's eighteen-year-old bottom. What consternation in her eyes now! She bit her lip not to cry out, though her seat and thighs squirmed with anguish. She clearly regarded the humiliation of pony-girl discipline with a mixture of dread and defiance!

Ibrahim's smile broadened. He gave a second and third stroke of the cane across her young arse. His schoolgirl pony yelled wildly at the atrocious smart and tried to kick backwards. His mouth tightened in disapproval. Karim, the valet, at his master's signal, cured this violence. He walked across, took the bamboo, and gave two thrashing strokes across the backs of Elaine's bare, sturdy thighs, keen enough to raise gooseflesh upon them.

What a change came over the young rebel now! The broad oval of Elaine's face was a picture of repentance. The narrow eyes brimmed with tears and the mouth wailed forlornly. She was almost more the whipped child of eighteen than the hardened young strumpet. Smiling, Ibrahim diddled her between her tomboy bottom-cheeks and thighs.

"Now your obedience training begins, Elaine Cox! You're sturdy enough to be my pony-girl—and impudent enough to need the whip across your bare bottom! Pull forward, Elaine!"

Smack! went the bamboo across her broad, young backside. 'Round went the wheels, with Elaine straining with every muscle of her robust young thighs and hips. The ornamental garden carriage trundled along the lakeside path, past banks of flowers rising like walls upon the dark-leaved shrubs.

Ibrahim had no eyes for the beauties of a garden. His gaze followed the squirming adolescent hips, the arching and rounding of Elaine's bum-cheeks, as she pulled forward. Her fatly offered adolescent seat bore the long, swelling weals of the bamboo's tapestry. At each step forward, with leg lifted, her hips went farther over the crossbar. With each stride, she lay almost bottom-upwards over the bar, buttocks enticingly parted in a full rear view. Elaine's backside tempted punishment like any fifth-form tomboy over the desk, awaiting the teacher's bamboo. The sight stiffened Ibrahim's disciplinary zeal. His cane rang out across the squirming, robust cheeks of Elaine's bottom, like a ringmaster's whip. Several times he required his minions to detain her in this pose while he added six or eight wicked strokes across the weals with which he had already embroidered Elaine's seat.

I will not weary you with an account of every detail. Suffice it to say that no act of a sexual nature was performed on this remarkable outing. The obedience lesson to which Elaine was submitted was, in essentials, of a kind thoroughly approved by England's moral educators.

As the sun waned over the pleasure gardens, the equipage came to an incline in the path, running up to the finest of the temples. Even a sturdy youngster of eighteen was tested in all her sinews to pull the carriage forward. Her momentum flattered. Ibrahim chose a woven, snakeskin pony-lash. Smack! went the whip across the broadened cheeks of Elaine's backside. Frantically she writhed her robust young thighs, struggling wildly upwards, arse over the harness bar. How seductively and lewdly Elaine's adolescent rump squirmed in this posture.

Ibrahim rose in his seat, teeth set with disciplinary zeal. *Smack!* The pony-lash sought the lower fatness of Elaine Cox's tomboy bottom-cheeks. Smack! Whip-smack! Whip-crack-smack! Surely her screams were justified by the ruby beads punctuating the lash marks, trickling down and spending themselves on her thighs.

I had some misgivings at the severity employed to ensure that she accomplished the last and most arduous part of her lesson. Yet one must consider Ibrahim's view. The slope of the path and the labor required caused the seat and hips of Elaine to arch out and squirm in the most lewd and tantalizing manner. It almost seemed that Elaine was deliberately thrusting her eighteen-year-old backside in his face, arching and rounding its fattened cheeks at every step. As her sturdy young legs strained forward, she alternately showed the love-pouch at her thighs and then her widely opened arse-valley. No teacher who had Elaine bending thus before the class could resist giving exemplary chastisement for the moral improvement of the others.

A gate was closed across the path, its keeper standing by. Ibrahim diddled his finger impatiently between the buttocks of his sturdy fifth-form schoolgirl.

"Sound your little post-horn for the gate to open, Elaine!'

When she hesitated, a crack of the snakeskin lash across her bum-cheeks strengthened the force of the command. She was beyond modesty, anyhow. With a cry of compliance, Elaine Cox farted as only a vulgar tomboy of her age knew how. The witty gatekeeper chose to be deaf. Again the snakeskin kissed Elaine's strapping young buttocks. She emitted two of the rudest carriage notes ever heard in the history of equitation. And so the gate opened.

So the obedience lesson ended. What controversies would attend it outside the harem walls! Yet it contained one advantage. Before it began, Elaine seemed a hard, impudent rebel. One felt pitiless in dealing with her, as if she were an insolent and vulgar grown woman of eighteen. Now the snub-nosed impudence of the broad oval of her face was dissolved in tears, she wailed for pity. Now one could soften towards her. She was a college girl of eighteen, pitilessly whipped for her offence. Of course one smiled and teased her gently about the whipping, to ensure that she did not forget its purpose. Yet now one could fondle Elaine gently and affectionately, knowing that she would respond with the tearful gratitude of a schoolgirl whipped and pardoned.

The two valets unfastened her and led her away. Elaine walked with her skirt and knickers in her hand, unable to wear them in her present state. The forlorn young mouth relaxed from its sobbing dejection and the weeping was less copious. Her head was still bowed a little in self-pity, her gentler wailing accompanied by the brushing-away tears with the edge of her hand. She walked slowly and uncomfortably. One could not begin to count the number of swollen weals from the bamboo that crossed her tomboy buttocks.

As she passed the onlookers, Ibrahim explained that another such punishment lesson would be given her in a few weeks' time.

You may imagine Elaine looking 'round at us, the broad oval of her face a study in dismay, as she tossed back her long fair hair. Make no mistake, several of the spectators craned forward to catch her gaze. It seems they wanted Elaine to see their eyes wide and mouths open in amazement and delight at what was going to happen to her.

Do you deplore this as the vindictive lechery of the harem? Believe me, Tim, it is no less common among our educators and moralists at home. As Lord Byron remarks to them when they execute vengeance upon a pair of shapely buttocks, "'Tis well your cassocks hide your rising lust." Had you but seen the sight in the reformatory punishment room on the night before Elaine was shipped into harem slavery, you would need no further argument. On that last evening, she was strapped over the block on all fours, as if for judicial caning. The justices sat smiling in their chairs to watch. The master, grave-faced in his shirtsleeves, carried the bamboo.

You might have thought it a lesson in moral discipline. And so it was but for one thing. Elaine would be going to a place from which she would never return to tell tales! All restraint upon the moralists was removed. It was a year ago when she had much the appearance she has now.

The eight magistrates were rotund figures of about fifty. They went in two by two at first. Elaine's skirt and pants were lowered. By talk of whips and cigar tips, she was made compliant. One man knelt before her and she sucked his grey-haired cock. The other knelt at the rear, seduced by the full, pale cheeks of Elaine Cox's eighteen-year-old bottom. Four in succession

Anna & Tim

sodomised the schoolgirl tomboy, four more obliging her to swallow love's potion. Her virginity was kept for the market-place.

Three dozen with the cane across her sturdy, bare backside. Then, since no one would ever know, the pony-lash! A savage half-hour. Elaine Cox, screaming and twisting, saw only stiff, grey-haired pricks and smiles of delight. Such is the influence of moral discipline! Lads from the adjoining boys' reformatory risked life and limb, shinning up to peer in at the high, barred windows. As the thirty-six allotted bamboo strokes were given across the cheeks of Elaine's arse, the lads grinned knowingly at her. She was the permitted spy at their masturbation rituals, the young slut who sucked off the winner of the bare-knuckle boxing. When, her buttocks wealed by the bamboo, the whip was chosen in addition, not one of them would have gone to her aid. They too were longing to see Elaine taken all the way into that darker region which lies far beyond the limit of any punishment. To her screams as her bottom was skinned they replied with priapic delirium, each lad pumping his organ until his eyes rolled back and the gruel jetted wildly out. Was this truly superior to the example of the harem?

At dinner we were waited upon by two of Ibrahim's eighteen-year-old nymphs. Valerie was a slim gamine, with a short, auburn crop and a slender figure. Linda appeared so a soft, sensuous little blonde, with sly, blue eyes, a short mane of fair hair, and a sniggering manner. I cannot say which of these two slipped a note under my plate informing me that they and other beauties had been abducted and were now unwilling bed slaves of the pasha. I was beseeched to convey this news to London. A gunboat might then blast the palace of Ibrahim to pieces and carry home the little minxes in triumph!

Be sure I know my duty! I handed the note to Ibrahim at once. He thanked me gravely, promising me that, in the coming night, Linda and Valerie should be birched for five minutes each time the clock struck. I begged only that he would make it ten minutes!

You approve my action, Tim? Think what a scandal would result from the note written by these little sluts! The pashas are our loyalist allies! Imagine the fate of poor Papa—and he only just accoutered with an ambassador's cocked hat and plumes! Britannia may have her faults, but she knows better than lesser nations the importance of avoiding such imprudent disclosures!

I was not much disturbed that night by agreeable images of the plump, pearly little moons of Linda's bottom under the bamboo. It is no worse than discipline in many an English home. Thus I take my adoring leave of you, dearest Tim. Your next news is eagerly awaited by

Your ever-loving Anna

* * *

Greystones, 20 My 1904

My own dearest Anna,

My heart leapt for joy when an envelope came bearing upon it your own unmistakable hand. I read your bold account of the good Sultan Ibrahim and his novel method of carriage propulsion! It is true, my sweet, there are young termagants like Elaine who, by every moral right, should be put to discipline of this kind. Almost all the educators and justices of England would agree with me in that.

By the same token, one respects a wife who is loyal to her husband and duties. Once she transgresses, however, is there any reason for trying to shield her from the ravishing of the world?

In my own small way, I too have had a victory over a recalcitrant girl. I speak of our young trollop Noreen. But what insolence still dwells in those hard, pale features and brown eyes.

The other night, Miss Martinet, aided by her staff, was awarding discipline to certain strapping young wenches like Noreen. The procedure for this is, indeed, singular. There is a long bench over which the girls kneel, presenting a row of tightly clad backsides. Their wrists are strapped to a rail on the far side, so that they kneel over the bench on all fours. Lastly, a long screen is lowered from a rail to the backs of their waists, so that they cannot see who stands behind them.

That night it was Miss Martinet who walked down the row. She indicated the fate of each delinquent, for the benefit of the grooms, by chalking on the tightly clad seat-cheeks. Thus a number chalked on the left cheek indicated strokes to be given by the person responsible. A number on the other half showed the preliminary to be given by a groom with a gym-shoe heel.

I vowed to curb Noreen's ill-mannered conduct. So, as Miss M. walked down the line, I watched closely. She strolled up and down the row several times. Pausing she applied the chalk to the robust young cheeks of Katie's seat and inscribed the numbers twenty and twelve. A moment more and she drew thirty and twelve where a pan of tight, grey pants was strained over the full, young cheeks of Susan Underwood's bottom. Sue, with her soft, blond beauty, was a girl whom it would be a pleasure to get into trouble. So it went on until the tour of duty was complete. To my dismay, however, Noreen was un-chalked!

The remedy for that was simple. The curtain had been arranged so that the culprits could not see who was chalking them. It was also intended to prevent a groom with a grudge from adding to the punishment of a girl with whom he had a quarrel. In this case, however, Noreen was easily identifiable. The collar length of her dark hair was concealed as she lay over the bench. Yet, in kneeling over it, she offered an unmistakable alternative profile. The pale jeans seat was taut across her firm, statuesque buttocks, the central seam drawn taut and deep into her arse-crack. The lower softness of her bum-cheeks almost closing over the seam could belong to only one of the miscreants.

I stood there, as if I might Miss M., or whoever had been deputed to this task. Then I ran a hand over the thin, taut denim, which sheathed Noreen's backside. As I did so, she caught her breath, knowing that she was about to be marked with the chalk which lay conveniently to hand. Under my stroking hand I could feel the tensing of her buttocks and her taut, young thighs.

Perhaps it was because she had believed herself safe, having escaped the weekly reckoning, that she now reacted with such consternation. I ran a hand between the rear opening of her thighs and gave her cunt-pouch a good feel through the tight cloth. I continued so long that I began to feel Noreen moistening herself in the clinging pants despite her predicament.

I drew my hand away and left her in suspended animation, so near and yet so far from her fulfillment. My hands were now busy again with the firm, sturdy cheeks of Noreen's arse, stroking, parting, and thumbing. She pushed back impatiently with her hips but, much as she urged it, she could not quite bring herself to beg for the masturbation to continue.

Then I took the chalk, and she was tense and still so that she would be able to feel the shape of the numbers written. On one cheek, I wrote twelve for the groom with the hard-heeled rubber gym-slipper. Noreen cried out, "No!" in a protest at this preliminary discipline. Then, on the other cheek, I chalked a thirty-six. She cried out in alarm, for she had good reason to know what that would mean.

Greatly looking forward to the night ahead, I now tiptoed away to my room and awaited events. I sat in the easy chair, reading the fancies of the

Sporting Times and smoking a thoughtful pipe, as if I had been there all the evening.

Presently I was aware of a disturbance in the next room, to which the grooms had taken my culprit. Noreen still displayed her firm-faced indifference, no more than a flick of her dark fringe or a stare from her impudent brown eyes. They had, I think, held her over a tall stool with her pants undone and pulled down to her ankles.

From the gasping and protests I concluded that one of them was fiddling with her as she was secured. They could not, of course, unbutton themselves and do what they wanted in this situation. Yet it was impossible to believe that they would not play "dirty girl" between her legs with their fingers and between the cheeks of her backside.

The laughter and smiling stopped. One groom spat lightly on the rubber gym-shoe heel. There was a *whack*! and a *smack*! To judge from the sharp intake of breath, it had stung her hard, for her pale bottom-cheeks were jumping and quivering like spanked jelly under the impacts.

One could tell that Noreen was biting her lip not to cry out, as if seeking to deny the groom his triumph over her. He, on the other hand, was grinning back at her, sensing his victory in her tensing seat-cheeks and loud, uneven breath. She held out as the gym-slipper tanned her twice more, and then let out a long gasp.

"Now the first cheek all over again, Noreen," smiled the groom. "No, don't squirm your seat like that, you young trollop! We'll see to it that Mr. Timothy's cane has something to work on!"

I gathered that even when the discipline was finished there was further hostility. A sound of struggling was caused by one groom working the singlet up in order to play with Noreen's tits. The other positively could not draw his fingers away from between her legs and bum-cheeks.

At last they brought her in, wearing only the white singlet, which ended at her waist. In the customary manner, she was made to stand in the corner with her back to the room like a spanked schoolgirl in disgrace. She was not permitted to speak until spoken to, nor to move until ordered to do so. I was to keep her there in that posture until it was convenient for me to complete the discipline. Her wrists were strapped together in front of her, but she was not otherwise restrained.

So I sat there and read the racing column over and over while I smoked a pipe and drank another glass of hock and seltzer. Or so it appeared. In truth, for the next half hour or more, my eyes peeped over the edge of the *Sporting Times*. I simply could not draw my gaze from the deliciously provoking view which a young slut like Noreen offers in this situation. To keep her waiting was also a means of heightening the drama—comedy or tragedy, according to one's view. They had left the stout, leather belt of her riding jeans strapped tightly 'round her waist, narrowing her there and emphasizing the proud swell of her hips and seat.

What was rather appealing was the way in which she stood with head bowed, the dark hair just lifted clear of her collar at the back. I was able to admire her strong and straight young back, the firm robust young thighs, the cheeks of her well-made bottom, still blushing deeply from her tanning and marked in several places by the muddy print of the gym-shoe heel.

I noticed that, as a half-hour ended, Noreen grew increasingly restive. How shall I describe it? Her thighs seemed to shift and tense together a little. The cheeks of her bottom pressed together spasmodically, reducing her arse-cleft to a thin, tight line.

I stood up and walked across to reprimand such willful disobedience. "You were ordered to stand *still*, Noreen! Since you seem to find such difficulty in obeying a simple command, we must enforce that instruction with the cane! Perhaps that will cure you of fidgeting. Bend over! Right over! Do you hesitate, you young slut? Obey the command! At once!"

Rather awkwardly, as it seemed to me, and breathing audibly, Noreen bent to touch her toes. I went down on one knee behind her and my hands made a brief but intimate examination of her strapping young backside. Then I turned away to take the cane from its cupboard.

As I did so, I heard from behind me the sound of a loud and vulgar raspberry. I swung 'round. I must admit that Noreen, her mouth open in alarm, did not look like a girl who had just pressed her tongue between her lips and blown off that street-urchin rudeness. Yet I can hardly believe that my ears deceived me at such close range! Moreover, the young strumpet certainly showed open defiance. Though her pale, firm-featured face was suffused with consternation, she had straightened up and was standing with one hand pressed to her behind. I had certainly given no permission for such a change in posture.

"Very well, Noreen," I said quietly, "if you will have it so, you will. I should very much like to give your backside a long session with the pony-lash tonight. Unfortunately, such extreme discipline must be approved by Miss

Martinet. Be assured I shall apply to her in the morning. Tonight you shall have the cane."

In order that I might enjoy the retribution fully, I thought it prudent to require her to pull her pants up and to have her escorted to the stable-block, well out of earshot. Would I not be approved of by those passing admirers who had seen the strapping young wench standing slack-hipped as a whore? When the grooms had secured her on all fours over the padded birching stool, would not those admirers have stood agog at the same sight? The pale-blue jeans seat was splitting tight over the strong, well-made cheeks of Noreen's backside. A flick of her dark hair and she was staring back with the same firm-faced impudence which had greeted their admiration of her in this pose.

I undid her at the waist and pushed the pants to her knees, adding one more strap to pinion her sturdy legs together just at the base of her thighs. My finger teased the rear pout of her vaginal lips. My hands fondled the pale, sturdy swell of her bottom-cheeks. My fingers fiddled remorselessly between those cheeks for several minutes, despite the tensing and shifting of her seat.

"Thirty-six strokes of the bamboo across your behind, Noreen. That is your allotted penalty for a week's misconduct. After that, we must add something for your disgraceful conduct in the other room."

Now, under the level fringe of dark hair, her eyes filled with dismay. Yet I had endured enough of her impudence and was resolved.

"You fear you will not be able to bear it, Noreen? Fortunately, the choice is not yours. You will be made to bear it all the same."

She could not take her eyes off the long, rippling bamboo. I was determined to subdue her quickly. She gave a gasp of fright as I measured the first stroke very low, across the light creases which divided Noreen's statuesque buttocks and thighs, a supremely sensitive area.

"Six strokes in succession across there, Noreen, to teach you manners!"

The first lash of the bamboo across that path made her fingers clench and thighs press hard together. A flat *smack*! of the cane across the same track brought a half-suppressed cry. With wicked but righteous accuracy, I landed two more on top of those. Noreen screamed as the last two whipped the swelling bamboo print of the others.

"And two more across there, Noreen. Just where the edge of the chair comes. Remember this when next you are tempted to be insolent."

Twice more I caught her there. Noreen's bottom-cheeks were writhing, as if she were seated bare on a red-hot saddle. What a tale of woe might be read in that hard young face now; Noreen's tears were brimming and coursing down. I touched the cane across the crowns of her buttocks, where she was so broad. "Eight strokes here, Noreen. Right where you sit." Wide-eyed and wild-mouthed, she made the rafters ring. I allowed her a pause after the second batch. Then I put my lips to her ear. "And now, Noreen, your thirty-six." At nineteen, Noreen is so strongly built I quite thought she would break the straps in her frenzy at learning this. But they held her. I continued to murmur to her—for my bark was to prove worse then my bite—explaining the leniency of such discipline. There were countries in the world, I told her, where such insolence by a slave girl to her master would be rewarded by one last night. There, too, she would be

on all fours, though strapped down astride the traditional bench, her thighs conveniently parted and rump-cheeks spread. The grave-faced vizier would watch the two burly, lion-clothed minions during the long night. The whips and the implements of the brazier would be eagerly employed upon Noreen's bottom there, no less than between her thighs. Monstrous devices would impale her both ways. Without remorse, dawn would bring the belly skewer to nineteen-year-old Noreen and the leather collar would be tightened inexorably. The final scene would reveal Noreen tumbled arse-upwards in a dark pit, the food for predators.

Such words do more good than all the canes in the world. With the thrashing at last finished, I undid the straps which held her ankles and legs.

If you imagine her lashing back at me with her feet kicking wildly, you are quite wrong. Noreen set her knees wide apart with frantic haste, thrust her hips back, and begged for love in the humblest and most pleading terms. She sobbed for it, if only as a temporary respite from correction. What could I do? Laying down the cane I knelt behind her and unbuttoned myself. Then my stiffness parted the way through her love-pouch from behind and into her warm, receptive depths. Gently at first, then harder, we rode together until the bomb of passion burst and I flooded her most copiously.

How she feared now that the caning might resume! Lowering her shoulders and straight dark hair, she raised her seat and begged for love another way. When I said that she deserved to be caned for suggesting such a thing, she pleaded all the harder, most vulgarly offering me her "arse" and promising "a good time" with it.

My finger soaped her tight portal of Sodom. "Too late to recant now, Noreen!" I said, smiling at her. "Will you still think it worth the excitement when I cane you for this afterwards? Now lie more tightly over the scroll."

I did not, of course, punish her as I threatened. Taking her breasts in my hands as the guide, I rode Noreen's arse in the grand manner, spending copiously inside it. When it was over, she knew that the caning might follow. I could scarcely believe her next request. I undid her and staggered to the chair, from which I have not had the strength to rise since being squeezed from Noreen's rear. Yet I gave my consent to her suggestion. As I pen these last lines, she kneels before me and takes in her mouth my stiffening... My darling Anna, I can write no further... Ah, Noreen, you delicious young whore! Your tongue—use it again like that! Ah!

... A leather strap round your throat, Noreen, that I may guide you by its reins... Rise now, turn, and bend... Sit upon the love-lance... Deep in your behind. Noreen! Move up and down gently... And thus, my sweet Anna... Harder, Noreen, you young bitch!

Believe me, Anna, your own adoring Timothy.

* * *

31 July 1904

My darling Anna,

Catastrophe has come upon us! I write at the first opportunity, knowing not where I am, and having only a general notion of the day of the month.

You will scarcely believe what has occurred—the audacity and the impudence of the young whore who has brought such things about! When I wrote my last adoring letter to you, I was, you may well believe, in a state of nervous excitement after my night of fun with Noreen. I was still lightly distracted and, therefore, made a fair copy of the letter in which I corrected all those small errors one makes under such circumstances. The rough copy, with all its blots and scorings out, I discarded in the waste-paper basket. Why did I not burn it—I would surely have done so within the hour?

I went to post my letter to you. When I returned, the basket had been emptied by the servant, and the paper had gone. I thought no more of this. What could it matter? On the following day, Miss Martinet and I received a visitor—an inspector of constabulary! Noreen, in a wild passion of vengeance for being thrashed, had stolen the copy of my letter and smuggled it out to the local newspaper! The proprietor of the paper, an officious penny-a-liner oaf, had gone with it to the police station!

Here was a pretty pickle! The inspector was friendship itself, and most respectful to one of my standing in society.

"The pity of it is, sir," he said, supping the tea which Miss Martinet had poured, "that something cannot be done about such young whores as Noreen! They get above themselves and imagine it is their privilege to abuse their superiors! If I had my way, such sluts would be taken to the strictest prison and there birched raw twice a week. If they were never set at liberty to make mischief again, it would not greatly trouble me."

This gave me hopes that I should come off well.

"Unfortunately, sir," he went on, "now that this has come to the notice of the newspaper and the police, it cannot well be ignored. If there were any way to prevent it coming to court, it should be done. Alas, sir, it cannot now be done. Even without any generous consideration from yourself and Miss Martinet, I would strive to prevent it. But that is beyond my power now. Be sure we shall have our eyes upon the newspaper fellow and shall prosecute him at the first chance. But what good will that do you, sir?"

I opened my pocket-book, drew out several bank notes, and made his visit well worth his while. Next day came Colonel Whackford, the chief constable of the county. He was full of the same regrets.

"There must be a prosecution, Mr. Timothy," he said, shaking his old grey head sadly, "but count upon me for one thing. It shall be delayed a day or two. Make the best of your chance. It would be a timely thing if you could manage to make yourself scarce the next two or three years. The young bitch who caused the trouble might also be transferred elsewhere."

The chairman of the local justices also paid us a call—going away with his pockets fuller. Wringing his hands, he swore that next day he would be obliged to sign a warrant for my arrest and another for Noreen's detention as a witness. He had tried to prevent this but the Lord Chancellor, his master, had been adamant. It was not that the Lord Chancellor too could not be bribed—being only a politician, after all—but rather that his price came too steep for us.

Next morning, Miss Martinet told me to pack my things at once: the officers of the law were coming for me. I was to be taken in custody to the Isle of Wight, where there was a prison for such creatures as I until the time of our trial. Certain of the girls from Greystones were to be sent to a reformatory in the same neighborhood, it seemed, and would be accompanied by the officers.

The inspector arrived. He arrested me with so many winks and nods that I thought him nervously afflicted. Two constables escorted Noreen, Vanessa, Jackie, Julie, and several other delinquents to the large, closed van. Thus I took a final fond farewell of Greystones and Miss Martinet. You may be sure I distributed all my remaining funds to the officers of the law—twenty each to the two constables and fifty sovs for the inspector.

Deuced civil they were in return, providing food and glasses of dark, foaming ale on the way. The inspector confided to me that Noreen's treason had been carried by Vanessa. I looked at her. For the convenience of the journey she had been put aboard in the white singlet and tight, blue riding jeans which she had been wearing when summoned. No sign now of the innocent-looking blouse, tie, and demure skirt of her uniform.

There was still, I thought, a mockery in the face of this fourth-form schoolgirl! The brown hair worn straight to the collar with parted fringe was not unlike Noreen's, as if she aped the older girl. What of the firm, lightly sun browned face, with its clear-cut features, high cheekbones, and laughing blue eyes? Such innocence indeed!

As if to pile misery upon me, the inspector—with the nervous wink and nod of a man in the grip of St. Virus jig—assured me that Vanessa must receive a reward for her cleverness. How downcast this left me! Presently the inspector said we must stop, though I did not see why, for we were miles from anywhere, on a wooded road. All the girls but Vanessa were handcuffed to the detention rail in the van. The young traitor and one of the two constables got out with the inspector and me. Vanessa is not big-hipped or fat-bottomed at eighteen, but she has the slight ungainly puppy fat at the hips and the seat of a goose who has yet to become a swan. As I watched her walk into the trees, the pale-blue tightness of the riding jeans gave an almost slovenly weight to Vanessa's eighteen-year-old arse-cheeks, and to her hips generally.

It seems that the length of the journey had put Vanessa in the plight of a pupil kept in class too long by the teacher, and now needing to squat in the ladylike privacy of the trees and piss for a full minute or two. Imagine the desperate and vindictive mood I was in, Anna—as you would have been on my behalf. Given the chance I would have allowed Vanessa to remove her riding pants but not the tight, white-cotton knickers. Would I have allowed visits to the trees? Be sure I would not! I would have set up the folding table and made her lie on her side upon it, her back to the watching girls and officers, her hips and seat in the cotton pants arching towards them.

Anna & Tim

As a mere prelude to my vengeance, I would have commanded Vanessa to wet her pants in front of the onlookers, enforcing the injunction by tantalizing the little water-spout between her legs with finger-tickling. She would soak herself before I was done. I imagine the officers, at least, would have been vastly intrigued to see this little temptress, though a grownup, fourth form girl, wet her pants in this manner.

It was, of course, out of the question. The inspector and the constable led her to a place among the trees. I waited. Presently the inspector reappeared and summoned me with his nervous wink and jerk of the head. I followed him to a small opening among the trees—and what do you think I saw, Anna?

A tree had been felled across the glade—a stout trunk. Vanessa was kneeling over it, still fully dressed, the tight and heavy-cheeked seat of her riding jeans well raised. She had not assumed the posture voluntarily for the constable knelt with her shoulders clamped between his burly thighs. The obliging inspector cut a long, slim switch from an ash sapling and handed it to me.

"Take your time, sir," he said courteously, "we need not resume our journey just yet. If I may be so bold as to suggest, Vanessa's bum-cheeks will be more responsive if bare. I feel sure that would be the wish of a teacher at her school."

I was, you may imagine, flabbergasted by the suggestion. Though I had paid the officers of the law handsomely, I had never supposed I would be given this last liberty of taking revenge upon the little minxes who had brought me to this present pass. Yet, my dear Anna, you may believe that I was not slow to seize the opportunity.

Half-expecting them to stop me, I undid the riding jeans and tugged them awkwardly to her knees. Vanessa twisted a little, but the constable's hold of her shoulders was strong and secure. Vanessa's knickers were, indeed, the tight, schoolgirl kind of white cotton. I lowered these too, noting how she tensed against the intrusion of ringers inside her pants! I was more than a little nervous, never having had to deal with an adolescent girl pupil before. I craned my head down and examined the slight adolescent heaviness, the almost muddy pallor of Vanessa's fourth-form bottom! To prevent wriggling, I drew off my belt and strapped her legs together just above the knees, then trussed her ankles with another lent by the inspector. Her light-haired young cunt was just peeping between her thighs. There was no point—and indeed no time—to lecture the delinquent on her offence. I warned her briefly.

"You know you're going to have your arse thrashed, Vanessa. For what you've done, you must be hurt, and, believe me, you will be."

Can you imagine it, Anna? Such stern words from one whose life has been passed in pleasure. Ah, but life was pleasant no longer! I will not weary you with Vanessa's desperate pleading, the reasons advanced why she should not be whipped, her inability to endure it on her bare bottom, her urgent need to let her fountain gush, her promises to be good, never to offend again. Urged on by the officers of the law, I touched the ash switch across her squirming seat-cheeks, took aim, and thrashed hard.

For the next ten minutes, it was dance time for Vanessa, or at least for the adolescent puppy-fat cheeks of her muddy-white bottom. Her thighs are still quite slim, and I took care not to execute judgment upon them. Yet the taut elasticity of Vanessa's fourth-form bum-cheeks was severely dealt with. It is hard to judge, I suppose, when whipping the bare backside of a eighteen-year-old high-school girl on the frontier of sophistication and feminine beauty, whether to treat her as a young woman or a little girl. Had she not committed a woman's crime? Thinking of this I cast restraint aside and thrashed the slim switch across Vanessa's bottom-cheeks!

How she screamed! Yet I guessed the sly minx was acting a part. There were as yet only two raised and burning stripes across her innocently immature bum-cheeks—both marks low down—which convinced me that they had taken effect well. I resolved to ignore her hysterics, the wild promises of repentance and amendment, the shrill imploring of those, now miles away, who might save her from her fate. I would judge only by the state of Vanessa's arse-cheeks.

When I stopped, and looked at the inspector, he gave me a quizzical glance and directed my attention to Vanessa's behind, as if to say, "Finished already? Come, now! Please continue!" I think there were three rather stiff members in that woodland glade at the sight of Vanessa's backside being tanned! So I gave her a last bout, first stooping to her ear.

"Since I shall soon be within prison walls, Vanessa, and since you will have helped to put me there, I want you to know that I am enjoying thrashing your bottom very much indeed. Now, much worse this time!"

When it was over, Vanessa was allowed into the trees for a weep, a gulping of final tears, and a release of bladder water. I was gratified that she preferred to complete the journey in the van without her pants on and sitting sideways on her hip.

So we came safe, in the arms of the law, to the prison ferry at Portsmouth.

The young female delinquents were taken aboard. Before I started down the gangway, the two constables saluted me smartly, congratulated me again on the striping and bruising of Vanessa's bottom, and thanked me for my "great generosity" to them. The inspector came aboard as my escort.

It was now dark, yet I was surprised how gaily lit the prison ferry seemed to be. It had the size and look of an ocean-going steam-yacht. The inspector escorted me to a comfortable chair in the forward saloon and commanded a hock and seltzer for me from a warder who looked for all the world like a mess steward. I began to hope that my sentence might be served in such agreeable conditions. I asked the inspector the name of this prison hulk.

"Do you not know, sir?" said he, "it is the steam-yacht *Brandon*."

You being less of a duffer than I, Anna, will have guessed the truth ere now. My wily Uncle Brandon had seen just such a difficulty as mine and had laid his plans. Not only did he enjoy the Greystones girls but contrived to ship many of them to lands where harem beauties are bought on the auction block! Thus he had made his fortune and, with the cargo I now possessed, he put me in the way of making my own. As for the inspector, Uncle Brandon had bought him as a mere constable. The zealous officer had, many a time, acted as master of ceremonies on these occasions.

I vow, Anna, to tell the story of ray escape thus far exhausts me. Forgive me, my dearest, if I now take a fond leave of you and lay my head for the night on the pillow of a fugitive.

And so the morning comes and finds me refreshed again. I have husbanded my energies in order to tell you the most comical thing that ever happened to me. Whoever the fellow was who said that life at sea is worse than confinement in prison would eat his words if could see me now.

On our first day out, I cast an eye upon the girls to see which should divert me between the sheets during our voyage. I was rather taken with Julie, nineteen years old. Do you recall her?

I chose a morning when she was ordered to don her singlet and working trousers for deck-washing. How well one could observe her now. Unlike Vanessa, a little girl with a woman's appeal, Julie is petite and slim— a woman in child's shape. With tall heels on her shoes, she is still diminutive. Her golden-blond hair is worn in a loose sweep from her high crown, lying on her back to the top of her shoulder blades. A somewhat sulky little face is marked by rather a crude nose and weak chin, hazel eyes with darkened lashes.

She is, to talk colloquially, what is known as a penis-teaser. The blue denim of the working trousers is worn tight and smooth as a skin. One views, as if she were naked, the slender thighs, which, even at their tops, are scarcely thicker than a man's upper arm. She has that taut belly and backward jut of hips which is characteristic of girl children rather than young women. Her breasts are small and her bottom, though its cheeks are quite slim and tightly rounded, has a soft, feminine fatness in proportion to her other curves.

Thus I watched her. To speak the truth, the tight denim trousers were not entirely smooth. The straining of the skin-tight denim caused sheaves of creases across the backs of her knees and, indeed, across the backs of her childishly slim upper thighs. The tight seam under her legs visibly parted her love-lips. I have read somewhere of girls who can frig themselves by the tightness of such clothes. Did Julie masturbate on the cord seam as she walked? When she bent over, her bottom-cheeks became two tight, distinct rounds with a deep and widely open arse-valley between. What a sight if the denim trousers had not impeded the view!

Yet to what purpose was all this? Who would bed a sulky little penis-teaser for preference? I said as much to the inspector. He at once promised me that Julie should prove as eager to please me as if her life depended on it, but he would not tell me why or how. Believe this who may, says I to myself! Yet, in the course of the day, I caught many a flutter from the lashes of those dark, hazel eyes, and often a vacant, hopeful smile. How was this, I wondered?

Late that night, I rang the bell in my cabin for my brandy and soda. Instead of the steward, it was Julie who tiptoed in, darkened eyelashes fluttering. The sulky little face made a visible effort to be alluring. As I tossed back my brandy, she stood before me, squirming her tight-denimed thighs together—indeed frigging herself on the seam!—giving out imploring little sighs and whimpers. Next she perched on my knee, thighs still squirming, and led my hand under the gusset of her pants.

"Please!" It was a little girl's whimpering half-sob, demanding to be indulged.

"Get your pants off, then, Julie! Astride my thighs, facing me, as I sit here! That way you'll get the shaft nice and deep between your legs!"

How eagerly she stripped off her pants? Julie's knickers came next, and she gingerly lowered herself onto the erection. How she rode! As if her life indeed depended on winning this race! Jig! Jig! Jig! she went, rising and falling in the saddle like a true equestrienne. Her tongue was more active in my mouth than almost any other girl I have encountered. Nor was this a single bout. After the first pumping of my lust into Julie's cunt, we retired to the bed and there repeated the rogering of her love-pouch three times during the night in various postures.

I was not surprised when she appeared the next night, though a surprise was indeed in store. When I suggested a repetition, a cunt-ride on the prick, Julie gave a sulky little wail.

"We did that last night!"

Never before had I heard that such things were allowed on one night only. A moment more, however, and she was on her knees before me, unbuttoning my trousers. Though Julie's knickers came off, she would do nothing but suck the penis and swallow its tribute, which she did twice more during the night.

The third evening, she would do nothing but make love to herself for my diversion, her bare thighs wide open, knees bent, the nails of her slim fingers painted so that the effect of her masturbation was more dramatic.

On the fourth night, she again insisted on something new. How long could this continue? Turning her back to my chair, she bent over, and I admired the tight, denim seat molding her taut, well-separated bum-cheeks and the open valley between. So that I might see her face better, I made her plait her hair and pin it in a top-knot. What a little madam she looked! Off came the pants and knickers. She bent with knees tucked a little forward and parted. The tight, slim cheeks of her bottom, her narrow hips, the dark anus-bud, seemed so fragile to look at. Prudently, I took a slim, glass pencil-squirt of liquid soap, inserted it in Julie's behind, and pressed the bulb, giving her half an hour of in-and-out with the slender rod.

"I fear I must stretch you hard now, Julie," I said, adjusting my stiffness to her. Then presently, "I think you like a man to bugger you, don't you, Julie? You know you're going to a harem master? The man who's bought you will give you plenty of this!"

Once again, the pleasure was repeated during the night.

The mystery grew deeper. Next night, Julie came to my cabin but resisted all my approaches. This was too much! I seized her wrist as I sat there and so drew her forcibly to kneel by my chair. Gently but deliberately, she twisted her head, set her pretty little teeth to my wrist, and bit me softly. As she did so, the dark hazel eyes looked up at me.

"I must be whipped for that!" she said quietly.

Before I could deny it, she had gone to the cupboard and come back with a single-cord whip, some two feet long. She handed it to me, took off her pants and knickers again, and bent over, her slim buttocks tightly and separately rounded. She had chosen to bend over a tall stool equipped with attaching-straps. In this posture too I required her mane of blond hair to be plaited and pinned in a top-knot that I might see her young face more easily. Seen from the rear, her thighs seemed almost fragile in their slenderness. The neat, demure cheeks of Julie's nineteen-year-old bottom were tightly rounded and well parted as a result of her petite shape. She had chosen to bend diagonally over the top of the stool—corner to corner—which seemed unusual. Yet what difference could it make, since the straps held her arms and legs so tightly?

"I shall make a note for the pasha who has bought you, Julie," I said, "recommending frequent harem discipline on those bare bum-cheeks of yours."

I thought she might be grateful—even excited. But she cried in her whining voice, "No! Please, don't do that! Oh, please!"

Here was a mystery to be sure! However, I caressed briefly between the trim, saucy little cheeks of her arse and then went to work with the whipcord. No harem whipping would ever lodge in her memory vividly than this, I swore. Her slim neck and the fine blond hair upswept to her top-knot twisted urgently from side to side. The woven cord whipped—and whipped—and whipped—across the taut little rounds of Julie's bottom-cheeks, sometimes catching the inner edges.

Why had the sulky little face with its vacant mouth, petulant air, and whining manner asked for this? The plum-colored tracery of lash marks soon embroidered Julie's fair-skinned little seat-cheeks and there were such forlorn cries and desperate squirming. Yet the cries were not as shrill or frantic as one might expect. It was then that I noticed what the little tart was doing. She had the edge of the stool between her thighs and was frigging herself between the legs upon it! Though it did not, of course, enter her cunt, she was able to squeeze her clitoris upon it and rub it between her love-lips. No doubt she had learnt such tricks from Katie!

All my scruples were now overcome. I cracked the cord across Julie's pert backside a dozen more times, and then a dozen again. Towards the end, she gave a short, aching cry of longing and then with a shuddering and limpness underwent her orgasm before my very eyes.

Tim

Anna & Tim

* * *

Port Rif, 1 August 1904

My dearest Anna,

I send this briefest of notes to tell you that I am now safely arrived on the continent which holds within it your own sweet self! How long it will be before I see you again, I dare not say. It may be many weeks or, by a happy chance, I may overtake this very letter with the wings of adoration! It depends much on the disposal of my "cargo" and the state of my late Uncle Brandon's affairs here.

I will, however, regale you a moment with the events of the last night of our voyage. The inspector, who has now quite deserted his post in England for some more lucrative employment here among the traders, continued in his role of master of ceremonies. He devised what he promised would be a Rabelesian banquet for our final dinner: the best food, the finest vintages, and a bevy of nude damsels to attend to our every desire! You may well believe that not one of his invitations was declined! The result was both inexpressibly randy and yet comic at the same time.

We entered the main saloon with its silks and cut glass. I vow, Anna, I experienced a combination of sensations unknown to me before: a stiffening penis and a desire to roar with laughter. Separately, these are common enough. Together, they must be rare indeed.

Ahead of me was the banquet table at which the inspector, the Captain, and I were to sit. It consisted of a light, wooden surface, some six feet long and two feet across, and a hole cut in the middle through which the lighting column rose. What is so curious, then, you ask? The table was supported at either end, not by legs but on the backs of two figures kneeling on all fours. Well, you say, such carvings are not unusual. Ah, but these were not carved figures. The nude flesh of Katie and Noreen was more succulently molded! The stools over which they were strapped supported them in turn and the tabletop was secured by a harness 'round their waists and shoulders. A man who sat on one side would have Katie's blond head protruding on his left-hand side, from under the table end, and the pale spread of Noreen's strapping young hips on his right. Those who sat opposite would have Noreen's face and Katie's rump either side of their chairs!

The lighting was more ingenious still. Our good inspector had had cause to arrest three loudmouthed street girls, some eighteen years old, for their noisy conduct. He had carefully ensured that they should be among our cargo in order that he might have some stock to drive to market.

Mandy, Tracy, and Sal (as Sally preferred to be known) stood naked upon the central platform of the table and provided our candelabra. Their wrists were joined in the leather cuffs above. It was Sal who provided the light for me and to whom I gave the most attention. What a pint-sized little strumpet she was at eighteen or nineteen! Imagine a broad, high boned face with rouge on the cheeks. Picture the snub little nose and the dark, defiant eyes. Add to it a collar-length crop of fair, tousled, wavy hair. In her figure, she was not tall, even for her age. Unlike the elegance of Tracy's skirts, Sal's costume for roaming the streets included the tight denim of her working trousers. Picture the two as they must have been—almost like boy and girl!—the firm tomboy thighs and the fat little cheeks of Sal's bottom rolling as she walked, filling the tight jeans cloth so heavily!

Now, like her two young friends, she posed naked on the pedestal. Like them, too, she had an ingenious dildo threaded in her cunt, curving out in the front to become a triple candle holder with its three tall flames twelve inches or so from her belly. At the rear, an identical candelabrum had been firmly inserted between the fat little cheeks of her arse!

Vanessa and the other girls attended as our charming naked waitresses. As we awaited the first course, the inspector told us humorously of his arrest of the three street girls. How they had gone through the quiet middle-class thoroughfares, Sal bawling her war song: "I go out on Saturday night, and I look for a fucking fight!" How she had insolently begged for a cigarette—"Got any fags?"—and how she had surrendered to the riff-raff melting pot of society. Having apprehended the three young strumpets, he was struck at once by the thought of being a partner in Uncle Brandon's business rather than a mere assistant.

Six waitresses entered, almost staggering under the weight of the huge salver, whose cover still hid from us our banquet. The splendid piece was loaded onto the table and the cover removed. Can you guess, my sweet?

It was twenty-five-year-old Jackie, the promiscuous young slut with her bell of blond hair, impudent blue eyes, sullen jaw, and fattish hips. Have no fear, she was not the meal itself, merely the delectable platter. Upon her breasts were arranged the hors d'oeuvres, so that her nipples appeared as the cherries atop them, for she was entirely naked. Jackie's sluttish young body was to provide all the plate and glass we required. We took wine by pouring it into her mouth and she turned her blond head obediently to the imbiber and gave him the draught from her mouth into his, nicely mulled.

Our fingers worked eagerly on the salad of the hors d'oeuvres, the slightly acid tingling of the salad dressing causing Jackie's nipples to stiffen remarkably. Finger bowls were not needed: glancing down at the firm, pale insolence of Noreen's face, I had only to hold my fingers to her mouth and command her tongue to do the work. There were some very firm bananas in the fruit bowl and you will believe I could resist taking one in my other hand. Katie's blond hair, as well as her crude, pale features, were reflected for me in a mirror. As I coaxed the banana into Kate's young cunt, she was as eager as I. Then her tongue washed the Captain's fingers lovingly.

Was Noreen more or less fortunate? In her case, the inspector took a different aim. The banana entered between the pale, strapping cheeks of Noreen's nineteen-year-old bottom. That left only one receptacle for the olive stones of the salad. In my own case—for I enjoy a meal of olives—I judged it uncouth to litter floor and table. To recompense my young blonde, with her firmly broadened buttocks and thighs, I first gave her a frig-jig with the banana. Then, one by one, I popped the olive stones up her arse-hole. We now went on to the salmon mayonnaise and asparagus.

The main dish was served upon the proud curve of Jackie's young belly, though the asparagus stalks were tucked deeply into her love-pouch, protruding between her thighs, which gave them a most novel savor. We ate heartily, but did not forget the hunger of those who supported us. In my case, it was possible only to feed Noreen from my hand. She hesitated at first but the folly of refusing such delicious morsels was soon shown her. In the end, she ate with relish some of the asparagus impregnated with Jackie's own girl taste.

I will not weary you with every course and wine we enjoyed. The dessert was of pancakes, and for this we required a clean platter. It required only Jackie to turn over on her mayonnais-covered belly in order for the pancakes to be served upon her seat-cheeks. They were hot enough to make her stir a little but not excessively so. The advantage of the pale, fattish cheeks of Jackie's arse was that they provided a convenient central cleavage for the droplets of lemon and sugar. To dunk each bit of pancake between Jackie's sluttish bum-cheeks was most lewdly enjoyable.

Our banquet ended with fruit of the season: grapes accompanied by peaches and plums. Jackie would take the grapes in her mouth, pop them open, remove the pips with her tongue, then feed the fruit into the mouth of the man whose open lips covered hers. Plums she treated similarly but, turning her head, Jackie was of course obliged to spit the stone lightly into the man's hand. Katie shook her blond fringe indifferently, but there was some apprehension in her blue-green eyes. A plum stone, after all, is a size larger than that of an olive. Alas for Katie! How easy it is to eat those sweet, syrupy plums voraciously. I thought of those men who had pressed at the Greystones stable window to goggle at the young blond saddle-dresser as she worked with her nonchalant sluttishness in tight riding jeans. Imagine their delight now, had they been able to see the intruding banana, the waste bowl presented to Katie's bottom, and the slow, measured clatter of falling plum and olive stones.

I thought how inexpressibly randy and delicious it was to have one's dinner impregnated by the skin flavors of a girl's most intimate body surfaces. We pushed back our chairs a little and lit our cheroots. This was charmingly done: it was young Sal who was my human candelabrum. Once I had the weed between my teeth, she backed a little towards me and bent over so that the rear triple candle was presented. She had to tuck her knees forward a little, for Sal, of course, stood above me. You may be sure I detained her a moment in this posture.

When the meal was over, the inspector begged our indulgence. He would take his three young street girls to another saloon, for an Arab harem buyer was coming out in his barge this evening, with a view to purchasing all three for his collection. You may be sure that the Captain and I took up positions outside the door, listening and endeavoring to catch keyhole glimpses.

With an eye to a good profit, the inspector once again dressed Sally as a young slut of the streets, in her black, waist-length jerkin and the tight, pale-blue denim of her working trousers. The harem owner murmured approvingly. He said he liked young hoydens of eighteen or so who challenged him by disobedience. Such ill-bred defiance was plain in Sal's broad and high-boned face, dark eyes, and shock of fair hair. He spoke eagerly of sturdy little hips and firm thighs. Had she been trained by sport and exercise?

Perhaps she struggled a little as the two valets held her by either arm and his hand ran under the gusset of jeans cloth. Was Sal a virgin? The inspector could not claim that, but he hastily assured the harem master that it had only been boys of Sal's own age. In the passageways of the town, Sal would also suck the penis of older men in exchange for cigarettes.

The harem buyer did not seem unduly displeased to learn of her experience in such a craft. Seduced by the swagger of Sal's fat little bottom as she walked, he required the valets next to turn and bend the young strumpet. He inquired if the virginity of Sal's young arse had been taken. The inspector vouched it had not. The harem buyer thus became master of all three girls and was left alone with them, assisted by the two valets.

"Away with your skirts and pants, my three hours! Excellent! Mandy—on the bed and make love to yourself! Tracy—join her! Sally, bottom upwards over the pillows, if you please. Why, the top of your head scarcely reaches a man's shoulder, and yet how many you have made to lust after you, Sal, as you walked through the streets, rolling your fat little bottom-cheeks in working jeans!"

At his command the valets tightened the wrist straps on his young mistress. "How often have you made respectable husbands follow you, Sally? How often have cameras clicked upon your face and your rear view to add gems to their private collections? Why, you even intrude into the marriage bed, I dare-say! As they do their duty to their wives, their minds are elsewhere. They dream of taking you down to the county wine vaults or the monks' rendezvous in the old churchyard. They dream of such fucking, even of buggering Sal's fat little bottom at eighteen or nineteen years old!"

There was a pause and then he continued more breathlessly. "Absurd to refuse me your rear virginity, Sally! Your attempt merely earns you a reprimand afterwards! Were you so haughty with the yokel boys who kept your company in the merchant's passage? Bite the pillow, Sally, to give you greater endurance! Ah, how copiously I shall spend my seed on this hot, infertile soil!" Ten minutes later, his furious cries confirmed that he had pumped his lust into Sal's backside, where no unwanted progeny is engendered.

"Now, Sally," he murmured, "there is one other joy which the men who admired you in the streets would have relished. It requires this whip with the lash of woven snakeskin. Karim, my fine fellow! Teach the young slut a lesson! Let me see the cheeks of Sal's bottom resemble a pair of skinned tomatoes!"

The sounds that rose from Sally, though a vulgar young strumpet, can well be imagined. As it happened, I had a rendezvous with Katie in my own cabin just then. It was the last before she, too, was sold to the highest bidder at the auction block. The Captain and the inspector, however, were privileged to spy through the crack of the door where Sally sprawled on her belly over the divan.

There were many, worthy citizens of the elegant city who would have wished such a loud-mouthed young slut punished. Karim did not disappoint them, I was assured. By the time he had visited the fat, squirming little cheeks of Sal's bottom with his lash, she could not have endured sitting on the lightest feather cushion without a cry! The Captain and the inspector watched, mouths open with amazement and delight at Sally's shrill descant. There was much satisfaction that such a master should have purchased her.

Thus we came safe ashore this morning, my dearest Anna. I was not sorry to part with the Captain and the inspector, for their vindictiveness towards the rebels among the girls suits ill my own more softly lascivious tastes. However, who can say that young Sally did not need some whipping of the kind? As for Noreen, I had no compunction over the "scolding" which the Captain, with his leisurely Havana, had administered to her strapping young seat!

In a day or two the last of our business will be done. Events make it impossible that I should return to England, even were I so inclined. All my thoughts now turn towards you. Be sure, my love, that the final journey between us shall be accomplished with the minimum of delay by your own adoring

Tim

* * *

Ramallah, 5 August 1904

My very own Timothy,

I write at once to tell you of a most remarkable spectacle, which is continuing even as I pen these words. It is an experimental lecture performed on the person of an attractive young Englishwoman, in front of an invited audience. Dr. Jacobus, a crony of the Pasha, is to demonstrate the sexual anatomy and functions of this young wife.

Two days ago the Pasha mentioned it to me. An examination table was to be set out under bright lights on a dais in the walled courtyard. Twenty of his friends, connoisseurs of the female body and owners of private harems, would dine with him. After dinner they would adjourn to the outdoor "lecture theatre," where the learned Dr. Jacobus would illustrate every form of sexual enjoyment which the young woman could offer. It was expected that the lecture would continue long after midnight.

"But, surely," I objected, "no woman would consent unless she were a slave and was given no choice? Yet, if she were a slave, her master would scarcely abandon her to such a purpose?"

"True," smiled the Pasha, "however, in Lesley's case, she has just lost her freedom but has not yet been sold by the trader. She is thus the ideal subject for the good Dr. Jacobus."

My curiosity was afire! I was determined, if possible, to be one of the learned audience at the experimental lecture! It was, for obvious reasons, confined to men of great trust who would not regret anything that Lesley might undergo.

How well our cunning Pasha guessed my intention, Tim! I slipped into the courtyard while they were at dinner and inspected the arrangements. The large marble table was on the dais, a cupboard of accessories standing behind it. The seats rose slightly in three tiers, curved to give each occupant a perfect view, no more than ten feet from the demonstration table. To speak the truth, my dearest, they were more old-fashioned sedan chairs than seats, each having tall, curtained sides so that no spectator could see another. During her ordeal, of course, Lesley would be able to see them all. Why such privacy? In each booth was a girl to minister to the occupant's needs as the lecture provoked them.

Mathematics was never your strong point, my beloved. Yet think. Twenty spectators and twenty-one seats! Were I seen at this demonstration, what a scandal there must be! So, our thoughtful Pasha had provided an extra place for my concealment. I moved to the empty booth at the end of the first row and took my perch.

Who was the slave girl in the next seat? I could not help furtively peeking through the curtaining enough to peep. Behold, it was Patrizia, the eighteen-year-old Italian bride. She is short and sturdy as tomboy, dark-brown hair worn straight to her collar and parted on her forehead, like a medieval page. Such olive-skinned appeal, wide cheekbones under dark eyes, and a firm line to mouth and jaw!

Now the Pasha and his guests came out into the courtyard, he directing them away from the booth which concealed me. "That is set aside, gentlemen! The rest are at your disposal!"

Smiling at his cunning, I peeped into the next booth. A fair-skinned man of fifty or so with silvered hair and moustaches was the guest. Patrizia stood before him in a blue blouse and matching drawers, skin-tight from waist to knees, worn with a belt of pale-brown leather. Still such a playful but innocent girl, her eyes widened with astonishment when he made her sit on his knee and kiss him. Unbuttoning her blouse, he molded her full, Italian breasts with his hands. Then, standing her up, he admired her firm, though somewhat stocky, thighs. He turned her 'round. From the rear, her hips sloped downward and outward, giving her a delightful, broad-bottomed tomboy look. Though not fat in the seat, her rear-cheeks have a voluptuous weight. The tight pants' crease behind her knees and across the back of her thighs. Deeper folds curve from between her legs under the full, olive-skinned cheeks of Patrizia Luis's bottom.

The murmur of voices fell silent as Dr. Jacobus came onto the dais, where the lights shone bright as noon. He was a very smartly dressed man of Latin appearance. About forty-five years old, he seemed the dark-haired medical scholar, with knowing eyes. "This evening, gentlemen, we are fortunate in our subject," said he, sharing the amusement of his listeners. "Lesley is a young, married woman, twenty-eight years old. Until recently, she led a life of promiscuous sexual emancipation. You need have no compunction, then, over what is done to her here. She is well used to the penis, both in marriage and outside it, being willful and selfish in her lusts. Moreover, child-rearing has given her a firmly controlled maturity of figure, enabling her to bear far more than could be inflicted on a college girl of eighteen or nineteen."

The learned doctor glanced 'round at us and continued. "Lesley is an educated young wife, emancipated and self-possessed. Yet her arrogant and disdainful manner makes her a more exciting challenge. How remorselessly we shall pursue extreme possibilities in dealing with her backside!" He lowered his voice confidentially. "Some of the ordeals which Lesley will presently undergo would be frankly impossible if she were still free and able to tell tales. Fortunately, she is already destined for a life of sexual slavery in a place from which no complaints are ever heard. When Lesley lived freely with husband and lovers, the mere unwanted display of a stranger's penis to her was an offence! The use of it on her without her grudging consent was a crime! The whip across her bare bottom was deemed torture! Happily, such words are meaningless here, where her master's pleasure is the law."

Two of the Pasha's soldiers brought her on to the dais. How shall I describe the young woman? Lesley is quite tall and, at twenty-eight years old, her body is kept nicely trim. Her straight, fair hair is cropped almost boyishly short at the nape, shaped close to her head from its high crown to her jaw line, and parted in a long fringe on her forehead. Aloof blue eyes are matched by firm, fair-skinned features, with a sulky downward turn of mouth and sullen chin. She is a girl of English good looks, well bred, but spoilt by her moody expression. How her figure would thrill you!

"Turn over and show me your behind. Ah, yes! I think our guests will find the next hour or two of the lecture most stimulating!"

I report the very words, Tim, spoken not an hour since, for in my innocence I had no notion of what to expect. When the curtain was drawn back and Dr. Jacobus stepped forward on the dais again, the scene had changed a little. Lesley was re-attired in tights and singlet, but now she lay face down over a stout leather bolster. Her seat was well raised and broadened by this. Her hands were held at full stretch ahead of her by the wrist cuffs. Leather anklets held her long, trim legs to the opposite rim of the marble demonstration table.

"Gentlemen," said Dr. Jacobus, "let us consider posterior possibilities."

In her present pose, the tantalizing film of the tights showed Lesley's seat-cheeks swelling firmly, and marked the dusky cleft between them. Dr. Jacobus drew his lecture cane over these contours, which contracted instinctively at the touch. The learned doctor showed how an active young woman in her middle twenties, her maturity firmly controlled, was often at her best in this area of her charms.

"In Lesley's case," he remarked, "regular penis exercise in the marriage bed and carefully controlled pregnancy has given a taut, proud maturity to her bottom-cheeks without making her in the least flabby."

I could not see the other guests, of course, as Lesley turned her moody, fair-skinned face with a shake of her fringe. Yet, from the sudden look of apprehension in her blue eyes, I believe she must have seen the twenty middle-aged gentlemen looking expectantly at her, each displaying his own interest at the ordeal she was about to undergo.

"In nature," said Dr. Jacobus, "Lesley's bottom has three uses. For a man, the most important is performed by her anus, which is made as a tight and enjoyable entry for the penis. Those who prize such tightness, and those who enjoy spending in a girl's body without fear of engendering a baby, will make good use of her in that way."

At this point one of the scholars interrupted with a question.

"Risks?" said Dr. Jacobus thoughtfully. "When she chose to bear a child, Lesley thereby diminished the tightness of her cunt. Some men who value tightness will now, understandably, demand the use of her anus. Lesley surely has only herself to blame! She was eager for her husband's penis and so became pregnant. Carrying a baby in her belly made her prone to certain trivial afflictions of her rear dimple. Perhaps she remains vulnerable there. Yet that was the cause of her own randiness. Lesley must not expect to deny us our pleasures because of the consequences of hers!"

Dr. Jacobus returned to his theme. "The second purpose of Lesley's backside is to receive chastisement. Scholars through the ages are of one mind that no part of the female anatomy is better suited to this than the buttocks. Since Lesley will never be set at liberty from her fate as a slave girl, we need have no hypocrisy here. She will be chastised by her master on her bare buttocks and the duration of this will be determined solely by his enjoyment."

Lesley pulled vainly at the leather anklets and wrist cuffs with a wail of protest.

"Finally," said Dr. Jacobus, "her behind was made for woman's ease as well as man's pleasure. That subject concerns us only in so far as she may plead her needs as a pretext. It is, of course, a simple matter to deny such a performance or, indeed, to compel it by means of a loaded squirt. Yet she will no doubt try to end a caning or prevent her master's entry by protesting the urgency of her situation. Happily this may be easily checked."

Now he turned to Lesley and took hold of the waistband of her tights. As he drew it down to her knees, the pale hip flesh swelled free a little. Now we looked down on the slight, taut maturity of her pale hips, the gentle firming-out of her bottom-cheeks, and her long, trim thighs. Despite her twenty-eight years and her promiscuous ways, the young wife lowered her face from our sight, for now Dr. Jacobus pressed her two rear moons apart and displayed Lesley's anus. The tight, dark bud shrank from his finger's touch.

"Lesley pleads that she has never had a man that way," he explained. "Alas, she does not realize how greatly that will make the buyers covet her in the slave girl market!"

He stroked Lesley's fair urchin crop as if to calm her. Then he took a glass squirt about eight inches long and slim as a pencil, with a rubber bulb at one end. He filled it from a bottle of liquid soap. Next he sat on the table's edge, firmly circling Lesley's waist with one arm, and looking down at the taut swell

Anna & Tim

of her seat. The skin of the cheeks, where they curved in to meet at her anus, was ivory-yellow, in contrast to the pallor of her buttocks.

The neat inward dimple of Lesley's arse tightened with alarm at the touch of the cold glass squirt. Dr. Jacobus laid the squirt down. With all his power, he delivered a series of ringing smacks upon the full, pale moons of Lesley's bottom. The promiscuous young wife was soon gasping, tensing, and shifting her seat-cheeks desperately. Then she bowed her head, hiding her face, and yielded her anus to the slim probe.

"Opinions vary," said Dr. Jacobus, "as to whether Vaseline or liquid soap will best prepare a young woman like Lesley for love. For her lover, the convenience of merely using Vaseline is clear. In the present case, where we are dealing with an adulterous young wife, there is an element of punishment. The length of the glass squirt and the jet it expels will stimulate needs and sensations deep in Lesley's backside. Also the light perfume will cause a slight erotic irritation."

The full length of the squirt was now sheathed in Lesley's bum, only the black rubber bulb nestling between her hind-cheeks.

"Lie quite still, Lesley," said Dr. Jacobus calmly. "You must learn to accept these measures of harem hygiene."

Those who had suffered the arrogance of the young wife would have relished the face which Dr. Jacobus obliged her to turn to us. The arrogance had gone from the blue eyes. Where was the sulky, self-possession of her clear, fair-skinned features and firm mouth? He squeezed the black bulb lightly and her body tensed at the first muffled squirt. There was a sudden wild-eyed and open-mouthed alarm in her face. Our haughty young woman seemed to scan the rows of chairs imploringly for someone who might intercede on her behalf. She saw only twenty eager faces. Dr. Jacobus tightened his arm 'round her waist. He pressed the bulb hard and repeatedly. With a forlorn cry, Lesley jammed her legs harder together and tensed her pale bum-cheeks on his busy fingers. When he had done, he withdrew the glass probe. Lesley's anus went desperately tight and small as the glass tip came clear.

"First, gentlemen, let us consider the amorous use of Lesley's behind. By her promiscuous conduct, she has lost all right to object to its use in this manner. Having surrendered herself to her urges, it is only right that she must surrender to those of others."

There was a ready murmur of assent to the justice of these remarks, for who could dispute so moral an argument? Dr. Jacobus resumed. "We are fortunate in having as our demonstrator one whom I will call the Schoolmaster.

He has long been an admirer of Lesley's backside as she bent to some task in a pair of tight riding jeans. Then, alas, she was not a slave girl and his lust had to be curbed. Let us concede, however, that he is not a favorite with her. He lately administered severe chastisement with his cane to the bare buttocks of a favorite of hers, her daughter-nymph, while our boyishly cropped Venus was obliged to listen in the next room!"

This at once made the situation more provoking! The Schoolmaster appeared in a mask and a waist-length leather jerkin. His phallus, understandably stiff with expectation, stood out and nodded as he walked. He adjusted a mirror so that he would be able to see Lesley's face while he ravished her arse. Sitting on the side of the table, he circled her waist with one arm and looked down on the full, pale swelling of Lesley's wifely young seat-cheeks. "Your face to the mirror, Lesley," he murmured. "Watch yourself being prepared. Try to imagine how much a man enjoys doing it!"

He took a large blob of Vaseline from a jar and slowly spread it on her tight inward rear dimple. In her agitation, Lesley twisted her head, looking back at him beseechingly. Her blue eyes interceded forlornly. The sulky mouth whispered peevishly those reasons which made her behind so vulnerable to ravishing. He smiled at her with amusement.

"That's your problem, Lesley! My prick is so stiff that I could not desist merely because you may be inconvenienced for a day or two! Such shrewishness, Lesley! Your right to choose who beds you? Your body belongs to you? Surely you forget where you are! Such mischievous nonsense is never tolerated from a harem slave-wife!""

His finger diddled the urchin-cropped Venus between her buttocks as she lay on her belly over the rubber cushions. He fondled the smooth, erotic maturity of Lesley's bottom-moons, which were swelled out and broadened by the cushions under her loins. "Be sensible, Lesley!" he murmured, "it won't be the first time you've been sodomised, will it? You still pretend your husband never dared it in a fit of honeymoon passion? None of your lovers during marriage? Ah, but do not deny that the two Arab traders performed the act on you during your night in their captivity. True, we heard you refuse their suggestion indignantly. But Karim waited long enough to hear you getting it anyway, Lesley! Such cries at first—and then soft sighs. A furtive and guilty thrill as they probed your rear depths, Lesley? A promiscuous young woman soon learns to enjoy it!"

"They *forced* me!" Her resentment had a spoilt child's petulance.

Anna & Tim

"Your consent is irrelevant here, Lesley. Your master's right over your backside and the rest of you is absolute. Did those two rogues get you into bad habits? I follow their example without compunction!"

"But I can't! I daren't!... I won't!" He stooped, kissing each of Lesley's proud, pale bottom-cheeks.

"The days are past, Lesley, for walking out on marriage and duty to gratify your urges with a lover. The little metal prod heats in the brazier coals. Every poor frustrated harem eunuch longs for the order to draw it out and tantalize your bare bottom with it where my lips now browse! Ah! Your buttocks tighten with alarm at that!"

He paused, then resumed, smiling at her with wicked promise.

"Your rear valley and its tight little crater, Lesley! My lips salute you there... and there. Ah, you have underestimated its seductive appeal! At high school and college, did you never imagine a man for whom this would be your great centre of interest?"

"No!" A peevish wail, petulant yet imploring.

"Ah!" Touching Lesley's anus with his finger, he seemed to guess the truth. "Why so tense and tight, Lesley? Too proud to confess the cause? I believe that my shapely young hen is shy of the cock because she wants to lay? Let us see!"

While Lesley's mouth turned down in a woebegone manner, he took a slim, twelve-inch glass rod and slid it gently but deeply into her backside. The young wife gave a little cry as it reached its full depth. The Schoolmaster withdrew it carefully.

"Ah, yes. Not truly desperate, but beginning to be so. Take the rod carefully by this end, footman, and show it to the spectators."

"Oh, please... no!" It was Lesley's hopeless protest at seeing the state of her behind thus displayed to the amusement of the onlookers.

"Turn your fringe, Lesley! I must kiss those arrogant blue eyes! Lesley, my love, I taste your first tears upon my tongue! Now, my sweet, the phi-head of the marker is glowing. I shall enjoy caressing you with it between your buttocks, Lesley, unless you can divert me by your submission."

I am sure he would never have done so, Tim—would he? But the effect of his words was enough.

"That's better, Lesley! Arch your seat out like that! A little farther! I believe you want it after all! Now, let me kneel astride your thighs—my knob to your anus, Lesley! Ahhhhh!"

He pressed the tight rear dimple inwards until the young wife yielded her arse to him with a short, hollow cry. The Schoolmaster's penis shaft slid deeply in-between the proud, white cheeks of Lesley's bottom. He drew back a little and plunged again in a vigorous in-and-out. His loins slapped rhythmically upon Lesley's buttocks, his penis driving with all its power into the arse of this promiscuous young wife, punishing her adultery.

"So tense, Lesley? What? Whisper it to me! Ah, the added bulk of the tool compounds your urgency, does it? Put such things from your mind. Tighten your rear muscle rhythmically on my shaft. Exquisite!"

He rode her triumphantly for about ten minutes, at which point Lesley begged him to end the ravishing quickly.

"You abandoned marriage for your own pleasures, Lesley," said he, "now you must abandon yourself to mine. Lie still a moment! My lust shall not boil over for half an hour yet!"

Soon he began again, and later paused. Another beginning, a pause, and so on. Presently, while they lay still and his loins covered Lesley's backside, an involuntary jet of his passion escaped deep in her rear. She made a faint sound of distaste in her throat. He kissed her bare back and was severely logical.

"So prudish, Lesley? The thick warm discharge disgusts you? Such hypocrisy! Why, it is the very substance you begged from your lovers in the warm adulterous passion of your loins! Not quite so snooty about it then, were you, Lesley?"

"I was in love!" Such a sulky schoolgirl wail again.

It was curious, perhaps, that the balm which consummated her illicit passion should so revolt Lesley when squirted into her behind by a man whom she detested. Yet he kissed the crown of her head and his movements began once more.

"You went whoring, Lesley," he murmured, "you deserted the penis of your husband, who had sole legal right to you. Now you shall be punished by mine. Justice requires it!"

"I was in love!" she wailed peevishly, just as before, and as if this excused her.

"You shall be loved here, Lesley," he promised. "The valets will always be waiting in the tiled closet when you needs must go and take your knickers down in there. Karim and Saleh are both lovers of the female backside. Be prepared to bend to their whims before you are permitted to attend to your own."

Anna & Tim

So the moral agent of retribution rode to his triumph. "Lie still now, Lesley, but arch your bottom out a little farther. I feel the flood breaking the barrier! Lesley, darling! I believe my passion for you is hotter than husband or lover ever felt! Do you feel the squirting in your rear, Lesley? The pulse in your throat beats faster! Ah, you're getting to like it, Lesley, aren't you?"

He lay upon her, not yet drawing his tool from her bum, whispering gently in her ear. To judge from her dismay, he may have been assuring her of his obsessive love for her in this way. Or did her wide eyes testify to how he frightened her with the bogey tales of the harem?—the ultimate demand which lay in wait for her; the underground room, musicians playing outside to prevent the escape of a chance sound. The pale moons of Lesley's bottom were presented for this last rite as if on a pagan sacrificial altar, for even in extremities his obsession would choose this way. Whatever the subject, his last words were audible.

"You shiver, Lesley? Did you never wonder if such things must not happen behind harem walls?"

When the young wife gave a little cry of alarm, it was because she felt how his own words had hardened him again in her behind. In vain, the boyishly cropped Venus tried to expel the flaccid serpent. But Lesley's arse movements, squeezing upon it, had only stiffened it once more.

"Ready for it again, Lesley? You liked an encore from your lovers!"

The movements of sodomy resumed. Lesley shook her parted fringe back to twist her head 'round and plead that she could scarcely contain the volume of his first tribute in addition to her own load and the heavy penis muzzle. There was a faint show of resistance, a smack or two on her legs, his smile meeting her forlornness as she yielded with a soft cry.

"For your own sake, Lesley, you must be broken in to this pleasure thoroughly in a few weeks, so that you may overcome timidity and enjoy it. My valets shall accompany your morning visit to the tiled closet. This exercise shall be part of your routine in there."

She gave a plaintive and yearning little cry at last, as a morbid and hectic thrill was stirred by the penis in her bowels. Several of the audience chuckled and vowed the young bitch was getting a taste for it. Meanwhile, a soldier had Shawn bending over with knickers' round her ankles. He kissed the full lips and the tight-lidded dark eyes of this eighteen-year-old. He kissed his way up the length of her long, elegant, coffee-skinned legs. He kissed the West Indian beauty between her thighs, then on her tautly rounded bum-cheeks.

He pressed apart the tawny-gold cheeks of Shawn's bottom and presented his knob to her anus. The way was too narrow without the aid of some unguent. He applied this, pressed her waist down, and spanked hard on Shawn's buttocks. After that, she received him with a wild willingness, randily supplying the movements for her own ravishing.

Peeping through the curtains beside me, I also glimpsed my silver-haired neighbor and his young concubine. Patrizia was bending forward over the rail in front of the seat. He made her keep her face turned so that he might enjoy the appeal of her wide, brown eyes, broad, warm-skinned cheekbones, and dark page-style hair. This appealing Italian tomboy no longer boasted the tight pants whose seat she had filled so broadly and roundly. Now one could admire the bare olive-skinned voluptuousness, the slight heaviness in the cheeks of Patrizia Luis's bottom. Her eyes were fixed upon her elderly lover's swelling knob. "No is possible!" she gasped, in her charming broken English.

His answer was to stroke scented lubrication between her buttocks. He took his lance in both hands, aimed it, and thrust home. I guessed that her little friend Regina was undergoing a similar ordeal in the next seat. Beyond that, perhaps, was blond Francesca, with her elegant coiffure. Francesca's costume of short, belted tunic in red silk and tight, plum-colored riding trousers of shiny leather would seal her fate. So, while Patrizia was buggered next to me, sharp-featured little Regina matched her ordeal. Beyond her, blond and sophisticated Francesca bent over, her wifely young anus stretched round her admirer's weapon. Thus, my dear Tim, I take my leave of you as our learned Dr. Jacobus pauses before the final part of his stupendous experimental lecture.

A bientot,
Your loving Anna

* * *

Ramallah, 5 August 1904
My dearest Tim,
I now find leisure to write—even as the events still unfold—to tell you of the conclusion of the lecture by our learned moral philosopher, Dr. Jacobus. Though past midnight, the courtyard was brightly lit. The attention of the assembled scholars never once wandered from the theme.

Lesley remained secured on her belly over the leather bolster. Her behind was still the centre of attention. Though discipline now replaced passion, the pale, yellow-grey gobs of Vaseline were still visible, like honey in the comb, between the cheeks of Lesley's bottom. A broad smear of the unguent crossed one of her seat-cheeks, marking the track of the Schoolmaster's penis as he withdrew it from her.

"Gentlemen," said Dr. Jacobus solemnly, "we now come to a scene which must be set in somber colors, a theme cast in a minor key. I speak of chastisement. You need, however, have no misgivings. You will see Lesley punished for adultery in a manner which law and morality have upheld since the dawn of civilization. The whipping of an adulterous young wife is an act in which almost all men of sense and honor would concur. Her husband, even the lovers she deserted her marriage for, would want to see the penalty inflicted. In the Arab world our punishment of the whip is lenient by comparison with the vindictive discipline of branding needle or impaling cucumber for Lesley's backside. By the law of many pashas, such retributions are followed by the inexorable tightening of the leather 'Collar of Justice' about the throat. Here we deal more lightly with her."

You may imagine the fright which filled Lesley's arrogant blue eyes under her little-boy fringe at this. Yet she would not suffer more than the ultimate discipline of the prison or school.

Lesley will use every subterfuge to escape justice," continued Dr. Jacobus. "Exaggerated screams to win pity are most common. Unnecessary degrees of twisting and writhing are also intended to mislead. Urgent entreaties will be made to perform certain acts whose needs can no longer be denied. Yet we may defeat such ruses!"

What could he mean? I had no idea.

"We judge by the state of Lesley's bottom," said he. "Therefore we curb her writhing a little. An extra pinion strap above the knees, another at the waist. A gag of damp wadded cotton, held by a thin strap between the teeth and secured at the nape, is doubly advantageous. It reduces the temptation to unnecessary shrillness and protects her teeth against chipping as she clenches in pain."

There was a moment of resistance—pressed lips, mewing, and head-twisting—like a little girl refusing the medicine spoon. But soon the wadded cotton and strap were in place.

"Lastly," said the learned Dr. Jacobus, "in her frantic endeavor to end the thrashing, she will lose all the self-possessed arrogance of an educated and emancipated young woman. She will perform as shamelessly as a desperate young woman of eighteen or nineteen. Of course, the little fountain between her legs has played to exhaustion. Yet Lesley has also implored for some hours a few moments of urgent privacy for another reason. You will, I am sure approve the refusal of such requests, for the ordeal of her punishment is to be increased rather than lightened."

There was a murmur of approval. Dr. Jacobus smiled.

"Indeed, gentlemen, in so distinguished an audience as this, there may be scholars who wish to see the performance of such curious acts. It is prudent, then, to have Lesley in a state where she can display any function of her rear anatomy commanded by you."

He then responded to a ripple of amusement.

"Despite this young woman's appearance of arrogance, she may secretly hope that such commands are given. You may be sure that Lesley would respond to such an order with a show of repugnance and defiance. Her self-respect requires that. Several strokes of the cane would be needed. However greatly she may wish to do it anyway, Lesley will escape the ultimate self-humiliation, if she appears to yield only under the compulsion of the whip."

Like a conjurer, Dr. Jacobus stood before us with a china egg between finger and thumb. It was not quite large enough to tightly fit the necessary place, but it would not be easily dislodged. Lesley twisted her head 'round urgently to watch him, the light catching the fair, straight cut of her crop from its high crown to the severe cutting of it level with her jaw. Dr. Jacobus slid a hand under her, supporting her bare belly. He pressed the oval china egg between her buttocks, the narrower end foremost. There was a tensing of seat-cheeks, and a keening through wadded cotton, while the scholar's mouth set firm and the veins in his forehead stood out more prominently. Lesley's tight inward dimple yielded and closed again over the china oval as it passed up into her behind.

"Observe, gentlemen!" Dr. Jacobus stood back with a flourish. "See how hard and rapid the pulse beat in her throat is. Can it be sexual arousal at the thought of being chastised—or is it no more than a young woman's desperate fright? It matters not at all. Either emotion will generate a pitch of excitement. Lesley feels butterflies in her tummy, as the saying goes, and the flutter of panic in her bowels. The cheeks of her arse are no doubt crawling with such apprehension that they almost itch with it!"

Lesley gave a shake of her little-boy fringe in order to look back at him over her shoulder. It seemed as if the once-disdainful blue eyes were trying to ask a question she could not utter. Her clear, pale features were a study in the most fearful anticipation.

"Ah!" Dr. Jacobus smiled knowingly at her. "Lesley is tormented by a last doubt! Will there be any restriction on the instrument of punishment? Any limit to the number of strokes? I think she can already guess that the answer is in the negative!"

How Lesley tugged at her straps—and all in vain! How she turned her blue eyes and fringe urgently to the audience! Whatever disapproval one may feel for Dr. Jacobus, he had a good deal of reason on his side. Lesley is a mature young woman. Her hips and seat have that slight firming-out which enables her to undergo chastisements that would be unthinkable for a school-girl. She has endured regular penis exercise in the marriage bed, the labor of child-bearing, the demands of her lovers. Having willingly incurred such extremes of pleasure and pain, she was scarcely able to object to a whipped bottom as punishment for her infidelities. Indeed, by cutting her fair hair in a rather boyish manner, she was surely asking to be given the sort of thrashing well known in some boys' prisons.

"Presently you will be caned, Lesley," said Dr. Jacobus quietly, "but first I shall mark my personal disapproval of your marital treason by twelve strokes with a snakeskin pony-lash."

Lesley was truly frantic at this. She twisted her head and scanned about her, with blue eyes wide and desperate. In vain, she jerked at the restraining straps. The gag reduced her protests to the same shrill keening, but her pale seat-cheeks were tensing urgently.

Dr. Jacobus took the whip, which consisted of a handle and slim, woven-lash about eighteen inches long. He ran his hand briefly over the full moons of Lesley's bottom, smiling at the pale Vaseline blobs between them and the peeping vaginal pouch between the rear of her thighs.

"You had your fun with your lovers, Lesley," he said gently. "Was it nice? Was it? Did you wriggle on the adulterer's penis until you almost swooned with the joy of it? Now you shall pay a cruel price for it, you young whore!"

His right arm went back and Ms lips tightened. The cheeks of Lesley's bottom shifted and squirmed uncontrollably. With an ear-stunning crack, the slim, black-lash snaked down, curling and clinging to the bare cheeks of Lesley's backside. A split second's pause was followed by wild mewing and buttocks contorting urgently to contain the naked smart of the leather whip. A scarlet stripe appeared, an S-shaped curve across Lesley's bum-cheeks, dotted by two ruby droplets. Lesley had the firm, young seat-swell of a Spartan soldier-girl. Perhaps it was this which caused such breathless excitement among the audience as she was whipped. Or perhaps it was merely the satisfaction of seeing the boyishly cropped wife punished for her promiscuity and for being an arrogant young bitch. Who can say?

Dr. Jacobus made the whip ring out repeatedly with a savage accuracy across Lesley's bottom-cheeks. Soon her pale buttocks were embroidered by plum-red loops and curlicues. Two! Three! Four! The strokes sang out like pistol shots, each stinging Lesley's arse with a scorpion viciousness. Even the fiery kiss of the leather whip was but a prelude to the swelling torment as the impact of the stroke searched her lingeringly for several seconds afterwards. Vainly she tried to take the strokes on her flanks to spare her bottom. But her hips were too well pinned down for that. She tried to turn each buttock uppermost in turn, but neither of them could elude the lash. She tightened them desperately, until her arse-crack was a thin, compressed line.

Dr. Jacobus put a stop to this by an upward stroke of the woven lash, catching the fatter undercurve of Lesley's seat-cheeks just above her thighs. Frantic to writhe away the anguish, the promiscuous young wife thrust her rump out in a complete display of her rear anatomy. It was at this point that the eyes of Dr. Jacobus gleamed. He aimed the lash with vindictive precision between the cheeks of Lesley's bottom. No refuge was left to her as the whip cracked out again. Eight! Nine! Ten! All the self-possessed sophistication taught her at school and college was stripped from Lesley now. Twice the whip's command was printed between the cheeks of her arse. Neither this, nor the flooding tears in the blue eyes, moved the onlookers to intercede.

One must concede, of course, that Lesley was being punished for the great harm done to others by her conduct. To desert marital duty for illicit pleasures is a crime which law and custom has always punished in this manner. Almost every man—and perhaps most women—would have been pitiless with Lesley now. Under the long, fair parting of her little-boy fringe, Lesley's eyes—once so aloof and dismissive—implored her master vainly.

Smack! Whip-smack! Crack-smack! As the lash caught the inward curve of Lesley's bottom-moons again, every muscle in her thighs went taut and her toes curled with the intensity of the discipline. Once or twice Dr. Jacobus moved to block our view a little, and he paused. An Arab boy ran on and held something to the young wife's nose. The scent of ammonia suggested smelling salts. Who can say? During this process, Lesley's face was level with the boy's loins. Like us, she must have seen the scrap of his loincloth bulging with the stiffness inside. No doubt there was many a wicked smile and knowing whisper from the frisky boy, assuring her of his enthusiasm for seeing her punished.

Indeed, as I glanced up at the windows overlooking the scene, I could make out the faces of the Arab boys pressing eagerly at each one. Here and there a lad stood alone, the movement of his upper arm suggesting that he was busily polishing some object in his hand.

"The justice of chastisement is absolute," said Dr. Jacobus, as he finished. "Lesley has made others suffer in order that she might enjoy her lecheries. What she endures now is a modest retribution."

Lesley twisted her head wild-eyed in dismay, for now the Schoolmaster appeared, cane in hand. Already Lesley's bottom-cheeks blushed deeply, the whip prints raised in slight contours across her backside and the rear of her upper thighs. The boyishly cropped Venus-wife sprawled in her straps like an overgrown schoolgirl or page boy over the cushions of the teacher's sofa.

The Schoolmaster removed the gag, allowing her to lie flatter as well. "I shall not need such expedients," he said. "Besides which, when I cane a bottom, I like to see it writhe! How many canings your parents and teachers neglected, Lesley! How many punishment lessons to make up for before we have trained you to loyalty and submission!"

Lesley emitted a shrill protest, but the Schoolmaster dismissed it. "Come now, Lesley! You have tasted the pony-whip! What greater objection can there be to a reformatory cane? Remember, I have already severely bamboo'd the bare buttocks of your eighteen-year-old filly. Surely that entitles me to thrash the backside of the young mare with my cane, as well?"

There was a good deal of general amusement at this. When the murmurs of laughter died away, the supple bamboo rang out across Lesley's bottom, the weals rising straight across the curving prints of the lash. You may imagine the frenzy of Lesley's screams, deeply gratifying to the moralists who watched her thrashed for adultery. He caned her across the backs of her thighs half a dozen times and then returned to the cheeks of her statuesque young seat.

The Schoolmaster was worthy of the great tradition of pedagogues. Each lash of the cane was given with stern vindictiveness. I doubt if the thirteen-year-old nymph wept more violently under the bamboo than the boyishly cropped young Venus of twenty-eight was doing now. Lesley's backside writhed over the leather bolster in a manner which was positively lewd. You might have thought, from its sinuous squirming, that her behind was trying to seduce the chastiser into other pleasures.

In the warm night, the young wife's proud bare belly slithered on the leather bolster as she squirmed. There was a faint dry squeak of the restraining straps as she pulled vainly at her bonds. Under the caning, the firm, mature cheeks of Lesley's bottom met and parted in their writhing with a slippery kissing sound caused by the thickly smeared Vaseline between them.

How would it end? How *could* it end? The Schoolmaster's disciplinary zeal seemed unabated, and it was impossible to imagine what would satisfy his punitive skill. His resolve stood out stiffly as ever for all to see. Yet now Lesley twisted her head round. She seemed to be trying to look down the length of her spine at her own bottom. In truth, she was directing the Schoolmaster's gaze to that place! The reply was an expertly aimed lash of bamboo, drawing blood in pinpricks across several of her earlier weals. Such frenzy was provoked by it! The atrocious smart of the bamboo caused the rounded end of the china egg to peep out between Lesley's bottom-cheeks! Was she about to use the only subterfuge remaining by which she could halt her punishment, if only for a moment?

The Schoolmaster, admirable moralist that he is, was not to be deflected from his duty by the reappearance of the china egg, which Dr. Jacobus had inserted in the young wife's behind. Again and again and supple bamboo lashed across Lesley's buttocks. The egg grew rounder and larger as it emerged, until it rolled free from Lesley's anus, down her bare legs, and across the demonstration table. An ear-splitting smack of the cane across her statuesque backside brought a frantic pleading to her face again. As the Schoolmaster caned her again and again it seemed that this promiscuous twenty-eight-year-old wife disgraced herself deliberately. The blemish swelled out between her buttocks and hung in a lewd curve down the left cheek of Lesley's bottom!

What of the Schoolmaster when he saw this outrage to discipline? His lips parted in a paroxysm of moral outrage—or was it a grin of delight?—and he gave two more strokes of the cane across Lesley's backside with all his skill. A second swelling blemish dislodged the first. Had one not known how strict a moralist the Schoolmaster was, it might seem that, having seen Lesley's eighteen-year-old filly lift her tail under chastisement, he was determined to drive the young mare to the same extreme.

For all her educated arrogance and emancipated self-possession, Lesley perhaps guessed at the strange vices which bedevil mankind. Her college education, several years of marriage, and a few lovers, had surely taught her some bawdy truths. Did she hope to excite the Schoolmaster to completion by performing the most lewd and utter self-abasement of which her bottom she was capable?

To be sure, it had an effect upon him. The cane dropped from his hand, for he was now obliged to clutch his own stiffness. Lesley turned her brimming eyes and woebegone mouth—a vision in itself enough to cause his orgasm. She was in time to see the Schoolmaster's weapon explode in mid-air, uncontrollably, with the pure exhilaration of his triumph. Thick lusty jets spat forward and liberally bespangled Lesley's backside with arcs of spawn. Who knows? Perhaps the slippery balm soothed her at last.

The Schoolmaster staggered with the exertion of his display. Murmurs of concern for him rose among the spectators, as two soldiers ran forward and supported the valiant pedagogue from the dais. In a spontaneous tribute, the assembled scholars broke into applause. Happily, the Schoolmaster was able to return in a moment. Weeping contritely for her misconduct, Lesley implored him not to cane her again. He knelt to pick up the bamboo. As he did so, Lesley twisted her urchin-crop 'round violently and with tongue fully extended just managed to lick at the Schoolmaster's knob. Her arrogance was conquered now, for we heard her plead like a little girl.

"Please! Please, let me! Oh, please!"

He permitted it, teasing her over her reluctance to perform the same lip service to her husband. At the same tune, he left her in no doubt that she was earning a temporary respite at the cost of humiliation presently. As the curtain fell upon the dais, his voice was audible behind it.

"Your tongue under the foreskin as you suck, Lesley! What delights await you when the shaft grows hard again. So randy even in your present state, Lesley? A moment more and I shall make you do something which will shock you profoundly. Can you guess it, Lesley? Yes! I believe you can! The promise of chastisement alone shall ensure your obedience this time."

Dr. Jacobus in turn was the object of prolonged applause. He was recalled repeatedly, smiling and bowing his thanks to the guests. Our generous host, the Pasha of Ramallah, has put his own private bedroom at my disposal. Its secret windows look into adjoining suites, including that of Dr. Jacobus. Now I make my way thither to see what I shall see. Be sure, dearest Tim, you shall have a full report of the proceedings from your own adoring

Anna

ROSA & ANN

My Dear Girl,

I know I have long promised you an account of the reason for my penchant for the rod, which, in my estimation, is one of the most delicious institutions of private life, especially to a supposed highly respectable old maid like your esteemed friend. Alas, treaties must be carried out, and promises kept, or how can I ever hope for the pleasure of making you taste my little green tickler again? Writing, and especially a confession of my voluptuous weakness, is a most unpleasant task. I feel as shamefaced in putting these things on paper as when my grandfather's housekeeper first bared my poor, blushing little bottom to his ruthless attack. My only consolation at commencing is the hope that I shall warm to the subject as it progresses in my endeavor to depict, for your gratification, some of the luscious episodes of my early days.

The man I refer to as "my grandfather" was, as you well know, the celebrated General Sir Eyre Foster, almost as well-known for his eight-penny fiasco with the Bluecoat boys as for his services to the Hon. E. I. Company. He was a confirmed disciplinarian and nothing delighted him so much as a good opportunity for the use of the whip. But I cannot tell you anything about that, as that was before my time. My first recollection of him is after the aforesaid City scandal, when he had to retire from public life in comparative disgrace. My parents both died when I was just eighteen years of age, and the old General, who had no other relatives to care for, took charge of me. I add now, though it is early in my tale, that at his death I was left his sole heiress, and mistress of nearly £3,000 per annum.

He resided in a quiet country house some twenty miles from London. It was there I spent the first few months of my orphaned life, with only his housekeeper, Mrs. Mansell, and the two servants, Ann and Jemima to act as guardians. The old General had spirited himself away to Holland searching, so I afterwards heard, for original editions respecting the curious practices of Cornelius Hadrien, a father confessor who delighted in the flagellation of religious penitents.

It was the middle of summer when he returned, and I soon found the liberty I had been enjoying considerably restricted. Orders not to pluck the flowers, or the fruit in the garden, descended upon me with frightful swiftness, as did the perceived need for a regular lesson. It was to be administered by the old autocrat himself. At first the teachings were tolerably simple, but gradually increased in difficulty. Now, in after years, I can plainly understand the General's wolf and lamb tactics, by which I must eventually fall under his assumed just displeasure.

What gave me considerable pleasure at this time was his decided objection to mourning, or anything at all somber in my dress. He said my parents had been shown every possible respect in that I had worn black for months, and that I must now be dressed as became a young lady of good expectations.

Although we scarcely ever received company, and then only some old fogy of his military acquaintance, I was provided with a profusion of new and elegant dresses, as well as beautiful shoes, slippers, drawers, and under-linen, all trimmed with finest lace. Nor did the lascivious wretch even forget to provide some very beautiful garters, a pair of which he would insist upon putting on me, taking no notice of my blushing confusion as he pretended to arrange my drawers and skirts afterwards. He would merely remark what a fine figure I should make if they need ever strip me for punishment.

Soon my lessons came harder than I could fairly manage. One day after I had stumbled badly, the General expostulated, "Oh, Rosa! Rosa! Why don't you try to be a better girl? I don't want to punish you."

"But grandfather," I replied, "how can I learn so much of that horrid French every day? I'm sure no one else could do it."

"Hold your tongue, Miss Pert. I must be a better judge than a little girl like you."

"But, grandfather dear," I would tell him in all my innocence, "You know I do love you, and I do try my best."

"Well, prove your love and diligence in the future, or your posterior must feel the sting of the whip I shall have ready for you," he said sternly.

Confused and hurt, I would merely nod my acquiescence with tears near to springing from my eyes.

Another week passed, during which I could not help observe an unusual fire and sparkle in his eyes whenever I appeared in evening dress at the dinner table. (We always dined in quiet state.) He would also suggest that I wear a choice little bouquet of fresh flowers in my bosom, to set off my complexion.

But the climax was approaching; I was not to escape long. He again found fault at the most minor of offenses and gave me what he gravely called my last chance. My eyes filled with tears, and I trembled to look at his stern old face. I knew as well that any remonstrance on my part would be useless.

The prospect of punishment made me so nervous it was with the greatest difficulty I could attend to my lessons, and the second day after, I broke down entirely.

"So, it's come to this has it, Rosie?" said the old gentleman.

"Nothing will do but that you must be punished." Ringing the bell for Mrs. Mansell, he told her to have the punishment room and the servants ready for when he should want them. Mrs. Mansell's eyes were sympathetic as the General continued his diatribe: "Miss Rosa has been idle, and has been getting worse and worse with her lessons every day. She must now be taken severely in hand or she will be spoiled for life."

"Now, you bad girl," said he, once the housekeeper retired, "go to your room and reflect upon what your idleness has brought to you."

Full of indignation, confusion, and shame, I rushed to my chamber and bolted the door, determined they should break the door down before I would submit to such a public exposure before the two servants. I threw myself on the bed, giving vent to my tears for an hour or more, expecting at any moment the dreadful summons to attend the old man's punishment drill. But no one disturbed me, and I at last came to the conclusion it was only a plan of his to frighten me. I fell into a soothing sleep.

Later a voice at the door awakened me. It was Ann summoning me to dinner.

"No dinner for me, Ann" I said sadly. "I'm going to be punished. Go away, leave me alone," I whispered through the keyhole. "Oh, Miss Rosie, the General's been in the garden all the afternoon, quite good-tempered," she said encouragingly. "Perhaps he's forgotten it all; don't make him angry by not being ready for dinner. Let me in and we'll have you dressed before the appointed time."

So I cautiously drew the bolt. Ann entered smiling.

"Cheer up, Miss Rosie. Go down as if nothing has happened and most likely all will be forgotten. His memory will be short, especially if you put in your bosom this sweet little nosegay to please him." Thus encouraged, I met my grandfather with a good appetite. His mood was bright and I began to believe that the bitterness was past, little suspecting the devious turn of his mind.

The dinner passed most pleasantly for such a formal affair as my grandfather made it. He took several glasses of wine, and in the middle of the dessert seemed to contemplate me with unusual interest. At last, suddenly seeming to notice the little bouquet of damask and white roses, he said, "That's a good girl, Rosa; I see you have carried out my suggestion of a nosegay between your budding breasts at last; it quite improves your appearance." Then he smiled like a child about to enjoy a sweet. "But it's nothing to what my birch will effect on your naughty bottom. Soon it will look like one of these fine peaches," he said, holding up and admiring the fruit. He stroked his chin and laughed, then rang the bell he kept close to hand. Almost distracted, and ready to faint, I rushed for the door, but only in time to fall into the strong arms of Jemima.

"Now for the punishment drill; march on, Jemima. Hold fast the culprit and keep her safe." He gestured to Mrs. Mansell and Ann.

"Come along," he said to them, "you must see this as well."

Resistance was useless. I was soon carried into a room I had never entered; it contained very little furniture, only a carpet and one comfortable easy chair. But on the walls hung several bunches of twigs, and in one corner stood a device like a stepladder. It was covered with red baize, and fitted with six rings – two halfway up, two at the bottom, and two at the top.

"Tie her to the horse and get ready for business," said the General. He plopped himself in the chair to look on at his ease. He frowned and shook his head at the sound of my whimpers.

"Come, Rosa dear, don't be troublesome and make your grandfather more angry," said Mrs. Mansell, unfastening my waistband. "Slip off your dress while the girls put the horse in the middle of the room."

"No! No! I won't be whipped," I screamed. "Oh! Sir! Oh! Grandfather, do have mercy," said I, throwing myself on my knees before the old man.

"Come, come, it's no use showing the white feather," he said with a kindness that belied his intention. "It's for your own good, you know. Now no more nonsense. Mrs. Mansell, do your duty, and let us get the painful business over with; she isn't fit to serve in my troops if she doesn't show her pluck when it comes to the pinch."

The three women tried to lift me, but I kicked, scratched, and bit all round, and for a moment or two, almost beat them off in my fury. But my strength was soon exhausted, and Jemima, smarting from a severe bite, dragged me in vengeful triumph to the dreaded machine.

Quick as thought, my hands and feet were secured to the upper and lower rings; the horse widening towards the ground caused my legs to be well apart when drawn up closely to the rings at my ankles. I could hear Sir Eyre chuckle with delight at my squirming.

"By God! She's a vixen," he exclaimed. "She's a Foster all over. Bravo, Rosie! Now get her ready quickly."

I submitted in sullen despair, while my torn dress and underskirts were turned up and pinned round my shoulders. But when they began to loosen my drawers, my rage burst out afresh. Turning my head, I saw the old man, his stern face beaming with pleased animation as he whisked in his right hand a small bunch of fresh birchen twigs. My blood was in a boil, and my bottom tingled in anticipation of the strokes, especially when Jemima pulled the drawers nearly down to my knees and gave me a smart little slap on the sly. Malicious and wicked, she wanted me to know what I might soon expect. In my anger I fairly shouted, "You must be a cruel old beast to let them treat me so."

"Old beast, indeed!" said the General, jumping up in a passion.

"We'll see about that, Miss; perhaps you'll be glad to apologize before long."

I saw him stepping forward. "Oh! Mercy! Mercy! Sir! I didn't mean it. They've hurt me so I couldn't help what I said."

"This is a serious case," he said, apparently addressing the others.

"She's idle, violently vicious, and even insulting to me, her only natural guardian, instead of treating me with the proper respect. There can be no alternative. The only remedy, however painful the scene may be to those of us who must inflict the punishment, is to carry it out. It is a matter of duty, or the girl will be ruined. She has never been under proper control all her life."

"Oh! Grandfather, punish me any way but this," I sobbed out through my tears. "I know I can't bear it; it's so dreadfully cruel."

"My child, such crocodile tears have no effect on me; you must be made to feel the smart. If we let you off now, you would be laughing at it all, and go on worse than before." He came ahead. "Stand aside, Ann, we can't waste any more time." So saying, he made a flourish with the rod, so as to make an audible "whisk" in the air. I suppose it was only to clear the way, as it did not touch me. In fact, up to this time, he had treated me like a cat which knows the poor mousey cannot escape, but may be pounced upon at any time.

I could see the tears in Ann's eyes, but Jemima had a malicious smile on her face. Mrs. Mansell looked very grave.

No time was allowed for further reflection. The next instant I felt a smart, but not-very-heavy stroke right across my loins, then another, and another, in rather quick succession, but not too fast for me to think that perhaps after all it would not be so dreadful as I feared. So setting my teeth firmly, I determined to give as little indication as possible of my feelings. All this and a great deal more flashed through my brain before a handful of strokes had been administered. My bottom tingled all over, and the blood seemed to rush like lightning through my veins at every blow.

"Now, you idle puss," said the General, "you begin to feel the fruits of your conduct. Now you know the price of your sloth and impertinence!" With each ejaculation he laid on a harder stroke.

My courage still sustained my resolution not to cry out, but only seemed to make him more angry.

"Sulky-tempered and obstinate, by Jove!" he roared. "We must draw it out of you. Don't think, Miss, I'm to be beaten by a little wench like you; take that, and that, and that," he said, whisking me with still greater energy, concluding with a tremendous whack which drew up the skin to bursting tension. I felt another like it would make the blood spurt forth, but he suddenly paused in his fury, as if for want of breath. I now know too well, it was only to prolong his own exquisite pleasure.

Thinking all was over, I entreated them to let me go, but to my sorrow soon realized my mistake.

"Not yet, not yet, you bad girl, you're not half punished for all your biting, scratching, and impudence," exclaimed Sir Eyre.

Again the hateful birch hissed through the air, cutting into my bruised flesh. My buttocks and thighs suffered and smarted in agony, but he seemed to be taking some care not to draw blood. I was, however, not to escape; it was only his deliberate plan of attack, so as not to exhaust his poor victim too soon.

"You'll not bite, and scratch, and fight against my orders again, will you child? You'll know next time what to expect." He shook with near-apoplectic excitement and rage. "You deserve no mercy. Your idleness was bad enough, but your murderous conduct is intolerable; I believe you would have killed anyone in your passion had you the chance. Bite, scratch, and fight, eh? Bite, will you?" Thus lectured the old man, warming to the business at hand till he'd nearly made corduroy of my poor thighs.

I was in dreadful agony at every cut and must have fainted, but his lecturing seemed to sustain me like a cordial. Besides, with the pain I experienced a most pleasurable warmth and excitability that is impossible to describe, but which, doubtless, you, my dear, have felt for yourself when under my discipline.

But all my fortitude could not much longer suppress my sighs and moans, and at last I felt as if I must die under the torture, in spite of the exquisite sensation which mingled with it. Notwithstanding my ohs and ahs, and stifled cries, I would not ask for mercy again; my thoughts ran solely upon the desire for vengeance, and how I should like to whip and cut them all to pieces, especially the General and Jemima, and even poor, tearful Ann.

Sir Eyre seemed to forget his age and continued to work away in frightful excitement. Nor could the generous line of his breeches conceal the aroused swell of his manhood.

"Damn you, won't you cry for mercy? Won't you apologize, you young hussy?" he hissed between his teeth. "You're tougher and more obstinate than any of the family, a real chip off the old block. But to be beaten by such as you... I'll not have it. There! There! There!" cried he as if in the climactic throes of passion; and at last the worn-out stump of the rod fell from his hand. He sank back quite exhausted into his chair.

"Mrs. Mansell," he gasped, "give her half-a-dozen good stripes with a new rod to finish her off, and let her know that although she may exhaust an old man, there are other strong arms that can dispense justice to her impudent rump."

The housekeeper, in obedience to the command, took up a fine fresh birch and cut deliberately, counting in clear voice, "One, two, three, four, five, six." Her blows were heavy, but did not seem to sting so cruelly as those given by Sir Eyre. "There, Miss Rosa," she said sympathetically in a near whisper, "I might have laid it on more heavily, but for pity's sake I could not."

Although victorious, I was nearly dead and frightfully cut up. I had to be carried to my room. But what victory could I enjoy? I was all torn and bleeding, and I had the certainty that the old General would renew his attack at the first favorable opportunity.

Poor Ann laughed and cried over my lacerated posteriors as she tenderly washed me with cold arnica and water. She seemed so used to the business that when we retired to rest (for I got her to sleep with me), I asked her if she had not often attended bruised bottoms before.

"Yes, Miss Rosie," she replied, "but you must keep the secret and not pretend to know anything. I have been whipped myself, but not so harshly as you were. Although it's cruel, we all rather like it after the first time or two, especially if we are not cut up too much. Next time you should cry for mercy. It pleases the old man and will temper his fury," she giggled. "He was so exhausted with whipping you, Mrs. Mansell was going to send for the doctor. But Jemima said a good birching would do him more good and would draw the blood away from his head; so they pickled him finely till he quite came to himself and begged hard to be let off." At that we both laughed.

"It won't do for you to wear a shift tonight, Miss Rosa," Ann said shyly, "or the unguents may rub off. You'd do best to lie as you are and let the air caress your skin and grant whatever relief my hands cannot."

Even at my tender age and in the blush of my innocence, the look and invitation in Ann's eyes was unmistakable. Perhaps it was my weakened state, or perhaps it was my tumultuous state of mind, but I lay back and succumbed to Ann's gentle ministrations.

The contact of my cruelly striped buttocks with even the cool silkiness of the sheets caused me great discomfort, but I soon forgot it at the touch of Ann's fingers. It was a wonder the sensations they elicited at their skilled plying of my body.

Ann concentrated first on my developing breasts, running her fingertips oh-so-lightly along their swell and circling purposefully the edge of the sweet pink nipples. I could feel those rosy tips swelling to meet her touch, and I sighed contentedly at the ensuing shiver of pleasure I experienced.

Unknowing that there was better still to come, my eyes snapped open when Ann's hands quested lower and lower over first my stomach, then my belly.

"Oh, it is so white and flat," she cooed with admiration, kissing the snowy expanse.

Then her fingers found their knowing way to my mount, and caressed and teased the virgin folds of pink skin. Peeling back my hood, she tickled and caressed my sensitive clitoris while I writhed and squirmed beneath her hands. It was heavenly, and the warmth that suffused my poor aching body was a great consolation to me. Dear Ann demanded nothing in return, and, as I was tiring, she ended her ministrations.

Thus ended my first lesson in the art of the rod... and the art of love. In further letters, you shall hear how I got on with Ann, continued the contest with the General, of my adventures at school, and of my own domestic discipline since left to myself. Believe me, Dear Christine...

Your affectionate friend,
Rosa Belinda Foster

ANN

My Dear Christine,
I'll deny you no longer the continuation of my tale. To resume where I left off, Ann and I had some further conversation the following morning in the dreamy afterglow of our night's activities. "So, Ann," I asked, "you have been whipped, have you? What was your offense?" I was feeling considerably better by then, the faint throbbing of my wounds the only persistent reminder of my punishment of the afternoon before.

"The first time was for being seen walking from church with a young man," she sighed, arching her back with languorous sensuality.

"The General said I had never been religious and only pretended to be so for the chance of gadding about with young fellows. He said this must be checked, or I should be ruined."

"Humph," I snorted, rather enjoying my view of her long, pale limbs and the way her pert nipples jutted toward the ceiling. "Didn't you feel revengeful at being whipped for that?"

"So I did, but forgot all about it in the delight I had in seeing Jemima cut up as well. Oh, she did just catch it, I can tell you; but she's as strong and hard as leather."

Ann

"So I could forget and forgive too, had I not been the sole recipient of the General's strokes. I've got a good mind to share some of it with you, Ann," I laughed, "when I don't feel quite so sore." I ruefully ran my fingertips along the weals and welts that crisscrossed my tender buttocks. Some of the swelling had already subsided, though I would bear the angry red marks for days.

"Ah! But I know you hate Jemima, and would rather see her lashed naked to the horse. Perhaps we shall be able to get her into a scrape and earn her the General's anger if we put our heads together."

I wagged a finger at her. "Oh! You sly girl. Don't you think I'll let you off, much as I long to repay the others. Just wait till I feel well enough, and I'll settle with you first. There will be plenty of opportunities, as you are to sleep with me in my room every night. I haven't forgotten how you persuaded me to dress for dinner when you knew, all the time, what lay in store for me." The color rose in Ann's cheeks at her distress. "Dear Miss Rosie, I couldn't help it. Mrs. Mansell sent me up to dress you. The old General put it off till after dinner, as he likes to see the culprits dressed as nicely as possible. Whenever he punished any of us, we would have to attend the punishment drill in our very best clothes. And if they got damaged, Mrs. Mansell soon fit us out again, so we didn't lose much by a good birching. I have known Jemima to get into trouble so as to damage her things and get new clothes, but Sir Eyre made her smart well for them."

I casually dropped the matter then and there to ease Ann of her anxiety. Nonetheless, I planned with secret glee to even the score at the first opportunity. Though very sore for several days, I managed to make and secrete a fine bunch of twigs, ready for Miss Ann when she would little expect it. In fact, she did not know I had been into the garden or out of the house. Of course, she was a much stronger and bigger girl than I, so I should have to secure her by some crafty stratagem.

I let her think I had quite forgotten my threat, but one evening, just as we were both undressed for bed, I asked, "Ann, did Mrs. Mansell or Jemima ever birch you without grandfather knowing it?" She continued turning down the covers, thinking nothing of what was behind my innocent question.

"Yes, Miss Rosie, they've served me out shamefully, more than once."

"How did they manage that?"

"Why, I was tied by my hands to the foot of the bedstead," said she, "a helpless slave to their wishes was I, nor did I cry for the General as well I might have."

I clapped my hands and ran over to her. "Oh! Do show me, and let me tie you up to see how it all looked."

She looked wary, but shrugged her shoulders and nodded at my expression of innocence. "Very well; if it's any pleasure to you, Miss." Dear Ann of the white skin and burnished copper hair; she was so obtuse and trusting at times.

"What shall I tie you up with? You're as strong as Samson."

"A couple of handkerchiefs will do, and there's a small comforter to tie my legs."

By following her directions, I soon had her hands tied to the two knobs at the foot of the bed. Her feet, stretched out a little behind, were secured to the legs of the table.

"Oh! My!" exclaimed Ann. "You have fixed me tight. Why did you tie me so securely? I can't get away till you release me." She squirmed in vain against her bonds.

"Stay! Stay!" I cried. "I must see you quite prepared now that you are properly fixed up." I quickly turned up her nightdress and secured it well above her waist so as to expose her plump bottom and delicately mossed front to my eager gaze.

"Oh! What a beauty you are, Ann," said I, kissing her lightly on the lips. "You know I love you, but your naughty little bum-be-dee must be punished. It is a painful duty, but I'll let you see it's no joke, Miss. Why look, what a fine swish tail I've got," I teased, producing my rod from its place of concealment.

"Mercy! Mercy!" cried Ann. "Dear Miss Rosie, you won't beat me; I've always been so kind to you!"

"It won't do, Ann," I said regretfully. "I must do my duty. You were one of the lot against me, and the first I can catch. It may be years before I can pay off the others."

The sight of her beautiful posteriors filled me with a gloating desire to exercise my skill upon them, and see a little of what I'd been forced to feel myself. Without further delay, I nervously grasped my birch and commenced the assault by some sharp strokes, each blow deepening the rosy tints on Ann's delectable cheeks to a deeper red.

"Ah! Ah! What a shame," she wailed, smarting from the blows.

"You're as bad as the old General, you little witch, to take me so by surprise."

"You don't seem at all sorry, Miss," I cried, "but I'll try and curb your impudence. In fact, I begin to think you are one of the worst of them, and only acted the hypocrite with your pretended compassion, when you were, in reality, in on it all the time. But it's my turn now. Of course, you were too strong for me, unless I had trapped you so nicely. How do you like it, Miss Ann?" All this time I kept on, whisk, whisk, whisk, in quick succession, till her bottom began to look quite interesting. I felt my young body quickening at the sight of the oh-so-helpless morsel before me.

"You little wretch! You vixen!" gasped Ann. "Your grandfather shall hear of this."

"That's your game, is it, Miss Telltale? At any rate, you'll be well paid first," I replied. The sight of her buttocks only seemed to add to my energy, and it was quite a thrill of pleasure when I first saw the blood flushing under her skin. She writhed and wriggled with suppressed sighs and moans, but each time she gave utterance to any expression, it seemed only for the purpose of irritating me more and more. My excitement became intense, the cruel havoc seemed to be an immense satisfaction to me, and her bottom really was in a deplorable state through my inconsiderate fury. At last, quite worn out and fatigued, I could hold the rod no longer, and my passion melted into love and pity as I saw her in an apparently listless and fainting condition, with drooping head, eyes closed, and hands clenched.

The worn-out birch was dropped, and kissing her tenderly, I sobbed out, "Ann, dear Ann, I both love and forgive you now, and you will find me as tender to you as you were to me after my flogging."

Her hands and feet were soon released. To my astonishment, she threw her arms round my neck, and with sparkling eyes and a luscious kiss she said softly, "And I forgive you too, Miss Rosie, for you don't know what pleasure you have given me. The last few moments have been bliss indeed."

This was all a puzzle to me at the time, but I understood it well enough afterwards. She made quite light of her bruised bottom, saying, "What was awful to you was nothing to me, Miss Rosie, I am so much older and tougher. Besides," she said huskily as she assisted with the removal of my nightdress, "the first time is always the worst. It was too bad of Sir Eyre to cut you up as he did, but your obstinacy made him forget himself; you'll grow to like it as I do."

Determined to do for Ann as she had done for me after my flagellation, I encouraged her to recline. I bathed and salved her wounds, murmuring all the while how sorry I was to have raised such welts on her pretty bottom.

Needless to say I was not sorry at all, though I truly didn't wish to cause her discomfort.

"Ah, your touch is a healing balm, Miss Rosie," she sighed as she rolled upon her back. The sight of her pendulous globes heaving with each breath filled me with desire and I took her in my arms. I caressed their large brown nipples with my teeth and tongue, tugging and licking until they became pebble-like and hard. All the while my fingers had been entwined in the fine hair on her mount, stroking and prodding and seeking to penetrate the secret of her womanhood. I succeeded first with one finger, then two, then three, as Ann veritably flopped beneath me with pleasure.

Her fluids lubricated my hand and I continued my assault with youthful vigor. I so enjoyed the sounds of her moans and sighs as I manipulated her clitty with one finger and thrust into her with those of my opposite hand. Finally she stiffened and cried out and I lay back to my well-deserved rest, but not before Ann crushed her lips to my own.

When we had finished, we bathed and I further soothed the irritated parts of her back. We finally fell asleep with a promise from me to let her give me a pleasant lesson of similar kind in a day or two.

Things went on smoothly for a few days – my punishment had been too severe for me to lightly dare a second engagement with the General. Still, I burned for a chance to avenge myself on anyone but Ann, who was now my bosom friend. We discussed all sorts of schemes for getting Jemima and Mrs. Mansell into trouble, but to no purpose. The old gentleman often cautioned me in passing to take care, as the next time he should not fail to make me cry, "Peccavi."

One fine afternoon, however, being in the garden with the housekeeper, I remarked to her, "What a pity it is grandfather lets the nectarines hang and spoil, and no one is allowed to taste them."

"My dear," said Mrs. Mansell, "if you take two or three, he'll never miss them, only you must not tell that I said so. It's such a shame to let them rot."

"But, Mrs. Mansell, that would be stealing," I replied innocently.

"When nothing's lost, nothing can have been stolen," she instructed.

"Only a false sense of honesty would lead you to admit such a guileless act. Besides, you are the little mistress of the house." I shrugged. "Well, you are the serpent, and I'm Eve, I suppose. They really do look delicious, and you won't tell, will you?" I asked with simple naiveté. So the fruit was plucked, and Mrs. Mansell helped to eat it, which put me quite at my ease.

Ann

Just before dinner the next day, we were surprised by the General calling us all into his sitting-room. "How's this, Mrs. Mansell?" he growled, looking fearfully angry. "I can't leave my keys in the lock of that cabinet without someone tasting my rum; I've long known there was a sly-sipping thief about, so I have been sly, too. Finding it was the rum that was most approved, the last time the decanter was filled I put a little scratch with my diamond ring to mark the height of the liquor in the bottle, and have since only used the brandy for myself.

Look! Whoever it is has got through nearly a pint in three or four days." His eyes bore into us as if by that alone he could uncover the felon. "Come here, Rosa, now Mrs. Mansell, and now Jemima," said he, sternly, smelling the breath of each of us in turn.

"Woman," he said, as Jemima faltered and hesitated to undergo this ordeal, "I didn't think you were a sneaking thief. If you really wanted a little spirit, I dare say Mrs. Mansell would have let you have it. You have, after all, been with us some years. But you chose instead to play the wolf in the garden. Very well, you shall be cured of it tomorrow. You should be well thrashed at once, but we have a friend to dinner this evening and your services are required. Also, it will do you good to wait and think upon what's coming. Be off now, and mind the dinner's served up properly, or you'll catch it in Indian style tomorrow, and be a curried chicken if ever you were."

Jemima scampered off fearfully as I secretly applauded this unexpected turn of events. As to our visitor, he was an old foxhunting colonel, our nearest neighbor, and my spirits continued to be so elated at the prospect of Jemima's impending punishment that the evening seemed to me the most pleasant one I had ever spent in that house.

All next day grandfather spent looking over the garden, and a presentiment came over me that the nectarines would be missed; if he had been so cunning in one thing, he might be in another. My fears were only too well founded, for catching sight of me with the housekeeper, cutting a nosegay for Jemima's wear, he said, "Mrs. Mansell, you had better make another bouquet while you are about it. Someone has been at the nectarines." He faced me and arched his eyebrows. "Do you know anything about it, Rosa?"

I fought to keep the color from my face as I stood in his enormous shadow. He was like a huge dark cloud blocking the sun from which thunderbolts might strike at any moment. "Grandfather, you know I was strictly forbidden to touch the fruit," said I as sweetly as possible.

"Humph. Mrs. Mansell, do you know anything of it, as the girl won't give a direct answer?" he questioned, eyeing me with knowing disapproval.

I was covered with confusion, and to make it worse, Mrs. Mansell, with affected reluctance to tell an untruth, confessed the whole affair.

"'Upon my word, a nice honest lot you all are, as I dare say Ann is like the rest. Mrs. Mansell, I'm astonished at you," he said, shaking his head sadly. "I think, however, it will be enough for you to stand and watch and consider how seriously I look upon such things. But as to Rosa, my head spins at the enormity of her offense. Such cunning in one so young is frightful. But we'll settle Jemima first, and then think of what's to be done." With that he was off.

Left in this state of uncertainty, I fled to Ann for consolation, who assured me it was a good thing Jemima stood first. She told me the old man would get exhausted and perhaps let me off lightly if I screamed and begged for mercy.

Thus encouraged, for I was young and trusting and unaware of the depths to which a soul could sink, I managed to eat a good dinner. I even took an extra glass of wine on the sly. Thus fortified, I marched to the punishment drill with great confidence, especially as I so wished to see Jemima well thrashed.

When first I set eyes upon her, as she curtseyed to the General already seated in his chair, rod in hand, her appearance struck me with admiration. She was rather above medium height, had hair as dark as night, skin the color of fine, light chocolate, and proud hazel eyes. Her dark blue silk dress was low-cut, almost revealing the splendors of her full-rounded bosom. The large nosegay was fixed rather on one side under her chin; she had short sleeves, but fawn-colored gloves of kid, and a delicate net that covered her arms to the elbows and hid the coarseness of her skin and hands. Pink satin high-heeled shoes with silver buckles completed her attire.

"Prepare her at once," said the General. "She knows too well all I would say. Here, Rosie, hand me down that big bunch of birch; this little one is no use for her fat rump. Ha! Ha! This is better," said he, whisking it about after he snatched it from my hands.

Ann and the housekeeper had already stripped off the blue silk, and were proceeding to remove the underskirts of white linen trimmed with broad lace; the bouquet had fallen to the floor. Presently the submissive victim stood with only chemise and drawers. What a glimpse I had of her splendid brown neck and bosom, what deliciously full and rounded legs, with pink silk stockings and hand-

Ann

some garters (for the General was very strict as to the costume of his penitents).

I assisted in tying Jemima up, then unfastened her drawers and drew them well down. While Mrs. Mansell pinned up her chemise, the opportunity was presented to me to fondle Jemima's private parts, shielded as I was behind the horse and by Jemima's own body. What a fine manse of curly black hair she had covering the area below her belly. She made no sound as I ran my fingers along the pink wetness of her slit, then inserted one digit between the folds of skin. Her eyes opened wide and her lips pursed in surprise and pleasure, and I could feel her muscles tighten around my probe.

By now Mrs. Mansell had completed her ministrations and had fully exposed the broad expanse of Jemima's glorious buttocks, the darkness of her skin standing out in sharp contrast to the dazzling glare of the well-lighted room. I withdrew my finger and gave her two or three smart pats of approval just to let her know I hadn't forgotten the slap she gave me, then drew aside to make way for Sir Eyre.

My thoughts were so entirely absorbed by the fascinating spectacle that I foolishly lost all remembrance of my own impending turn. Whack! came the big birch, with a force to have made Jemima jump out of her skin if possible. Only a stifled moan and a broad, red mark that deepened the color of her skin were the results. The blood mounted to her face and she seemed to hold her breath for each blow as it came. But the rod was so stout, and the old General so excessively severe, that in less than a dozen strokes there were bits of birch flying in all directions. "Ah! Ah!! Oh!" she screamed. "Do have mercy, sir; I can't stand it. Oh! Oh! Indeed I can't."

"You sly thief, don't think I'll let you off lightly, even if it means you won't be able to sit down for a week? If I don't cure you now, I shall lose a good servant," exclaimed Sir Eyre, cutting away.

My blood boiled with excitement of a most pleasurable kind. Young as I was, and cruel as I knew it to be, no pity for the victim entered my breast; it is a sensation only to be experienced by true lovers of the rod.

"You like rum, do you, Miss?" said the General. "Did you take it raw or mixed? By God, I'll make your bottom raw." He thrashed with merry abandon.

The poor old man was finally obliged to sit down for want of breath. Mrs. Mansell, understanding his wishes, at once took his place with a fresh birch, not giving the victim any respite.

"She must, indeed, be well punished, sir," said she, with a stern relentless face. In fact, after a stroke or two, her light-brown hair was all in disorder from the exertion, and her flashing green eyes and well-turned figure made me think her a goddess of vengeance. "Will you? Will you do so again? You ungrateful thief," she kept on saying, with a blow to accompany each question.

Poor Jemima moaned, sobbed, and sometimes cried out for mercy. But the housekeeper seemed determined to hear nothing, and Sir Eyre was in a selfish ecstasy of gloating and sexual euphoria.

The punishment could not continue long, however strong the victim might be. Becoming exhausted with her accumulated sensations, Jemima at last fairly fainted, and we had to dash cold water over her face to recover her. Then we covered her with a cloak and led her off to her room where she was left to herself.

"Now, Rosa," said the General, holding out a light-green bunch of fresh birch, "kiss the rod and get ready for your turn."

Hardly knowing what I was about, I inclined my head and gave the required kiss. Mrs. Mansell and Ann had me prepared in no time, as I was quite passive; and as soon as I was fairly exposed and spread-eagled on the horse, the old General rose to his task. His stern eyes raked my nakedness, settling momentarily on my young breasts capped by their blushing nipples, and on the growth of hair between my legs. He walked around to the other side to address my back and my poor, barely-healed buttocks.

"You have seen how severe I can be, by Jemima's punishment," said he. "But, perhaps, you did not think your answer to me yesterday was any offense. I am almost inclined to forgive you, but remember in the future, if you get off lightly this time, a plain lie is better than a mediated one." He stroked his chin as he prepared to stroke me. "I think the last flogging must have done you great good, for your conduct is quite different tonight. But remember – remember – remember!" he cried again and again, giving sharp, cutting hacks with each word. My poor bottom tingled with agony, but I didn't cry out for mercy, beyond promising to be strictly truthful in the future. In truth, I was pleased to discover my own strength, which he called stubbornness. After about twenty strokes, he said: "You may go this time," finishing me off with a particularly vicious remembrance which fairly shook me when it fell. You may imagine I had some fine tender weals afterward!

This must finish my second letter. Believe me my true-born child of the rod...

Your loving friend,
Rosa Belinda Foster

JEMINA

My Dear Christine,

I told you in my last letter how easily for me the affair of the nectarines passed over, but I was not long to go free with a whole skin. The General had evidently booked me in his mind for a good dressing the first time I should give him a pretext for punishment. Strange to say, my first terrible punishment and the dreadful cutting up of poor Jemima, related in my last letter, had very little effect on me, except, if it were possible, to render me rather more of a daredevil. I longed to pay off both Sir Eyre and Mrs. Mansell, but could think of no possible plan for exacting my revenge satisfactorily.

If I could but do it properly, I was quite indifferent to what they might wreak upon me. Ann could offer no suggestion, so I resolved to act entirely alone and pretended to let it all drop. However, sundry little annoyances began afflicting different members of the family, even to your own Rosa. The General was very angered by it all, and became particularly furious when one day he found some of his flagellation books seriously torn and damaged. He could fix the blame on no one, but I rather fancy he strongly suspected Jemima had done it out of revenge. Next Mrs. Mansell got her feet well stung one night by nettles placed in her bed. She and Sir Eyre always were the principal sufferers. Almost as a climax, two or three days after Mrs. Mansell's mishap, the General got his flesh considerably scratched and pricked by some pieces of bramble, cleverly hid in his bed. They'd been placed under the sheet so as to be felt before they could be seen, it being his practice to throw back the upper bed clothes, and then, laying himself full length, pull them over him again. His backside first felt the pricks, which made him suddenly start from the spot, only to get his hands, feet, legs, and all parts of his body well lacerated before he could get off the bed. I saw the sheet next day all spotted with blood, for he was fearfully scratched and pieces of the thorns stuck in his flesh. From the stridency of his yells one would have thought he'd been stricken by the most dire of calamities.

Mrs. Mansell had to get out of bed in a hurry to attend the poor old fellow, and was occupied a long time in putting him to rights. She retired in about an hour's time, and making haste into bed, was quite unsuspicious of any lurking danger. After all, she had already been in it prior to the General's alarm. She was barely settled when, prick – prick – prick… "Ah! My God!" she screamed. "The devil's been here while I was away." Jemima, Ann, and I ran to her room and found her terribly scratched, especially on her knees. There were suppressed smiles on all our faces, although Jemima looked pleased most of all.

"Ah! What a shame to serve me so," Mrs. Mansell cried. "It's one of you three done this, and I readily believe it's Jemima."

The accused's arms flew into the air in a gesture of protest and innocence. "I couldn't help smiling, ma'am. You did scream so, and I thought you had no feeling."

"You impudent hussy," Mrs. Mansell spat bitterly. "Sir Eyre shall know of this."

The three of us declared our innocence, but in vain; there evidently would soon be a grand punishment drill for Jemima, if not for all. The housekeeper and the General were both too sore for nearly a week, and, in fact, many of the thorns remained in their flesh. One in Mrs. Mansell's knee kept her very lame and I can't say I was sorry of it. Sir Eyre had to wait ten days before he could enter into any kind of an investigation.

But at last the awful day arrived. We were all mustered in the punishment room, the General seated in his chair (it was after dinner, as usual), and we in evening costume.

"You all know why I have called you together," he said matter-of-factly.

"Such an outrage as Mrs. Mansell and I have suffered cannot be passed over. If I cannot get to the bottom of this, if neither Miss Rosa, Jemima, nor Ann will confess to the crime, I have resolved to punish all three severely, so as to be sure the real culprit gets her desserts. Now, Rosa, was it you? For if not you, then surely it was one of the others."

"No grandfather," I replied demurely. "Besides, you know all sorts of tricks have been played upon me."

"Very well then." He turned away with a frown. "Jemima, what do you say, yes or no?"

"Good Lord, sir!" she stammered. "I never touched such thorns in my life."

He began to see the futility of his approach, but continued nonetheless. "Ann, are you guilty or not, or do you know anything of it?"

"Oh! Dear! No, sir! Indeed, I don't!"

"Be damned, all of you," the General blustered. "One of you must be a confounded storyteller. Rosa, as youngest lady, I shall punish you first. Perhaps we may get a confession from one of you before we're done."

Then turning to Mrs. Mansell, he said, "Prepare my grandchild; she didn't get such a birching as she ought to have had the other day, but if it takes all night, the three of them shall be well trounced. Ann and Jemima lend a hand and anticipate well the coming strokes."

My thoughts were not so much upon what I should soon feel myself, as they were upon the anticipation of the fine sight the others would present. I hoped to again realize the pleasant sensations I had experienced when Jemima was so severely punished. They soon removed my blue silk dress and fixed me to the horse, but the General interposed; he had a different idea.

"Stop! Stop!" he cried. "Let Jemima horse her." So I was released, and having my petticoats well fastened over my back, I was at once mounted on her strong stout back, my arms round her neck, being firmly held by the wrists in front, and my legs also tied together under her waist, leaving me beautifully exposed and bent so as to tighten the skin. Mrs. Mansell was about to open my drawers when Sir Eyre said: "No! No! I'm going to use this driving whip. Jemima, just trot around the room. I can reach her now."

Then, giving a sharp flick with the whip, which quite convinced me of its efficacy, he commenced his interrogation.

"Now, miss! What have you to say for yourself? I believe you know all about it." Slash! Slash! He laid on with the whip, as Jemima, evidently enjoying it, capered round the room. Each cut made my poor bottom smart with agony, and each jounce and bounce upon Jemima's back magnified it twofold.

"Oh! Oh! Ah! Grandfather!" I cried. "It's a shame to punish me when you know I'm innocent. Oh!" He slashed me without mercy. I could feel I was getting wealed all over, but my drawers prevented the flesh from being cut.

Presently he ordered a halt, saying, "Now, Mrs. Mansell, let's have a look at her naughty bottom, to see if the whip has done any good."

Mrs. Mansell, carefully opening my drawers behind, exclaimed, "Look, look, sir, you've touched her up nicely. What beautiful weals, and how rosy her bottom looks."

"Aye, aye, it's a beautiful sight," the General breathed, all worked up, "but not half pretty enough yet." I could feel his coarse hands roving over my flesh, his thumb pausing at and probing my virgin bottom-hole. "Mrs. Mansell, do finish her off with the birch."

I felt assured of catching it in good earnest now. The General lit a cigar and composed himself in his easy chair to enjoy the scene. Mrs. Mansell selected a fine birch of long, thin, green twigs, and leaving my drawers open behind, ordered Jemima to stand in front of her.

Mrs. Mansell, whisking her birch, said, "I feel sure this young lady is in on the secret, but we shall get nothing out of her since she is so obstinate. I will try my best, Sir Eyre." She turned to me, her eyes flinty. "Now, Miss Rosa, tell the truth if you want to save your bottom; are you quite as sure as ever of your own innocence?" She whisked and slashed me smartly and with great deliberation, making the blows fall with a whacking sound. My poor bottom smarted and tingled terrifically at each cut.

"Oh! Ah! How unjust," I screamed, hoping to relieve myself as much as possible. "If I do know I can't tell; it's a secret. Oh! Have mercy!" Thus I tried to serve a double purpose – to be let off lightly myself by making them think someone else did it, and to transfer their fury to Ann and Jemima, whose whipping I hoped to enjoy.

"Ha!" crowed Mrs. Mansell. "'Tis wonderful how the birch has improved you, my dear Miss Rosa. You're not nearly so obstinate as you were. But if you won't tell, you must be punished as an accessory. I'm sorry to do it, but it doesn't hurt you quite so awfully, does it?" All the while she continued to thrash away without a moment's respite. My cheeks were beginning to be finely pickled, and I could feel a cold sweat trickling down my legs inside my drawers.

"Hold! Hold!" cried the General excitedly. "If it's anyone, it's that devil Jemima. You've punished Rosa enough; try Ann next. If she knows anything, we'll make her confess, and then the impudent raven-haired Jemima shall catch it finely. We're getting at the truth, Mrs. Mansell."

I was let down, and the General ordered Ann to take my place on the stout back. I let my clothes down with a thrill of excitement, thanking Sir Eyre for his kindness. At once I made myself busy helping arrange poor Ann's posteriors for the slaughter, pinning up her skirts to her shoulders, exposing her fine, plump bottom and beautiful thighs and legs, the latter encased in pink silk stockings, nicely set off by red satin slippers and blue garters with silver buckles.

"How now, Ann, you hussy," he spluttered. "Do you dare to come into my presence without drawers? How indecent; you'd do no worse telling me to wax your arse." His indignation was really quite laughable. "You impudent girl; how do you like that?" He gave her a tremendous undercut so that the birch fairly well wealed the flesh right up to her mossy crack. "It's all very well in the heat of a birching, but to expose your nakedness like that so impudently is quite another thing," he said, continuing to cut away in righteous anger.

"Ah! Mercy," she wailed. "My God, sir, have pity. Mrs. Mansell didn't allow us time to dress, and in the hurry I couldn't find my drawers to put on. She was so angrily calling me to come and not keep her waiting, I thought duty must be considered before decency. Oh! Oh! Sir, you are cruel. Have mercy; I'm as innocent as a babe!"

She was in terrible agony from the undercuts, already darkly bruising her delicate skin. She writhed and struggled piteously so that Jemima could hardly remain upright.

"Well, well, I'm inclined to forgive you about the drawers," mused the General, "as I always like everybody to consider duty before everything. But how about the thorns in the beds? You must know about that, and it is your duty to confess." He continued his rough treatment all the while. I rather suspected his efforts to stroke Ann's privates with the switch were a thinly disguised substitute for his desire to penetrate them with his own fleshy rod.

"Oh! Ah!" she cried. "I can't tell about the thorns, sir. I'm innocent. How can I split upon another? Oh, you'll kill me, sir! I shall be confined to my bed for weeks if you cut me up so!"

"Fiddlesticks! Bottoms get well quicker than that, Ann." He raised the switch threateningly. "But I shall punish you a good deal more if you don't confess it was Jemima who did it. Now, was it, or was it not Jemima? Was it Jemima? Was it?" he thundered at her with both voice and rod.

The victim was by then almost ready to faint. Still I could see the usual indications of voluptuous excitement notwithstanding the agony she must have been in. But at last she seemed quite exhausted, and ceased to writhe and wriggle as if she no longer felt the cruel blows. Her shrieks died down to a quiet sob of, "Yes, yes! Oh, yes. It was Jemima."

"Ha! Ha! Ha!" laughed Sir Eyre in anticipation of getting the real culprit. "Yes! Yes! She's confessed at last. Let her down now, poor thing." He threw away the stump of the worn out rod. "She took a lot before she would give way, but it was bound to come out."

Poor Ann was let down in a pitiable condition, and was quickly replaced with Jemima who hissed something about "lying chit" between her teeth. I assisted Mrs. Mansell in tying her to the horse.

My excitement grew as I pinned up her skirts and opened her drawers so as fully to expose the earthen beauties of her fine rump.

"Open them as wide as possible, Rosa," instructed the General.

"The mean creature meant to let others suffer for her own crime, and even took delight in helping to punish them."

"It's all a lie, Sir Eyre," protested the new victim. "I never had anything to do with it, and they have turned round on me so that they might enjoy the sight of my flogging. Oh, this is a cruel house. Pay me my wages and let me go."

Sir Eyre chuckled. "You'll get your wages, or at least your just desserts, you sneaking wretch."

Jemima's face darkened further with shame and fury. "I'm not so much a sneak as somebody else who's done it, and I'll die before I own up to something I never did."

"Don't let us waste any more time on the obstinate hussy. Let's see what a good birch will do," he exclaimed, slashing her two or three times severely on her bottom to bring out the flush all over the coffee colored surface of its firm broad cheeks.

"See how her bottom blushes for her," laughed the General. "Better she had blushed for herself, before her conduct brought her to this pass." He increased the force of his blows, drawing weals at every stroke.

"Sir Eyre!" Jemima screamed. "How can you believe a lying girl like

Ann? Won't I box her ears for her when I get over this, the spiteful thing, to say it's me!"

"You're the spiteful one," responded her tormentor. "Will you box her ears? Do you really mean that, you strong, impudent donkey! I shall soon have to try something better than a birch on you. It's not severe enough. You shall beg Ann's pardon before I've done with you; you may be strong and tough, but we'll master that somehow. How do you like it? I hope you don't feel it, Jemima. I don't think you do, or you would be more penitent," said he in a fury. "I wish I had a good bramble here to tear your bottom with... perhaps you might feel that."

"Oh! No! Pray don't. I didn't do it, and wouldn't have done such a thing to my worst enemy. Oh! Oh! Sir! Have mercy. I'm being murdered. You'll kill me."

"You're too bad to be easily killed. Why don't you confess, you wicked creature?" Then, turning to Mrs. Mansell: "Don't you think, madam, she's got too many things on? I am not given to cruelty, but this is a case requiring greater severity than usual."

Mrs. Mansell nodded sternly. "Shall we reduce her to her chemise and drawers, so that you can administer the extreme penalty?"

"Yes! Yes! It will give me a little time to recover my breath. She's taken all the strength out of me."

They then stripped all Jemima's petticoats off and undid her stays, fully displaying the large, fine plump globes of her splendid bosom with their huge brown nipples. At once she was fastened up again and made to stand with her wrists fastened well above her head. She had her fawn-colored kid gloves, and the net, as usual, up to her elbows, so as to set off her arms and hands to the best advantage. She had nothing but chemise and drawers to hide her fine figure; but before commencing again, the General ordered the latter to be entirely removed and her chemise to be pinned up to the shoulders.

Then turning to me, he said, "Rosa, my dear, it's all because of that wicked young woman that you have been punished. I don't wish to teach anyone to avenge themselves, but as Mrs. Mansell is hardly well enough, and I am in want of a little more rest, I think you should take this whip." He handed me a fine ladies' switch with a little piece of knotted cord at the end. "You know how to use it; don't spare any part of her bottom or thighs."

This was just what I had been longing for, but did not like to volunteer. With a glance of triumph towards poor Ann (who had recovered enough, after her own punishment, to begin to take interest in what was going forward), I took the whip and placed myself in position to commence. What a beautiful sight my victim presented, her splendid plump back, loins, and buttocks fully exposed to view, while the red-wealed flesh of her bottom now contrasted so nicely with her unmarked belly in front, ornamented on the Mons Veneris with a profusion of taut curly hair of a dusky color. Her legs being fixed widely apart, I could see her pink bottom-hole, and the pouting lips of her cunny just underneath; further down stretched the splendid expanse of her well-developed thighs, as smooth as her belly. She was also dressed in crimson silk stockings, pretty garters, and fawn colored slippers to match her gloves. My blood seemed to boil at the sight of so much loveliness.

"Go on, Rosie, what makes you so slow to begin? You can't do too much to such an obstinate thing; try and make her beg Ann's pardon."

"She looks very nice, but I'm afraid the whip will cut her up so, Grandfather. Now, Jemima, I'm going to begin. Does that hurt you?"

I gave her a light cut on her tender thighs, where the tip of the whip left a faint red mark.

"Oh! Miss Rosa, be merciful," she pleaded. "I've never been unkind to you. How nicely I rode you on my back when you were punished."

"Yes! And enjoyed the fun all the time, you cruel thing. You knew what I was getting, but I could tell you were delighted to horse me." I gave three or four smart cuts across her loins. Each one registered with a fine, angry-looking weal. "There! There! There! Ask my pardon, and Ann's pardon for your threats. Box her ears, will you?" I cut sharply at every question in some unexpected part; no two strokes followed each other in the same place.

"Have mercy," Jemima wailed. "I was sorry for you, Miss Rosie. Oh! You're as hard as Sir Eyre. You'll cut me to pieces with that whip," she sobbed out, her face dark with the conflicting emotions of fear, rage, and obstinacy.

"Now, Jemima," I said tolerantly, "your only chance is to beg our pardon, and confess your crime. You know you did it; you know you did it, you obstinate wench." I laid on in every direction, making up in my vengeful enthusiasm what I lacked in experience and skill. She writhed and shrieked with pain at every blow, but refused to admit her fault, or beg pardon, any more than I had done before. The sight of her sufferings seemed to nerve my arm and add to my excitement. Her flushed, well-striped skin seemed delicious in my eyes, and I gradually worked myself up until I felt such thrilling sensations as quite overcame me.

I dropped the whip in exhaustion and sank back on a seat in a kind of lethargic stupor, yet quite conscious of all that was going on. So this was what my guardian felt at such moments? The nasty hypocrite! I quite saw the point of the whole exercise.

The General frowned in disappointment. "Why, Rosie, I thought you were stronger than that. Poor thing, your punishment was too much for you. I'll finish off the culprit; just see if she won't confess!" He snatched up another whip, heavier than the one I had used, with three tips of cord on the end. "You won't confess, will you, you obstinate wicked creature? My blood boils when I think how I punished the other two innocent girls," he exclaimed, whipping Jemima fearfully on the calves of her legs, knocking the delicate silk of the stockings to pieces. She couldn't plunge about, as her ankles were fastened, but she moaned and shrieked and sobbed in turns at this attack, to excellent effect. The General seemed beside himself with rage, though after my own recent pleasure, I had my doubts about the precise nature of his emotions.

"I shall murder her!" he yelped. "I can't help it; she's made me quite mad!" His blows wound round her ribs and even made forays into the beauties of her splendid bosom, though any marks thus inflicted were scarcely visible. Yet still her nipples stood out in excited defiance.

Jemima was screaming openly, "Oh! Oh! Mercy! Let me die! Don't torture an innocent thing like me any longer." When her eyes rolled up in her head, Mrs. Mansell interposed herself, saying simply, "It is enough."

Sir Eyre, gasping for breath, lowered his whip and wiped the sweat from his face. "I know you are right to take me away. One of these days, either she or I will expire in medias res."

Jemima was a pitiable sight as we released her from the ladder. She was wet and trembling, scarcely able to stand. We had to administer a cordial before she could be supported to her room, where we saw to it that she kept to her bed for several days.

I had now had almost all the revenge I had been so anxious to inflict, except upon the General himself. But that soon followed, since, unlike Jemima, he could not be ordered to bed for a good long rest. The great avenger of all soon removed the old man from this world, and left me once again an orphan. Being still very young, my guardians under Sir Eyre's will placed me at Miss Flaybum's Academy to finish my education, and the old home was broken up, the inmates scattered.

I shall send you some of my school experiences in my next missive, and remain...

Yours affectionately,
Rosa Belinda Foster

LAURA

My Dear Christine,

I vowed in my last to relate a few of my school experiences, so now I will try and redeem the promise.

Miss Flaybum's finishing school was situated at Edmonton, so famous for John Gilpin's ride. It was a large, spacious mansion, formerly belonging to some nobleman, and stood on its own grounds. What were called the private gardens, next to the house, were all enclosed by high walls to prevent the possibility of any elopements. Beyond these, in a ring fence, there were several paddocks for grazing purposes in which Miss Flaybum kept her cows and turned the carriage horses when not in use. This was all the week, for we only took coach, carriage, or whatever the conveyance might be, on Sundays when we were twice regularly driven to the village church, nearly one-and-a-half miles distant. Of course, Miss Flaybum's ladies could not be permitted, upon even the finest days, to walk there. We always called the vehicles coaches, although they were a kind of nondescript transport. Having nearly three dozen young ladies in the establishment, we filled three of them, and formed quite a grand procession as we drove up to the church door.

Laura

There was generally quite a little crowd to see us alight or take our departure, and, as the more worldly girls assured us, it was only to see if we showed our legs, or displayed rather more ankle than usual. We were very particular as to silk stockings and the finest and most fashionable boots we could get to set off our limbs to greatest advantage. In wet weather, when we were obliged to hold up our dresses, the spectators, as it seemed to us, were mostly the eldest gentlemen of the place. They evidently were as anxious to keep their sons away from the sight of our blandishments as Miss Flaybum could possibly wish. At any rate, it seemed to be understood to be highly improper for any young gentleman ever to present himself at what we called our Sunday levee.

We were never allowed to walk in the country roads. But on half holidays or any special occasions, in fine weather, our governess would escort us into paddocks. There, within a little wood of three or four acres which was included within the ring fence, we were permitted to indulge in a variety of games free from observation.

The school was very select – none but the daughters of the aristocracy or officers of the army or navy being admitted to the establishment. Even the professions were barred by Miss Flaybum, who was a middle-aged maiden lady and a very strict martinet. Before I went to this school, I always thought such places were conducted with the greatest possible propriety as to morals, but soon found that it was only an outward show of decorum. In reality, the private arrangements admitted of a variety of very questionable doings, not at all conducive to the future morality of the pupils; and at any rate, being young ladies we were far less biddable than scrubby schoolgirls. If other fashionable schools are all conducted upon the same principles, it easily accounts for that aristocratic indifference to virtue so prevalent in these days.

The very first night I was in the house (we slept, half-a-dozen of us, in a fine large room), I had not been settled in bed with my partner more than an hour before quite a dozen girls invaded the room. They pulled me out of bed to be made free of the establishment, as they called it.

They laid me across one of the beds, stuffed a handkerchief in my mouth to stifle my cries, and every one of them slapped my naked bottom three times. Some of them did it very spitefully, so that my poor rump tingled and smarted as if I had had a good birching. Laura Sandon, my bedfellow, who was a very nice kindhearted girl of eighteen, comforted and assured me that all the girls had to go through the same ordeal as soon as they came to the school. I asked her if the birch was ever used in the establishment.

"Bless you, yes," she replied. "You are a dear love of a girl, and I shall be sorry to see you catch it." She kissed me and rubbed my smarting bottom. "How hot the skin is; let's throw off the bedclothes and cool it," she added.

I was quite surprised by this, but silently allowed myself to be divested of my shift. Laura was quick to discard hers and we were soon naked upon the sheets spread as it were before the eager eyes of the other girls.

"Never you mind them," Laura said, kneading my body with her hands. She began by caressing my bottom gently, pausing only to cover the reddened and swollen cheeks with tender kisses. Then she turned me over and repeated the treatment on my breasts, which I can tell you caused my nipples to fairly jump from my skin. She tugged on them as if suckling, causing me to moan in pain and pleasure.

"What a very pretty mount you have," she complimented me, turning her attention to my most sensitive of spots. Her fingers played along the V formed by my upper thighs where they joined to my belly, then crept to the entrance to my secret grotto. Several of the digits plunged within to the applause of the spectators.

"Make her spend herself for us," someone called. "Her pussy is so sweet, dear Laura, and would make such a pretty sight all wet and dripping." All this while I writhed and thrashed upon the bed in a near frenzy.

"I think not," said my bedmate, "for I think we'll reserve that pleasure for another." She withdrew her fingers and lay back to receive my attentions.

Eager to perform for the satisfaction of all, I ministered to Laura in like kind, covering her face and bosom with kisses and roving freely with my hands. Laura's mount was a delight, covered as it was by fine curly hair that invited exploration. I combed it thoroughly with my fingers before opening the way and penetrating love's crevasse. The others oohed and aahed at the workings of my fingers while Laura hugged her breasts and moaned her satisfaction.

When we had quite finished and were spent from our exertions, the other girls drifted closer. "Let's look at her poor bottom," said Miss Louise Van Tromp, a fine fair Dutch girl. "Shall we have a game of slaps before Mademoiselle Fosse comes to bed?" Mlle. Fosse was the French governess who roomed with us.

"Yes, come, Rosa dear," said Laura. "You'll like it. It will make you forget your own smarts. Come along Cecile and Clara for a romp," she addressed the Hon. Miss Cecile Deben and Lady Clara Wavering, who with our governess made up the six occupants of our room. "You know Mlle. won't say anything if she catches us."

We were soon out of bed with our nightdresses thrown off, and all quite naked: Laura, thin and fair, with the soft blue eyes that often indicate an amorous disposition; Cecile, a nice, plump little dear with chestnut hair and darker blue eyes; Lady Clara, who was dark, rather above the middle height and well-proportioned, with languid, pensive hazel eyes; and Louise Van Tromp, a splendidly strong, fleshy, well-developed miss, with clear gray eyes and a radiant complexion.

It was a beautiful sight, for they were all very pretty. None of them showed any shamefacedness over their nudity, evidently being quite used to the game. They all gathered round me, and patted and kissed my bottom, Cecile saying, "Rosie, I'm so glad you've no hair on your pussy yet, you will keep me company. These other girls think so much of their hairiness, as if they were old women. What's the use of it, Laura, now you have got it?" she asked, playing with the soft fair down of Miss Sandon's pussy.

"You silly thing," Laura replied, "don't tickle so. You'll be proud enough when you get it."

"Cecile, dear," said Lady Clara, "you've only to rub your belly on mine a little more than you do. That's how Laura got hers."

"Rosie, you shall rub your belly on mine," Louise chimed in.

"Clara is too fond of Cecile. I can make yours grow for you, my dear." So saying, she kissed me and felt my mount in a very loving way, pausing every so often to insert a finger past the taut lips. I could feel the stirrings in my loins as my cunny moistened.

"Listen to Gray Eyes Greedy Guts," exclaimed Laura. "You'd think none of us ever played with the Van Tromp. Rosie, you belong to me."

We now commenced the game of slaps, which in reality was similar to a common children's sport called "touch." Ours was a very large room, the three beds, dressing tables, washstands and all, arranged around the sides, leaving a good clear space in the center.

Lady Clara took charge. "I'll be 'Slappee' to begin," she volunteered, taking her station in the middle of the room.

Each girl then placed herself with one hand touching a bedstead or some article of furniture, and as Clara turned her back to any of us we would slip slyly up behind and give a fine spanking slap on her bottom, making it assume a rosy flush all over. But if she could succeed in returning the slap to anyone before they regained their touch, the one that was caught had to take her place as 'Slappee.'

It was grand fun and we all joined heartily in the game, keeping up a constant sound of slaps, advancing and retreating, or slipping up now and then to vary the amusement, in which case the unfortunate one got a general slapping from all the players before she could recover herself, making great fun and laughter. You would think such games would soon be checked by the governess, but the rule was never to interfere with any games amongst the pupils in their bedrooms.

Just as our sport was at its height the door opened, and Mlle. Fosse entered, exclaiming, "*Ma foi*, you rude girls, all out of bed slapping one another, and the lamp never put out. What indelicate young ladies to expose yourselves so. Mlle. Flaybum does not like to check you out of school, so it's no business of mine; but you want slapping, do you? How would you like to be cut with this, Mlle. Foster?" she inquired, showing me a very pretty little birch rod of long thin twigs, tied up with blue velvet and ribbons. "It would tickle very differently from hand slapping."

"Ah, Mademoiselle, I've felt much worse than that three times the size and weight. My poor old grandfather, the General, was a dreadful flogger," I replied.

Mlle. Fosse lowered the rod, her brow wrinkling. "I thought girls were only whipped at school. You must tell me all about it, Miss Rosa."

"With great pleasure," I said, happy to be the center of attention. "I don't suppose any of you have seen such punishment inflicted as I could tell you of," I began.

The young French lady rapidly undressed herself as I unraveled my unhappy tale. She had very dark, black hair over a rather low forehead, with a most pleasing expression of face, and fine sparkling eyes hid under what struck me as uncommonly bushy eyebrows. She unlaced her corset, fully exposing a beautiful snowy bosom, ornamented with a pair of lovely round globes, capped with dark nipples. Her skin, although so white, had a remarkable contrast to our fairer flesh. There seemed to be a tinge of black somewhere, whereas our white complexion must have been from an original pink source, infinitely diluted.

"You, Van Tromp, *ou est ma robe de chambre?* Have you hidden it?"

Louise clapped her hands. "Oh! Pray strip and have a game with us. You shan't have the nightdress yet."

Mademoiselle Fosse wagged a finger in response to the invitation.

"You shall catch it if you make me play; your bottom shall smart for it."

We all gathered round her, and although she playfully resisted, she was soon denuded of every remaining rag of clothing. We pulled off her boots and stockings. What a beautiful sight she was, apparently about twenty-six, with nicely rounded limbs. Her glorious profusion of hair, now let loose, hung down her back in a dense mass and quite covered her bottom, so that she might have sat on the end of it. Of her belly, it is almost impossible to describe, except to call it a veritable "Forest Noire." The glossy, black curling hair extended all over her mount, up to her navel, and hung several inches down between her thighs.

"There, Mlle. Rosa," she exclaimed, sitting on the edge of her bed, "did you ever see anyone so hairy as I am? It's a sign of a loving nature, my dear," nipping my bottom and kissing me as she hugged my naked figure to hers. "How I love to caress darling little birdies like you. You shall sleep with me sometimes. The Van Tromp will be glad to change me for Laura."

At this point she reclined fully upon the nearest bed and spread her legs before our appreciative eyes.

She hesitated not at all, moistening her middle finger with her tongue, then inserting it fully into her slit. Her hand was quite lost in all the luxurious hair that adorned her private spot, but it wasn't sufficient to conceal the in-and-out motion that she maintained with lustful concentration. She thrust her belly up with every downward stroke to better enjoy her self-induced pleasure, seemingly eager to present the spectacle to our eyes. Her breasts bounced and swayed in their glorious fullness until I could restrain myself no longer.

Stepping forward, I took them in my hands and added my own crushing manipulations to their natural motion.

"Ho, we cannot allow more of that," cried two or three of the others together. "Now you shall be 'Slappee' with your birch, Mlle."

"Very well," said the lively French lady, rising from her pleasures.

"You'll get well touched up if I do catch any of you."

Then we commenced our game again and she switched us finely, leaving long red marks on our bottoms when she succeeded in making a hit. Her own bottom must have smarted from our smacks, but she seemed quite excited and delighted with the amusement, till at last she said, "Oh! I must be birched myself. Now who will be the schoolmistress?"

"Oh! Let Rosa!" cried Laura. "She will lecture you as if you were a culprit, and give us an idea of good, earnest punishment. Will you, Rosa? It will amuse us all. Just try if you can't make Mademoiselle ask your pardon for taking liberties with you."

"Yes! Yes! That will be fine," cried the others, especially Lady Clara, who was already seated on her bed with Cecile as her partner.

They began their own activities as I took birch in hand. Their tongues were as snakes, darting and flicking on all the passion-inducing parts of their bodies. I watched appreciatively before turning to my task, enjoying the sight of those taut young bodies so much like my own entwined in the throes of lust. Their eagerness to use their tongues on their partner's pink little slits especially fascinated me, though I wasn't permitted the time to consider the matter further.

"Yes," laughed Louise, "Mlle. wants Rosa for her bedfellow tonight, so let her tickle her up with the birch. Don't spare her, Rosie, she's so hard to hurt." Then she took Laura's hand. "Come Laura, let us enjoy the night together."

Thus urged I flourished the rod lightly in the air, judging its strength. "I indeed know how to use it properly, especially on naughty bottoms of those who have the impudence to challenge me. Now, Mlle., present your bottom on the edge of the bed with your legs well apart just touching the floor. But I must have two of them to hold you down; come, Laura and Louise, each of you hold one arm, and keep her body well down on the bed. There," I said, when they were all settled, "that will do just so. Hold her securely; don't let her get up till I've fairly done."

I turned my full attention to my panting victim. "Mlle. Fosse, you are a very wicked young lady to behave so rudely to me as you have done. Will you beg my pardon and promise never to act again in such a fashion? Do you feel that and that?" I gave a couple of stinging little switches across her loins.

"Oh! No! I won't apologize," she rasped. "I do love impudent little chits like you!"

"You call me a chit, do you? I'll teach you a little more respect for your schoolmistress. Is that too hard? Or perhaps you like that better," I admonished, giving a couple of slashing cuts on her rounded buttocks. They left long red marks and made her wriggle with pain.

"Ah! Ah! That's too hard. Oh! Oh! You do cut, you little devil," she cried as I went on sharper and sharper at every stroke. She writhed and wriggled under the tingling switches which marked her bottom in every direction. Her

241

full breasts bounced deliciously with the movement, and her nipples rose under my assault.

"Little devil, indeed," I hissed. "You shall beg my pardon for that too, you insulting young lady. How dare you express yourself so to your governess; your bottom must be cut to pieces if I can't subdue such a proud spirit. There – there – there!" I cut away, each stroke going in on the tender parts of her inner thighs. "Will you be rude again? Will you insult me again, eh? Ha! Ha! Ha! You don't seem quite to approve of this, judging by the motions of your impudent bottom." I flailed away all the while I was speaking, directing each stroke with deliberation on some unexpected place till her bum was rosy all over and marked with a profusion of deep red weals. Mademoiselle made desperate efforts to release herself, but Lady Clara and Cecile helped to keep her down, all apparently highly excited by the sight of her excoriated bottom. They added their encouragement with each new stroke: "Bravo, bravo, Rosie, you didn't think she would catch it so. How delightful to see her writhe and plunge in pain, to hear her scream, and help to keep her down. At last, Mlle. Fosse begged and prayed for pardon, crying to be let off with tears in her eyes. We let her up with murmured endearments and tender hands.

This was the end of the night's amusements, for all now resumed their night chemises and prepared to retire. Mlle. took me to sleep with her. "Ah! Ma Cherie," she exclaimed as the lamp was put out and I found myself in her arms, "how cruelly you have warmed my poor bottom. Have you really seen worse than that, Rosie?"

"Far, far worse, Mlle., I've seen the blood flow freely from cut up bottoms," I replied, at the same time repaying her caresses and running my hand through the thick curly hair of her mount as she was feeling and tickling my pussy.

"There, there," she whispered breathlessly, "nip me, squeeze that little bit of flesh." My hand wandered to the lips of her hairy retreat. I willingly plunged to the task, probing and fondling with all the energy I could muster. The act was still new to me – my being in the blush of my youth – and the reactions my penetrating fingers could induce were still a wonder to me. Meanwhile, she tickled and rubbed the entrance of my slit in a most exciting manner, and suddenly she clasped me close to her naked body (our chemises were turned up so we might feel each other's naked flesh). She kissed my lips in such a rapturous, luscious manner as to send a thrill of ecstasy through my whole quivering frame. Her fingers worked nervously in my crack, and I felt quite a sudden gush of something from me, wetting her fingers and all my secret parts, while she pressed me more and more, wriggling and sighing, "Oh! Oh! Rosa, go on, rub, rub." Then suddenly, she stiffened herself out straight and seemed almost rigid as I felt my hand deluged with a profusion of warm, thick, sticky stuff. After resting a few moments, she recovered herself and said to me,

"Listen! Listen! The others are all doing the same. Can't you hear their sighs? Oh! Isn't it nice, Rosa dear?"

"Yes! Yes!" I whispered in a shamefaced manner, for I was unsure if we had indulged in some improper proceeding. "Mademoiselle, do they all do it? It's so nice of you to play with me so."

"Of course they do," she assured me. "It's the only pleasure we can have in school. Ah! You should be with Lady Clara or the Van Tromp; how they spend and go on in their ecstasy."

"What is spending?" I asked. "Is that the wet I felt on my fingers when you stiffened yourself out?"

"Yes, and you spent too, little bashful. Didn't the relentless birchings you received at home make you feel funny?"

I nodded. "Even when I had been cut so viciously that I vowed eternal revenge, at last I suddenly got dulled to the pain and shivered all over with a delicious, hot, burning, melting feeling which drowned every other sensation."

"Rosa, you're a little darling," Mlle. Fosse cooed. "Would you like to feel it over again? I know another way, if you only do to me exactly as I do to you. Will you?"

I willingly assented to the lovely governess, who, reversing our positions, laid on her back, and made me lay my body on hers, head downwards. Our chemises were turned up close under our arms, so as to fully enjoy the contact of our naked bodies. I found my face buried in the beautiful mossy forest on her mount, and felt Mademoiselle, with her face between my thighs, tickling my little slit with something soft and warm, which I soon realized was her tongue. She passed it lovingly along the crack and inside as far as it would reach, while one of her fingers invaded my bottom-hole and worked in and out in a most exciting way. In all my experiences with Ann at the General's house, I had never experienced such feelings as this.

Not to be behind hand, I imitated all her movements, and burying my face between her thighs, reveled with my tongue and fingers in every secret place. She wriggled and tossed her bottom up and down, especially after I had succeeded in forcing a finger well up the little hole and worked it about, as she was doing to me. Although it was all still so new to me, there was something exciting and luscious in it all; to handle, feel, and manipulate such a luxuriously covered pussy and bottom excited me more and more every moment. Then the fiery touches of her tongue on my own burning orifices so worked me up that I spent all over her mouth, pressing my slit down upon her in the most lascivious manner, just as her own affair rewarded me in the same manner. After a little time we composed ourselves to sleep with many loving expressions and promises of future enjoyment.

This was my experience the first night of my school life, and I need not weary you with repetitions of the same kind of scene. I'll simply tell you that it was enacted almost every night, and that we constantly changed our partners. I expect it was the cause of my acquiring such a penchant for female bedfellows... especially when they have been previously well warmed by a little preparatory flagellation.

Miss Flaybum was a stern disciplinarian in her school, and we often came under her hands. She wielded the birch with great effect, generally having the culprit horsed on the back of a strong maidservant who evidently delighted in her occupation. I must be drawing this letter to a close, but will give you one illustration of how we were punished in my time.

I cannot exactly remember the nature of my offense, but it was probably impertinence to Miss Herbert, the English governess, a strict maiden lady of thirty who never overlooked the slightest mark of disrespect to herself.

Miss Flaybum had seated herself in state upon a kind of raised dais, where she usually sat when she was in the schoolroom. Miss Herbert then dragged me before this tribunal and introduced me thusly:

"Madame, this is Miss Foster, who has been disrespectful to me and said I was an old frump."

"That is a most improper word to be used by young ladies," said Miss Flaybum. "You have only to take away the 'f' and what remains but a word I would never pronounce with my lips, it being too vulgar. Miss Rosa Belinda Foster (she always addressed culprits by their full name), I shall chastise you with the rod; call Maria to prepare for the punishment."

The stout and strong Maria immediately appeared and conducted me into a kind of small vestry sacred to the goddess of flagellation, if there is such a deity. There she stripped off all my clothes, except chemise and drawers, and made me put on a kind of penitential dress consisting of a white mobcap and a long white garment, something like a nightdress. It fitted close up round the throat, with a little plain frill round the neck and down the front being fastened by a band round the waist.

Maria then ushered me again into the presence of Miss Flaybum, all blushing as I was at the degrading costume and ridiculous figure I thought I must look to my schoolfellows, who were all in a titter. Maria placed a fine bunch of fresh birch twigs (especially tied up with ribbons) at my feet, which I then picked up and kissed in a most respectful manner, it being the way of things at the school. Next I asked my schoolmistress to chastise me properly with it. All this was frightfully humiliating, especially the first time. For however free we might have been with one another in our bedrooms, there was such a sense of mortifying shame to this that was sure to be felt all through the proceedings.

Miss Flaybum rose with great dignity from her seat, motioning with her hand. Miss Herbert and the German governess, Frau Bildaur, at once mounted me on Maria's broad back. They pinned my dress above my waist. Then Miss Herbert, with evident pleasure, opened my drawers behind so as to expose my bare bottom, while the softhearted young German showed her sympathy by eyes brimming with tears.

"I shall administer a dozen sharp cuts, and then insist upon your begging Miss Herbert's pardon," said the schoolmistress. She commenced to count the strokes one by one as she whisked steadily, but with great force. Every blow fell with a loud "whack," and made my bottom smart and tingle with pain and assured me of a plentiful crop of weals. My red blushing bottom must have been a most edifying sight to the pupils, and a regular caution to timid offenders, two or three more of whom might expect their turn in a day or two. And although I screamed and cried out in apparent anguish, it was nothing to what I had suffered at the hands of Sir Eyre or Mrs. Mansell. The worst part of the punishment was the degrading ceremony and the charity-girl costume the victim had to assume. The dozen duly inflicted, I had first to beg Miss Herbert's pardon, and after again having kissed the rod, I thanked Miss Flaybum for what she called her loving correction. I was then allowed to retire and resume my own apparel. I could tell you about many punishment scenes, but in my next letter I shall record only one other before recounting the grand finale to my school life, and how we paid off Miss Flaybum and the English governess before leaving. I remain, dear Christine,

Your ever loving,
Rosa Belinda Foster

MADEMOISELLE FOSSE

Dearest Christine,

Harried as I am for time on this occasion – being shortly bound for London on business of a pressing nature – I will relate a brief aside on how we idled away the springs and summers at Miss Flaybum's school.

You were already aware of the fine grounds upon which the establishment was situated. Indeed the walls enclosed some elegant gardens that splashed our immediate surroundings with vibrant colors. Beyond the walls and paddocks, however, the trees encroached closely and extended several miles to the next closest estate. Within these woods were found rolling meadows and shadowy glens suited perfectly to picnicking and the aggressive dispositions of young ladies such as ourselves.

It was never easy gaining leave of Miss Flaybum to take our little excursions. More often than not we would use the pretext of studying nature at its closest for our science lessons. Our schoolmistress would only be well satisfied when Mlle. Fosse would agree to accompany us and act as proper chaperone.

We were especially conscious of the newly-leafed trees in spring when our own blood ran hot with the changing of the season. At such times those

Mademoiselle Fosse

of us who were prone to wander – usually myself, Laura, the Van Tromp, and of course, Mlle. Fosse – would arrange a basket and set out upon the adventure.

As we walked we would delight in each other's company and in the diversity of the leaves. The moss underfoot would muffle our footfalls, though our laughter echoed endlessly from bole to bole. When we arrived at our destination, usually a small clearing well away from the perimeter of the woods nearest the school, we would empty the basket and indulge in a lunch of the fruits and cheese we'd brought, as well as the champagne Mademoiselle would filch from the cellars.

One such time we continued the tradition, and having dispensed with the amenities of sustaining ourselves, prepared for our "Rite of Nature" as we called it. With the blood pounding in our ears – long suppressed by the cruel restrictions of winter – we cast aside our clothes and cavorted naked among the leaves. Oh, we were a fine gaggle of wood-nymphs, white of skin and free of our inhibitions, giving vent to our longings for the caress of the sun and the wind on our bare breasts and upturned nipples. Mlle. Fosse especially – she of the thick tresses and dense forest noire between her legs – appeared nothing less than some primal earth-goddess.

We spent the afternoon in such state, lounging as we would or rising occasionally to engage in a game of slaps or hide-in-the-woods. The fact that we were bereft of our clothing (and perhaps our reason as well) only added to the wicked excitement of our pursuits. When we tired of frivolities we drew sticks; she of the shortest stick would be ministered to by the others upon a bed of leaves. As luck would have it, my own draw was the lucky one. As I waited with all the patience my excitement would allow, Laura, Mlle. Fosse and Louise gathered the required leaves and spread them in a spot bedewed by a warming lancet of sunlight. They then gathered me by the hands and made me lie down upon this softest of mattresses.

When I was recumbent, they descended on me like bees to the honey, for is that not the sweet nectar 'tween all ladies' legs? Laura busied herself with kneading my globes, twisting and massaging them till the nipples fairly jumped up at her touch and at the coolness of the afternoon breeze. She then replaced fingers with tongue, and drew circles around the pink aureoles that induced in me a great weakness of limb.

Louise had settled herself near to my head, consenting herself with brushing her pouting lips against my own before guiding her free-swinging breasts to my mouth. I accepted them eagerly and sucked and pulled like a newborn. Her nipples covered the entire ends of her globes, the sight of that pink expanse so close before my eyes raising me to increased heights of excitement. For my part, I employed one questing hand to fondle the taut folds of her pussy, probing tentatively now, then again, with this finger or that.

Mademoiselle, however, had buried her face between my quivering legs, knowing full well the pleasure her expert tongue elicited from me. She began at my mount, painting the borders like some impassioned artiste. Then she nibbled at the little pink clit that peered shyly from its place of concealment. But there was no hiding from her strokes. She lapped at the bud until I writhed upon the ground scattering leaves this way and that. Only when I allowed a moan to escape my lips did she plunge her tongue full into the pinkness of my harbor. She stabbed again and again while the others held me down and worked my body with their own hands and tongues.

The tears were rolling down my cheeks when Laura looked up from her work. "My, I believe our dear Rosie is about to spend herself. See how the flush spreads from her belly to her neck?" Upon hearing that, Mlle. Fosse withdrew her tongue and substituted instead as many fingers as my gaping pussy would hold. I spent immediately, soaking the frenzied digits with the unspent flood of my youthful passion and crying out in a voice that was lost in the breezes that traveled the forest avenues.

There was much hugging and kissing following this completion of our ritual, but unbeknownst to me, my companions had additional pleasures in store. When I made to rise, the three of them held me down while Louise withdrew a quartet of sturdy vines from its place of concealment.

"And what's this?" I gasped. "Are we to alter our grand traditions without the benefit of consultation with our peers?"

"The ritual remains unaltered, dear Rosie," Laura assured me.

"This is a special surprise we felt sure you would enjoy. In fact, we must admit to having conspired earlier to assure you'd draw the short stick. We would not have you spoil our planning by seeing our attentions fall upon the wrong party."

I was speechless at this and could only submit humbly as they looped one length of the vine about my wrists and drew them together. Additional lengths were secured to each ankle and I was led to a close pair of saplings within reach of my legs when spread. My hands Mademoiselle secured to a branch overhead so that I was stretched like a victim upon the rack; my feet were bound each to one of the infant trees.

"And now," commenced the Van Tromp, "it is only fitting that we initiate the new season with a proper sacrifice of virgin blood." So saying, she produced a handsome switch of fresh-cut birch, still green and resilient as was evident when she whipped it though the air. Laura and Mlle. Fosse situated themselves on each side for the most advantageous view of my bottom as Louise laid on the first strokes. Swish – swish – swish. They were not heavy, but coming as soon as they did after the delightful treatment I'd received not moments before, they reduced me to a limpid husk waiting to be filled with the most fiery of emotions.

"Yes! Yes!" I moaned, caught up in the feverish cadence of the strokes. Louise echoed my words as she cut harder and harder, raising the fine red weals along my back and bottom. She seemed determined to raise my blood as she'd promised, and it wasn't long before I could feel a faint scarlet trickle working its way down my back, then meandering along my thighs.

The sensation was heavenly, and the only matter that led to a disappointing cessation of the strokes was the bowing of the sun. It wouldn't do to have Miss Flaybum inquire too closely of our activities should we arrive past the appointed hour.

So I was summarily cut down and tenderly attended, all agreeing that a sufficient and memorable offering had been made to whatever spirits loomed in the wood.

This must hold you till my next, dear Christine. I promise a longer account of my final days at Miss Flaybum's institution, and promise as well a speedy return so as not to needlessly render still greater suspense.

Yours with affection,

Rosa Belinda Foster

MISS FLAYBURN

My Dear Christine,

I was some time with Miss Flaybum before my education was declared complete, a consummation I had done my best to avoid for some while. But by the time the last half year arrived, you may be sure I looked forward to my emancipation from the thralldom of Miss Herbert and her mistress. Lady Clara, Laura, and the Van Tromp had all left. Cecile was now my bosom friend, and I loved Mademoiselle Fosse so dearly that my guardians had arranged with her to live with me as a companion in the future, as they intended making me a sufficient allowance to set up a genteel household of my own – I being now, quite undeniably, a woman, no matter how much I enjoyed becoming "finished."

Besides myself and Cecile, there were at school no less than nine or ten young ladies who, like Mademoiselle, would leave for good when we broke up for the approaching holidays. Miss Flaybum seemed to be much annoyed at the prospect of losing quite a third of her pupils all at once. She became decidedly spiteful in her little tyranny and in the punishments inflicted, seeming to take an especial delight in horsing the biggest girls. We were birched – often three and four at a time – for the most trifling offenses. Such

Miss Flayburn

doings could not fail to breed resentment in our breasts, and we all longed for some chance of revenge. I had become quite a leader in the school, and, with the other girls, often made what we called sacrifices to the rod. Our victims were usually the younger pupils, who dared not complain to Miss Flaybum for fear of worse happening to them.

The last few days were approaching, and in less than a week I hoped to take leave of old Edmonton for good. Not wishing to abandon the field without paying off old scores, I had a consultation with Mlle. and Cecile as to the practicality of wreaking our revenge. We decided to engage all the big girls who were leaving to help us, besides taking about a dozen more of the others into our confidence. They promised, at the very least, to remain neutral, frightened spectators.

Miss Flaybum in her careful wisdom had all the servants except Maria sleep in a distant part of the house. A heavily barred door prevented all access by them to us at night.

Miss Flaybum also invariably gave the young ladies a breaking-up party the evening before they were to go home, so we determined to make it an event that would be well remembered. Our plan required us to bribe Maria to forfeit her allegiance and aid in our treason; our intention being that at the end of the evening's entertainment, we would seize Miss Flaybum, Miss Herbert, and Frau Bildaur, and well birch them all – especially the two former tyrants. We had no difficulty with Maria who had recently drawn most of her wages. I promised her a handsome douceur and a place in my own establishment, which she gladly accepted, being, as she said, quite tired out with the Misses' tantrums.

She also agreed to provide everything necessary for our purpose – cords and especially three of the penitential dresses to put on our victims.

The eventful evening arrived. The conspirators had agreed between themselves to irritate Miss Flaybum by making very free with her champagne, which upon such occasions was made a great display of, but very sparingly served out to the company.

Maria, assisted by two other servants, was principal waitress, and at supper, by her connivance, nearly all of us took about three glasses of the sparkling gooseberry instead of the usual one. Miss Flaybum opened her eyes in astonishment as she saw us indulging in a second glass, but when she saw us still further encroaching on her profuse hospitality, she fairly exploded.

"Miss Foster, Miss Deben, I'm astonished at you! How dare you,

Mademoiselle, to encourage those young ladies in such intemperance." She rose from her seat in a rage, bellowing, "Half of my pupils will get intoxicated. Maria, remove those bottles this instant; you must have lost your head."

Maria, who had watched the storm brewing, had, just the previous instant, succeeded in dismissing the other two servants and well bolted the door leading to the domestics' quarters after them. This, of course, after having provided them with a considerable amount of refreshment with which they could regale themselves.

Perceiving the field was all clear, I rose up, glass in hand, saying, with a bow of mock deference, "Wait a moment Maria, we are not quite ready to dispense with the champagne. Miss Flaybum, Miss Herbert, young ladies, we shall, many of us, part tomorrow morning, never to return to this happy establishment. I, for one, feel sure you will all join with me in drinking a real bumper to the health of our much respected and beloved schoolmistress."

Miss Flaybum gasped with agitation, but subsided into her chair as if resigned to her fate and apparently unable to help herself. The young ladies all received the proposal with rapturous applause; glasses were filled without stint.

"Now, then," I exclaimed, stepping onto my chair and placing one foot on the table, "we must drink to the health of such an illustrious and amiable lady, in the Scotch fashion, with all honors, one foot on the table. Throw your glasses over your shoulders as you drain them to the bottom, in her honor. To the health of Miss Audrey Clementine Flaybum –

For she's a jolly good fellow,
For she's a jolly good fellow,
For she's a jolly good fellow,
And so say all of us.
And so say all of us,
And so say all of us,
With a hip, hip, hurrah,
With a hip, hip, hurrah,
Hurrah, hurrah, hurrah."

My confederates joined and gave the health in regular chorus and, I must say, in rather a masculine manner. Glasses rained upon the floor.

"My God! My God!" screamed Miss Flaybum as the carnage to crystal continued. "The young ladies are all drunk. What shall I do, Miss Herbert? How awful, where did they learn all this pot-house slang?"

Feigning indignation, I gestured for silence. "What an insult!" I exclaimed. "Are we drunk, young ladies? Cecile, Mlle. Fosse, will you stand still and be stigmatized as drunkards?" We all crowded round Miss Flaybum and the English and German governesses, the two former red with passion, while Frau Bildaur trembled with fear.

"This is no laughing matter," I continued. "We have all been insulted. Miss Audrey Clementine Flaybum, our turn has now come. You shall be made to smart for this, and you will make a most abject apology for insulting a number of young ladies of the highest aristocracy." My accusing finger found the English governess. "And you, Miss Dido Herbert, shall be punished as well because you evidently approved it all. I think we will begin with Frau Bildaur, but I won't be hard on her, as she is rather tenderhearted. Maria, do your duty. No retiring now. Strip them and put the penitential garments on them before us all here."

By now Miss Flaybum had quite lost the color in her face. "How dare you address me so! Maria, clear the room of these impudent young ladies at once; they are all flushed with wine."

Her appeals to Maria were all in vain. Disregarding her former mistress, she first stripped and robed Frau Bildaur; the poor creature, ready to faint with fear and shame, offered no resistance. Miss Herbert however, was indignant, and resisted strenuously, while Miss Flaybum was held down in her chair by half-a-dozen strong young ladies.

"Never mind about dressing that old frump," I exclaimed of Miss Herbert. "Stretch her on the table first of all and turn up her clothes."

Almost by magic the supper table was half cleared, all the debris of the entertainment swept to the other end of the table. The struggling victim was powerless as soon as Maria, with the assistance of Cecile and Mlle. Fosse, resolutely dragged her to the table. Immediately Miss Herbert was stretched over the mahogany. Mlle. Fosse, having turned up her clothes and pinned them well up, sat on her shoulders to keep her down, while one or two others held her arms. Chortling with glee, Cecile opened her drawers and exposed a rather thin bottom.

"She's not very plump, dear Rosa, but no doubt you can make her squeak."

I was of no mind to be merciful. "Tear off her drawers and fully expose her," I ordered. "I must pay off all scores at once." This was speedily done, while poor Miss Herbert appealed for mercy and exclaimed against such indecency. Miss Flaybum looked on in speechless horror, gasping and sighing with indignation, doubtless thinking of the shameful indignities that were in store for her.

I commenced by laying a light swish on the exposed rump. "Have you got any feeling, Miss Dido Herbert? I hope this won't hurt you much, but you've been a spiteful old thing to us for a long time." Swish, swish, swish. I stroked harder and harder till the devoted bum began to get quite rosy. "Will you beg our pardon and promise to be kinder to your pupils in future?" I gave a whack with all my force, which wealed and almost drew the blood from that scrawny bum.

Miss Herbert howled in pain and anger. "Oh! Oh! We never punished like that! Oh, shameful, Miss Foster!"

"How dare you, Miss Dido, tell me it's shameful? Do you really mean what you say?" I slashed away in earnest, soon making little drops of blood begin to ooze from the bruised weals.

My target sobbed hysterically. "Oh! Oh! I didn't mean to say that. Oh! Have mercy! My God! How cruelly you cut!"

"I thought you would come round, Miss Dido; pray," I said, "pray, don't you admire my style of birching? Don't you wish me to do it a little harder?" I taunted her to the applause of the other girls, all of whom clustered around to see. Their cheeks were flushed with excitement, their eyes bright. I kept up a vigorous stroke all the time, and began to make quite a beautiful display of raw buttocks.

Miss Herbert shrieked with agony and cried for help.

"Yes," I crooned, "you may scream. It's delightful to hear it. It shows you have some feeling after all. Will you beg our pardons now?"

"Oh! Yes! Yes! I will. I will," cried the hapless woman. "Oh! Oh! Pray stop. Have mercy. I'll never be unkind any more!" she gabbled hysterically. "Oh, dear! Oh, dear! I shall faint; I know I'm bleeding! Oh, dear Miss Foster, how can you be so cruel?"

"Do you think we're any of us intoxicated? Don't you think it was very improper and unladylike of Miss Flaybum to say what she did, and insult us so, just as we had done her a great honor?" I prodded her with the birch. "What do you think of it, Miss Dido?"

"Oh! Ah! Ah! Ah! Yes. It was so wrong of her! Oh! I do apologize. Oh! Let me go. Mercy!" She writhed and twisted in the most agonizing manner.

"Very well," said I. "But first you must thank me, and promise to retire quietly to your room when you are allowed to go, and profit by the lesson you have received. Remember, it was not half so bad as it might have been." I gave her a couple of slashing undercuts between her thighs for good measure. "Kneel down and kiss the rod, and thank me."

"Ah! Ah! Dreadful. Oh! I shall die! Oh! Have pity," she sobbed and moaned. Upon her release, she kneeled and kissed the rod, and made most humble thanks, apologies, and promises, to the infinite delight of the audience who thoroughly enjoyed her humiliation. Then they bade her farewell with a storm of hisses as she hobbled from the room crestfallen and smarting with her degradation. I turned, a vengeful goddess. "Now, Miss Aubrey Clementine Flaybum, it's your turn. Resist us, and you shall be punished ten times worse than that woman Herbert."

The schoolmistress was quite cowed by the previous scene. She begged for mercy and pleaded not to be degraded before the whole school, but we were determined and relentless.

Maria slowly stripped her mistress, who was a fine-looking woman of the fat, fair and forty class, with quite prominent blue eyes and flaxen hair. The disrobing process displayed in turn her fine neck and bosom, crimson with shame and heaving with agitation, while tears of bitter vexation coursed down her cheeks. Soon she stood clad in only chemise and drawers, the latter so well filled out as to give promise of a splendid bottom within. The drawers were the finest – beautifully trimmed with expensive lace, capping flesh-colored silk stockings and high-heeled shoes with jeweled buckles. But when the penitential dress and mobcap were put on her, she looked quite the jester.

"There," I said, "she's wise not to resist. Let her stand and see Frau Bildaur receive her punishment, and I will rest, too. You dear Cecile, take a new rod and punish her lightly."

It was a beautiful sight to see the chestnut-haired, plump, merry looking Cecile as she prepared to whisk her birch against the trembling Frau. The woman was presently horsed on Maria's back, and with drawers let down and skirts up, was soon ready for her punishment, displaying a very fine, full bottom on which to operate.

"Frau Augusta Bildaur," said Cecile, "I will only give you a dozen smart cuts. I will let you go after you have kissed the rod and thanked me for chastising you." Thus saying, she slowly counted the number of each blow. She struck well-aimed, deliberate cuts, which quickly raised all the exposed surface to a warm, rosy tint, and left a lot of very red marks.

Frau Bildaur received her punishment very firmly, with closed lips all the while, but when released was very profuse in her thanks as she kissed the instrument of her flagellation. Her timid look was gone, and instead of the tears, her eyes were lighted up with a warm sensual light. To our satisfaction, she begged in a whisper, to be allowed to witness Miss Flaybum's castigation. I consented, kissing her roundly on the lips.

"What a pity there is no proper whipping post to tie Miss Flaybum up to," I said. "We must make shift with the table. Put her up in the same way as you did Miss Herbert. And mind that I would have her naked altogether."

Miss Flaybum thought better than to resist, seeing it was quite hopeless and would only entail greater pain to herself. We tore the penitential-dress and her drawers from her, displaying a beautiful plump bottom and white belly, ornamented by a fine Mons Veneris covered with a profusion of light curly hair. The tip of a luscious looking clitoris just peeped out between the lips of her pussy.

Then we spread-eagled her on the table, four girls holding her legs wide apart, while others secured her arms.

"What a fine sight," said I as I played the tip of the birch along the edges of the forest between her legs. "And these–" I shifted the end of the rod to her firm breasts, plumb globes now rosy from fear and shame – "who would have thought such healthy examples of womanhood lay hid beneath those stern frocks and jackets?" I laid down my switch and grabbed both her breasts with my hands, squeezing and molding them till the pink nipples rose in barely suppressed excitement.

"Exquisite melons, these. Ripeness such as this should not go untasted." The schoolmistress gasped as I lowered my lips to her nipples, worrying them gently with my teeth. The girls applauded vigorously and snickered at Miss Flaybum's discomfort.

"Oh, shame! To think one of my girls should so consign herself to the fiery pits by her actions," the woman groaned.

I laughed with delight. "Come now. Surely there's worse to be done to be deserving of such a fate." I clutched her quivering mounds as I ran my tongue down her stomach to the juncture of her legs.

"And what fate then would you mete out for this?" I buried my face and stabbing tongue in the profusion of curly hair, lapping at the clitoris that had so enticed me. Miss Flaybum bucked and moaned, her buttocks rising off the table though she was heavily restrained.

"We'll see how much woman's here before the switching," I declared. The girls yelled encouragement as I set to once again at the pink border of her pussy lips, licking and nibbling and penetrating her with my tongue. Her cries became more and more frenzied until I felt sure the torrent was about to be unleashed. Then I denied her the release and raised my head to her mumbled protests and pleas.

"Oh no, my dear Miss Flaybum. Not for you that ecstasy," I pouted in mock sorrow. "We have other things in store."

I stood up and had Maria turn her over to present us her healthy plump buttocks. "How delightful to subdue the spirit belonging to such a splendid figure. Miss Audrey Clementine Flaybum, you have been guilty of grossly insulting myself and other young ladies." I took up my rod. "You must retract all your accusations of drunkenness. Do I whip you like a drunkard, or were you not rather intoxicated with passion when you said so?" I whipped her slowly at first. "Did we use pot-house slang? I hope I don't hurt your poor delicate bottom, it begins to look rather flushed, but perhaps it's only blushing at our rudeness." I warmed to my work and slashed away in good earnest.

Miss Flaybum's face showed the depth of her indignation, while her fat, plump bottom writhed at every stroke. She moved about so violently it was all the young ladies could do to hold her legs. At first she seemed determined not to cry out, but I increased her pain with such skillful and maliciously planted strokes that she was compelled at last to sigh for relief.

"Ha! Ha! Ha!" I rejoiced. "She's obstinate and won't answer as we would wish. She wishes me to cut harder. Maria, get another good heavy birch ready, this one won't last long. I begin to think Miss Audrey Clementine Flaybum is really drunk herself, or she would have the sense to apologize. But I'll bring her to her sober senses. How do you like that, and that, and that." I aimed each stroke to go in well between the cheeks of her bottom and touch the pouting lips of her pussy, which could be quite plainly seen behind; they were indeed painful cuts and elicited sharp cries of pain that drew laughter and applause from the gathered throng.

"Ah! Ah! How cruel," Miss Flaybum screamed. "What fiendish creatures to cut me up so!"

I laughed again. "Look! She's just beginning to get sober; a little more will thrash all the champagne out of her." I joyously cut up her bottom and made the blood run in little streams, so that it soon began to run down her thighs and drip from the hairs of her pussy. I began to be quite excited at the spectacle, as did the observers, but not the least in sympathy with the victim, whose sufferings seemed to afford us all exquisite voluptuous sensations. In fact, many of the elder girls were stretched out on the floor together, or had assumed positions of sensual enjoyment.

I have never seen such frenzied probing of cunnies, such licking and prodding and rubbing, such sheer indulgence in the bacchanal, as I did that afternoon and later again that evening. All inhibitions were shed as easily as the girls cast away their vestments. They were inverted one upon the other, heads dipping with each stoke of the tongue, or lay side by side and indulged in mutual manual manipulation. All this while I had continued to flail away with gusto.

Miss Flaybum, by now, began to scream for mercy. "Have pity, Miss Foster. Oh! Oh! I shall faint; I shall die."

But I was in a fearful state of excitement. "No, no, no fear of your dying. Your fat bottom will stand a good deal more yet. You are too obstinate to be let off; the birch will keep you from fainting. Now, will – you – apologize?" I gave a terrific undercut between the tender surface of her thighs at each word of the question, making the poor schoolmistress gasp and moan in agony. Still her proud spirit refused to do what was required of her.

She was almost fainting when I, getting rather tired with my exertions, called for a bottle of champagne. "Now then girls," I exclaimed, "she's so plucky we must drink to her health again." In response to this call, half-a-dozen of the young ladies took a bottle each, and at my signal, discharged all the corks at Miss Flaybum's bleeding bottom. It presented a fabulous mark and elicited peals of laughter at the joke, after which everyone drank to "the plucky old girl." This unexpected indignity deepened further the color in her face, and deepened as well the extent of my pleasure at it. Refreshed, I threw away the stump of the birch I had been using and took up another heavy swish tail. "This is a sturdier rod. Will you now, Miss Audrey Clementine Flaybum, beg our pardon, and own you were drunk yourself, or must I cut your fat rump in pieces?" She smarted at that. "Aha! That's the vulgar word you would never allow your lips to mention. Perhaps you did not think you had such a thing as a rump yourself when you used to birch and humiliate us." Whacking away with great earnestness, I lectured the victim all the while. She screamed and shouted in agony as the thundering strokes of the fresh heavy rod crashed on her bottom, scratching and tearing the already bruised and bleeding skin in a frightful manner.

Miss Flaybum was almost done for, and really thought she was going to die, and in an agony of fear and pain forgot the indignity of her position as well as her firm resolve never to debase herself before her pupils. She screamed for mercy.

"I beg you," she sobbed. "Let me go now, dear Miss Foster. Oh! I will beg your pardon. I must have been intoxicated myself. Oh! Forgive me, and I'll never say a word about this. Indeed I won't if you spare my life," she cried in a quietly hysterical voice. "And you will forgive us all, and thank us for making you sober again? Fie! Fie! Miss Flaybum. You were indeed overcome. Was it not so?" I gave her a sharp cut right up under her pussy to keep her from fainting and steady her to her promises.

"Yes! Yes!" the miserable woman howled. "I'm sorry to have forgotten myself, and – and – I do thank you for correcting me with firmness. Oh! Oh! Have mercy now; let me kneel and kiss the rod."

What a pitiable object she looked, kneeling in front of me as she kissed the broken stump of the birch which was now well dyed in her own blood. Such a sight of abject terror and degraded, humiliated pride she presented. Her burning shame was evident to all – her cheeks were stained with tears, and her face and neck blushed nearly as red as her still-exposed bottom; for, to humiliate her as much as possible, we had made her kneel with her clothes still pinned up behind.

I don't know what possessed me, but I felt such extraordinary excitement that I hardly knew what I was doing; my only idea being that she was getting off too easily. So, suddenly stooping, I said, "Ha! Ha! Miss Audrey Clementine Flaybum, you know what a good birching is like now. I must look and see how I have pickled your delicate rump for you. I haven't cut it up too much," I reported, passing my hand all over the raw lacerated posteriors. "It will be well in a week, although there is a good deal of blood. Do you see?" I wiped my hand all over her face, to her intense shame and disgust, just as she was beginning to slightly recover herself. This was the last indignity before we allowed her to retreat to her room.

As to ourselves, we were indeed intoxicated with success, so that I shall never forget the goings on of that last night at school. The girls all rushed about to each other's rooms and indulged in every kind of lasciviousness one with another. Sleep was banished from our eyes, and nothing but the advent of breaking-up day put an end to our orgy of sensuality.

I suppose the icons of society would have declared our behavior shameful. But it was in truth nothing more than a youthful expression of freedom from our intolerable thralldom.

The sights of the evening remain buried in my memory to this very day. Writhing bodies were strewn from one end of Miss Flaybum's establishment to the other. Here three had descended on one and carnally explored every orifice; there a veritable group was linked head to cunny licking furiously amid sighs and moans. Never were more fair daughters deflowered than were that night by members of their own sex.

I, myself, fingered and licked such ripe pink slits in numbers that fairly escape memory, and was in turn so handled. We, all of us, gave ourselves up fully to the frenzy, spending each other till little energy remained.

Miss Flaybum was not visible next day, and the only reference she ever made to our memorable scene of retributive justice was an enormous charge for damaged glass she appended to my school bill. This will end my letter for the present, dear Christine. But when I return from my tour, perhaps I can tell you a little more of my experiences.

Your affectionate friend,
Rosa Belinda Foster

MINNIE & LUCY

My Dear Christine,

During my late tour in Italy and Germany I often amused myself with making notes for further letters to you on my return to England, collecting all the incidents I could think of or remember as likely to interest you. Now that I am at home once more, I will amuse myself on dull evenings by writing you another series of letters. Well, then, to begin.

When I left school my guardians entrusted me to the care of Mlle. Fosse, and we were soon settled in a house of my own in the western suburbs of London. My establishment consisted of ourselves, Ann (my late grandfather's servant who acted as our lady's-maid), a cook called Margaret, and two housemaids – Mary and Polly, besides a nice young page, a sort of foster-brother of Ann's, who was called Charlie.

My guardians judged that we could dispense with a footman or coachman, and hire from time to time such carriages as we might require to visit our friends or go shopping, or sally to the theatres. I did not object to this. My allowance was limited to £1000 a year, out of which Mademoiselle had a liberal salary of £200, which I never begrudged in the least; she was such

Minnie & Lucy

a dear, loving soul, and always did all she could to further my amusements and keep me out of serious mischief.

Mademoiselle and I occupied separate bedrooms communicating with each other, so that we could, if we wished, enjoy each other's company by night as well as day. The cook and Mary occupied a room at the top of the house, while the page had a little cell of a room to himself on the same corridor as our bedrooms. Ann and Polly were also in a room on the same floor, which also contained a couple of spare rooms for visitors.

On the top floor there were several spare rooms, one of which was very large, and after consultation with Mademoiselle I determined to fit it up as a punishment chamber. Wishing to maintain strict discipline in my family, I had hooks fixed in the ceiling, and also provided a complete paraphernalia of ropes, blocks, and pulleys, a whipping post and ladder, as well as a kind of stocks in which to fix a body so as only to expose the legs and bottom behind and prevent the victim from seeing who was punishing her.

Thereafter, Mademoiselle and I frequently indulged in our "*Soirees Lubriques*" as she called them. For an occasional extra excitement we got Ann, and either birched her in our bedrooms, or got her to assist us in birching one another, for I was now thoroughly given to the pleasures of the rod and the excitement to be raised by its application. Unfortunately, these little bits of fun were wanting in that piquancy so appreciable when the victim is a thorough stranger to the birch and feels its tickling effects for the first time. This made us particularly on the lookout for some culprit whom we might immolate to our prurient desires.

Our gardener was a steady man, rather over forty, and his wife, a very pretty woman of about thirty. They had charming twin daughters as delicate and pretty as china dolls, and lived in a pleasant cottage at the back entrance of our garden, which was pretty large. Mrs. White, the gardener's wife, was very fond of finery, and her husband's wages not being sufficient to satisfy her cravings in that respect, she hit upon the ingenious plan of supplying some of our neighbors (who were not so well off for garden produce as we were) with some of the fruit and vegetables which otherwise would have been wasted. Why waste, she thought, what might as well be sold for her own profit? The gardener did not see much harm in it. As he afterwards said, Miss Foster was so good and generous, she did not seem to mind what they took for themselves.

The daughters, Minnie and Lucy, were employed by their parents to carry things out at the back gate, but they happened to be seen by Ann early one morning, who duly reported to me.

I had long an unaccountable wish to birch these angels, but could think of no excuse how to bring it about, so that Ann's report was most welcome.

In company with Mademoiselle, early in the morning, we repaired by a roundabout way to the back entrance of my garden, and placed ourselves so as to see exactly what was going on. We were soon rewarded for our trouble by seeing Minnie and Lucy carry several baskets of fruits into their mother's cottage.

Having satisfied ourselves as to the facts of the case, I returned to the house and ordered the gardener and all his family to be summoned to my presence.

In company with Mademoiselle, I received them in the drawing room, White and his wife and his daughters all together. He made a respectful obeisance and enquired the reason of my sending for them.

"Your pretended innocence is well assumed," I said with arched eyebrows. "How is it, White, that your daughters apparently carry away quantities of fruit from the garden every morning?"

This set the gardener stammering in great confusion. "We only have a little for ourselves, Miss."

"You're only adding falsehood to theft. White, your wife does not get all her finery out of your wages."

"Oh, Sally," he said to his wife, "Pray speak. I don't know anything about it."

Mrs. White already was scarlet with shame and near to bursting into tears. "Oh! It's all my fault. William didn't know I ever sold anything, and the dear children are innocent. Pray forgive me, Miss Foster."

"He must know," I said sternly. "He's as bad as you. Meanwhile, your daughters are scarcely children. I'm quite well aware that they're of legal age, and more than old enough to know what they're doing!"

White and his wife and daughters all went on their knees, imploring me for mercy and protesting that very little had been sold.

"Nonsense! You make me think you even worse, because I know it has been going on for some time. Now make your choice. Shall I punish you severely myself, or have you taken before a magistrate? You know they will be severe with both you and your girls; and I will have no choice but to refuse to give you a character in the future." Of course I would not have done any such thing, but how else was I to manifest my purpose?

White and his wife both implored for mercy and begged me to punish them any way I might think best. "Only, pray Miss Foster, spare the dear little things," the wife cried, gesturing at Minnie and Lucy. "They're such good girls! They only did what we told them."

"You are wise to leave it to me," I said sagely. "I may have some mercy; the law has none for poor, wretched thieves. I don't know how to punish you, White. As you are a man, and responsible for your family's well-being. I will forgive you and let you worry for all their futures. But Minnie, Lucy, and your wife must be corrected. They will attend me here, dressed in their Sunday clothes, at seven o'clock this evening. Now you understand. Go home till then. I will cure them of thieving, or my name's not Rosa Foster."

Poor White and his wife retired in the throes of consternation and confusion, while I congratulated Mlle. Fosse on our good fortune in securing such virgin victims.

At seven o'clock I was ready in the punishment chamber to receive the culprits. They entered with a very dejected appearance, although they were dressed smartly in the highest style of rustic fashion with their bouquets.

"I am glad, for your sake, Mrs. White, you have left me to punish you, as I hope after this you will be thoroughly trustworthy," I said. "Mademoiselle Fosse, will you assist Ann in preparing Minnie for the birch? But first tie Mrs. White to the ladder, or her motherly feelings may cause her to interfere. Then get Lucy ready also. If they haven't got drawers on, we must find a pair for each of them."

"Oh, Miss Foster, my dear young lady, don't be too hard on them," Mrs. White begged with tears in her eyes. "Cut me to pieces rather." She was soon tied by her wrists to the ladder. Then Ann and Mlle. Fosse stripped little Minnie and Lucy, and exposed their prettily rounded, womanly figures to our gaze. Despite their age – which I more accurately judged when I saw them unclothed – they had been zealously protected by their mother from all contaminating knowledge. This gave them an innocent hesitancy which, combined with their lovely fair skin and delicate build, made the twins seem like a pair of lovely china shepherdesses brought to life.

Mademoiselle bent Lucy over her knee, and I did the same with Minnie. The darling creatures were all blushes and quite crimson with shame as we turned them on our laps bottom-upwards. I laughed at the sight, truly meaning them no great harm. "How you do blush, my dear; are you afraid I shall hurt you so much? What a lovely plump little bottom. Does your mother still slap it when you're naughty?" I gave two or three fair spanks, which very much improved the lovely color of the firm flesh and made the little thing twist about beautifully as she felt the smart.

"Pray don't!" cried Minnie. "How you hurt me! I can't bear it, Miss Foster." She began to cry, the pearly tears dropping on my lap.

"So, you sold fruit for your mother, did you, Lucy?" interrogated Mlle. Fosse.

"Father gave it to us to carry home," her victim replied.

"Ah, the old story of Adam and Eve. One tempted the other. So it was all father; your mother quite innocent, eh?"

"I think I can make Minnie tell us a different tale to that, Mlle. Fosse," I said. "They are little storytellers as well as thieves." I gave Minnie a good slap on the bottom with my open hand. "Just try my plan, Mademoiselle."

Minnie shrieked and kicked about in pain as I tanned away, and Mademoiselle did the same by Lucy, till both their bottoms were as rosy as peaches. Both of them screamed loudly for mercy, laying the blame first on their father, and then on their mother as they found it no use to deny it.

"Now, Ann," I instructed, "hand us a couple of light birches. We must thoroughly cure them before they are let off." Then taking hold of the birch, I directed Ann to tie both victims to the whipping post and put a tight pair of drawers on each to hide their blushing rumps. Ann tied them up, side by side, by their wrists, the arms well stretched above their heads and their toes only just reaching the floor. Then she produced two pairs of very thin lawn drawers almost as delicate as muslin, so that the rosy flesh was slightly perceptible through the material. They were, if anything, rather too small, and fitted quite tightly because those fleshy, resilient bottoms were so finely developed. But they left a space of nearly three inches wide behind, where they gave a delightfully seductive view of the pink roseate flesh. Their shamefaced confusion and distress, as they gracefully lifted their legs into the drawers and went through the positions Ann managed to put them in as she fastidiously arranged them for sacrifice, was a most delightful sight to me. I thrilled in anticipation of the pleasure the whipping would be sure to afford. "Now, Mademoiselle," I said, "will you assist me in the whipping? I will do all the talking."

Mrs. White was so distressed at the sight of her daughters tied up for whipping that she tried to fall on her knees, but soon remembered herself when her tied hands thwarted her intention. "Oh, Miss Foster, do have mercy on my little daughters," she sobbed. "To think I should have brought this on them."

"Hold your foolish noise, woman. I'm just going to begin. How do you like it, Minnie? How is it, Lucy?" I began to switch them finely, soon making a lot of thin red marks all over their backs and bottoms. "Will you ever take my fruit again, you little hussies? Warm their bottoms well for them, Mademoiselle. Take the thieving impudence out of their posteriors."

The victims shrieked in a series of shrill screams, their faces scarlet, and the tears rolled in a little stream down their pretty, pitiful faces as they begged and prayed to be let off. "Oh! Oh! We will be good. Please! Mercy!"

Mademoiselle and I were delighted; the sight was so stimulating that our blood rushed through our veins and raised our voluptuous feelings of sensuality to the highest pitch. The cries of pain were so much music to our ears, and we went on with a will – though with no great severity – until their bottoms glowed a healthy pink. Meanwhile, the squealing of their mother only added to our enjoyment. She felt every blow, of course, and cried and sobbed as if her heart would break.

"Look at the silly woman," Mlle. Fosse said. "You're distressing your daughters far more successfully than you're exciting our sympathies, Mrs. White."

The girls' drawers were soaked with sweat after the thrashing. The birches themselves were in good condition, having received minor, almost ceremonial use. Forgetting ourselves, we would have gone on longer, but Ann coolly interrupted us, pointing out that Minnie and Lucie were far less familiar with such proceedings than we were. We untied them, and with a little water and pungent smelling salts soon revived the little one. Then all three were refreshed by some of that useful medication, champagne.

Mrs. White, who had also been released, clasped her daughters to her bosom in proper theatrical style, caressing and kissing them, crying and hysterically sobbing over their sore bottoms. "Poor little dears! Oh, Miss Foster, you have been cruel to the innocent things!"

"They may look like perfect angels, but they are two sturdy young women who should know better than to steal! How dare you call them 'innocent things'? If they are, it's only because you taught them to be thieves, and so neglected their moral education that they that they saw no fault in obeying you. I'll make you confess your own guilt next!"

Realizing her presumption, she began to tremble. "My heart bleeds for their poor rumps. I can't help what I say."

"Take them away," I directed Ann, "and let Mary see to their grief. Then come back and help us to cheer up the mother a little; she's dreadfully depressed, poor thing." Ann soon returned and began to prepare the mother for her punishment.

"Stretch her properly on the ladder; she's the worst of the lot, first tempting her husband and then making the children help to steal."

"Truly, I didn't think you cared about the garden stuff," she explained. "It would have been spoilt."

"Then why didn't your husband ask me what to do with it? Did you not use the money to buy ribbons and dresses?"

The poor woman groaned in shame and had nothing to say for herself. So Ann and Mademoiselle pulled off her bright blue dress and exposed a fine pair of white shoulders, showing that her blushes extended all down her neck, which was slightly flushed as they uncovered it. She was a fine woman with reddish brown hair and hazel eyes, fine plump arms, and hands which didn't look as if they worked too hard at home. Her underclothing, skirts, and petticoats, although not of the finest material, were beautifully white and tastefully trimmed with cheap lace.

We had soon removed everything and found her quite sans culottes. The poor woman blushed scarlet at the exposure of all her luscious charms, her splendid prominent mount being covered with a profusion of long, curly hair, similar to what she had on her head.

"My gracious, Mrs. White, how could you come here for a whipping and have nothing on to cover your modesty? It's shockingly indelicate. What can we do?" I addressed the others.

"I guessed what would happen," said Mlle. Fosse. "Look here, Miss Foster, I amused myself before dinner and have made her an apron of fresh vine leaves. How pretty they will look on her, and set off the pink flesh."

The poor woman fairly sobbed with shame at our remarks and laughing jokes about what a fine set of rump steaks she had, and how nicely they would be grilled for her. My assistants adjusted the apron of vine leaves very tastefully about her loins, and then presented her to me so that she could kiss the rod. Oh, it was a fine heavy bunch of long, green, fresh birchen twigs, tastefully ornamented with gaily colored ribbons.

Mrs. White was made to kneel and give the required kiss. Then she stammered out as whispered in her ear by Ann, "Oh, my dear young lady, Miss Foster, do – do – whip me – soundly – for I have been a wicked, dishonest woman. Oh, forgive me; don't be too hard," she exclaimed, forgetting the orders.

Trembling in fear and anticipation, the tears streamed down her scarlet cheeks as she got up on her feet. They laid her at full length along the ladder, which was at a great angle, so that both arms and feet were stretched out as far as possible. She was tied tightly so she could scarcely move her bottom or wiggle in the least. All was in readiness.

"You have only half confessed your guilt, but your bottom well-warmed will bring you to a full sense of it," I said as I waved the tremendous rod about. It fairly hissed through the air, keeping my victim in agitated expectation for several seconds. Then – whack – whack – whack. The three ensuing blows resounded through the room. Mrs. White's bottom immediately showed the result of a confused appearance of long red marks and weals, while the green leaves went flying in all directions.

The culprit screamed in dreadful pain. "Ah! Oh! I can't bear it! Oh! Spare me; have mercy!" The muscles of her back and loins showed by their contortions the agonizing sensations caused by the cuts in her distended and distressing position.

"How she screams!" I observed. "Where's your courage? Why, your daughters bore it better than you do. But scream away if you must; it will keep you from thinking too much of the pain. I'm only just beginning and have not got warm to my work yet." I went on – whack – whack – swish – swish, all the while.

"Oh! Oh! It's frightful! You'll kill me!" screamed the woman. "Do have mercy now."

"You're a bad one!" I chided. "Will you be a thief again? Will you bring up your offspring to be honest in the future? What do you think of a good birching? Does it make your posteriors feel warm?" I struck blow after blow with great deliberation. The poor woman was utterly distraught, more terrified than pained, and sobbed and moaned in her distress.

"I know I deserve it," said she. "I will never do it again. Oh! How terrible. I feel like I'm being burnt with hot irons!" I guessed from this that neither parents nor husband had ever given her severe punishment. Caught up in my excitement, I varied the blows so as to inflict the greatest possible anticipatory dread on the poor woman by thonging her round the loins, making long stripes over the lower part of her belly, and occasionally even stinging her front, but for all the number and diversity of the blows, none was very hard. It was almost as though I were whipping her imagination more than her body. Then I let my instrument play across the tender thighs, making the tips of the birch go in between her legs, leaving her in a perfect agony of apprehension.

The fig leaves of her apron were by now all cut off and scattered, making the stems which had been interlaced look like exploded fireworks as they still hung about her roseate loins and buttocks. Meanwhile, I continued to work myself up into a magnificent state of pleasure. I flailed away regardless of my victim's protestations, upbraiding her continually and making her promise to take her daughters to church regularly every Sunday in the future, and telling her to pay particular attention to the seventh commandment, "Thou shalt not steal," and much other nonsense besides. Mrs. White was almost too far gone to appreciate the half of this, but managed to moan, "Oh, my God, I shall faint. Let me die in mercy. 'Thou shalt not steal.' My God, how I am punished!" She fairly swooned under the rod, to the great pleasure of Ann and Mademoiselle, who were exquisitely enjoying the scene.

"Enough then!" I said, tossing away the birch.

The victim was released, having incurred no wound more severe than the marks on her wrists and ankles where she'd thrown herself against the cords. Her bottom and thighs and loins presented a lovely mixture of pink and red marks; apparently she possessed the same delicately transparent skin so evident in her daughters.

Ann and Mary and Polly sponged and relieved the poor woman as well as they could, and revived her by plenty of cold water and fresh air. Then they sent her home refreshed by a little more champagne, along with an extra bottle wrapped up in a basket in case she had some urgent medicinal need for further doses of it later that evening. Next day, as I was walking the garden with my dear Mademoiselle, we asked White how his wife fared after her whipping. Being a blunt man, he gave us a rather indelicate answer that, afterwards, gave us quite a laugh.

"I'm darned, Miss, I never had such a night before. I was abed and asleep before she got home with the daughters. But she was so hot she left them to shift for themselves, and mounted me as you often see the cow do to the bull when she wants him to do his duty. She didn't care how tired I was with my day's work; she was off and on all night. I can't understand her being so on heat, for we always leave that to quiet days like Sundays, but she said it was delightful. Darn me, though, if I liked it quite so much. We shall be having twins again, or three or four at once, after such a tarnation game as that."

He seemed pleased enough though, as you might guess. I have offered to help him dower Minnie and Lucie, and if marriage puts them forever beyond my reach, still, White and his wife will be able to further their acquaintance (how delicate I'm being here!) without fear of interruption or audience, the other six days of the week; so you see in the end it was a good deed I did there.

I will send another letter soon. How much there is to tell!

Yours affectionately,

Rosa Belinda Foster

SELINA

My Dear Christine,

In my last letter you had an account of some everyday larceny, but in this one you will read about a pretty young lady who was also a thief by nature, not from any necessity. In fact, it was a case of what they call in these degenerate days kleptomania; when downright thieving is called by such an outlandish name it is no wonder that milk-and-water people have almost succeeded in abolishing the good old institution of the rod.

Miss Selina Richards was a cousin of Laura Sandon, my old schoolfellow and first bedfellow at Miss Flaybum's. Bye-the-bye, can you explain or did you ever understand how girls can be fellows? But I know of no other term which will apply to the relationship in question. Is there no feminine to that word? It certainly is a defect of the English language.

Well, being on a visit to Laura when I was about eighteen, she mentioned the case to me, saying that her cousin Selina was such an inveterate thief that her family was positively afraid to let her go anywhere from home for fear she should get into trouble. Her parents were obliged to confine her to her room when they had visitors in the house, as the young thief would snatch any trifles, more especially jewelry, she could lay her hands upon.

"And you know, Rosa," Laura said to me, "what an awful disgrace it would be to all the family if she should ever be accused of such a thing."

"But have they never punished her properly, to try and eradicate the vice?" I asked.

"Well," she said, "they confine her to her room, and often keep her on bread and water for a week. But all the starving and lecturing in the world doesn't seem to do any good."

"Have they never tried a good whipping?"

"It never seems to have entered the stupid heads of her father and mother; they are too tender-hearted for anything of that kind." I put my arm around her shoulders. "Laura, dear, I don't mind confessing to you I should dearly love to birch the little thieving mouse. Ever since I left school, our last grand séance at the breaking up party has quite fascinated me, especially when I think over the beautiful sight of the red bleeding posteriors, the blushes of shame and indignation of the victims, and above all the enjoyment of their distress at being so humiliated and disgraced before others. You and I often reenact our old school birchings in private, and a little while ago I administered the most amusing whipping to our gardener's wife and her two daughters for stealing my fruit. I effected quite a cure, let me tell you; they are strictly honest now. You are coming to see us soon – can't you persuade your uncle and aunt to entrust Selina to your care with the promise that I am to be thoroughly informed of her evil propensity? On second thought, I think you should say you have told me, and that I offered to try and cure the girl, if they will only give me a carte blanche to punish her in my own way. You will have a great treat," I promised. "We shall shock the girl's modesty by stripping and exposing her, and you will see how delightful the sight of her pretty form is added to the distressing sense of humiliation we will make her feel. The real lovers of the birch watch and enjoy all the expressions of the victim's face, doing all they can to increase the sense of degradation, as well as to inflict the optimal degree of torture by skillful appliance of the rod. Delightful, too, is the placing of the victim in the painfully unnatural, distended positions to receive her chastisement."

Laura feigned shock and disapproval. "What an ogress of cruelty you have become, Rosa!"

I kissed her on her brow, then fully on the lips. "So will you, my dear, with a little more experience. You are much older than me, but really younger in that respect. By judicious use of the rod, a club of ladies could enjoy every sensual feeling of pleasure without the society of men. I mean to marry the birch – in fact I am already wedded to it – and retain my fortune as well as my independence."

"What a paragon of virtue," she said quite out of breath. "Do I really understand you pander to your sensuality without intercourse with men?"

"Come and see. That is my only answer to such a dear skeptic. Only manage to bring the pretty thief with you and you will have every reason to be satisfied with your visit."

I needed encourage her no more. Laura was quite successful in her application to the parents of Selina. They thought the visit might perhaps result in some good to their daughter, and readily gave all the required assurances as to the liberty of inflicting punishment for any little dishonesty we might detect.

Not many days afterward, they arrived at our house. Selina was allotted a small room to herself, while Laura asked and was allowed to be my bedfellow again. Nothing had been put out of the way, as I was so thoroughly assured of the honesty of all about me. I felt certain that if Miss Selina did steal anything, she could only secrete it and would have no opportunity to dispose of the plunder, so we might be sure to recover all of our lost property.

Selina Richards had received a very careful education, and, in general, was a most interesting young lady, apparently very modest and retiring.

Several days passed very pleasantly, and it almost seemed as if her fingers had forgotten their cunning. I was just beginning to fear we might lose our victim for want of a fair opportunity, but the delay turned out to be only a kind of natural shyness which soon disappeared when she found herself quite at home. Things began to vanish. My jewelry seemed much preferred – first a small diamond ring, then an opal brooch set with pearls. Gloves, scarves, and any small article walked off mysteriously, but no one could ever detect her even setting her foot in my room in the daytime. So Laura and I determined to watch at night after our usual visit to Selina's room the last thing before retiring ourselves.

Our resolve was put in practice the first night, and about two hours after we were supposed to be safely asleep, the creaking hinge of the door gave us a slight warning of someone's stealthy approach. We could hear no footstep, but caught a glimpse of Miss Richards putting her head just inside the door to see all was right.

We were motionless, our heads being well within the shade of the bed curtains, while a dim moonlight partially lighted up the rest of the chamber. The little mouse, as stealthily as a Red Indian, actually crawled on her hands and knees to the dressing table, and then without raising her body, groped with her hand on the top of the table for anything that might be lying about. In fact, we could see nothing of her as we were in bed, but could plainly hear the slight movement of the articles as they were touched or moved.

Off went our bedclothes with a cry, "Now we have her safe, the sly thief!" I sprang to the door and cut off her retreat, while Laura acted the policeman by sternly arresting the confused prisoner.

Turning the key in the lock, we at once laid her over the foot of our bed with her feet resting on the floor. Turning up her nightdress, we administered with our hands a good spanking till she fairly screamed for mercy.

"Oh! Pray, Miss Foster, forgive me. Let me go; I won't come here again. Oh! Indeed I won't." She struggled and writhed under our smarting slaps. We could see even by the faint light how red her bottom was, and at last we released her with the assurance of a full enquiry the next day and advised her to give up all she had stolen or it would be worse for her.

By my orders, she was confined to her room in the morning; Ann acted as guard. After dinner, about six o'clock, she brought the prisoner before me in the punishment room.

To make my proceedings more impressive, all the establishment had been invited, except Charlie the page. Being a male, I did not think it would be decent to have him admitted.

I looked down at the thief from my chair. "Selina Richards, you stand before me a convicted thief caught in the act. Have you restored all your booty, you sly young cat?"

With a crimson face and downcast eyes she replied, "Oh! I have indeed. Ask Ann. She has searched the room and can't find any more but what I gave up to her. Miss Foster, I don't know how I could have done it; I'm so ashamed of myself and sorry to have been so wicked. Oh! What shall I do?" She seemed quite overcome and burst into tears.

"If you please Miss," said Ann, "I've got everything but your ring. That I can't find anywhere."

"You bad girl. I know your character; don't think you can deceive me by your feigned tears and repentance. What have you done with my ring, eh?"

"I have never seen it," appealed Selina in apparent distress.

"Indeed, I didn't take that, Miss Foster. Ah, you must believe me, I am so degraded to feel how guilty I am. I had the brooch, but have given that and everything else up to Ann."

"I don't believe what you say about the ring," I sniffed, "and will birch you well till you really confess the truth. Now strip the little thief and examine every article of clothing as it is taken off. Shake out all the braids of her hair as she may have it there."

Notwithstanding her confusion, I noticed a slight gleam of satisfaction pass across her countenance, which, at the time, I was puzzled to see.

Mlle. Fosse and Ann proceeded with the undressing, and I could not help noticing Selina's continued satisfaction as each garment was overhauled, as much as to say, "You haven't found it yet." This convinced me she had the ring very cunningly secreted somewhere, but for the life of me, I was quite at a loss to think how she could have disposed of it. Ann assured me there was not a chink in her room where it could possibly be put; she had even ripped up the bed in her search.

At last they let down all the braids of her hair and she stood only in her chemise, blushing crimson at the exposure, her usually damask cheeks as rosy as ripe cherries. She evidently now considered the search at an end as she kicked off the drawers, protesting against my order to "remove the last rag."

"Oh! Pray don't expose me," she begged. "There can't be anything in that."

"But there may be somewhere else," I said with narrowed eyes.

The suddenly abashed look that came over her face convinced me I was now getting near a discovery. Her legs were closely nipped together and she covered her tidily-furred mount with her hands, though she couldn't conceal those sweet pink lips from my penetrating gaze.

"Give me a birch Ann; I'll make her jump." I took the switch in hand and cut smartly over Miss Selina's knuckles. "Remove your hands, Miss Prig. Jump, will you." I repeated the blow on her naked bottom with such effect that the poor girl screamed with pain, but still kept her legs close. Again the rod descended with a terrific undercut.

"Open your legs and jump, Miss." This time it was effective. With a fearful scream the victim threw herself down on the carpet, but she was unable to prevent the escape of the ring which rolled out on the floor.

It would be impossible to describe the poor girl's distress and confusion now that her guilt was so thoroughly established. She was crimson all over, and tried to hide her face in her hands as she cried for shame. Her bottom had some fine-looking red marks, and also in between her thighs, which the last cut had inflicted.

"Look at the little thief," I sneered. "She thinks to hide herself by covering her face. She doesn't care about exposing all her private parts, or using them to hide my ring. What a disgustingly clever trick. Ann, put on her chemise and drawers. If she does not care, I do, and like to do birching decently with all propriety."

Ann and Polly lifted her up and put on the required articles. Then, as she stood before me still sobbing with shame and pain, I admired my delicious-looking victim. She had such a beautiful brunette complexion; her almost-black hair hung all down her back to her loins; pretty, white, rounded globes with dark brown nipples looked impudently above her chemisette, which only reached a little way down her thighs; it was tastefully trimmed with lace all round, and drew attention to her beautiful thighs and legs, the latter set off by blue silk stockings with handsome garters and lovely boots. Ann whispered in the culprit's ear, and Selina humbly knelt before me, saying in a broken voice, "How can I speak to you, dear Miss Foster. I – I – have so disgraced – myself. Will – will – you ever forgive me? What shall I do? – Will you punish me properly and cut – the – the – awful propensity out of me? – indeed, dear Miss Foster – I can't help myself – my fingers – my fingers take the things – even – when I don't – want them." She kissed the rod and burst into a torrent of hysterical tears.

By my orders the victim was well stretched out on the ladder, as I generally preferred it to the whipping post. Having armed myself with a very light rod made of fine pieces of whalebone, which would sting awfully without doing serious damage, I went up to the ladder for a commencement. But first I made them loosen Selina a bit, and place a thick sofa bolster under her loins, then fasten her tightly again with her bottom well presented. The drawers were pinned back on each side and her chemise rolled up and secured under her arms.

Poor Selina seemed to know well enough what was coming. It checked her tears, but she begged and screamed piteously for me to forgive and wait and see if she ever stole anything again.

I laughed. "Why, what a little coward you are. I should have thought such a bold thief would have more spirit, and I have hardly touched you yet. Don't worry, you won't be hurt more than you can fairly bear; you would do it again directly if I don't beat it out of you now."

Poor girl; she didn't seem to see the need for further punishment.

"My arms and limbs are so dreadfully stretched, and my poor behind still smarts from the three whacks you gave. Have pity! Have mercy dear Miss Foster."

"Now, now," I reproached her. "Enough of such childish nonsense. You're both a thief and a dreadful liar, Miss Selina. You'll not – do it – again." I laid in with four smart, stinging cuts, the whalebone fairly hissing through the air as I flourished it before each stroke to make it sound more effective.

"God in Heaven!" the girl screamed. "I can't bear it. You're thrashing me with wires; the blows are red hot. Oh! Oh! I'll never, never do it again!" Her bottom was finely streaked already with thin red lines, the painful agony being greatly increased by the strain on her wrists and ankles as she failed to restrain her writhing at each cut.

"You don't seem to like it, Selina, but indeed it's for your good," I continued. "There – there – there, you've only had six yet, but you do howl miserably, you silly girl!"

My words did nothing to help her bear up. "You're killing me. I shall soon die!" Her bottom reddened delightfully.

"You'll have a full dozen whalebone strokes," I said, counting and cutting deliberately till I called twelve. Then I gave a little pause as if finished – to let the victim compose herself with a sigh of relief. And just then I gave another thundering whack, exclaiming, "Ah, ha, ha, ha! You thought I had finished, did you Miss Prig? It was a baker's dozen you were to get; I always give thirteen as twelve for fear of having missed one, and like to give the last just as my target thinks it is all over."

Selina, hopeful of release, tried a different, penitent approach. "I know it's well deserved, but your treatment is so cruel. You will let me go now, won't you? Pray forgive me. Indeed, you may depend upon me in the future." She was still sighing and quivering from the effects of the last blow.

I wagged a finger. "You're not to get off so easily, Miss Prig. Your bottom would be all right in a few minutes, and then you would only laugh when you thought of it. The real rod is to come." I held up a veritable branch. "Look at this bum-tickler. It's the real birch grown in my own grounds, and well pickled in brine these last two days to be ready for when you were caught. It will bring your crime to mind in a more awful light, and leave marks to make you remember it for days to come."

Selina's eyes widened at sight of that terrible switch. "Pray let me have a drink if I must suffer so much more. My tongue is as dry as a board, Miss Foster. You are cruel; I am not stout enough to bear such torture."

"Be quiet! You shall have a drink of champagne, but refrain from any talk about your small stature… you wouldn't be such an accomplished sneak-thief if you were larger and noisier, nor is it any credit to you to have mastered that art by your eighteenth year." She gulped the refreshing draught and the rod resumed its sway.

"You have been wicked, deliberately wicked, and you know it perfectly well. Your bottom shall be marked for many a day; I'll wager you won't steal as long as the marks remain. Two dozen's the punishment, and then we'll see to your bruises and put you to bed. One – two – three – four…" I increased the force of the blows with each cut, and soon saw the marks I administered rise up into weals.

"Mother! Mother!" she screamed. "I shall die. Oh, kill me quickly if you won't have mercy." She writhed in such agony that her muscles stood out like whipcord, and by their continued quivering, straining action, testified to the intensity of her pain. At the same time her luscious youthful nipples jutted forth like pointers, and I determined to provide them sensation that would strain them to the bursting point.

"That's right, call your mother; you know how much she'll help you." I laughed a little, for effect. "She couldn't think how I was going to cure you. Your papa, on the other hand, gave his consent for me to punish you in whatever way I like. Five, six, seven…" I continued counting. "You must admit, Selina," I remarked, "I actually care whether you steal or not – I dare say you can see that!"

I thrashed the poor girl over the back, ribs, loins, and thighs, as well as on her posterior, wealing her everywhere. All the spectators were greatly moved, and seemed to enjoy the sight. I must admit my own enjoyment; my excitement was quite as great as anyone's, as the wetness between my legs would attest.

The victim had not sufficient strength to stand such thrashing very long. Her head drooped and she was too weak even to scream. Her moans and sighs grew fainter and fainter, till at last she fairly swooned.

By the twenty-second stroke I was fairly exhausted with my exertions, and sank down on a sofa to refresh myself in Laura's embraces.

I described to her all the thrilling sensations I enjoyed during the operation. Her flushed cheeks and sparkling blue eyes showed she was beginning to duly appreciate my methods and my pleasures. As this was going on, my hands were beneath her shift, giving vent to the excitement that had built within me. She was quick to reciprocate, and soon each had the other's fingers twined in the elegant hair that had long ago sprung copiously between our legs.

It would not do for Selina to see us further progress beyond this preliminary teasing, so we remained satisfied with whiling away those few moments with such circumspect activity. The practiced motions of Laura's hands were quite restorative and I was soon ready to return my attention to the task at hand.

Mademoiselle Fosse and the servants released Selina on the floor and sprinkled her face with water, while one of them used a very large fan most effectively. Her lacerated bottom was sponged with strong salt and water, and she soon showed signs of regaining animation.

"Where, where am I?" she sobbed. "Oh! I remember; Miss Foster has cut my bottom terribly. Oh! Oh! Ah! How it smarts and burns!"

They poured a little liqueur down her throat, and she was soon quite conscious again, crying hysterically over her pickled state.

"Now for the finishing touch," said Mlle. Fosse. "Mary, fetch that pot from the kitchen, and bring the bag of feathers."

Selina cried piteously, "Haven't you finished yet? What have I to suffer?" She wrung her hands in apprehension.

"Ah, here it is. We won't keep you in suspense." Mlle. Fosse took the brush from a pot of warm tar held by Mary. "This will heal your bruises and prevent the flies getting at your sore bottom."

They made her stand up, and Mademoiselle painted all over Selina's posteriors, the lower part of her belly inside her thighs, and even the crack of her bottom with the hot stuff, regardless of the great pain she inflicted.

Selina shrieked in fearful distress and shame at this final degradation. "This is worse than all; you're actually scalding me. My skin will peel off," she wailed, dancing about in excruciating agony.

Mademoiselle laughed at these antics. "My dear, it is to heal and keep your skin on. We're going to cover you with nice warm feathers. You never felt so comfortable in your life as you will presently." The ceremony was both amusing and exciting, but it would be impossible to describe the poor girl's misery and dreadful shame. Her shrieks and appeals of "Oh! Ah! It will never come off," especially as they lifted her up and rolled her bottom and front in

Selina

a great heap of feathers, were especially gratifying. We took great care to shove them in everywhere, so as to thoroughly cover all the tar.

This was the finale, and Selina was led from the scene of her punishment and degradation. But that was not all; every day for nearly three weeks she had to strip and exhibit her feathery bum for inspection and laughing remarks. I need scarcely say the ordeal she went through effected a radical cure of her kleptomania.

Do you not think, dear Christine, my plan would cure the kleptomaniacs of the present day? It would be well worth a trial. Yours affectionately,

Rosa Belinda Foster

LUCRETIA

My Dear Christine,
     I do not intend to trouble you with all the little incidents of domestic discipline which my strict regulations so often brought under notice, and required the exercise of the beloved rod, but only write out for your amusement a few of my most remarkable recollections. The cure of Selina Richards brought me very considerable fame amongst a large circle of acquaintances and friends. The miracle I had effected also resulted in a flood of offers and requests that I perform similar magic on this or that *mauvais sujet*, often for substantial sums of money. But I steadily refused to take charge of any more poorly behaved children and devoted myself instead to promoting a Ladies Club exclusively for the admirers of Birch Discipline. The meetings were to be held at my house, where my servants would be sworn to secrecy and would act as sub-members, not on an equality with the ladies of our Club.

The rules specially enjoined utmost secrecy on every member, so that novices might not obtain the slightest inkling of the ordeal they would have to undergo when initiated into the mysteries of Lady Rodney's Club, as it was called. Our object was to make our séances for the receiving of new members the means of affording us the most exquisite enjoyment. We would do this by bringing out all their modest bashfulness and studying their distress and horror at finding themselves stripped and exposed for flagellation before all the sisters of the rod.

My old schoolfellows, Laura Sandon, Louise Van Tromp, Hon. Miss Cecile Deben, Lady Clara Wavering, and three other ladies besides Mlle. Fosse and myself, as president and manager, were the first members. Two of them had married, but we agreed that everyone should be known to the other sisters by her maiden name only. Lady Clara was the first to propose a novice for admission to the Club. It was a younger sister of hers, who she informed us had a great penchant for young gentlemen, having several times seriously misconducted herself with youthful friends of the opposite sex. Her lecture and castigation would be of a most piquant description.

We fixed an evening for her introduction, and were all present to inaugurate the Club's first séance of admission.

Our large punishment room was tastefully draped all around with elegant curtains, and was brilliantly illuminated by clusters of wax candles projecting from the walls. Above these were handsome mirrors set in bouquets of lovely flowers.

The ladies of the Club were all dressed in the same costume – blue silk corsets with scarlet silk laces, and short skirts of white tulle, only coming a little below the knee so as to show all the beautiful legs in pink silk stockings and high-heeled Parisian boots. All were in these short skirts, the outer dresses being discarded to allow a greater freedom of action. They also allowed the display of the glorious necks and bosoms of the members, who were every one young and beautiful, flushed with excitement and anticipation, their snow-white breasts heaving at each breath and set off to the greatest advantage by bouquets of red roses adjusted between the lovely hillocks of love. As president, I was seated in a chair of state, supported on either side by four ladies, while Ann and Mary stood behind me.

The moment of initiation arrived with a knock at the door. Lady Clara advanced to open it and introduced her sister, Lady Lucretia Wavering. The novice was about eighteen, but otherwise a very counterpart of Lady Clara – dark, well-proportioned, rather above the medium height, having languid expression and large, pensive hazel eyes. She held a beautiful bouquet in one hand and was dressed in simple white.

Advancing right up to where I was seated, she made a profound bow.

Lady Clara said, "Permit me, Miss President and ladies of the Lady Rodney Club, to introduce to you my sister, Lady Lucretia, who is desirous of being admitted a member."

I inclined my head in royal greeting. "Lady Lucretia, we welcome you to our sisterhood. Are you willing to take the oaths of secrecy and be initiated into the mysteries of the rod?"

"Yes, and to be submissive to all your rules and regulations," answered she.

"Very well. You must now strip and assume the costume of a member, and must truthfully answer any questions I may put to you."

Ann and Mary as servants assisted to disrobe the novice, who blushed slightly as they proceeded to remove her skirts after taking away her dress.

Lucretia turned to me in surprise. "You surely don't strip us quite naked. I thought I had only to change the dress."

"Yes, you must discard everything," I explained, "because you have to taste the birch before assuming our costume."

She blushed deeply. "Oh! I never expected that; it's so indecent."

"Make haste," I ordered. "Such improper remarks must be checked, Sister Lucretia. You have already broken the rules by objecting to lawful commands. Your bottom shall smart soundly for it."

Lucretia stammered in a faltering voice. "Pray permit me to apologize, I had no idea the members were liable to chastisement, but thought they amused themselves whipping charity children sent up by schools for punishment."

"You will have to apologize under the rod. We are quite above abusing school children here for the amusement of the idly curious, although it is the duty of every member to exercise wise and proper discipline in any house or place where she may have authority." Lucretia was silent, but the scarlet face and nervous twitchings of the corners of her mouth attested to how she felt about the approaching taste of the rod. Her eyes were cast down in shame, and presently, with nothing but her drawers, chemise, boots, and stockings on, they led her to the ladder, everyone rising and clustering round the victim.

"Have the ladder nearly upright," I instructed. "Secure her wrists high up, and let her toes only just touch the floor. Woe to her bum if she dares to step on the bottom rung of the ladder without orders." With tears of shame and apprehension Lucretia protested against this disposition of her body as being too painful. She cried out for mercy as she felt her chemise rolled up and fastened under her armpits, and her unbuttoned drawers pulled down to her knees. "Ah! Ah! Oh! You would never be so bad as that to a novice! Have mercy, dear Miss Foster. Sister, how can you stand idle for this?"

"Don't show the white feather, young lady," I said to her. "And don't beg the help of you sister… You'll find none. We're going to initiate you into a most delightful society. You will soon be one of the most active members of the sisterhood." I took from Ann a very elegantly tied-up rod, ornamented with blue and gold ribbons, then just lightly switching the victim's bare bottom. "Now ask me to birch you properly and beg pardon for your frivolous objections."

Lucretia, in a tremor of fear, said with a faltering voice, "Is there no getting off? Why must I be cruelly whipped?"

I became angered at that and delivered a smart cut across her beautiful buttocks, which at once brought the roses to the surface.

"There, that's a slight taste you stupid, obstinate girl. I can't waste more time. There, there and there." I gave three more sharp cuts in succession, each leaving their respective long red marks. "Perhaps in a minute or two you will think it worth while to obey orders, and beg pardon." I delivered one more that curled under to stroke the delicate pink lips of her pussy.

"Ah!" Lucretia screamed. "It is cruel. I am sorry for saying so, but the cuts smart so it's impossible to think what one is saying. Oh! Pray forgive me and punish me properly. But – but – oh! Be merciful." As she writhed and wriggled under the painful strokes which had already begun to weal her snowy, tender skin.

"Very well, you've done it after a fashion, I admitted. But now as you're becoming one of our members, pray have you got a sweetheart?" I gave her an extra sharp cut.

"Oh! I can't bear it; it's like a hot knife cutting the skin! Indeed, I have not got a lover, if that's not allowed!" She put her feet on the rungs of the ladder to ease the painful strain on her wrists. I gave her a tremendous whack across the calves of the legs, which made Miss Lucretia fairly spring with agony. "How dare you alter my disposition of your body by putting your feet on the ladder?" I switched her legs again and again with great heavy cuts, till the poor girl capered like a cat on hot bricks. "Perhaps you won't do that again, but wait till I give you the order presently. Now about lovers, of course you have had one, if not just at present?"

Lucretia nodded painfully. "My poor legs! Yes! Yes! But I gave him up six months ago. Have mercy, or how can I speak to answer your questions?"

I shook my head in mock disappointment. "Out of order again, Sister Lucretia. Your rosy-looking bottom must be enjoying the fun, or you would never keep questioning my discretion as you do. How do you like it? Does it smart very much? Tell us a little more about your lover, if you please."

"My wrists are breaking, and my bottom – my bottom burns and smarts so!" She writhed in agony. "You want to know about my lover. I gave him up because – because he behaved improperly to me."

I tapped her lightly with the rod. "Are you speaking the truth, Sister Lucretia? That is a most essential thing with us. We call the birch the Rod of Truth, for it is sure to bring everything out. What did he do to you? Cry out if you are in great pain. We like to hear it, and it will do you good." I undercut once again. Lucretia's agonized response was immediate.

"Ah, indeed! I must shriek! You cut me so dreadfully. Oh! He took liberties with me, and put his hands up my clothes to feel my breasts, that's all. Ah! Have mercy! You don't give time for me to get my breath."

"Are you sure that's not a bit of a fib?" I slackened a little with the rod.

A look of relief crossed her face as she thought she was to be let off. "It's quite true, my dear Miss Foster. That's what he did." She so obviously began to feel a deliciously voluptuous warmth and lubricity in her sensitive parts, for she shut her eyes while a sensuous smile betrayed her pleasurable emotions.

"What are you thinking of, Sister Lucretia, with that satisfied smile?" I enquired. "How your buttocks seem to quiver with some curious emotion. Has my question about your lover revived anything in your mind of past enjoyments? Out with the truth. I believe you have been telling a lot of fibs." I renewed cutting her with a perfect shower of blows, which wealed and brought blood for the first time. My rage caught her by surprise. "Oh! Oh! Ah! Ah! How cruel! Just as I thought it was all over and began to feel a delicious warmth in my posteriors. Indeed, I was not thinking of my lover." She cast down her eyes and blushed more than ever in a very confused manner.

"How dare you persist in telling so many fibs," I said sternly. "We happen to know a little of your goings-on with young Aubrey. Speak the truth at once, or I will cut your impudent bottom into ribbons! You can't deceive us; we know the effects of the rod and the voluptuous feelings it induces." All the while my strokes with the birch echoed in the room – whack – whack – whack – as they ruthlessly cut and wealed the victim's bottom. I admit I was getting

Lucretia

quite excited and felt every thrilling sensation of the punishment I administered. Each stroke had an electrical effect on my nerves; the cries and screams
of Lucretia seemed most delightful to me and all the spectators were in
ecstasies of voluptuous emotions. Lucretia fairly shrieked in agony; she
writhed her body about, displaying her lovely figure in a variety of contortions, shifting continually at every scathing touch of the birch. I especially
enjoyed the bounce and quiver of her delightful breasts, and the shaking of
her buttocks at the contact of the rod.

The ladies at first watched the scene with rapt attention, but gradually the
blood coursed in warm excitement through their veins, mantling their cheeks
with a flesh-like bloom. Their eyes sparkled with unusual animation, and at
last, by a common impulse, the eight ladies, with Ann and Mary, each took a
fine, long, light rod of green twigs and formed a circle round me as I continued to flagellate Lucretia on the ladder. Each raised her skirts under her arms
so as to leave all exposed from the waist downwards. For a moment there was
a lovely scene of plump white buttocks and thighs, fascinating legs encased in
silk stockings, pretty garters and attractive elegant shoes set off with jeweled
buckles, and, above all, such an inviting collection of impudent-looking cunnies, ornamented with every shade of *chevelure*... black, auburn, or light
brown.

Then all was motion. The birch rods soon put a rosy polish on the pretty bums, each one doing her best to repay on the bottom in front of her the
smarting cuts she felt behind. Laughter, shrieks, and ejaculations filled the
apartment, and their motions were so rapid as to make quite a rainbow of
frenzied activity round the central figures. This luscious scene only lasted
three or four minutes. Lucretia, under my rod, had got quite exhausted. Her
shrieks had sunk into sobs, and at last she sighed lower and lower until she
fairly fainted. Her head hung helplessly back; her limp form was a picture of
weals and blood which oozed from the cuts and slowly trickled down the
white flesh of her thighs.

I threw aside my broken and used-up rod. "There ladies, stop your game
and all help to bring her round." I looked her over and nodded with satisfaction. "She'll soon recover. How pretty your rosy bottoms look; I shall join in
the next ring that is formed."

The victim was loosed from the ladder, and by use of a large fan, she soon
showed signs of returning animation. Her eyes opened and she looked
around in bewilderment. "Where am I? What a beautiful dream!" she mur-

mured in a low voice. Then, a little more refreshed by a strong cordial that was poured down her throat, she sat up painfully. "Ah! I remember, my bottom smarts so!" Putting her hand down to feel her posteriors, she looked at the blood which stained her fingers and sobbed hysterically, "What a cruel girl that Miss Foster must be, and how she seemed to dote over my sufferings. Let me only handle the tickler over her bum someday."

At this we all burst out into a loud laugh and thoroughly enjoyed poor Lucretia's shame and confusion.

"Cheer up, Sister Lucretia," I said. "You have only to do what we call stepping the ladder. Someday you will have a chance of revenge, but first you will find Louise Van Tromp quite as cruel as I am when she uses the birch in her skillful style on your half-cooked bum. Come, Ann; I think she is ready for the second edition of her punishment."

The Van Tromp saluted smartly and grinned. "Ah! Trust me, Sister Rosa, to do my duty. She has not half confessed to us yet." She took up and switched a fine birch rod, making it fairly hiss through the air, to the evident terror of the victim.

Lucretia was thoroughly overcome with fear. Sobs and tears ran in streams down her cheeks. "Oh! Oh! How horrible. Will you never have mercy? My bottom is so sore I really can't bear it to be touched." She shrank back as Ann tried to draw her to the ladder. "Oh! No! Not again on that awful thing!"

Louise brought down her rod with a tremendous whack across the poor girl's bare shoulders, exclaiming, "What are you hanging back for? Look sharp, quick, or I'll cut your shoulders again." She looked with delight on the red marks her cut had left on the white flesh of the victim.

"Oh! Oh! I will, I will!" Lucretia shrieked, holding up her wrists for Ann to secure them, which was quickly done.

"Now, step on the rungs of the ladder one at a time as I call out the number beginning at the bottom. If you take two at once you must do it over again," warned Louise. "Now, one" – she gave a terrible whack on Lucretia's bruised rump.

The poor girl howled in terrible agony as the birch cut into the already lacerated skin. But careful only to take one step. Louise made her birch flourish through the air with a hissing noise.

"Pretty well, now – now – now," keeping her in trembling suspense. "Two – three" – she administered a couple of crashing strokes with a good interval

Lucretia

between them, to make the victim feel the effect as much as possible.

Lucretia let loose a fearful shriek at each cut, and sobbed out hysterically, "Ah! How dreadful, the skin of my bottom will burst; it's getting so tight."

"Glad you enjoy it so, dear; I'm sorry to hurt you much," said Louise, looking delightedly round at the other members. "Now – now – now–" another flourish "–four – five," each blow drawing the blood afresh from the already crimsoned surface and putting the spectators into a flutter of excitement.

Lucretia fairly groaned, but only once made a false step, which she corrected before Louise could find fault. "Only two more," she sighed, as if calculating the steps yet to be done.

"Steady, keep your bottom well out," called Louise, switching her lightly underneath so as to tickle the exposed pussy before laying on another grand flourish. "Six – seven…" These were awful crackers, but Lucretia kept herself steady, and her pluck was greeted by clapping of hands all round. Ann took advantage of the opportunity to secure the victim's ankles so that she was fixed in a most inviting attitude for further flagellation.

"Thanks, Ann, very thoughtful of you," said Louise. "Now, Sister Lucretia, before you are let off, you must tell us all about yourself and young Aubrey. Miss Foster did not half get it out of you." She whisked the tightly bent bottom in a playful way with her rod, but the victim was evidently so sore that even light strokes made twinges of pain pass across her scarlet face.

"Oh! Oh! Pray don't begin again. I told you he took liberties with me. What more can I say? Oh! Oh! Don't touch me; the least whisk of that thing gives awful pain."

"Then, you silly girl, why do you persist in keeping back the truth? Did you not encourage him?" Louise made the victim writhe under her painful touches, which, although not very heavy, seemed to have great effect on the raw bottom in such a tightly bent position.

Lucretia seemed to crimson all over at the thought of her degradation before them all. "Oh! Oh! Spare me! If you know all, have mercy. Consider my feelings, how painful such a confession must be. You are shameful girls to enjoy my pain and shame so," she sobbed as if her heart would break.

"Come! Come!" encouraged Louise. "It is not so bad as that. Make a clean breast and be one of us now and always. You will enjoy such scenes yourself when the next novice is admitted. But I can't play with you any longer. There – there – there!" she cut three brisk strokes on the bent bottom.

These elicited wonderful shrieks. "Ah! Oh! Oh! I shall faint again. It's like burning with red hot irons. Ah! You know he seduced me, and – I must confess I did not resist as I ought. Something tempted me to taste the sweets of love, and your President's birching brought all the thrilling sensations – the pounding of my blood, hardening of my nipples, the wetness of my loins – back to me. When I fainted, my dream was all about the bliss enjoyed in my lover's arms."

Louise prodded with her rod. "A little better, and getting nearer the truth, but you still prevaricate so in trying to excuse your own fault. Now, did you not seduce the youth instead of his taking advantage of you?"

"Oh! Pity me," she said crimson-faced. "I saw him lying asleep on the grass in a secluded part of the garden. He was so sleepy that I failed to wake him, but I since believe he was shamming. Noticing a lump of something in his breeches, I gently pressed it with my fingers to see what it was, when it gradually swelled under my pressure and became like a hard stick throbbing under the cloth. My blood was fired. I can't tell how I did it, but presently, when he opened his eyes and laughed at me, I found myself with his exposed shaft in my hand. Before I knew what he was about, he had taken my head gently in his hands and lowered it to the throbbing organ. It was huge and veined, and its head was such a pretty pink and smooth as silk. I had never quite seen its like before and hesitated not at all before nestling it in my mouth. He sighed pleasurably at the workings of my lips and tongue as I laved its entire length. I even caressed his sac with my tongue, taking first one, then the other of his manly fruits in my mouth."

The girls were all breathless and rapt with attention at this description.

"When I returned to the head of his shaft, I worked it with my hand and could see that its color had deepened to an angry purple. It swelled still further until it veritably filled my mouth and near-butted against my palate at the juncture of the throat. Then he cried out and filled my mouth with his salty fluid in a seemingly never-ending spurting stream." Her eyes had glazed over at the recollection and I could see that her nipples were erect and rock hard. "I swallowed as much as I could, yet still some escaped past the edges of my lips. It seemed to pleasure him.

He jumped up, sprang upon me, and taking advantage of my confusion, I own he had an easy conquest. He had my skirts off before I was barely conscious of it. So hot was his blood that his shaft had remained tremendous and firm, despite him having just spent himself. He penetrated me with one quick thrust and hammered at me till I thought I should split. But the sensations were heavenly, I do admit, as I felt every inch of his fleshy pole sliding past my gaping cunny lips. The juices ran from me and mixed with his own as he spent yet again. All the while he had crushed my mouth with his own and fondled my globes with greedy hands. Something of the sort will happen to every loving girl at some time or other," she said with shame in her voice. "Now I have told you all, have pity and let me go." She sobbed and looked dreadfully confused and distressed. She was let down and we all crowded round her, giving affectionate kisses and welcoming her to be a real sister of Lady Rodney's Club.

The poor girl was very sore and sobbed over her poor bruised bottom. "Oh! Oh! I can't sit down; it will be weeks before I can do anything with comfort. Ah! You pretend to be kind now after all that dreadful cruelty. I only wish we could get Aubrey and give him a good thrashing; it would do the impetuous boy good." We had another laugh at this, but assured her our rules didn't provide for admitting any of the opposite sex to the séances of the Club. But in my next, you shall see what happened, and how Lucretia tricked us by introducing young Aubrey as a young lady novice desirous of admission to our Society. Till then, I remain, dear Christine…

Yours affectionately,

Rosa Belinda Foster

MARIA

My Dear Christine,

I have been looking over some of my grandfather's papers, and found the following curious little bit written by his brother Dean Foster:

Remarks on the Influence of Female Beauty

I shall reverse the general practice, and instead of beginning with the head, commence with the leg, and hope to get credit for so doing. A pretty face, sparkling eyes, rosy cheeks, delicate complexion, smiles, dimples, hair dark, auburn or blonde, have all, it is acknowledged, great weight in the business of love; but still let me inquire of every impartial and unprejudiced observer, which he is most curious to behold – the legs or the face of his favorite lady. Whether does the face or the legs of a pretty girl that is clambering over a style, or mounting a ladder, most attract our notice and regard? What is it that causes my lord to smack his chops in that wanton lecherous manner as he is sauntering up and down the lounge in Bond Street, with his glass in hand, to watch the ladies getting in and out of their carriages? And what is it that draws together such vast crowds of the holiday gentry at Easter and Whitsuntide to see the merry rose faced lasses running down the hill in Greenwich Park?

What is it that causes such a roar of laughter and applause when a merry girl happens to overset in her career and kick her heels in the air?

Lastly, as the parsons all say, what is it that makes the theatrical ballets so popular?

It has frequently been remarked by travelers that in no nation of the world are the ladies more nice and curious about their legs than in England. And to do them justice, there is perhaps no nation in the world where the ladies have greater reason to show them like pretty girls in dirty weather when the fear of passing for drag tails causes the pretty creatures to hold their petticoats up behind and display their lovely calves and ankles above par. But I am infinitely more delighted with my muddy walk than were I making an excursion in the finest sunshiny day imaginable. There is a kind of magic in the sight of a handsome female leg, which is not in the power of language to describe. To be conceived, it must be felt.

We read in the memoirs of Brantome of a certain illustrious lady who was so fully sensible of the vast importance of a handsome leg and once had the misfortune to break one of hers by a fall from a horse. The surgeon, by some inadvertency or other, failed to set the bone straight. Well, so grieved was she at this accident that she actually had the fortitude to snap it across a second time on purpose and with design, then sent for a more skillful doctor, who took care to have her leg carefully reset. By this means was her leg restored to its former grace and loveliness.

Some of my readers may, perhaps, condemn this conduct in the lady. For my part, I cannot but greatly admire both the soundness of her judgment and the amazing strength of her mind. But too well am I acquainted, from experience, with the magic which centers in a pretty leg, a delicate ankle, and well-proportioned calf.

The first time that I was in love (I perfectly well remember the circumstances as if it occurred but yesterday), the first time I could ever be said to feel what love is, I had to thank a pretty leg for it. I was then in my late-teens, as harmless and innocent a young fellow as needs be. My friends were of the strictest sect of religion. I was, willingly or not, brought up in their principles. Plays, novels, and all kinds of books which treat upon the subject of love were denied me; my parents were ambitious that I should be a second Joseph. They had partly succeeded in this pious design, when one single unlucky circumstance completely baffled all their endeavors.

It was a beautiful summer's day. I had strolled into the wood, laying myself down in a copse of young hazel trees, and alternately musing and dozing away, when my curiosity was excited by a rustling noise close to the spot where I lay concealed. I was all attention. Directing my inquisitive eyes to the quarter from whence the noise proceeded, I discovered a lovely rosy-cheeked girl, who lay basking, as it were, in the sun, and deeming herself sufficiently remote from observation, was under no restraint in her motions. Presently up she whipped her coats and garter-free stockings, then contemplated her legs, turned them this way and that way, and in short practiced a thousand maneuvers, which I have not at present leisure to expatiate upon. Suffice it to say not a single movement was lost upon me, and from that hour to the present moment, I never see a pretty leg that I feel certain unutterable emotions within me, which seem to realize the observations of the poet:

Should some fair youth, the charming sight explore, In rapture lost he'll gaze, and wish for something more! The inestimable Dean Foster was quite right in his pretty delicate remarks about the influence of the leg. Although I am only a woman, the same magic influence affects me; when I see a pretty pair of calves in silk stockings it makes me long to look higher, and have the bottom which belongs to them under a nice birch rod.

To return to my experiences, novices were rather shy of offering themselves as candidates for admission to Lady Rodney's Club. I rather suspected they heard something of the rites of passage. But one day, two or three weeks after the séance described in my last letter, Lucretia called upon me, apparently very much excited. Her errand was to tell me that Maria Aubrey, the sister of her former lover, wished to join us, and asked me to fix a day for her admission. Knowing the young lady to be a very desirable subject, and to belong to a most aristocratic family, I could make no objections. I expressed my pleasure at the acquisition I hoped she would prove to the sisterhood, and appointed that same day one week later for the reception of the novice.

When I mentioned the proposal to Lady Clara and asked what she knew of the young lady, she assured me that she had not yet the pleasure of her acquaintance as the young lady had been at school in Germany for some years, and was only just returned home. Lucretia kept away from me till the eventful evening, but arrived punctually at seven o'clock with her protégée, who appeared slightly taller than herself, rather slim, with blue eyes. She was dressed in white for the occasion; in fact, Maria seemed a very quiet, good looking girl, the only thing specially attractive about her being a remarkable merry twinkle of her eyes, which seemed to look everywhere and enjoy the sight of everything.

We were all present, with myself as usual seated as President, surrounded by the others. Lady Lucretia presented the novice without delay, taking her by the hand and leading her close up to the chair. Then she bowed, saying, "Allow me, dear Miss Foster and sisters of Lady Rodney's Club, to present to you Miss Maria Aubrey, a dear friend of mine, who wishes to be admitted to your society." I cast my sternest gaze upon her. "Miss Maria Aubrey, are you willing to submit to our initiative ordeal and swear to obey the rules enacted by a majority of the members?"

"Yes, I am anxious to be admitted," said she. "We had so much of the birch in Germany that I am an enthusiast in the use of the rod." "Let her be sworn as usual," I intoned. "Now Sister Maria, you will have to strip and assume the regular costume which we have provided for you."

The novice blushed deeply, and seemed quite at a loss about what to say, and I noticed that Lucretia was hugely enjoying the scene. From some secret cause she whispered something to Lady Clara, and the latter to Mlle. Fosse, who imparted the information to me that our novice was not in reality Maria Aubrey, but her brother Frank, Lucretia's lover, whom she had persuaded to impersonate his sister. She had done this without in the least letting him know what he would have to go through, and he no doubt was quite nonplussed at the idea of being stripped and exposed.

I must confess that I felt quite a flush of anger at learning the trick Lucretia had put upon all of us, but by the whispered advice of Mlle. Fosse, I proceeded as if nothing was untoward. "Come Sister Maria, begin to disrobe yourself; here, Ann and Mary assist the young lady."

"Oh! No! No!" she gasped. "I can't be stripped. I didn't know you did that." She blushed more than ever and pushed the servants away from her. "Give me the things and I will retire to make the change, but not before you all."

"Already disobeying the regulations; you must strip this instant or the birch will be used without mercy, and we shall see if you are so fond of it."

She threw herself at my feet. "Ah! I beg your pardon, but you really must excuse me from undressing before so many."

Unseen by the deceiver, I took up a most formidable rod, made of a thick bunch of long birch twigs and elegantly tied together with red and blue ribbons. Then, upon my signal, Ann and Mary, assisted by four or five others, pounced upon the victim, dragged her to the ladder, and in spite of desperate struggles, secured both ankles and wrists with cord which were passed through the rings of the ladder. 'Miss Maria' found herself quite helpless before she was well aware of what was going to be done.

I advanced to her/him, rod in hand. "Ah! I see, this is a case of serious obstinacy; rip off that dress and pull up her skirts. The sooner we begin to initiate her a little the better."

They all helped to tear off the dress, and some of the garments beneath. Our victim was scarlet with shame and shrieked out, "Ah! Oh! Pray don't, I have been deceived. I am not a girl at all; do not expose me." Tears of mortification ran down his cheeks.

"What's this?" I said authoritatively. "Who may you be? Are you a male, or a hermaphrodite?"

The spectators all laughed at this question, and seeing his tongue-tied confusion, they cried out, "Go on, go on, Miss Foster; give the impudent fellow a taste of your tickler. He must confess everything, and take an oath of secrecy, or we'll whip him to death."

Lucretia's one-time paramour looked about with wild eyes. "My God, what a scrape I'm in. These devils of girls will murder me. Let me go and I will swear never to tell anything."

"You'll have plenty of time for that bye-and-bye," I assured him.

"You're not going to get off quite so easily after your impudent conspiracy with Lady Lucretia. You shall both see each other well whipped. You won't be shocked at seeing the bottom we know you are so well acquainted with. You're secure enough." I spun around and pointed at Lucretia with my rod. "Ann, prepare Sister Lucretia for punishment, so that this one may know what to expect for himself."

"Ah! No!" Lucretia cried out in protest. "I never meant anything but a little fun. You know I wished to birch him, and this was the only way I could manage it."

"Very well, Miss," I responded. "We'll take that all into consideration, and perhaps let you put the finishing touches to his bottom bye-and-bye. Put her posteriors in the stocks, Ann." Leaving the young gentleman securely fixed to the ladder, they seized upon his lady love, who knew better than to resist. In a few moments Frank had the pleasure of seeing her blooming bottom and beautiful legs projecting from the wooden stocks in which she was so fixed that only the lower half of her person could be seen.

"Now Mlle. Fosse will administer a proper correction for the insult

Lucretia has put upon the Club by introducing a person of another gender amongst us."

Mlle. Fosse had already armed herself with an excellent bum-tickler of well-pickled birch. "I didn't think the impudent hussy was half punished when we admitted her, or the soreness of her bottom would surely have kept her out of this." Then whack – whack – whack – she gave four very smart strokes with great deliberation.

"How do you like that? Is my arm heavier than Miss Foster's?"

Lucretia screamed and kicked her legs about in great pain. "Ah! Oh! Oh! I beg – I beg pardon. Indeed, I thought a young gentleman would be a most agreeable accession to the Club. Oh! Ah! How you cut; it's dreadful!" The blows continued to fall with great effect and precision, each one leaving its long crimson and blood-red marks and weals.

"I must be quick, as it will take some time to punish Master Frank," said the mistress of the whip. "I hope he is enjoying the sight of your castigation. Is it as nice as it was before? Let us know when your prurient ideas are satisfied by that feeling of sensuous pleasure you told us you experienced then." She swept the tips of her birch in under Lucretia's exposed pussy, and between the tender inner surfaces of her upper thighs.

Frank's face was flushed with excitement at the sight of his lady's punishment. I had little trouble discerning how every blow seemed to thrill through his system, and put him into such a state of feeling as he had never experienced before, bringing out all the sensuality of his disposition as he watched the scene with rapt attention. Mademoiselle plied her rod so vigorously that the blood soon began fairly to trickle over Lucretia's bottom and thighs. "Ah! Oh! I shall faint. I shall die!" she sobbed, writhing and twisting beautifully under the continued flagellation.

"You shall do neither," I scoffed, coming forward with my rod. "I think Master Frank is longing to taste what it is like. Pin up his skirts as decently as possible. I only want to see his bottom; we don't want the other thing introduced to our notice." The others tittered long and well at that.

Frank was so absorbed in watching the beautiful sight of Lucretia's whipping that he never knew his own skirts were pinned up. Then my tremendous whack on his own bum awaked him in a most lively manner to a sense of his forlorn condition. He winced and bit his lips. The tears started to his eyes, and an extra crimson gushed over his face, convincing us of his renewed humiliation.

Again and again I made my blows sound through the apartment, but not till seven or eight weals had been raised on his posteriors would Master Frank gratify us with anything in the least approaching a cry. Then, with a tremendous crack which fairly drew the blood, I said to him, "I'll make you beg our pardon, sir. Will you ever insult us by coming here as a girl again?"

Frank, trying to bear it pluckily, and ashamed to cry out before a lot of girls, writhed his lovely buttocks in agony, and still bit his lips in silence till they fairly bled.

I looked in surprise around the assemblage. "Obstinate, eh? So much the more fun for us, my boy. Will you beg pardon, and swear never to tell anyone of this spree of yours?" I cut his white bottom with all my might, each blow scoring the flesh and making it raw.

Finally, "Ah! I must call out; it's awful. Oh! Don't quite murder me ladies." He yelled quite nicely at my next stroke.

"Will you come here again, you impudent fellow? Will you take the oath now to keep our secret?" I kept him in constant agony by my well-applied strokes.

Frank's cries and Lucretia's sobs, in addition to the sight of two well-pickled bottoms, made the ladies all quite excited. Each one took up a birch, and as mademoiselle and I retired, they relieved each other in short spells of birching on the posteriors of the two victims. It was not long till Lucretia was nearly spent; she had become oblivious to the pain and seemed lost in a kind of lethargic stupor.

They let her down and applied restoratives, which soon brought her to herself again. Frank, meanwhile, had been imploring for mercy, and prayed to be sworn to secrecy through the entire latter portion of his punishment. At last he was allowed to take the required oath, but was greeted with renewed laughter when he begged pitifully to be released and allowed to go home.

"Ha! Ha!" I laughed secretly to the others. "He thinks we shall let him go now. But surely he can't object to Lucretia finishing him off when she's a little recovered."

"It was all her fault," Frank continued. "I should never have come, only she assured me of a warm welcome."

We all laughed good naturedly. "That's fine, ladies, is it not? And Master Frank, you can't say we haven't given you one. But it must be warmer still before we let you go."

Lucretia swallowed some stimulating cordial, and with sparkling eyes announced herself as ready to assume the rod. We handed her an elegant new one and she took her position, evidently minded to give him a little after the fashion of Louise Van Tromp's style of birching.

"Do you," said she, "dare to insinuate that I tempted you to come here, sir?" She flourished the rod over her head so that he could hear it hissing through the air.

Frank began to tremble. "Ah! Ah! Lucretia, will you also prolong my torture, now I have promised everything?"

Lucretia, bringing down her rod in earnest, made his bottom wince and writhe under the stroke as she continued, "Then you don't withdraw that insinuation, sir." Whisk – whisk – whisk. Each blow came harder than the last. She became excited more and more, as the cuts seemed to make the blood boil more tumultuously in her own veins. "Is it not true that you ravished me, sir? These ladies know all about your shameful conduct to me."

Frank was in a fine agony and desperate at this renewed torture.

"Ah! Oh! Ah! I'm hanged if I own all that. Why, you know you had my – my – you know what I mean – in your hands and mouth first."

Oh, we began to enjoy the scene immensely.

Lucretia responded angrily. "Don't mention the disgusting monster." She cut him desperately across the shoulders. "Hold your wicked tongue, sir, if you are only going to asperse my character."

She again paid her attention to his raw-looking bum. Frank, who had now lost his false hair by twisting his head about too much, looked a little more manly. He was a very fair youth withal, although his rump was not so finely developed as it would have been in a girl.

Lucretia, who felt all the stimulating warmth of her own flagellation, cut away in fury. "See, see," she cried, "that unmentionable thing of his is quite rampant, and sticks out under his shirt in front. It's impossible to hide the disgusting creature." She struck more and more round his buttocks, which so disarranged his shirt that we continually got glimpses of a very formidable-looking weapon projecting six or seven inches from a bed of curly light hair at the bottom of his belly. The youth's eyes rolled in a kind of erotic frenzy, and every thought of pain and shame had evidently given away to his sensuous feelings as he writhed and twisted his bottom in a most lascivious manner at every stroke. To our delight, his shaft throbbed and grew before our eyes till it extended well beyond the bounds of his shirt.

The flagellatrix was also beside herself, the sight of his bleeding bottom and erotic emotion increased her fury more and more. "Ah," she cried, "he not only tries to make me out worse than himself, but see how insultingly he is exposing himself to us all." She cut the next stroke so as to reach the offending member. This she did again and again, causing such intense pain and excitement that at last the poor fellow shouted out, "Oh! Oh! My God! I shall burst. It's awful, and yet gives the most delicious sensations." He yelled loudly, and then he seemed to die away in an excess of voluptuous emotion. At the same time his questing flesh-pole jerked and spasmed and released an intermittent stream of white sticky fluid that puddled upon the floor in small gobs. The ladies first screamed, then laughed and applauded such show.

Lucretia suspended her rod for a few instants and then suddenly woke him up again with two or three tremendous whacks upon his sore posteriors, exclaiming, "Wake up, sir, we've had enough of that. Your exhibition, though unknowing, we found offensive and disgusting. You will now withdraw your insinuations against me. Did you not take advantage of my confusion when I found you so exposed in the garden?" She followed up her question by a lively application of her rod till the blood fairly trickled down Master Frank's thighs.

Frank, now that his erotic excitement had passed off for the moment but again in awful pain and ashamed to think how he had been exposed, said, "Ah! You she-devil. Who could believe you could cut me up so after your loving caresses and assertions of your affection for me. Ah! Miss Foster, save me from her; have mercy ladies!" The tears of shame and agonized mortification ran down his crimson face.

"Not yet, you impudent boy," said his tormentor. "Will you withdraw your assertions about me, or must I literally skin your bottom before you get let off?"

"How cruel of you, Lucretia, to force me to tell a lie." He writhed under the shower of smarting strokes, although the stirring of his manhood evidenced the return of his voluptuous feelings.

"Your cries are delightful. I enjoy it so much more, knowing how we love each other. Will – will you withdraw your wicked assertions? You have made these ladies think me a monster of lasciviousness. Do you hear, sir?" She cut well up under the crack of his bottom, so that the tips of the birch might sting him in the most tender and most private parts.

"Ah! Oh! Oh! My God! You'll kill me." He seemed almost ready to faint with the suddenly excruciating pain.

Maria

"Then why do you obstinately persist in refusing the satisfaction I ask of you? Why say I want to make you tell lies, you wicked fellow? I'll murder you with the birch if you don't retract your vile insinuations." She whisked him terribly everywhere she fancied he could feel the most pain.

It had the desired effect, as Frank was in terrible agony. "Oh! What – what must I say? All those stories about us are quite untrue; we never did anything wrong." He writhed about and hardly knew what he said in his anxiety to get away from his torture. Lucretia laid on a furious blow which almost took his breath away.

"Hold, hold, now, sir. You go to the other extreme. I only want you to confess you took advantage of me. Your brain is confused. What a strange thing that after all this whipping and wealing, the blood should still fly to your head."

Frank sobbed with mortification. "Indeed – indeed, I remember now how I put my hand under your clothes when you were so overcome you could not resist me. Ah! Oh! Oh! Let me off. You never need fear I shall tell the secret of my own humiliation!" He was fairly broken down. Lucretia dropped her worn-out birch as tears of sympathy rose in her large loving eyes. "Poor fellow," she sobbed. "Poor fellow, what made you so obstinate?"

"Let him down," I instructed, "and make him kneel before me and beg our pardon for the indelicate scandal he has caused amongst us, as I can feel and see what painful emotions the sight has caused in every lady's breast."

He was released, and Frank, humbly kneeling, declared his sorrow for having so shamefully intruded upon our private proceedings. He again promised faithfully to keep our secret, and begged with fresh tears in his eyes to be allowed to remain a member after his painful initiation.

This was most favorably received, and I soon found out that Lady Clara was at the bottom of a plot for introducing the male element into our society.

I hastily closed the séance, and never knew how or what means they used to ease his sore bottom. The next day, by advice of Mlle. Fosse, I intimated to them all a dissolution of the Club, as I could not possibly join in or allow my house to be used for birching orgies in connection with the opposite sex. My next and last letter on this subject will relate more nearly to myself.

Yours affectionately,
Rosa Belinda Foster

MARY

My Dear Christine,

I have found a curious letter from a lady, espousing the most antiquated sentiments, amongst grandfather's papers. It may afford you some small amusement, and so I begin this letter with some excerpts from it:

Dear Sir Eyre,

We live in an age so dissolute, that if young girls are not kept under some sort of restraint and punished when they deserve it, we shall see bye-and-bye nothing but women of the town, parading the streets and public places. God knows, there are already but too many of them. When fair means have been used, proper corrections free from cruelty should be administered. What punishment can be more efficacious than birch discipline?

Physicians strongly recommend the use of birch for faults which appear to proceed from a heavy or indolent disposition, as nothing tends more to promote the circulation of the blood than a good rod made of new birch, and well applied to the posteriors. (I may add my own opinion that the rod is equally good in its effects on quick, excitable temperaments.)

Birch breaks no bones; used temperately causes no great harm; the harm it does is very trifling when put in comparison with the evils which it can prevent. I know it is pretty well used amongst what are called genteel people...

I called last week on a friend of mine, an eminent gown-maker in the city, whom I found in a violent passion.

On enquiring the cause, she told me that one of her apprentices had stolen a large silver spoon. Just as she was going to send her maid to jail on suspicion of the crime, she received a letter from an honest person to whom the culprit had sold it. He intimated he had suspected his customer, and so followed the girl to her house. He concluded by offering to return the article.

"Now," said my friend, "I generally correct my apprentices with the birch, but I have just bought this horsewhip (showing me a large, heavy carter's whip) to flog the hussy with. I will strip her and horsewhip her, till every bit of her skin is marked with it." "Pray don't use that murderous thing," I expostulated in reply. "You might be punished for it; people have not yet forgotten Mother Brownrigg's case, who whipped her apprentices to death for the fun and cruelty of the thing."

It was with the utmost difficulty I could prevail upon her to substitute a good birch rod for that cruel whip. However, on my persistently representing to her the cruelty of chastising a girl with a horsewhip (although I am sorry to say I have actually seen it done in many families, where those in authority were inconsiderate and hasty in their tempers and would use the first thing that came to hand), she consented to do the whipping with a good birch.

Domestic discipline, to be most effective, ought always to be carried out calmly. All show of temper in inflicting punishment ought especially to be avoided, as likely to conduce to a want of respect in the delinquents.

A cart full of birch brooms, just cut from the trees, happened to pass by at that moment. She sent one of the servants to purchase a couple of them.

We both went upstairs to the back garret where the apprentice was confined. She appeared to me exceedingly pretty, with a beautifully white and delicate skin.

At the desire of my friend, I stripped her of her clothes except her shift, and then the girl was ordered to seat herself on the floor. The two brooms were thrown down in front of her and she was made to select the finest pieces of birch herself and tie them up into a rod, her mistress all the while pointing out particularly fine bits as most suitable for her thievish bottom. This put the girl into the greatest possible shame and confusion, the presence of a stranger like myself evidently adding immensely to her mortification.

When the rod was finished, she tied her to one of the posts of the bed and began to whip the young pilferer's posteriors and thighs with all her strength.

"Oh, you hussy!" she exclaimed. "Will you ever steal anything again? Will you? Will you? Will you? I will teach you to be honest! I'll whip it into your system."

"Oh, God! Oh, gracious heaven! Oh, mistress! Oh, mistress!" screamed the girl, wriggling and twisting like a little devil on feeling the smarting cuts of the new birch. "Do forgive me. I will never steal any more for the rest of my life. Oh! Oh! Oh! Indeed I won't!"

The mistress had been so foaming with rage, in such transports, that I half expected her to go on flogging the unfortunate young woman with unremitting fury till the rod was worn out. As it happened, she had to drop it from sheer exhaustion. Then she called another servant and ordered her to wash the apprentice's weals and bruises.

She has threatened to give her every Saturday during the month just such another whipping. I think she was quite right to do so, as it may very well deter her from ever stealing again, protecting both the holders of property and the apprentice herself, since she would likely fall into the unmerciful hands of the magistrates.

When we left, the girl had been ordered by her mistress to amuse herself during the week by making four more good useful rods from the brooms which were left with her. She was actually doing so, and looked so terrified and contrite that the further promised beatings might well prove superfluous.

I have myself three daughters grown up. The eldest is about twenty-three. She was addicted to telling lies when she was young, but I whipped that quite out of her. My second daughter I also entirely cured of some very dirty habits. The youngest, who has just finished her schooling, is not only idle and obstinate, but has an exceedingly mischievous temperament. I have apprehended her in no wrongdoing, but if that should happen, I am determined that she shall feel the stings of the birch, till she amends. Believe me, dear Sir Eyre…

Yours faithfully,

Mary Wilson

Now for my own adventure promised in my last letter. You will remember that in giving some account of my establishment I mentioned Charlie the page, childhood friend and foster-brother of my favorite servant, Ann.

Well, Charlie was such a nice boy as to be a universal favorite in the house.

Mary

He was just nineteen, with the guileless blushes of a girl. His voice was soft and he was in all things very willing and agreeable. In fact, he was such a good-looking youth as to make quite an impression upon me, but I resolutely kept that secret buried in my own bosom.

In my second letter I told all about my regard for Ann, and it was often my practice, especially when I awoke too early of a bright summer's morning, to get up in my nightdress and slip unseen into Ann's chamber to satisfy my restlessness by a luscious embrace in the arms of my favorite.

I had by this time become quite expert in the use of the tongue, and knew well the pleasure it could provide another. When I exercised this magnificent instrument upon Ann's eager slit, she was a veritable slave to me, eager only to respond to my every instruction so as to heighten her pleasure. I would swirl it through the burnished hair adorning her mount, then trace a path to the very doorstep of love's abode. There I would slash and sweep as though my tongue were itself a rod, and scour every inch of flesh before darting to the bud of her clit. Under my ministrations it would present itself to my teeth, whereupon I would gently worry it while Ann moaned and thrashed beneath me.

This treatment was nearly more than she could bear, as Ann often told me, and I was brashly confident of the bond that we had forged. But one morning as I approached the door, which was slightly ajar, I heard a suppressed sigh. Cautiously peeping in, I to my infinite astonishment, saw Master Charlie with nothing but his shirt on, and that drawn up almost under his arms, on the top of Ann, who was equally nude. His lips were pressed to hers in the ardor of intercourse, and her legs were thrown over his loins.

My first impulse was to withdraw as silently as I had come, but the luscious sight rooted me to the spot. Like Moses at the burning bush, I felt constrained to witness the wonderful sight. There was his youthful shaft, almost as big as that of Mr. Aubrey mentioned in my last. It looked as hard and smooth as ivory, and I was forced to fix my attention on its rapid pushing and withdrawing motion, which she seemed to encourage and meet by the heaving of her bottom to every rapid shove.

The door was close to the foot of the bed, and as they were quite unconscious of my presence, I knelt down to avoid being seen and enjoy the voluptuous sight to the end.

I felt awfully agitated and all of a tremble. It was so new to me, and so unexpected; I had grown used to thinking of them as being almost brother and sister – as indeed they had hitherto appeared to regard each other.

Ah, how they seemed to love and enjoy each other now! They clung to each other in ecstasy, and the lips of her vagina seemed literally to cling to his shaft, holding on and protruding in a most luscious manner at each withdrawing motion. But it soon came to an end, as both died away in a mutual flood of bliss, while a warm gush from my own cunny bedewed my thighs with an overflow of what was as yet a truly maiden emission.

Hot, flushed, and confused, I silently withdrew from the scene unobserved, fully determined to punish Mr. Charlie for his seduction of my own dear Ann, and if possible secure him for my own enjoyment. The temptation was irresistible; the more I thought and strove to banish it from my thoughts, the more would my blood boil and throb through my veins at the thoughts of what I had seen, and must experience for myself. It was no use; I could not struggle against the fascination of the thing.

It was a Sunday morning. Mlle. Fosse was going to Moorfields to her father confessor and to attend an afternoon lecture. So as soon as I had done luncheon, I told Ann and the other two servants they might go out for the afternoon and return by half-past six or seven. I would dispense with dinner if Margaret the cook would have something nice for supper, and Charlie could answer my bell if anything was wanted. As soon as the house was clear, and I knew the cook liked the society of her pots and pans too much to think of leaving the precincts of the kitchen, I rang for my page. I ordered him to bring a lemon, some iced water and sugar. Seeing that he had dressed himself with scrupulous care in case I summoned him, I said, "Charlie, I'm glad to see you are particular about your appearance, although there is no one at home."

He replied with great modesty, "But you, Miss, are my mistress, and I always wish to show you the greatest possible respect even when you are quite alone."

"Indeed, sir, you profess great respect for me, and seem afraid hardly to lift your eyes, as if I was too awful to look at. But I have my doubts about your goodness. Will you please fetch me a rather long packet you will find wrapped in paper on the library table?"

He soon returned with the parcel, and I proceeded to open it as he stood before me awaiting his dismissal or further orders. The paper was removed, and I flourished before his face (which rather flushed at the sight) a good long rod of fresh green birch, tied up with scarlet ribbons. "Do you know what this is for, sir?" I asked the astonished boy.

Mary

Charlie's face reddened still more in some little confusion. "Ah! Oh! I don't know – unless it's what's used for whipping young ladies at school."

"And why not boys, you stupid lad?" I demanded.

"Ah! Miss Rosa, you're making fun of me," he stammered. "They use canes and straps on boys – but – but–"

"Out with what you are going to say. I'm the only one that can hear it."

"Why – why–" he turned quite scarlet, "the thought came into my head that you might be going to whip me."

I said with a smile. "Well, that shows that at least you must know you have been doing something very bad."

"Oh! It was only a silly thought," was his rejoinder, "and I didn't mean I knew I deserved it."

"That's a clever answer, Master Charlie. Now, answer me. Am I your only mistress?"

He cast down his eyes, but managed to stammer out, "Why, of course you are, Miss, as I am in your service alone." I snapped the rod on a nearby table. "Now you bad boy, I prepared this rod for you on purpose; can't you guess what I saw early this morning in Ann's room?"

Charlie seemed as if shot; he fell on his knees before me in the deepest shame and distress, covering his face with his hands, as he exclaimed, "Oh, God! How wicked of me. I ought to have known I should be sure to be caught. Be merciful, Miss Rosa. Don't expose us; it shall never happen again. Punish us anyhow rather than let anyone know of it."

"It is indeed awful, but I'm inclined to keep your secret, and be merciful," I responded gently. "You are both guilty of fornication, but has it not occurred to you that if this were to come out, it is poor Ann who would lose her reputation?"

"What? For that?" he sobbed. "I only went to kiss her last night, and then laid down by her side; somehow our kisses and the heat of our bodies led from one liberty to another till – till – I stopped all night, and you found me there this morning."

"You must both smart for this. I will whip you well myself to cure such behavior. But if ever it happens again, remember you shall suffer for it. Now, sir, off with your coat and vest, and let down your breeches with your behind toward me."

He was terribly shamefaced over doing as I ordered him, but too frightened of the consequences to remonstrate. Turning his back to me, he soon stood in his shirt with his breeches well pulled down.

"Now, sir," I said, "draw up that chair and kneel upon it with your face over the back. Then just pull up your shirt so as to properly offer your uncovered rump to the rod. Mind you bear it like a man, and keep as I order you, or I will have you thrown out of the house." "Oh, Miss, I won't even call out if I can help it." Charlie promised in a broken voice. "Punish me as much as you like, only don't betray poor Ann."

"Well sir, you'll find my hand rather heavy, but you must smart well for your carelessness." I gave him a couple of good stinging strokes which made their red marks and suffused the white flesh of his pretty bum with a rosy tint all over. "Will you commit such wickedness again with a woman who trusts you as if you were her brother? I can't cut half hard enough to express my horror of the thing!" exclaimed I, striking every blow with great deliberation. I managed, as I walked round his posteriors in the exercise of the rod, to see that his face was a deep scarlet, but his lips were firmly closed. The sight of his bottom just beginning to trickle with blood so excited me that my arms seemed to be strengthened at every cut to give a heavier stroke next time.

"Ah! Oh! Oh! I will never do it again," he screamed. "Forgive me, mistress. I can't keep my mouth shut any longer. It's awful. Oh! Oh! How it burns into my flesh." He was compelled to writhe and wriggle under my fearful cuts.

This went on for about twenty minutes. Now and then I had to slacken a little for want of breath, but his sighs and suppressed cries urged me on. It was a most delicious sensation to me; the idea of flogging a pretty youth fired my blood so much more than if the victim had been a girl. The rod seemed to bind me in voluptuous sympathy with the boy, although I was in perfect ecstasy at the sight of his sufferings.

At last I sank back on a sofa quite exhausted with my exertions, and presently found him kneeling in front of me, kissing my hand, which still held the birch, exclaiming, "Ah! Miss Rosa, how you have pickled me. But I'm sure to do something bad again to make you whip me another time. It's so beautiful I can't describe what I feel. All the pain was at last drowned in the most lovely emotions."

"Oh! Charlie," said I in a faint voice, "how wicked of you. You shan't kiss my hand; my foot is good enough for you to beg pardon of."

"My God! Miss Rosa, may I kiss that dainty little trotter of yours?" he said rapturously, seizing one of my feet and pressing his lips to my slightly exposed calf. His touch was like a spark to a train of powder. I sank quite back on the sofa in a listless state, unable to repel his liberties and leaving my leg at his mercy. I felt his roving hand on the flesh of my thighs under the drawers, but the nearer he approached to the sacred spot, the less able was I to resist. His hands went higher and higher; the heat of unsatisfied desire consumed me. At last with an effort I whispered, "Oh! Oh! For shame, Charlie. What are you doing? Come, let my leg go, I want to tell you something. Ah! The punishing of you has been the undoing of me. I am indeed afraid of you." I hid my face in my hands just as he raised his beautiful scarlet visage close to mine, and one of my feet also just touched something projecting in front under his shirt.

"Oh my! What's that in front of you Charlie?" I gasped.

"Oh, dear Miss, it's what Ann calls 'the boy,' and gives such pleasure that Aaron's Rod could not equal its magic power," he said softly.

"Oh! Charlie, will you be good and true to me? My life, my honor are in your power. You must never use my confusion, the secret that my impulsive nature cannot restrain. You naughty boy, the sight of your performance with your sister fired my imagination so that I determined to score your bottom well for you. But, alas, the sight has been too much for the sensuality of my disposition."

I could not continue what I had to say, but the dear boy covered my face and bosom with kisses, his searching hands finding out and taking possession of all my secret charms, while I could not restrain my own hands from being equally free, and repaid his hot burning kisses with interest. Our lips were too busy to give utterance to words.

I had to taste him and stripped him quickly of his shirt until he stood before me clad as God intended.

I tore myself away from his lips and moved downward to the smooth plane of his stomach, then still lower to his glorious pulsating shaft. Mindless with passion, I circled the head with my eager tongue. I know, dear Christine, that you must shake your head at my lack of restraint, but I was unable to hold back. I moved my head up and down, ceaselessly pumping, while Charlie lay there slowly moving his slim hips. His gasps of ecstasy were music to me. Then, suddenly, he could wait no longer and had me on my back. He spread my legs wide after tearing my skirts and drawers from me. Pausing only a moment to admire the beauty of my mount, he rammed the massive member into me. Of course I experienced the painful tension and laceration of my hymen, but all was soon forgotten in the flood of bliss which ensued.

I raised my hips to meet each of his thrusts. He was so large; each movement sent shivers through my body. As he quickened his pace I could feel the tightness building in my stomach. When the glorious spasms came, they quite engulfed me from my head to my toes, centering in my pussy.

In short, I surrendered everything to the dear boy, and we swam in the delights of love. His efforts exhausted him, and I resorted to the rod to procure myself a repetition of our joys. Finally, when I feared the dear youth might perhaps be seriously injured if I exacted from him more than nature could sustain, I prevailed upon him to use the birch on my own bottom, so as to keep my voluptuous sensations from abating. Ah! The rod is delicious if skillfully applied after the delights of coition. The dear boy wanted to renew his attack, but I would not permit it, promising he should come to my room at night for another feast of love, but insisting upon his being rested for the present.

I enjoyed a most voluptuous liaison with my page for three or four years, till I was constrained to part with him on account of his manly appearance. By my advice and assistance he married well, entered into business, and became a thriving man. From time to time, as long as he lived, we secretly enjoyed the sweets of each other's society. You have often wanted to know why I never married; the truth is, two things combined to prevent it. The first being my love of independence and aversion to being subject to anyone, however I might love him. This I might perhaps have brought myself to give up. But the second reason was insurmountable. I could not get a new maidenhead, and positively gave up all idea of marriage without that article. Poor Charlie died in the prime of his life, at thirty-five, but before his decease gave me a packet of papers relating to his amorous adventures. I found he was not very faithful to me, even when in my service, but I only know I loved him when I had him. Perhaps someday I may put his memoirs into some shape for your perusal, but this letter is the finis of these selections from my own experience.

Your affectionate friend,
Rosa Belinda Foster
Finis

AMY BROWN

When her widowed aunt, with whom she had been living for several years in Yorkshire, died, Miss Amy Brown was sent off to live with her nearest relative and guardian at his house in Suffolk. The change from a small house in a bleak and lonely part of the West Riding to a Baronet's establishment was hailed with rapture by the handsome and healthy girl of eighteen. The only, or at any rate, the principal advantage gained by her life with her aunt was one she scarcely appreciated. Her life in the country, the bracing air, the long walks, and the rigorous punctuality of the old lady had allowed Miss Brown to fully develop all the physical charms which so distinguished her. Add to that her fresh complexion, laughing brown eyes, the magnificent contour of her form and her limbs and you may begin to see what a rare beauty Amy possessed. But she also had a distracting air of reckless ingenuousness, picked up, no doubt, in her moorland scampers. Although unconscious of her charms, she sighed for the pomp and vanity of the world, even though they were held up to her by her aunt as perils of the deadliest description—a view regarded by Amy with skeptical curiosity. Her solitude only increased her imaginative faculty, and the fascination it attached to balls, parties, and life generally in the world, was greater than their charm actually warranted, as Amy subsequently found out. The only disquiet she had experienced arose from a vague longing which was satisfied by none of the small events in her puritanical life. She was modest even to prudishness; had long worn dresses of such a length as to make them remarkable; had never in her life had on one of the fashionable low-cut variety. She blushed at the mention of an ankle, and would have fainted at the sight of one. The matter of sex was a perpetual puzzle to her, but she was perfectly unembarrassed in her interaction with men, and quite unconscious of the desire she excited in them. All she knew of her guardian, Sir Charles Bosmere of Bosmere Hall, was that he was her trustee and that he was a widower much older than herself, a cousin some degrees removed from her, but that notwithstanding, she called him "Uncle."

Thither then she went. Sir Charles turned out to be a man of about fifty; very determined in his manner, powerfully built, and of a medium height. But what surprised Amy most was to find herself introduced to a tall, dark girl who looked about two and twenty, who was introduced as his housekeeper. She was dressed in exquisite fashion, but Amy thought most indecently. Even more shocking, she, too, called Sir Charles, "Uncle."

The first few days were taken up in making acquaintance, but Amy was surprised one morning at breakfast to see the housekeeper, Maud, grow very pale when told by Sir Charles that she was to go to the yellow room after breakfast, and that she was to go straight there. This direction apparently was directly as a consequence of some cutlets which were served at the meal slightly overcooked. When Amy again saw Maud, she was flushed and excited, and appeared to have been crying her eyes out. In some consternation, she inquired what the yellow room was. Her curiosity wasn't to be satisfied, though, as the only reply she obtained was that she would find out soon enough. On the same occasion, after Maud had left the breakfast-room, Sir Charles, who had by that time quite accepted Amy into his household, told her he thought she dressed in a very dowdy fashion, and said he had given directions to their maid to provide a more suitable wardrobe for her. Amy was quite flustered. She was covered with blushes and confusion as she listened to her Uncle speak of having her dressed like Maud. She was most disconcerted, for Maud showed a great deal of leg—as well as other charms. So Amy tried to pull herself together and replied that she really could do no such thing. Sir Charles looked at her in a very peculiar way and said he felt sure her present mode of dress hid the loveliest neck and limbs in the world. He went on to ask whether she did not admire Maud's style of dress, and if she had noticed her stockings and drawers.

"I have indeed, uncle; but I could never wear anything like them."

"And why not, pray?"

"I should be so ashamed."

"We will soon cure you of that. We punish prudish young women here by shortening their petticoats. How do you like that idea?"

"I like it not at all; and I will not have anything of the sort done to me."

"I am afraid, miss, you want a whipping."

"I should like," Amy declared defiantly, "to know who would dare such a thing."

Sir Charles again looked at her in a peculiar manner, but said nothing more on the subject. Instead, her guardian went on to tell her of his belief that young women should learn how to manage a house before they had one of their own and found themselves not knowing what to do with it. As part of her training as a proper young lady, she and Maud were to take weekly turns in the management of his household. A week from that day she would take the running of the household in hand.

"In the meantime, my dear, you had better learn as much as you can from Maud; especially not to let them burn cutlets like these." Saying which, he left the room.

At this point the narrative can best be continued from the diary of Amy Brown herself:

Wednesday, July 3, 1883

As soon as uncle had left the breakfast-table, I felt quite disturbed, but on the whole determined to go on as if nothing had happened. A message from Maud came a little later, delivered by our maid, Janet. The note said that she could not go out riding that morning as we had arranged. What a terrible woman our 'maid' is! Why on earth does uncle have a Scotchwoman with so terrible a disposition for two young girls? She makes me quake if she only looks at me. Well, I made up my mind to go alone, and rode off very soon after.

On my return I met Maud, very red-faced, and looking as though she had been crying dreadfully. I asked her what was in the room to which uncle had sent her. She would not tell me what had happened, although I was struck with an icy chill down my spine when she told me that I should soon learn the secrets of the yellow room for myself.

The rest of the day passed in the usual way. We drove out after lunch, paid some visits, received several, and dressed for dinner. While waiting for the gong to sound, Maud came to me, and to my horror took up precisely the same subject Sir Charles had so thoroughly embarrassed me about at breakfast.

"Uncle does not approve of your dresses, you little prude, and Janet has another one for you."

"If Janet," said I, "has a dress for me that shows my neck and breasts and back, as well as my feet, my ankles, my legs—I mean, if she has one for me that is like yours—I declare flatly, I won't wear it."

"Don't be a fool, dear. I am mistress this week; you will be next week, as uncle has explained to you, and if you do not get rid of your ridiculous shame, you will be soundly punished. You may be thankful if you are only obliged to show your legs up to your knees and your bosom down to your breasts."

"I do not care. I have never been punished."

"Very well," said Maud, "have your own way. You will soon know better."

When I arrived for dinner, uncle and Maud were there with three or four young men. Some very handsome women were also present; every one in low dresses. I was the only one in a high dress. Uncle said something to Maud, who in turn whispered to me that I was to go with her. As soon as we got into the hall, she told me I was to be taken to the yellow room and that I was a goose. When I asked her why, she only laughed. Once we arrived there, she said she was very sorry, but that she must obey orders. She then strapped my hands firmly behind my back. My struggles were useless in the end, but kept her so long that she said, "I shall take care that you shall have an extra half-dozen for this." I could not think what she meant but I had plenty of time to ponder the strange comment, for I was left alone in that room for a considerable time. It got darker and still no one came. The yellow room was in an out-of-the-way wing, and I could hear not any activity from the party which I knew was still in the dining room. In fact, I heard nothing until the faint sound of the tower clock striking ten reached my ears. My hands tied tight behind me and ached with a dull, throbbing pain. I began to lose my temper. I wondered how long I was to be kept there, and then I wondered who had the right to keep me, trussed up in such a manner. I had nothing to occupy my time so I made a study of my surroundings. I suppose it was called the yellow room because the bed-curtains, the curtains on the windows, and the valances were all yellow damask. I found myself staring at the ottoman and wondering what such an enormous one was doing here, in company with a heavy oak table. That wasn't the only oddity about the room. There was a bar swinging from the ceiling! I puzzled over that for quite awhile and, then, overcome with vexation and impatience, I went to sleep.

I was awakened at about half-past eleven by the sound of carriages driving off. It was pitch dark and the curtains had been drawn. I know it was about half-past eleven because about half-an-hour later midnight struck. There was a footstep in the corridor, and uncle came in.

Before I could express my anger at being treated in such a manner, my uncle addressed me in a clipped angry voice. "I am extremely surprised at your insubordination, miss, and for that I am about to punish you." What followed I cannot write.

* * *

So much for that part of the diary. Later on, by way of penance, as the sequel will show, Miss Amy Brown was compelled to write out the minutest description of her punishments and her sensations and secret thoughts.

What happened was this: Sir Charles Bosmere at once informed Amy that he would have no more prudish nonsense. He explained that he was going to strip her and flog her soundly. "But you must first promise to take off your own drawers. That is a very important humiliation to which a proud young beauty such as yourself has to be subjected."

She protested in the most vehement manner.

"You have no right to whip me," she said in a cold, tight little voice. She was trying hard to keep control of her speech. She tried not to screech or let her voice tremble, as that would tell him that he had the power to frighten her. "I will not be whipped by any man or anyone else. Undo my hands at once," she said in what she thought was an authoritative voice. "Being kept all the evening in this room without any dinner is quite punishment enough. And what have I done that calls for punishment? Refusing to wear horrid dresses which only serve to make nakedness conspicuous? If I am to be treated in this way, I shall leave tomorrow. As for promising to take off my own drawers before my own uncle, you must be mad, Sir, to think of such a thing. I would rather die first."

She looked lovely in her fury, and an alteration in the surface of Sir

Charles's trousers showed his appreciation of her beauty. He longed to see her naked and all her charms revealed.

"I will not dispute with you, you saucy miss, and as your face is too pretty to slap, I will settle accounts with your bottom—yes, your bottom, and a pretty plump white bottom I have no doubt it is. I can promise you, however, it won't be white long. Now lie across that ottoman on your face. What? You won't? Well, across my knee will do as well, and perhaps better."

Putting his arm round her waist, he dragged her with him to the sofa, telling her that her shrieks and struggles in that heavily curtained and thickly carpeted room would bring her no assistance; that even if they were heard no one would pay attention to them. In fact, he told her, the only result, if she persisted, would be to double her punishment. He did not, however, at that moment wish to do more than examine the charms that were so jealously concealed, the magnificence of which might be easily guessed from the little that did appear of her figure. He walked her to the sofa and sat down upon it, still holding her by the waist, and then, putting her between his legs, pulled her down across his left one. Her power of resistance was very much lessened because her hands were strapped behind her, but still she managed to slide down upon her knees in front of him instead of being laid across his lap. He then held her tightly between his knees and proceeded to unfasten the neck of her dress. Since the buttons were at the back, he was obliged to put his arms round her and draw her so close that he felt her warm pressure upon him. The passion he felt was intensified, and the girl then, for the first time, seemed in a hazy sort of wonder as to whether the treatment she was undergoing was altogether unpleasant. So shocked was she by this unconscious thought, she ceased her useless resistance. At length the buttons were all undone to the waist. The dress was pulled down in front as far as her arms— still strapped behind her back—would allow. It was sufficient, however, to disclose a neck as white as snow and the upper surfaces of two swelling, firm globes. Sir Charles immediately, placed his left arm under his victim's armpit and round her shoulders, and drew her closer to him, spreading his legs wider. Notwithstanding her pretty cries for him to desist, he inserted his right hand in her bosom. At last, succeeding in loosening her corset, he was able to caress the scarlet center of the lovely, palpitating breast while its owner lay in most bewitching disorder in his lap. Her hair had partly fallen; her bosom was exposed by the dress three parts down and the loose corset—her eyes swam, and her color was heightened.

"Oh, stop! Uncle; oh, do, do, do stop! I never felt like this before. Whatever will become of me? I cannot bear the sensation. You have no business to pull me about so."

"Do you not like the sensation, Amy?" asked he, stooping and putting his face into her bosom, "and being kissed like this, and this, and this? And is this not nice?" Taking her red teat between his lips, he gently played with it, using his tongue and his teeth until she was quite overtaken by strange feelings, the like of which she had never experienced or even imagined.

"Oh! Uncle! Whatever are you doing to me?" said the girl, flushing crimson all over, her eyes opening wide with amazement while her knees fell wider apart as she fell slightly back upon his right knee.

"Is it nice? Do you like it? Does it give you sensations anywhere else?" asked he, glancing at her waist—and then, a moment after, putting his hand down outside her dress, asked, "Here, for instance?"

She flushed a still deeper crimson shame, but there was a gleam of rapture after the momentary pressure, followed by the exclamation: "How dare you?"

"How dare I, miss? We shall see. Now you will please lie on your face across my knee. You can rest on the sofa."

"Oh, I suppose, you are now going to button up my dress," she said with some disappointment in her tone.

"Am I?"

"Then what are you going to do?"

"Make you obey me, and without any more resistance, or you shall have double punishment. Lie down at once, miss."

"Oh, uncle, don't look at my legs! Oh, do not, do not strip me. Oh, if I am to be whipped, whip my hands or shoulders; just not—not t-there."

"You are a very naughty, obstinate girl, with too much prudishness about you. But when you yourself have been forced to expose all you possess in the most unconcealed manner, and have been kept some days in short frocks with no drawers, there will, no doubt, be an improvement. And, as I said before, I shall flog your bare bottom soundly, Miss Amy, and fairly often if you do not mend your ways. Lash your arms and shoulders? Indeed! I shall lash your legs and thighs. Lie down this instant."

The poor girl, although she sensed resistance was useless, made not a move, but the arm put round her back soon cured her inaction. She lay across her uncle's left leg and under his left arm, which he had well round her waist.

"Now," said he, tightening his grasp, "we shall see what we have all along so carefully hidden; eh, miss?" He pulled up her dress behind, despite her struggles and reiterated prayers to him to desist.

"No use struggling, miss," he went on, slipping his hand up her legs and proceeding at once to that organ in front which women delight in having touched.

"Oh, uncle! Oh, leave off. How dare you? How dare you outrage me in this manner? Oh! Take your hand away! Oh! Oh! Oh!"

"So you are a little wet," he said, feeling the hairs moistened by the voluptuous sensations he had caused her by caressing her breasts, "and you hoped that no one would know, no doubt. Now just let me stroke these legs." He ran his free hand up and down her silky thighs; his left arm was still draped over her back, holding her across his lap, although it could be argued that he could have used both hands to explore her form as it was doubtful that she had the strength or inclination to escape. "What a nice fine pair they are," he exclaimed, turning the robe above her waist. "And what a pretty, what a perfectly lovely bottom!" he said, opening her drawers. "What a crime to hide it from me. However, you will make amends for that by taking your drawers off presently."

"Never! Never while I live! You monster! You wretch! If ever I get out of this room alive, I will expose you!"

"My dear, let me try a little gentle persuasion, a novel sensation. If that does not suffice, I can find some better, more striking, argument."

And again, he pressed her down upon him and slipped his hand up along her thighs. He deviated for a moment to caress her fine plump bottom-cheeks, but he wasn't long distracted from his true purpose. He moved his hand down once more and, while putting his finger in her virgin orifice in front, he positioned his thumb over her rear opening. Upon feeling his finger at the lips of her cunny, she jerked herself upwards, heaving herself off his lap as high as she could manage. Although her movement did manage to dislodge his finger somewhat from her front, she soon realized that she had just facilitated the invasion of her bottom-hole, for as she rose up, his thumb, which had been carefully positioned to take advantage of this very reaction, went in. Then, with a little scream, Amy again bounced forward and his finger slid into her cunny as far as her maidenhead would admit. She could do nothing to dislodge either invader, for her hands were all the time still tied. Besides which, she was mortified that she had so unthinkingly assisted in her own undoing.

While she was held motionless by her shock and embarrassment, her uncle kept up a severe use of both his finger and thumb for some moments, moving in and out of the two openings with surprising ease. Soon she was unable to contain herself, and was ultimately obliged to abandon herself to the sensations he provoked. Her legs were stretched out and wide apart; her bottom rose and fell regularly; her lovely neck and shoulders, which were still exposed to his sight, increased his rapture and her dismay; and at last, when the crisis had arrived—pretty nearly at the same moment did it overtake them both—she lay panting and sobbing, almost dead with shame, but for the time subdued.

"Well, dear, how do you like your new experience?"

"Oh, uncle, it is awful, simply awful! I am beside myself."

"When you have rested a moment, will you stand up and take off your drawers before me?"

No answer.

"Answer directly, miss."

"No, I won't! I won't, and I shall not allow you do take them from me."

"I have no intention of removing the pretty garment myself," he said with a wicked twinkle in his eyes. "I believe I can convince you to follow my orders."

Getting up, he went to a chest of drawers, and opening one, took out a riding-whip. Silently, and notwithstanding her violent resistance, he again got the refractory girl over his knee, with his arm round her, her dress up, and her bottom as bare as her drawers would admit. Across the linen and the bare part he gave her a vigorous cut, making the whip whistle through the air. It fell, leaving a livid mark across the delicate white flesh and causing her to yell in shocked pain. Again he raised it and brought it down—another yell and more desperate contortions.

"Oh, uncle, don't! Oh! No more! No more! Oh! I can't bear it. I will be good. I will obey."

Although he had succeeded in wresting from her the promise he sought, Sir Charles paid no attention. Instead, he raised the whip, made it whistle a third time through the air. A more piercing shriek.

"It is not enough for you to promise to obey; you must be punished and cured of your obstinacy. Here's your reward for calling me a wretch and monster"—swish—swish!

"Oh! Oh! Oh! Don't! Oh, don't! Oh, you are not a wretch! I say you are not anything but what—oh! Oh! Put down that whip. Oh! Please, dear uncle! You are not a wretch or monster! I was very naughty to call you so, and I liked what you did to me, only I was ashamed to say it. I will take my drawers off before you if you like! I will do anything, only don't whip me any more."

"You shall have your dozen, miss"—swish. "So you liked my tickling your clitty, did you, better than"—swish—"tickling your bottom with this whip, eh?"—swish—swish. "You will expose me if you escape alive, will you?"—swish—swish.

"Oh, stop, stop! You have given me thirteen. For heaven's sake, stop!"

"I have given you a baker's dozen, and"—swish—"there is another because you complained."

Sir Charles was carried away by the passions excited by the punishment he was inflicting upon this lovely girl, and her yells as he brought the whip down again, cutting into her delicate flesh, only stirred his own passion to greater heights. Still holding her, he asked the sobbing girl whether she would be good.

"Yes. Indeed, indeed I will."

"There is a very satisfactory magic in this wand. Now, if I unfasten your hands, will you stand up and take your drawers off so that I may birch your bottom for refusing to wear a proper evening dress?"

"Oh, uncle, you have whipped me already, and punished me severely, too, by what you did to me with your f-fingers. Why should I be put to more shame?"

"Shame! Nonsense. You should be proud of your charms and glad to show them. What I did should give you pleasure. Anyhow, will you take off your drawers?"

"Oh!" she said, flushing and in despair, "however can I? I should have to lift my dress quite up, and I should be all exposed. Besides, it is so humiliating."

"Precisely. You yourself must bare all your hidden fascinations. And the humiliation is to chastise you for your prudishness. You must do it. You had better be a good, obedient girl, as you promised you would be just now."

"Very well. I will then."

"That is a good girl. You shall have a kiss for reward," and, putting his lips on her beautiful mouth, Sir Charles gave her a long and thrilling kiss, and inserted his tongue between her lips until it came into contact with hers.

"What a delicious kiss," she said, shuddering with delight and coyly adding, "I shall not so much mind taking off my—my—my drawers now," she said in a hushed tone, her eyes averted from him.

"That is right, dear. Now let me undo your hands. There. Now stand before that mirror and let me arrange the light so that it may fall full upon you. You must do this unassisted; I shall sit here."

Miss Amy Brown walked over to the mirror in a graceful and stately fashion, and started as she saw herself. She turned round and looked shyly at her master, but said nothing. Stooping down, she gathered up her gown and petticoats in her arms and slowly lifted them to her waist. The act revealed a slender and graceful pair of ankles and calves, but the knees were hidden by the garment she was about to remove. She fumbled with the buttons about her waist. They increased her confusion by not readily unbuttoning, at which she, in a charming little rage, stamped angrily once or twice, making the drawers tumble down.

"Keep up your petticoats," cried Sir Charles, "and step out of your drawers. Keep them up," said he, rising, "until I tell you you may let them down. What lovely thighs! What splendid hips! What a lovely, round bottom! Look at it, Amy, in the glass."

"Oh," she said, startled, "I am so glad you think so. I have never looked at myself before."

He laughed at this revelation and stroked the satin skin with his hand, rubbing her limbs in front and behind and all over her bottom until, at last, when he had gradually stroked her all the way up, he put his hand between the cheeks of her backside right through to her cunt. He rubbed that passage also, and kept gently stroking for some minutes until she fell limply against him, uttering inarticulate sounds of delight.

"There," he said at length, "that will do for tonight. You may let your clothes down now. It is so late that the birching shall be postponed until the morning."

"May I take my drawers with me?"

"No, my dear; it will be some time before I shall allow you to wear them again. Not as long as you are still a maiden," he added significantly.

"Oh, that will be years."

"Will it?" he inquired, innocently. "Come," he said, "I will take you to your room. You will, in the future, occupy the one I will now take you to, and not your old one."

"Why, uncle? All my things are in the old one."

"That does not matter, my dear. I must keep you under my eye until you are reduced to abject submission."

The room to which he took her was cheery and warm. Although the month was July, a fire had been lighted and had evidently been recently stirred. And on a small table near the hearth stood a biscuit box and a small bottle of Dry Monopole. Amy would have preferred a sweeter wine, but was told that this was better for her. It was quite plain that either uncle had told someone the precise hour at which he would bring her to the room, or that someone had been watching, for the wine was still frothing in the glass and therefore must have been poured out the very moment before she entered. What a terrible thought—could anyone have been watching her and have seen her nakedness? Her uncle could not have known at what hour he would take her there. She was for an instant paralyzed at the notion, but the next moment, accidentally catching sight of a bare breast and arm, it caused her a certain voluptuous thrill to think she had been seen by someone besides Sir Charles. As she slowly undressed herself, her uncle having gone off, shutting the door behind him, it struck her that she would herself, for her own satisfaction, have a peep at all she had been compelled to expose to him. Having resolved to so look at herself, she felt delightfully immoral. She stood before one of the large glasses with which her room was furnished, and after letting down her wealth of brown hair, she divested herself of all but her chemise. She stood staring at herself in the glass for a time before she allowed that last garment to slip off her shoulders and arms. She gazed at her naked charms in the glass. But only for an instant. She was then overcome by a flood of shame at her nakedness and, after fully realizing what she had been doing, she hurriedly averted her eyes and looked about for her nightdress. That she could not find, and she then recollected that the room she was in was not the same one she had previously used. She supposed they must have forgotten to bring her things. No, here was her dressing gown. She would put it on, and go to her old room for her nightdress.

She went to the door, and to her utter amazement, found that there was no handle inside! She was a prisoner. She looked about, but there was no other door anywhere to be seen.

"Very well," she said to herself; "I shall have to sleep in my chemise."

She was naked underneath, so taking off her dressing gown made her feel immodest. She didn't feel much better once she had her chemise on as it was cut very low in the neck and left her arms bare. She felt more immodest still when she remembered what she had undergone and was to undergo later in the morning.

Before she got into bed she looked about for the article ladies generally use. There was nothing of the kind in the room, and there was no bell. Then it struck her that the deprivation of her nightdress and of the utensil she now needed to make use of, must have been done deliberately by Sir Charles, and the idea that he had thought of such things so intimately connected with her person gave her a fresh delightful glow of sensuality as she plunged into the cold, silky, linen sheets. The necessary effort to retain her urine, the sense that she was being punished by being made to retain it, and the knowledge that her uncle knew all about it and so was punishing her, excited her to such an extent that she went to bed a very naughty girl indeed.

Circumstances had been such that she found it impossible, even though she closed her eyes, to fall asleep. Her mind was racing with the memories of what had happened to her just a short time ago. As she tossed and turned in her bed in this strange room, unfamiliar sensations again stabbed through her as her sore bottom scraped against the sheets with only the thin chemise to protect her. The feelings that overtook her were new and different, yet strangely similar to what she had experienced when Sir Charles had touched her so intimately. How could she sleep when so many thoughts rushed through her head? It was difficult to believe that she had gone down to dinner just a few short hours ago and, now, only a little while later, she felt as if her whole world had changed. She blushed just thinking about how Sir Charles had touched her. She had been shocked and embarrassed, yet, at the same time, the feelings he had inspired in her had been enjoyable.

In fact, now—as she thought of it—her bottom-hole squeezed, gripping a finger that was no longer there. But, strangely, she could still feel it. Never before had she passed one moment thinking of that embarrassingly personal area. But now, since her uncle's finger had delved inside, she could not help but think of it, imagining again how the tiny hole had expanded to accept his thumb, how it resisted only a little as he pushed in, and then closed again as his digit was removed; closed, but felt surprisingly open still, wanting, waiting to be filled again.

She started awakening, drifting back out of her thought-filled slumber. "I must stop these wicked thoughts," she chastised herself. "I must clear my mind and sleep."

But each time she closed her eyes she imagined her uncle's hands roam-

Amy Brown

ing once more over her naked limbs. Her breath caught in her throat as her thoughts drifted to the memory of his lips closing over her breasts. Her nipples swelled as she remembered how her heart leapt in her breast at the sensation. Her thoughts ran wild again and she imagined his tongue encircling her nipple, his teeth nibbling at the bud of flesh. She moaned at the thought and her nipples tautened at the memory. She was amazed that her body, so recently awakened to these sensations, could react so physically to the mere memory of what had taken place. Even as she wondered at this phenomenon, she felt a sudden gush of wetness between her thighs and an intense heat radiated upwards. She blushed at her body's betrayal, even though no one else knew of her shame. She thought of her recently deceased aunt and how she had raged at the sins associated with pleasures of the flesh. She shuddered to think what the prudish old lady would have thought of tonight's activities. Her thoughts didn't rest long, though, on that frigid woman. The reactions of her own body, the throbbing ache and the wetness between her thighs, soon brought her back to the present. Not caring about the propriety of her actions, Amy slid her hand under the sheets and tugged on her chemise until it rested above her belly. She worked her hand between her legs, mimicking the actions her uncle had performed earlier. She slipped one finger into her opening and began to work it in and out. The moisture she had felt earlier facilitated her movements and soon her finger was coated with the slick, warm stuff. Her heart was pounding in her breast and a moan escaped her before she closed her mouth to muffle the sound, wondering if anyone had heard her. Again, as had happened earlier, her legs stiffened and she felt a warmth spread quickly through her. Her back arched as her finger slid furiously over the slick folds of flesh. She tried jamming further into the still-tight opening and was rewarded with an intense shot of pleasure that was quickly followed by a sharp stab of pain. Her finger could go no further within, but exploring deeper did not seem necessary, since the feelings she had unleashed in her explorations were fast coming to an earth-shattering conclusion. She worked her hand even faster between her thighs, switching to a circular motion so that her finger came in contact with the entire circumference of her opening as it made its journey around. Her juices flowed more freely and her hand slipped during yet another joyous trip around. Suddenly, Amy was overcome and her body was wracked with tremors. Her back arched still more until, exhausted, she relaxed back into the soft bed and fell fast asleep.

326

* * *

Awakening next morning about nine o'clock, she caught herself wondering what the whipping would be like, and how it would be administered, and was filled with a delightful sense of shame when she recollected the part of her body that would receive the castigation and she imagined the exposure it would inevitably entail. The thought or anticipation of this did not disturb her much. She even contemplated with pleasure how her legs and thighs would be exposed. She also realized that more would be exposed, specifically that part of her which she could not name to herself. Even though she had been made quite free with that area as she lay in bed the night before, and suffered the examination by her uncle, she could not now, in the bright morning light, bring herself to name it, considering the word immodest; but she did trust that her uncle would not flog her very severely.

As she lay thus occupied with these thoughts, there was a tap at the door. Since there was no handle on her side of the door, she sat up in the bed, covering herself as best she could with the sheet, and waited. Within moments, the door swung open and Janet entered carrying a cup of tea and some buttered bread.

"You have just an hour for dressing, miss," she announced, "for breakfast will be served at half-past ten in the blue sitting-room—the one which overlooks the park. Miss Maud will come to show you where it is."

"Thank you, Janet," said Amy, the sheet drawn close about her neck. "There are several things I shall want from my old room—linen and a dress. Will you please bring them?"

"I have the clothes you are to wear all ready, miss, and will bring them to you."

"What do you mean, Janet? I should like to choose my own dress."

Janet did not reply, grimly leaving the girl to find out for herself.

The maid returned presently with an armful of clothing, which she deposited on a sofa.

In the meantime, Amy had jumped up and donned the dressing-gown. She then found it necessary to again look about for that piece of furniture which is a feature in most bedrooms. Alas, she could not find it anywhere. She did not know, however, how to broach the subject to Janet, and while she

Amy Brown

was wondering how to accomplish it, that amiable domestic had left the room. Amy had told her to return in about half an hour to do her hair, and the reply was that her hair was not to be done up that morning—a circumstance which, recalling what was before her, made her blush deeply. Then Janet departed, shutting the door and again leaving her trapped since the door only opened from the outside. Amy, resigning herself to the idea that her bodily needs would have to wait until she was on the way to breakfast, proceeded to wash. In the wall, close to the washstand, was a black marble knob with the word 'Bath' inscribed upon it in gold letters. It was exactly what she wanted at the moment. Putting her hand upon it, she pressed slightly. To her surprise, a panel slid aside and revealed a marble-floored room surrounded by looking-glasses. There were several large slabs of cork for standing on, and a large bath of green Irish marble in the center. Proceeding to it, she found that the same knob that had opened the room, filled the bath with water. She soon found the water to be not only perfumed, but deliciously softened. The champagne she had refreshed herself with the previous night and the tea she had just finished made her wish again that she could have got rid of the water she herself contained, but she could not make out how the water ran away or was emptied from the bath—so that little idea was knocked on the head. While bathing, she caught sight of herself continually in the glasses about her, and fell in love with her round, plump limbs and frame. She briefly wondered why she had never looked at herself before. She also noticed with indignation the red marks her uncle had made across her bottom with the cruel whip. She dried herself with the deliciously woolly and warmed towels, as she remembered that she had yet another flogging to undergo. She shuddered as she came to the conclusion that her disobedience deserved punishment; and felt naughty, as she confessed to herself that she really deserved to be whipped.

She had just made this determination when she found her obedience again put to the test. Proceeding to dress, she found that the clothes she had been provided were far worse than the dress she had refused to wear the evening before. They were unfit even for a girl of ten. The chemise was cut abominably low both behind and before, and the petticoats were quite short. So was the dress. And the petticoats were starched in such a way as to stand almost straight out. In other words, instead of hiding her limbs, they would display them. And there were no drawers. What was she to do? Sir Charles was rigid in his expectation of punctuality at meals. If she waited until Maud came, she would be too late, and probably receive a worse flogging; besides, in all probability, Maud would only laugh at her again. So, a little indignantly, she dressed herself in the white silk stockings, which reached just halfway up her thighs, fastened them with the rose-colored garters above her knee, put on the patent leather low-cut shoes, the black and yellow corset, and the white frock with a rose-colored sash. She tied her hair with a ribbon of the same color, and then looked at herself. She looked like a great, overgrown schoolgirl, but, she could not help owning to herself, a very lovely one. Her arms were bare and the frock was so low that she noticed with horror that it would only just conceal her red teats from someone looking at her from straight in front. But if someone were to look straight down from her shoulder, they would be quite visible. And the dress stopped at her knees; no amount of tugging or pulling could make it longer. And the petticoats made it stick out so. The only comfort was her hair, which did help to hide her naked back. Dressed at last, but feeling worse than naked, she sat down to wait for Maud. To her horror, she noticed, by looking in a glass opposite her, that the dress stuck out to such an extent that not only could her leg be seen to the top of the stocking, but that the rosy flesh beyond was quite visible. After a trial or two she discovered that if she was not very careful how she sat, not only would the whole of both legs be displayed, but the juncture between her thighs would be clearly visible as well. She wondered how she could go about, and whether she would have to; and at last the costume so excited her passions that she was compelled to walk up and down, and became so naughty that she did not know how to contain herself or the water she had been unable to get rid of. While fidgeting about the room in this state of agitation, Maud entered, and immediately applauded.

"How perfectly lovely you are, Amy, with that blush-rose flush!" she exclaimed in the most disingenuous manner. "What a splendid bust! Good gracious! Do let me look at them. What lovely straight beautifully-shaped legs," she giggled, catching hold of the skirt of the frock. "Oh, do let me see!"

"Oh! Don't, Maud! Don't!"

"Very well, dear. But you have not done up your hair. That won't do."

"Janet told me I was not to."

"Yes, I know. But that was a mistake. It hides too much."

"That is just why I like it down."

"And just why I do not, dear. You must let me roll it up for you so that your back and neck and shoulders may be fully shown. There; now you look a perfect darling. I thought I should find you quite cured of your anxiety to hide your charms. Do you not now wish you had taken my advice?"

"Yes."

"But," she went on, "it is not of much consequence; for if you had not rebelled, some other excuse would have been made for punishing you."

"Indeed?"

"Yes, and you deserved it, Amy."

As Amy had herself come to this conclusion, she only blushed.

Feeling her bare legs, she said, "Oh, Maud, do you know I have no draw-ers on, and that when I sit down my legs a-and-and everything else will show? Shall I have to go about in this dress? How long shall I have to wear it?"

"That depends upon how you take your punishment. Until you are given other garments to wear, you will certainly have to go about the house and grounds with it. I suppose you wish you had drawers on?"

"Indeed you may suppose so. Oh, Maud, however can I…"

"We must be going, Amy," Maud interrupted, "or we shall be late."

"Oh, Maud, do tell me, does uncle whip very hard?"

"I should have thought," and Maud's eyes flashed, "you could have answered that question yourself."

"Yes. He hurt me dreadfully with the riding-whip. Have you been birched?"

"Yes. I have."

"Was it very bad?"

"In a few hours you will be able to judge for yourself."

"Where did he birch you?"

"Here," said Maud, slyly putting her hand under Amy's petticoats upon her bare bottom.

"Oh, don't, Maud."

"Silly child, you should be obliged to me for the sensation. Do come along to breakfast."

"Oh, Maud, there is something I want to ask you, but how to do it I do not know. Perhaps," she said with a deep blush, "the best way is to say they have forgotten to put something in my room."

"I know very well what you mean, Amy. You mean you have no pot and you want to pee. All I can say is that I hope you do not want to very badly, because it is not at all likely that you will be allowed to do so until after your flogging. But, of course, you can ask uncle."

"However could I ask him?" replied Amy, aghast and pale at the notion and the prospect of what she would have to endure. "Does he know that this room is so lacking in the necessary furniture?" remembering her thought of the night.

"Yes. Of course he knows, and he does it to punish you and to help to make you feel naughty. Do you feel naughty, dear?" asked Maud, again putting her hand under Amy's petticoats. This time she did not allow Amy to brush her hand away; indeed, she began tickling the shocked girl's clitoris.

"Oh, don't! Maud. Oh, pray don't! Oh, you will make me wet myself if you do. Oh, can't you let me go to your room?"

"My dear girl, if I were to let you pee without permission I would probably be forbidden to do so myself more often than twice a day for a week or a fortnight. And I advise you to say nothing about it to uncle, for if he finds out that you want to very badly, he will probably make you wait another hour. It is a very favorite punishment of his."

"Why?"

"Oh, I don't know, except that it is a severe one. And it is awfully humiliating to a girl to have to ask, but it certainly makes one feel naughty."

"Yes, it does. Do you know I was nearly doing it in the bath?"

"Lucky for you that you did not. It would certainly have been found out, and you would have caught it. But, Amy, why do you say 'doing it' instead of 'peeing' when you refer to it. When you do ask, you will have to use plain language."

"Oh, Maud!"

"Yes, and most likely you will have to do it in front of uncle. One more note of warning: If he finds out you squirm about saying things and calling them by their names, he will make you say the most outrageous things, and write them also. Now hurry, there's the clock chiming half-past ten. Come along."

When they got to the blue room—on the way to which they passed, to Amy's intense consternation, several servants who gazed intently at her—they found Sir Charles there in a velvet coat and kilt. He greeted them cheerily. The view across the park, in the glades of which the fallow deer could be seen grazing, was lovely; the sunshine was flooding the room, and the soft, warm summer air carried the perfume of the flowers in through the wide-open windows from the beds below. Amy was so struck by the view that for a moment she forgot to notice how her uncle was gazing at her. She forgot how she was dressed until she felt the air on her legs, and it provoked a consciousness at which she blushed.

"How do you like your frock, my dear? It becomes you admirably."

"Does it, uncle?" She looked coyly at him. "I am glad you like it."

"I am glad to see you are a sensible girl after all. We shall make something of you."

"How long am I to wear it, uncle?"

"For a week."

"For a fortnight," corrected Maud, maliciously. "She is to be mistress next week."

Maud knew very well how difficult it would be to give orders to the staff dressed like that. She reveled in the notion of getting Amy soundly punished.

Sir Charles noticed with a gleam of amusement how fidgety Amy became towards the end of the meal, and Maud smiled gently to herself. Amy thought that after breakfast she would have a chance to relieve herself. She was disappointed. Sir Charles then said, in a severe tone, "I think, Miss Amy, we have a little business to settle together. Your disobedience cannot be overlooked. You must come with me. Your short skirts will punish your prudishness, but the birch is the best corrector of a disobedient girl's bottom." She grew quite pale and trembled all over, both with fright and at being spoken to so before Maud, who, reposing calmly in her chair, was steadily gazing at her.

She got up. When her uncle had finished speaking, he came up to her and took hold of her left ear with his right hand, and saying, "Come along, miss, to be flogged," he marched her off to the yellow room.

There, to her consternation, she saw straps and pillows on the oak table. In a perfect fright, she said: "Oh, pray do not strap me up, uncle; pray do not. I will submit."

"Undress yourself," he said, having closed the door; "leave on your stockings only."

"Oh, uncle!"

"You had better obey, miss, or you shall have a double dose. Take off your frock this instant."

"Now your petticoat bodice."

"Now your petticoats. Now your corset and chemise. Now, my proud young beauty, how do you feel?"

He had not seen her to such advantage the evening before. She had kept her long dress on the whole time, and while punishing her he had only uncovered a small portion of her legs. It is true she afterwards had been made to take off her drawers; but the skirt and petticoats gathered about her hips had still concealed much. Now she was naked from the crown of her head to her rose-colored garters. Burning with shame, she put her hands up to her face, and remained standing and silent, while Sir Charles feasted his eyes upon the contemplation of every beautiful curve of the lovely little head poised so beautifully upon a perfect throat; of the dimpled back and beautifully rounded shoulders; of the arms; of the breasts and hips and thighs. She was the most lovely girl he had seen, he said to himself, and then, seating himself, he added aloud, "Come here, miss. Kneel down: there, between my knees; clasp your hands, and say after me: Uncle, I have been…"

"Uncle, I have been…"

"A naughty, disobedient girl."

"A n-naughty, disobedient girl."

"And deserve to be soundly birched."

"And deserve to be s-sound-soundly birched."

"Please, therefore…"

"Please, therefore…"

"Strap me down…"

"Oh, no! Oh, no! Oh, please don't strap me down!"

"Say what I tell you at once, miss, or it will be worse for you."

"Strap me down…"

"To the table…"

"Oh! Oh! Oh! To the table…"

"With my legs well apart…"

"Oh, dear! I can't. With—with—I can't. With my—oh, uncle!"

"An extra half-dozen for this."

"Oh, uncle!"

"Say at once: With my legs well apart."

"With my—my oh!—legs…" she struggled with the words shuddering deliciously and blushed bewilderingly, "well apart,"

"And give me…"

"And give me…"

"Please…"

"Please…"

"A dozen and a half."

Amy Brown

"Oh, uncle! Please, not so much!" she cried, recollecting the baker's dozen with the riding-whip.

"You will have more if you do not say it at once."

"A dozen and a half…"

"On my bare bottom."

"Oh! that!—my—I can never say"

"You must."

"My bare?"

"You had better say it. Stop; I will improve it. You must say: On my girl's bare bottom."

"Oh, uncle!" she said, looking at him and seeing his eyes doting upon her and devouring her beauty, and the lust and fire in them, she immediately turned hers away.

"Now, Amy, 'On my girl's bare bottom.'"

"On my girl's b-bare b-bottom."

He moved as he said this, and Amy noticed that he adjusted something under his kilt.

"Well laid on."

"Well laid on."

"Yes, I will, my dear. I will warm your bottom for you as well as any girl ever had her bottom warmed. I will set it on fire for you. You will curse the moment you were disobedient. I will cure you of disobedience and all your silly nonsense. Come along to the table. There, stand at that end"—Amy began to sob—"put the cushion before you, so. Now lie over it, right down on the table. No resistance."

As he fixed the strap round her shoulders, she made a slight attempt at remonstrance. The strap went round her and the table, and once it was buckled she could not, of course, get up. He then buckled on two wristlets, and with two other straps fastened her wrists to the right and left legs of the table; then another broad strap was put round the table and the small of her back. This was pretty tight, as were also those that fastened her at the knees and ankles. Her legs were wide apart, fixed to the legs of the table. She was spread-eagled, and her bottom, the tender skin between its cheeks, her cunt, and her legs were most completely exposed.

"Now, my dear, you will remain in that position half an hour and contemplate your offenses, and then you shall have as sound a flogging as I have ever given a girl."

334

"Oh, uncle, before you flog me, do let me do something. Maud told me I should have to tell you, but I do not know how to. I will come back directly and be strapped down again if you will only let me. And, oh! Please do not leave me in this dreadful position for half an hour."

"You must say what it is that you want."

"Oh, uncle," feeling it was all or nothing, she whispered, "do let me go and pee before I am flogged. I want to, oh, so dreadfully. I have not been able to all the morning, nor all night."

"So you want to very dreadfully, do you, miss?" and going up to her, he put his hand between her legs from behind and severely tickled the opening through which the stream was burning to rush. It was all that Amy could do to retain it.

"Oh, don't! Oh! If you do I shall wet myself. I shall not be able to help it. Oh, uncle, pray, pray don't! Oh, pray let me go!"

"No, miss, I certainly shall not. It is a part of your punishment. There was an unnatural coldness about these parts of yours which this will help to warm up. Have you not felt more naughty since you have had all that hot water inside you?"

"And you are beginning to see how ridiculous prudishness is. Now, just you think about your conduct and your disobedience until I return to whip you, and remember you owe your present position to those shameful attributes."

Saying this, Sir Charles left the room. Poor Amy, left to herself, all naked save for her stockings; her arms stretched out above her head and tightly strapped; her legs divided and fastened wide apart; the most secret portions of her frame made the most conspicuous in order that they might be punished by a man, did feel her position acutely. She considered it and felt it to be most shameful. Her cheeks burned with a hot, red glow. But all concealment was absolutely impossible; the haughty beauty felt herself prostrate before and at the mercy of her master, and experienced again an exquisite sensual thrill at the thought that she really deserved to have her bottom whipped by her uncle.

Presently Maud came into the room in a low-necked dress, with a large bouquet.

"Well, Amy," she said, "I hope you enjoy your position and the prospect before you."

"Oh, Maud; go away. I can't bear you to see me in this position. I won't be punished before you."

"Silly goose! Young ladies strapped down naked and stretched out spread-eagle for punishment, are not entitled to say shall or shan't. What a lovely skin and back, Amy. Alas! Before long that pretty, plump, white bottom will present a very altered appearance. How many are you to have?"

"I was made to ask for a dozen and a half, well laid on."

"And you may depend upon it, you will have them, my dear, most mercilessly laid on," Maud cooed, stroking her legs and thighs, which caused Amy to catch her breath and shrink away from the pleasure Maud's hand gave her. Maud asked her whether she had tried to induce her uncle to let her go somewhere.

"Yes," replied Amy. "I did. But he would not."

"And I suppose you want to very badly," went on Maud, maliciously placing her fingers on the very spot.

"Yes, I do. Oh, don't, Maud, or you'll make me…"

"Now mind, Amy, whatever you do, hold out till your birching is over. If you do not, I warn you that you will catch it."

"I think it is a very, very cruel, horrid punishment," said Amy, whimpering.

"It is severe, I know, and it is far better not to be prudish than to incur it. But here comes uncle."

"Now, you bold, disobedient girl, I hope you feel ashamed of yourself," said Sir Charles, entering the room and shutting the door. "Maud will witness your punishment as a warning to her of what she will receive if she is disobedient."

Going up to the wardrobe, he selected three well-pickled birches, which had evidently never been used, for there were numbers of buds on them. They were elastic and well spread, and made a most ominous switching sound as, one by one, Sir Charles switched them through the air. Amy shuddered and Maud's eyes gleamed.

"Oh, pray, pray, uncle, do not be very severe. Remember it is almost my first whipping. It is awful!"

"Maud had changed the dress she had worn at breakfast and, as already mentioned, now had on one cut very low in the body; her arms were bare and her skirts short. Between her breasts was placed a bouquet of roses.

"Hold these," said Sir Charles, giving her the rods.

He then put his left arm round Amy, and said: "Now, you saucy, disobedient miss, your bottom will expiate your offenses, and by way of preface…"—smack, smack with his right hand, smack, smack, smack. "Ah, it is already becoming a little rosy."

"Oh, uncle! Oh, how you hurt! Oh, how your hand stings! Oh! Oh! Oh!"

"Yes. A bold girl's bottom must be well stung. It teaches her obedience and submission"—smack! "What a lovely, soft bottom!"—smack, smack, smack.

Maud's eyes gleamed and her face flushed as Amy, wriggling about as much as the straps allowed, cried softly to herself. When her uncle had warmed her sufficiently, he removed his arm and moved about two feet away from the girl, whose confusion at the invasion of her charms by the rough hand of a man increased her loveliness tenfold. Maud held one birch in her right hand. She, too, looked divine. Her dark eyes flashing, her lovely bosom heaving, she handed it, retaining the other two in her left hand, to her uncle. Amy could not see that as she gave him the birch. As soon as her hand was free she slipped it under her uncle's kilt from the back, and the instant increase of his passion and excitement left no doubt as to the use she was making of it. Sir Charles stood at the left side of his refractory ward. He drew the birch, lecturing her as he did so, three or four times upwards and downwards from back to front and from front to back between the cheeks of the girl's bottom, producing a voluptuous movement of the lovely thighs and little exclamations that he found delightful.

"Oh! Oh! Oh! Don't do that! Oh! Oh! How dreadful! Oh, please, uncle!" she shrieked, trying to turn round, which, of course, the straps prevented. He next proceeded to birch her gently all over, the strokes increasing in vigor, but being always confined to the bottom.

"Oh, uncle, you hurt! Oh! How the horrid thing stings! Oh! It is worse than your hand! Oh! Stop! Have I not had enough?"

"We will begin now, miss," said he, having given her a cut severe enough to provoke a slight cry of real pain; "and Maud will count."

Lifting up the rod at right angles to the table on which she was bound down, he brought it down with a tremendous swish through the air across the upper parts of her hips.

"One," said the mellow voice of Maud—her right hand and a portion of her arm hidden under her uncle's kilt, the movements of its muscles under the delicate skin and the wriggles of the Baronet showing that Maud had hold of and was kneading a sensitive portion of his frame. The bottom grew crimson where the stroke had fallen, and the culprit emitted a yell and gasped for breath. With the regularity of a steam hammer, he again raised the rod well above his shoulder, and again making it whistle through the air, he gave her another very severe stroke.

"Two," said Maud quietly.

A shriek. "Oh! Stop! Oh! Stop! Oh! Stop!"

Swish. "Three," calmly observed Maud.

"Oh! You will kill me. Oh! I can't—I can't"

Swish. "Four, uncle."

"Oh, ah! Oh, I can't bear it! Oh, I will be good! Oh, Maud, ask him to stop."

Swish. "Five."

Maud had given her uncle an extra pull when Amy had appealed to her, and this stroke was harder in consequence. Spots of blood began to appear where the ends of the birch and its buds fell, especially on the outside of the thigh. The yell which followed number five was more piercing, and choking sobs ensued; but Sir Charles, merely observing that she would run a very good chance of extra punishment if she made so much noise, without heeding her tears or contortions or choking, mercilessly and relentlessly gave her six, seven, eight, and nine, each being counted by Maud's clear gentle voice.

"Now, miss, you've had half of your punishment…"

"Half! Oh! Oh! Oh! I can't bear more! Oh, I can't bear more! Oh, let me off! You will kill me! Oh, let me off! I will—I will—I will indeed be good."

"I suppose you begin to regret your disobedience."

"Oh, don't punish me any more," cried the girl, wriggling and struggling to get free—of course ineffectually, but looking perfectly lovely in her pain.

"Yes! You must receive the whole number. It is not enough to promise to obey now; you should have thought of this before. You are now having your bottom punished, not only to make you better in the future, but for your past offenses."

And Sir Charles walked round to the right side of his niece, and there, in the same place, but from right to left, gave her three sharp cuts. Amy yelled and screamed and roared and rolled about as much as she possibly could, perfectly reckless as to what she showed.

The next three were given lengthwise between her legs. Her bottom being well up, and the legs well apart, the strokes fell upon the tender skin between them, and the long, lithe ends of the rod curled round her cunt, causing her a great deal of pain.

"There is nothing like a good birching for a girl." Swish.

"One," said Maud, moving voluptuously. "Oh! Oh! Yah! Oh! My bottom! Oh! My legs! Oh! How it hurts! Oh! Oh! Oh!"

"They are all the better for the pain!" Swish.

"Two," said Maud.

"Oh! Oh! Oh! Oh, don't strike me there!" as the birch curled round her cunt.

"And the exposure. I do not think you will disobey." Swish.

"Three," said Maud, apparently beside herself, her eyes swimming.

"Oh! Oh! Oh! Yah! Oh! I shall die! I shall faint! Oh! Dear uncle! I will—please forgive me—I will never disobey. I will do anything—anything—ANYTHING!"

"I daresay you will, miss; but I shall not let you off"—swish"there's another for your cunt."

"Four," said Maud.

"Oh! Oh! Not there! Oh! I am beside myself! I shall go mad! I shall die or go mad!"

"You will not do anything of the sort, and you must bear your punishment." Swish.

"Five," counted Maud.

The cries gradually lessened, and the culprit seemed to become entranced, whereupon the uncle, at whom Maud looked significantly, directed the single remaining stroke to the insides of her thighs, leaving the palpitating red rose between them free from further blows, for the present.

Amy's moans were then succeeded by piercing shrieks, but her uncle, perfectly deaf to them, continued the flogging. When the eighteenth stroke, given lengthwise, had been completed, Sir Charles put down the birch he had used and took a second from Maud.

Seeing this, Amy earnestly implored him to let her go, since the promised dozen and a half strokes had already been administered.

For reply, he again took up his station at her left side, saying: "No, miss; I shall certainly not unstrap you; you have been far too naughty. I will punish you, and your lovely legs and bottom, to the fullest extent. I'll teach you to be good, you bold hussy! I'll give you a lesson you won't forget in a hurry." He gave her nine more blows; but this time, instead of being administered on the upper part of her bottom, perpendicularly, they were given almost horizontally on its lower part, where it joins the thigh. Amy's renewed shrieks were to no avail. In her agony, she lifted up her head, her shoulders being fastened down with the strap, and prayed her uncle, in the name of heaven, to spare her. But the relentless rod still continued to cut into her tender flesh, as she was told she would receive no mercy.

The girl's head dropped again. "No mercy," she whispered, "no, nor justice either, nor even fair play. Indeed, why pretend at all?"

Maud's even voice continued to number the strokes, and Maud herself seemed aflame, and the sight of the agony her uncle was inflicting seemed to excite her sensuality in an extraordinary degree. Her lips were moist; her eyes swam; the eyelids drooped; and all the indications of a very lovesick girl appeared in her. The bleeding bottom, the tightly strapped limbs, the piercing cries, and the relentlessly inflicted punishment excited her strongest passions. She could have torn Amy limb from limb; and she encouraged her uncle, by rolling his balls and pulling and squeezing his prick, to continue the punishment in the severest manner.

She gloated over the numbers as she called them out.

Sir Charles, too, seemed beside himself. His eyes were as two flames as he watched every motion of Amy's body; gloated upon all she displayed. He could have made his teeth meet in her delicate flesh, which he lacerated with the rod yet more severely as his organ, already excited to an enormous size, was still further enlarged by Maud's hand.

At length he judged that, Amy's lower bottom having been striped from right to left as well as from left to right, there remained but nine last lengthwise strokes to be given.

For these, Sir Charles took the third birch from Maud, who by this time was standing with her legs wide apart, uttering little sounds and breathing little sighs of almost uncontrollable desire.

The unhappy culprit's yells had somewhat lessened, for shock had relieved pain; it had been so severe that her sensitiveness to it had much diminished. But now, feeling the rod curling round her cunt, which, being pulled open, was more exposed than ever, she yelled in a perfectly delirious manner.

After some few of these strokes had been given, her uncle asked her whether he was a wretch and a monster, as she had called him last night, she replied with vehement denials:

"No! Oh, no! Oh! Oh! Oh! Oh, no! Not a monster! Not a wretch! My own dear uncle, whom I love! Oh! Oh! Oh! My bottom burns! Oh! Oh! It is on fire!"

"Will you be a good, obedient girl miss?"

"Yes! Yes! Yes! Oh! Indeed"

"And thank me for whipping you?"

"Yes, indeed I do."

"Whip well in, uncle," said Maud quietly in her rich voice.

And he did so. Amy, thus betrayed, shrieked; flooded the floor with urine, and fainted!

Maud, beside herself, threw herself backwards on the long and broad divan, her breasts jiggling, her legs—unhampered by drawers—thrown wide open. Sir Charles, throwing down the birch, fell upon her with a fury. He inserted his enormous appurtenance into her burning cunt, sighing as the lengthy tool was eagerly accepted and drawn deep within the panting girl. Once he had made his entrance, he began fucking her so violently that she almost fainted from delight. As Sir Charles worked himself against her body, Maud looked kindly upon the still unconscious Amy, knowing that the punishment she had undergone was responsible for the pleasure Maud herself was now receiving. Maud sighed delightedly and wrapped her long legs around Sir Charles's back, allowing him to penetrate still deeper within her heaving body. After the long pleasurable minutes spent whipping his beautiful niece, Sir Charles could not long contain himself. His body was wracked with shudders as he grabbed Maud's hips and slammed into her even more furiously. They both exploded and collapsed in a heap on the couch.

When Amy came round, Sir Charles rose from Maud's breast, and then Maud said, in slightly breathless tones:

"Uncle, I told Amy yesterday evening, when she kept me so long before I could succeed in tying her hands, that I would take care it secured her an extra half-dozen."

"Oh, uncle! I beg Maud's pardon. Oh! After all I have gone through, let me off that half-dozen. Oh, dear Maud! Do ask uncle to let me off. Oh, do! If I am birched any more I shall go mad! I shall—I shall indeed!"

Maud, still lying backwards on the couch, supported by a big, square pillow, said nothing. Her hands were clasped behind her head. But Sir Charles said, "No miss; you can never be let off! You must have the half-dozen. It will be a lesson to you." And taking up the birch, he gave her six severe strokes, distributed evenly all over her bottom.

As they were being administered, Maud's left hand stole down to her waist and found its way between her legs.

While Amy was smothering her sobs and cries after her last half-dozen,

Sir Charles again threw himself upon Maud and enjoyed her.

About ten minutes or a quarter of an hour later, he proceeded to unstrap Amy.

She could not stand without Maud's help. The cushion and carpet were soaked with her urine.

"You will tomorrow have a dozen on the trapeze, miss, for disgracing yourself in this beastly manner; you will write out fifty times, 'I peed like a mare before my uncle.' And for the next fortnight you will only pee twice every twenty-four hours. And now come and kiss the rod and say: 'Thank you, my dear uncle, for the flogging you have given me.'"

Quite docilely she knelt down before him, kissed the rod he held to her lips, and repeated the words.

"Will you be a good, obedient girl in future?"

"Yes, dear uncle; indeed I will!"

"That's a good thing. There is, you see, nothing like a good, sound flogging for a girl. Were the rod more in use, how very much better women we should have. Now go with Maud and get some refreshment. I have various engagements, and shall not be in 'till dinner. After lunch you had better have a sleep." And so saying, he packed the two girls off to Amy's room, shut the door to the yellow room, and ringing for a footman, gave orders that the estate steward and horses should be in attendance at the front door in half an hour.

Maud and Amy went to the latter's new room. By Maud's advice, Amy, who was so sore that she could scarcely move, got into bed and had some strong broth and Burgundy, and presently fell asleep. Maud spent her afternoon at an open window reclining in a lounge chair, pretending to read a novel, but in reality reveling in the reminiscences of the morning and meditating upon its delights—and wondering when she would get whipped next herself. The afternoon passed in this manner until she was disturbed by some afternoon visitors.

* * *

It was a beautiful summer's night. The air was heavily laden with the sweet perfume of the flowers in the garden below the windows, which were thrown wide open. There were, besides, several china vases, or rather bowls, standing about the room, full of roses of shades varying from the deepest crimson to the softest blush scarcely more than suggested upon the delicate petal. The only sounds were the gentle rustle of the summer zephyr amongst the trees and the weird hoot of the owls. The deeply-shaded lamps gave animation to the rosy tints of the boudoir. They were emphasized by the yellow flame of the fire which, notwithstanding the season, crackled merrily in the grate.

(A fire upon a summer's night is an agreeable thing.) Between it and Amy there at once appeared to be something in common. She and the fire were the only two black and gold things in the rosy apartment. The fierce flame struck Amy as being a very adequate expression of the love she felt seething in her veins. She felt intoxicated with passion and desire, and capable of the most immoral deeds, the more shocking the better.

This naughty lust was soon to have at least some gratification. Maud had seated herself at the piano, an exquisite instrument in a Louis Seize case—and had played softly some snatches of Schubert's airs, and Amy had been reclining some minutes on a rose-colored couch—a beautiful spot of black and yellow, kept in countenance by the fire—showing two long yellow legs, when Sir Charles noticed that every time she altered her position she endeavored, with a slightly tinged cheek, to pull her frock down. Of course he had been gazing at the shapely limbs and trying to avail himself of every motion, which could not fail to disclose more—the frock being very short—to see above her knee. He thought once that he had succeeded in catching a glimpse of the pink flesh above the yellow stocking.

Amy, sensible of her uncle's steadfast observation, was more and more overwhelmed with the most bewitching confusion; her coy and timid glances, her fruitless efforts to hide herself, only serving to make her more attractive.

Maud looked on with amusement from the music stool where she sat pouring liquid melody from her pretty fingers, and mutely wondering whatever had come over Amy, and whatever had become of the healthy delight in displaying her charms of which she had boasted before dinner. Maud felt very curious to know how it would end.

"Amy," her uncle said at last with a movement of impatience, "have you begun to write out that sentence I told you to write out fifty times?"

"Oh, no, uncle! I have not."

"Well, my dear, you had better set to work. It will suggest wholesome reflections."

So Amy got up and got some ruled paper, an ink stand, and a quill pen;

then, seating herself at a Chippendale table, began to fiddle with the pen and ink.

Her uncle continued to watch her intently. Maud had ceased to play and had thrown herself carelessly on the couch which Amy had just left. Maud's dress, too, was quite low and very short; but in the most artless way she flung herself backwards upon the sofa and clasped her hands behind her head, thus showing her arms, neck, bust, and breast to the fullest advantage; and pulling her left foot up to her thigh, made a rest with the left knee for the right leg, which she placed across it, thus fully displaying her legs in their open-work stockings and her thighs encased in loose flesh-colored silk drawers with crimson ribbons. Her attitude and abandon were not lost upon Sir Charles.

Amy's sensations were dreadful. How could she, there, under her uncle's eye, write that she had peed? And not only peed, but with shame and anger she recollected the sentence ran, "like a mare!"—like an animal; like a beast as she had seen them in the street. And all "before her uncle." Whatever would become of her if she had to write this terrible sentence; to put so awful a confession into her own handwriting; to confide such a secret fifty times over with her own hand to paper? If it was ever found out, she would be ruined—her reputation would be gone—no one would have anything to say to her—she would have to fly to the mountains and the caves. She had not realized, until it came to actually writing it out, how difficult, how terrible, how impossible it was for her to do it. If her uncle knew, surely he would not insist. He could not wish her to humiliate herself to such an extent, to ruin and destroy herself with her own handwriting; neither could he have realized what it would be for her to write such a thing. While these thoughts were passing through her mind, she kept unconsciously pulling and dragging at her frock. If only she could cover herself up. So much of her legs showed, and the long yellow stockings made them so conspicuous under her black frock. Although they were above her knee, unless she kept her legs close together she could not help showing her black garters. And her arms and her neck and her breasts were all bare. She began to feel almost sulky.

"Well, Amy," at length said her uncle, "when are you going to begin?"

"Oh, uncle! It is dreadful to have to say such a thing in my own handwriting—I am sure you have never thought how dreadful."

"You must chronicle in your own handwriting what you did, miss. Writing what you did is not so bad as doing it. And you will not only write it, but you shall sign it with your name, so that everyone may know what a naughty girl you were."

"Oh, uncle! Oh, uncle! I can't. You will burn it when it is done; won't you?"

"No. Certainly not. It shall be kept as a proof of how naughty you can be."

And as she kept tugging at her frock and not writing, her uncle said, "Maud, will you fetch the dress-suspender? It will keep her dress out of her way."

Maud discharged her errand with alacrity. In less than three minutes she returned with a band of black silk from which hung four long, black silk ribbons. Making Amy stand up, Maud slipped her arms under her petticoats and put the band round Amy's waist next to her skin, buckling it behind, and edged it up as high as the corset, which Janet had not left loose, would allow. The four ribbons hung down far below the frock, two at the right and two at the left hip—one ribbon in front, the other at the back.

Maud then walked Amy over into the full blaze of the fire. Putting her arms round her and bending down, she took the ribbons at Amy's left side, one in each hand, and then pulled them up and joined them on Amy's right shoulder in a bow. The effect, of course, was to bundle half Amy's petticoats and dress up about her waist, disclosing her left leg, naked, from the end of the stocking. Maud, with little ceremony, then turned her round, and, taking the ribbons at her right side, tied them across her left shoulder, thus removing the other half of Amy's covering and displaying the right leg. She then carefully arranged the frock and petticoats, smoothing them out, tightening the ribbons, and settling the bows. And by the time she had finished, from the black band round her waist nearly to her garters, Amy was in front and behind perfectly naked—her breasts and arms and thighs and navel and buttocks. The lower petticoat was, it will be remembered, lined with yellow, and the inside was turned out. It and the stockings and the two black bands intensified her nakedness. She would sooner have been, she felt, stripped entirely of every shred of clothing on her than have had those garments huddled about her waist, and those stockings, which, she instinctively knew, only heightened the exhibition of her form and directed the gaze to all she most wished to conceal.

"Now, miss," said her uncle, "this will save you the trouble of vain and silly efforts to conceal yourself."

"Oh, uncle! Uncle! How can you disgrace me so?"

"Disgrace you, my dear? What nonsense! You are not deformed. You are perfectly exquisite. With," he continued, passing his hand over her, "a skin like satin."

Feeling his hand, Amy experienced a delicious thrill, which her uncle noticing, recommended her to sit down and write out her imposition a task which was now a hundred times more difficult. However could she, seated in a garb which only displayed her nakedness in the most glaring manner, write such words?

"Amy," said he, "you are again becoming refractory."

Putting his arm round her, he sat down and put her face downwards across his left knee. "You must have your bottom smacked. That will bring you to your senses." Smack—smack—smack—smack—smack—smack.

"Oh, uncle! Don't! Oh!" she said struggling. "I will write anything!"—smack—"Oh! How you sting!"—smack—smack—"Oh! Oh! Oh! Your hand is so hard."

Then, slipping his hand between her legs, he tickled her clitoris until she cooed and declared she would take a delight in saying and writing and doing the "most shocking things."

"Very well, miss! Then go and write out what I told you; sign it; and bring it to me when it is finished."

So Amy seated herself—the straw seat of the chair pricking her bottom—resolved, however, to brazen out her nakedness, and wrote with a trembling hand: "I peed like a mare before my uncle; I peed like a mare before my uncle; I peed like a mare before my uncle." Before she had half completed her task, she was so excited and to such an extent under the influence of sensual and voluptuous feelings that she could not remain still, and she felt the delicate hair in front about her cunt grow moist. Before she had completed the fiftieth line, she was almost beside herself.

At last, for the fiftieth time, she wrote: "I peed like a mare before my uncle." And with a shudder, signed it, Amy Brown.

During her task Maud had looked at what she was writing over her shoulder, and Amy glowed with shame. So had her uncle; but Amy was surprised to find she rather liked his seeing her disgrace, and felt inclined to nestle close up to him.

Now Maud had gone to bed, and she was to take her task to her uncle.

He was seated in a great chair near the fire, looking very wide awake indeed. He might have been expected to have been dozing. But there was too lovely a girl in the room for that. He looked wide awake indeed, and there was a fierce sparkle in his eye as his beautiful ward, in her long yellow stockings and low dress, her petticoats turned up to her shoulders, and blushing deeply, approached him with her accomplished penance.

She handed it to him.

"So you did, Amy," said he, "so you did," sitting bolt upright, "pee like a mare before me, and here is, I see," turning over a page or two, "your own signature to the confession."

"Oh, uncle, it is true, but do not let anyone know. I know I disgraced myself and behaved like a beast, but I am so sorry."

"But you deserved your punishment."

"Yes; I know I did. Only too well."

He drew her down upon his knee and placed his right arm round her waist while he tickled her legs and her groin and her abdomen, and lastly her clitoris, with his hand and fingers.

He let her, when she was almost overcome by the violence of her sensations, slip down between his knees, and as she was seeking how most effectually to caress him, he directed her hands to his penis and his testicles. In a moment of frenzy she tore open his trousers, lifted his shirt, and saw the excited organ, the goal and Ultima Thule of feminine delight. He pressed down her head, and, despite the resistance she at first made, the inflamed and distended virility was very quickly placed between the burning lips of her mouth. Its taste, and the transport she was in, induced her to suck it violently. On her knees before her uncle, tickling, sucking, licking his penis, then looking up into his face and recommencing, the sweet girl's hands again very quickly found their way to his balls.

At last, excited beyond his self control, gazing through his half-closed lids at the splendid form of his niece at his feet—her bare back and shoulders—the breasts which, sloping downwards from her position, he yet could see—her bare arms—the hands twiddling and manipulating and kneading with affection and appreciation his balls; his legs far apart, himself thrown back gasping in his arm chair; his own most sensitive and highly excited organ in the dear girl's hot mouth, tickled with the tip of her dear tongue and pinched with her dear, pretty, cruel ivory teeth—Sir Charles could contain himself no longer and, grasping Amy's head with both his hands, he pushed his weapon well into her mouth and spent down her throat. He lay back in a swoon of delight, and the girl, as wet as she could be, leaned her head against his knee, almost choked by the violence of the delightful emission, and stunned by the mystery revealed to her. How she loved him! How she dandled that sweet fellow! How she fondled him. What surreptitious licks she gave him! She could have eaten her uncle.

In about twenty minutes he had recovered sufficiently to speak, and she sat with her head resting against the inside of his right leg, looking up into his face; her own legs stretched out underneath his left one as she was still sitting on the floor.

"Amy, you bold, bad girl, to pee like a mare. I hope you feel punished now."

"Oh no, uncle, it was delightful. Does it give you pleasure? I will suck you again, if you wish," she said, taking his penis, to his great excitement, again in her warm little palm.

"My dear, do you want to pee?"

"Yes, before I go to bed."

Then here is the key. Run along and go to bed."

"Oh, I would rather stay with you."

"Although I have whipped you and birched you and smacked you and made you disgrace yourself?"

"Yes, dear uncle. It has done me good. Don't send me away."

"Go, Amy, to bed. I will come to you there."

"Oh, you dear uncle, how nice. Oh, do let down my things for me before I go. Some of the servants may see me. And," she continued after an instant's pause with a blush and looking down, "I want to be for you alone."

Touched by her devotion, her uncle loosed the ribbons, let fall, as far as they would, her frock and petticoats, and giving her a kiss, and not forgetting to use his hand under her clothes in a manner which caused her again to cry out with delight, allowed her to trip off to her bedroom. But not without the remark that she had induced him to do that which did not add to her appearance; for the rich, full, and well developed girlish form had been simply resplendent with loveliness in the garments huddled about her waist; the petticoat lining of yellow silk relieved by the black bands from her waist to her shoulder crossing each other, and bits of her black frock, with its large yellow spots, appearing here and there. And as the eye traveled downwards from the pink flesh of the swelling breasts to the smooth pink thighs, it noted with rapture that the clothes concealed only what needed not concealment, and revealed with the greatest effect what did; and, still descending, dwelt entranced upon the well-turned limbs, whose outlines and curves the tight stockings so clearly defined.

Sir Charles, who had made her stand facing him, and also with her back to him, was much puzzled, although so warm a devotee of the Venus Callipyge, whether he preferred the back view of her lovely legs, thighs, bottom, back, neck, and queenly little head, with its suggestion of fierce and cruel delight; or the front, showing the mount and grotto of Venus, the tender breasts, the dimpled chin and sparkling eyes, with the imaginations of soft pleasures and melting trances which the sloping and divided thighs suggested and invited.

The first thing which Amy noticed upon reaching her room was the little supper table laid for two; and the next that there were black silk sheets on her bed. The sight of the supper—the chocolate, the tempting cakes and biscuits, the rich wines in gold mounted jugs, the Nuremburg glasses, the bonbons, the crystallized fruit, the delicate omelet delighted her; but the black sheets had a somewhat funereal and depressing effect.

"What can Maud have been thinking of, my dear, to put black sheets on the bed; and tonight of all nights in the year?" asked Sir Charles angrily the instant he entered the apartment, and hastily returning to the sitting-room, he rang and ordered Janet up. She was directed to send Miss Maud to "my niece's room, and in a quarter of an hour to put pink silk sheets on the bed there."

Then Sir Charles returned, and giving Amy some sparkling white wine, which with sweet biscuits she said she would like better than anything else, he helped himself to a bumper of red—standing—expecting Maud's appearance. Amy was seated in a cozy chair, toasting her toes.

Presently Maud arrived in a lovely dishabille, her rich dark hair tumbling about her shoulders, the dressing-gown not at all concealing the richly embroidered *robe de nuit* beneath it, and the two garments clinging closely to her form, setting off her lovely svelte figure to perfection. Her little feet were encased in low scarlet slippers embroidered with gold, so low cut as to show the whole of the white instep.

Her manner was hurried and startled, but this pretty dismay increased her attractions.

"Maud," asked her uncle, "what do you mean by having black sheets put on this bed when I distinctly said they were to be pink?"

"Indeed, indeed, uncle, you said black."

Amy Brown

"How dare you contradict me, miss, and so add to your offense? You have been of late very careless indeed. You shall be soundly punished. Go straight to the yellow room," he went on to the trembling girl. "I will follow you in a few moments and flog you in a way that you will recollect. Eighteen stripes with my riding whip and a dozen with the cat-o'-nine-tails."

"Oh, uncle," she gasped.

"Go along, miss."

Amy, to her surprise, although she had some little feeling of distress for Maud, felt quite naughty at the idea of her punishment; and, noticing her uncle's excitement, concluded instinctively that he also felt similar sensations. She was, consequently, bold enough, without rising, to stretch out her hand and to press outside his clothes the gentleman underneath with whom she had already formed so intimate an acquaintance, asking as she did so whether he was going to be very severe.

"Yes," he replied, moving to and fro (notwithstanding which she kept her hand well pressed on him). "I shall lash her bottom until it bleeds and she yells for mercy."

"Oh, uncle!" said Amy, quivering with a strange thrill.

"Go to the room, Amy. I shall follow in a moment."

Poor Maud was in tears, and Amy, much affected at this sight, attempted to condole with her.

"The riding-whip is terribly severe; however I shall bear it I can't tell; and then that terrible cat afterwards; it will drive me mad."

"Oh, Maud, I am so sorry."

"And I made no mistake. He said black sheets. The fact is, your beauty has infuriated him and he wants to tear me to pieces."

Sir Charles returned without trousers, wearing a kilt.

"Now come over here, you careless hussy," and indicating two rings in the floor quite three feet apart, he made her stretch her legs wide, so as to place her feet near the rings, to which Amy was made to strap them by the ankles. "I will cure you of your carelessness and inattention to orders. Your delicate flesh will feel this rod's cuts for days. Off with your dressing-gown; off with your night-dress." Amy was dazzled by her nakedness, the ripeness of her charms, the whiteness of her skin, the plump, soft, round bottom, across which Sir Charles laid a few playful cuts, making the girl call out, for, fixed as she was, she could not struggle.

Amy then, by her uncle's direction, placed before Maud a trestle, the top of which was stuffed and covered with leather, and which reached just to her middle. Across this she was made to lie, and two rings on the other side were drawn down and fixed her elbows so that her head was almost on the floor, and her bottom, with its skin tight, well up in the air. Her legs, of course, were well apart. The cruelty of the attitude inflamed Amy.

"Give me the whip," said her uncle. As she handed the heavy weapon to him, he added, "Stand close to me while I flog her, and," slipping his hand up her petticoats on to her inflamed and moist organ, "keep your hand upon me while I do so."

Amy gave a little spring as he touched her. Her own animal feelings told her what was required of her.

Maud was crying softly.

"Now, miss," as the whip cut through the air, "it is your turn"—swish—a great red weal formed across her bottom, and she writhed in agony. "You careless"—swish—"wicked"—swish—"disobedient"—swish—"obstinate girl."

"Oh, uncle! Oh! Oh! Oh! Oh! I am sorry, oh, forgive…"—swish—"no, miss"—swish—"no forgiveness. Black sheets, indeed"—swish—swish— swish—"I will cure you, my beauty."

Maud did her best to stifle her groans, but it was clear that she was almost demented with the exquisite torture the whip caused her every time it cut with relentless vigor into her bleeding flesh. Sir Charles did not spare her. The rod fell each time with unmitigated energy.

"Spare the rod and spoil you, miss. Better to spoil your bold, big bottom than that," he observed as he pursued the punishment. The more cruel it became, the greater Amy found grew her uncle's and her own excitement, until at best she scarcely knew how to contain herself. At the ninth stripe, Sir Charles crossed over to Maud's right to give the remaining nine the other way across.

Swish—swish—swish—fell the heavy whip, the victim's moans and prayers absolutely unheeded.

"A girl must have her bare bottom whipped"—swish—"occasionally; there is nothing"—swish—"so excellent for her"—swish—"it teaches her to mind what is told her"—swish—"it knocks all false shame"—swish—"out of her; there is no mock modesty left about a young lady after"—swish—"she has had her bottom under the lash."

Amy trembled when she saw the cat-o'-nine-tails, made of hard, tightly twisted whip-cords, each tail bearing several knots, and when she looked at the bleeding bottom, she grew sick and pale. But when her uncle began to lecture Maud as he caressingly drew the terrible scourge through his fingers, and to tell her that for a hardened girl such as she, such a whip was insufficient punishment, and that she must also be subjected to the cat's claws, Amy began to revive, and she noticed that, while Sir Charles again approached boiling point, Maud gave as much lascivious movement as her tight bonds permitted.

But the first three strokes, given from left to right, evoked piercing yells and shrieks; the next three, given across the other way, cries and howls of the wildest despair, followed by low sobs. The purplish-red marks thus given swelled immediately above the surface of the skin.

"You will not forget again, I know," said Sir Charles as he wielded the terrible instrument. "You careless, naughty girl, how grateful you should be to me for taking the trouble to chastise you thus. The cat has quite irresistible arguments, has she not?"

The last six were given lengthwise, first along the legs, then round the bottom, and lastly on the cunt. Maud's roars and yells were redoubled, but in an ecstasy of delight, she lost her senses at the last blow.

Amy, too, was mad with excitement. Rushing off, as directed, to her room, she, as her uncle had also bid her do, tore off all her clothing and dived into the pink sheets, rolling about with the passion the sight of the whipping had stimulated to an uncontrollable degree.

Sir Charles, having summoned Janet to attend Maud, hastened to follow Amy.

Divesting himself of all his clothing, he tore the bedclothes off the naked girl, who lay on her back, inviting him to her arms, and to the embrace of which she was still ignorant, by the posture nature dictated to her, and looking against the pink sheet a perfect rose of loveliness. Sir Charles sprang upon her in a rush and surge of passion which bore him onwards with the irresistible force of a flowing sea. In a moment he, notwithstanding her cries, was between her already separated legs, clasping her to him, while he directed, with his one free hand, his inflamed and enormous penis to her virgin cunt. Already it had passed the lips and was forcing its way onwards, impelled by the reiterated plunges of Sir Charles, before Amy could realize what was happening. At last she turned a little pale, and her eyes opened wide and stared slightly in alarm, while, finding that her motion increased the assault and the slight stretching of her cunt, she remained still. But the next moment, remembering what had occurred when it was in her mouth, it struck her that the same throbbing and shooting and deliciously warm and wet emission might be repeated in the lower and more secret part of her body, and that if, as she hoped and prayed it might be, it was, she would expire of joy. These ideas caused a delightful tremor and a few movements of the buttocks, which increased Sir Charles's pleasure and enabled him to make some progress. But at length, the swelling of his organ and his march into the interior began to hurt, and she became almost anxious to withdraw from the amorous encounter. His arms, however, held her tight. She could not get him from between her legs, and she was being pierced in the most tender portion of her body by a man's great thing, like a horse's. Oh, how naughty she felt! And yet how it hurt! How dreadful it was that he should be able to probe her with it and detect all her sensations by means of it, while on the other hand, she was made sensible there, and by means of it, of all he felt.

"Oh! Uncle! Oh! Dear, dear uncle! Oh! Oh! Oh! Oh! Wait one minute! Oh! Not so hard! Oh, dear, don't push any further—oh, it is so nice; but it hurts! Oh, do stop! Don't press so hard! Oh! Oh! Oh! Oh! Please don't! Oh! It hurts! Oh! I shall die! You are tearing me open! You are indeed! Oh! Oh! Oh!"

"If you don't"—push—push—"hold me tight and push against me, Amy, I will—yes, that's better—flog your bottom until you howl like a dog at the moon, you bold girl. No, you shan't get away. I will get right into you. Don't," said he, clawing her bottom with his hands and pinching its cheeks severely, "slip back. Push forward."

"Oh! I shall die! Oh! Oh! Oh!" as she felt the pinches and jerked forward, enabling Sir Charles to make considerable advance. "Oh! I shall faint; I shall die! Oh, stop! Oh!" as she continued her involuntary motion upwards and downwards, "you hurt excruciatingly."

He folded her more closely to him, and, altogether disregarding her loud cries, proceeded to divest her of her maidenhead, telling her that if she did not fight bravely he would punish her till she thought she was being flayed alive; that he would tear her bottom for her with hooks; and he slipped a hand down behind her and got the middle finger well into her arse.

After this, victory was assured. A few more shrieks and spasms of mingled pleasure and pain, when Sir Charles, who had forced himself up to the hymen and had made two or three shrewd thrusts at it, evoking loud gasps and cries from his lovely ward, drew a long sigh, and with a final determined push sunk down on her bosom, while she, emitting one sharp cry, found her suffering changed into a transport of delight. She clasped her uncle with frenzy to her breast, and throbbed and shook in perfect unison with him while giving little cries of rapture and panting—with half-closed lids, from under which rolled a diamond tear or two—for the breath of which her ecstasy had robbed her.

Several moments passed, the silence interrupted only by inarticulate sounds of gratification. Sir Charles's mouth was glued to hers, and his tongue found its way between its ruby lips and sought hers. Overcoming her coyness, the lovely girl allowed him to find it, and no sooner had they touched than an electric thrill shot through her; Sir Charles's penis, which had never been removed, again began to swell; he recommenced his (and she her) upward and downward movements and again the delightful crisis occurred—this time without the intense pain Amy had at first experienced, and with very much greater appreciation of the shock, which thrilled her from head to foot and seemed to penetrate and permeate the innermost recesses of her being.

Never had she experienced, or even in her fondest moments conceived, the possibility of such transports. She had longed for the possession of her uncle; she had longed to eat him, to become absorbed in him, and she now found the appetite gratified to the fullest extent in a manner incredibly sweet. To feel his weight upon the front of her thighs—to feel him between her legs, her legs making each of his a captive; the most secret and sensitive and essentially masculine organ of his body inside that part of hers of which she still could not think without a blush; and the mutual excitement, the knowledge and consciousness each had of the other's most intimate sensations, threw her into an ecstasy. How delicious it was to be a girl; how she enjoyed the contemplation of her charms; how supremely, overpoweringly delightful it was to have a lover in her embrace to appreciate and enjoy them! How delicious was love!

Sir Charles, gratified at length, rose and congratulated Amy upon her newborn womanhood; kissed her, and thanked her for the intense pleasure she had given him.

After some refreshment, as he bade her good-night, the love-sick girl once more twined her arms about him while slipping her legs onto the edge of the bed. She lay across it and managed to get him between them; then, drawing him down to her bosom, cried, "Once more, dear uncle; once more before you go."

"You naughty girl," he answered, slightly excited. "Well, I will if you ask me."

"Oh, please, do, uncle. Please do it again."

"Do what again?"

"Oh! It. You know… What—what—what," hiding her face sweetly, "you have done to me twice already."

"Don't you know what it is called?"

"No. I haven't the slightest idea."

"It is called 'fucking.' Now, if you want it done again, you must ask to be fucked," said he, his instrument assuming giant proportions.

"Oh, dear, I do want it ever so; but however I can ask for it—once more before you go!" and she lay back and extended her legs before him in the most divine fashion.

In a moment he was between them; his prick inserted, his lips again upon hers, and in a few moments more they were again simultaneously overcome by that ecstasy of supernatural exquisiteness of which unbridled passion has alone attempted to fathom the depths, and that, without reaching them.

Exhausted mentally and physically by her experiences and the exercises of the evening, Amy, as she felt the lessening throbs of her uncle's engine, found she was losing herself and her consciousness in drowsiness. Her uncle placed her in a comfortable posture upon the great pillow, and throwing the sheet over her, heard her murmured words of thanks and love as she fell asleep with a smile upon her face. Janet came and tucked her up comfortably. And she slept profoundly.

* * *

Amy lay awake next morning listening to the birds in a sweet trance as the recollection on which she dwelt of what she had passed through the night before. She felt completely changed, and could she have seen the dark stains upon the crimson sheet under her, she would have known that she really was so.

She met Maud in the breakfast-room and was warmly greeted by her.

"Well, love; well, Amy?" cried she, clasping both her hands in her own and gazing into her face with a glance in which there was deep meaning.

"Oh, Maud!" ejaculated Amy, blushing, and then, to turn the subject, "how are you, dear, after that terrible flogging? I could almost have cried at what you suffered one moment, and yet I could have made uncle tear you in pieces the next."

"Yes," said Maud; "I have experienced the feeling. The result was that you and your uncle enjoyed yourselves the more. Now, wasn't it?"

After breakfast Amy remembered that she had to go straight to the yellow room. She did so without much dread, feeling that she could not have worse to go through than she had already suffered, although one or two chance expressions of Maud had made her doubtful of this conclusion, and the cold sternness of her uncle startled and alarmed her after his warmth and tenderness of the preceding evening. When he met her and wished her good morning in the breakfast room, he was apparently absolutely unconscious, and certainly totally forgetful, of what had passed.

Amy went with Maud arm-in-arm to the yellow room, wondering what the trapeze would be like.

Her uncle soon followed her and locked the door. He had a long carriage-whip and some sheets of paper which she recognized in his hand.

"You are Miss Amy Brown, and this is your handwriting and signature?" asked he severely, showing the papers to her.

"Oh yes, uncle, they are," answered the girl, trembling with fright.

"You peed like a mare before your uncle, eh, miss?"

"I-I-I couldn't help it."

"Did you?"

"Y-ye-yes?"

"Well, you shall be flogged like a mare. Strip yourself."

"Oh, uncle!"

"Strip yourself absolutely naked, or," he said, raising the whip and lightly slashing it about her legs, for her frock only came down to her knees, "you shall have double."

She jumped as she felt the lash sting her calves, and drew up her legs one after another.

Then, seeing her uncle's arm again raised, she began to quickly undo her bodice and slip off her frock; her petticoats and corset soon followed, and, lastly, slipping off her chemise, she stood naked except for her long stockings, and covered with a most bewildering air of shame, not knowing whether to cover her face or not, or how to dispose of her hands and arms."

"Take off your shoes and stockings," said her uncle.

She had to do so seated in her nakedness, and the action added extremely to her confusion.

Sir Charles then went to a bracket or flat piece of wood screwed on the wall on which were two hooks fixed back to back and some distance apart; round them was fastened a thick crimson silk cord. As he unwound it, Amy saw that it communicated with a pulley in the ceiling over which it hung, and dangling from which was a bar of wood, about two-and-a-half feet long, the cord dividing about three feet above it, and being fastened to each of its ends.

"Now, Maud," said Sir Charles, "put her in position and fix her wrists."

Maud walked up to Amy and led her beneath the pulley. Sir Charles allowed the bar to descend to a level with the top of her shoulders. Maud then took the naked girl's right wrist and fastened it by a strap ready prepared to one end of the bar, so that the back of the hand was against it. And then she did the same with the left hand.

"Ready?" asked Sir Charles.

"Ready," answered Maud.

Whereupon he pulled the cord, availing himself of the hooks to get a purchase, until Amy's arms were stretched high above her head, and her whole body was well drawn up, the balls of her feet only resting on the floor.

"Oh, uncle! Oh, uncle! Oh, please! Oh! Not so high! Oh! My arms will be dislocated! Oh! It hurts my wrists!" and, involuntarily moving, she found very little would swing her off her feet.

Sir Charles, finding her sufficiently drawn up, fixed the cord, and, taking the whip in his right hand, played with the lash with his left as he gloated upon the exquisite naked girl, her extended arms, her shoulders, her breasts, her stomach, her navel, her abdomen, her back, her thighs, her buttocks, her legs, all displayed and glowing with shame and beauty.

At last, raising his whip as he stood at her left, he said, "So we 'peed like a mare before uncle,' and are now going to be flogged like a mare."

Amy, in silent terror, drew up first one leg and then the other, showing off the exquisitely molded limbs, and giving more than a glimpse of other charms.

"And," went on her uncle, "on the very part guilty of the offense."

He had raised the whip, swinging out the lash, and brought it down with full force across the front of the girl's thighs, the lash striking her fair on the cunt. For a moment she was speechless, but the next elicited a piercing yell as she threw her head back and struggled to be free.

Sir Charles's arm was now across him.

Whisp, whisple went the whip as he gave the return stroke severely across her bottom, making her dance with anguish and leaving a red weal.

Whisp, whisple went the whip with merciless precision back again.

Amy's gymnastics were of the most frantic description. She jumped and threw out her legs and swung to and fro, showing every atom of her form, in utter recklessness of what she showed or of what she concealed.

When three strokes had been administered backwards and forwards from the left side, Sir Charles went round to the right. There her bottom received the forward and her front the back strokes, and well laid on they were. Sir Charles delighted in the infliction of a punishment which left his victim no reserve or concealment whatever, and he made the whip cut into the flesh.

Amy, almost suffocated with her cries and sobs, writhed for several minutes after the last stroke. At last her agony became less intense and her sobs fewer.

A high stool was then put before her and on it a pot.

It was pushed close up to her, and Sir Charles inserted his hand from behind and tickled and frigged her cunt, saying, "Yesterday you peed to please yourself. Today you shall do so to please me."

Amy, beside herself, knew not what to do. She had not relieved herself since the night before. At last, with a shudder, a copious flood burst out, partly over her uncle's hand, and she gave a groan as she realized the manner in which she had been made to disgrace herself.

Her uncle then loosened the rope sufficiently to let her heels rest on the ground, and calling Maud to the sofa, which was immediately in front of Amy, he threw her back on it, while she quickly unfastened and pulled down his trousers, exposing his back view entirely to Amy. Maud, too, whose petticoats were up to her waist, threw wide her legs, and Sir Charles, prostrating himself upon her, fucked her violently before Amy.

Never was Amy so conscious of her nakedness as then.

Never, apparently, did Maud enjoy the pleasure of a good fucking more than she did in the presence of that naked and tied-up girl.

And never did Sir Charles acquit himself with greater prowess.

Amy's movements, as she saw her uncle's exertions in Maud's arms, and his strong, sinewy, bare and hairy legs, and his testicles hanging down, and heard his deep breathing and Maud's gasps and sighs began again, but this time from pleasure instead of pain. She could not, however, as she longed to, get her hands to her cunt, and could only imitate the motions of the impassioned pair before her by a sympathetic movement to and fro which expressed, but did not assuage her desires—and by little exclamations of longing.

At length the crisis was reached, and Sir Charles sank into Maud's embrace, while Amy could see, and imagined almost that she could hear, the throb, throb, throb that was sending thrill after thrill through Maud, and was causing her such a transport of delight that she seemed about to faint from it.

And then he untied her, and was about to leave them, when Amy said, in a most bewitching way: "Could you not 'f-fuck' me just once, dear uncle?" her face was covered with a deep blush.

Her half-closed eyes, her splendid form, her nakedness, reawakened her uncle's love and reinvigorated his bestowal of those sensible proofs of it in which bodies so delight. He replied, "Maud has made me work pretty hard, my dear; but," he said, putting one hand upon her shoulder as she faced him, "as you honor me with such a command, I should be an ungallant knight were I not to execute it—or at any rate to make an effort to do so," added he as he led the beautiful girl, nothing loath, to the couch whereon he had enjoyed Maud, and gently pushed her backwards. Amid her cries and exclamations and involuntary but pretty reluctance, he inserted himself into her embrace. She inundated him at once, and Maud, perceiving it, slipped her hand between his thighs. This help soon worked the cavalier up to a proper appreciation of the situation in which he lay and to a due expression of his sense of it, to the body's intense gratification especially as her forces were sufficient to enable her to, a second time—and this time at exactly the right instant

Tumble down,

And break her crown

and, fortunately, not "come tumbling after" Jack, as Jill does in the story.

Although her uncle gave her these marks of affection, he did not relent in severity. She was kept without drawers the whole fortnight—a severe punishment! And the stiff white petticoats kept what skirts she had well off her legs, so that, when she was seated, all could not fail to be seen.

And, indeed, after the lashing on the trapeze, she was not allowed any garment at all that day.

She had been given a notebook in which she was compelled to make an entry of every fault and the punishment she was to receive for it.

Amy Brown

In her room on that particular day, aghast at her own nakedness, and thinking herself alone, she had taken up a pair of drawers which, by accident or design, were left there—she had gone to get ready for luncheon—and put them on, when suddenly Sir Charles entered the room.

"What do you mean, miss, by putting on those things? Did I not tell you you were to remain naked the whole of today?"

"I only put them on for a moment. I felt so ashamed of being naked."

"Take out your book and write: "For being ashamed of being naked, and for disobedience to my uncle, I am to ask him to give me two dozen with the tawse across his knee after supper this evening, and I am to remain stark naked for three days."

"Oh! Oh! Oh! Forgive me, dear uncle. I won't be ashamed anymore. I won't disobey you any more. I won't indeed."

But it was no use.

At luncheon she had to sit down naked. All the afternoon she had to go about so. If only she might have had one scrap of clothing on! At dinner she could not dress, absolutely naked again, not even shoes or slippers permitted. And that to last three days more! All the evening naked, and as she thought of it she rolled over onto the pillow of the couch and hid her face, but notwithstanding, felt naked still.

After supper came those terrible two dozen with the tawse. The tawse is a Scotch instrument of punishment and in special favor with Scotch ladies, who know how to lay it on soundly. It is made of a hard and seasoned piece of leather about two feet long, narrow in the handle and at the other end about four inches broad, cut into narrow strips from about six to nine inches in length.

Amy had never seen, much less felt one.

She was commanded to bring it to her uncle, and had to go for it naked—not even a fan was allowed! How could she conceal the least of her emotions? Oh, this nakedness was an awful, awful thing!

She brought it, and opened her book and knelt down and said: "Please, uncle, give me two dozen with the tawse for being ashamed and trying to cover my nakedness, and for my disobedience."

"Across my knee."

"Across your knee."

"Very well. Get up. Stand sideways close up to me. Now," taking the tawse in his right hand and putting his left arm round her waist, "lean right down, your head on the carpet, miss," and holding her legs with his left one, he slowly and deliberately laid on her sore bottom two dozen well-applied stripes. Then letting her go, she rolled sprawling on the carpet with pain and exhaustion.

The three days' nakedness were rigorously enforced.

They entirely overcame and quenched every spark of shame that was left about her, and she was much the more charming. Her silly simplicity, her country ignorance, were replaced by an artless coquetry and a self-possession which took away the breath and struck those in her presence with irresistible admiration.

Other punishments, too, she had to endure, some of them of a fantastic character.

The fortnight passed rapidly, but the last week, during which she was mistress, was a trying one for her. The servants scarcely heeded a baby in short frocks with bare legs except for her long stockings, and became careless.

Many a smacking she received across her uncle's knee in the dining-room, or wherever they might happen to be, for some short coming; often was she sent away hungry from the table and locked up in a black hole for hours because she had not ordered this or that, or someone had done what he disapproved of. And after supper every evening, and all night if he was in the humor, she was required to be at his disposal and to give him pleasure in every form his endless ingenuity could invent. At the end of the week, when her drawers were restored to her, she scarcely cared for them; but had not worn them long when the recollection of having been so much without them gave her the sweetest sense of shame possible.

JESSICA CANE

Jessica Cane adjusted the folds of her blue velvet gown and gazed curiously around her as she descended from her carriage assisted by a footman who had hastened down the broad stone steps of the country manor. Never before had Jessica made a social call on her own, but this first sight of *Hardcastle*—as the manor was called—pleased her. Its stone walls, latticed by Nature with ivy, had long mellowed with age, as if to avow their proud permanence in the county of Buckinghamshire. Glittering in the afternoon sunlight, the trellised windows offered their discreet greeting.

Unaccustomed to hurrying, the aristocratic young lady slowly ascended the steps, where a housemaid awaited her.

'Lady Tingle waits in the drawing room to welcome you, Miss'.

'Very well, you may show me through', replied Jessica languidly, dangling a small, blue parasol from her wrist.

The house was cool, smelling pleasantly of lavender and wood polish. The fragrance of newly baked bread wafted through from some distant kitchen, making Jessica's finely cut nostrils twitch agreeably. Opening two inner doors—since Society will oddly have it that it is impolite for servants to knock before entering drawing rooms—the maid announced Jessica briefly and then left her to be welcomed by her hostess.

Lady Tingle, who had just entered her fortieth year was a woman of imposing figure. A little above medium height, she bore herself like a queen. She was attired in a black gown whose somberness was relieved by a subtle patterning of silvery threads interwoven in the material. Her auburn hair was bunched high, her swan-like neck adorned with a black-velvet choker set in the middle with a single diamond. Her bust, being prominent, announced a rich firmness of flesh beneath, as did the arrogant thrusting of her derriere.

'You are most welcome, my dear', Lady Tingle said in a voice as soft as a dove's feathers. Without seeming to, her eyes drank in the svelte curves which the clinging of Jessica's dress accentuated. Slender, and of equal stature to her hostess, Jessica was in her twenty-third year. Her complexion was marble smooth and clear, with a pretty hint of pink in her face that was enhanced by the noble lines of her cheekbones. Her mouth was full, her lower lip being particularly voluptuous. An aquiline nose, neither long nor short, large hazel eyes, and an abundance of soft, d ark hair completed the most pleasing nubile curves of her figure.

'I fear that I know little enough of the purpose of my visit, save what Mama wrote to me', Jessica said.

'We must have tea and talk', Edith Tingle answered comfortably, and motioned her guest to a chair. 'You need experience no embarrassment, my dear, at the fact that we have not previously been introduced. Your dear Mama is in Switzerland, of course, and, I gather, may remain there for some time. She has naturally been concerned as to your future. You are, after all, the oldest of her daughters and the one whom she cherishes the most. Ah, here is the tea!'

The afternoon comforts of the well-to-do having been served, and the Indian tea being of the finest, Jessica was set a little more at ease, though not a wrinkle of her clear brow betrayed the uncertainty she felt at journeying to make this visit as her mother had requested.

'I know not how long I can stay', Jessica said, failing no more than her hostess to drink in all that she saw, whether of Lady Tingle herself or of the superbly appointed drawing room with its glittering chandelier, its grey and blue silks, and the numerous pretty ornaments that lay everywhere. In particular, the eyes of her hostess attracted her glances, for they seemed to glitter with hidden lights.

'It will depend on your progress, my dear. From the little I have seen of you up to this moment, I would say that a month would suffice—perhaps less. You are here to be introduced to a world of disciplinary experiences all of which will benefit you as much as your dear Mama intends they shall'.

At this, Jessica's mouth dropped, for she could not believe that she had heard what she thought she had, all of Lady Tingle's words being uttered in the most casual fashion.

'I fear I do not quite understand', she responded.

'You have a fine, proud look, Jessica—I am pleased with that. You will not succumb easily, but then it is for the best if you do not, as will come clear to you. Those who do, often prove useless'. Rising, Edith placed her hand beneath Jessica's chin and lifted it. 'Marie, the maid, will show you to your room', she added.

Appearing at first lost for words, Jessica returned her gaze with total wonderment. 'I… I fail to understand, Lady Tingle. I cannot possibly stay more than a day or two. Uncle expects…'.

'What your Uncle expects and what he receives are possibly two different things, Jessica. Do, please, call me Edith. Your clothes will have been wardrobed by now and you will naturally wish to change after your journey. We have much to talk of. There are few enough young men and young women who are sent to me for whom I have any true affection. In your case, I believe I find immediately a charming exception. Ah, Marie— yes, come in. Escort Miss Cane to her room'.

'Yes, Ma'am'.

The maid had entered so silently that Jessica started and then gazed all about her as though in a dream.

'I cannot believe that Mama had any intentions other than that I should make a social call upon you', she said stiffly.

'An extremely social call, yes', Edith laughed, 'but perhaps rather more prolonged than you anticipated and certainly of a nature that you least expected. Marie, I think you had best call Tom. The young lady appears unwilling to rise. You will both assist her upstairs'.

'Madam—no!' gasped Jessica, rising quickly and utterly bewildered. 'I believe you fail to understand who I am. If you will be so kind as to have my carriage recalled, I shall leave'.

'Your carriage has long left, my dear. There is no way that you are going to leave until I judge you fit to do so. Now, Marie and Tom, take her up!'

'How dare you! No!' screamed Jessica, who in that moment found herself in the close presence of a burly male servant and Marie. Unheard of as it was to be touched by mere servants, she felt the outrage of having her wrists seized and drawn behind her by Tom, whose grip she could find no way of escaping from without utter indignity. At the same tune, Marie took her elbow.

'To be bathed, Ma'am?' Marie asked her mistress.

'Yes, you and Amy will see to it. Have me called when it is done', Edith replied to screams from Jessica who was being propelled towards the double doors of the drawing room. Hustled into the great hallway, Jessica fought bitterly against the hands that, as she felt then, were impelling her to her doom.

'Release me! Ah, you beasts, how dare you lay hands on me!' she screeched to no avail. Bundled slowly upstairs, her feet kicked frantically until Tom wheeled her about and, with no more effort than it would take to lift a kitten, slung her over his shoulder. 'No! No! No!' moaned Jessica, beating with her fists upon his broad back the while that he reached the first landing, with Marie following. He then bore her towards a bedroom.

Meanwhile Lady Tingle languidly lit a Turkish cigarette and took from a small chest of drawers a letter which bore a Swiss stamp and which she had already perused several tunes. Jessica's cries reached her but faintly as she unfolded the delicately scented pages and regained her seat to engage herself anew in the message.

'My dearest Edith', she read, 'I write to you with a purpose that you have for several years wished and which we have not infrequently discussed. My sojourn here will be considerably extended, for the air and all about suits me as well as does that engaging rascal, Rudolph, for whose sake I have put England behind me. He and I are of mutual mind, as you well know, and thoroughly enjoy what you are occasionally pleased to call our "sporting activities" together. He is as thorough, my dear, with the strap, the cane, and the crop as ever you were, though his own sturdy buttocks are put to such in turn when I am so minded.

'His daughters, Amanda and Rose, are perfect darlings, the former being now twenty and her sister just attaining her eighteenth year. The little devils have been well bottom-trained, I can tell you. 'Tis a pure delight to unveil their lovely round derrieres and apply the strap or birch or what you will to their refulgent cheeks. Rose is naturally a trifle more hesitant than her sister and occasionally must be held. In such matters your frequent counsels to me are well taken. "An air of mystery should attend all", I hear you saying. For this purpose an upper room of the house is set aside, all daylight being excluded by thick drapes. How delightfully the soft glow of but three oil lamps casts its subdued glimmerings over their naughty bottoms!

'Rose is not yet broken in. I would have it so in a few weeks time upon her nineteenth birthday. As yet the dear girl knows only the occasional brushing of my lips over her heated nether cheeks when the birch has swished across them a full dozen times. In coddling her afterwards, I have naturally soothed her blubberings by moving my mouth lightly upon her own. Her eyes in that mysterious gloom beseech a little more, but 'tis best to keep her for the nonce on tenterhooks. I have but flirted my fingers about her moist cunny once. How ardently her hips writhed, though naturally this sensuous movement was understood to be solely the result of her birching!

'Amanda is quite other. We are as sisters of occasion. Her pleasure in being bound tightly, attired in a short chemise, stockings, and shoes, and with her drawers lowered just sufficiently to display the pretty muff of her pubis, is quite delightful. Thus secured, I bring her to lie upon the bed in the self-same room of mystery, and, having kissed her once or twice upon her ruby lips, I leave her to her anticipations, frequently for a full hour or more. Her waist is slender, as are her calves and ankles, but she is otherwise plumpish, which pleases me, for she beds well thus under a male. Her nipples are thick and conical, her mouth sultry, her titties exceedingly full and firm. You would find it a rare pleasure to possess her.

'But before I am lost in such diverting details, I hasten to the matter of my darling Jessica, whose education in all these respects has been too long neglected. I need scarcely repeat what I have so often said, that my husband, Ralph, is a weakling and totally unimaginative in all matters as concern you and me intimately. Can you conceive, Edith, that, unlike his sterner brethren, he has never once put the girls to the birch? In all such respects they are complete muffs who know not the lingering pleasures that bind the more knowing of us together. As to Jessica herself, she has the core of strength that you will not fail to recognize and must take her place among such womanly ranks as you and I realize to be the only ones worthy of attainment.

'Take her, train her, my love, as you yourself once trained me in my state of unknowing. To no other could I entrust such a mission. She will emerge from the fire well tempered and perfectly understanding of the future delights to which you will have awoken her. Judging the moment as you will, you may then return her home. I expect not to hear from her until then, by which time she will surely be among the chosen, as imperious to give as she is willing to receive. That you will privately apprise me of her progress I doubt not. For the moment I must attend to that of Amanda and Rose. Deprived of the prick for a full week, Amanda's mouth has a deliciously sulky look. Her bottom must be attended to with the martinet before she receives again the manly weapon. As to Rose, I shall leave it to her Uncle to spank her, for he truly adores bouncing his palm off those resilient cheeks. Once he has concluded that entertaining chore, he will be in a fine, stiff condition to perform his next!

'*Au 'voir*, my darling Edith. I wait breathlessly upon your first report'.

Your ever adoring,

Cynthia

Bringing the perfumed pages to her lips in a token salute, Edith smiled reminiscently. It was she indeed who more than twenty years before had first put Lady Cynthia Cane's bottom to the crop before it received its first libation of sperm. Ever before Edith's eyes was the sight of Cynthia's red-streaked bottom, her howls and cries resounding through the stable to which she had been taken. Wrists bound—'to prevent any nonsense', as Edith put it—Cynthia had been hauled over a bale of straw, drawers at the ankles, and her skirts piled well up above her hips.

'No, Edith, no—oh my God, you cannot!' Cynthia had screeched to no avail whatever while a silent housemaid held her down and the first slicing cut of the crop swished across her bared cheeks. 'AAAARGH!' had come Cynthia's agonized shriek, though each swish was controlled with such moderation as marked but did not otherwise harm the luscious moon which her naked bottom presented. Bucking, sobbing, and protesting, Cynthia had received the full dozen before the rubicund knob of a prick was urged between her heated, throbbing cheeks, the possessor of that initiating penis being none other than Edith's older brother, Henry, who had become totally subservient to her whims.

Tight as the entry was, he had affected it until Cynthia's scorched bottom was held rammed to his stomach. The maid was then dismissed and Edith held and coaxed her friend, whose tear-streaked face swung from side to side as she endeavored to contain the throbbing weapon.

'Forty strokes, Henry', Edith had then commanded crisply, holding her left hand clamped down firmly over the nape of Cynthia's neck. Groaning at the sheer bliss of being so tightly ensconced in a bottom he had often eyed but had never seen unveiled before, Henry had commenced his duty, ramming his fiery shaft slowly back and forth within Cynthia's clinging orifice while Edith—beholding all with an expression of great calm— failed not to count each forward plunge as silently as he.

Well-rewarded for her silence upon the matter, the housemaid had thereafter attended frequently upon Cynthia's training. She took such a taste for it that within a month she had bedded with the two friends and become the object of their lascivious toying. By then Cynthia had brought herself more willingly to all that Edith had taught her to suffer and enjoy, and had been so frequently spermed by all the subservient males of the household, that she could, as Edith of times said, have bathed her in the throbbing liquour, had been preserved.

Now from her musings of the past, Edith rose and smoothed her faultless coiffure. Jessica's cries still came from above, as she had expected. It was time for her first lesson.

* * *

Jessica's experiences in the time that had passed since she had been carried upstairs had brought her almost to a point of dumbness. At home, her personal maid, Mary, frequently assisted her in her boudoir, lacing her corsets and such. Not infrequently Mary would dare to allow her warm palms to linger around the smooth silky globe of her young mistress's bottom, while adjusting the straps of Jessica's corsets to her stockings or smoothing out her drawers. Jessica suffered such touches, though they would sometimes cause her to flush and to stir her hips as the delicate fingertips assailed her naked cheeks, bringing curious longings to her mind.

Never before, however, had Jessica been stripped by force, as Marie and Amy now saw to it that she was. Thankful only that the manservant had been dismissed, Jessica spat and hissed while the remaining garment of her white-batiste drawers was removed.

'You beasts, you shall suffer for this!' Jessica moaned, though her protests were now so feeble that she was but as a limp doll. She permitted herself to be weakly along the corridor to a bathroom of such curious aspect as Jessica had never seen before.

The bath itself was marble and like no other she had encountered. It so shallow that it seemed but a trough of elongated oval shape set upon four short and gilded plinths. Warm and scented water lay already within it to a depth of scarce more than eighteen inches. Immediately above the bath hung gilded chains which extended down from hooks. On seeing these, Jessica uttered a cry of alarm and would have urged herself back again towards the door had not the two maids forced her into the bath holding her in a standing posture. Marie clasped her tightly about her slender waist, while her companion took the chains and fastened them with circlets of iron about Jessica's wrists. Held upright thus, Jessica commenced beseeching the pair as she would never otherwise have deigned to do with servants.

'Let me go, I beg you! My uncle will reward you well! Oh, why am I chained?'

'Tut, tut, how the young lady questions things', laughed Marie, taking a fine, large sponge and lathering it well with perfumed soap. 'Whether your Uncle will reward you or you him is something for the future to decide. As to your bonds, they are but to keep you still while you are bathed. Open your legs now, Miss!'

Uttering a rattling cry, Jessica could but hang her head back in quivering shame and wonder as the warm sponge laved her legs, moving ever upwards until its sensuous surface was worked by Marie's subtle hand beneath her dell. Feeling the warm water, Jessica haplessly rotated her bottom. The sensations she had already endured under Edith's caresses had been exquisite, yet that they were the devil's work she was convinced and strove still to suppress them.

'What would I not give to kiss her!' Amy exclaimed, while she herself saw to the additional sponging of Jessica's body above her hips.

'Madam will be very angry if you do', Marie scolded, though she herself could not resist slipping her middle finger up past the sponge and letting it brush beneath the lips of Jessica's cunt, making her quiver adorably. Occasionally Lady Tingle permitted them to sport with some of the girls who were brought to *Hardcastle* for training, but only those whom their mistress considered to be naughty but submissive, having no streaks of arrogance in them and being fit only for 'harem games', as her Ladyship would declare. Instinctively, Marie had already divined that Miss Jessica Cane was not one such. Had she been, Lady Tingle might well have birched her first, for it was thought to be 'as fine a way of bringing a young lady on as any. That she had accorded Jessica much more intimate attentions was a sign of more loving devotion.

Jessica by now had ceased to protest, knowing well enough that there was no purpose to it. Thoroughly washed, she was dried and powdered in the bath before the chains were released and her aching arms allowed to fall. That she would soon enough escape she had no doubt and therefore permitted herself to be taken in silence back to the boudoir, where her hostess had been amusing herself by reading a novelette of a kind that may only be purchased in Paris or from certain discreet establishments in London. The change of expression in Jessica's face amused her but did not surprise her. The mettle of her mama showed more clearly now, save for a slight trembling of Jessica's fingers as she was sat upon the bed.

Edith's nostrils twitched at the fresh and perfumed aromas that exuded from the young woman's naked body. 'Your first experience, my dear, has, I trust, not been too alarming?' Edith asked without a trace of irony in her voice. Women were ever more intriguing to handle than males, for the subtlety of their minds was greater and their instincts more finely attuned. A battle of mind and soul with a male could be won briefly by a determined female. With her own kind the matter was often different.

'Will they not leave?' Jessica asked in as calm a voice as she could muster, for she sat now at least untouched.

'If you will have it so', Edith sighed. She had no illusions that Jessica might attempt to overpower her. It had been attempted but once before by a young aristocrat who had fought like a tigress for a minute until the snarling of a whip around her naked bottom had finally quelled her. 'You will not mind if I take precautions, Jessica?' she asked, letting her book fall upon her chair as she rose. Jessica's momentary curiosity in that moment was her undoing, for her eyes chanced to fall upon an illustration which the open book revealed. In so doing, a fierce blush rose into her cheeks since that which she saw seemed to her the most infinitely shameful thing she had ever encountered.

Alas, that moment of inattention proved her further undoing, for in a trice Marie and Amy were upon her, binding her arms to her sides with a fine rope which had lain in readiness under the bed. While Jessica, now laid full-length, screamed her protests, which were as much of anger as humiliation, her long and beautiful legs were similarly secured until she lay completely trussed and panting.

'That will do', Edith declared, having watched the struggle with passionate interest.

'Oh, my God, you will surely suffer for this! The moment that Uncle learns of how shamefully you have treated me he will…'.

'He will do nothing', her hostess declared, seating herself beside the writhing girl and quelling her further words by placing her hand over her mouth while Jessica's noble eyes blazed into hers. 'Cry and scream as you will, my love, for no one will hear you, save those whose pleasure it is to do so. I refer to the servants, of course. They are completely in my thrall, as are you now, Jessica, until it pleases me to release you. Listen and listen well, girl. You are not here to be tortured, as you appear to think. Did my tongue torture you? Only to a point of exquisite delight, yes. Were the chains in the bathroom rough? They but held you still and prevented unseemly struggling. You do not wish to appear undignified, I am sure, whatever trials you may be put to. There is a purpose to them which you will soon enough understand. Be civilized, Jessica, for I mean to bring you nothing but pleasure and enduring happiness'.

'Don't! No! Ah!' Jessica spluttered, for in that selfsame moment Edith removed her hand and held her ripe mouth down firmly over the young woman's while gripping her chin so that her lips were unable to escape the wanton salute. Little by little, under the squashing of Edith's mouth, Jessica's upper lip rolled back, her white teeth parting haplessly to receive the gliding of Edith's tongue within. Therewith, pinching the girl's nostrils, Edith ensured that Jessica's mouth remained open while her tongue swirled about hers.

Long, long did this kiss of illicit passion last, while Jessica quivered in her every vein. Not even her dear mama had kissed her upon the mouth before and the experience flooded her mind with unwonted pleasure against which she still willfully fought. Knowing her victim better even than she did herself, however, Edith relinquished her grip upon Jessica's chin and allowed her palm to float lightly and in the most teasing manner over the rosebud nipples, which peeped amid the binding ropes.

Her nose still pinched twixt Edith's finger and thumb, Jessica gurgled and twisted. Their saliva mingled as did their tongues. Electric thrills coursed through her tits, which the bonds caused to swell even more. Her nipples rose like thorns and her scented cunt moistened anew. Bubbling out her breath, she gave a long, low sob that throbbed with untold passions, as Edith slowly withdrew her mouth and hands.

'A kiss between women—is it not the most voluptuous thing?' Edith asked softly while yet Jessica endeavored to gather both her breath and her mind. Before she could do either, Edith had rolled her over so that she lay helpless upon her belly.

'You must, must, must let me go—please, oh please!' Jessica whimpered.

'No., my dear, that is the last thing I shall do. Rather, I shall bring you to me, but these are words you will not understand yet, for your mind and your soul are not yet broken away from the dull, meddlesome world you would otherwise have inhabited'.

So saying, Edith slowly divested herself of her gown, beneath which she wore naught but a black waist corset which left her mammalian beauties completely bared, and patterned stockings of the sheerest black silk. Going then to an armoire, she drew forth a martinet whose thongs hissed menacingly as they sleeked down one noble thigh.

'Has no part of your adorable body been caressed before, Jessica?' she asked.

'My God, no—how dare you ask me such a thing! YEEE-AAAARGH!' screeched the tightly bound young woman, as, without further ado, the thongs hissed across her naked bottom cheeks, leaving in their path a fierce singeing of fire.

'Never, Jessica? By no one?' came Edith's voice insistently. "Think carefully before you reply. Let me give you something to stir your thoughts, my pet'.

'OW-OUCH! NEEE-YNNNNG! Stop it! Don't Ah, it burns! You beast, you beast—OUCH!'

Again and again the martinet sang its song now, sweeping this way and that as the tortured orb of Jessica's bottom writhed and jerked. Streaks of white fire seemed to be invading her ardent buttocks, the long tongues of heat reaching into her every crevice.

'NEVER, Jessica? Mark carefully your reply or a dozen more will fall!'

'BOO-BOO-BOO-BOOO!' Jessica sobbed, for with each word the thongs hissed their paths across her blazing cheeks, which tightened visibly at every stroke. 'Ah! AH! Ah, God, stop, Yes! My… my… MY maid… she… she has touched my bottom in assisting m… me to dress. YOOOOH!'

'Indelicately, nicely, has she touched you, Jessica?'

'YA-AH-AAAAH! Oh, stop, please, stop, YES! She f… f… feels me there—oh, I am ashamed to tell it! OH!'

Sobbing uncontrollably, Jessica was spun over once more onto her back, her scorched bottom throbbing and jerking to the unwonted contact with the silky bedcover upon which Edith nevertheless firmly pressed her so that Jessica's agonized and weeping eyes stared up into her own.

'You are not untruthful, then', Edith purred. 'No, do not struggle, my girl, for a hot bottom is best alleviated by being pressed into something—preferably the torso of a male with a hard prick. The sensation is torturous but yet quite delicious when the waiting knob slips in. Every wriggle of the bottom but assists the invasion that follows. It is called corking, or sheathing, or ramming, or what you will—exactly as in the drawing in my book upon which your eyes fell. Look again, Jessica!' Edith commanded, picking up the volume and holding it before the young woman's bleared eyes.

'It is h… hateful, wicked, oh, I cannot! Take it away!' Jessica pleaded while with a taunting smile Edith traced the outlines of the drawing with her finger. Perfectly delineated, it showed a young woman bent over the back of a chair in the seat of which knelt an older one holding her arms. On the floor lay a cane whose handiwork was evinced by the parallel stripes marking the girl's round bottom. To the rear of her, his knees slightly bent and his trousers at his ankles, crouched a man whose rearing penis was pointed directly between her nether cheeks.

'Wicked, indeed! Such pleasures', Edith laughed throatily, and then, with a sinuous wriggle, slid full down upon Jessica so that every inch of their warm bodies curved into one another's.

'No! Please, no!' Jessica sobbed. Unable now to squirm her blazing bottom as she wished, she was forced to lie still under the heavy, voluptuous weight of Edith, whose stiff nipples rubbed upon her own and whose hairy bush was couched upon hers. 'Lie still, lie still, and say nothing. NOTHING, do you hear? Or I shall whip you more fiercely, my naughty one', Edith both chided and soothed in the same breath.

'I c… cannot! It is wicked, wicked, wicked!' Jessica choked. Her cheeks, wet with tears, were stroked by Edith's hand. Edith's mouth brushed hers softly.

'Many are the delights of the world that are wicked, my love. Be certain only that mine will eventually prove the most delightful. In but a moment, when the warmth of my breasts and belly and thighs and the hungry heat of my cunt have fully invaded you, I shall leave you here to lie still. Wine and food will be brought to you and then you will sleep. When you awake it will be to find yourself as helplessly bound as you are now'.

'No, no! Oh, Lady Tingle—Edith—let me go, let me go home, please! I swear to say nothing of this if only you will!'

'SHUSH!' Edith commanded her softly. 'There is much for you to learn. Think upon it, Jessica. You will not know what will happen to you when you awake, though it shall not be dire. You will remain a victim of my pleasures until you discover your own'.

'NO-OH!' Jessica's wail came then, but, even as her cry echoed through the sumptuous boudoir, so Edith gathered up her gown and departed smoothly and silently, closing and locking the door behind her.

Eyes glazed and bottom cheeks still twitching from their unaccustomed basting, Jessica wriggled, and then with a sobbing sigh lay still once more. With the closing of the door a terrible silence reigned about her. Once or twice she fancied that she heard muffled footsteps and a murmuring of voices. Each time they appeared to approach, she stiffened within herself and then relaxed again. The stinging feeling in her nether cheeks changed gradually to a warm glow that infused even her sticky quim. From moment to moment, she felt as though she were falling into dreams of her maid's hands soothing subtly under the bare flesh of her bottom. After a seeming eternity, the door opened and her haunted state went to the door. Marie and Amy entered, Marie carrying a large silver tray of food and wine which she rested upon her knees as she sat close to Jessica.

Lifted into a sitting position by Amy, who stroked her hair fondly, Jessica dumbly allowed herself to be fed with smoked salmon and other delicacies. Between bites, wine was gurgled down her throat.

'She eats well—that is the best of signs', Marie said contentedly when Jessica was laid back again, her head on a pillow, her eyes closed. The draught she had been given would ensure that she slept for an hour at least. Her pretty lips quivered and then were still. Falling, as it seemed to her, down a long, black-velvet tunnel she slept.

* * *

Later, Jessica awoke to the sight of Edith looking at her from the doorway. The tray that she had eaten from still sat where it had been left. How long had she slept? How long had Edith been watching her, waiting? Reaching out to the bell pull, Edith drew upon it, summoning a waiting Amy within. 'Turn her about and hold her down, Amy!'

'NO!' Jessica shrieked, but all in vain, for even as the wine spilled over her thighs and her small plate clattered to the floor, the maid pressed her back and spun her over, landing with a thump on her shoulders. From a wardrobe Edith hastened to produce a whip of many thongs, whose black-ivory handle was formed in the shape of a huge penis. 'YEEE-OW!' Jessica shrieked as within seconds the hissing thongs assailed her pouting derriere.

'You disobeyed my injunctions, girl? You will rebel?' asked Edith scornfully, sweeping in the whip once more in such wise that a thousand streaks of fire seemed to course through the girl's bottom, making it heave and writhe.

'HOO-HOO-HOOO!' Jessica sobbed, feeling more and more like a schoolgirl. 'Will you stop? Oh, stop, I cannot bear it!'

'What a ninny she is!' Amy laughed incautiously, receiving such a glare from her mistress that she blenched and fell quiet. She was riding like a jockey on the heaving back of Jessica, whose bottom-cheeks reddened anew as the thongs bit into her as might a passing horde of bees.

'YEE-EEE-EEEK!' she screeched again and again, her cries going completely unheeded by Edith, who thoroughly adored whipping a bottom as round and desirable as Jessica's. Twisting the small whip this way and that, she ensured that not an inch of that luscious flesh was left unassailed. Spots of pink appeared on the flawless half-moons, merging them into an overall glow. 'HAAAAR! I cannot b... b... bear it!' sobbed Jessica, quite unable to unsaddle Amy. The maid's own cunny had in fact moistened much during the delightful conflict, and by positioning herself more artfully she was able to rub it through her dress against Jessica's spine.

Having at last afforded the writhing maiden a good thirty strokes, which left her bottom glowing, Edith tossed aside the whip and slid from beneath one of the pillows close to Jessica's head a slender, velvet-covered dildo, which she sprinkled with sweet oil from a little phial on the bedside cabinet. At that, Amy flung herself forward, and to Jessica's utter, screeching dismay, held the springy cheeks of her hot bottom well apart to expose the crinkled hole that was now Edith's target.

To a thin, high scream from Jessica, the smooth round knob of the enticing instrument was introduced into her virgin sphincter, its passage being so soothed by the oil that in but a few seconds it had burrowed up within. Jessica felt as if all the air were being expelled from her body. Clamping her knees on either side of the girl's waist, Amy held her firmly, watching with greedy eyes the now unimpeded progress of the imitation prick until over six inches of it were sheathed.

'NOOO-OOOH-OOOH! Take it OUT!' Jessica shrieked, as Amy's palms settled firmly down into the small of her back, forcing her bottom to orb up to the wicked offering. The slow insertion and withdrawal of the dildo burned and itched, complementing strangely the agonized burning in her cheeks and causing her belly to ripple and her mouth to sag. Such cries as she subsequently uttered in the increasingly rhythmic pumping of the luring instrument were then more muffled. Shamefully screwing up and then closing her eyes, she worked her derriere fretfully to each in-and-out motion of the dildo, now and then issuing a sob or a gasp as her sensations mounted.

Wise to every tiny movement of the girl's hips, as also to the tenor of her cries, Edith motioned with her head to Amy, who thereupon slid completely off and stood by the bedside. The maid knew, too,, that Jessica had passed the first barriers to pleasure and was now about to ride on the crest. Clawing at the bedcover in her newly found freedom, Jessica nevertheless did little enough to escape the steady pumping of the smooth, persuasive dildo which was affording her certain exquisite sensations she had never previously known. In her momentary frenzy, her teeth bit into the silk bedspread beneath her. Her nostrils flared. Breath hissed from her mouth and nose.

'She is about to come! Quickly, now!'

Amy moved swiftly at Edith's command. It was not the first time that she would have helped her mistress accomplish such a feat as. With the dildo buried full within her sphincter, Jessica found herself twisted about until, laid on her back, her legs were slung over the shoulders of the maid, whose long, wet tongue sought the bubbling crevice of her cunt. Lying beside Jessica and holding the dildo in beneath her, Edith commenced again working it back and forth.

'WHO-OH!' Jessica moaned, assailed now in both her parts. Her face lolled sideways as Edith cupped her chin. Her lips parted, receiving Edith's tongue. Their lips meshed. Jessica's hips worked violently, seeking as though to receive as deeply as possible both tongue and dildo. Violent tremors shook her and a gurgling sounded from Amy, whose flashing tongue was of a sudden coated and splattered with a salty rain sparkling like a brook from Jessica's slit. 'B... b... b ...!' Jessica mumbled incoherently. Her legs, hooked over Amy's shoulders, jerked, her arms enfolded Edith's neck. Extreme quivers rippled through her, another salty effusion flowed into Amy's mouth, and then all was still. With a faint 'PLOP!' the dildo was slowly withdrawn. Amy rose to her feet, leaving the girl's legs to slump lazily down. Edith was kissing Jessica still. Their mouths worked dreamily together.

* * *

When, some weeks later, she returned home, Jessica found only Jemima there, curled up in a chair and looking somewhat fretful. Concerned lest her pretty little sister should be of dull spirits, Jessica sat on the arm of her chair and kissed her fondly.

'Are you well, Jemima? You look a little peaked'.

'I am well, really, Jessica, but life is so boring, isn't it? Scarce anyone comes to call, and Uncle seems especially broody so that there is nothing to be got out of him at all'.

'Well, darling, I intend to see that changes are made about the house now and that we shall indeed have a merrier life. As for Uncle, you may be sure that we shall get plenty out of him. I mean to make it my duty to see so. Did Patricia tell Crissie about my dress?'

'No, she didn't. She is all of a mood, too, and said she did not see why she should have to do it for you'.

'Not to fret, Jemima, I will ensure that she is put into a better frame of mind. Be a good girl and go and tell Crissie for me. Before you do, there is a package I hid behind the stand in the hall. Will you fetch it?'

'Are there presents in it?' Jemima asked excitedly, but before Jessica could reply she had run into the hall and returned carrying a small, black-leather valise. 'What is in it—oh, do tell me! Is it a secret?'

'It is rather one, pet, but I will show you first. Come, let us go up to your room for we shall be more private there and need have no fear of interruptions'.

All aglow with interest, Jemima followed her sister upstairs. Having entered the bedroom and locked the door, to the great intrigue of Jemima, the bag was opened and its contents laid out. Jemima's expression took on one of astonishment. 'Oh, what funny, horrid looking things!' she exclaimed.

'Really, Jemima, they are not horrid at all. Come, sit with me and I will explain. First we have these two pairs of leather cuffs, which fit closely but comfortably around the wrists or ankles. Then we have this broad leather strap, which is called a tawse. The end is split into two, and makes a fine slapping noise. There are several lengths of cord, as you can see, some longer straps for the body, and finally this little whip, which has a full twenty thongs, all very slim, with the ends are tied in a knot'.

'Oh, Jessica, are they for naughty girls?'

'For naughty girls and naughty boys, dear. Have you been naughty while I've been away? I'm sure you have a little. Let's pretend you have and play a game. I will just slip these cuffs around your wrists, so. No, don't struggle, silly, or it will spoil things'.

'Really, what are you doing! I don't want to! Why are you pulling my dress up? Oh, stop!'

'Shush, Jemima! You must not make so much noise—that is one of the rules of the game. If you struggle so hard I shall really spank you. I am just getting your drawers down for a moment. There! What an adorable bottom! To think that Uncle has never so much as smacked it'.

'OUCH! What are you doing? How hateful you are, Jessica! I shall tell Uncle of this, and Patricia, too!' squealed Jemima, as Jessica drew her across her lap and gave her two quite light smacks landed on the resilient cheeks of her chubby bottom. The cheeks were prettily dimpled and of perfect whiteness. Beneath the cleft orb showed an already promising fluff of curls, the whole seeming to invite such titillation as Jessica intended to give it. SMACK! fell her palm again, the impress of her hand leaving a most attractive imprint upon the plump little half-moons. This brought a further yelp from Jemima, who wriggled madly, though, her wrists being bound behind her back, she could little to effect her escape. 'BOO-HOO!' she sobbed, and would have rolled off Jessica's lap had Jessica not caught her. 'If you don't st… st… stop, I shall scream and scream!'

'Very well, Miss, if that is to be the case I shall have to dun your cries, will I not?' With that, Jessica took a black cloth from the valise, which lay open at her side, and promptly gagged Jemima, rolled her upon the bed, and made her draw up her knees.

'No, no, NO!' her sister endeavored to screech but only a thin sound came from behind the gag while her dress and chemise were drawn up high over her hips and her bottom more fully bared. With that, Jessica reached for the little whip of many thongs and began swishing it quite gently across Jemima's bottom, for she had no desire whatever to cause her pain but only to let her feel the first urging of the burning tips, the tiny knots at the ends ensuring that they nipped like bees.

'OOOOH-WAH!' Jemima could hear her own voice echoing in her ears. Her back being clamped down firmly by her sister's hand, her bottom squirmed and bounced while the tips seemed to seek between her cheeks and even occasionally beneath, to tickle her cunny. It did not hurt her half as much as she thought it would, but it was a most funny sensation, and made her nether cheeks grow hot all over as again and again— and now and then with a little more force—the thongs swirled like striking snakes all about her delightful posterior.

'Now, Miss, I propose to give you a fine sixer to polish you off', declared Jessica, who was delighted to see what charming hues of strawberries and cream her efforts were producing. It would do no harm at all for Jemima to be well heated, she decided suddenly, and by no means against her better judgment, for she knew she could wield the thongs as delicately as any or as strongly as might be wished.

'NEEE-YNNNNG!' came Jemima's muffled cry. SWEEE-ISSSH! came the thongs again and again, causing Jemima hips to rotate delightfully while all over her bottom appeared splotches of pink. Her knees jerked, her face grew ever more flushed, and her bubbles seemed to swell until the sharp tips of her nipples pressed through the cotton of her dress. SWEE-ISSSH! WEEEE-ISSSH! SWEE-ISSSSH!.

'Up with it, Miss—come on—two more!' Jessica sang with a most bewitching smile playing about her lips. No sooner had she accorded them, and brought her sister's bottom to a full, rosy glow, then she acted with all such speed as she knew was required. Slipping a sobbing Jemima's gag, she fell on the bed beside her which, being narrow, caused them to lie closely together.

'OH-WOH-WOH!' Jemima blubbered, while Jessica, cupping her hot bottom firmly, held her tight against her so that their titties together and her mouth softly silenced her sister's cries. Feeling smothered and squirming still from the stinging, Jemima sobbed into Jessica's mouth the while that Jessica reached far under her bottom to tickle and tease her cunny.

'BLUB!' mouthed Jemima, who was now seized by so many different sensations at once that she felt even hotter and headier. Little by little as Jessica's persuasive finger moved and, while her tongue twirled all about in Jemima's mouth, her sister quivered, gasped, and then began to cling to her as with her free hand Jessica loosed the cuffs.

'There, darling, there—does it not feel nice now?' Jessica soothed. 'Lift your leg up, darling, so that I can feel your pussy better. There! Ooooh, how moist it is! Don't be afraid for I am going to make something very nice happen. Ah, now I can feel your clitty. What an adorable little bud it is! Shall I rub it more while I hold your bottom?'

'NOOOO! Y... yes... yes! Oh! I feel I'm melting!'

'You are coming, pet, you are coming. Lie on your back now and open your legs well. There's a good girl! Give me your tongue now! Ah, how you are gushing! How lovely and sticky-wicky it feels all over my fingers'.

'GOOOOO!' quivered Jemima. The hot stinging of the thong tips made her bottom bounce still, which of course is exactly what that instrument is designed to do, so that the maiden is brought to respond to the delights that follow. Her legs, held wide open, straightened, and her toes curled while Jessica so artfully kept on brushing her clitty with the lightest of fingertips. Jemima once more spurted and then again until, with a huge contented sigh, she lay still, her eyes wide open in an expression of innocent delight.

'You see? Was it not nice? Keep squirming your bottom, dear, for you may come again, if you wish. Come—tell me that you liked it, for I know you did'.

'It st... st... stung me—oh!' replied Jemima, blushing but at the same time keeping her pretty legs apart.

'It is meant to, for it brings you on. What a delicious little mouth you have—fresh as a peach. Confess to me, you little minx, that you enjoyed it despite all'.

Jemima giggled and hid her face, for she felt both naughty and excited at the same time. 'Yeth!' she lisped, and gurgled quite happily as Jessica passed her lips suavely across her own while feeling the straining of her nipples through her dress. 'You must not do it again though, Jessica, must you?' Jemima asked naively.

'On the contrary, I will return shortly and do it to you again.'

For the next hours, Jemima lay under her covers waiting, impassive even when Uncle came in to gaze at her distraught and violated body. Upon Jessica's return, she huddled up tighter and was completely invisible, forming a shapely hump beneath the covers. Jemima remained still while uttering a little cry as she sheet was drawn down to reveal her flushed face.

'I am disgraced forever! What am I to do now that Uncle has seen me!'

'Consider yourself well looked upon and some benefit perhaps to come from it. All is well now, Jemima. You have taken your punishment and I have no doubt are all the better for it'.

'Why did you whip me? Oh, that I should be held down by a common servant!'

'Hush! We will have no more questions nor remonstrances nor objections. These are three rules by which you are to abide, Jemima. Come, let us lie together as we were doing before I had to correct your rebellious behavior. Place yourself on your back with your arms behind your head. There, now, you are more acquiescent, are you not?'

Jemima's eyes blinked. Relentlessly once more her dress was being drawn up to her hips until, still without her drawers, she lay naked from her navel down. Feeling the tip of Jessica's forefinger brushing about her clitty, she wriggled but did not otherwise move. Her lips pursed together, a soft whistling sound emitted as by hazard from them as the finger teased. Caressing her fondly, Jessica passed her free hand beneath her sister's bottom and felt its throbbing warmth. Thereat, Jemima jerked and would have brought her arms down but was stayed by a warning murmur.

'D… d… d…! You are p… putting your finger in there!' came a stutter.

'Yes, my darling, where the Major put his prick. Do not pretend to me any longer that it is not to your liking. Roll upon your hip now and pass your upper leg over mine that I can attend to you. Wind your arms about my neck but loosely and pass your tongue between my lips. Your bottom is pleasantly hot for the exercise, my love'.

Hissing through her nostrils with an excitement she could no longer deny herself, Jemima kissed, tongued, and worked her hips lewdly as simultaneously Jessica's fingers inserted themselves, the one in her bottom and the other in her slit. Warmly their breaths flowed together, the moisture from their lips and mouths sweet to one another's.

'Uncle had his cock well up for you, my sweet. It is the best of signs'.

'Jessica! Nooooo! Oh, do not speak of… AAAH! OOOOH!'

'His eyes were languid with desire, his balls full. He spoke of your bottom, your cunt, your thighs. Had I remained in the study a moment longer with him he would have delved into my drawers. How wicked of him! I have locked him in'.

'HAAAAAR!' Jemima sobbed. Her legs straightened full down, her toes straining. She held Jessica's finger in her rosehole full to the second knuckle while her sister's other hand beneath her quim brought her to the very peak of fulfillment. Just as it is said that a drowning person sees his whole life flash before him, so Jemima obtained the most vivid glimpses of the licentious behavior into which she had been driven with the Major. All now had changed in her life and to nothing but the present could she retreat. Licking the pink, wet tip of her tongue against Jessica's, she released the spilling flow of her juices with utter abandon, heated the more by the insensate whisperings of her sister into her pleasure-wobbling mouth.

BERTHA STEPHENS

The Story of a Woman's Part
in the Struggle to Free the Slaves

An Account of the Whippings, Rapes, and Violences that Preceded the Civil War in America, With Curious Anthropological Observations on the Radical Diversities in the Conformation of the Female Bottom and the Way Different Women endure Chastisement

In *The Memoirs of Bertha Stephens,* the true adventures of the brave women of the "underground railway" are related with a candor and a graphic beauty rarely encountered in any literature.

CHAPTER ONE:

A young girl's humiliating experiences, death of my father; how I made Miss Ruth Matthews's acquaintance and what came of it; helping to free the slaves.

My name is Bertha Stephens, I am just twenty-six years of age and I was born in Philadelphia, where my father was a clerk in a bank. I was his only

Bertha Stevens

child and my mother died when I was two years old, so I have no remembrance of her. My father's salary was small, but he gave me as good an education as his means would allow, his intention being that I should gain my living as a school teacher.

He was a silent, stern, reserved man, who perhaps may have been fond of me in his way: but he never showed any outward sign of affection, and he always kept me under strict discipline. Whenever I committed a fault, he would lay me across his knees, turn up my short petticoats, take down my drawers and spank me soundly with a broad piece of leather. I was a plump, soft, thin-skinned girl who felt pain acutely, and I used to shriek and kick up my heels and beg for mercy —which however, I never received, for he would calmly go on spanking me till my poor little bottom was as red as fire and I was hoarse with screaming. Then when the punishment was over and my trembling fingers had buttoned up my drawers, I would slink away with smarting bottom and streaming eyes ° our old servant who had been my nurse, and she would sympathize with me and comfort me till the smart of the spanking had passed off.

Our life was a rather lonely one; we had no relatives, my father did not care for society of any sort and I had very few girl friends of my own age; but I was strong and healthy, my disposition was cheerful and, fortunately, I was fond of reading, so, though I often felt very dull, I was not absolutely unhappy as a child.

And so the years rolled on, quietly and uneventfully. My childhood passed, I was eighteen years of age and had grown to my full height of five feet, four inches; my figure was well rounded, and I was quite a woman in appearance. I had begun to chafe at the monotony and repression of my life, and was sometimes very willful and disobedient. But I always suffered on such occasions, for my father still continued to treat me as a child, taking me across his knees and spanking me whenever I offended him. Moreover, he informed me that he would spank me every time I misbehaved until I was twenty years old. This was very humiliating to a girl of my age, especially since I had become rather romantic and had begun to think of sweethearts. But I never dreamed of resisting my father's authority, so I took my spankings —which, I must confess, were sometimes well deserved—with as much fortitude as I could muster up.

But a change in my life was soon to come. My father was seized with an attack of pneumonia, to which he succumbed after a few days' illness.

I was stunned at first by the suddenness of the blow, but I cannot say that I felt much grief at my loss. My father had never made a companion of me, and, whenever I had tried to interest him in my little affairs, he had invariably shown himself utterly unsympathetic. However I had not much time to think over the past; my position r s it was at that moment had to be faced, and a most unfortunate one it was.

My father had died in debt, and the creditors were pressing for payment. I had no money, so the furniture of the house was sold by auction, and, when everything had been settled, I found myself without a cent, homeless and quite alone in the world.

I lived for a month with my old nurse. She would have kept me with her always, had she been able but she had her own living to make, so she was obliged to go into service again. Then I would have been compelled to seek shelter in the poor house had it not been for the kindness of a lady who, hearing of my friendless and forlorn condition, took me into her house.

Her name was Miss Ruth Matthews, and she was at that period thirty years of age. She belonged to the Quaker sect, or, as she called it, "The Society of Friends." She was a virgin, she had no lovers, she was her own mistress and she lived in a large house about two miles from the city. She was well off and she made good use of her money, spending most of it in charity. Her time was chiefly occupied in philanthropic work of all sorts, and she was always ready to give a helping hand to anyone who needed a start in Me.

As time passed Miss Matthews became like an elder sister to me. I likewise grew very fond of her. She admired my face and figure, and always liked to see me nicely dressed, so she gave me lace-trimmed petticoats, drawers and chemises, and also several pretty frocks, though she herself was content with the plainest of under-linen and she always wore the Quaker costume, a plain bodice with a straight-cut skirt of drab, dove-colored material.

As a matter of course, Miss Matthews hated the institution of slavery and was an ardent member of the abolitionist party. She supplied funds to and was in constant communication with "Friends" in the Southern States who were in charge of "underground stations," and she frequently received into her house escaped slaves of both sexes whom she kept till they got employment. She could harbor the fugitives openly because Pennsylvania was a free state, but we later headed to another house further south.

Bertha Stevens

CHAPTER TWO:

My new style of life; redeeming the slave; our first runaways and how we passed them "underground".

The house we lived in was well-adapted for our purpose, owing to its isolated position. Our nearest neighbor lived three miles away and the little town of Hampton, whence we got our supplies, was also three miles distant. The weather was quite warm; however, it agreed with me, and I was in splendid health and condition. Dressed in a plain linen costume with a broad-brimmed straw hat on my head I daily roamed about the country, soon making the acquaintance of a number of plantation slaves, who, seeing that I took an interest in them, were always glad to talk to me; they used to bring me presents of bits of "possum" and "coon," two animals which the Negroes are very fond of, but neither Miss Matthews nor I could touch the meat.

I sometimes visited the slaves' quarters on the plantations and always was heartily welcomed. But I was obliged to pay my visits very secretly, for, if the owners of the slaves or the ordinary white folks in the neighborhood had discovered that I was visiting the quarters, my motives would at once have been suspected. (Though the Negroes whose acquaintance we had made never hinted at the subject, I felt pretty sure that they all guessed why we had taken up our abode in their midst.)

Three months passed, and during the whole of that period the work at our station had gone on smoothly. Sometimes in one week we would have two or three fugitives; on other occasions several days would pass without a single runaway arriving. Whatever the case, they always came after dark to the back of the house and the first thing we did was to give them a good meal, then put them in the barn for the night. Next day we fed them well, and, as soon as it was dark, we supplied them with a packet of provisions and they started off for the next station, walking all night and hiding in the woods during the day. (If, as sometimes happened, the fugitive was a woman who was too tired to go on after only one night's rest, we kept her till she felt able to continue her journey.)

The runaways were of all sorts: old men and young men, old women and girls, and sometimes a woman with a baby in her arms. Some of the fugitives were in good condition and decently clothed, others were gaunt and ragged, having come long distances and having been many days on the road. Some had come even from the extreme South of Florida. Many were scarred with the marks of the lash, some bore marks of the branding iron, and others had open or half-healed wounds on their bodies. But all the poor creatures who passed through our hands were intensely grateful to us, and we often heard their stories, which were in many cases most pitiful. I need not enter further into details of our management of the station, but I will give you a short account of one of the cases which came under our notice.

One night Miss Matthews and I were sitting as usual in the parlor, chatting and sewing. The lamps had been lit, the curtains had been drawn and everything was quiet and snug. There had been no arrivals for upwards of a week, and Miss Matthews had just said: "I wonder if anyone will come tonight." Then, suddenly, we heard a low tapping at one of the windows.

I ran to the door and opened it, and, as I did, a girl staggered up to the threshold, then fell fainting at my feet. I called to Miss Matthews, who, with Martha, at once came to my assistance. We carried the girl into the parlor and laid her on the sofa.

She was a very light-colored quadroon, with a pretty face and long, wavy, dark brown hair, which was flowing in disorder over her shoulders. Her age appeared to be about sixteen, but her figure was fully developed, the rounded contours of her bosom showing plainly under her thin bodice. (Females of her race soon mature.) She was evidently not a field slave, as her hands did not show signs of hard work, and her clothes were of good material, though they were draggled and torn to rags. She was wearing a neat pair of shoes, but they, as well as her stockings, were covered with mud. We soon brought her round, and she opened her great brown eyes which had a hunted look in them, while her face wore an expression of pain and weariness. We gave her a bowl of soup, and some bread and meat, which she ate ravenously, telling us that she had had nothing for twenty-four hours.

Because the girl was so weak and ill, we did not send her to the barn. Instead, as soon as she had finished her supper, I took her upstairs to the spare room, telling her to undress and go to bed. She looked bashfully at me, but after a moment's hesitation took off her frock and petticoats. She wore no drawers, and I noticed immediately that the back of her chemise was plentifully stained with spots of dried blood. I knew what that meant! Going up to the girl, I raised her chemise and looked at her bottom. The whole surface was covered with livid weals, and the skin was cut in a great many places.

I soon got her to tell me why she had been so severely whipped. It was the old story. She belonged to a planter, a married man with young children, who lived about twenty-five miles away. She was one of his wife's maids. Her master had taken a fancy to her and had ordered her to be in his dressing room at a certain hour one evening. She was a virgin, and she disobeyed the order. Next day she was sent with a note to one of the overseers who took her to the shed used as a place of punishment. He then informed her that her master had sent her to be whipped for disobedience.

She was stretched over the whipping block. Her wrists and ankles were held by two male slaves. Then the overseer laid bare her bottom and whipped her with a hickory switch till the blood trickled down her thighs. She then was allowed to go, being told that if she did not obey her master she would find herself on the whipping block again.

But she was a plucky girl, and she determined not to surrender her maidenhead. So she ran away that night, sore and bleeding as she was, and made her way for twenty-five miles through the woods and byways until she reached our house. She had heard that we were kind to slaves, and she thought that we would hide her from her master.

We did hide her, keeping her for a week. Then we sent her on to the next station along with a man who happened to arrive just at the right time.

Now I will return to my own story, and that of Miss Matthews, for our fates at this period became linked together even more closely than they had been.

Time passed and everything continued to go on quietly. Miss Matthews was still full of enthusiasm for the work, but I had got rather sick of it. The stories of cruelty I constantly was hearing and the sights which I sometimes saw made my heart ache. Moreover I was tired of the loneliness of my life. I wanted some companions with whom I could laugh and chatter freely and frivolously. Though Miss Matthews was always sweet and amiable, her conversation was not of a light sort.

Occasionally, too, a feeling of fear would come over me: we might be found out. I did not feel so brave as formerly. I dreaded being put in jail and having my hair cut. And I did not like the idea of the hard labor and the scanty fare.

However, so far, I had had no cause for alarm. We had come to be well known by the people in the neighborhood, but no one suspected that the two quiet women living by themselves in the lonely house were engaged in unlawful practices. There had never been an instance known of an "underground station" being run by women.

The ordinary white people—and by that expression I mean the white folks who did not own slaves—were always civil to us whenever we had anything to do with them. Many of them were very rough-looking fellows, and there were some lazy loafers. But there were also a number of respectable, hardworking men with wives and families. Strange to say, all these whites, though not one of them owned a Negro, were staunch upholders of slavery. They sold us venison, wild turkeys, and fish, all of which were welcome additions to our usual homely fare.

CHAPTER THREE:

The results of my resistance; the inutility of goodness; an unwelcome visit, which leads to the humiliation of our persons and the ravishment of my virgin state.

As soon as he was out of sight, I twisted up my hair and arranged the disorder of my attire as much as was possible; then I hurried home, and fortunately got up to my room without being seen by either Miss Matthews or Martha.

Locking the door, I undressed, for my clothes were in a dreadful state; my frock, a white one, was torn at the gathers nearly all the way round, and the back was stained green; the strings of my petticoats were broken, my chemise was torn and my drawers were hanging in ribbons about my legs; my thighs were covered with black marks made by the pressure of the man's fingers, and I was sore and bruised all over.

After I had put on clean things I threw myself on the bed, buried my face in the pillow and cried. But my tears now were angry ones, for the keenness of my shame had somewhat worn off.

I was enraged at my foolishness in having trusted myself alone with Zachary, for whom I had a feeling of distrust ever since he had expressed to me his low opinion of the virtue of women. I also felt degraded in my own estimation that he should have taken for granted that I was the sort of girl who would give herself up to a man for the asking. I am sure that I had never given him the least encouragement.

Bertha Stevens

Then I remembered that he had said that I would be sorry for not accepting his offer. I had made an enemy of him, so most probably he would give information about us to the police.

It was not pleasant to think of. I felt that I ought to let Miss Matthews know that we had been found out, but, had I done so, I should have been obliged to enter into all the details of my affair with Zachary. And I could not bear to tell her of the outrage which I had been subjected to. Altogether, through my imprudence, we were in a dreadful fix, and there was nothing to be done but wait miserably for the end, which would be in the jail. (Already in my mind I pictured Miss Matthews and myself clad in coarse prison garments, and with our hair cropped short, toiling at some hard labor.)

Presently Martha knocked at the door to tell me that tea was ready; so I had to pull myself together and go down to the parlor. I could not eat much, and Miss Matthews noticed at once my want of appetite; she also saw that my face was pale and my eyes red, and she asked me what was the matter.

I told her that I had a bad headache, which was the truth. On hearing that, the kind-hearted woman made me lie on the sofa while she bathed my forehead with *eau de Cologne*. Then she recommended that I go to bed, so that I might have a long night's rest and sleep off the headache.

But I did not sleep well. My rest was broken by a succession of horrid dreams in which I fancied that I was struggling in the arms of a man with an enormous member, who always succeeded in overcoming my resistance and taking my maidenhead. In the morning, while dressing, I wondered where we should be in twenty-four hours' time, for I fully expected that Miss Matthews and I would be arrested before the night came.

The day wore slowly away. I was uneasy and restless, I could not settle down to my usual routine of work. I was constantly peeping out of the window watching for the arrival of the police.

They did not come. But, at nine o'clock, a runaway made his appearance in a starving condition, and, in attending to the poor creature's wants, I forgot for the time, my own precarious position.

Several days went by quietly and I began to think that Zachary after all was not going to be so mean as to inform on us. But all the same I was very anxious to get out of the state of Virginia, so I said to Miss Matthews that I thought we had now done our share of the work and that we ought to go back to Philadelphia. Miss Matthews however would not hear of such a thing. She said we were doing good work and that we must go on with it, for some time longer at any rate.

Another fortnight passed, during which period three fugitives had arrived, two men and a woman, all of whom we had sent on to the next station without, as far as I knew, exciting any suspicion, and, since nothing had occurred to alarm me, my spirits rose and I became quite myself again.

I had not seen Zachary since the day he had assaulted me, but I often had thought of the shameful affair, the recollection of it always sending the blood in a hot flood to my cheeks. I had a hatred for the man and hoped that I should never again set eyes on him.

But, alas! I was fated to see him before long, under the most painful circumstances. One afternoon, about five o'clock, we were sitting in the veranda at the front of the house. Miss Matthews, looking very sweet and pretty in a dove-colored dress, was as usual usefully employed in making shirts for the runaways, while I was engaged in trimming a hat for myself. Martha was in the kitchen washing up plates and dishes, for we had just finished tea.

I was in good spirits, and as I worked I sang to myself in a low voice a plantation song I had learned from the Negroes, called "Carry Me Back To Ole Virginny." It was strange that I should have been singing that particular song, for I was very anxious to get away from "Ole Virginny" and had I been out of that state I certainly would not have asked anyone to carry me back to it.

Presently the stillness of the evening was broken by the clatter of horses' hoofs mingled with the sound of loud voices in the distance, and, on looking down the lane, I saw a number of men, some of them mounted, some on foot, coming towards the house. Miss Matthews and I gazed at them as they came along, and we wondered where they were all going; people very rarely entered our secluded lane.

To our surprise, the party stopped at the house, the men on horseback dismounting and hitching their horses to the fence. Then the whole crowd came into the veranda and gathered round us as we sat, in silent astonishment, on our chairs. I noticed however, that there was a hard stern look on the face of every man, while some of them scowled at us with angry glances.

There were fifteen men, all of whom were quite unknown to me, even by sight. Most of them were bearded, rough looking fellows, dressed in coarse cotton shirts of various colors, with their trousers tucked into boots reaching to the knees, and wearing slouch hats on their heads. But there were some men better dressed, and evidently of a higher class.

Bertha Stevens

My heart began to flutter, and a vague foreboding of evil came over me, for, though I had not the least suspicion of what the men's intentions were, I guessed from their looks that they had not come to pay us a friendly visit.

One of the intruders, a man about forty years of age, who was addressed by the others as Jake Taylor and who appeared to be the leader of the band, stepped forward, and laying his hand on Miss Matthews's shoulder, at the same time looking at me, said sternly: "Stand up you two, I've got sumthin' to say to you."

We both rose to our feet, and Miss Matthews asked in a quiet tone: "Why have you and your companions invaded my house in this rough manner?"

The man laughed scornfully, saying, "Well, I should say you ought to pretty well guess what's brought us here. You ain't so innocent as you look, by a long chalk." Then, with an oath, he went on: "It has come to the knowledge of the white folks in these parts that you are keeping an 'underground station.' Since you have been here you have got away a great many slaves. Now I jest tell you that we Southerners don't allow no derned Northern abolitionists to run off our slaves. When we ketches abolitionists we makes it hot for them, and now that we've ketched you and your assistant, we are going to bring you before Judge Lynch's court. The boys who have come here with me are the gentlemen of the jury. Isn't that the right talk boys?" he said to the men round him.

"Yes, yes, Jake. That's the talk. You've put it the right way," shouted several voices.

I sank down on my chair, horribly frightened. I had heard dreadful stories of the cruelties perpetrated under the name of "Lynch."

Miss Matthews again spoke calmly: "If you have found out that we have broken the law of the State, why have you not informed the police? You have no right to take the law into your own hands."

There was an angry movement among the men, and a hubbub of voices rose. "We've got the right to do as we please." "Lynch Law is good enough for the likes of you." "Shut your mouth." "Don't waste any more time talking to her, Jake. Let's get to business," was shouted.

"All right boys," said Taylor, "we'll go into the garden right away and settle what shall be done with the prisoners. We know they're guilty, so we've only got to sentence them, and then we'll proceed to carry out the sentence of the court."

Miss Matthews and I were left on the veranda while the men, all trooping out into the garden, gathered in a cluster and began to talk; but they were too far off for us to hear what was being said.

I sat huddled up in my chair, with a dreadful sinking at my heart. "Oh Miss Matthews," I wailed, "what will they do to us?"

"I do not know dear," she replied, coming over to me and taking my hand. "I am not very much concerned about myself, but, oh, my poor girl, I am so sorry for you. I never should have allowed you to come here."

Too miserable to say another word, I sat pale and silent. The men continued talking together, and there seemed to be differences of opinion among them, but I could not catch a word that was said. The suspense to me was dreadful, my mouth was parched and I turned alternately hot and cold. But Miss Matthews, who still held my hand, occasionally pressing it, was quite calm.

At last the men seemed to have agreed, and they all returned to the veranda. Then Taylor, assuming a sort of judicial manner, addressed us, saying: "The sentence of the court upon you two is that you are each to receive a whipping with a hickory switch on the bare bottom, then you are both to be made to ride a rail for two hours, and, further, you are warned to leave the state of Virginny within forty-eight hours. If at the end of that time you are found in the State, Judge Lynch will have something more to say to you."

When I heard the shameful and cruel sentence which the lynchers had passed upon us, my blood ran cold and I trembled all over. There was a singing in my ears, and a mist came before my eyes. I rose from my seat, my legs shaking under me so much that I had to hold the back of my chair to support myself.

"Oh, you surely don't mean to whip us!" I exclaimed in piteous accents, stretching out my arms appealingly to the men. "Oh, don't put us to such awful shame and pain. Have pity on us. Oh, do have pity on us."

But there was not the least sign of pity on any of the faces surrounding us. All were stern, or frowning, or stolid. And one man called out: "Serves you right, you darned little abolitionist. You both ought to be stripped naked and tarred and feathered after the whipping and then perched on the rail. You would look like a queer brace of birds."

At this coarse joke, there was a burst of laughter from the other men and I again sank down on my chair wringing my hands in despair while the tears streamed down my white cheeks. Miss Matthews, however, faced the men boldly. She turned very pale, but her eyes were bright and she showed no signs of fear. Addressing the leader, she said without a tremor in her voice: "I have often been told that the Southerners were chivalrous in their treatment of women, but I find that I have been misinformed. Chivalrous men do not whip women."

"I don't know nothing about chivalrous," said Taylor gruffly, "but when women acts like men and sets to running an 'underground station' they must take the consequences."

The men in various terms, garnished with oaths, expressed their approval of what their leader had said.

Miss Matthews calmly continued: "I wish you all to know that I am the only person in this house responsible for what has been done. The young lady is not to blame in any way. She is my paid companion and has acted entirely under my orders. You must let her go free."

"Oh no we won't," exclaimed several voices at once. "She must have her share of the switch."

"Let me do the talking," said Taylor. "We know very well, Miss Matthews, that you are the boss of this yer show, but the girl has been helpin' you to run it, so she's got to be whipped. But she won't git such a smart touchin' up as you will. Isn't that right boys?" he asked.

"Yes." "Yes." "That's all right," some of them answered. "Let the gal off a bit easier than the woman." Just then one of the men called out: "Whar's the hired woman? She ought to have her bottom switched, and get a ride on the rail as well as the others."

"Certainly she ought," said Taylor. "A couple of you go and bring her here. I guess she's hiding somewhere in the house." Two of the men went into the house and while they were away the others talked and laughed with each other, making ribald remarks that caused me to blush and shiver. But Miss Matthews did not appear to hear what was being said. She stood quite still, her hands loosely clasped in front of her and a far-off look in her great, soft, brown eyes.

In about five minutes' time, the two men returned and one of them said with an oath: "We can't find the bitch anywhere in the house, though we have looked well. She must have run off into the woods."

"It's a pity she's got away," said Taylor, "but anyhow we've got the two leading ladies of the show, and I guess we'll make them both feel sorry that they ever took a hand in the game."

"You bet we will, Jake," shouted the men. "We'll make them sorry they ever came to Virginny. Let's get to work at once."

"Very well," said Taylor. "Bill, you run to the barn and fetch the ladder you'll find there. Pete and Sam, you go and cut a couple of good, long, springy hick'ry switches and trim them ready for me to use." Then he added with a laugh: "I daresay these yere northern ladies have often eaten hick'ry nuts, but I reckon they never thought they would feel a hick'ry switch on their bare bottoms." The men all joined in the laugh, while I shuddered and my heart swelled with bitterness at our utter helplessness.

The ladder and the switches were brought, then all the men went into the garden. The ladder then was fixed in a sloping position against the rail of the veranda on the outside, and Taylor took up his position near it, holding one of the switches in his hand, while the other men stood round in a ring so that they might all have a good look at what was going to be done.

"Bring out the prisoners," said Taylor. Some of the men took hold of us by the arms and led us out of the veranda to receive the cruel and indecent punishment. I was trembling and crying; but Miss Matthews was calm and silent.

Taylor said to her: "Since you're the boss, you shall be whipped first. Tie her up, boys."

She immediately was seized by two men and laid upon the ladder. Her arms were stretched out to their full extent above her head and her wrists were tied with thick cords to the rungs of the ladder. Her ankles were securely fastened the same way. She had not shown the least resistance nor had she uttered a word while being tied up, but now she turned her head and looking over her shoulder at Taylor said: "Can you not whip me without removing my clothes?"

"No, certainly not," he replied. "You was sentenced to be whipped on the bare bottom. Turn up her clothes, boys."

Her skirt, petticoats and chemise were rolled high above her waist and tucked under her body so that they could not fall down. She had not on the ordinary drawers with a slit behind, such as are usually worn by women, but was wearing long pantelettes which were buttoned up all round, fitting rather closely to her legs and reaching down to her ankles, around which the little frills at the end of the garment were drawn in with narrow ribbons.

"Why darn me, if she ain't got on white trousers!" ejaculated Taylor in a tone of astonishment. "I never seen such things on a woman before."

The other men also seemed surprised and very much amused at the sight of the trousers, and various remarks were made by some of the spectators. I suppose that women of their class in that part of the country never wore drawers of any sort. "Take down her trousers," said Taylor. Again Miss Matthews looked around. "Please leave me my pantalettes. They won't protect me much. Do not expose my nakedness to all these men," she pleaded earnestly.

But no attention was paid to her entreaty. One of the men roughly put his hands in front of her belly and after some fumbling unbuttoned the pantalettes and pulled them down to her ankles, leaving her person naked from the waist to the tops of her black silk stockings.

When her last garment had been removed, her pale cheeks blushed scarlet. Even the nape of her neck and her ears became red. A shudder shook her body from head to foot, she bent her head down and she closed her eyes. I was being held by two men close to the ladder, so I could not help seeing everything.

Miss Matthews, as I have before said, was a tall, slim, slightly built woman. Her hips were very narrow and her bottom very small, but it was round, well shaped and fairly plump; her thighs and legs also were well formed though slender; her skin was of a delicate ivory tint, smooth, and fine in texture.

The men pressed closer to the ladder, and I could see their eyes glisten as they fixed them with lecherous looks on Miss Matthews's half-naked body. Taylor, after gazing for a moment or two at her straight figure, exclaimed with a laugh: "Je-ru-sa-lem! What a little bottom she's got. It ain't no bigger than a man's. By gosh, boys! Perhaps she is a man!" This was meant as a joke. It amused the men and they all laughed, one of them calling out: "Well Jake, you can easily find out whether she's a woman or not."

"Why, so I can, now that you have put it in my head," drawled Taylor, grinning and pretending to be surprised at the suggestion. Then he thrust his hand between her thighs.

Miss Matthews flinched convulsively, uttering a startled cry. Then, looking round at the man with an expression of intense horror on her face and with her eyes flashing, she exclaimed: "How dare you touch me like that?! Take your hand away! Oh, whip me and let me go!"

She writhed and twisted, but the man kept his hand in the cleft of her thighs, saying with a coarse laugh: "She's a woman sure enough, boys. I've got my hand on her slit."

Then he said to her: "My hand won't hurt you. But if I and these other gentlemen were not decent sort of chaps who only intend to carry out the sentence of Judge Lynch, you would soon find something different to a hand between your legs. Now I'll whip you right away, and I guess you'll soon be begging me to stop whipping you."

He withdrew his hand, and Miss Matthews ceased struggling. Her head drooped forward. She again closed her eyes and lay silently awaiting the shameful punishment.

Taylor raised the switch and flicked it about so as to make it hiss in the air. Then he brought it down with considerable force across the upper part of her bottom, the tough hickory spray making a sharp crack as it struck the firm flesh which quivered involuntarily under the stinging stroke.

Miss Matthews winced, drawing her breath through her teeth with a hissing sound. A long red weal instantly rose on her delicate skin.

Swinging the switch high, Taylor went on whipping, laying each stroke below the preceding one so that her skin soon was striped in regular lines. Each stroke smacked loudly on her flesh, and each one raised a fresh, red weal which stretched across both sides of her quivering bottom.

She began to writhe, and she clenched her teeth so tightly that I could see the outlines of her jaws through her cheeks, but no sound came from her lips. The man laid on the strokes with severity, and I wondered how she could bear the pain in silence. I felt inclined to scream, and I shuddered every time that I heard the horrid sound made by the switch as it fell on her flesh.

Taylor continued to whip her ruthlessly and slowly, pausing between each stroke. The weals increased in number and her skin grew redder until at last there was not a trace of white to be seen on the whole surface of her bottom. Her flesh twitched, she winced more sharply, she writhed more and she jerked her loins from side to side as the hissing strokes fell. Then, raising her head and looking over her shoulder, she fixed her eyes, which had become dilated and wild looking, on the switch every time it rose in the air.

Her lips were quivering, her pretty face was distorted with pain, the big tears were streaming down her scarlet cheeks and she began to moan. Still Taylor plied the hickory. Drops of blood began to show all over the surface of the skin. Her contortions became more violent and she uttered a groan every time the switch raised a fresh weal on her bleeding bottom. But the brave woman never once screamed, nor did she make an appeal for mercy. Her fortitude amazed me.

At last Taylor stopped whipping and threw down the switch which had become quite frayed at the end. Then, bending down, he closely examined the marks of his handiwork on the sufferer's bottom.

I also gazed at it, shuddering. The whole surface from the loins to the thighs was a dark red color; it was covered with livid weals crossing and re-crossing each other in all directions, and it was plentifully spotted with blood. It was dreadfully sore looking and its extreme redness contrasted with the ivory-like whiteness of the untouched skin of the thighs. She had been most severely whipped. I think she must have received forty or fifty strokes.

"There boys," said Taylor, looking round at the spectators, "I guess that will do for her. I touched her up pretty smartly, as you can see by the state of her bottom. She won't be able to sit down comfortable for two or three days, and I don't think the marks of the whipping will ever be quite rubbed off her skin."

He then pulled down her clothes and unfastened her wrists and ankles. She stood up, twisting her loins in pain, with her pantalettes hanging about her feet. Her face now was pale and drawn with suffering, her bosom was heaving, her tears were flowing and she was sobbing.

She seemed oblivious of everything except her pain. But, after a few moments, she recovered herself a little and, taking her handkerchief from her pocket, wiped the tears from her eyes. Then she pulled up her pantalettes and with some difficulty—for she was trembling very much—buttoned them around her waist, her cheeks again reddening when she noticed the grinning faces and leering looks of the men standing round her.

Two of the men then took her by the arms and led her into the veranda, where they left her. She laid herself down at full length upon a couch and hid her face in the cushion, weeping.

CHAPTER FOUR:

I am stripped naked and receive a most terrible whipping; the coarse observations of the men; my shame and terror, showing from experience that chastisement by the opposite sex awakens sensations sometimes far from pleasurable.

I have told you all these things precisely as they happened, and I have used the exact words and phrases which were spoken by the band of lynchers who tortured us that day. I daresay you wonder at my remembering all the little details. But such an experience can never be forgotten: all the incidents which occurred during that dreadful period were indelibly printed on my memory so that I have still a vivid recollection of them.

But to resume. You can imagine my feelings as I listened to the coarse language of the men, language such as I had never before heard, and as I watched the proceedings at once so cruel and so utterly revolting the feminine delicacy. I was torn with various emotions. I was horrified at what I had heard and seen; I was filled with pity for Miss Matthews; I was consumed with impotent rage against the men in whose power we were; I dreaded the coming exposure of my person, and I was awfully afraid of the whipping before me. I never could bear pain with any fortitude. In fact, I must confess that I am morally and physically a great coward.

Taylor picked up the unused switch and straightened it by drawing it through the fingers of his left hand. "Now boys," he said, "put the gal on the ladder and tie her up but let me do the stripping."

The awful moment had come, and I became quite frantic at the thought of the shame and pain which I was about to undergo. An insane idea that I might escape came into my head. The men were holding me loosely, so I easily slipped from their grasp and made a dash for the garden gate. Several of the men gave chase, and, though I exerted myself to the utmost, I soon was caught and dragged to the ladder, shrieking, struggling and begging them not to whip me. But my entreaties evoked only laughter. I was lifted up, was placed in position with outstretched arms and was securely bound at the wrists and the ankles.

Taylor now began to strip me and seemed to take as long a time over the work as possible, slowly rolling my garments up one by one till he came to my drawers. Then he paused. I was wearing the usual feminine drawers that are open behind.

"Look, boys," he observed, "this gal has got on trousers too, but they are different from the ones the woman wore. These are loose, and are real dandy ones, all pretty frills and lace and ribbons. And, you see, there is a big slit at the back. I suppose that's there so her sweetheart can get at her without taking down her trousers."

The men all laughed loudly, while I, on hearing the shameful words, shrank as if I had received a blow.

Taylor now untied the strings of my drawers and pulled them down to my knees. I could feel the breeze fanning my naked bottom and thighs. A sensation of unutterable shame overwhelmed me. To be exposed in such a way before fifteen men!

And such men! Oh! It was horrible! I knew that they were all gloating over my nakedness, and I seemed actually to feel their lascivious glances on my flesh. I was hot with shame, yet I shivered as with cold.

But worse was yet to come. Taylor put his hand on my bottom, stroking it all over and squeezing the flesh with his fingers, making me thrill and quiver with disgust. In fact, my feelings of shame and horror at the moment were far greater than they had been when Zachary assaulted me.

"Ah!" said Taylor, chuckling and continuing to feel me with his rough hand, "this gal has got something like a bottom. My! Ain't it jest plump and firm and broad. There's plenty of room here for the switch, and her skin is as soft and smooth as velvet. You can see how white it is. I've never before had my hand on such a scrumptious bottom. It's worth feeling, and no mistake,"

I writhed and moaned. He went on: "I should like all of you to have a feel of it, but as leader of this yer party, I can't allow you to touch the gal for fear some of you might want to do more than feel her, and that would lead to difficulties among us. Now, as to the punishment of the gal. I propose to give her a dozen strokes, but not to draw blood. Remember, she's only an assistant in the business."

The men were divided in opinion. Some said that I ought to be whipped just the same as the "missis"; but the majority was in favor of my receiving only twelve strokes. And so it was settled. Even in my fear and shame, I felt a wave of relief at hearing that I was not going to be whipped so severely as Miss Matthews had been.

One of the men called out: "Mind you, lay on the dozen right smart, Jake. Make the young bitch wriggle her bottom."

"You bet I'll lay them on smart, and you'll see how she'll move. I know how to handle a hick'ry switch, and I'll rule a dozen lines across her bottom that'll make it look like the American flag, striped red and white. And when I've done with her I guess she'll be pretty sore behind, but you'll see that I won't draw a drop of blood. Yes, gentlemen, I tell you again that I know how to whip. I was an overseer in Georgia for five years."

All the time that Taylor was holding forth I lay shame-stricken at my nakedness and shivering in awful suspense, the flesh of my bottom creeping and the scalding tears trickling down my red cheeks. Finally he raised the switch and flourished it over me, while I held my breath and contracted the muscles of my bottom in dread of the coming stroke.

It fell with a loud swishing noise. Oh! It was awful! The pain was even worse than I had anticipated. It took my breath away for a moment and made me gasp. Then I uttered a loud shriek, writhing and twisting my loins in agony.

Taylor went on whipping me very slowly, so that I felt the full sting of each stroke before the next one fell. Every stroke felt as if a red-hot iron was being drawn across my bottom. I winced and squirmed each time the horrid switch fell sharply on my quivering flesh. I shrieked and screamed and I swung my hips from side to side, arching my loins at one moment and then flattening myself down on the ladder, while, between my shrieks, I begged and prayed the man to stop whipping me.

I had forgotten all about my nakedness now. The only sensation I had at the moment was one of intense pain. When the twelve strokes had been inflicted, I was in a half-fainting state.

I was left lying on the ladder with upturned petticoats while the men all gathered round me and looked at me. Because I was a strong healthy girl, the faintness soon passed off, as also did the first intense smart of the whipping. But my whole bottom was sore, and the weals throbbed painfully.

The feeling of shame again came over me as I began to notice the way the men were looking at my naked body, and I tearfully begged them to pull down my clothes. No one did so, however, and Taylor, pointing to me said: "There boys, look at her bottom. You see how regularly the white skin is striped with long red weals? But there is not a drop of blood. That's what I call a prettily-whipped bottom. But the gal ain't got a bit of grit in her. Any nigger wench would have taken double the number of strokes without making half the noise. Now the other woman is a plucky one, she took her whippin' well."

He then pulled up my drawers and tied the strings round my waist, saying with a laugh: "This is the first time I've ever fixed up a woman's trousers, and it's the first time I've ever whipped women who wore trousers."

Pulling down my clothes, he now loosened me from the ladder and led me, crying, sore and miserable, back to the veranda where Miss Matthews was still lying on her side upon the couch with her hands over her face. He then went off to the other men, a few of whom I saw were engaged in work of some sort near the fence.

But I was so thankful at having got out of their hands and sight that I did not particularly notice what they were doing. I thought they would soon go away and that all our troubles were over. I had quite forgotten that Taylor had said we would have to ride a rail for two hours after being whipped.

Miss Matthews looked mournfully at me. Her sweet face was very pale and her soft eyes were full of tears but the tears were not for herself, they were for me. She beckoned to me, and, when I went to her, she folded me in her arms, pressing me to her bosom.

"Oh! My poor, poor girl," she murmured in tones full of compassion. "How I have felt for you! Your shrieks pierced my heart. Oh! The cruel, cruel man, to whip you so severely!" (She seemed to have quite forgotten the shame and pain of her own whipping in her pity for me.)

"He did not whip me nearly so severely as he did you," I said. "He gave me only a dozen strokes and no blood has come. But I could not help screaming. I am not so brave as you are." Then we kissed and cried and sympathized with each other, comparing notes as to our feelings while we had been on the ladder exposed to the eyes of the men.

After a moment or two I put my hand under my petticoats and touched my smarting bottom, feeling the weals which had been raised on the flesh by the switch. They were exquisitely tender and I could hardly bear to touch them.

"Oh! Dear me!" I wailed, "How dreadfully sore I am. But you must be much sorer."

"I certainly am very sore," said Miss Matthews, wiping her eyes. "I can neither sit down nor lie on my back. My bottom is still bleeding, I think, and my pantalettes are sticking to my flesh. But, oh, oh! The awful exposure, and the shameful touch of the man's hand was worse than the whipping!" she exclaimed, wringing her hands while the tears again began to trickle down her cheeks.

I pressed her hand in sympathy, and she went on: "Our sufferings are not over yet, Dorothy. Don't you remember that the man said we would have to ride a rail for two hours?"

I now did call to mind what Taylor had said about our riding a rail, but I was not much frightened at having to do so. Of course, I knew that it would be very uncomfortable—if not downright painful—to have to sit with a sore and smarting bottom on a rail for two hours. But that was all I thought about the matter at the moment. Ah! I little knew what a terrible torture riding a rail would prove to be! I don't know whether Miss Matthews had any notion of what it actually was, but anyway she did not say a word more on the subject, and we stood, both of us being too sore to sit down in comfort, with our arms round each other, weeping silently and waiting miserably for the men to come for us.

We had not long to wait. In a couple of minutes, four of the band came and, taking us by the arms, led us out of the veranda to the fence beside which the other men were standing, some of them holding pieces of rope in their hands. The fence was about five feet high and of the ordinary pattern, made of split rails, the upper edge of each rail being wedge-shaped and sharp.

Taylor, with a cruel smile on his face, said: "Now you are going to receive the rest of your punishment, a two-hour ride on the rail. I guess your bottoms must be very hot jest now, but they'll have plenty of time to cool while you are having your ride. And to prevent you from falling off your horses, well tie you on them. Get them ready, boys."

I thought that we merely would be tied in a sitting posture on the fence with our clothes down. But I was soon undeceived! We were each seized by two men who held our arms while a third man raised our petticoats and pulled our drawers entirely off our legs. Then our skirts were held high above our waists so that the whole lower parts of our persons, both behind and before, were exposed to the lustful eyes of the horrid men. Since they had already seen our bottoms, they all crowded in front of us, gloating over the secret "spots" of our respective bodies, while we, crimson with shame greater than ever, struggled and wept and entreated the wretches to cover our nakedness. But they only laughed, and two or three of them put their hands on the "spots." The touch of their fingers making us start and shrink with a horrible feeling of disgust.

Taylor stopped them by saying: "No, no, boys, you must not touch the prisoners, but you may look at them as much as you like."

And the men did look, making remarks, speculating as to whether we were virgins or not, pointing the difference in the shape of our figures and observing the color of the hair on our respective "spots," while we blushed and cried with shame.

You have seen my "spot" and know what it is like; there is nothing remarkable about it. But Miss Matthews's "spot" was somewhat remarkable. I had never seen it before, and I could not help looking at it with astonishment. It was covered with a thick forest of glossy, dark-brown hair which extended some distance up her belly and descended between her thighs in curly locks nearly two inches long. The fissure was completely hidden and not a trace of the lips could be seen.

One man, after a prolonged stare, exclaimed: "By Gosh! I've never seen such a fleece between a woman's legs in my life! Darn me if she wouldn't have to be sheared before a man could get into her."

The men roared with laughter at the remark, while Miss Matthews groaned and writhed in the bitterness of her shame.

After looking at our naked bodies for fully five minutes, the men went on with their work. A long piece of rope was passed several times round our bodies so that our arms and wrists were lashed closely to our sides. We then were lifted bodily up and, to my intense horror, seated astride one of the topmost rails of the fence, facing each other and about six feet apart.

The rail passed between our naked thighs, and our bare bottoms rested on the sharp edge of it. On each side of the fence and close to it the men had driven stakes into the ground, and to these stakes our ankles ' were securely tied. When the men had fixed us in this painful position, they allowed our clothes to fall about our legs. Our nakedness was covered, but our torture had begun.

Taylor looked at us with a grin on his face, saying: "There now; you are properly mounted on your horses. We're done with you and we're all going away. But at the end of two hours one of us will come back and loosen you. And I reckon you'll both be mighty stiff after your ride."

Then the band of lynchers took their departure, laughing and shouting coarse jokes which made us, even in our pain, grow hot with shame. The clatter of the horses' hoofs and the loud laughter of the men gradually died away in the distance. Then all was perfectly still.

CHAPTER FIVE:

On the rack; moral torture is allied to physical; I make the great decision of my life and consent to become Zachary's mistress; his revolting cynicism.

It was a beautiful, calm, bright evening. The sun was just setting and the house, the garden and our two unfortunate selves were bathed in a flood of amber light At first I had entertained a faint hope that Martha would come back once the men had gone and would release us. However, she never came, and there did not seem to be the slightest chance of anyone else's coming to the house at that hour. Thus, escape being seen as impossible, I resigned myself to the thought that Miss Matthews and I would be forced to undergo the whole of our dreadful punishment.

From the first moment of our being placed astride the rail we had been suffering pain. Now it was increasing every minute. We did not speak to one another—our sufferings were too great!—so we just sat in silence with the tears, which we could not wipe off, trickling down our pale cheeks, while every now and then a shuddering sob or a groan of anguish would break from our parched lips.

Since our legs were rather widely stretched apart, the rail was imbedded in the cleft between our thighs and the weight of our bodies forced the sharp edge deeply into the division between the cheeks of our bottoms. Consequently the most delicate part of our persons was hurt by the pressure. Just imagine our positions and think what it meant to individuals of the female sex! Miss Matthews, throughout the whole time we were on the rail, bore her sufferings bravely. Alas, I, for my part, could not.

As the minutes slowly parsed, the pain grew more and more excruciating. In addition, my bottom still was smarting and the weals on it still were throbbing. I felt as if the wedge-shaped rail were slowly splitting me.

Sharp, lancing pains darted through my loins and up my back. Since my ankles were tightly fastened to the stake, I could not alter my position in the slightest degree. If my arms had not been bound to my sides, I might have gained a little temporary ease by resting my hands on the rail and thus taking some of the weight off my bottom. But the men, in their devilish ingenuity, had taken care that we should not have even a moment's respite from our tortures. Even if we had fainted, we would not have fallen off the fence: the upper part of our bodies would have dropped either forward or backward, but our legs, tied to the stakes, would have remained straddled over the rail, and the sharp edge still would have remained between the cheeks of our bottoms.

Before long, every nerve in my body was throbbing with agony. A cold dew of perspiration had broken out on my forehead. I groaned and writhed and twisted about, but the more I did so, the more firmly the sharp rail was imbedded in my tender cleft.

I began to scream, and, but for the grace of God, might even have cursed. Miss Matthews, meanwhile, was crying, and her face showed the anguish which she felt. However, she made no outcry.

A few minutes more of agony slowly passed. Then I saw a man enter the lane and come towards the house. He was not one of the lynchers, so my heart bounded with joy. We should be released in a few moments!

I redoubled my cries, begging him to come quickly to our assistance. However, he did not hurry himself in the least. He walked deliberately and slowly up the path, and, alas, when he got a little nearer, I saw that he was none other than Zachary.

A few days previously I had hoped never to set eyes on him again. But now I was intensely delighted to see him. "Oh, Mr. Zachary!" I gasped out in a choking voice, with tears streaming down my cheeks. "Take me down! Oh! Take me down quickly!"

He came close to the fence and stood looking down at Miss Matthews and me. He had a smile on his face.

"Oh dear, Mr. Zachary!" I again wailed. 'Take me down! Do be quick and take me down!"

But, to my horror, he did not move. "Well," he said mockingly, "if it isn't Miss Ruth Matthews and Miss Dorothy Stephens. This is what slave-running has brought you. And it is to me that you owe your present position. I let the 'white' people know of your doings, and you have been rightly and smartly punished. I told you, Bertha, that we should meet again, and we have met. I knew that the men were coming to pay you a visit this evening, so I came with them, and, though you did not see me, I saw both of you getting your bottoms whipped. I must say, Bertha, you squealed just like a pig being killed."

He paused to laugh, and a sickening feeling of despair came over me. The cruel man, not content with having set the lynchers on us, had come to mock us in our agony.

He continued: "I am afraid that your bottoms— especially yours, Miss Matthews—must be very tender after the smart switching, and I am sure that you both must be extremely uncomfortable on your present seats. The edges are sharp, and I have no doubt that they are pressing sorely on a certain delicate 'spot' between your thighs."

Miss Matthews's face was working with pain and her eyes were full of tears. But, when she heard Zachary's coarse and indecent words, she put aside her suffering and was consumed with indignation. Her pale cheeks grew red.

Looking at me, she said in a quavering voice: "Dorothy, do you know this boor?"

Zachary answered for me: "Oh yes she does! Miss Stephens and I once were great friends. But we had a little tiff one day and she told me to go away. Is that not the case, Bertha?"

I hated the man, but at that moment the dreadful pain which I was suffering overpowered every other feeling. "Yes! Yes! That is the case!" I exclaimed fretfully. "But don't stand there talking! Take us down at once!"

Zachary smiled, but did not make a move to release us.

"Oh! Oh!" I shrieked with pain, enraged at his utter callousness. "How can you stand there and watch two poor women suffering agony? Oh! Why don't you release us? Have you no mercy or pity?"

"I am not a merciful man," he replied coolly. "I am a Southerner. As a rule I have no pity for abolitionists when they get into trouble for interfering with our slaves." Then, grinning lasciviously, he added: "But I don't mind making an exception in your case, Bertha. I will take you down if you will promise to come and live with me." Upon hearing what he said, Miss Matthews again fixed

her eyes on me. She said earnestly: "Oh, Dorothy! Don't listen to the man! He is a cruel scoundrel to try to take advantage of your sufferings. But be brave, dear. Don't give way. I am suffering as much as—if not more than—you are, but I would not accept release on such disgraceful terms."

Zachary laughed scornfully. "I have not the least intention of offering the terms to you, Miss Matthews," he said. "As far as I am concerned, you may sit on the rail till the two hours are over. The view I had of your naked charms did not tempt me in the slightest. You have no figure. You are quite straight up and down. Your bottom is too narrow, your thighs are too small and your legs are too thin. I like a woman to have a broad bottom, plump thighs and good legs, such as Dorothy has."

"Oh! You hateful man!" exclaimed Miss Matthews angrily—for, after all, she was a woman, and no woman likes to hear her charms, whatever they may be, spoken of in disparaging terms.

But Zachary ignored her. "Now then, Bertha," he chuckled. "You have heard what I said. Do you intend to come home with me tonight?"

The coarse way he put the question shocked me, so I tried to pluck up a little spirit. I partly succeeded. "No, no, I won't go home with you," I said. But, I fear, my tone of voice was far from determined.

"Very well then," replied he. "Stay where you are. You have an hour and a half more to sit on your perch. By that time you'll be in a terrible state between the legs. And you'll be half-dead with pain. Rather a dreadful prospect, isn't it?"

Alas, it was! I moaned and shuddered at the thought of the long period of agony before me. Again I piteously entreated him to take me down.

He made no answer, but coolly lit a cigar and began to smoke. Then, leaning against the middle of the rail, he looked first to his right at Miss Matthews, then to his left at me. His physiognomy was a study in perfect unconcern as we writhed, wept and groaned in anguish—and as the sharp edge of the rail pressed harder and harder against the tender flesh between the cheeks of our bottoms.

For a few minutes more, I bore the pain, which was growing more and more intense. Then I gave way utterly. I could no longer endure the anguish. I said to myself: "What does anything matter, so long as I can escape from this terrible torture?! I can't bear it for another hour and a half I'll go raving mad, or die!"

No doubt it was weak of me, but I was in a half-fainting state, and, as I have told you before, I am physically and morally a coward. "Oh!" I cried. "Oh! Take me down! Take me down at once, and I promise to go home with you!"

When Miss Matthews heard me promise to go with Zachary, she said: "Don't! Oh, don't go with him Dorothy! Don't wreck your life! Try to bear your sufferings! They soon will be over! If I were you I would rather die than yield my body to the man."

"You are not she, Miss Matthews," Zachary said curtly. Then, turning to me, he asked: "Have you quite made up your mind, Bertha?" And, so saying, he touched his hand to the knot of the rope binding my arms.

"Yes! Yes!" I cried impatiently. "Oh! Do be quick and release me!"

"Oh, Dorothy!" sighed Miss Matthews in a sorrowful tone. "Oh, you poor girl! I pity you! You do not know the horror and shame which lie before you!"

Zachary soon untied the ropes which fastened my arms and ankles. Then, putting his arms around my waist, he lifted me off the rail, carried me into the veranda and laid me, limp and faint, on the couch. I was stiff and sore and aching from head to foot, but I was not suffering much pain. And, oh, the intense relief to find myself no longer astride the sharp rail!

When I was situated comfortably, Zachary fetched me a glass of water, which I drank thirstily, for my mouth was parched and I was quite feverish from the torture which I had undergone. Then, when I had recovered a little, I thought of Miss Matthews and I asked Zachary to release her. However, he was very bitterly set against her, and would hear nothing of my pleas. It was not until after I had begged for her with all the pathos at my command that he finally consented to release her before we went away.

"Now, Bertha," he said, "I'll go for the buggy. I left it just around the corner of the lane. I shan't be gone long, so you lie here quietly until I come back." Then he added meaningfully: "You had better not attempt to escape, for the men still are somewhere in the neighborhood and if they see you they'll put you back on the rail." So saying, he took his leave.

The thought of escape never entered my head. At that moment I was so weak and frightened that all my senses were in a half-torpid state. I did not fully realize the horrors which lay ahead of me, and I lay languidly on the couch, thinking only that it was so delightful to be free at last from pain.

Presently Zachary drove up with the buggy and, after hitching the horse to the garden gate, came to the couch, "Now then, Bertha," he said to me, "come along. Never mind your things. My women can supply you with everything necessary for the night, and I will send for your trunks tomorrow morning. Can you walk to the buggy, or shall I carry you?"

I replied that I could walk. But, on attempting to do so, I found myself so shaky and stiff that I could barely put one foot before the other. Noticing how feeble I was, Zachary lifted me up in his arms and carried me to the buggy. Then he placed me inside and wrapped a rug around my knees. I reminded him of his promise to free Miss Matthews before we left, and he dutifully went to the fence and untied her bonds. However, he did not take the trouble to help her off her painful perch; the poor creature was forced to climb from the rail without assistance of any sort.

Miss Matthews was weak, pale and suffering. Her feebleness was such that she had to lean against the fence for support. But her thoughts still were for me. "Don't go with that man, Dorothy," she said again, her tone urgent and earnest. "Never mind your promise. It was extracted from you by torture, so you are not morally obliged to keep it. Stay with me."

I did not want to go with Zachary, and I would have been only too glad to stay with her. But my cowardice ruled the day. Afraid of being placed once more astride the rail, I could only cry out feebly: "Oh, I must go with him, my dear friend. I am in his power."

"Yes, indeed you are," Zachary observed. "And if you were to attempt to break your promise you would very soon find yourself back 'in the saddle.'" Then, addressing Miss Matthews, he went on: "Remember, Ruth, what the men told you. If you are not out of the state before forty-eight hours have expired, you will receive another visit from 'Judge Lynch.'" He then got into the buggy beside me, and, as he did so, I shrank as far away from him as possible, hating him and despising myself even more.

Zachary touched the horse with his whip and we drove off, leaving Miss Matthews standing with drooping head by the fence. After we had gone a short distance, I looked back and saw her lonely figure still in the same position. She did not move, and I kept my eyes fixed upon her until the buggy turned the corner of the lane. Then I sank back on the seat and, covering my face with my hands, wept bitterly. I had parted with the only friend I had in the world.

CHAPTER SIX:

The slaves get to know me; voluptuous effects of flagellation; my maid, Rosa, is whipped for impertinence; description of her bottom and legs; Zachary's opinions on the right to rape colored women; Zachary puts me on the sofa and does the "usual thing."

The weeks slipped away. My health remained good, my spirits revived and I was not unhappy. I had plenty of books to read, I rode nearly every day—sometimes alone, sometimes with Zachary—and I often took a long buggy ride.

We occasionally spent a few days in Richmond, staying at the best hotel and going every night to the theatre or to some other place of amusement. Before that time, I never had been in a theatre, so I enjoyed the performances immensely and wished very much that I could go on the stage. I told Zachary one day, but he only laughed, telling me that I was "a little goose" and that I had not enough "go" in me to make an actress.

At Woodlands I often amused myself by roaming about the plantation, which was very extensive. There were upwards of two-hundred field hands, male and female, all of whom were engaged in cultivating the cotton. Zachary fed his slaves well and did not overwork them, but otherwise he was a hard master. His four overseers had orders never to pass over a fault or to allow the least shirking of work; consequently, the strap, switch and paddle constantly were being used on both men and women.

The slaves' quarters were divided into three blocks of "cabins," as they were called; one block was for the married couples, another for the single men and the third for the unmarried women and girls. But as soon as work was over for the day, all the slaves of both sexes met together round a fire, where they spent most of the night dancing, singing and playing the banjo.

As a matter of course there was a great deal of poking. However, no notice was taken of what slaves did among themselves at night, so long as they were present the next morning when roll was called by the overseers.

The slaves soon got to know me well, and, since I took an interest in them and often was able to do them little kindnesses, they all became fond of me. I liked these poor, good-natured creatures who were always lighthearted except when they happened to be smarting from a whipping.

Although I often had seen the marks of the lash on the bodies of the run-aways who had passed through our station, I hitherto had never seen a slave whipped Dinah, in her capacity of housekeeper, maintained strict discipline, so she often brought one of the women or one of the girls before Zachary for neglecting her work or some other offense, and sometimes he himself gave the offender a whipping on her bottom with the switch. I occasionally had heard the squeaks of a culprit, but I always had avoided being present at the punishment.

Whipping a girl seemed to have an exciting effect on Zachary, for, after switching one, he invariably used to come to me, wherever I happened to be, and poke me with great vigor. I thought it strange at the time, but I since have found out that men's passions are inflamed by whipping the bottom of a female until she cries and writhes with pain, and, if they can't do it themselves, they like seeing it done. This is a curious, but undoubted fact, and it shows what cruel creatures men are.

I have already mentioned that an octoroon girl named Rosa had been appointed to act as my maid. This girl formerly had been Zachary's favorite, but, since my arrival at Woodlands, he had had nothing to do with her. When Rosa found that she was entirely neglected and that she was obliged to serve as my maid, she had been filled with bitter resentment. In fact, the girl was bitterly jealous.

She had shown her vexation from the first, by constant sullenness, and at times she was very impertinent to me. But I had borne with her ill temper and had always been kind to her, trying to make her like me, for I pitied her and all the other slave girls. However, nothing which I could do had any effect in softening the girl; she continued to be sulky and disrespectful, though I had managed to make all the other women and girls fond of me.

I knew that if I reported Rosa to Zachary he would have punished her, but, since I did not wish to get her into trouble, I did not say a word. Rosa was twenty years of age, tall, handsome and not darker than an ordinary brunette, her complexion being a clear olive with a tinge of pink showing on her cheeks. She had a well-rounded figure, with full bust and broad hips. Her feet were small and her hands were smooth, for she never had done any hard work. She had a profusion of long, wavy, dark brown hair. Her eyes also were brown, large, and soft. She had white, regular teeth and full, red, moist lips. Her voice was low and musical, but she was perfectly uneducated, not being able either to read or to write, and she spoke in the usual "nigger" way.

One morning when she was helping me dress, she appeared to be in worse temper than usual, and, while brushing my hair, pulled it so roughly that I several times had to tell her to be more careful. I spoke gently, but my remonstrances seemed only to irritate her.

Tossing her head and giving my hair a nasty pull, she said in a most saucy way: "I oughtened to be brushin yo' hair at all. Becos you is white, you tinks you is a very fine lady but you is not a bit better dan me. You isn't married to de Massa, yet you sleeps wid him every night."

I flushed with anger. Rising from my seat, I ordered the girl to leave the room. She did so, laughing.

The tears came into my eyes. My heart swelled and I felt a deep sense of degradation. It was humiliating that, owing to a series of misfortunes, I should have come to be spoken to in such a coarse way by a slave girl.

But, alas! What she had said was the truth. I really was no better than she.

After a moment or two, I put up my hair, finished dressing and went down to breakfast. I had not intended to say anything to Zachary, but he noticed that I was depressed and asked me what was the matter.

"Oh, nothing much," I replied. "Rosa has been a little impertinent to me."

Not being satisfied with my answer, he insisted on knowing what the girl had said to me.

Unable to contain my hurt any longer, I told him exactly what had occurred, adding that Rosa had always been more or less impertinent to me, and I suggested that, if he spoke to her, she probably would be more respectful to me in the future.

"I will speak to her presently," he said. Then he went on quietly with his breakfast.

I thought no more of the affair, and, when the meal was over, we left the room and went into an adjoining apartment, where I amused myself reading the newspaper while Zachary smoked his cigar. When he had finished, he rang the bell, which was answered by one of the parlor maids, Jane.

"Go tell Dinah and Rosa that I want them here, then come back yourself," he said to the girl.

She went away, returning in about five minutes accompanied by the other two women. Zachary rose from his seat with a stern expression on his face and, turning to Rosa, who was looking rather frightened, said angrily:

"You young hussy! I have been hearing about your conduct. How dare you speak to your mistress like that? Did you think I would let you insult a white lady? You are getting too saucy, but I will take the sauce out of you. I am going to whip you."

Rosa turned as pale as her olive complexion would allow. A frightened expression came into her eyes and she burst into tears.

"Oh! Massa!" she exclaimed. "Don't whip me! Oh! Please don't whip me! I'se very sorry I was sassy to de Missis. Oh! Do let me off an' I will be a good gal and never be sassy again." Then turning to me she said imploringly: "Oh! Missus. Forgive me, an' ask de Massa not to whip me dis time."

I did not want the girl to be whipped, so I asked Zachary to let her go away, saying that I was sure that she was sorry for what she had said and that I did not think she would offend again. But her master was very angry with her and would not consent to let her off. Turning to Dinah, he said curtly: "Take her up."

I had no idea what was meant by the words, but Dinah knew what to do. She often had "taken up" naughty slave girls on her broad, strong back. Going up to Rosa, she seized her by the wrists, and, turning round, drew the girl's arms over her shoulders Then, bending well forward, she raised the culprit's feet off the floor so that her body was brought into a curved position.

Not wishing to see the punishment inflicted, I walked towards the door. But Zachary peremptorily ordered me to remain in the room. "Turn up her clothes, Jane, and, mind you, hold them well out of the way," he said.

Jane went to the right side of the delinquent, and, rolling up her skirt, petticoats and chemise, held them high above her waist. The girl's under-linen was perfectly clean, but she wore no drawers—none of the slave women possessed drawers. She had a fine, big, well-shaped bottom and, owing to the curved position in which she was being held, the large, plump round cheeks swelled out in high relief at a most convenient angle for receiving the switch. Her olive-tinted skin was perfectly smooth, her thighs were large and well-rounded, her legs were shapely and her ankles were trim. She was wearing white stockings, gartered with bows of blue ribbon, and she had on neat shoes.

Zachary went to a cabinet from which he took a hickory switch—he kept a switch in nearly every room —then, placing himself at the left side of the culprit, said: "Now, I'll teach you to respect your mistress. I have not whipped you for some time, but I'm going to make your bottom smart now."

Rosa had not struggled or uttered a word while she was being "taken up" and prepared for the switch. But now she turned her head, looking at Zachary with a dog-like expression of appeal in her great, brown eyes, and said beseechingly, while the tears ran down her cheeks: "Oh, Massa, don't whip poor Rosa hard."

He began to whip her, laying on the strokes smartly and as calmly as if he were merely beating a dog. The girl winced, drawing the cheeks of her bottom with a jerk each time the switch fell. Long, red weals rose on her skin. Her plump flesh quivered and she kicked up her feet, squealing shrilly and exclaiming in gasps:

"Oh, Massa! — Oh, Massa! — Don't whip — me — so — hard—! Oh! Massa! Oh!—Good Massa, please—don't whip — me — so — hard! Oh! Oh! Stop Massa! Oh! Please—please—stop. My bottom—is—so—sore—I Oh! Oh!"

The switch continued to stripe her writhing bottom, extracting loud cries from her, making her struggle and plunge violently. But Dinah, slightly separating her legs and bending well forward, easily held the shrieking girl in position while Zachary whipped away steadily. Jane held up the girl's petticoats and Dinah gripped her wrists tightly while Rosa, squealing and twisting herself about, drew up her legs one after the other, then kicked them out in all directions, and, in her contortions opened her thighs so that I could see the curly dark brown hair shading the "spot"—and every now and then I caught a glimpse of the bright pink orifice.

Rosa's skin was rather fine, and she appeared to feel the pain acutely, begging piteously for mercy. But Zachary, utterly regardless of her cries and entreaties, went on whipping till the surface of her bottom, from the loins to the thighs, was covered with red weals. Then, throwing down the switch, he said: "Let her go."

Jane let the sufferer's petticoats fall and Dinah released her wrists. Then Rosa stood on her feet, twisting her lips and wailing with pain while she wiped the fast-flowing tears from her eyes with her apron.

"There, Rosa," said Zachary, "I have let you off rather easily this time, but if I ever again hear that you have been saucy to your mistress, I will whip you till the blood runs down your thighs. Now you can all go back to your work."

Rosa, still wailing, slunk out of the room with her hand pressed to her smarting bottom; the other two women followed, and Zachary and I were left alone. He put away the switch, then, turning to me, said: I don't think she'll give you any more trouble, but if she does let me know."

"Oh, George!" I said. "How could you bring yourself to whip the girl so severely. She is a pretty creature and I know you often have had her."

He laughed. "Yes. I have often "had" her and will "have" her again if ever I feel inclined to. But I will also whip her again whenever she requires punishment. She is only a nigger, though she is so light in color. You are a Northern girl, so you don't understand how we Southerners look upon our slave women. When they take our fancy we amuse ourselves with them, but we feel no compunction in whipping them whenever they misbehave. Their bodies belong to us, so we can use them in any way we please. Personally, I have no more regard for my slaves than for my dogs and horses."

Though I had got to know Zachary pretty well by that time, I felt rather shocked by his unfeeling sentiments. However, I made no remark. He was standing in front of me, and I noticed that there was a protuberance in a certain part of his trousers. I guessed what was coming.

He went on: "You know, Bertha, whipping a girl always excites me, so I am going to have you." Then, laying me on the couch, he pulled up my petticoats, took down my drawers and entered me with more than usual vigor. Whipping Rosa's bottom certainly had acted on him as a powerful aphrodisiac!

When all was over and I had fastened my drawers, we went to our respective rooms and made ourselves tidy. Then he ordered the buggy and we went for a long drive in the country, lunching at a farm house and not returning home until it was time to dress for dinner.

When I got to my room I found Rosa there, as usual, waiting to assist me in making my toilet. She was looking very subdued and her manner was humble and submissive. She had received a severe whipping, and her bottom must have been very sore. I felt for her, knowing as I did how dreadfully the switch could sting. "I am sorry for you Rosa," I said. "Did the whipping hurt you very much?"

"Oh! Yes Missis," she answered, giving a little shudder at the remembrance, "it did hurt me most drefful. De Massa never give me such a hard whippin before. Dinah has rubbed my bottom with possum fat, an' dat has taken de sting out of de weals som, but I'se very sore an' I can't sit down easy."

She helped me to dress, seeming very anxious to please me in every way, and always speaking most respectfully. From that day she was a changed girl so far as regarded her behavior to me. I never had occasion to find fault with her again during the rest of my stay at Woodlands.

CHAPTER SEVEN:

Zachary's fresh "amours"; he starts for Europe; my last spanking; the only reminiscence of "tenderness"; I begin housekeeping.

As the days passed, I saw less and less of Zachary, and, even when he was with me, he never touched me in any way. Meanwhile, his manner towards me became very cold, though he never was actually rude to me. I guessed what it all meant. He had grown tired of me, and I had a presentiment that he soon would turn me adrift. However, I always had known that our relations would come to an end sooner or later, and that then I should have to do what many a woman has had to do when she has found herself deserted by the man by whom she has been ruined.

Before long, Zachary gave me the news which I had been expecting. One morning, after an absence of three days, he came to me and said that he had something to tell me. My heart gave a jump. I knew what he was about to say, but I made no remark.

He said: "I am going to Europe with a party of friends, so I cannot take you with me. In fact, Bertha, the time has come for us to part altogether. But, though I am leaving you, it is not through any fault of yours. You have always been a good-natured girl and you have done whatever I asked you. Therefore I wish to do the best I can for you. I intend to buy you a little house and to furnish it well for you. I also will give you a sum of money to start with. You are only twenty-two years of age, you have a pretty face and a very good figure. You also have lots of good clothes and a quantity of jewelry. You soon will make friends and I am quite sure that you will manage to get on very well here in New York."

It was a hard way of putting the matter before me and the tears rose to my eyes. But nevertheless I felt a certain amount of gratitude to him for what he intended to do for me. He had ruined me, but he might have cast me off with nothing at all. I thanked him, and he gave me a short kiss, saying that he would take me out next day to look for a house. He then went away, leaving me to think over my future prospects.

The prospects did not seem very bright at that moment. But they might have been worse, so I made up my mind to face my position as bravely as I could. I did not see Zachary any more that day or night, but the next day, after lunch, he came for me and we looked at several houses in various parts of the city.

I shall not lengthen my story by telling you of our house hunting; it will suffice to say that eventually he bought this house, furnished it throughout and engaged a couple of white female servants. I afterwards sent them away and got two colored women, whom I have at this moment in my service. I find them much easier to get on with, and also far more faithful than white servants.

When everything was in order, Zachary brought me here one afternoon, handed over the title deeds of the house and gave me a thousand dollars. We then sat down and had a chat while he drank a glass of wine and smoked a cigar. When he had finished, he rose from his seat, saying with a laugh:

"You know, Bertha, that I am fond of whipping a woman's bottom. Now I don't suppose that I shall ever have a chance of doing such a thing in Europe, so you must let me give you a farewell spanking, a real smart one.

I did not like the idea at all, and a cold shiver ran down my back, for I knew that he would hurt me dreadfully. But I had not the strength of mind to refuse his farewell request, so, in a rather faint voice, I said: "I will let you spank me, but do not be too hard upon me. You know that I cannot bear pain."

Taking a handkerchief from his pocket, he tied my wrists together, a proceeding which alarmed me. "Oh don't tie me!" I exclaimed.

He laughed, saying: "I am going to whip you as if you were a naughty slave girl, so your hands must be tied to prevent your putting them over your bottom during the spanking."

Thoroughly frightened, I made some feeble remonstrances, but he seized me and, sitting down on a chair, placed me in the orthodox position across his knees. Then he turned up my petticoats and took down my drawers.

"Now," he said, stroking my bottom, "don't make too much noise, or the servants will hear you."

Then, holding me firmly, he began to spank me very severely. Oh how hard his hand was, and how it did sting!

I burst into tears, wriggling and squirming about on his thighs. I could distinctly feel his stiff member pressing against my belly. Clenching my teeth and holding my breath, I suppressed for a short time the cries which rose to my lips. But at last the stinging pain became so intense that I began to squeal shrilly, kicking my legs about in anguish and begging him to stop.

He went on spanking me until my bottom burned and throbbed in a most agonizing way and I screamed out as loudly as I could. Then he stopped, and, laying me in a stooping position over the end of the sofa, he poked me while I was still crying and smarting with the pain of the horrid spanking.

When all was over, he untied my wrists and laid me on the sofa, while he stood beside it, looking down at me with a smile on his face as I lay with the tears trickling down my cheeks, all my clothes rumpled and my drawers hanging about my ankles. My face was red, but I am sure that my poor bottom must have been much redder judging from the way it was throbbing and tingling. (It was black-and-blue the next day.)

Bending down he gave me a kiss, saying laughingly: "There, Bertha, that is the last spanking—and the last poke you will ever get from me."

"It was very cruel of you to have spanked me so severely," I said tearfully. "I cannot understand why you should have taken pleasure in giving me such dreadful pain."

He was not a bit sorry for having whipped me with such wanton severity. He said: "Oh, you soon will find that many other men besides me are fond of spanking a woman till she squeals." (I since have found that such indeed is the case: many men are very fond of taking a woman across their knees. I often have been asked to allow myself to be spanked, but I have never consented. Zachary is the only man who ever has taken me on his knees for a spanking.)

He went on, laughing at his own poor joke: "You know, Bertha, when a man sets up a new establishment, he generally gives a housewarming. Well, I have given you a bottom-warming instead. I have always admired your bottom, and I shall always have a pleasing recollection of it as it appeared today.

It looked very pretty while the plump white cheeks were blushing at the touch of my hand."

He then kissed me again on my tear-bedabbled face, bade me goodbye and calmly left the house, leaving me lying on the sofa, sore, angry and indignant. Fortunately, the servants had not heard the shrieks which I had uttered while being spanked.

I lay there quietly till the intense smarting pain of my bottom had somewhat subsided, then I fastened up my drawers and, going into the bedroom, bathed my flushed face, thinking to myself what an utterly heartless man Zachary was. There certainly had never been any sentiment in the relations between us, but I thought that he might have parted with me in a more tender way. However, I had no tender feeling for him after the way he had treated me, and so the only "tenderness" there was about our parting was the "tenderness" of my sorely spanked bottom.

Zachary sailed for Europe the next day. I have neither seen him nor heard from him since. But I know that he remained abroad until the war was over, then returned to Woodlands, and I believe that he is there now.

THE END

CHICAGO

Preface

In this long-banned 1907 chronicle of scandalous goings-on behind-the scenes of turn-of-the-century America has been acclaimed as an erotic and literary classic and an important historical document. Supposedly penned by Lord Winston, a peer of the British realm, on a tour of the U.S., the book makes clear just how widespread and deeply-rooted the pleasures and practice of bondage always has been in this country.

In the course of his travels, Winston visited two great metropolises, Chicago and Boston, and through his contacts discovered the underground world of the caned and caner alive and well in each. Winston wrote a separate book about his experiences in each of these cities

In Volume I, set in what Chicago (which he calls Porkopolis), Lord Winston finds himself the subject of birchings by several refined, handsome ladies. In Volume II, he visits Mrs. Palmerston of Boston, and other leaders of the town's aristocratic Puritan blue bloods.

FOREWORD

The passion for flagellation counts numerous votaries all over the world.

Chicago

Birching lust flourishes in Austria, Hungary, Germany, and Russia. In all these countries, womankind is fully alive to the thrilling charm of the rod and its extraordinary effects upon the masculine organization. Innumerable are the lovers of the twigs in high society and amidst artists and intellectual folks. It is in the United States that birching discipline is best-known and most popular, being carried out with artistic, poetical sentiment until it becomes the inseparable, supreme refinement of love.

In France, flagellation has many followers, if one may judge by the fact that there are very few courtesans in Paris or the principal provincial towns who do not possess in a corner of their mirrored wardrobes a goodly selection of whipping instruments which are used by these *complaisant cocottes* almost every day.

Many Parisian closed and shuttered houses of love can show special rooms fitted up with everything needful for the application of flogging pleasure. As priestesses, these mysterious temples are provided with most adorable, beautiful charmers, who exercise their art with finished skill, being perfectly able to lead the man who kneels before them through every delicious by-path of sublime and intoxicating voluptuousness.

The love of birching, active or passive, also exists in the upper circles of Paris. When, now and again, some sensual scandal is revealed, indiscreet newspapers lift a corner of the veil hiding these private practices, and the general public is strangely stirred. Such propensities are generally put down as bordering on weird insanity. When voluptuous flagellation is brought into play, it is nothing more than sublime exacerbation of tender affection, forcing a fervent lover to reach the highest pitch of adoration for the weaker sex. In that case, any pain inflicted by the female of his choice becomes a source of joy. There are certainly many men and even women who cannot understand or permit such proceedings. To fully realize the enthralling influence of the birch, one must be predisposed by nature, instinct, temperament or education; or else specially destined to drain this cup of ineffable delight by some happy hazard of environment. The women of France are not successful when trying to enact the part of a domineering queen. Young Parisian beauties, delightful types of femininity though they be, care for naught else in love but the simple frolic and merry laughter.

Austria, Hungary, Russia, and even Germany have given birth to haughty, superb females, such as Catherine the Great and Maria Theresa, fated to bend the lords of creation beneath their yoke, curbing manly pride by the power of an inexorable scepter grasped in the small white hand of a woman.

Petticoated despots are still to be found in these lands. Empresses from the cradle, they have proud dispositions, and when in the flower of woman-hood and wonderfully handsome, appreciative men are wafted into a terres-trial paradise, as they humble themselves before such tyrannical, capricious mistresses.

Sacher-Masoch, the powerful Hungarian novelist, used to delight in pic-turing implacable and haughty women. He is the author of a long series of thrilling tales and romances, where his dominating heroines pass in proces-sion, as ruthless as Roman Empresses and as beautiful as Olympian goddess-es. They are all cruel tigresses, but their excessive severity, joined to the fas-cination of their bodily beauty, causes in men the excessive exaggeration of loving pain, called "masochism."

Nevertheless, we must distinguish between a "masochist" and a volup-tuous flagellant. The latter is an ardent poet, awake to all delirious artistic manifestations, a fervent admirer of women, adoring his sweetheart with an ardor which gives rise to the greatest excesses of throbbing sensuous worship.

A masochist, on the contrary, is always depressed. Beauty without cruelty does not impress him. He never kisses the girl he adores, and his sole delight is to show her that his servility reaches the uttermost limits of disgusting ignominy. The more his mistress forces him to execute nauseating and infa-mous tasks, the happier he is – a repulsive and unfortunate slavish being.

Mentally diseased, he often finishes in a madhouse. His desires are unin-teresting; his cravings loathsome, and he can never please his female partner. She pities him, and he affords her but little pleasure. A voluptuous lover of the rod is generally much sought after by women of refined tastes.

He is a most agreeable sample of a suitor; good-humored, full of gaiety, and brimming over with delicate attention for his companion. Artistic are his tastes; he is a lover of music and verse; his voice is daily lifted skywards, inton-ing a tuneful hymn in praise of sunny nature, and womankind made brighter and more comely by reciprocal tenderness. Like all that is good and beauti-ful in loving passion, voluptuous flagellation has been handed down to us from ancient Greece, whence came penetrating kisses, maddening caresses, and the mystic lasciviousness of Lesbos.

Clyso, an adorable priestess of Venus, first caused the passion of flagellation to arise in Athens. She was one of the most entrancing and renowned courte-sans at the epoch when the divine sculptor Praxiteles gave to the world his ideal types of marble beauty. The story goes that an inhabitant of Creos, a village adjoining the fair city of Athens, had come into town to sell the produce of his fields, when he chanced to meet Clyso, the delicious wanton. Straightway, he fell in love with her, and so mad was his yearning that he offered her the half of his worldly possessions for one hour in her arms. Clyso consented.

He was the happiest of men. Clyso was not only endowed with rare, surpassing beauty, but she was intellectually gifted. Being of an inquiring mind, she asked the peasant, as he shared her couch, a thousand questions relating to his homestead. She gleaned from his frank and honest answers that the cult of Venus was completely forgotten and neglected. Few sacrifices were made on the alter of love, although Creos was inhabited by robust, healthy males; and many women, as comely as Aphrodite incarnate.

Despite their bodily rigor, these men were stirred by no violent desires when they looked upon the scarcely-veiled nudity of their wives or girlish companions. Never did the frigid village lads seek to pluck the half-open rosebuds ready to their hands.

The senses of the maidens were also dulled by this indifference and the quadruple pink petals of their secret love-blossoms slowly faded and withered, deprived as they were of the divine dew of passionate ecstasy.

Such dreadful news saddened sort-hearted Clyso. Her sole aim in life was the radiant embrace in which her soul mounted to realms of indescribable bliss. She had sworn to Venus to devote her existence to the propagation of the religion of love among mankind, so that the bodies of mortals should quiver in the giddy vortex of deep sensual joy. She was inexpressibly grieved to learn that at Creos, men as well proportioned as Apollo, and women equaling Aphrodite in grace and allurement could pass their time on earth without seeking to fathom the mysteries of love.

With a heavy heart, away went saddened Clyso, tripping to the temple of her goddess. The fair priestess carried two trembling doves closely clasped to the tepid twin glories of her young bosom, as she prayed for help and inspiration. While the blood of the poor, white, feathered things gushed forth beneath the knife of the sacrificer, a branch fell from one of the trees of the sacred grove. As it dropped, the twig rebounded from Clyso's tiny, naked foot. It struck her white, firm flesh like a blow from the lash of a whip, but far from hurting her, seemed to vivify the whole frame of the gentle courtesan, causing her young blood to course through her veins with new and powerful ardor.

Recognizing an omen of the gracious goddess, Clyso picked up the branch, and taking it with her, was absorbed in deep meditation as she wended her way homeward.

Gathering all her handmaidens around her, she returned with them to Creos. But before entering the hamlet, she ordered her devoted servant lasses to cut a great quantity of branches resembling the one consecrated to Venus, furthermore telling the girls to tie them into bundles, thus forming rods.

She next summoned all the inhabitants of the village to the market-place and whipped them – one after the other. The effect of this birching was magical; and new life-blood, as fierce and fiery as boiling lava, flowed in the veins of the lazy males. Their senses broke through all barriers. They threw themselves madly on their lovely wives, covering them with burning kisses; overwhelming them with the most intoxicating caresses; forcing their surprised and delighted companions to experience the most profound, sweet spasms of lustful felicity.

Clyso was happy at last, and when she went back to Athens, offered up another pair of white doves, immolating them in devout thankfulness to the beneficent goddess.

Athens was soon astir with the tidings of the miracle of Creos. There was not a Greek but who desired to taste the sweets of the love-philter sent on earth by Venus.

Young or old, all men rushed to throw themselves at Clyso's feet, offering their muscular bodies to be flagellated, so that they might be strengthened and rejoiced by the divine nectar instilled through her stinging, magic rods.

The whole of Athens reveled in a splendid love-feast beneath the fire of the miraculous talisman – birchen twigs awakening desire, increasing manly vigor and causing the flame of lubricity to burn brightly in the veins.

Clyso had not rods enough to lash all the writhing bodies prostrate before her, quivering impatiently to be fortified by the strokes of her bewitching birch. So her sister courtesans of Athens furnished themselves likewise with an ample store of supple green twigs. Under the aphrodisiacal influence of divine flagellation, old men acquired rejuvenation, and youths and middle-aged males found their amorous fury increased tenfold. Thus was voluptuous flagellation discovered by Clyso, and taking firm root at Athens, it gradually spread through the entire kingdom of Greece. Flourishing mightily, the worship of the rod passed into the Roman

Chicago

Empire, where young courtesans and harridan harlots were never without a bundle of whistling birch wherewith to invigorate their lovers and cause them to increase the force and number of their caresses, clippings, and intertwinings of soft sexual conjunction.

I

I knew that voluptuous flagellation flourished in North America, but I had no idea of the delightful way in which it was practiced.

From the standpoint of charm and poetical feeling, there are in that country exceptional opportunities for amateurs of birching discipline. I made a two months' trip through the United States during the spring of 1905. My delightful journey was one long triumphal march, as far as entrancing whipping pleasure is concerned. From my boyhood's days, I have been a fervent worshipper of birching, and I found fresh surprises in every town of the vast continent, while I was continually marveling at the beauty and enthralling charm of the divine priestesses of love who preside over the alter of the birch.

America is the promised land of flagellation. On every tree grow supple twigs, used daily in schools. Floggings are frequent in families, where children as well as adults are severely corrected.

When President MacKinley spoke of the Cuban war, he used a typical expression. "We don't want to exterminate the Spaniards," he said, "our sole desire is to give them a good birching."

That word "birching," crops up in every conversation, and is to be found in newspapers, stories, and songs. Teachers flog; the whip is wielded in houses of correction; the cowhide is an instrument of revenge; the free citizen of Columbia is birched for health's sake, or he submits to a thrashing because he likes it.

I had been two days at Chicago, when some advertisements in the daily papers attracted my attention by their enigmatical phrasing:

"Miss Nelly specialty massage, from noon to 9 p.m."

"Miss Esther, severe disciplinary treatment, 10 a.m. to 10 p.m."

"Miss Clara, scientific massage, from 9 a.m. to 10 p.m."

These announcements puzzled me not a little, but I called to mind something similar in the Parisian Press, relating to "English educational methods for unruly pupils."

Such appeals to public curiosity are made by charming cocottes who birch their adorers with fierce voluptuousness. I had often worshipped at their shrines in the Gay City, being as I have said, a fervent lover of lascivious lashing sport.

When very young, I had an adventure that caused this passion to arise in my being, and as I grew up, my longing for the rod greatly increased. No doubt the seed fell on a soil already well prepared, for as far back as I can remember, corporal punishment exercised a peculiar dominating influence on my disposition.

Belonging to a family of Scotch origin, in which the tradition of birching discipline had always been maintained I was soon acquainted with the furious, mystic caress of the supple twigs. Every time I was punished by a full dose, the tickle-toby being applied with a firm hand by my harsh governess, I fell under the spell of a strange sensation which I could hardly define. It possessed a certain pleasurable charm, and soon I sought, not to avoid my penance, but to provoke it, especially when my nerves, strung to the highest pitch, seemed to clamor for the beneficent shower of cuts.

When I was twelve years of age, there came a change in the organization of our household, and I was no longer whipped. As a consequence of this enforced calm and repose, I had almost forgotten my weird and agreeable feelings under the birch, when a couple years later, an incident took place which enslaved me body and soul to the extraordinary, besetting passion of flagellation.

* * *

My parents thought it would be good for me to pass my holidays in England, so as to enable me to speak the language of Shakespeare better than I could by learning it at school in Paris. I was sent to stop with a family of friends who lived in a pretty cottage at Richmond, not far from the celebrated park.

I was cordially welcomed by the mistress of the house, a young widow about thirty-five. Her name was Mrs. Smythe, and she had two charming daughters, fifteen and thirteen years of age, and a little boy of ten.

I soon noticed that my hostess ruled her tiny army with great rigor. The slightest fault was punished by birching.

When, in an adjacent room, I heard the noise of the rod brushing tender flesh, and the cries of my tiny playmates, my blood boiled. I was overwhelmed by a strong emotional feeling.

These corrections were generally inflicted in the bath-room, where a stock of fine, sturdy rods was always kept soaking in a pail, in order to that they might remain lithe and supple. When I was left alone in this room, shut in while I performed my ablutions, I could not refrain from touching the bundles of birch, old friends of mine by whom I was now abandoned. As I stepped naked out of the water in the morning, seeing them dripping on a chair, I often tried to calm my craving by dealing myself a few stingers, but I regretted not being able to hit hard for fear the noise should be overheard.

When I left the bath-room, I would put the rods back in the water, never daring to think that one day the hand of the charming lady of the house would brandish them relentlessly over my loins.

This impossible dream, filling me simultaneously with joy and terror, was however soon realized. I perceived that I was no more exempt from the ardent touch of the bath-room birch than was sweet Maud, the handsome and fair fifteen-year-old girlie, delicious Lizzie, her auburn sister, just thirteen, or sprightly Master Bob, only ten. I made Lizzie accompany me to the end of the garden, to help me to demolish an ant-hill I had discovered. The little insects scampered away in all directions, much to our joint amusement, and they lost no time crawling up Lizzie's legs, as she squatted near the scene of mischievous eviction. She jumped up, shaking her short skirts and shrieking.

To quiet her and help her to get rid of the ants, I led her to the neighboring summer-house. I was overjoyed at this lucky accident, allowing me an excuse to explore the undergarments of the handsome hoyden whose naked calves were extremely alluring to my young senses. I was not long before pulling off her tiny white linen knickers, and as I ran my eye over her delicate rosy limbs, and plump, round posterior, my budding, boyish passions rose to fever heat. With joy my hands smoothed her satin skin. Maddened by this unknown rapture, I fastened my burning lips to a divine mysterious cleft I had never seen before.

I should have liked to prolong this exquisite kiss of the pink grotto of her sex, shaded with slight silky down, and have licked her all over indefinitely. It was all so novel for me! Lizzie liked it too. But I felt myself violently tugged at from behind. A hand pulled my long curly hair. I tumbled over on my back, and saw Mrs. Smythe standing erect over me.

She was trembling with rage, and as I sprang up to my feet, gave me two stout slaps in the face, nearly knocking my little head off. I saw a shower of sparks. She then turned to Lizzie and dealt her a similar brace of smacks; afterward driving us both brutally before her into the house.

Without another word, I was at once bundled into an empty room. The door was locked, and I was left for an hour to reflect upon my dreadful plight. I may was well confess at once that I felt no remorse. On the contrary, I was delighted at my discovery. I could think of nothing but the image of the radiant slit, so miraculously revealed. The veil of my youthful cecity concerning sexual differences was lifted at last. Mentally, I compared feminine and masculine bodies and I was pleased to mark that God must be a lusty lover and a delicate artist to have formed the secret cranny of the fair sex like the calyx of a flower. I made a vow to devote myself fanatically to the worship of the mystic blossom and adore it fervently as long as I lived.

My daydreams were disturbed by the entrance of the housemaid who took me straight to the bath-room.

As I entered, I saw the worn stump of a rod on the ground, amid a quantity of broken twigs, from which I concluded that before I had been fetched Lizzie had passed a rough half-hour.

I pitied the poor girl who was innocent after all, but Mrs. Smythe's harsh tones cut my musings short.

"Young man," she said, "I can find no words to qualify the act you have committed. Your crime is so monstrous that I ought really to send you packing back home to Paris at once. I do not wish, however, to grieve your kind parents. They have delegated to me all their rights over you while you reside under my roof, comprising permission to punish you as I may think fit when you deserve to be corrected. I have therefore decided that your wrong-doing shall be expiated by corporal punishment as proportionally severe as your great fault deserves. You will thus learn that an Englishman respects all women, and more than any, an innocent young girl. I warn you that I shall flog your naughty bottom mercilessly. I also tell you at once that it will be best for you to submit with due humility to your deserved punishment. Should you resist my authority, I shall take forcible measures to restrain you. Here I have everything necessary for subduing a young scamp such as you are!"

I uttered not a word in reply, feeling quite dazed, not knowing whether I ought to be overjoyed at tasting at last the caress of the magic rod, or be alarmed at the rigor of the chastisement the young mother threatened in such despotic terms.

My impassibility seemed to increase her ill-temper.

"Undress!" she commanded, clutching my arm, and shaking me furiously.

Suiting the action to the word, she helped me to obey by tearing off my garments.

I was soon in my shirt, blushing to have to stand thus, half-nude, in the presence of this beautiful woman, who looked quite young. My shame, however, was not devoid of lascivious pleasure.

She pushed me toward a heavy armchair and made me lean over its seat. They she fastened me securely to this piece of furniture, in the proper position for enduring my torture. I could not take my eyes off my lovely hostess, whose irritation increased the beauty of her features. Giving fresh life to her good looks, causing her to appear bold and fearless. Every time her silk skirt touched my naked flesh or her soft hand skimmed over my skin, a delicious thrill ran through my frame.

From the pail, she chose a long rod, and after having shook the superfluous moisture from it, she wiped it on a towel, and made it whiz through the air, as if to try its elasticity.

"You'll now see," she said, coming close to me, "what happens to a boy of your age who takes indecent liberties with a young lady!" The rod began its wild saraband on my buttocks. I throbbed and bounded beneath the ruthless onslaught, unable to prevent myself from groaning with real pain.

My lamentations evidently excited the rage of my severe flogging hostess, and she kept on hitting me with still greater force. I trembled in every limb, making desperate efforts to get loose. But I was tightly tied, entirely at the mercy of cruel young *mater familias* who continued to birch me with a firm hand, unheeding my cries and prayers for forgiveness.

When her birch had been worn away to a stump, she desisted – but not till then. The violence of her beating had caused every twig of the bundle to be broken. My fright increased, because I saw her return to the fatal bucket, and I greatly feared that she was about to take another rod and continue my martyrdom. But she only dipped her practiced hand in the cold water for a few seconds; her fingers being numbed by the tension of her grip, and her palm slight scratched by the thorny ends of the branches forming the handle.

When she finally undid the ropes that held me captive, I ached all over and was quite exhausted. There was blood on my thighs, and the tail of my shirt stuck to my raw bottom.

The young widow did not deal me a second dose, and a few days afterward, when the traces of her severe treatment had disappeared, all that remained of this adventure was a most entrancing remembrance. I fell under the imperious obsession of a curious feeling which impelled me to long for the sting of the rod grasped by the firm hand of the lovely widowed Mrs. Smythe.

My yearning remained unsatisfied, and I said goodbye to Lizzie's mother with deep regret. Up to the moment of my departure, I had hoped that something would happen to curb me again under her bewitching blows.

At home again in Paris, the memory of the torture undergone at Richmond remained in my brain like some faraway disturbing dream.

For many years, I lived with the seed of flagellating passionate lasciviousness germinating in my inmost soul. In the society of capricious and refined queens of Parisian fashion, I tried fruitlessly to find a woman who understood my haunting ideas. But the lust of the rod being practiced in secret, prevents confidential discussion. I read all the exciting works of Sacher-Masoch, and my young, ardent imagination grew more and more inflamed by the perusal of his novels and tales which filled my mind with enticing pictures where I saw myself in the power of beautiful, hot blooded, ferocious females. Soon, however, reality granted me delights surpassing my most extravagant fancies.

II

As soon as I was manly enough to freely frequent any female I fancied, my love of flagellation, so far only a dream, blossomed into tangibility.

In the lounge of one of the principal Parisian variety halls, I became acquainted with a fine-looking, haughty brunette who at first sight made a deep impression on me.

A born *Parisienne*, having first seen the light in the outlying district of La Chapelle, she had started life as an apprentice to a manufacturing jeweler, before trying to sell her charms to the highest bidder. Despite her humble beginning, she was one of those heroines Sacher-Masoch loved to depict. It is not indispensable that a woman should come into the world in a sumptuous castle of the so-called blue Danube to posses an ardent and imperious disposition.

This splendid dark woman bearing the prosaic name of Julie, might have been a twin sister to some cruel Wanda, or terrible Sarolta dear to my favorite novelist. Julie's obscure birth and early workshop career did not prevent her carrying herself like a true patrician dame and even in her most tender, yielding moments, her manner was brutally despotic. She was selfish while enjoying carnal conjunction, and full of pride. I was quite stirred by her overbearing moods. I should never have dared to have approached her on the subject of flogging, if I had not accidentally discovered that she was a fervent expert in this salacious science. Entering her bedroom one day unannounced, I caught her with a long, flexible birch in her hand, and she deftly hid the whipping implement as she saw me. The revelation came upon me like a clap of thunder, and mastering my emotion as best I could, I asked her huskily how it was she had a rod in her possession.

"Does that surprise you, my dear boy?" she replied. "I love to whip men!"

Her words rang in my ears like celestial chimes, and my joy was so immense that I felt as if I was going to faint.

Without speaking, I lead the young *cocotte* to the corner where she had hidden her magic wands.

"Oh, I know what you are going to say!" she explained. "It's very funny, but I guessed your feelings the first time you had me. I was awfully astonished when you came to see me often and never unburdened yourself about your sweet mania. You're in luck's way to-day, for you've no idea how excited I am! Only handling that bunch of twigs that I've got ready for one of my gentleman friends who ought to have been here an hour ago, has made me feel as wicked and barbarous as possible! Come, darling, let that rod of mine writhe like a living thing on your stout bottom! Make haste, I entreat you!"

Never waiting for my reply, she began tearing my clothes off my back. When I stood naked before her, she slipped out of her dressing gown, the only garment veiling the secrets of her delicious body, and like a madwoman, the fascinating flogging harlot threw herself upon me, pinching my flesh with both hands, and making her teeth almost meet in the nipples of my breast and the muscles of my arms. Clutching the rod with her right hand, she enlaced me with her legs and her left arm, squeezing me in a vice-like grip, in such a way as to present my plump young bum most advantageously to the approach of her blows which she rained down furiously.

Flooded by the fiery waves of her frenzied birching cuts; electrified by the close contact of her firm flesh, I writhed and twisted in an infinite lewd spasm of wild enjoyment. Her frame followed the movements of mine, as she still held me clasped to her, unceasingly applying with sure hand and great skill a series of stinging cuts causing atrocious pain. The elastic birch rebounded like a metal spring, and its hissing ends always touched upon the same sensitive spots just at the lower part of my bottom, at the top of my thighs. My twin hinder cheeks quivered and trembled at the incandescent kisses of the supple instrument of torturing passion.

Making a desperate effort to escape from the fatal embrace, and avoid the awful stinging stripes, I fell, turning right over, dragging my implacable dominating mistress with me.

With one bound, she sprang to her feet, and throwing her whole weight – that of a tall, fine woman – upon me, she bent one knee on the nape of my neck, seizing my arm in her nervous hand. She had thus found a posture that suited her; where she had full command over my backside, and so she kept on striking at it, never stopping.

"I must flog you! I must! I must!" she cried, and her words burnt into my brain, as she accompanied her exclamation with formidable blows.

A prisoner under her precious, but inexorable yoke, I felt the full force of her descending blows, as I shuddered all over. I yelled with the pain of her attack, but she occupied an inexpugnable position and profited by it to keep on birching me, covering my bruised buttocks with a never-ending shower of fearful strokes.

She only stopped when the rod failed her. Half its branches were broken, and littered every part of her room. Throwing away the remains of her birch, Julie fell upon me like a wild beast, shaking me and biting me, until at last she forced upon my eager, willing mouth the dewy rosebud of her sex which opened itself and palpitated beneath my moist kiss and titillating tongue.

The furious copulation that followed transported us in heavenly ecstasy, taking our senses away in a reciprocal swoon of delight. I left her dwelling, with a staggering walk resembling that of a drunkard, my backside afire from the bristling twigs, and my flesh tingling from the insensate joy of our delirious bout of love.

I had discovered the divinity I longed for. She showered upon me the sweet warm rain of voluptuous sensual enjoyment. Many a time and oft did I howl and rave under the adorable pain of Julie's bewitching birch.

Thus it was that my lecherous love for voluptuous flagellation took a thoroughly defined shape in my mind, and possessed me for ever. As time went on, I found out other clever torturing beauties, among courtesans as well as in the ranks of the most aristocratic ladies of high standing in Parisian society.

Among the latter, the most striking was a young girl of seventeen who did not look more than thirteen, so slight was she – fair, fresh, and delicate, with a child's voice and a baby's face. One of our most famous procuresses, Madame Suzanne de Dreux, told me that she knew a real female phenomenon, a tit-bit for an amateur. The meeting and the bout took place in a sumptuously furnished flat, *Rue de la Victoire*, where there was a room specially arranged, fitted up with every kind of apparatus pertaining to the practice of flagellation in all its branches.

I was surprised to see a little slip of a girl enter the whipping chamber. I felt inclined to propose a game of marbles, when, in curt tones, she put a stop to my attempts at joking.

With the utmost deftness, she tied me across a bench, and when I was powerless, birched me with extraordinary cleverness. She was as much a mistress of her rod as a violin-player is master of his bow, and led me up and down the gamut of voluptuous pain, the torturing path leading to heaven through hellish purgatory, transporting me finally into a luminous paradise of lubricity where I felt myself dying with ineffable bliss. The inspired goddess, who had brought about my spermatic delirium, writhing on the ground in a vibrating paroxysm of indescribable meretricious voluptuousness, her secret sluices replying in solitude to the gush of my wellspring of manhood.

As we were both exhausted, I called for champagne, and the wonderful wee lassie consented to confide to me how her passionate love of whipping had been born in her.

In babyish accents, but with the malicious wit of a precocious girlie, she told me that her brother, two years her senior, had contracted a desire to be birched after having studied at a college where the master, a decrepit clergyman, allowed his young and robust better half to whip the boarders.

When the youthful collegian returned to Paris, he visited prostitutes to satisfy his yearnings which had become a pressing need, but his mother and father kept him from gadding about and he was obliged t flog himself on the sly.

His sister caught him birching his own bottom one day, and the young lover of the rod revealed the hidden secret of his lust to her, leading her to follow him into the birching vortex. Compassionate and full of tender pity, she determined that her brother should not be deprived any longer and offered her services immediately. He accepted eagerly, and happiness reigned in both their hearts ever since. At first, it was in the parental dwelling that they indulged in their favorite sport, the fear of detection proving an additional charm. Later on, free to do as they liked, they built a discreet nest to shelter the incestuous mysteries of their mutual splendid letch. In a little villa, hidden amidst trees and flowers at Neuilly, the young lass improved her mind and trained her hand so that she became a perfect flagellating artist.

I was afterwards informed by an American girl who had been a governess in a fashionable Boston boarding school, that corporal punishment was quite common throughout the United States in governmental schools, and families. She insinuated that flagellating passions flourished also. That was all she said, drawing back when she found how ardently I pressed her to reply to my interrogatories concerning the use of the rod. She was quite shocked. Her words were soon afterward corroborated by a rich member of the *demimonde* to whom a Yankee lover had recited, in picturesque bold language, glowing stories of the satisfaction he obtained by means of voluptuous flagellation in his free country, where the art of birching was taught by divine wenches.

I therefore resolved to explore this paradise of the rod and having inherited a fortune through the death of a generous uncle, I thought I would treat myself to a voyage through America and devote a royal sum of money to the indulgence of my passion.

In March, 1905, I embarked at Cherbourg on an Atlantic greyhound bound for New York, where I experienced such a unique and fairy-like pleasure that I intend to live my birching adventures over again, and so immortalize their memory in these pages.

III

The first few days after my arrival, I was greatly interested by the novel sight of the Yankee monstrous agglomeration of feverish, busy, go-ahead workers, and the only way I nourished my devouring hunger for flagellating joys was by listening to conversations wherein I was often startled to find allusions to corporal punishment.

In the columns devoted to current events in a leading New York daily, I read about a boy and a girl, caught in an indecent position under a doorway, playing at the game of "pa and ma." The precocious couple was soon arrested and severely birched by a policeman's wife, officially entrusted with the duty of whipping sentenced to culprits. I regretted not being able to go and play at this forbidden game sheltered by some wide portal, so as to be given over to the municipal female flogger, who, I imagined, must be a first class flagellant. Finding no immediate birching satisfaction, my letch began to jar my nerves seriously, and the image of the birching police virago trotted daily in my mind, until the idea struck me that it would not be amiss to introduce myself to her, so that she could whip me in return for a monetary gift.

I therefore charged one of my hotel commissionaires to obtain an interview for me with the flogging female of my dreams. He succeeded in making an appointment on my behalf in a neighboring square. I was delighted at this result, hoping at last to begin my task of gaining practical experience of American whipping methods. The day came, and at the appointed spot, I met a woman of low class extraction, but with a certain air of bold authority, eminently suited to her functions.

I told her what I wanted in plain words, but directly she grasped the meaning of my request, she stopped me.

"That's not my business," she said. "I only birch women and children; my husband punishes the men. I know what you require. You'd better try a massage institute."

She departed, obstinately refusing the five-dollar bill I tried to slip into her big fist to reward her for her loss of time. I was highly excited at having been in the company of this implacable birching dame, so independent in her talk and manner.

During the afternoon, strolling through the populous streets, I caught sight of a door-plate with the mention, "Massage Institute."

"The very thing!" I exclaimed.

Delighted at being able to follow the advice of the magisterial flogging female so quickly, I ran up to the second floor, where the same kind of plate fixed on a door.

A page-boy showed me into a room where I saw a tall, buxom lady, far from ugly, but with little or no gentility in her bearing. She was dressed like a hospital nurse, with her sleeves rolled up to the elbow.

"Massage?" she said. "All right – two dollars! Undress!"

She pointed to a low sofa covered with a linen sheet.

I was soon stripped, looking about me as I pulled off my clothes. There were bottles, sponges, and horsehair gloves, but no signs of birchen twigs.

As soon as I was on my back on the couch, the obliging female got to work. She patted, rubbed and pinched me all over. It was really most excellent shampooing.

After a short interval, I ventured to ask her without mincing matters if she went in for flagellation.

"No!" was all she said, continuing her massage.

I kept questioning her, refusing to believe her statements.

"That's not my graft!" she added still kneading my limbs.

"But I've been told that I could get whipped at all massage establishments," I insinuated.

"Yes," she replied, "gentlemen do get birched by women who call themselves 'masseuses.' They've got no diplomas. It costs ten or twenty dollars for a few cuts from a rod. I work like a horse for two dollars, but I'm a real, certified masseuse."

Her forefinger, shining with Vaseline, pointed out a big parchment covered with seals and stamps. It was hanging on the wall in a fine gold frame.

"Not a stone's throw from here," she added, "on the other side of the street, two blocks away, you'll see a sign which says 'Special Massage.' That's where you'll locate the artful creatures you need!" quite satisfied with the information, if not with the way in which it was conveyed, I waited impatiently for the painstaking masseuse to put an end to her rough rubbing, although its stimulation prepared my body for more efficacious action.

I soon found the establishment in question, and the scene presented to my gaze was quite different to anything I had as yet to see on this side of the Atlantic. In a comfortable parlor, sat an elderly lady, dressed in deep black, and wearing gold-rimmed spectacles, giving her an owl-like appearance. She was busy embroidering a pair of slippers. On a sofa-bench which ran along the whole of one side of the room, four young women lolled in lazy attitudes.

They were all very pretty. One was a haughty blonde with luxuriant yellow hair; next to her reclined an auburn darling with curly locks – an uncommon type, resembling a courtesan of ancient Venice; and this brace of beauties was flanked by a pair of saucy-eyed brunettes, doubtless of Irish descent, with fine fair skins. They were all dressed alike, in loose robes, that had flowing sleeves like Japanese kimonos, cut very low in front, and terminating in a V-shaped point, so that the girls' firm white breasts could be viewed almost in their entirety. The quartette's little white feet, innocent of stockings, were encased in small shoes, having high gilt heels.

As I entered, the old woman threw her work on one side, and advanced curtseying.

"You want a birching?" she asked.

"Yes," I replied.

"Bully for you! You're the right man in the right place. How will you take it – easy, mild, or strong?"

"Rather strong, if you please."

"Not afraid of surrendering to a whipping girl who is crazy on flogging a man? She's very hot on the job, rather cruel, and sometimes loses her head. In that case, she goes a bit too far for most gents. Don't say afterwards I didn't warn you!"

"I'm not frightened! She won't kill me!" I exclaimed. "That's just the treatment I prefer!"

"I reckon you'll get about your bellyful," was the matron's dry rejoinder. "Miss Cora will spank you pretty, and there'll be nary laugh about it!"

At these words, the lass with the golden locks rose majestically, tossed her head in the air, arched her loins, and looked at me scornfully.

"It's ten dollars," continued the old procuress eagerly, and in a jiffy she seized the bank-note I handed her.

"Pass on – in front of me! Hurry up!" said my tall imperious queen, and she pushed me rather brutally toward a short passage leading to a small room.

I found myself in a real arsenal of flagellation implements. A large enameled zinc tub contained quantities of birch-rods in all sizes and lengths, soaking in water. On a table were loose twigs ready to be selected and tied in bundles. On the walls hung various kinds of martinets with thongs of leather and cord. I also remarked a collection of whips. A shelf was stocked with riding-whips of whalebone and twisted catgut; all slender, elegant, and flexible. A servant-girl in a white apron was making rods, and the floor was littered with the green leaves she had stripped from the branches. "I've tumbled into a wholesale flagellating firm," said I to myself, as I glanced round at the enormous number of instruments of torture.

"Bottoms are cut up here, I should say, by dozens – nay, by the gross!"

My thoughts were interrupted by my fair-haired, conquering Cora speaking to the hired girl.

"Choose two good rods, Molly! The longest and strongest you've got! I don't know what's the matter with me to-day! I'm quite unnerved and fretful. I'm just dying to hear a man howl!"

"If you feel that way, Miss Cora," said Molly, "I guess you'd better take a stinging little riding-whip. That'll make him yell louder still!"

"Yes, I'll not forget the whip," responded Cora warmly, "but I want two rods as well, so as to tan his hide before I weal it till it bursts!"

This bloodthirsty little speech was uttered in sharp, biting accents, followed by a tigress-like flashing side-look at your humble servant, causing a voluptuous shiver to run through the whole of his body. While the servant carefully wiped two long, supple, stout rods, Miss Cora selected a whip, after trying several on her open pink palm. She chose one of elastic black whale-bone, as straight and tapering as the steel top of a lightning-conductor.

"Look alive! Get along!" she said to me, as, grasping her rods and whip, she drove me before her, out of the room.

IV

Roughly, with brutally nervous movements, the young woman took me a few steps down the passage, and then sent me spinning into another room, deliberately bolting the door, which she hid by heavy hangings.

The floor of this chamber was covered with a soft carpet, and I could not help seeing a kind of post, breast-high. It was fixed in the middle of the room, and covered with velvet. At the top of it was a bright copper ring through which ran a silken cord, the end reaching to the ground.

"Strip!" exclaimed martial Miss Cora. "Wait a bit. You seem rather dull! I'll wake you up, my lad!"

I had just taken off my morning coat, and as she spoke, she gave me such a fearful stinger from her whip across the back of my waistcoat that I almost lost my footing.

Before I could utter a syllable, the cruel flogging lass threw herself upon me, and tore off the rest of my clothes with skilful strength quite uncommon in a woman. It was not without a throb of pleasure that I submitted to the strenuous efforts of the implacable and vigorous feminine fingers which impressed me with the power of petticoat tyranny. So, ready to endure any suffering Cora felt inclined to inflict, I offered her my naked body.

With a coquettish gesture, Cora flung off her delicate little shoes, and the whiteness of her tiny feet – like a pair of spotless doves – showed up gloriously enhanced by the dark red background of the Smyrna carpet.

She dragged off my shirt and under vest, and throwing me on the ground, trampled on me, as she seized a rod. Threatening me with it, she made me lay prostrate while she thrust her toes to my lips. "Lick!" she shouted, and down came her rod with a loud crash, swishing my shrinking rump without the slightest idea of moderation, while my mouth feasted greedily on her exquisite pink and white pedal extremities, perfumed like some strange tropical flower and as agreeable to the taste as fruit from the gardens of paradise.

I writhed in agony under the fiery cuts of Cora's busy birch, and as, by the irregularity of my contortions, I let her foot escape from between my lips, she dealt me a startling blow, with renewed rage.

"I'll give you the whip, if you let my foot go again!" she exclaimed. "Take it entirely in your mouth!" she added, not ceasing to birch me rigorously while giving her orders.

Her delicious tiny toes – five rose-petals – passed beyond my lips to be sucked by my mouth and tickled by my tongue. Her foot half choked me, but I groaned with rapture, which the searing stripes of the painful birch were powerless to overcome.

My adorable charmer passed round to the other side of my body, so as to whip in the contrary direction, and she thrust out her other foot for me to kiss. I rolled on the carpet, unknowingly describing a circle in order to try and evade the awful blows of the sharp twigs. I took good heed, however, not to let Cora's exquisite wee toes escape from my clinging mouth. One devilish, white-hot stinger caused the tit-bit to slip from the touch of my tongue. My efforts to regain possession of the fairy foot were in vain, for the alert young female threw her rod away and fell back on the sofa.

I breathed freely, relieved at no longer experiencing the dreadful burning smart of the rode. I stretched my limbs, and contemplated my tormentress.

"How was it? Great, eh? Had a good time?" she asked roguishly, with a smile. "Lucky chap to have a free lunch off women's natty feet!"

Then suddenly rising, she grew serious again.

"Come here! Now, I'm going to whip you!" she said harshly. I hardly understood her. For the last half-hour I had been writhing on the ground under the flaming cuts of her stinging birchen caresses and now she spoke as if only just about to begin flogging me!

I begged her to spare me. My prayers – alas! – only made her burst out with a long peal of silvery laughter.

"What a fool you are! Let you off?" she merrily said. "I haven't whipped you yet. I've only just started! Come along and make no fuss about it!" she picked up the silk cord, and tying my wrists, dragged me to the post, fixing my bound wrists to the ring at the top. I was captive by the arms and entirely at her mercy.

Cora's flowing robe, loose from top to bottom, had opened itself during our struggles, showing the treasures of her fair-skinned frame; her hard, white breasts tipped with pink buds; her flat polished ivory belly, finished off by the mysterious golden curls of her sexual fleece; and her perfectly-shaped legs terminating in a pair of adorable little feet, still moist from my hot servile kisses.

She rolled up her sleeves, pinning them to her shoulders. I could see her lovely, white, dimpled arms, while she seized the second, unused rod, and clutched me under her left arm. I felt a thrill of enjoyment by reason of the contact of her tepid skin, but my delight was quickly dispelled when such force that I started in real excruciating pain.

The rod hissed serpent-like through the air, and spreading out like a released steel spring, slashed deeply on both buttocks, as the torturing creature held me with her strong arm to prevent me moving. With sonorous swishing sounds, the shower of blows fell on my aching posteriors. Unable to support the acute suffering, I began to groan.

"Yell, you devil!" she exclaimed. "I love to listen to men who howl! Louder! Louder!"

with another outburst of hysterical merriment, she struck at me with all the strength she could muster, birching me with might and main. My backside, bruised and bleeding, seemed ablaze. I arched my trembling body beneath this frenzied assault, and all at once freed myself from the grip of her arm, turning half round.

She cast the rod from her. I heaved a sigh of relief.

"Don't holloa till you've out of the wood," she said. "I've not done with you yet!"

Picking up her birch, she once more encircled my loins with her lovely, powerful arm. I almost swooned with delight when she lifted one leg from the folds of her open kimono, twisting her shapely lower limb round one of mine, so as to hold me tighter to her. And once again the biting birch resumed its diabolical dance all over my palpitating backside.

"Howl away1" she shrieked, noticing that I clenched my teeth, and was silent under the scalding shower of stinging stripes.

I was soon unable to restrain from yelling. My cries seemed to amuse her. Her nervous laughter rang through the room like the sound of some clarion of victory, as her nervous fingers never ceased brandishing the rod which rebounded from my scarlet rump like a sword-blade.

I made renewed despairing efforts to escape, but her arm and leg held me fast, tightening against my trembling body with a solid and delicious grip.

Cora at last grew tired. Throwing away her rod, worn to a jagged stump on my poor bottom, she thought fit to rest herself for a moment. She now took the riding-whip. Forcing me to assume a bowed posture, masterful Cora stood a little way off. Lifting her weapon as if saluting with a fencing foil, she gave me about ten awful cuts in rapid succession. They were well-aimed, and so terribly painful on my bruised stern that I fell to the ground with a long shriek under the influence of such atrocious pain that I quivered all over.

When I left the fantastical temple of torture, my head whirled giddily. A thousand hot branding-irons seemed to have made my posterior hiss as if broiled.

This violent flagellation appeased my lustful longings for a several days. My raw rump needed rest. Such a vigorous birching had cut me to pieces. The most harm had arisen from the formidable lady's whip. It had raised a series of red weals, full of blood, and smartly pricking at the least touch.

I left New York for Chicago. As time went on, the energetic discipline of my yellow-haired birching beauty left naught in my brain but a voluptuous remembrance. Her luxurious comeliness; her authoritative disposition and inexorable manner were charming for me to think about.

I passed a week visiting the marvels of Chicago – its manufactories and stockyards – until my lubricity was once more awakened by the goad of my secret yearning for flagellation.

I had discovered in a daily newspaper mystic advertisements, relating to "severe and special massage treatment," emanating beyond a doubt from the radiant priestesses officiating at the altar of the occult religion of voluptuous flagellation, of which I had been afforded a foretaste by capricious Cora of the golden locks. My wayward imagination, ever eager for the unknown, soon prompted me to try fresh experiments. I cut out and collected with care all the announcements that appeared in the press and seemed to relate to the rod, hoping, in my rambles round the crowded city to make interesting discoveries throughout the birching world, so attractive to me.

V

One fine, sunny afternoon, I determined to begin my visit to the "specialty masseuses". "Miss Nelly" came first at the top of the advertisement column in the leading Chicago daily, so I boarded a car, and soon reached the street where she lived.

I found myself in a fine, new house where a magnificent elevator, guilt like a Chinese pagoda, landed me at bewildering speed on the fourth floor.

A tall, stout negress, dressed in blue silk with yellow trimmings – a laughing black girl with a fine figure – led me into a large drawing room. The ceiling was supported with stucco columns, standing on golden pedestals. This saloon was furnished with striking luxury, being full of artistic furniture, statuary, and rare curiosities. Soon I saw appear between the pillars a dazzling creature, remarkably handsome – Venus incarnate, half naked in a white peplum. Quite fascinated, I admired the pure contours of her beautiful arms, seemingly fashioned out of pink marble; her big, melting, intelligent blue eyes; and her wealth of hair of the hue of ripe corn. Her locks were twisted into a heavy knot, resting low down on the nape of her rounded straight neck.

"Come, friend," she said with affable familiarity, drawing me near to her on a soft couch, "and tell me all your troubles."

I was delighted at such an affable welcome and painted my admiration for he loveliness in glowing colors. The blue and yellow coon-girl then brought in a tray full of splendid crystal glasses and flagons of liqueurs; sweets, cakes and Turkish cigarettes.

"Friend," said my adorable blonde hostess, "do you know the duties a fervent lover owes his mistress?" And she added: "He should be the originator of a thousand delights and imagine new tricks of voluptuous joy – all for her! He must surround her with an atmosphere of immense sensuality; pay her refined, detailed delicate attention, besides being willing, submissive, caressing and inventive. His mistress will be all in all to him. She will embody the whole universe, becoming his unique idol. He respects her like the holy Madonna; and adores her as of divine essence. Every inch of her sweet body will be known to him. For each spot of her fame he will inaugurate special worship and magical caresses, forcing her to laugh until she weeps for very excess of sensuous joy. Her lovely limbs will be covered by him with fragrant flowers. He will kiss her darling feet, kneeling to her as to a statue of the Virgin Mary. Ardent lover and attentive slave, he will always bow to her commands. Ever ready with compliments; never tired of praising her beauty, grace and condescension, he will sing to her songs of passion describing the adoration that burns his blood; charming her, too, by, scientific tender kisses and touches. Prostrate at her feet, he will be curbed beneath the yoke of her caprice, to accept and endure any pain she may be pleased to force him to endure. Tell me, friend, do you know greater happiness than to die and resuscitate in sensuous enjoyment by the aid of the birch's burning caress, while you are captive at the knee of a charming and implacable mistress, who shatters your resistance by the crushing weight of her powerful domination?"

For a long time she spoke in similar strains, with fiery words, the sound of he mellow voice lulling my senses as in a delicious soothing dream.

Then her tiny, girlish fingers, with their pink nails, squeezed my hand. Under the softness of her satin skin, great strength laid dormant, and I felt my digits gripped as in a vice.

"Come, friend," she sighed. "Come quickly, and taste the delights with which you have cradled your thought s in visions of desire." Unable to move, I was as one possessed. I wished to hear her melodious voice continue singing her hymns of love.

"Let us remain her, divinity," I replied. "I enjoy by the brain, and love to evoke a golden chimera in the flames of my musing daydreams."

"Now come with me," she murmured, "and I will show thee the altar of mystic torture."

She forced me to follow her into an adjoining room, full of freshly cut flowers giving out intoxicating fragrance. The walls of this chamber were completely hidden by red velvet hangings. In the middle of the vast hall was a long padded bench, on which, in the center, were two cushions, one on top of the other, held in this position by ropes of twisted gold thread.

There was no doubt but what this piece of furniture was destined for flag-ellating purposes. Several straps, nailed to its sculptured frame, were evidently intended to keep the lucky victim fixed in one position, when his body would be obliged to affect an arched shape, by reason of the cushions forced under his stomach. The posteriors would thus jut out, advantageously exposed to the descending rod. Not far from the bench of torment was a small table, covered with a white cloth, trimmed with lace. On the spotless damask were a dozen birch-rods, slender and well-selected, the handles ornamented with bunches of multi-colored ribbon.

"see," said my adorable goddess, "the supple implements whence I cause heavy sparks to fly, electrifying the man who begs for the beneficent application of the miraculous twigs. Never do I use whips or martinets. Their action is brutish and uncouth – devoid of the slightest charm. But rods are my resounding harps. They chant the lilting lay of passive submission and impotent rebellion; their resonant strings are stretched to breaking-point. And then they are still, tuneless through excess of melting voluptuousness."

There was a pause.

"Come!" she cooed.

"No, divinity," I responded, retreating. "Let your grand words live in my brain and sink deeply into my thoughts for many days. Soon will I be here and throw myself at your feet, beseeching you to let me hearken to the mystic melody of your harp-strings."

She led me back to the hall of pillars and stretched herself on the sofa.

I knelt at her feet, where lost in silence, I contemplated for some time this sphinx-like, supernatural apparition.

In our time, the goddesses, formerly immortalized by Phidias and Praxiteles, have taken up their abode in the United States and thus do I explain this fact, which at first sight seems absurd.

In the balmy days of the Grecian Empire, that nation held the first rank.

Chicago

Its galleys ploughed the sea, and from all parts of the known world brought back the most courageous men and the finest of women. Numerous colonies gave up to the Greeks the pick of their populations, and these varied races, by breeding and mixing many strains of blood, engendered and brought forth the type of mortal perfection.

Nowadays, the Greeks are a decadent race. The harbors of their lovely land are deserted or choked up and its people are feeble and degenerate. The Greece of our epoch is in America. The heroes who have conquered the New World were also the choicest flowers of heroism in the old continents. Only bold and robust travelers dared affront the perils of the unknown country. Bold weaklings died off rapidly on a foreign soil. Thus was formed a selected set of inhabitants, to whom the United States owe their splendid women, admirably proportioned, and haughty bearing; whose perfectly molded figures are aesthetically equal to the most ancient Grecian ideal standard. The same causes have led to the production of a race of enterprising robust men, brimming over with vital energy.

"What do they call you, divinity?" I asked the sorceress.

"Nelly Lamb," she answered. "My father was a Kansas farmer."

"How did a goddess, such as you are, grow up on a farm in the wilds of North America?"

"We were eleven children in all," she graciously rejoined, "all proud, Herculean men, and tall, noble-minded women."

I took my leave, delighted with my charming conquest. Leaving her a roll of bills, I swore I would soon return.

My solemn promise was needless; we both knew full well the invincible attraction we felt toward each other; bound by fate to meet again.

VI

I was no sooner in the street, where I was carried along by the hustling throng than I regretted having refused the offer of such divine dew as I knew must be distilled from the be-ribboned birch of Nelly Lamb.

Doubtless, she was a perfect mistress of the flagellating art, but the state of feverish excitement I had been in, exacerbated my need of some violent upheaval to calm my nerves; the influence of the adorable woman's marvelous beauty; her cajoling, graceful ways – all this had combined to confuse my ideas, their present trend being towards some energetic action.

When, therefore, I recovered self-control, I felt inclined to continue my voyage of discovery, hoping to find, among other Chicagoan female floggers, the inexorable and authoritative domineering woman, who, conquering my will-power, would know how to force me to submit to the severe birching correction I so greatly required. Before pursuing my exploration, I was obliged to return to the boarding-house, where I had taken up residence, to get a cheque-book my bankers had promised to send me.

By one of those mysterious hazards of life, an event took place as I returned to my lodgings which caused my inward excited feelings to be increased to the highest neurotic pitch. More oil was thrown on the fire of my secret passions.

A young hired girl, a fat wench of twenty, had been detected in an act of petty pilfering. From a lady boarder, she had stolen a scrap of lace which had been found in her room. The married couple who ran the establishment proposed their ultimatum to the wretched servant girl: a complaint would e maid to the police and she would go to prison, or she was to submit with docility to severe corporal chastisement.

The silly lass was dreadfully frightened at the vision of a stone cell, and with much weeping, elected to endure castigation. Her master and mistress decided that she should undergo her whipping at the hands of a disciplinarian governess of a neighboring school. She consented to carry out this private execution at the boarding-house, in return for her customary fee of one dollar.

As I returned, I saw the formidable person destined to dispense birching justice. The mere sight of her caused me to experience a thrill of deep emotion. This governess was a fine, tall woman, getting on for forty. Her frigid stare and imperious bearing made me shiver. She was not alone, being accompanied by one of her young pupils carrying a bundle of rods wrapped up in a newspaper. Dragging her sobbing victim into a room on the first story, the severe matron locked herself in.

Urged on by an invincible inquisitive craving, I stealthily glided down the dark passage, until I reached a little cupboard-like chamber adjoining the room where the punitive drama was to be enacted. My narrow retreat was separated from the whipping room by a light partition. I could see nothing, but it was easy to hear distinctly all that took place. My heart beat heavily at

Chicago

the sounds that fell upon my ears.

First, there was a long interval of silence, broken only by the loud sobs of the young minx. Then came a curt order from the governess, telling the girl to undress. I heard her garments fall, one by one, on the floor.

"Don't give me any trouble or bother," said the stern disciplinarian. "You know you're only getting what you richly deserve."

I felt sure that while she spoke thus, she was tying the culprit to some heavy piece of furniture. A long wait followed, full of anxiety for me, until the rod began to hiss in the air before falling with its loud "click, clack," on the firm young posteriors; the blows being applied in rapid succession.

The wretched maid-servant began to moan, and soon howled dismally, but the implacable twigs continued their task of expiation most mercilessly.

Suddenly, I heard the rod fall to the ground. There were hurried steps, as if someone moving about. The chambermaid uttered a shriek of affright.

"No, no, ma'am! Oh, don't, I pray you! I'll hold my tongue! I won't shriek any more!"

The voice of the guilty girl gave way. Choking, smothered sounds issued from her throat. The implacable schoolmistress had surely forced a gag into her victim's mouth, preventing her crying out. Then the saraband of the whistling, crashing twigs was started once more, terrible to listen to, in the midst of gruesome stillness.

I gasped with anguish, hearkening to the whistling rod cutting and lacerating the hussey's plump buttocks where it would leave bleeding traces.

It seemed as if the flogging harridan would never stop. I plainly made out her hoarse, "Ugh!" as she made each successive slashing effort, putting her maximum of strength into all her stinging swishes. I trembled from head to foot, shuddering at the echo of every smarting cut, as if I had received it on my own backside.

I cannot tell how long this poignant scene lasted. I was maddened and bewildered, when I caught sight of the terrible flogging woman leaving the locked room. Her face was full of animation. Her eyes sparkled. She was followed by her wretched victim, who, crying bitterly, could scarce drag her faltering steps along.

There rose in me a mad wish to accost the flogging governess and beseech her to treat me with the same rigor, but before I had quite made up my mind, she was gone, and my excited feelings were more tumultuous than before, as I had found I had missed her.

Forgetting all about my cheques, I jumped into the first cab that passed, ordering the man to drive to the address of a masseuse who had used the word "severe" in her advertisement.

I was shown into a flat which did not in the least resemble that of entrancing Nelly Lamb. The parlor, furnished with sober good taste, appeared as if it was also used as an office. A roll-top desk, encumbered with heaps of books and papers, made me fancy for an instant that I had made a mistake in the address.

My doubts increased when I was confronted by a young and remarkably pretty woman who came into the room. She was very ladylike, dressed in a becoming, rich frock of pearl-grey silk, fitting admirably and closely to her fine figure. She looked like a wealthy, middle-class tradesman's wife. Nothing in her manner or appearance betokened the "severe masseuse."

With rather more ceremonious gravity than was necessary, she saluted me politely, and begging me to take a seat, asked me very solemnly what was the object of my visit?

"I hope I have made no mistake," I said. "This is the dwelling of Miss Esther, 'severe masseuse,' is it not?"

"You are perfectly right, sir," was her reply. "I am Miss Esther.

Now I have given you that information, it's time to come to a showdown. I reckon you are an amateur of flagellation?"

"Your surmise is correct," I rejoined.

"In that case, my dear sir," she went on, "I may as well tell you at once that I don't go in for voluptuous birching, like many women who mix up coaxing caresses with whipping, thereby destroying the true character of corporal punishment. I don't try to give pleasure. My aim is not to provoke lascivious feeling by progressive artful fingering and vile kisses.

"I am a normal bircher – almost administrative, I must say – and the punishments I inflict are intended to create in a guilty person the impression of enforced chastisement from which there is no escape once he has elected to endure it. My chastisement is of two kinds: ordinary correction, consisting of sixty strokes of the rod, applied in two series of thirty cuts each, with a short interval between each series, so as to allow the culprit to collect his thoughts. My fee is ten dollars.

"The second kind is very severe indeed. It consists in the employment of a martinet with leather thongs. The blows are distributed all over the body, with the exception of the posteriors, where are reserved for active treatment, comprising one hundred blows of the birch in two series of fifty strokes each, and twenty cuts from a riding-whip – also divided into two series.

"My severe punishment costs twenty-five dollars and I assure you it is well worth the money. Such are my two chastisements. I do nothing else. I have an equal and regular way of whipping, peculiarly my own. My hand never trembles, nor does it change style of mechanical infliction for any reason whatever, so that you may be sure to get good and loyal measure. Should you wish to try ordinary punishment, you will be able to judge for yourself."

"I shall be delighted!" I exclaimed.

"Oh, delighted?" she replied with a skeptical smile. "It's not a laughing matter. My rods are splendid and I have strong, untiring arms."

Her last remark did not frighten me, but caused my yearnings to reach their uttermost limits, so I begged the young woman to operate on me at once.

"That will be ten dollars," she said.

I handed over the bill, which she put in a drawer of her desk.

VII

I was indeed charmed by the intelligent, ladylike, and straightforward manners of this young woman, treating flagellation from an "administrative? And commercial standpoint. Nothing about her smacked of the professional birching lady I had hitherto met – the sort of swishing siren who generally tried to infuse a sensuous flavor into the birching bargain and ordeal. Miss Esther treated the whole thing coldly and financially, without betraying the least feeling, real or feigned.

It pleased me to add to my flagellating knowledge, and fix in the museum of my mind this specimen of a "normal" flogging woman. I was impatient to see and feel her at work.

After having closed the drawer, wherein she had slipped my banknote, the birching queen struck a bell on the table twice. At this signal, a charming young girl, certainly not over eighteen, came into the room. She was simply, but coquettishly dressed in a simple dark frock with a white apron. On her shapely little head, she carried a tiny, pleated lace cap.

"Get this gentleman ready for ordinary punishment," said Miss Esther to her youthful assistant.

"Yes, miss," replied the winsome lass. "Follow me, sir, please," she added, addressing herself to me.

She led me into a large room, quite square, and shut the door behind her. There was very little furniture. In the middle, a plain wooden form of thick unvarnished oak. Close to it, a small table; a couch in an angle against the wall; and in another corner, a large trough, where rods, of all the same length and size, were in soak. On a flower-stand, near the sofa, were several whale-bone riding-whips, flanked by martinets with wooden handles to which were nailed ten or twelve leather thongs.

"This is what you must do, sir," said the engaging damsel. "You must take off your jacket, let down your braces, if you have any, or if not, take off your belt and lie face down ward on that bench. I'll do the rest."

I followed her instructions to the letter.

She took a wide strap, furnished with a buckle, and clasped it round my body in the middle of the back, fastening me securely to the hard wood. Then, with silken cords, she tied my wrists and ankles, binding them to the upper and lower ends of the form.

It was not without delight that I felt her pretty, little, cool, pink fingers rummaging round my waist, pulling my trousers and drawers down to my feet, afterwards throwing up the hinder tail of my shirt which she fixed to my shoulders wit pins she took from her bodice. I blushed with shame as I thus exposed the most secret parts of my frame to this sweet girlie – so engaging and so young. She, however, betrayed no emotion of any kind; no rosy flush invaded the fresh bloom of her cheeks, and her innocent eyes glanced calm-ly at me, as if she was accomplishing some natural task or ordinary household duty.

Going to the trough, she took out two rods, shook the moisture from them, wiped them on a towel, and placed one on a chair at each side of the bench.

"Miss Esther will be with you in a minute," she said, and then with a whirl of her slight skirts, she flew lightly out of the room, like a bird.

Her simplicity was delightful.

I was alone full five minutes, securely tied down on my bench, when the door was thrown open at last and the beautiful flogging female advanced to where I was. She had changed her dress, and now wore a tight-fitting black silk frock, very high in the neck, but sleeveless, showing the entire length of her marble, muscular arm." "Sir," she declared, "I am now about to deal you sixty strokes with a birch; thirty at once in one direction, and after a moment's rest, thirty more in the contrary direction. I hope you will endure your punishment courageously. It is quite useless to cry out or pray to me, as I am obliged to give you your full number of cuts without stopping for any reason whatsoever. Look out!" she added.

The first blow fell noisily on my hinder cheeks, the other cuts following quickly, without a break. She did truly flog with clockwork regularity, aiming to cover the two posterior spheres at once. The pointed ends of the twigs spread out like fiery tongues, searing my bottom all over with their flames.

The skillful lashing lady, her features impassible, stood as erect as a statue, her arm rising and falling with almost automatic precision. I groaned and twisted about under the consecutive cuts, falling fast and sturdily on my suffering stern, torn by the scratching ends of the branches.

At the thirtieth blow, Miss Esther cast away her instrument of torture, and sat down, as she crossed her legs, in a waiting attitude. I admired her clear-cut profile and the outline of her fine figure, terminating in small pointed, patent-leather shoes peeping out from under her skirt. I marveled at her unimpassioned disposition, permitting her to remain indifferent to such a sensational occurrence as the flagellation of a man. She soon rose to her feet, and crossed over to the other side of the oak bench.

"Look out!" she said again, emphasizing her ironical warning with the first blow of the second dose.

The rod continued to cut my throbbing skin. It's "swish, swish," was mechanically regular, and the sharp ends hurt me terribly, smartly applied to the side of my bottom which had the least suffered during the first half of the castigation. My whole backside ached with scalding pain.

I now began to feel as if bright flames were licking my stern, but the vigorous biceps of the nonchalant young woman was still active and I was flogged atrociously; the strokes descending in cadence as if proceeding from a motor.

The second rod was thrown to where laid the stump of the first, and my beautiful flagellating lady, as calm and as cold as ever, dropped a curtsey.

"All over!" she exclaimed.

I caught sight of the train of her black dress disappearing through the doorway, and I was very nearly regretting that I no longer felt her cruel birching touches so suddenly cut short. They had set my flesh on fire, without extinguishing my devouring desires.

Another minute, and the graceful girl came back. In the same deliberate way as her mistress, she unbuckled the strap, cast off the ropes, and pointed to an adjoining dressing-room.

As soon as I was alone in this feminine toilet retreat, full of subtle womanly perfume, my sense of eroticism manifested itself in furious fashion. The scientific and regular flagellation just endured, and that had not been terminated by any outburst of manly enjoyment as was the usual custom with lustful, ladies, seemed to me as if some powerful engine had been suddenly brought to a standstill. Something was wanting. It was exactly what a frenzied lover would feel, if interrupted during copulation, just as he reaches the ecstatic goal. With my hands, I rubbed my excoriated bottom, which was scarcely scratched. My burning flesh was languishing for more energetic caresses of the rod.

When the girl came to show me out, I followed her mechanically, but as I reached the hall, I hesitated. I was loath to leave the house where lovely, supple rods were always ready, and putting out my foot to prevent the girl closing the door, I pushed her gently aside. I boldly walked into the combined parlor and office.

My beautiful flogging female had resumed her grey costume, and seated in an armchair, was reading an evening paper.

"Are you going, sir?" she said, as she saw me enter.

"No, miss," I replied. "On the contrary, I have returned."

"I thought you would!" she said, quietly, and rising, dropped her newspaper.

"I immediately handed her two bank notes, amounting in all to twenty-five dollars. Without asking me to explain matters further, she put them in her drawer, striking the bell as before.

"Prepare the gentleman for severe punishment," she said, as soon as the young girl answered her summons.

"All right, miss," said the maid, at once leading me back into the room which I had only left a few minutes before.

I was about to obtain complete satisfaction and get a taste of one of those lithe whalebone riding-whips, that sting so terribly.

"This is what you've got to do," said the pretty maid, sending me into the dressing room. "You'll undress quite naked, without a rag left on your body, and put on the belt I'll give you."

She pulled out a drawer in a chiffonier and soon put her hand on a strange sort of girdle, fashioned in black elastic silk.

"Now, I'll leave you to yourself. I shall be back in five minutes. Mind you're ready."

I was not long stripping until I was in the same state as Adam before he was tempted. I examined the most original black belt. I had never seen anything like it before.

It was a narrow elastic ribbon, encircling the loins like an ordinary belt, closing in front by means of a buckle. When it was on, a second elastic band dropped down vertically. This strip of material was wider in the middle, forming a kind of pocket; and then it gradually grew more narrow until it was finished off by another buckle. I understood that this last ribbon had to be passed between the thighs, and its extremity brought up on the belly to rejoin the waist-buckle.

This invention, like all other Yankee notions, was excessively ingenious. The weird girdle fulfilled a twofold purpose. A man wearing it could stand naked before a woman without putting her to the blush, because his private parts were packed away, hidden in the rounded pocket. On the other hand certain delicate manly organs were sheltered from the contact of the rod, and the vertical ribbon separating the two posterior gloves, enhanced those hinder portions of the masculine frame specially destined to receive the cutting caress of the painful twigs.

I could do naught else than inwardly congratulate the unknown inventor of this most practical belt, of great service to birching – or rather birched – amateurs.

Thus armored, I bravely showed myself to the young servant-girl who paid no more attention to me than if I had been in evening dress. She stood on a chair, and released a rope hanging over a pulley that I had not hitherto remarked in the centre of the ceiling. She then took two leathern bracelets garnished with eyelet holes and laces, such as are use by athletes. Each of these cuffs was finished off with a metal ring. Fastening these gauntlets tightly round my wrists, she passed the end of the cord dangling over my head through the two iron circlets, and hauled me up. I was hanging with my arms in the air and my feet just off the ground, in such a way that I could turn about in every direction, but without being able to stoop or get away.

"Miss Esther will attend to you in a moment," was the stereotyped remark of the lovely little creature, as she disappeared with a frisky step.

VIII

There was a large mirror in the room of punishment. I could see myself from head to foot, suspended by the arms; quite naked, with the exception of the peculiar belt, tracing deep black lines on my body; splitting my hind quarters into two well-defined halves. I must have looked like an acrobat hanging from his trapeze apparatus. Turning slowly round to inspect myself on all sides, I saw that my freshly-birched, dark red buttocks stood out in deep contrast to the dead-white tint of the rest of my skin. Nevertheless, I hungered still for the burning smart that I had not fully experienced, and I gloated over the sight of two new, grand rods that the pretty girl had placed on a chair, side by side with a riding-whip.

The door opened. The superb female executioner came in, again attired in her tight black dress which clung so deliciously to her perfect frame.

"I am about to prepare you for punishment! Look out!"

So saying, she came near to me with a firm step, holding a martinet in each hand.

Scarcely were the words out of her mouth, when I felt myself enwrapped with a shower of hot blows. The heavy lashing of the two martinets was bestowed upon my flesh with unparalleled velocity, sweeping all over me with their numerous thongs, from shoulders to loins; then thighs to feet, on which I hopped despairingly, first on the right then on the left.

I twisted round and round like a mad dervish, under the rain of the white-hot serpents that stung me with their painful darts on all sides, and the clever whipping creature laid on her blows with mathematical precision, cut following cut with scarcely an interval. Every part of my body was inflamed, with the sole exception of the very spot where I wished to feel the fustigation.

In vain I turned toward the cruel flogging female those hinder parts of mine that palpitated with the desire to be assaulted. She cunningly avoided striking my backside. Both her martinets were plied above and below, so as to cause my suffering to increase. I stamped and howled, in a sudden fit of real rage, trying to place myself in such a way as to receive a stroke of relief on my poor bottom. I never succeeded, and my fury thus grew more frenzied.

All of a sudden, my flagellating lady threw her martinets from her, and left the room without speaking. I felt stupefied, not knowing what to think. The young chambermaid now appeared. Climbing on a chair, she freed my arms.

"Lie down – flat on your face – on that bench," she told me. By this I guessed at last that the whipping woman was coming back to quench the feverish thirst that tortured and devoured me. This long interval was infinitely terrible. I could hardly put up with it. While waiting, it seemed as if every inch of my skin was burning with flames even more ardent than when Miss Esther had flogged me with her martinets. The parts she had spared felt swollen, like big balloons. Every pore was open – a thousand tiny mouths seeking for breath.

The pretty minx had concluded her work of tying me down. She made as if about to go. Feeling myself under the spell of insensate desire, I begged the obliging maid to take pity on me and give me a few stout cuts with a whip before leaving the room.

"I'm sorry, sir" she said dryly, "but that's not my business."

Sketching a stiff curtsey, she flew out of the chamber.

When finally the door did open, I saw the irreproachable mistress of the house again. I thought that the archangel Gabriel had arrived in person, to save me from hell, and take me straight into paradise. "I'm now going to apply one hundred strokes of the birch, and twenty cuts with my whip," she said.

Her words fell on my ears like celestial music.

"Look out!"

The first blows, rained down with her usual firmness, cutting and lacerating my buttocks, were a sublime relief. I arched my loins, enjoying the heavenly dew of birching blows that refreshed my body athirst for flagellation. Oh, what a beautiful birch-rod it was! How divinely did it beat me, wounding me with its incandescent points and bounding off again, like a storm of boiling raindrops.

The beautiful flogging woman kept on castigating me, beating time to some unknown measure in her mind; dealing me the fifty blows, the barbarous, beautiful creature took a few moments' well-earned rest. She was impassible and calm; her eyes full of a faraway expression as she appeared to be plunged in some profound reverie of remembrance.

She then drew herself up to her full height, and passed round to the other side of my prostrate body. The regular swishing of the second rod tingled my bottom in its turn, torturing me with its sharp ends. It was terrible and delicious, at one and the same time. Maddening pain, mingled with ineffable sensual joy, made my flesh throb and beat with strange lewd pulsations.

I yelled, and twisted myself about, thousands of incandescent sparks sinking deep into the skin of my stern, while the rod never ceased slashing away at me with its harmonious and inflexible rhythm.

When Miss Esther dropped her second rod, I was on fire. My body was contorted like that of a sufferer of epilepsy. She seized the whip. I heard it hiss through the air and then with a sonorous, slashing sound, it came down dealing terrible cuts on my bruised bum. I writhed under the awful avalanche of blows. Every one of my joints ached. The rigid queen of flagellation, crossing over to the other side of the bench, let me have the remaining ten cuts, dealt with unchanging vigor. The last put an end to all the straining efforts of my tormented body. I lay inert, after one superhuman bounding effort, casing the bench to rock like a boat in a storm.

The moment after, my awe-inspiring mistress of the martinet had disappeared. The young girl came in, and liberated me from my bonds. She begged me not to get up, as she wished to attend to my a little.

Fetching tepid water and a sponge, she wiped away the flow of blood that stood out in ruby beads on my bruised flesh. After that she made me take off the black belt, and bringing a pot of ointment from the dressing room, spread some over my posteriors, covering the greased flesh with a piece of soft cambric.

"As you're a lover of flagellation," she said, "you ought always to have a pot of this nice cream handy. It heals the skin admirably, quickly effacing all marks of the rod or whip. It's called Cowper's Cucumber Pomade, and is sold in all drugstores."

While I was putting on my clothes in the dressing-closet, she brought me a glass of very good port. It ran through my veins like liquid fire, bracing me up after the strong succession of shocks I had experienced.

Dinner-hour was now nigh, so I was not long driving to a first class restaurant, where I invigorated myself completely.

My whole body burnt still with thousands of flames, while delightful reaction threw me into a state of voluptuous beatitude, the well-earned reward of passionate sensualists who dash headlong into the furnace of rods, martinets and whips. This reaction is not sought for nor expected. It is only the happy result of punishment. The votary of the rod, without thinking of the consequences, seeks only at starting to quench the mad thirsting desire that eats up his soul; that imperious craving to feel on his martyred flesh those cutting caresses which bruise and wound.

IX

The passion leading a man to long to be flagellated is a need quite as tyrannical for those engrossed by it as for others who cannot subsist without alcohol, opium or morphine. I was led to note the effect of this besetting idea on myself, for, although still feeling quite sore all over as a result of the terrible castigation to which I has allowed myself to be subjected, my imagination began to stray toward fictive regions where I pictured adventures in which rod or whip played important parts. My flesh cried out again for the beneficent bite of the birch.

A print seller, trading under the rose in most spicy specimens of artistic photography, showed me some very suggestive group which contributed to excite my salacity still further.

With astonishing fidelity to nature, these representations of living models showed various scenes of flagellation, where charming, young women abandoned themselves with voluptuous frenzy to the delight of whipping masculine backsides of all conditions and ages. One series was devoted to the punishment of a youthful pupil by a strict governess. This long suite of postures was reproduced with cinematographic exactness. A boy could be seen undressing; lying down tied to a bench. The birching game began. The authoritative, stern look of the school mistress and the struggles of her pupil writhing under the hail of blows had been dexterously caught by the operator, so that by looking at these photographs it was easy to feel the inward emotion that only such a truthful image can arouse. The punishment could be followed in all its phases; even the progressive effect of the rod on the lad's fleshy buttocks growing darker and darker as they became covered with scratches and weals.

Another most characteristic picture was that of a naked man, rolling on the ground at his mistress's feet. He was howling, covering with both hands his aching bottom, which the cruel nymph had just caused to bleed. She stood over him erect and triumphant, having thrown down the stump of the rod she had just used. She gazed at her victim with a lifelike, expressive glance of mocking scorn. The dealer assured me that this was the portrait of a renowned Boston birching beauty.

I purchased a copy, and several others as well. One that pleased me greatly portrayed a lad about to receive a flogging. He was ingeniously bound to an ordinary chair. It was overturned, its back on the floor. Kneeling on the back rail, the young fellow bends over the edge of the seat, in such a way that his shoulders reach to the extremity of the front legs. A long strap holds him fast in this posture which causes his backside to jut out high up, while his teacher birches him with all the strength she can muster.

These photographs had played sad havoc with my sense of eroticism, still more heightened by a most naughty conversation I had with I came home, with Miss Rosey, the female bookkeeper and cashier of my boarding-house.

I had remarked her the first day I arrived and felt irresistibly drawn toward her. She was a most lovely young woman, twenty-four years of age, with chestnut hair and eyes of a sapphire-like blue. Her entire bearing was full of graceful gentility, added to a light touch of offhanded independence which suited her very well.

I sought an opportunity for becoming intimately acquainted with her. She furnished me herself with the means of being more than friendly, since, to my great delight, she stood revealed as loving passionately to flog.

While I was looking at my photographs, Miss Rosey entered my room. Despite my instinctive movement to hide them from her, her keen furtive glance sufficed to fully acquaint her with the true meaning of the salacious scenes depicted. She made no sign, however, as she began to stow some linen away in a cupboard generally kept locked, and that I had requested the proprietors of the house not to empty on my account, as I had plenty of space for my belongings without that receptacle being handed over to me. I profited by Miss Rosey's presence to ask her how poor little Anna, the chambermaid who had been birched, had got on after her recent chastisement.

"Oh, first-rate!" the bewitching bookkeeper replied. "Her bottom being cut up did her good. She's more alert and active now. The rod is a grand remedy for sassy or heavy dull girls of her sort. If I was mistress here, I'd whip her often!"

"So, Miss Rosey," I said, "you stand for corporal punishment?"

"You bet! It's the most elegant thing on this old earth!"

"Have you often been whipped?" I asked.

"Nary! But I've given many a licking!"

"How – when?"

"I used to be housekeeper to a bachelor who loved to be flogged. You may guess I didn't make any fuss about birching him when he asked me."

"Most interesting! Tell me how you set about it?"

"It's a funny story," she replied. "I don't mind spinning the yarn, because I kinder fancy you're up against the same tough flogging proposition, too!"

The sharp young darling darted a sharp eye toward the photograph that I had turned face downward on the table, at the moment of her entrance.

"My chap," she went on, "used to flog himself every morning in front of a mirror, when he got out of bed. He was bound to do it, otherwise he was all abroad and as nervous as a kitten the whole day. But from time to time – once or twice a week – he felt inclined for a stronger shock. That I had to give him. You may be sure he got all he wanted!"

"This is the most delightful news for me, Miss Rosey!" I exclaimed. "How did you manage to turn on this powerful current?"

"I cut some rods in the garden, from an old, silvery birch-tree. Age had made the branches very tough. Then I tied my master on his bed; his wrists strapped to the head-rails and his ankles to the foot. Gee! It was a dance! Real elegant! I knew what was good for his complaint, and no matter how he raved and stormed, I whipped away as long as there was a twig intact on my rod, or a white bit of skin on his – ahem! Afterward, he would lie down on the carpet, and when he had taken my boots and stockings off, kiss my feet for hours, covering them with knowing, fiery caresses. That was how he showed his gratitude."

"How delicious, Miss Rosey! said I. "No martyrdom could be too great if followed by the favor of kissing your ravishing wee tootsies. Did this succession of violent emotions agree with him?"

"Why, certainly! He swore this treatment made him younger and stronger, being much better than any prolonged and tedious course of electric baths, and so on."

"What were your feelings while your obedient bachelor groaned under the fiery scourging of your heavenly birch?"

"My sensations were exquisite, maddening; carrying me off to a fairyland of unspeakable enjoyment."

"You must miss these pleasures greatly, Miss Rosey!" I remarked after a short pause.

"I try not to think about such things," she answered. "There are days, I must say, when I felt so excited and overwrought that I'd flog anything or anybody. But I have to restrain myself. I can't confess my longings to the first person I meet, can I?"

"Suppose, Miss Rosey," I said, "you were to fall across some one who would esteem himself the happiest man in the world, if you condescended to curb him beneath your cutting rod?"

"I shouldn't think of refusing my services, especially as I should have pleasure in whipping him."

We understood each other. As I stared at her with mute appealing looks, she broke out in a laugh.

"You great goose!" she exclaimed. "I see your drift. Anyway, it's impossible here, and my day off isn't till next Thursday. You must find some decent house where we could meet."

I promised to arrange matters, offering up a prayer of sincere thanksgiving to Providence for sending me such an adorable little birching elf, with whom I was sure of tasting ineffable joys.

Six days had still to elapse until that blessed Thursday, when Miss Rosey was to offer me the feast of love and flagellation. To me, these six days seemed an eternity.

Whenever the lovely young woman passed me in the passages or staircase, we would exchange tender, friendly glances, and we never saluted each other politely, with the usual commonplace greetings, without experiencing the enthralling emotion of lovers who have made mutual promises of reciprocal abandonment for the near future. In my case, this feeling was rendered still more keen by my imperious desire to have my bottom throbbing under a burning birch, brandished by Miss Rosey.

My yearning became intensified through a fortuitous meeting in the street with the school-mistress who had been summoned to the boarding-house to chastise the maid. The austere governess was accompanied as before, by one of her pupils carrying a parcel of which it was not difficult to divine the contents. The female disciplinarian was probably on her way to some family to exercise her severity on a young and pretty pair of plump posteriors. I followed her a few blocks, racking my brain to find an excuse for entering into conversation with her. Before I had arranged a few neat sentences, she disappeared into a respectable private house. I stood paralyzed on the sidewalk, quite disappointed.

In my thoughts, I turned over all the addresses of flagellating female charmers, of whom I might have ventured to demand instantaneous appeasement.

I was too undecided to select any of those I knew, preferring adventurous exploration, leading me to new faces and feelings.

X

Returning to my boarding-house, an untoward circumstance extricated me from my dilemma. Miss Rosey, full of joy, met me as soon as I went in, telling me she could grant me a few hours in her company that very evening. She had a ticket for the play, and permission to go out.

Having already seen the piece, she did not care to profit by her free admission to the playhouse, and besides, felt sure she would get much more fun out of a little flagellation.

So she decided to sacrifice scenic delights, preferring to meet me in some quiet retreat where, from nine o'clock until midnight, we could revel in the pleasures of our secret birching passion.

I was enchanted at the news, fitting in so well with my desires. We arranged an appointment at the door of the theatre, and I was off at once to discover the nest where we could take refuge to perform the rites of our religion. In a large town, such cozy nooks for lovers would surely abound, I thought.

There were yet three hours for me to pass before the hour of meeting. I made out that I had lots of time for my quest. As soon as I began my investigations, I found it was not so easy after all. Some inconvenience or the other prevented me from making a definite selection. Time went by like lightning, and my peregrinations were fruitless. The hour of the tryst drew nigh. I was on the verge of despair.

It was half-past seven when my luck changed at last. I was offered a little self-contained flat. There were three rooms, sumptuously furnished. I took it without haggling, for I only just had time to rush off and rejoin my sweet companion.

She was punctual at the spot agreed upon; neatly dressed; and as happy as a baby at the idea of our risky escapade.

"Have you brought some good rods?" was her first question.

"Great Caesar, no! I've quite forgotten them! It is really stupid of me! How was it I had not dreamt of the birches, although the teasing twigs continually haunted my thoughts? It's the first thing I ought to have thought of! Now, it's too late. Where on earth could we buy birch-rods at nine o'clock in the evening?

All the shops were shut. Florists, horticulturists, fruiters – had put their shutters up an hour or more ago. The only tradesmen open were chemists, whose colored lamps I could see from where I stood. I was downcast, and felt very silly. Miss Rosey began to pout. "We might find a riding-whip perhaps?" I suggested.

"There's not the slightest chance of that," she rejoined. "Saddlers close at seven. Let's go look round a drug-store. We may light upon some implement or the other."

At a couple of chemists, we found nothing to suit our purpose. Miss Rosey, not wishing to trouble the apothecaries for nothing, made me purchase some boxes of lozenges and chewing gum. Passing in front of a third druggist's emporium, Miss Rosey clapped her hands. "The very thing!" she exclaimed, showing me in the window a packet of gutta-percha probes, having some vague resemblance to riding-whips.

I made haste to buy four, and Miss Rosey, her good humor returning, insisted on carrying them herself.

"At last!" she said. "I've found good implements and I'll teach you, sir, to forget to bring a birch. Your bottom will pay for your negligence."

"My bottom," I replied, "quivers with delight at the idea of expiating my wrong-doing at the hands of the most adorable lady cashier in the States!"

"Laugh away," she rejoined, "while you can. By and by, your bum will certainly quiver, but it won't be with delight. Of that you may be sure!"

In the cozy apartment, brilliantly illuminated by the electric lights, Miss Rosey jumped for joy, like a schoolgirl out for a holiday. When, however, she tried the probes we had bought, by striking them on her hand, she doubted their efficacy.

"These things don't seem much good," she said ruefully. "Let's look through the furniture. We might tumble on to a rod or a whip."

She opened all the cupboards, searched in every drawer – there was nothing.

"It's dreadful," she said. "Hasn't anybody ever been whipped in this place? Never mind, sir, get undressed quickly. We'll try the effect of rubber probes on your wicked skin."

In the bedroom, garnished with rugs, curtains and hangings, a large, low bed was ready, offering us a comfortable exercise-ground. "Get on that coun-terpane, and bare your big bum," she said. "Now come to think of it – how am I to tie you down? You've thought of nothing! No rods; no ropes or straps to bind the victim! How am I to whip you? You deserve double punishment and I've got no reliable instrument with which I can apply it!"

Naked to my shirt, I was lying on my stomach, on the rich coverlet of the comfortable couch. She arranged my linen so as to expose my rump advan-tageously for punishment, and taking one of the probes, started beating me boldly. The India-rubber piping made a great noise, but I could support, without the least discomfort, the soft sonorous blows that the charming young woman dealt me, fatiguing herself greatly with little or no result.

Losing patience at my indifference, she took all the four probes in her lit-tle hand, and pulling up her sleeve put forth all her strength, flogging me as hard as she could.

The effect of her punishment was not a wit more terrible. On the con-trary, the four probes made the blows duller and heavier. United, they cer-tainly hurt much less.

As I saw the impotent efforts of my pretty girl, trying her utmost to make my penance perfect, I could not refrain from roaring with laughter.

"Ah, you grin, do you?" she exclaimed, as throwing the probes to the other end of the room, she fell upon me like a fury, driving her sharp finger-nails into my flesh; biting and pinching my buttocks. I was thrilled with intense joy, from the warmth of her mouth and the electric touch of her hands. I made no resistance, intoxicated by her celestial contact.

In her mad efforts, she rolled to the ground. It was my turn to rush to her assistance. Picking her up like a child, I carried her to the bed, gently laying her in the place I had just occupied.

"Let me be!" she said. "You are a monster to have got me into this excit-ed state. I'm sick! I guess I'm going to have a nervous attack." I undid her shirtwaist. Two lovely white, plump gloves appeared to my dazzled eyes. I lost my head, and dared to cover the twin glories of her breast with gluttonous kisses.

"Leave me alone!" she said, struggling in my embrace. "What you've done to me is awful! You worked me up to the highest pitch of naughtiness! I felt quite lewd! And then you left me in the lurch without satisfying my craving for the birch. I order you to come here on Thursday. Then I'll bring some rods. We'll see whether you'll laugh under my lashing!"

She jumped off the bed, again in a pet. Her rage was comic. It was like a child's sullen fury.

"My word!" she shouted, stamping her little feet; "can't I find something I here to cut up your horrid old bum with?"

Again, she opened every cupboard, fumbling in all the drawers, but with the same ill-luck.

"Ah! A good idea strikes me!" she exclaimed, suddenly. "Take a napkin, roll it up tight – as tightly as you can. Then wet it to make it harder, and I'll see if I can't tame you!"

I plaited and twisted one of the fine linen towels until it assumed the form of a thin, ling, white snake. It looked a useful sort of assaulting article, and Miss Rosey seemed satisfied. She dipped this strange improvised scourge in the water jug, and after she had wrung it out, it looked strong and serviceable.

"Take your places for the quadrille! commanded Miss Rosey, quite delighted.

I stretched myself once more on the bed. She began to flog me with great and renewed energy. The spotless snake fell noisily on my bare hinder cheeks, at first causing me to shiver, for the towel was cold and damp. Miss Rosey, seeing me shudder, thought she hurt me very much, and was greatly pleased. She kept on striking me as hard as she could, with much graceful flourishing of her pretty arm. The twisted towel got harder as it dried. It now stung a little. My flesh took on a rosy hue. Encouraged by this result, she grew more active, dealing me some rare stripes, skillfully applied. I was deliciously enthralled by the beating which inflamed the flesh of my rump and excited my senses of voluptuousness. I could willingly have submitted to more violent discipline.

Suddenly, the towel unrolled itself like a flag, and my young lady, deeply vexed, cast it far from her.

"It was going on so nicely – and now it's all stopped again. No, you've no heart nor conscience to play me such a trick! I had formed such hopes of enjoyment, as I thought of birching you! Oh, I do wish I'd gone to the theatre!"

"Dear Miss Rosey, " said I, trying to soothe her, "why trouble, when you'll get your own back on Thursday –"

"The deuce take Thursday!" she interrupted. "It was this evening that I wanted to flay you alive! I wonder if you know how to kiss a woman's feet, with new and unexpected caresses? Take my shoes off, quickly!"

With a great rustling whirl of silk and lace, she threw herself on the bed. Pulling her skirts up very high, she exposed to my enraptured gaze, her shapely legs, encased in black, transparent silk hose, and her little feet tightly clasped by pretty, patent-leather baby shoes. I could not control my joy at the prospect of kissing her dainty, tiny tootsies, and after having unlaced her shoes with trembling fingers, I thrust my daring hands far into her silk petticoats, amid filmy lace, while the heady musk scent emanating from her underneath mysteries mounted to my brain and made me dizzy. I had been forced to be so audacious since I had to undo her broad garters which she wore above the knee. Gently, I pulled at her long stockings, as light as cobwebs, and soon I feasted my enchanted eyes on her naked rosy limbs and lovely pink feet.

I had never seen such magnificent, divine pedal extremities. They were chiseled like marvelous artistic statuary; perfect and delicate in line, color and shape. Standing away from its companions, the big toe was cocked up saucily like an impudent nose, and the whole row of wee pink coral digits were tapered like fingers, with microscopically nails, rounded in the form of some pearly seashell. My eager mouth devoured them. It was a divine tit-bit of delicious, fresh-flavored fruit, such as must have grown in the garden of Eden.

"Again! Again! Keep on! You do it so nicely!" sighed my adorable creature, in a dying murmur of deep delight.

My greedy lips and tongue rendered due homage to this priceless pair of feet, licking, sucking and tonguing – first one and then the other; and lastly, both at once, until I had to hark back again, not knowing in which marvelous little nook I ought to stop and concentrate all the delight I tried to impart and the vast, sensuous, mad pleasure I kept on experiencing.

Her heels were finely molded. The skin of her feet was soft and tender; smooth as satin and of a rosy shade. Here and there, the tint was deeper. At the root of the toes, on the ball of the foot, were amber splashes of color, akin to the hue of old carved ivory. The instep, high and proudly arched, was crossed by an almost imperceptible bluish vein, meandering – a capricious arabesque – on the white surface; but the supreme wonders were her miniature, tiny toes, worthy of adoration, looking like a row of newborn Christ-like babes slumbering in cradles of lily-white silk.

My eyes and mouth were insatiable. I groaned with excess of lust. No man could have been more happy.

XI

"Oh, it was fine!" exclaimed my companion, rearranging her rumpled petticoats. "I don't regret having missed the play, after all. I suppose you got me here to show me how clever you are with your naughty mouth? What time is it?"

"Eleven," I replied.

"Gracious! Hurry up! I must be in by midnight at the latest," she said. "I'll have my revenge on Thursday. You'll lose nothing by having to wait!"

Like school children having played truant, we got home at once. I let her go in first, allowing a quarter of an hour to elapse before returning. We had also alighted from our cab a few blocks away from the boarding-house.

The night passed after that grand evening was filled with radiant dreams. I desisted from drinking or smoking a cigarette before getting into bed so as to jealously keep on my lips as long as possible the fresh, fruity perfume of Miss Rosey's adorable little feet. I was still under the charm of the surprise I had felt at seeing such unhoped-for marvels revealed from out of the shoes of a simple book-keeping lassie.

I ought not to have marveled, knowing as I did that the female foot was the object of devout worship in the United States. I had heard of the untiring minute care that young American girls take of that delicious hidden part of their desirable bodies. I had been told, too that betrothed maidens, during meetings of acknowledged courtship, abandoned their naked feet to the admiration and exquisite kissing titillation of their future husbands, who highly prize this favor.

My countrywomen, the *universally-admired* Parisienne, is renowned for her little, fairy feet, but – alas! – many a time and oft, her *gentil petit pied* should be described by the words, "pretty little boot."

So long as the high-heeled *bottine* is small, tight, narrow, and elegant, the beauty of the City of Light thinks she has a pretty foot.

* * *

Everybody round her encourages her in her error. She lets her tootsies twinkle in and out of her skirts, for the men to admire and pay her compliments thereon. Nobody troubles to ask what is enclosed by the dainty footgear, so slim and pointed.

In many cases, and I know more than one, the object imprisoned in the

Chicago

Cinderella shoe, which arouses our sensual longings as it trips along the wood-pavement or is seen stepping in and out of the motorcar, cannot even lay claim to be considered as a foot. It is nothing more than a shapeless stump. So as to be able to reduce the size of her boot by one number and sport tight and tiny footwear, many females have no hesitation in sacrificing divine extremities originally fashioned by Providence to be one of the principal ornaments of woman's sacred body. The toes are forced together, until they are pressed one above the other. Jammed out of their natural direction, they bend over, shoved remorselessly in a bunch toward the shining toe-cap. The continual pressure to which they are subjected makes the little martyred digits become square-shape, without counting that they are always inflicted with a sickening series of hard and soft corns, and bunions. As to the nails – what a disaster! Some disappear entirely; the remainder are deformed. The silly lady of fashion is happy nevertheless, because from under her pretty petticoat she can thrust forth a microscopic shoe, to which her admirers bow down and do homage.

The Parisian Venus is always represented in naked splendor, but with black stockings. Following the same aesthetic ruling, the courtesan and the patrician pet alike, when undressing in the presence of a lover, keep on their stockings. They are to be congratulated for doing so, as the modern French female is a delightful statue, chipped at its base.

Things are different in America. There flourishes the cult of the hand as well as that of the foot. Yankee boots are rationally modeled, allowing the toes to spread out with ease; giving space for natural development, according to admitted academic outlines. No American woman consents to put up with the torture of tight boots under any pretext whatever. She is rewarded by being without agonizing corns or other excruciatingly painful excrescences of the same family. She takes as much care of her feet as of her hands, and when she kicks off her slippers, lover and artist feel unalloyed delight. "Foot-flirtation" is the lascivious coquetry of the beautiful up-to-date Stars and Stripes siren, offering to the gluttonous, loving lips of her betrothed sweetheart or her chosen suitor that maddening, intimate plaything – her naked foot.

The smart set in New York often organize prize beauty contests for feminine feet. These "Tribly" competitions cause painters, sculptors and refined adorers of the fair sex to foregather enthusiastically. In a vast hall, the pretty competing charmers are unseen by a picked jury. The Yankee goddesses are behind a curtain. Their naked feet, resting on little cushions, are alone visible. The sight is a wonderful one – a delicate treat for connoisseurs of true feminine beauty. The ladies taking part in the contest, nearly all belong to the Four Hundred; or the high society of multi-millionaires; but middle class beauties are also eligible, as well as the pick of the basket of bejeweled "kept" women.

The jurymen are sometimes in a quandary. They have to award the prize – a heavy bangle of massive gold, incrusted with diamonds, forming an ornament to be worn round the ankle to the best pair of impeccable feet they can see, judged from an academic standpoint. The following important points are deserving of the highest award, when found united: white, smooth skin' absolute perfection of the nails, rounded and almond-shaped, like those of the hands; while the carnation of the heels and tops of the toes is also not to be overlooked. I ought to have advised Miss Rosey to take part in a New York "Tribly" contest, and among American women I have known, I often met with many adorable little feet, worthy of the suffrage of the most fastidious and exacting jury.

Every time I met ravishing Rosey in my lodgings, my whole frame was voluptuously stirred as I glanced at her little shoes hiding her delicious marvels. My mouth watered, impatient to drink in the intoxicating scented taste of paradisiacal fruit.

Day after day went by much too slowly for me, waiting impatiently for that happy Thursday when I was to sate my lascivious appetite during a long afternoon of joy, satisfying my furious cravings to be forced to suffer and start under the divine caress of the rod. "Now, boy," Miss Rosey told me, "don't worry all the time about those birches you forgot. One of my lady friends, whose husband is a fervent votary of flagellation and who she flogs daily, has promised me a few of her real good, green rods such as she gets for dutiful hubby. She's also going to buy me a riding-whip, exactly the same as she uses. It appears her old man howls and leaps in the air when she cuts him with it. I'm so happy! At last I shall be able to flog you properly!"

Miss Rosey's features were illuminated; her eyes sparkled joyously; still more intense pinky color came into her cheeks; and her little nostrils palpitated. Only to look at her and listen as she spoke made me beside myself. The promise of this festival of flagellation; the fulfillment of my most deeply-hidden desires was rendered more heavenly by the knowledge that this entrancing girl was as pleased as I was, if not more.

Chicago

Three days had yet to pass before the memorable day of joy. I had all my work cut out to support being deprived of my birching nourishment until then. To enable me to curb my impatience, I had paid a visit to the flat of Nelly Lamb. Her door was closed. The adorable goddess was away on a journey, and would only return the next day.

Another night and half a day of languishing expectation and I rushed to the hall of pillars.

Again I was permitted to gaze upon her enthroned in the sumptuous setting that suited her so well. Affable and smiling as ever, she was really wonderfully beautiful in a Greek peplum. She looked like a lining statue.

"Friend," she said, "could you sleep calmly all these ling nights without my image troubling your rest?"

"Divinity," I replied, "you deserted your temple. I returned and knocked at your door in vain."

"I allowed myself to be carried off by a handsome Russian prince," she said. "he took me to the borders to see the ocean."

She went on to tell that a Muscovite nobleman came to see her once a year, about this time of year. He always passed a few days with her in a superb villa that he hired on the sea-shore. Possessed by the passion of the birch, he forced himself to fly from her, so as not to die under her rod. She had to flog him for hours together. He was never tired of begging to be scourged. Luckily, she knew how to satisfy him, and to that end, displayed indefatigable energy.

At night, when he slept, she would lift off the bedclothes, and wielding the instrument of torture with artistic, delicate, make him moan for joy in the dreamland of flagellation. His nerves vibrated like the strings of a harp beneath the touch of her agile fingers, forcing him to experience such exquisite profound manly enjoyment, that she had to restrain herself and graduate the effect of her penance, so as to keep him always floating on the surface of the sensuous stream, not letting him fall into the hidden concupiscent caverns of the dangerous depths of too great voluptuous pain.

He would then set sail for Europe, exhausted by these successive shocks of unique and stirring salacity. Once at home in Russia, he used to write her letters which were real poems of passion accompanying his epistles with precious stones beyond price, dug from mines of his own in Siberia where he was master of ten thousand slaves. The prince was young and gloriously handsome – a demigod – diaphanously pale, like an agate, and flaming gold spangles sparkled in his eyes. Nelly loved him madly, but they did not dare live together. Their mutual sensual intoxication was so great that they must both have succumbed. To protect the lovers against the overflow of their great happiness, it was necessary that two continents and the ocean should separate them.

XII

My beautiful acquaintance, Nelly Lamb, threw herself back on the sofa. Her magnificent arms, folded under her neck, caused the undulating lines of her sinuous body to be seen to the greatest advantage.

Real healthy blood coursed beneath the marble of the divine figure. I could see her armpits, where no luxuriant tuft threw any dark shadow to mar the statue's purity.

In silence I gazed at her. She suddenly rose to her feet.

"Tender friend," she murmured, "today you'll not escape me. I will have you groaning at my feet, plunging as you feel the burning kisses of my rods. You need the birch. I see that in your eyes."

She thrust her lovely foot toward me.

"Untie my sandals, darling friend," she said, "so that I may shudder at the contact of your hot lips on my flesh."

I immediately rushed to undo the knotted, pale-blue ribbon, terminating in a bow above the ankle, and which separated her big toe from the others. Soon, the sweet, twin, pink marble wonders and their nails as brilliant as jewels appeared to my enthralled gaze in all the radiance of their beauty. Bowing down, my mouth pressed them, as if they were the feet of a saint in a holy tabernacle.

"No, my friend," she said, rapidly drawing them beyond the reach of my kiss, "the fire of the rod must first enliven you. Come quickly and be naked so that I may bathe you in myrrh and incense."

She led me to the red room where there was a wealth of fresh-cut flowers of vivid hues in an atmosphere saturated with aphrodisiacal perfume.

I discarded all clothing, and naked, I felt as if in a scented, tepid bath, drawing in lascivious excitement at every pore, provoking a tantalizing upheaval of my deepest lust.

With a cry of triumph, I fell on my knees, joining my hands in adoration.

The superb creature had slipped off her robe, and stood before me like

Chicago

Venus rising from the sea, exposing the whole of her naked body. It was the statue of Phidias incarnate. Aphrodite without her sex; pure because so beautiful; divine marble; the incomparable perfection of sublimity in art. No shady bush tinted the swelling curves of her mount. There was no curling tuft to hide the quadruple pink petals of the blossom of supreme voluptuousness. Whispering Virgil's lines: *Vera incessu patuit dea!* I fell giddily to the ground, and my avid lips clung to the marvelous feet I saw before me. At the same moment, the rod descended on my buttocks, skimming over my skin with its incandescent ends, showering sparks of fire upon me.

I groaned with joy under the scalding rain, as I vibrated with happiness at the foot of the living statue that flogged me. She was more beautiful than any dream of painter or poet.

She moved about, and my tongue, fearful of losing one single crumb of enjoyment, slavishly followed every step of her delicious feet, fleeing from me on the thick carpet. Her birch kept on striking and biting my backside with fierce precision, causing the fiery ardor of the twigs to penetrate into the marrow of my bones, while my thirsty mouth was refreshed by the ineffable delights of the divine marble feet, as I sucked the mother-o'-pearl toe-nails. I writhed and rolled on the ground, moaning and gasping in delirium, crawling all round the room, in my chase after these marvelous feet; pursued myself by the smarting swishes of the rod that inflamed my rump and quickened my desires.

The sublime statue, exhausted by this Homeric struggle and by the efforts of her arm brandishing the birch, fell prostrate near me, and I threw myself on her like a wild beast on its quarry.

My greedy mad mouth followed the luminous path of her marble legs, and guided by this pair of glorious columns, as if led through the Milky Way; urged on, too, by blissful intoxication caused by the faint fragrance of the sexual flower of woman-kind, I reached at last the holy chalice of supreme voluptuous pleasure.

It was now her turn to shudder in a torturing spermatic spasm, and opening her marvelous arms, she drew me upon her in an embrace which momentarily destroyed our reason.

When I came back to my senses, after this unlocking of the sluice gates of my virility, every drop of blood seemed to be drawn from my body. I was alone in the room. The statue had disappeared. I passed the palms of my hands over my body, stroking my poor hinder globes, burning from the onslaught of the cruel branches. My expert flogging Venus had so cunningly aimed her cuts, that despite our struggle and my wild gyrations, not one blow had gone astray. My buttocks blazed in agony. The silky rod, causing this irritation, far from calming me, had rendered my craving for energetic punishment still more vehement. I was sorry my beautiful flogging friend had so soon abandoned her royal scepter, and left me in solitude with my tormenting yearnings.

However, there was a surprise in store for me. After a few minutes, the door opened. I saw a lady come in. She was beautifully dressed in a black satin frock and she held in her hand two long, strong rods.

I recognized adorable Nelly in this new disguise. The formidable bundles of birch she carried left me without a doubt as to her intentions. From the bottom of my heart, I offered up thanks to this considerate and intelligent young woman, who comprehended my tortures, coming to succor me in the hour of need.

"Now, dear friend," she said softly, "I have to flog you most severely. Stretch yourself on that bench!"

I dragged myself slowly to the piece of furniture she pointed out, without uttering a word, so impatient was I for the sting of real, powerful rods on my inflamed bottom.

The two cushions, one on top of the other, securely fixed to the middle of the long settee without a back, forced the middle of the victim's body to jut out high up, this exposing the posteriors fully to the birchen caress, while the upper part of his frame and legs sloped down on either side of the little hillock.

In a jiffy, I felt myself fastened on the bench by means of thick straps buckled round my waist and encircling the top of my thighs, preventing me making the slightest movement. My queen then tied my hands and feet to bronze handles screwed at each end of the wooden frame. I sighed with happiness, because I kept repeating inwardly that I now felt myself in the power of my goddess, the living statue of angelical beauty.

Grasping one of the rods, she struck me squarely. The blow went home. A thousand sharp points pricked my flesh hungering for the torment; a thousand tiny jets of flame seared and grilled my backside. These were no longer the silky strokes that had caressed me with comparative tenderness while I had become as a drunken man by reason of the taste and fragrance of her pink marble feet, and velvet sexual grotto. The supple

Chicago

birch flogged on still, flaying my smarting skin. Its elastic leaping and bounding strokes drew groans of anguish from me. These firm, deliberate cuts, digging deeply down into the flesh of my posteriors to incrust their scalding lance-points, were the source of divine delightful sensations.

I admire the adorable flogging lady whose strength was masked by infinite grace. She was marvelously handsome in this costume that I saw for the first time. It metamorphosed the Grecian statue into a haughty Society lady, of distinguished bearing and rare elegance. My heart was full of pleasure; I was joyous and proud of her power. I thought no blow from her could be too heavy, so sublime was her beauty.

The warmth generated by her efforts acted on her, too, bringing fresh animation into her birching task, and the rod whistled shrilly before it fell and fell again on my writhing rump, that vibrated under the ruthless assault.

I moaned and writhed as the elastic twigs flogged me, so vigorously wielded was the rod by Nelly's practiced, muscular arm. The points of the twigs spread out fan-like all over my behind, covering the skin, tightly stretched my arched posture, with flaming weals and livid cuts.

The end came at last. The lovely young woman dropped her instrument of love and pain. With a sigh of relief, I looked upon her – a light of supplication in my eyes.

"Stifle your joy for a time," she said. "I've not done yet. You've only had half your dose."

She then clasped the new rod, and passing round to the other side, began again, striking harder than before. The fresh twigs hurt me horribly, striking on the bruised surfaces of my bottom-cheeks. Each deep indent of the cuts seemed to lay my flesh open. The strokes were inflicted with elastic force, as a loud swishing sound preceded each slash. I wriggled under the series of stripes, begging for pity and clemency, but inexorable whipping Nelly flogged me with insensate rage, unheeding my shrieks of agony.

She stopped quite suddenly, and I thought I should die of happiness, when I saw her throw up her scented skirts, showing me clouds of lace and silk. She strode over my head, straddling on the nape of my neck, and the warmth of her divine flesh penetrated into my whole being. engulfed in the delicious maze of her perfumed underworld, I sobbed and choked for sheer felicity, as lifting her rod high, my Amazon gave me ten awful, strong, well-aimed blows, directing the points of the twigs between my thighs. These scorching cuts, violating the precincts of my manhood, caused such penetrating voluptuous laceration of the sources of manhood, that in a violent spasm of sexual gushing rapture, my reservoirs of lust burst their dykes, thrilling me from head to foot and depriving me of my reason. So there I lay as if dead, swooning in repeated throes of the keenest spurting enjoyment.

Freed from my bonds, I knelt before my enchantress, covering her hands with kisses of delirious gratitude.

"You are a fairy and a sorceress," I said. "Thanks to you, I have experienced the greatest joys of life!"

XIII

As I left the mysterious flat of incomparable Nelly Lamb after having presented the birching sorceress with a cheque for an amount proportionate to my enthusiastic regard for her, I found myself once more in the populous streets, amidst hurrying passers-by. I was like a drunkard. My brain whirled. I staggered, overcome by too much enjoyment. Never had I emptied my blood-vessels in such violent spasms of sensuality. Hours after the divine sacrifice, the shock of the repeated orgasm still shook my frame, and I began to fathom the depth of the birching priestess's occult science and the dangers encompassing any man falling under the hidden sway of her mortal spells.

My robust constitution nevertheless conquered this momentary exhaustion of body and brain, and two days later, warm blood, like generous wine or liquid gold, coursed freely through my veins. I felt deeply grateful for the efforts of the celestial queen of the birch who had thrown open for me the gates of a new paradise. I thought that the banker's draft I had left with her was an insufficient reward for the joy with which she had overwhelmed me. I wanted to present her with a lasting remembrance, which at the same time should be an adornment for her marvelous body. So I sent her a regal diadem set with large diamonds and sapphires; accompanied by a delirious letter, respectful withal. In return, I received a perfumed note, with a seal representing Leda and the swan. In the language of the Latin poets, the whipping artiste thanked me, telling me that she would never forget. At the same time, she sent me a photograph of herself in the attitude of the sexless Venus to be seen in the Secret Museum of Naples. This picture resembled some marvelous masterpiece chiseled by Phidias of Praxiteles.

I felt sure that Nelly Lamb's bodily perfection was to be found in other types of the American race, and I sought everywhere for another modern Venus.

In society, at theatres, in the parks and streets, I was struck by the admirable proportions of splendid females, as tall as giants. I met women in profusion who were truly handsome, splendidly built; upright and good walkers; knowing how to carry themselves like goddesses. They could all boast of brilliant complexions, and their luxuriant locks were of varied golden shades; or else blue-black. They were real women, full of genuine feminine grace and allurement. They were quite devoid of the juvenile, mincing charm of the *Parisiennes*, who are lissome and trip along the Boulevards or in the Bois with serpentine movements. Their saucy, bold manner is enhanced by their clever style of natty costume. An artistic Don Juan admires and appreciates the pets of the Gay City as a *bric-a-brac* collector does a pretty little Dresden statuette, but when in the commanding presence of the splendid and impeccable figure – from and academic point of view – of an American beauty, he is greatly impressed, as he would be if viewing some sublime picture or work of art.

The young Yankee girl is a full-grown woman at fifteen. At that early age, her bosom is almost developed – and all the rest as well. Her youthful freshness appeals to our sensuality, for she is a blossoming bud; a flower whose captivating perfume mounts to the brain; an appetizing peach to make your mouth water. Such was the sensation I experienced when, strolling in the great park, I made the acquaintance of a ravishing fifteen-year-old maiden, her cheeks glowing with healthy bloom, her violet eyes sparkling like the waters of a mountain lake.

Mute with admiration, while looking at her, I felt the same enjoyment as a connoisseur enraptured with some rare object of art, but my delight was unbounded when I learnt that this white dove was, like me, crazy on flagellation, and that her plump flesh shivered with inordinate lasciviousness at the stroke of a rod.

Her name was Lucy Farman, and I often met her on the same park bench, in front of the flower-beds where the busy bees sucked the honey from gorgeous plants. She soon became the sweet comrade of my leisure hours, thanks to the unrestrained liberty enjoyed by the young lassies of the United States. They go about alone, wherever they like, making friends with any men who please them; difference of sex being no obstacle.

I interrogated her at great length concerning corporal punishment, as carried out in the boarding-school she had left but a few months before, and she described for my benefit some moving scenes, entering into minute details – without the least reticence. The birch was in great favor at the "East End College for Young Ladies," where my pretty maid graduated. Punishment was inflicted by a governess, who was rather young, but authoritative and inexorable. The head school-mistress herself did not disdain to penalize certain bottoms for which she felt some particular affection; but she birched so tenderly that her discipline was more agreeable than anything else.

Little Lucy was one of her favorites. Thus it came about that she was gently led into the path of sensuous flagellation, under the voluptuous swishing of her soft-hearted directress.

The boarders were birched every evening before dinner, expiating all faults committed during the day. In very grave cases, the penalty paid in the presence of the entire school assembled, and the chastisement formed a solemn spectacle.

The pupil's failings were noted in a book, afterward submitted to the mistress of the college. She then selected the culprits she desired to flog with her own hands. For the others, she wrote down how many strokes of the birch they were to receive from the rod of the disciplinarian governess. The book was then taken to the whipping room, where the birching lady was in attendance with two female servants, ready to lend a hand in case of need.

Culprits were called in one after the other. The sentence condemning them to so many cuts was read out, and the two servant girls at once seize the guilty girl. She was bound to a ladder, slopping against the wall; her feet on the first rung; her arms fastened above her head. A strap was buckled round her shoulders, to keep her body fixed in one position. Petticoats being pinned up to the waist, the victim's knickers were taken off entirely. The disciplinarian monitor now began to play her part, applying with firm and vigorous touch the prescribed number of strokes as set down in the birching-book by the head of the academy. The full amount was always dealt out, in spite of supplications and shrieks. The whipping woman often added a few extra stingers on her own account, if the girl on the ladder howled or struggles too much.

For ordinary penitential purposes, the strokes varied in number between ten and fifty, according to the age of the young person condemned and taking into consideration the gravity of her misdemeanor. Delinquents of fifteen always got thirty lashes, and the severe flogging governess, never erring on the side of mercy, was mostly ready to add a few more, saying that her young ladies required twice the fustigation they got. After fifty blows, the young minx's delicate skins were generally covered with open weals. The standing rule was that a new rod should be used to each pupil, and the birches being ling and supple hit terribly hard. It was the duty of the gardener t cut them from the trees in the grounds surrounding the college buildings. He had to renew his stock as often as necessary in order that the bundles of birchen twigs should always be strong and ripe – neither too green, nor too old and easy to snap and break. Birching for really serious faults was quite another thing – awe-inspiring and impressive. It took place in a large gymnasium where all the pupils and the governesses had to muster. The guilty girl was brought in, wearing a special dress, consisting of a long, unbleached linen smock, reaching to the ground. This was the victim's only garment. It buttoned up the back, and sleeves were knotted, like those of a strait waistcoat, to keep the arms from moving. The sinning lass's feet were chained together, while on her head was a paper cap, inscribed with the word, "Guilty."

She was then forced to stretch herself face downward on a heavy wooden bench, placed in the middle of the hall. The two servants tied her down with rough ropes in such away that it was impossible for her to make the least move. The smock frock was unbuttoned, baring the part of the body destined for the birch. Three governesses took it in turns to apply pitiless punishment; each of them dealing fifty heavy strokes. The girl roped to the bench yelled in heartrending fashion and her skin was soon broken and bleeding on both buttocks. The most terrible part of the torture was not this correction with long weighty rods. There was more to come. The disciplinary mistress stepped forward, and laid open the poor girl's swollen, wounded, gory bottom with ten sturdy, terrible, lashing cuts applied with a lady's riding whip. It often happened that the victim of such barbarous treatment fainted, and had to be carried away senseless to be cared for in the infirmary.

XIV

Sweet little Lucy's narrative made a great impression on me, especially the part relating to cruelty inflicted for serious faults. My lively companion, likewise, I could see, was much moved as she recalled the painful scene.

"And you, my dear girl – did you ever have to submit to such severe discipline?" I asked.

"Oh no, never!" she replied. "Extreme penalties were rarely imposed. All the time I was at the school, I only saw a maximum dose given once. As far as I am concerned, the whippings were inflicted by the lady who was at the head of the college, and I can evoke them as agreeable remembrances. Once, however, I was severely birched by the disciplinarian governess. I hasten to declare that I brought it on myself. I did all I could to be swished."

"What, really, Miss Lucy?" I exclaimed, with surprise. "You sought to be scourged? How interesting! I should like to hear all about it."

"I told you, " replied the charming young girl, "that I was always birched by the schoolmistress. She had a method of her own, handling the rod in a way which was more caressing than otherwise. It was no real punishment. Her birches were artistically arranged. They were curiosities, so to say. She made them up herself, with the greatest care. Choosing thin twigs among young birchen shoots, she filed down all rough ends and asperities. Then she polished them with white wax and chamois leather, to make them smooth and slippery. "She forced me to strip and took me under her arm, my legs tickled by her rustling skirts. The feeling of her grasp on my bare skin, and the warmth of her under-garments thrilled me deliciously. When the birch waged war on my behind, I was transported with delight. This small elastic rod brought a rosy blush to my posteriors, but without ever lacerating my skin. It was like a series of pulsating vibrations; an electric douche, if you like, which, concluding by benumbing my bum, threw me into an exquisite nervous state, full of unappeased desire."

"But how about the flogging governess?" I asked with some slight impatience. My amiable companion signed to me to be silent and listen to her.

"The directress was just off to spend a week away from home. Before leaving, she had given me one of her tantalizing birchings, leaving me more unnerved than I had ever felt before. It was a stormy day, and when there is thunder in the air, my senses are always strangely stirred. Not satisfied with an ordinary beating, she had rubbed my inflamed globes with her soft hand. This had excited me so dreadfully that I yearned for some unknown relief. I knew something was wanting – some serious strokes from a heavy rod, applied by a firm hand. I had a notion how to obtain the flogging I wanted.

I had but to gather some flowers in the garden, to be condemned to thirty cuts. In the absence of the head of the college, the flogging governess would have to accommodate me. I was certain of getting all I wanted from her. So I hesitated no longer. The hour of punishment was nigh. I was sent almost at once to the whipping room.

"I did not feel at all at my ease when I found myself a prisoner in the tenacious clutches of the two servants. They soon had me bound to the latter; my petticoats roughly pulled up. It was then that a great wave of shame broke over my entire being. I shut my eyes and tried to think that I was transported to the epoch when the Inquisition flourished, and that I was in the power of bloodthirsty tormentors.

The big birch crashed noisily on my tender bottom. I clenched my teeth, determined not to sue for pity. I had nobody to blame but myself, and resolved to suffer in silence. The cruel female executioner hit out at me as hard as she could, as if taking revenge on my trembling bum for all the sweetness usually showered upon it by her employer.

"I was getting more than I required. I started to groan. I asked to be pardoned, but the severe governess, probably waiting for this sign of weakness, flogged me harder still, raising weals and crossing her cuts to make my rump bleed freely.

"When she let me go, I had had a surfeit, having got more than I had bargained for. My bottom was awfully torn, but I could only reproach my own self. Besides, pain soon left me, and there was a delightful reaction. My nerves were calmed, and a sensation of comfort filled my soul. This unique brutal birching, which made me tremble in acute agony, seems an agreeable adventure when I think of it now. It is an enchanting memory."

"I should think, Lucy," I said, "that you must miss these queer sensations greatly, now that you have left school?"

"I was not long before finding what I wished. One of my girl friends, who is as fond of birching as I am, lets me have satisfaction whenever I like. She has a lovely style of lashing. It's sweet and violent at the same time. She knows how to make me happy while pleasing herself as well. Unfortunately, she is away in the country for a couple of months."

The color mounted to this bewitching damsel's cheeks as she talked of all the voluptuousness she had enjoyed under the fire of the rod, and I began to think that it would be a novel pleasure for me to share my fun with Miss Rosey with this artless, fifteen-year-old maiden. I was quite certain that the lady cashier would be delighted at the idea.

I hardly dared explain my plan, when Lucy knowingly helped me, by deploring the annoying absence of her partner.

"Dear Miss Lucy," said I, "I think I can manage to afford you your favorite pleasure while your little friend is away."

"What on earth have you got into your head, my dear fellow?" she said, with a start of fright. "Do you think I'd let myself be birched by a man? Thank you!"

"No, no, Lucy!" I hurried to reply. "You don't understand me."

Then I drew a vivid picture of Miss Rosey, assuring Miss Farman that my friend would perform the operation faultlessly and overwhelm her with all the delight the rod could bestow. I told of our coming meeting, describing our plans for the entrancing appointment, in glowing colors.

"Will you promise to leave me alone with this young woman?" asked Miss Lucy, anxiously.

I promised to obey her in every way, but she still hesitated. "It's very tempting," she sighed, "but I'm taking some risks. I don't know your young lady, and you – hardly at all!"

I did all I could to reassure her. I showed her my pocket-book, credentials and cheques. This was subtle diplomacy on my part and gave her confidence. It was the American way of introducing oneself. Nevertheless, she would not give me a direct answer. She wanted to thing things over. If she accepted, I should be sire to find her in the park, seated on the same bench, at the hour agreed upon for Thursday. As soon as I reached home, I hastened to acquaint Miss Rosey with the good news.

"Try all you can not to let her bolt at the last moment," said she, full of anticipatory delight. "I should be so disappointed! I'm already mad with joy at the thought of birching that innocent birdie. What a treat for me! But don't you think, sir," she added with solemn archness, "that you'll get off any the easier. You'll be flogged worse than ever for having flirted with that dear child!"

XV

At last the long-expected Thursday arrived! The weather was lovely – warm and sunny. I had passed a troubled night, disturbed by creams of enchanting delight. There were no signs of recent corrections on the skin of my buttocks, and my imagination was seething to boiling point.

Miss Rosey seemed quite as excited as I was. She had taken great pains with her dress. She wore a tightly-fitting art-blue frock, trimmed with costly lace. She sported a pretty picture hat, cocked saucily on her front "frizzes", and her delicious little feet were encased in boots of Russian tan, as supple as Suede leather.

My adorable young female preceded me, having left the private hotel a few minutes before I did, and then, in a carriage, we drove to the park. We were not disappointed, for the graceful silhouette of my girlish companion soon appeared to us.

It did not take long to introduce the two girls to each other, and they were good friends at once. My first care was to take them to a first-class restaurant. I chose Bisleti's, where I knew I should find good cooking; sound, real French claret, and all the toothsome sweet dishes that please the weaker sex.

Our meal was gay and lively. We lingered long over it. Our veins were full of hot blood, and I know not who of the trio was most excited and impatient to begin the sacred ceremonies.

Getting into our vehicle, we made a stoppage at the house of Miss Rosey's married friend, who, as desired, had prepared the instruments of flagellation – rods and riding-whips. Miss Rosey, sprightly as a gazelle, leaped out to fetch the implements.

"What do you think of my friend?" I asked, alone with delicate winsome Lucy in the carriage.

"She suits me. I like her. She seems quite expert in birching games and somewhat resembles my absent chum."

"You'll soon be able to sample her skill," I replied. "I don't think you'll have anything to grumble about."

Time passed and Miss Rosey did not return. What could she be about in that house? I knew she was not a gossip. Perhaps the rods were not ready, or did not please her, and she was having them remade?

"Suppose we go up in the elevator, and see what has become of her?" I proposed to Miss Lucy.

"Wait a few minutes more," said Lucy, "we're all right here – comfortably seated and watching the people go by."

Her face was flushed. She was under the influence of our bountiful repast, washed down by heady wines.

We had been seated in the carriage a good half-hour, when Miss Rosey reappeared at last, lively, merry, very agitated, and her eyes sparkling. She was followed by a young girl carrying a big paper parcel.

Our coachman whipped up his horse. Miss Rosey leant back on her cushioned seat and burst out laughing.

"You'll never guess what I did upstairs in that house! No, it's too funny for words! I've just cut a man's bum to ribbons!"

"The deuce you have! Tell us about it," I said, vastly amused.

"It's perfectly true," said Miss Rosey. "I had begged my friend to prepare me some good rods and a riding-whip, thinking that she ought to be a judge of these articles, as her husband is a lover of flagellation. She whips him daily with bundles of birch, which she prepares herself with great care. It appears that when her hubby heard that a flogging lady was coming to fetch birch-rods from his place, he worked himself up into such a state that he swore he should die if he wasn't birched there and then by me. My friend did not want to refuse him this favor, for a reason that she told me later, so she begged me to accede to her husband's wish, and give him a sound correction immediately. I accepted with pleasure. 'I pray you, dearie,' said she, 'flog him till the blood comes. Hit him with all your might and don't leave off till he is well wealed. You'll be doing me a great favor. I want to cure him of the habit he has of desiring to be whipped by every fresh female flagellant he hears of – as if his own wife wasn't sufficient for him!' she had got ready two special tickle-tobies, very ling, and made of tough, resisting branches. They had been all night in vinegar to make them still more formidable.

"The chap was already tied down on a bench when I went in, and my friend, leaving me alone with her liege lord, told me not to spare him. You may guess how I let myself go, enjoying the treat, and rendering a service to my jolly pal. So long as there remained a sound bit of wood on the two rods, I slashed away like a mad thing, putting in all my energy, quite reckless, and tearing all the skin off his backside. His wife came back at the finish, and while I got my breath, gave him, as a wind-up, ten cuts with the whip. She dealt them with real rage. Oh, I've had a royal old time! I'm quivering all over with naughtiness. I feel quite lewd!"

"My dear girl," said I reproachfully, "if you wear yourself out like this, what will be left for us?"

"Don't you worry," answered the adorable creature, squeezing my hand in her firm grip. "You'll both be properly treated, I swear it!" A few minutes more and we entered my discreet flat, which had witnessed my delicious games, when I kissed Miss Rosey's wee tootsies.

The first thing we did was to open the packet containing four splendid rods, long and flexible; a lithe lady's riding-whip, and some silk rope for binding victims. Miss Rosey had taken an extra rod for Lucy.

"Now I'm going to settle accounts with Miss Farman," said Rosey, with a malicious little wink.

"as for you, my old boy – off you go into the next room, where you'll be locked in. for you to assist at the unveiling of all kinds of pink and white hidden beauties, or to allow you to be a witness of certain subsequent mysterious proceedings would be too indecent. So try and be patient, without a word of complaint. Your turn will come next, and you'll get complete satisfaction."

The door of communication was shut in my face. I was at the keyhole at once, but the key, remaining in the lick, prevented me seeing anything at all. I tried to push the obstacle back with my penknife, but wary Rosey, guessing what I was about, scolded me through the door and hung a towel over the key.

All I could do was to press my ear to the panel. There was a long silent pause to begin with. Then I heard garments rustling and falling, followed by the hissing of the birch and the swish of the twigs on plump flesh. In my mind's eye, I conjured up the image of the young girl whose lovely round globes were quivering under the ardent contact of the rod. Soon, slight groans and tender signs rent the air. The rode stopped its regular "click, clack" for a few minutes, and then the birching sport went on again.

I gasped for breath as I hearkened to the noise of the elastic branches still continuing, and I fretted childishly, stamping my feet like some caged animal. The rod flogged, crashed, and swept resonantly over a darling invisible rump; while the swish of the birch was accompanied by tiny shrieks, uttered in a shrill treble. There was a long swooning sigh and then complete silence.

The door opened at last.

"Come, my dear friend," said Miss Rosey. "You who can appreciate the beauty of a female foot, look at those ravishing baby toes! Kiss them!"

I went in and saw Lucy, half-naked, on the tumbled bed. Her cheeks were suffused with blushes of shame and there were tears in her eyes. Her splendid legs were quite bare, and she had delicate, small feet, short and fat, exactly like those of an infant. My lips pressed every one of her wee toes, rounded and well-shaped, with their nails like pink pearls.

My gluttonous allegiance was interrupted much too soon by Miss Rosey who sent me back to the other room, so as to allow Lucy to get dressed.

I was frantically impatient to be alone with my sweet flogging lady, whose features were full of fresh excitement. As soon as Lucy was gone, after having kissed her new flogging friend with affectionate impetuosity betokening all Miss Farman's gratitude, Rosey turned toward me, darting her fine eyes into mine.

"At last I shall be able to flog you as much as I like! Come now, get your clothes off!" she hissed through her set teeth.

Her look, coupled with her threatening words, made me shudder. I undressed hastily, stretching myself obediently on the bed, impregnated with Lucy's delicious fragrant warmth.

Miss Rosey got the ropes and tied my feet and hands to the four corners of the couch on which my body formed the figure of a Maltese cross. Then, seizing a strong rod, she birched me without graduating her strokes. The first was dealt with an amount of vigor that proved she meant to give no quarter.

At every burning blow, I leaped and bounded, groaning deplorably.

"Aha, you don't laugh to-day, master!" said Rosey, happy to see me writhing and moaning.

Her switching rained down quicker and harder. I trembled in every limb, arching up and pressing down my loins each time my bottom came in for a terrible cut.

Miss Rosey had to rest in the middle of her task, to roll up her hair which had fallen down, covering her as with a veil in which the ends of the birch kept catching. She profited by her pause to take another rod, and it seemed that she had gained renewed vigor, for she began to whip me frenziedly, tearing shrieks of suffering from my hoarse throat.

I begged for pity, but the relentless queen of the birch shook her head, continuing to stripe my tortured backside, her eyes rolling madly. Her movements irregular and wild, like those of a bacchante. From her lissome frame, whirling in a delirious slashing saraband, issued waves of vibrating salacity that encircled me. Every nerve in my pained body throbbed, as the flames of her burning birch licked my gory posteriors, and drew me near to her soul, as it were, in a vortex of unparalleled voluptuousness.

Casting the rod from her – she must have seen the lascivious effect her tormenting twigs produced on her slave – she quickly gripped the whip, and sent a dozen or more fearful strokes of the dread instrument made me plunge, tearing at my bonds as I stiffened all my limbs under the shock of the gruesome commotion.

This supreme fustigating effort caused a sweet rush of swimming pleasure to invade the secret being of the whipping woman as she threw herself upon me, delightedly kissing the part she had bruised and wealed. She undid the ropes, and took my place on the bed, while I fell panting on my knees, actuated by a greedy wish to kiss her small feet.

Indolent and disdainful, she permitted me to take off her baby shoes and softly draw away her long, silk, openwork hose. Her delicious, tiny pedal extremities appeared in all their luminous splendor, and I had not enough kisses and licking caresses to devour them as they deserved with the gluttonous lips and tongue.

"I'm still hungry to flog you?" she said suddenly, leaping to her feet, wet and bare.

With a neurotic twist of her lascivious loins, she stooped and picked up a new rod while I, tamed and obedient, calling myself for the birch's terrible smart on my raw buttocks, was just about to lie down again. But she had a new idea, seating herself on the edge of our couch, and throwing me across her lap like a child.

In this position, her arm had not much room to swing the rod. I was very happy at finding myself tightly clasped in her embrace, feeling her body pressed against mine. But she grew tired at having to birch me, without finding me plunging or quivering.

So she lost all patience, and ordering me curtly to bend over the bed, she got her whip again. After a few barbarous strokes, dealt with the greatest possible violence, I writhed on the carpet at her feet in a superhuman spasm where acute pain produced the acme of manly felicity. The gush of blood from my mangled bottom kept time to the throbbing torrent of my essence of virility torn from me by the red-hot searing stripes of the whip.

Miss Rosey was perfectly exhausted. She reclined at full length, languidly on the bed. Her ravishing little feet were abandoned to my loving moist caresses. Seeing the adorable young creature close her eyes, I grew more bold. My fierce kisses of lust mounted in spiral garlands of wet tonguing delight all along her divine legs and massive thighs, until the sacred depths of paradise were reached.

My mouth officiated at the soft altar of female worship where every delight is centered. I greedily sucked the dewy rosebud, until Miss Rosy's soul melted between my clipping lips – and I once more joined her in the ineffable bliss of the highest degree of ecstasy to which man or woman can possibly reach.

XVI

The hours I passed with adorable Miss Rosey in our discreet apartment will always remain in my mind as imperishable memories, for she caused me to enjoy sensations that can never be forgotten. I now had to think of my departure. It was drawing nigh. I regretted to have to go. In Chicago, I had met the incomparable female flagellants: Miss Nelly Lamb, Miss Esther, and above all, Miss Rosey, the sweet little hotel-bookkeeper, who, beneath an appearance of candid simplicity, hid the soul of a bacchante and the sculptural form of a legendary princess. Where on earth should I ever find again such a casket of pearls? My passionate devotion to birching games had increased and developed through being enjoyed in the company of such ideal partners.

That lovely Thursday with Miss Rosey had been one long dream of radiant voluptuousness, but her rod unnerved me, when it ought to have appeased my craving. Her strokes, on the contrary, had awakened my desires, creating an impetuous inward need for some great, energetic shock. Therefore, before leaving the windy city, I sought for some severe punishment, which I thought should be inflicted on my shrinking stern, not by a lascivious flogging beauty, but by a severe governess, capable of inspiring me with awe. I was within an ace of going to see Miss Esther, when a fortuitous circumstance caused me to find something better. I luckily met once again the disciplinarian matron of the neighboring school, who, it will be remembered, had so rigorously birched the young chambermaid at my boarding-house. The flogging lady was alone at this time, and I had to summon up all my courage before I dared address her. I stammered out my request quite timidly, but I had hardly uttered a few words before she flatly refused. "No, sir, I don't whip men for their pleasure! There are heaps of women who make a business of this sort of thing. Go to them!" I persisted, telling he that I prized a beating at her hands, because she was no common whipping woman, and that to be punished by her was almost ah honor; a privilege possessing

Chicago

peculiar piquancy.

"No, no, I cannot consent," she said, "except on one condition. Had you committed some fault that really deserved chastisement, I might see things in a different light."

Her declaration caused a glimmer of hope. I fancied I had found a way to realize my secret longing idea by mentioning some trivial motive, but I had hardly opened my lips than she stopped me.

"You are about to invent some foolish story. It won't go down with me. If you should do something deserving of punishment, write to me at the school. I shall then reflect. If I judge that the nature of your backsliding permits me to intervene, I will drop you a line to that effect."

She turned on her heel and left me rather puzzled. I imagined a thousand things, rejecting them soon afterward one by one, until, at last, I recollected perfectly well that a few days before I had indeed been guilty of an error that was worthy of expiation.

I bought some gloves and neckties in a large drapery story, paying with a hundred-dollar bill. The young woman who served me had handed me fifteen dollars too much when she gave me my change. I saw the mistake soon after I left the shop, but out of sheer carelessness, I did not go back to reimburse the lady assistant. I therefore wrote to my stern governess accusing myself of this slight sin of heedlessness. I awaited a reply with a feeling of great anxiety, but a note soon reached me. It read thus:

"Sir," wrote the whipping matron, "what you call negligence is real larceny. You had discovered the mistake and knew who would have to suffer from it. Your education and your social position ought to have rendered you incapable of such lightheaded conduct, causing you to neglect to set that striking example a man of your rank in the world should always be able to show his inferiors. There is not the slightest doubt but that your duty is to return without a moment's delay the sum of money you dishonestly appropriated to the person to whom it belongs. I will chastise you. You deserve severe corporal punishment. In order to endure it, you will present yourself at the school to-morrow, Saturday, at three o'clock, after the pupils have left. The janitor will show you my office. My fee is one dollar."

I had attained my ends. I was to be deservedly birched by an official whipping matron, almost a legal flogging governess, if I may venture to say so. The modest figure of her emoluments proved that she deemed herself invested with honorable functions and did not seek to make money.

When I reached the school, a boy between twelve and thirteen, holding a letter in his hand, was talking to the janitor, who, as he lead me to the office of the disciplinarian schoolmistress, told the lad to follow him as well.

The flogging teacher, without troubling about me, except by replying to my respectful bow by a slight nod, glanced at the note brought by the youth.

"Quite well, Harry?" she said. "Your father and mother ask me to give you a good dressing down. Come along here, I shan't be long over it!"

On hearing these threatening words, the little chap started as if he had received a shock from an electric battery, and began to sob.

"Oh no, please ma'am! Don't whip me! Oh don't, I pray you!"

"I shan't be more than ten minutes birching this young fellow," she said coolly, addressing me. "I will attend to you immediately afterward."

She opened the door of an adjacent room and dragged the boy, still lamenting and struggling, in with her.

"Down with your pants!" was the order given to the weeping lad.

"Oh no, please forgive me, ma'am! I'll never do it again!" howled the child.

The door had been left ajar. I could see distinctly what was going on in the other room, where there was a heavy form and a heap of birch-rods piled up in a corner.

"Didn't I tell you to let down your pants!" repeated the matron in an authoritative tone.

"Yes, ma'am. But oh! – do pardon me. Never again will I be naughty!"

The wretched boy trembled like a leaf, and the impatient woman slapped his face with such force that his head waggled about his shoulders for a few seconds afterward.

"So you won't take down your breeches?" she said.

"I'm letting them down – really I am!" stuttered the youth.

Without allowing him to complete this necessary act of partial disrobing, the termagant, in a rage threw herself upon him. Gripping both his hands, she tied them together at the wrists. She then threw him brutally on to the bench, passing a thick rope over his loins so as to bind him securely face downward. She then tore off his trousers completely, and wound a second stout cord round his legs, while he never ceased struggling and howling.

Catching up a strong rod, she set about flogging him with might and main, hitting him with real vigor. The lad yelled as if mad, bounding and writhing, despite his bonds. The terrible birching lady paid no attention to anything but her task. It looked to me as if she had lost her wits, for putting her entire strength, she literally covered the brat's little bottom with formidable slashing strokes.

It was a thrilling sight – this tall female, as frenzied as an enraged lioness, mercilessly cutting these palpitating boyish buttocks with practiced, mighty blows of her stout birch. Her victim roared with acute pain. I trembled in every limb thinking how in a few minutes, I also should be bound down on that same bench, to be birched still more brutally, as I was older, and able to support still greater agony. Nevertheless, the sensation that benumbed my entire being was not devoid of infinite voluptuousness. I struggled against a natural impulse prompting me to fly from such severe correction, and yet I remained as if my feet were nailed to the floor, incapable of movement. I was actuated by a furious desire to endure the torturing ordeal.

The spectacle became very thrilling; the teacher going on with her fierce birching, and her captive twisting about under the burning twigs, as he uttered heartrending cries.

Bits of birch flew about all over the room, and when at last the female executioner threw away the work stump of her rod, I breathed again. She unfastened the ropes and bundled the boy outside, without even giving him time to adjust his disordered garments.

Passing in front of me, she gave me a look that made me shudder.

"Go in the corner and undress!" she said roughly.

Just as the little boy left, a girl of about fifteen years of age came in. she brought a letter that the governess glanced over after tearing it open impatiently.

"What! More punishment?" she exclaimed. "Can I never have a moment's peace? They won't let me alone even during play-time!" At the word 'punishment' the lass started.

"If you care, madam, to attend to this young lady before me, I can wait."

She turned toward me in a fit of temper, and again eyed me with her cruel, piercing glance.

"I told you to strip, did I not? Have you heard what I said?"

I retreated in fear, and rapidly divested myself of coat and trousers. I felt very awkward at having to undress in the presence of the young girl, who, in the next room, could see me quite plainly. The schoolmistress, without troubling about such a trifle, rummaged in the pile of rods, choosing a couple – the longest and strongest. She threw them on the floor near the bench, towards which she pushed me.

She tied a rope tightly round my back, winding another cord about my legs. They she bound my hands, without saying a word; her eyebrows knitted and her face distorted. Taking up the rod, she at once set it going smartly on my bare bottom. Blow succeeded blow at express rate, and I started and plunged, howling with pain. She flogged me with insensate exasperation, soon causing me to shriek in agony. I made useless desperate efforts to burst my bonds, but my struggles only caused the ropes to sink deeper into my flesh. The rod never ceased torturing me with its reiterated sting; swishing, cutting, mangling the sensitive skin of my posteriors. I groaned and choked, losing my breath under the excruciating avalanche of lashes that swept over my smarting rump like a torturing hurricane. The cruel monitor, caring nothing for my sufferings, never ceased flogging me pitilessly. Throwing down her rod, reduced to a mere stump, she grasped the second one, and my martyrdom continued without a moment's respite.

The fresh birch dug deeper than its predecessor into my raw rump, now bruised and tender. My blackened, swollen flesh quivered and pulsated at the renewed attack. I tugged at the ropes in despair, not knowing what to do to escape from such intense suffering. Each blow that flattened out the twigs with a tremendous crashing noise on my scalded stern, caused me to jump like a fish just hooked. Blow after blow fell with regular monotony. The torture seemed to have lasted hours. When it came to an end at last, and the disciplinarian governess had loosened my bonds, I could hardly stand, so weak was I. Passing my hand over my excoriated hindquarters, I found my fingers suffused with blood. When I returned home after this thrilling experience, I met Miss Rosey in the hall.

"What ails you?" she said stopping me. "You're quite pale! You seem quite upset."

"It's nothing," I replied. "Just a trifling bilious attack."

I had formed an idea that this brutal chastisement would perhaps have quenched my passionate thirst for birching torments, and even cure me entirely of my love for passive flagellation.

Nothing of the kind took place, and a night or two after this terrible punishment, my blood boiled again in my veins, carrying to every artery the burning lava that impelled me to seek for the ardent voluptuousness which can only be aroused by the influence of the rod.

BOSTON

CHAPTER I

left Chicago for Boston, and during the period of ten days I had set apart to be passed in that latter interesting city, I was able to add still further fresh experiences to my knowledge of the mysterious domains where the birch is devotedly worshipped.

After my wonderful discoveries in Chicago what more could I glean in Boston? Nothing, it seemed to me at first sight, but in reality the ultimate results surpassed my most sanguine anticipations.

I soon got to know that in the city of culture there was a Flagellant's Club. All its members, male and female, were ardent adepts in the mystic passion.

The circle was very select, difficult to locate, and reserved for gentle and refined amateurs, moving in the best society. I managed t worm out the address of the stronghold, but it took me two days of negotiation and diplomacy to be admitted as honorary member.

The club-house was situated in a superb building on Park Avenue. There were about one hundred and fifty members, including sixty ladies. Every male member was allowed to bring a female guest, so that when meetings were held, the feminine element was always in the ascendant. There was a lecture hall, fitted up with all needful flagellating adjuncts and a raised platform for practical experiments. Another vast saloon was used for flagellation in common. There was every convenience for flogging forty persons at the same time. Besides these two halls for public whipping, the club boasted of a good many private apartments, known as "separate rooms"; each furnished with the necessary instruments and apparatus for private birching. There was also a reading-room and library stocked with works in all languages concerning flagellation, and many portfolios full of pictures, photographs, and engravings relating to the same fascinating subject.

As in all American clubs, there was a capital kitchen, a ladies' café, and bars and smoking-rooms for the men.

Introduced by two gentlemen who kindly consented to be my sponsors, I was led into the presence of a most affable Lady President, the widow of Colonel Islington. She was marvelously beautiful, scarce thirty years of age.

The week's program was handed to me. It ran thus:

Monday. 3 pm. Lecture Hall.

Miss Anna Knigge. Concerning the Choice of Flagellating Instruments, and Sundry Effects Produced Thereby. With public experiments on male and female patients.

Tuesday. 3 pm. Lecture Hall.

Miss Jane Silke. The Rod as a Factor in Education. Demonstration with the aid of a pupil, fourteen years of age. Miss Silke will afterwards attend to members of either sex who may wish to be corrected in separate rooms.

Wednesday. 3 pm. Lecture Hall.

Conference on Conjugal Flagellation. Only persons ready to take an active part in these lessons will be allowed to attend.

Thursday. 3 pm. Lecture Hall.

Sisters Daisy and Alice Pimlico will speak on Voluptuous Flagellation. Experimental efforts on any persons in the auditorium who may volunteer. At the conclusion of the meeting, Misses Pimlico will be at the disposal of fellow-members requiring their services in separate rooms.

Thursday. 4 pm. Lecture Hall.

Miss Amelia Dora. Scientific Flagellation as a Means of Reviving Virile Strength in Man. Demonstrations by the assistance of willing brethren. At the close of her discourse, Miss Dora will be pleased and ready to retire, if requested, to the separate rooms.

Saturday. 2 pm. Flagellation Hall. (Large Room)

Miss Bob Clasper, lion-tamer, issues her challenger for the second time. She defies any man who likes to mount the stage, and declares she will undress and flog him for a stake of one hundred dollars.

Miss Clasper will conclude by offering her gracious assistance in the separate rooms.

The perusal of the meretricious menu threw me into a state of rutting fever. Every variety of flagellation was represented in this list, and the lady lecturers, I thought, must be delicious creatures. I remarked that all seemed eager and ready to meet amateurs in private after their speechifying, which probably greatly excited their listeners, awakening in them a pressing wish to taste the caress of a prickly birch. Such discipline, undergone in secret in the separate rooms, allowed refined votaries to glut their sensual appetite in company of the very woman who had so highly exacerbated their longing lust.

I registered a mental oath to go to every lecture and besiege the private boudoirs. I was as yet rather uneasy about my admission, for my introduction to the Lady President had not smoothed away every formality. The superb, soldierly woman plunged her eyes into mine, and then looked me up and down, and all over. After a prolonged scrutiny, she informed me that I should be summoned to her office, when she would tell me all about the conditions regulating my admittance.

I had hardly concluded reading the program when a page-boy came to let me know that the Lady President was waiting to see me. I at once followed the lad into her sanctum, which was a most elegantly furnished snuggery. The walls, hung with silk, were decorated by four oil paintings, from the brush of French eighteenth century artists representing different scenes of mythological flagellation. On carved and gilt consoles and light pieces of ancient marqueterie furniture were innumerable delicate bronzes, ivory and porcelain curiosities, all depicting some scene of the mystic passion, by means of adorable nude charms shown quivering beneath the divine rod. Everything in the luxurious chamber recalled secret flogging rites. On a table, were several bundles of birch, tied up with multi-colored ribbons, and I noticed, too, a couple of slender, gold-handled riding-whips. The Diana-like colonel's widow was seated at her desk, a Sevres vase full of flowers at her elbow. She returned my deep bow by a gracious nod, and motioned me to take a seat on the soft cushions of a big armchair by her side.

"You have asked, my dear sir," she said, "to be admitted to our club for a week, as a traveling member? I must inform you at once that we never grant such a favor save to advanced amateurs in the science of flagellation."

"Madame and President," I replied, "this admirable passion possesses no more fervent votary than I!"

"Very good!" she rejoined. "Our statues require that your statement should be corroborated. At all cost, we see, to prevent prying, profane strangers from penetrating among us. I allude to such as do not understand the true signification of our delightful religion, and who only come here to see novel sights. Above all, we fear incursion of journalists who would stoop at nothing to worm their way in and obtain matter for sensational articles. We have founded our club to give satisfaction to our family circle of loving sensual flagellants, and not with the object of offering the public a theatrical display of the sacred ceremonies of our cult. No member, even a temporary one, such as you, can be received unless we are certain he thinks and feels as we do."

"I am ready to give you any proof of my good faith you may desire, madam," was my prompt reply.

"How long is it since you were last punished?"

"About a week ago, President."

"Was the birching severe? By whom was it inflicted?"

"A lady disciplinarian of a large ladies' college flogged me terribly."

"That sounds feasible, sir," she then said. She rose, turned the key in the door, and returning to her seat, continued: "Allow me to see the effects of your last birching. If it was as thorough as you say, some traces must still remain on your person. Please arrange your underclothing, so that I can examine you completely. Lean over that chair."

With delightful sensations, my skin rippled into gooseflesh at the idea of partially undressing before this radiant young woman. It filled me with voluptuous exquisite emotion to think she ordered such an inspection. Obeying her commands, I put myself in the posture she suggested, and I blushed to feel her gaze and her little hands on my bare flesh. She passed her agile fingers over my buttocks, handling my skin like a coquettish careful feminine purchaser sampling silk in a shop. She then took from a drawer a large magnifying-glass, which she used leisurely.

"You spoke of a terrible beating, sir," she said at last, with a malicious smile. "If so, how do you explain that all traces of the rod have vanished from your body within a week? This proves that the castigation was not so severe as you choose to say. Button up. I regret I cannot sanction your admittance without your undergo an ordeal."

"I am ready, President, to submit to any ordeal you may deign to impose upon me."

"Our rules set forth thirty cuts with a riding-whip. If a candidate endures them from first to last without being bound or trying to evade any one blow, we then consider him to be a real passionate lover of flagellation, and open our doors to him forthwith."

"I am willing to endure the thirty cuts stoically – without stirring, madam!" I exclaimed enthusiastically.

"Just as you like," rejoined the charming lady. "I will give you a note for one of the lady members of our club. She will apply the whipping discipline. My decision will depend upon her written report, which you will bring me."

The Lady President took a sheet of sky-blue, perfumed paper, and after having written a few lines of upright bold script, she put it in an envelope, carefully gumming it down with a rosy, pointed tongue-tip thrust from between two rows of pearly teeth.

"Take this letter to its address," she said. "It is not far from here – Fourth Avenue, Mrs. Blanche Palmerstown. I've chosen you one of our most beautiful and expert lady flagellants, a delicious blonde. If you are really a passionate worshipper at the divine birching altar, you will experience the final joys of sensual pleasure beneath the thirty lashes from a lady's riding whip, applied with nervous strength. Go quickly! I shall await your visit with the reply, at half past two.

CHAPTER II

Overjoyed at the lucky hazard that led me to be birched by a Society lady, I jumped in the first cab I found and drove to the address on the Lady President's note.

Mrs. Palmerstown dwelt in a superb private house, standing in its own grounds. In the entrance-hall was a crowd of work-people with ladders. Some of the men were putting up curtains, others were busy moving pieces of furniture, or arranging shrubs in pots.

Boston

As soon as I had given the letter to a lady's maid, I was shown into a drawing-room where all was in great disorder. Tables and chairs were piled in a heap, and several upholsterer's assistants were nailing garlands and rows of electric lamps to the walls.

The door opened. The beautiful mistress of the house swept into the room. She was a tall, fair woman of wonderful beauty, wearing a loose kind of dressing-jacket trimmed with the finest lace. In her hand was my letter, its envelope torn open, and she signed to me to follow her into a small boudoir adjoining the reception room.

"Mrs. Colonel Islington is plumb crazy!" Why on earth she sends me a candidate to be whipped on a day like this, I can't imagine! She knows very well I'm giving a dance to-night, and that I haven't a minute to spare. It's quite too awfully stupid of her! We're sixty lady birchers at our club, and she picks me out – of all people!"

she wrung her hands despairingly and, her loose lace sleeves fell back, showing her magnificent naked, plump, white arms.

"See here," she went on, "I'll give you your does at express speed. I've got a whip in this room – somewhere."

All the blood in my body rushed to my head as I heard these words issuing from the arched lips of the delicious young woman, and I was tearing away at my braces when there came a violent knock at the door. A tall swarthy, thin woman – Mrs. Palmerstown's first lady's maid – made her entrance.

"The dressmaker has called, please!"

"My dressmaker!" exclaimed my flogging goddess, clutching at her hair with a worried gesture.

"Gee! I must hustle! My dear sir," she added, turning to me, "I must really beg your pardon, but you see it's impossible to be willing, despite all my endeavors. I'll have you whipped by my maid and write out your certificate while she's at work on your – ahem! That'll do just as well. Berth," she went on, speaking to her servant. "Take that gentleman to your room and give him thirty smart cuts with a riding-whip on his naked bottom. You've got your jockey's whip upstairs?"

"I guess I've got everything in that line, mem," replied the girl in a rather sulky way, "but the silversmith will soon be here, and I must count the spoons and forks with him."

"That's all very well, but it won't take you an hour to give thirty strokes with your whip. Get a move on you! Hurry up like lightning and if the man comes down with the plate before you've done, let Louisa whip the gentleman."

Mrs. Palmerstown flew off, cyclone-like, as she had come, and the tall brunette ordered me sharply to follow her. She led me up a never-ending staircase until we reached the last story, right under the roof.

"It's disgusting," murmured the maid to herself, "these stunts always fall to me. I have no fun whipping a man! I don't belong to their precious club, and I don't care a straw for their dirty flagellation. I'm in a greater hurry than madam. The dressmaker can wait; she won't run away. But as for the silver – that I must count, because if one item is lost, who'll be blamed – missus or me?"

By this time we were in the soubrette's bedroom, where everything was topsy-turvy; the furniture littered with odds and ends of feminine attire, and articles of underwear strewed on the ground.

"Make haste! Off with your trousers!" said the young woman. "And don't be an hour over it! I'll teach missus to send me the fellows she ought to flog her own self! You'll remember the thirty cuts I'm going to give you, my fine fellow!"

Nervously excited, she searched in drawers and cupboards for her whip, while I gazed intently at this commanding, brutal lass. Her thick eyebrows met at the top of her nose, giving her features a hard imperious look. I trembled as I thought of the terrible strokes with which she threatened me, as I feared that perhaps I should not be able to support the pain without moving, and thus lose all chance of admission to the club. A timid knock at the door, and an engaging young lady about fourteen or fifteen and of genteel bearing, glided into the room.

"Bertha," said the newcomer, "the silversmith's man is unpacking the plate. Please come down at once!"

"What did I tell you!" snapped the big brown creature. "Say, Loo, madam's orders are that this fellow here has to have thirty cuts with a whip on his bare behind. Give them to him as hard as you can! I'm off! Look around for my whip. It must be in one of these drawers!"

The servant ran away. I was alone with the lovely, golden-haired girlie.

"What luck!" she exclaimed, with a merry laugh. "I adore whipping men! I may hit hard, may I not? Where's that blamed whip?"

She looked everywhere, but found no trace of the instrument of torture.

"What a bore!" she said. "But look here, I'll spank you with my hand. That'll suit as well as anything! Take your place for the dance!"

These rapid changes, the whip of the adorable mistress of the house; that of the brutal serving-wench whose ruthless fustigation I already felt in imagination on the flesh of my behind; and now the white hands of this delicious fifteen-year-old baby flagellant – all this inflamed my lust. I bent over the bed, jutting out my big posterior ready to enjoy the slapping onslaught of the tender maiden's tiny palm.

"You must keep tally yourself," she told me. "When we get to thirty, you'll call out, and I'll stop. See?"

She started smacking me with her hands. It was delightful. I felt my heart bounding in my breast with wild joy under this caress, as she banged at my buttocks with all her might, spreading her tapering digits as far apart as she could. I should have liked to have remained for an hour reveling in the charm of her beating, and the thirty blows were doubled and trebled, but I still let her keep on spanking my entranced posteriors.

I turned round, making as if to rise, when she stopped.

"You're cheating!" she said. "I've only given you twenty-seven slaps: I can count as well as you!"

I took up my position again with pleasure. As hard as she could hit, she gave me three more smacks, with an interval between each.

"Let's be off!" she exclaimed. "I'm in a hurry, too!"

Downstairs, I met the tall dark woman, as disagreeable as ever. She handed me a microscopic envelope, where the gum was still wet. It was directed to the Lady President of the Flagellants' Club.

Once outside, before putting the letter in my pocket, I was indiscreet enough to lift up the flap of the envelope. Inside was a little card, whereon I read:

"My dear friend, "You many admit the bearer to our club. I have had thirty cuts applied with a whip by Bertha, my maid, who loves to work off her bad temper on a man's bare backside. You may be perfectly sure that your candidate has not been spared in any way."

"Thus is history written!" I said to myself, as, with a chuckle, I carefully fastened the envelope.

The soft, caressing touch of the amiable fair girl had made me eager for more flogging fun, and I regretted having escaped the whip of the Society beauty and the tender mercies of the shrewish lady's maid.

CHAPTER III

I went straight home to my hotel to change my clothes and have a good lunch. At half past two to the tick, I was back at the club, where without waiting, I was ushered into the presence of the Lady President.

She ran rapidly through her friend's note, and gave me a card of admission, good for one week. I thanked her effusively, and at a few minutes before three, I took my seat in the Lecture Hall.

There was a good assistance already, and people kept dropping in. Quite a select fashionable crowd, too; ladies beautifully dressed and well-groomed gentlemen neatly attired.

A bell tinkled. The lady orator, Miss Silke, appeared on the platform. She was a very young woman, not much over twenty, with a sprightly and mischievous air. Her shooting costume became her – short, pleated skirt, and gaiters of soft leather with silver buttons.

Her preamble, given in clear and musical tones, was very eloquent. "Ladies and gentlemen," she began, "I am happy to see that the system of education by the aid of the birch is still in favor in our free country. The use of the rod is maintained in every state, despite the efforts of a few enemies who are not true Americans.

"In France and Italy, chastisement by the rod is well-nigh extinct, but it flourishes in England, Germany, Austria, Hungary and Russia. We all know how favorably the twigs are looked upon in our own happy land. The rod forms part and parcel of our daily life, for is not the birch to be seen in all schools; and hanging up in every household?

"There is no more efficacious method of enforcing obedience and attention to studies with children than by the help of a good birch-rod. Its crackling cuts subdue the most unruly, obstinate boys and girls. Such correction is practical, rapid, and easy.

"Long written tasks, solitary confinement, bread and water diet, deprivation of recreation, and walks in the open air should never be resorted to, as they tend to miss the intended aim. Enforced extra work dulls a pupil's brain instead of enlivening his mind. The other means of coercion I mentioned are also to be condemned because they violate the most elementary laws of hygiene. To deprive a child of food and air as a punishment is a torturing invention worthy to be put in force by barbarians, but not by the emancipated citizens of our enlightened Republic. The birch, on the contrary, exercises salutary influence; quickening the circulation of the blood; generating healthy reaction; and developing the figure.

"The rod is as beneficial for infants as for growing children. I will say nothing about adults; other lady lecturers, more learned than I, are ready to prove to you by theory and practice, that the birch is a blessing for both the sexes at all ages.

"I could quote a thousand cases to show that the rod has worked miracles when all other punitive methods have ignominiously failed, but instead of wearying you with theories, I prefer to proceed at once to a practical demonstration. I shall have the honor of whipping before you a lad of fourteen who never obeys save under the rod."

The electric bell rang shrilly. Miss Jane Silke stepped back to a curtain masking a door at the back of the platform. A stripling appeared. Despite his resistance, she dragged him to the centre of the stage.

"Here we have a young scamp," she said, "with whom nothing can be done. The smart of a birching alone subdues him. He listens to no remonstrances, and is always insubordinate. You will now see. Jim, down on your knees and kiss my feet!"

Jim did not stir.

"Jim," she went on, "I order you once more to kneel and kiss my boots!"

The boy stood erect, impassible.

"Aha! We'll soon see who's master!" exclaimed the young woman, impatiently.

Taking a silken cord, she bound his hands at the wrists. Then she unbuttoned his trousers, dragging them down to his knees, and placing his head between her thighs, squeezing his neck, as in a vice, by the firm grip of her muscular legs, she caught hold of a rod close handy. At once, she started vigorously swishing his naked bottom, which, boldly exposed, was in a splendid position to feel the full strength of every blow.

Jim struggled hard and viciously, giving vent to lamentable howls, but the cutting ends of the birch came down with automatic precision, and never a stroke was wasted.

The poor chap seemed quite dazed when the lady at last let him loose.

"Now, Jim, down on your knees, and kiss my feet."

Jim was obdurate as before.

Furious, the flagellating goddess clutched him violently, shook him into the same humiliation posture again, and the birch was set going for the second time on his stout backside which now began to turn a brownish violet hue from the virulent shower of blows.

The young lady flogged forcibly. Her boyish victim yelled at the top of his voice, making desperate efforts to get his head from between the robust thighs of his tormenting benefactress.

When she finally gave him his freedom once more, he still refused to obey orders.

So, full of rage at seeing that as he resisted so much, her demonstration might fail, she chose a longer and more flexible rod. For the third time, she clutched the lad's head between her graceful, nervous legs.

"I'm curious to see who'll have the last word – you or I, young gentleman!"

This time she frisked the torturing twigs all over his bruised rump with Satanic skill. Blow followed blow with lightning speed. Bits of birch broke off, flying into the middle of the hall.

"Forgive me, miss!" howled the culprit, as his bum became streaked with red weals. "I'll obey! I really will! I'll do anything you tell me!"

The cruel, flogging, lecturing lady took no heed of his promises of repentance, but continued her pitiless discipline.

The spectators were thrilled by poignant emotion. Not a sound could be heard in the silent hall, save the whizzing of the birch, and as it stung the youthful stern, it's significant swishing noise mingled with the groans and supplications of suffering Jim.

I admired the female flogger. She was greatly excited. Her cheeks were scarlet and her eyes ablaze. I thought there was something eminently fascinating in her rapid and strenuous movements. I longed to be in the place of the young fellow, writhing between her thighs, and I impatiently awaited the moment when she should be at liberty to attend to club-members in the private rooms. It would then be my turn to revel in the inexorable cruelty of her castigation.

Jim struggled so wildly that he dragged Miss Silke all along the platform. She looked like some Amazonian beauty of the plains bestriding a bucking bronco.

The mad ride ceased at last. Jim, having become wondrously submissive, threw himself at full length on the ground, ardently kissing the neat footgear of the superb tamer of unruly youths. We all breathed freely once more, and the entire admiring audience applauded enthusiastically.

Miss Jane Silke made as if to step down from the stage, and as I wanted to be the first to engage her services for birching punishment in private, I went up to her and formulated my wish with great respect.

"Willingly," she replied. "My fee is ten dollars. You're first on the list!"

So saying, she came among the audience and was at once surrounded by a crowd of congratulating fellow-members of both sexes.

A few minutes later, she came back to me.

"I hope you won't mind giving up your turn to a lady who's in a desperate hurry? You'll be Number Two? That'll suit, won't it? I shan't be long. I can polish her off in ten minutes."

Of course, I consented, and addressing myself to a liveried attendant, he showed me into a vacant separate room, where was the complete paraphernalia of punishment.

My beautiful professor soon came in, for, exactly as she had said, her lady patient had been thoroughly swished under a quarter of an hour.

"I'm awfully hustle and behind schedule time," she told me. "You ought to have got stripped while you were waiting. I've four gentlemen expecting my rod. You must understand that the craving is much greater after the imagination is heated by my performance with Jim."

As she spoke, she busied herself drawing a bench into the middle of the room, and she selected some lengths of rope. I was soon undressed to my shirt, and threw myself on the padded form, impatient to taste the sting of the heavenly birch brandished over my head by the girl in a hurry. She appeared to me, close by my side, and more beautiful than on the platform. She was so young; her complexion was healthy and brilliant; and her ripe lips had a mocking twist that made her seem ten times more bewitching. She tied me down in a twinkling with incredible dexterity and picking up the first rod that came to her white hand, flogged me severely.

I soon felt that she meant to lose no time, by the quickness and strength of her blows, dealt with full force. She held the bundle of lithe twigs at arm's length, and stood a little distance from me, so that I got all the benefit of the lancet-like ends. My whole frame vibrated as if electrified, and I could not refrain from emitting slight groans at every blow I received. She then passed round to the other side of the bench, to birch me in the opposite direction and the broken ends of the branches pricked my skin excruciatingly. Unable to support any more suffering, I begged for quarter.

"Hold your tongue, sir!" she said curtly. "If I were not pressed for time, I'd have whipped you quite another way. You're not a boy of fifteen! A man ought to be able to stand strong birching without a murmur."

Her discipline grew more sprightly. She threw more vigor into her work, and I panted like a dying man.

"Wait a bit! I'll finish you with a nice riding-whip!" she exclaimed, as she threw away her rod and unhooked from the wall a long and elastic lady's whip of real whalebone.

She did indeed "finish me," gratifying my unwilling bruised posteriors with a dozen cuts at least which she let me have at top speed and as hard as she could give them. They made me strain, writhe, and roar with pain, until after a last unavailing effort to break my bonds, I fell exhausted, closing my eyes and clenching my teeth.

"Ten dollars, please! Don't forget!" she said, untying the ropes that held me.

As I stood erect, trembling all over under the emotive effects of this quick and terrible penance, I had forgotten all about payment. Miss Silk showed herself to be a typical American lady – never losing her memory when the Almighty Dollar is in question.

CHAPTER IV

The club program announced for the morrow – Wednesday – a lesson in conjugal correction. I felt very annoyed at not being able to witness the interesting performance, as male members by themselves were not admitted to this lecture, reserved for assorted couples.

Each member was privileged to invite a lady; the weaker sex not being forced to submit to the same formalities of admittance as the lords of creation. The famous representation did not begin until five o'clock in the afternoon and I had hopes of finding some obliging young person who would consent to play the part of my spouse. I regretfully thought of adorable Miss Rosey and little Lucy. They would have made ideal partners. There were, however, no lack of prize beauties at Boston, where the fashionable flagellating epidemic raged quite as strongly as at Porkopolis. After having enjoyed an elaborate luncheon, I audaciously set out to find the angel of my daydream, when an idea, which I fondly found perfectly luminous, struck me suddenly.

Where was the best spot to find the object of my desires? In the club itself, to be sure! Was not that the meeting-place of the most entrancing whipping darlings of Boston? There were sixty lady members; without counting the lovely lecturing ladies – a fine flock for me to choose from, by my faith!

But this hope was soon wrecked. The sixty birching beauties each had their regular escorting cavaliers, and the female orators only came to the hall when they had to give a lecture.

Confiding my dilemma to one of the attendants, he discreetly gave me an address in town. Off I sped at once, and tumbled into the hospitable parlor of a San Francisco pet. I will call her Miss Nora, if you will allow me. She was a thin brunette, lissome and serpentine. She was enchanted when I asked to be allowed to become her beau and take her to the club, of which she had heard, without ever having been there.

"But first of all," she said, "just to see what you are made of, I'm going to begin by giving you a nice little slap-bottom."

She took me into her bedroom and showed me some rods – a present from a lady friend, an expert wielder of the birch.

"Undress and lie down flat on that rug!"

Such was her brief order, and as soon as I obeyed, she strode over my prostrate body, straddling across my shoulders, with much whirling of her scented skirts.

Choosing her instrument of torture, she began to swish my hindquarters with short, recurring blows. They were not severe, and tickled my skin, provoking a delicious tingling sensation. Her movements caused her frock and petticoat to completely cover my head, and I thus found myself in intoxicating darkness, my senses flattered by the warm atmosphere perfumed by the sweet odor of her sex.

Her birching fun was continued in a series of rapid slight cuts, almost without interval, deadening my flesh by their electrical caress. The charm was broken much too soon, by a ring at the street-door bell, causing my young despotic divinity to get up and leave me, while I jumped into the bed to hide my nakedness.

My head was scarcely on the pillow, when Nora came back.

"It's only my friend Harriet, the clever bircher I told you about, who gave me the rods. I'll introduce you."

As she finished speaking, a fine young woman with a wealth of magnificent chestnut hair, a dashing appearance and proud carriage, strode into the room.

"I've just given this naughty boy a severe whipping," said Miss Nora. "Shouldn't reckon so, by the look of him!" replied Harriett dryly. "I know your style of birching, Nora dear. You just sweep over the skin with your rod, and that's all! Isn't that so, sir?" she added, appealing to me. "To tell the truth, she hasn't cut me up much," I answered, happy to make the acquaintance of such a charming creature.

"You see, Nora, I guessed right!" chirped haughty Harriet. "It's lucky I've come around to put things straight. Come on, sir, and let me birch you to a standstill – in a proper manner; the only true way a professional female flagellant out to cut up a masculine bottom!"

Such an offer transported me into the seventh heaven, for this new friend pleased me greatly. I fancied I should experience extraordinary sensations, thanks to her efforts.

"Let me have some rope to tie him with," she said to her friend. "In the parcel I've brought are two new green rods. They'll come in useful." Into the centre of the room, she pushed a long sofa, so as to have space to walk all round it, and asked me to stretch myself thereon, face downward. Having obeyed with alacrity, the tow girls bound me tightly to the couch. "Don't go away, Nora," said Harriet, "but notice how I use my rod."

She grasped the new, ripe birch. It was long, thin, and seemingly very flexible. With it, she dealt me a shower of swift blows which pricked my skin and jarred on my nerves. But her movements quickened; she hit harder; the rod whizzed through the air and stung my bum with a crash that echoed loudly through the room. She birched me with the flat ends of the twigs, which, spreading fan-like over my buttocks, seemed to produce a flow of burning lava. My body was on fire; my sighs of delight changed to groans of agony, but the expert birching sorceress kept on flogging me with untiring vigor.

"Give me the other rod!" she said, and without stopping, changed the old weapon for the fresh one that she used with still greater energy. I writhed under the terrible downpour of swinging strokes, searing my smarting stern like tongues of flame.

"Now, Nora," said Harriet, passing the rod to her, "try yourself, and don't be frightened to let him have it – rough! He hasn't got his fill yet!"

Nora evidently wanted to show me she had profited by her friend's example and birched me as hard as she could, Harriet looking on, and smiling approvingly.

For a few minutes, she allowed her young friend to exercise all her talent and strength, and then, taking the rod in her grasp once more, she became excited and maddened, whipping me in the most merciless manner, finishing by ten furious cuts, which caused me to lose all control over myself. When I had repaired the disorder of my dress, I complimented Harriet on her scientific method that had brought the castigation to a satisfactory voluptuous termination.

"When I was eighteen, I had already been chosen to occupy the post of disciplinary teacher in one of the best New York boarding-schools, where I exercised my art on the most aristocratic bottoms of Gotham," she informed me.

"But that isn't where you learnt to whip a man?" I objected.

"Certainly not," she rejoined. "My fame as a flagellant was noised abroad by the boarders gossiping in their homes. The girls' relations – brothers and best boys – were therefore soon all agog to try the effects of my birching. That is how I established a fine circle of manly clients in the ranks of the Four Hundred."

Miss Harriet seemed impatient and ill at ease. I guessed that she wanted me to leave, so that she might be alone with her chum. My birching beauty betrayed disappointment when she heard that Nora was to accompany me to the club lecture.

"Perhaps you have some other fun on?" I asked the two young women.

"Oh no," replied Harriet. "Nothing to prevent my friend going out with you, but if you must be put wise to everything, I don't mind telling you that the object of my visit was to birch Nora's saucy bottom. She needs punishment greatly, but I – I – I can't very well flog her before a man, can I?"

I comprehended that I was in the way. They did not care to lift the veil that shrouded the secrets of their customary diversions, but the thought that I might be granted a view of these two nymphs when delirious with the lusts of their passionately sensual sport, excited me so highly that I begged to be allowed to remain a passive onlooker, promising solemnly not to interfere in any way.

This they refused. Nothing could tempt them. They even denied me the privilege of letting me remain outside the door, where, without seeing them,

I merely asked to be allowed to listen blindfolded, my hands tied behind my back. Unable to persuade the inexorable couple, I repaired for an hour to a neighboring saloon, where I smoked a cigar and indulged in a long drink. The brace of birching queens were delighted to be freed from my presence. When I returned, I found that Miss Harriet seemed rather excited. She wore a look of satisfied conquest, which increased her allurement. As for Miss Nora, she was in bed, tired and listless. Her hair was streaming over her shoulders, and under her lustrous eyes were deep-black half-moons.

"Well, my dear Harriet," said I, "you've got your young pupil into a nice state!"

"Yes," murmured Nora, her eyelids drooping. "I'm done up. You would be real good if you took Harry along with you to the club, instead of poor me!"

I could lose nothing by the exchange. Harriet was a grand specimen of queenly grace, really handsome, of warm and impulsive disposition – the very partner I could dream of for the coming flogging festival.

With this latter lady on my arm, I therefore set out on my voyage of discovery, after having bestowed a substantial cash gift on little Nora, who desired but one thing that afternoon – a long spell of repose.

CHAPTER V

My entrance into the club was triumphant and sensational, the majestic damsel I escorted being greatly admired on all sides. She carried herself magnificently – like an empress; and she was dressed with elegant taste in the height of fashion.

Without the least difficulty, we reached the Great Hall of Flagellation. Many couples were already seated and others came in at intervals. Each pair of spectators had at their disposal a wooden bench, a coil of rope, and a new birch.

The spokeswoman was a tall, auburn lass with an arrogant manner. She wore a tight-fitting black silk dress which set off every curve of her fine figure. Her frock, cut close up to the neck, had no sleeves, and her pair of sculptural, muscular, dimpled arms contrasted delightfully with the somber background of her costume.

"Ladies and gentlemen," she began, "or rather I should say, loving couples united by a chain of love, Providence, with divine foresight, has made trees so that rods may be formed from their branches. The twigs of the silvery birch may be likened unto celestial manna, of which a store should be jealously hoarded in every household. Husbands shall sting wifely posteriors therewith, and dutiful helpmates swish their lords with the beneficent rod, so that harmony may reign in a world of reciprocal tenderness. Like all good things, the birch must not be unthinkingly and indiscriminately used. It is foolish to whip without rhyme or reason, or on the slightest pretext. Corporal punishment is only charming when really deserved.

"The rod, rationally employed, eradicates for ever deplorable fireside squabbles, which in time prevent peace in the home. Wifie sulks no longer; hubby never thinks of reaching for his hat and departing with a bang of the door. Every little difficulty, so painful when two people have to pass their lives together, is smoothed away without quarrelsome scenes, rage, or hysterical fits, by the simple and judicious application of a few good bottom spankings.

"Husband and wife agree to a covenant. They give their word of honor to submit reciprocally to a dose of birching discipline every time that one catches the other at fault. For instance: Master gets home an hour late for dinner. The mistress of the house is crazy with rage. The soup is cold; the joint burnt a cinder, and directly the husband comes in, the storm bursts. The wife, in a temper, breaks a few plates; her lord swears, huddles on his overcoat and spends his evening in front of a bar.

"Now appreciate my method as applied to the same pair. Master returns to the dovecote an hour after dinner-time. His wife is waiting for him patiently. She is calm, sever, and undaunted. 'My dear boy' she says, 'you are one hour late.' Out comes her consort's watch. He mumbles some excuse, but Wifie interrupts him. 'There is no excuse for you! You're late! Remember our agreement! You deserve thirty strokes of the birch. Hurry up and undress!' She ties him to a bench, and with a stout, fresh bundle of birch, gives him his disciplinary chastisement, without omitting one blow from the account.

"Immediately afterward, both sit down to dinner and enjoy their repast with an excellent appetite, aroused by the excellent birching upheaval, as salutary for the woman, for whom it is good exercise, as it is for the husband who profits by its usual delightful reaction." (Great applause from every part of the hall.)

"Another example," continues the brilliant lady orator. "A husband forbids his wife to encourage the visits of a young cousin who shows her too much attention. She receives him on the sly and her lord and master catches the couple flirting together. what would be the outcome of such friction in an ordinary household? A frightful scene. The infuriated husband bangs his fist on the table, knocks over chairs and flower-pots; yells, blusters, gesticulates, and vows he'll keep a mistress. Wilfie seeks refuge in a fainting-fit.

"The same household according to my teaching. The husband surprises the youthful flirting relative in his parlor. 'My dear little woman,' he says icily, 'I forbade you to let your cousin visit here any more. He has just left my house. You know our contract, and that such outrageous behavior must be paid for by fifty cuts of the rod. Go up to our room, I beg you, and strip. I will follow in five minutes and punish you immediately.' He binds his wife, preferably on the conjugal couch, and turning a deaf ear to her protests and lamentations, lets her have the half-hundred slashing strokes. After this excellent exercise, Master's sensual feelings are fully excited. Madam's nervous system has been splendidly shook up and both are admirably prepared for the thrilling embrace of loving copulation in which they are soon joined." (Frenzied cheers from the entire audience.)

"Ladies and gentlemen," she went on, as soon as silence was restored, "I have submitted my theories to your approval. You're applause, for which I am sincerely grateful, proves the justice of my views.

"I will now pass on to the lesson proper, which I divide into three parts: First, the choice of flagellating implements; secondly, how to bind the culprit; lastly, the way to apply the rod.

"The selection of punitive instruments is more important than one might suppose. On that depends for the most part the success of the corrective operation. The instrument must not be too formidable, nor too slight; it must neither cut nor wound, and yet it should hurt as much as possible. Therefore, the birch-rod is the ideal weapon. To have a good one, the twigs should be cut from an old tree, choosing the topmost branches, where the wood is harder and more supple. Young shoots of birch are soft, only fit for making rods for children's bottoms. For adults, mature branches are needful. They sting better. The twigs should be cut about a yard long; leaves and tiny offshoots carefully stripped off, and ten or twelve of these selected branches bound together form a splendid rod, especially if you remember to have them all of the same length. In this way, the rod does not finish a point which might become curved during the flagellation and cut the fine, delicate skin of hips and thighs, which it is useless to endanger. The end of the rod, held in the hand, may be wrapped round with velvet or any other material, so that it be soft to the palm, and easy to clutch – a precaution not to be despised during long or oft-repeated flogging bouts.

"Rods require great care. To produce their maximum effect, they should be new, not having been cut from the trees more than a fortnight. To ensure the maintenance of flexibility, they out to be kept soaked in water; either laid out flat, or if the vase is upright and narrow, with the handle-end downward. If the thin ends are upward, the weight of the rod does not spoil their shape. Dry and careless-chosen rods, made up of short and thick twigs, should be strictly rejected. They would needlessly and never produce the vibrating result on the skin, following on the use of picked bundles of birch.

"Sometimes it is difficult to put one's hand on a birch-rod. In default, other instruments may be used. First on the list comes the riding-whip. "No one should resort for flagellating purposes to the thick and heavy whip used by hunting men and jockeys. The slender and elegant switch know as a lady's riding-whip should alone be called into play. It is lithe and supple, made of whalebone, and covered with plaited, varnished flax. Before use, the little knotted silken lash, which harness-makers and saddlers generally fix on the end, should be taken off, as it lays the skin open. "The whip is to be feared in the hands of a flagellating female apt to lose her head while correcting a guilty person. It should be handled cautiously, for it stings most terribly. Expert flagellating goddesses always make play with their whips as a wind-up after a good course of birching, when ten or twelve strokes well laid on produce the delirious shuddering spasm which brings truly lustful penitent victims to the spermatic crisis.

"After the whip may be catalogued the infinite variety of 'martinets'. Such an instrument, with its strips of thin leather nailed to a wooden handle, is worthy of notice, although it flogs with greater heavy violence than the birchen twigs, which act more superficially on the outer skin. Whips may also be subdivided into many classes. Some there are with long or short thongs, from the dog-whip down to the horsewhip, not forgetting the Russian knout. Such instruments are mostly too frightful for ordinary use, and should only be resorted to on rare occasions, when energetic action is required, destined to strongly impress the floggee.

"To terminate my dissertation on the choice of flagellating instruments, I will call the attention to my dear whipping sisters, the pretty flogging girls

I see here before me, to a special kind of implement which they may easily make if necessary, supposing they should happen to find themselves without rod or whip handy. This summary 'martinet' can be rigged up at a moment's notice with the aid of bootlaces. In the smallest village, leather shoelaces, finished off by metal ends, can always be purchased. Take a dozen, fold them in half, and with a string tie them to a piece of wood, forming an extemporaneous handle. If the punishment is intended to be severe, leave the little metal ends as they are. Would you temper justice with mercy, cut off the tags, and the hastily-made 'martinet' will produce about the same effect as an ordinary rod. But again, I say nothing equals the divine birch!"

CHAPTER VI

Again the assembled audience applauded the interesting lady lecturer. She gracefully nodded her thanks and went on.

"Ladies and gentlemen, I now come to the second part of my lesson – how to bind the culprit. In order to fully demonstrate my methods, I shall pass from the domains of theory into those of practice.

"It is absolutely necessary that the guilty person should be rendered powerless during punishment. First, because the delinquent being forced to remain in one position allows a person applying the blows to aim with precision at the part destined to be struck, without wavering to right or left, which must be the case when the guilty one struggles. Moreover, such immobility affords the flogging female an opportunity of seeing what she is about. She can follow the results of the rod's action, either progressively increasing the vigor of her cuts, or diminishing their severity of needful. In short, her work is regular and efficacious. Besides, bonds impress the captive. He feels himself at the mercy of the flagellating lady who ceases to flog when she wishes, and not when her victim begs for mercy. The moral effect is thus excellent.

"The ideal piece of furniture for restraining the guilty person is a rough wooden bench, without a back. My earnest wish, ladies and gentlemen, is that such a simple settee should form part of the chattels in every home, where it ought to be looked upon as the most necessary article in all well ordained households. It may, of course, be rendered more sumptuous, so as not to seem out of place in rooms that are richly garnished. This end may be attained if it is covered in leather or any fancy material, but its plain design should be strictly adhered to. This bench enable s us to tie the guilty party down securely in a few seconds by means of common rope or silken cords. The flogger can move all round the floggee, applying the twigs in the contrary direction, or following the line of the body lengthwise, by standing at the victim's head, thus reaching correctly and more readily the part where the extreme points of the rod falls in the first instance.

"Should the bench be lacking, a strong chair can be requisitioned. Throw it down, its back on the ground. The delinquent kneels on the head-rails, leaning over the end of the seat, so that his shoulders touch the extremity of the chair's front legs. Bound in this position, the section of the body reserved for the rod's attack is fully exposed and well within the flagellant's reach. Here is a photograph representing a guilty person bound to the chair."

From a portfolio on the table, Miss Needle took a picture which, as it passed from hand to hand, excited no small amount of curiosity. A young man could be seen tied to an overturned chair according to the foregoing explanation. He was writhing under the application of a birch-rod, brandished by a severe-looking governess.

"A small iron or camp bedstead," continued Miss Needle, "is a capital piece of furniture for putting a guilty fellow in bondage. Hands and feet are fastened to the cross-bars, and a rope should be wound round the loins. In this way, the whole of the body is rendered powerless. Here we have a photograph of this posture."

Another large picture was passed round the auditorium. It was an enlarged snapshot of a gigantic Negro roped to a small iron bedstead. The black was being vigorously whipped by quite a young white lassie.

"A flagellating lady," Miss Needle continued, "is sometimes perplexed when she ahs only an ordinary wooden bedstead at her disposal. Nevertheless there is a capital way of utilizing a common couch. The guilty party, his feet touching the ground, leans over the bed, arms outstretched, his hands dropping over the other side. Once in that position, nothing is easier than to tie his legs to one of the slats and the hands to another, so that the entire body of the victim cannot budge. The posteriors are advantageously exposed, ready to receive the full benefit of the birch. I think ladies, that you have understood? At any rate, here is a photograph that will give you a better idea of birching on a bed."

This third photographic exhibit created a deep impression, and when her hearers had settled down again, Miss Needle took up the thread of her discourse.

"I think you all know, ladies, and probably practice, what I may call the Maltese Cross, or spread-eagle position. The victim's legs and arms are drawn asunder and bound to the four corners of the bedstead. Such a proceeding is elementary, and it would be a loss of time to send round any photographs of such a posture.

"I have not exhausted ways and means for tying up guilty males. There are many others, resorted to by professional flagellating women, in order to impress their sensually passionate clients. A noteworthy example is that of the ring screwed into the ceiling, to which hangs a pulley and rope, allowing the culprit to be strung up by the arms, or if desired, by the feet – the head resting on the ground.

"This last attitude is, it appears, highly prized by refined votaries of the birch. Another way to utilize the ring in the ceiling, gives a curious opportunity of suspension, which seems as if the victim was hanging in the air by the skin of his behind. To obtain this peculiar effect, the delinquent wears a strong belt furnished with a ring or swivel in front. The rope hanging down from above rejoins the stomach-ring after passing between the thighs. The hands are tied to a hook screwed into the flooring." The fair lecturing lady handed another photograph to her listeners and the spectators clustered eagerly to feast their eyes on the representation of a man hanging by a thick cord, which seemed, indeed, as if it issued from his fundament.

"In conclusion," said Miss Needle, "I must not forget to mention the ladder, greatly in favor all over England for flagellating purposes. It is reared slanting against a wall; laid flat and fastened to two chairs; or simply thrown on the ground, its rungs affording capital opportunities for binding a victim according to the flogger's caprice.

"Ladies and gentlemen, the theoretical portion of my lecture is finished. I now come to practical demonstrations. I beg that all the ladies among my audience should order their partners to undress."

Round after round of enthusiastic applause resounded in the vast amphitheatre, where the forty seats it contained were occupied by twenty couples. It was a strange sight. Every dark coat and vest was discarded. Trousers dropped off, and all the men present appeared in their shirts; their legs bare. I followed the example of all the other gentlemen, much to the amusement of Miss Harriet.

CHAPTER VII

All the audience had been greatly excited by the lecture, and the gentlemen – every one undressed – were waiting impatiently for the rods to be used.

"Ladies, please order each guilty man to place himself face downward on the bench."

There was a great bustle in the hall as this suggestion was adopted.

"Now, ladies all, take your pair of short ropes; join the feet of the delinquents, their arms dropping over either side of the bench. Let the wrists be tied under the bench, and the ankles above."

Our charming partners followed these instructions with alacrity.

"Very good ladies," said Miss Needle, seeing that every so-called lord of creation was securely bound. "You are all, I think, in possession of a third long cord? Throw it under the bench, bring up the two ends over your victim's back; pass one end in the slip-knot, and pull until the culprit's body is pressed against the wood. Now make a knot. Those ladies who are not strong enough can place one foot on the edge of the bench to enable them to tug at the rope and make it taut."

The amiable charmers busied themselves in earnest, some being very serious; others laughing over their work.

Adorable Harriet lifted her skirts and placed her dainty little boot against the edge of my bench, allowing me to get a glimpse of a neat ankle and a tightly-fighting stocking emerging from the frills and flounces of her silk, lace-trimmed underwear.

When all the ropes were knotted, Miss Needle came down from her platform to view and criticize the fastenings as arranged by her docile pupils. Returning to her table, she spoke thus:

"Ladies, I have explained to you as clearly as I could how to tie a guilty man so as to render it impossible for him to struggle and evade punishment. You have the necessary apparatus placed at your disposal. Please remark that the ropes are woven with silk and are exceptionally strong. I warn you that if a delinquent should happen to escape from your bonds, his partner will at once be brought up on the platform where I shall flog her before the assembled spectators, to teach her to take more pains in future."

"Miss Harriet," said I, trying to tease my companion, "I shall break loose!"

"There's no danger of that!" she replied.

She indeed roped me down cleverly. I could not move a limb.

"Ladies," said Miss Needle, "all the men present are in your power, tightly bound to their benches. We are now women together and have no reasons for sparing these fellows. Profit by your opportunity to bruise their bums thoroughly. Let the boys have something they will not easily forget. This is set down on the program and is inherent to the demonstration of my lesson concerning the proper way of applying the rod. The number of strokes that the culprits deserve will now be put to the vote."

"One hundred and fifty!" ejaculated a silvery-toned voice.

This high figure drew loud and general protests from the prisoners.

"One hundred!" clamored another feminine voice.

"Still too much!" said Miss Needle. "It is not advisable to draw blood. We must stop at the frontier. I propose fifty sturdy, swishing cuts."

"Fifty! Agreed! Let it go at that!" were the exclamations proceeding from numerous rosy female lips in different parts of the hall.

"We all concur –," repeated Miss Needle. "You will kindly proceed as follows: twenty whipped cuts from right to left; as many in the contrary direction; and the last ten bestowed while standing at your victim's head, letting your rods fall lengthwise. Strike hard at once, beginning with the first stroke; gradually increasing the spring of your slash, by lifting your arms very high in order that the last ten cuts may be given with all the strength you can muster. Lift the delinquent's shirt-tails, pin them to the shoulders and take your rods."

As if obeying a military command, the forty birching beauties each brandished their bunch of branches.

"I am going to count aloud," continued Miss Needle, "and you will strike together. Attention! One!"

Forty rods came down with a noise akin to that of a hailstorm. Blow followed blow in cadence, following the loudly outspoken orders of the lady orator. At first, there was silence. But as soon as the blows increased in vigor, sighs and slight groans were forced from the mouths of the martyred males.

After the twentieth cut, Miss Needle's voice was heard above all this tumult of pain, as she called out:

"Halt! Ladies," she added, "pass round to the other side of the your benches and flog harder. I see that one or two swish much softer than they ought. At the conclusion of the punishment, I shall walk through the hall to note the result thereof myself. Should I see that any of you have deliberately spared the backsides confided to your care, I shall add what is lacking. Attention, ladies! Twenty-one!"

Again the rods hissed through the air, rustling in measure. The beautiful flagellating fairies, encouraged by the lady lecturer, increased their speed and attacked the males with renewed strength. Lamentations and groans burst forth on all sides.

Miss Harriet was always to the fore, birching me earnestly, and in so lively a manner that I found relief in involuntary shrieks of pain. At last the fortieth cut had been counted.

"Halt!" Miss Needle once more called out. "Ladies," she went on, "I notice that some of your flogging is a farce. I will put things right in a moment. Now please take your places at the head of the culprits. Aim correctly, so as to whip well in the center of the buttocks; pricking the top of the thighs slightly with the pointed ends of your twigs. Put forth the entire strength of your pretty bodies. You've only men before you, confound it all! Anybody would think you were whipping an omelets!"

These last words caused a storm of silvery laughter.

"Let us get on, my dears!" said Miss Needle. "Forty-one, forty-two –" The final ten blows, given with rare energy by most of the lovely birching ladies, caused a cat's concert of howls and yells.

I was one of the best musicians, as Miss Harriet fully intended that I should appreciate the strength of her biceps. I uttered a strident shriek. My rump quivered, as I bounded under the smart swishing shower.

CHAPTER VIII

Faithful to her promise, as soon as the fiftieth blow had been dealt, Miss Needle, with a big rod in her fist, came down into the body of the hall. She passed close to me, examined the state of my buttocks and seemed satisfied. "You can set your man at liberty!" she said to Harriet.

I almost regretted having been so well flogged because I was thus deprived of the delight of receiving the charming female lecturer's supplementary interesting onslaught.

As for my pretty partner, she appeared to be tired and languid, while slowly releasing me from my bonds. Her eyes sparkled in the same manner as when, after a lust fight on the battlefield of Venus, a woman's looks betray the intense joy she has just felt.

The handsome lady orator, having approached a couple near Harriet and myself, spoke to them in quite another way.

"Madam," she said to the young spectators, "I've been watching you. I noticed that you hardly dared to lift your rod. Allow me to suppose that if you're here with your gentleman it is because he is an amateur of flagellation.

This is no joking matter. I'll show you how a man out to be birched." She applied a dozen strokes, dealt with nervous strength, on the bum of the young woman's partner. He was quite astounded at this sudden assault, squirming and setting up a dismal howl.

"That'll do him good!" said Miss Needle, and turning to the surprised lady, she added, "You'll be good enough to step up on the platform bye and bye. I intend to whip you – just to give you a lesson."

Miss Needle passed along the other whipping benches, applying a few rasping cuts to such masculine victims she deemed insufficiently punished, and then the conscientious lady returned to her post on the stage, where three young women were waiting their penalty.

I was pleased to be able to enjoy what was a novel and attractive sight for me – women being birched. I also felt some surprise to find that such charming young creatures allowed themselves to be publicly fustigated. But when Miss Birch, after having thrown up the petticoats of the exquisite little brunette as high as possible, began to handle the rod with grace and delicacy, it slowly dawned upon my understanding that sensual passion played a great part in this drama. In point of fact, the young females obtained salacious satisfaction. The birch appeased their most secret sexual longings.

The skillful flogging woman birched these willing bottoms with slight blows, enwrapping the whole surface of the swelling globes, until the satin skin was tinged with pink blushes. The delicious brunette sighed heavily, and her lovely, amber, plump crupper wriggled as if under the influence of a love-spasm.

After her, it was the turn of a sweet blonde, hardly out of her teens. She pulled up her own underclothing, like a girl about to bathe, offering a pair of small hemispheres, white and firm, to Miss Needle's birch. The lady lecturer seemed to experience some special artistic pleasure as she cleverly attended to this perfect pair of hinder cheeks. She showered down upon them a multitude of sustained, rapid, swishing cuts, sounding sharply on the tender skin. Beneath the pleasing shower, the lovely lass twisted her well-made body, as she gave utterance to a series of small, half suppressed shrieks. She was literally swooning with languorous pleasure, until Miss Needle, also overwhelmed with blushing emotion, pushed her gently away.

The third lady, a tall, thin, dark young person, with sleepy eyes, began to shudder deliciously directly the female birching professor took her in hand. The victim bent her head, whispering a few words in Miss Needle's ear. The expert flogger smiled, and seizing her victim, threw her on a bench, to which she tied her without letting her undress. Up went her skirts. Then the birch was applied without mercy, reddening the smooth surface of her shapely bum at once. She next dealt her a few flogging slashes with extreme violence that caused the culprit to moan and bound in cataclysm of delicious delirium.

The spectacle of three pretty women baring their backsides to the brutal contact of the birch caused great excitement to thrill the audience. All the ladies present followed the scene with the utmost emotive interest.

"Ladies and gentlemen," said Miss Needle, advancing to the edge of her platform, "in order that my demonstration be complete, it is necessary that I conclude by teaching the men here to-day how to whip a woman. I do not wish to force my lesson on all the males among my appreciative audience. Let those couples who intend to utilize my teaching come forward."

There was a movement in the hall. One couple stepped from the crowd. Their example was followed by another lady and gentleman. In all, five couples singled themselves out.

"How is this?" demanded Miss Needle. "Among the forty ladies comprising my hearers, there are only five who allow their husbands to birch them! Must we then conclude that in the noble sport of flagellation, woman wears the breeches? Nevertheless, I shall proceed with my lesson. Come, gentlemen, please place those ladies destined to be punished in front of you. Let the other couples stand back."

The five ladies and their cavaliers lined up in a row facing the stage.

"Gentlemen," continued the lecturing lady, "a woman is always whipped quite differently to a man. A female is nervous. She must not be wrought up to the needful degree of obedience by violence. Persistent, progressive, and gentle action must be brought to bear, until she submits as if conquered by prolonged caresses. A woman loving passive flagellation prefers to be birched by another woman, because she understands much better the sensations sought for by one of her own sex.

"Enough words! Let us proceed to acts. Gentlemen, strip your ladies. You will then apply thirty strokes of the birch – fifteen on one side and fifteen on the other."

In the front row was now heard a rustling of silk-lined, tailor-made masterpieces. The lovers were helping their sweethearts and wives to disrobe. Radiant nude charms were soon exposed to the searching light of day, and dainty chemises, cut very low, veiled naught of perfect breasts and sculptural arms.

Following Miss Needle's reiterated instructions, the ladies were quickly tied down, and five pairs of rotund gloves of different sizes, but all white, and hard, were bared to our enchanted glances.

I was as happy as a king at this lascivious view. I gloated over these fine bottoms, as I reclined comfortably in my stall. I had not been able to do so when the men were flogged. Miss Harriet, seated by my side, was as much amused as a boarding-school miss paying her first visit to the play.

"Take your rod!" commanded Miss Needle. "Attention! One!"

A loud whistling sound, followed by soft shrieks, broke the entranced stillness of the hall. The five birches were brandished in cadence, delicately handled as advised by Miss Needle. Two men, however, slashed away much harder, causing their tender victims to groan loudly.

"Halt!" cried Miss Needle, after counting the fifteenth blow. "Sir!" she went on, turning to one of the gentlemen. "You are inconceivably brutal! Is that how you birch a woman? It seems to me, upon my word, that you think you are lashing a mare! If I see you flog again in that way, I'll have you up on the platform and give you a hiding that'll be something to remember! Now then, gentlemen, step to the other side and apply the remaining fifteen strokes. Attention! Sixteen!"

The switching gallop began again on the satin gloves, already changed to a rosy hue. Tiny shrieks and miniature moan broke from the lips of all the birched beauties, accompanied by the hissing and crashing of the supple twigs.

When the thirtieth cut had been given and counted, Miss Needle, in a rage, collared the gentleman she had already warned.

"Now sir," she cried, "up on the platform and get your clothes off! Despite my remonstrances, you kept on lashing like a brute. I mean to punish you as you deserve! Your chastisement will be an example for all your fellow-men here!"

Boston

The birched girls dressed again with the help of their husbands. Miss Harriet offered her services to the young woman whose lover was now dragged on to the stage by Miss Needle. My amiable companion then returned to my side, telling me that the poor little girl's bottom was dripping with blood, and that her man deserved no pity, however severely he might be castigated.

He was already stretched half-naked on the bench. Miss Needle, shaking all over with indignation, was tying him down securely. Her movements were rapid and rough.

She selected a large, heavy rod, and flogged him with the greatest energy, from the very first cut onward. At the fourth stroke, dealt with noisy rigor, the guilty man began to howl. He gasped for breath, begged for clemency, and promised never to offend again. Miss Needle, deaf to all his entreaties and remorseful apologies, brandished her rod furiously.

It was a scene of bitter anguish. Miss Heart watched my agonized emotion out of the corners of her eyes.

The flogging lady birched her man in masterful style. The delinquent's skin was covered with long, curving, bleeding weals. Despite his bonds, he squirmed like a worm. Miss Needle never left off until her rod was broken to pieces, its twigs having been scattered far and near in tiny fragments. Poignant emotion engrossed all the onlookers, and when the indefatigable female flagellant deigned to drop her strong right arm, an involuntary sigh of relief escaped from all of us.

Miss Harriet had been strangely, deeply stirred. Her lustrous orbs were illuminated with a strange light. Her cheeks were very red. She confided to me how much she would have liked to have been in the shoes of the barbarous, birching, lecturing beauty. For my part, I did not mind confessing in reply that I would willingly have served as victim, for the tyrannical fustigation of this incomparable artist in flagellation had made an enormous impression on me.

"I wager, dear boy," said Miss Harriet, "that you are dying to be birched in private room by the beautiful woman who has just been delighting us all with her lecture."

"You've guessed my thoughts aright," I could not help replying.

"Then I forbid it!" said my adorable Harriet.

"If you think I did not birch you sufficiently severely today, I am ready to give you an exemplary thrashing at once in a private room. I guarantee you'll lose nothing by letting me birch you instead of Miss Needle!"

"Harriet, dear, your idea is great!" I answered quickly, "and fits in with my most cherished wishes!"

"Come along quick!" she said, dragging me, full of joy, toward the entrance to the private rooms.

Once there, great deception awaited us. Every secret snuggery was occupied – taken in advance by amateurs, who were all expecting to be attended to by the lecturing lady whose lessons had fired every brain. Miss Harriet was grievously disappointed. She yearned to celebrate the most mysterious rites of the divine birching cult as much as I did. But the dinner-hour was nigh, and I persuaded my throbbing companion to follow me to a first-class restaurant.

CHAPTER IX

My stock of flagellating knowledge had been greatly enriched by the two lectures I had attended.

In this most select assembly, a club where election was beset with difficulties, the strange flogging passion has openly avowed and enjoyed, but still there are so many members that they formed a high percentage of the population. I could not help being surprised at the frankness with which these birching adepts confessed their lustful longings and practiced openly. The clandestine flagellant, quenching his thirst for the rod under the rose, is a much more common type. Rare indeed are those who reach the highest pinnacle of enjoyment by being publicly whipped. The lessons taught in the Lecturing Hall allowed me to see how far women went when devoted to sporting with the bewitching birch.

I had yet more marvels to view.

The day after the memorable sitting, when pretty Miss Harriet had accompanied me, the program announced an interesting lecture, to be given by two twin sisters, Misses Daisy and Alice Pimlico. Sweet Harriet was unable to be with me, having been obliged to go to New York, where she went every Thursday on a visit to a great lover of the rod. He was a faithful subscriber to the clever bottom-slapping of this skillful flagellating female.

I intended to console myself for the absence of the delightful girl, as I hoped to profit by my freedom to make the acquaintance of the two lecturing lassies.

Boston

I entered the club a few minutes before three, so as not to lose a single detail of the interesting performance. The hall was soon filled; the fair sex mustering in great force. Nearly all the ladies present were handsome, young, and elegantly dressed.

The urban Lady President, superb Mrs. Colonel Islington, was enthroned in her high chair or honor. It stood in the centre of the front row of seats, not far from my stall. She signed to me to approach her, and with great affability asked me if I was having a good time at the club.

"My dearest Madam," I replied, "everything is fantastically delightful, surpassing my wildest dreams."

She seemed flattered, smiling with charming, unaffected grace.

"You're a Frenchman?" she asked, and my affirmative answer seemed to please her.

"Will you come and have a cup of tea at my house to-morrow at five?" she said, slipping a tiny visiting card in my hand.

I was pleased to find there was an opportunity for me to become more intimately acquainted with such an adorable creature, and I said so – with hot enthusiasm.

"I like French gentlemen," she rejoined. "They have special 'attentions' for us poor women."

She laid stress on the word 'attentions,' and her long eyelashes quivered with a movement which was almost, but not quite a wink, as if she meant to say 'caresses'.

I went back to my seat. It was a few minutes past three, and the vast amphitheatre was crammed. There must have been two hundred spectators. Besides the hundred and fifty members, many had brought ladies with them. An attendant announced Misses Daisy and Alice Pimlico who were to speak on voluptuous flagellation. A moment afterward, a couple of luminous damsels; two fair lilies with immense steel-grey eyes, luscious red lips, and heavy, plaited golden locks, faced my enraptured gaze.

Their costumes betrayed quite half of their nudity, showing their bodies of alabaster whiteness; the delicate swelling globes of their bosom; their fine arms, and marvelously well-turned legs. They wore wreaths of roses; their tiny feet were shod with sandals, simply composed of a leather sole tied on with ribbons. Heavy ruby necklaces encircled their swanlike throats, and their girdles were fashioned out of a thick band of plain gold, fastened in front by a diamond clasp.

One of these entrancing idols seated herself on a footstool in the center of the platform. The other stood behind her, embracing her with her thighs and caressing her hair as she began her discourse.

"Most lordly gentlemen and noble ladies, voluptuous flagellation is a constant thought in the minds of all refined votaries of Venus, while in high society this rapturous pastime gains ground daily. Let us be pleased at such progress, for 'tis the game of the gods! It is the supreme expression of a lover's adoration for a divine mistress; the ideal of mysterious intoxication. Woman is a mystic rose, and the man who loses his senses when inhaling the fragrance of the feminine flower, must also quiver naturally beneath the sharp prick of its thorns. What greater voluptuousness is there for a fervid lover than to bow down at his adored sweetheart's feet and vibrate beneath the magical caress of her rod?

"In such a case, do you know what are a suitor's sensations? He is deliciously tormented by contrary emotions dragging him hither and thither, so to speak, between the fear of the sacrifice and his ardent desire to submit to it. He trembles at the sight of the formidable implements with which his mistress threatens him; he retreats affrighted, and yet dazed with delight is impelled to throw himself into the furnace. All his will-power crumbles away in a fit of bewildering weakness, as he feels himself humbled and crushed. He rolls on the ground at the feet of his inexorable charmer who renders him powerless by binding him with ropes abolishing all resistance. Obediently, like an attentive and submissive slave, he awaits his doom. His mistress's will is his, and she, implacable, soon resorts to extreme measures.

Seizing the birch, she encircles him in flames, licking and burning his flesh. He tries to escape, or flee, but he cannot extricate himself from the grip that holds him fast. The imperious loving woman is actively plying her rod. Nothing can stay her hand – neither his prayers, not his shrieks. He must suffer, since she so wills it! Pain, however, inflicted by her – the radiant idol of his maddest dreams – is akin to joy, and suffering becomes voluptuous delirium. His posteriors quiver and twitch beneath the pitiless caress of the prickly twigs, but his soul is bathed in infinite ecstasy. His divine mistress is cruel, full of complicated and charming caprice, but after exercising her adorable criminal scientific skill, she invents new sins and discovers unknown joys."

Thunders of applause greeted these vivid words. The exquisite lady orator dropped a curtsey and took her sister's place on the footstool. The latter damsel stood up and addressed the public.

"Most courteous men and lovely women, my sister Daisy has set forth in seductive speech the feelings of a fervent lover swayed by the spell of the celestial birch. Let it be my turn now to tell of an adored mistress's sensations, such as have often moved me; for many fine young fellows have trembled at my feet, writhing under the ardent kiss of my rod.

"The ecstasy of a loving woman is none the less radiant. She feels unspeakable happiness at the knowledge that she has enslaved her lover. She forces her power upon him, destroying his superior strength that slowly fades when he is on his knees before her. Carried away by spirit-stirring fever, she inflames the flesh of his hinder parts that writhe and redden; she causes to arise in his being a new pleasure; the voluptuousness of pain, and this violence forcing her perturbed blood to boil, she accomplishes the act of loving adoration, pouring out her libation to Venus by the fact of searing her lover's flesh!"

Fresh tumultuous applause resounded, and the ladies in the auditorium, greatly wrought up, whispered to each other; enthusiastically praising the two ravishing young lady lecturers.

CHAPTER X

Miss "Daisy Pimlico rose from her low stool and enlacing her sister lovingly, spoke as follows:

"Most noble gentlemen," she said, "if any among you wish to try our sublime methods, let such willing males step on to the platform so that the ladies here to-day may learn how to flagellate their husbands and lovers voluptuously and skillfully. Afterward, my sister and I will attend in the private rooms, placing ourselves at the disposal of any amateurs desirous of tasting this divine pleasure. I shall now send a few of our magic instruments round the hall to temp fervent lovers of the birch."

An attendant brought in a roll of blue silk, containing a dozen pretty, small rods with be-ribboned handles. Miss Daisy Pimlico walked along the front of the stalls, distributing her beautiful birches.

"See, ladies," she continued, "they are sweet miniature gems. We gather them ourselves, choosing young and tender birching shoots. We carefully file down all asperities, and then we soak them for forty-eight hours in perfumed alcohol. They are as soft as silk; as springy as steel, and they give out sparks, producing an electrical effect."

At this moment, a young man, quite a youth, scarcely twenty, left his seat and went upon the stage. His name was quickly whispered in every corner of the hall. He was a pianist of immense talent, celebrated all over the world, although hardly out of his teens.

Miss Alice clapped her hands joyously together, as she looked at the handsome stripling.

"Nothing could be better!" she exclaimed. "The female portion of the audience will be enchanted at seeing our methods demonstrated by the aid of such a handsome subject."

The young fellow undressed himself. His undergarments were as sumptuous as those of a woman of fashion. He wore embroidered silk drawers and a shirt of natural silk. He drew off his black silk, gold-edged socks, so as to show his splendid, perfectly-shaped feet, enhanced by rings where two diamonds sparkled between the toes.

A bench was brought; its head being placed looking toward the back of the stage, and its foot reaching to the edge. In the middle of the low settee was a fine satin cushion. The delicate lad stretched himself face downward on this piece of furniture, and submitted to be tied to it with blue silken cords by the two whipping sisters. The young ladies placed him in such a way that his head could hardly be seen by the public, while his bare posteriors were fully exposed, elevated by the cushion, allowing every spectator to note the effect of the rod on his soft skin.

"Ladies," said Miss Daisy, addressing her enthralled audience, "I beg to call your attention to the following important detail.

"We apply the rod gradually. First, we birch by a series of small strokes, lightly swishing, with the design of warming and benumbing the flesh. We thus get it used to the caressing touch of the twigs; preparing it for more energetic action. A man must be led to wish to be flogged harder, and be worked up to a pitch of frenzy by waiting impatiently for a keener contact. In this way, when the wished-for stinging cut finally raises a ridge on his rump, he feels delicious relief, causing his pain to be voluptuous and leading to supreme intoxication. This is quite a different process to severe punishment, which, however, we also know how to bestow to any amateurs who may call for it at our hands in one of the private rooms."

Each of the twins took up one of the tiny slender rods, and standing, one on the right and the other on the left of the young man, Miss Daisy, who seemed to be in command, gave a signal and both birches went to work. As one implement was lifted, the other fell, right in the centre of the lad's plump buttocks. With a hissing noise and a rebounding smack, this action was kept up with great regularity for many long minutes, the youthful victim sighing and stretching as if he was enjoying a beneficent douche. Every female in the stalls looked on, highly interested. The strokes were easy to support and the pianist's white skin was gradually getting rosy under this hot and exciting swishing storm.

Miss daisy made another sign, and the dance of the rods grew brisker, whipping and stinging, waking up the youth at every stroke. His plump bottom rose up high in the air; the skin of his buttocks wrinkled and rippled as he drew them in; opening our again ready to receive the succeeding cut. Scarlet weals traced a zebra-like pattern on his hindquarters, and he writhed about, uttering hoarse shrieks. Each blow was dealt with more force than its predecessor. The lad wriggled and palpitated.

Suddenly, Miss Alice dashed her rod to the ground, and Miss Daisy increased the speed and vigor of her strokes, evidently maddened by her task. She began to flog all by herself with the utmost rigor, but not before she had exchanged her miniature rod for one that was long and supple, evidently a terrible stinger.

The boy, starting violently at this fresh attack, let incoherent words escape his lips; and he moaned while beaten firmly with the new, stiff birch. The ladies in the audience rose to their feet, to get a better view of the young fellow's bottom as it became covered with large red weals. He bounded and wriggled in contortions of despair, and then, as a conclusion, a few blows dealt on his mangled bum with frenzied violence made him loft the trembling tender cheeks as high as the ropes would let him. His red stern fell down again, and a long, low groan of voluptuous enjoyment burst from the entranced boy.

A storm of applause broke out all round the room. Ladies were much agitated and blushed with tender emotion. While Miss Alice unbound her handsome victim, who staggered like a drunken man, Miss Daisy addressed the audience.

"Are there any other gentlemen," she asked, "who would like to go through the same enjoyment on this platform? No? I see they prefer to submit to our rods in the private rooms."

"Miss Pimlico," said a female voice from the stalls, "are your heavenly rods for sale?"

"Certainly," rejoined Daisy. "They cost a dollar each."

"In that case," replied the voice, "I'll buy the magic implement that made your young chap groan with happiness. Here's the dollar."

Miss Daisy was about to pass the rod, that she picked from the ground, into the auditorium when another voice arose from the back seats.

"I'll give two dollars for it!"

"Three!"

"Four dollars!"

"Ten dollars!"

These cries came from all parts of the great room at once.

Miss Daisy pricked up her ears, guessing that a wave of public-auction madness was passing over the audience, as is often the case in the United States.

"I'll put the rod up to be knocked down by the highest bidder," she said, advancing to the edge of her platform, the coveted broken birch in her hand.

"Now, ladies and gentlemen, here's the pretty birch that dragged a cry of enjoyment from the young artiste. The biggest offer gets the prize. Ten dollars bid! Who says more?"

"Fifteen!"

"Twenty dollars!"

"Thirty!"

I was happy to be able to witness this struggle, showing me the Americans when swayed by one of their most peculiarly characteristic manias.

"Fifty dollars!" thundered a deep masculine voice.

This high figure created a profound sensation. It was followed by a hushed silence. Suddenly, a lady, her eyes sparkling and her cheeks a vivid vermilion, stood up and drawled coolly:

"Guess I'll give a hundred dollars!"

There was a general hum of stupefaction.

"One hundred dollars! Any advance on a hundred dollars? Going –"

"And ten!" clamored the same strong male tones as before.

"One hundred and twenty," said the woman moving neurotically up and down in her seat.

There were loud murmurs of astonishment among the spectators.

"One hundred and twenty dollars," continued Miss Daisy. "No more? No advance on one and twenty? Going – going – gone!"

The tall red-cheeked woman tore the rod from the little hand of the improvised auctioneer, and then pulling out of her reticule a fountain-pen and a cheque-book, she scribbled in it.

I found this scene full of real Yankee local color and was delighted to have seen it enacted before my eyes.

"Ladies and gentlemen," said Miss Daisy, once more addressing her audience, "my sister Alice will now go down in the hall and give a number to any person who wishes to be attended to in the separate rooms; either for voluptuous flagellation, of which you have just had an example before your eyes; or for severe punishment applied in relentless fashion. As to our fees, we leave that to our patients' generosity."

Miss Alice stepped into the stalls, carrying a crystal vase containing numbered checks. I was impatient to feel myself bare beneath the yoke of these divine idols, and rushed towards her. I was lucky enough to capture No. 2.

I was gloating with ardent gaze over the charms of this entrancing maiden, so lovely in her semi-nudity, and I could not help imprinting a burning kiss on her tiny hand with its pink bejeweled, manicured fingers, from which I took the precious check. All the audience crowded round her. The furious bids for the rod seemed to have set every brain on fire. All the numbers ere torn from the vase, and adorable Alice brought it back empty to the platform.

"Ladies and gentlemen," said Daisy, smiling as she saw what success she and her sister were achieving, "I thank you heartily one and all. We seem to please you. There are thirty numbers gone; six having been taken by ladies. Such a great quantity of checks being distributed, we shall not be able to work together as we do generally. It would take us up to midnight, and no doubt some of you would not care to wait so late. I therefore propose that my sister and I should dissolve partnership for the time being, and operate singly. You will be treated just as well, I give you my word of honor. My sister Alice will attend to the odd numbers. I will devote myself to the even ones. Does my arrangement suit you?"

"Yes! Yes!" shouted several voices in the body of the hall.

"Is your vote unanimous?" asked Alice.

"Yes!" was the answer.

"I thank you!" replied Miss Daisy, springing into the stalls, followed by her sister. "No. 1 is for Alice," she added. "No. 2 is for me."

I was the happy possessor of that latter check, and delighted with my double luck, I advance toward adorable Miss Daisy. I thus fell into the hands of the lovely twin who please me the most, and who had flogged the young piano-player so masterfully, transporting him to the seventh heaven. The adorable birching lassie took my arm. I left the hall with her, followed by the jealous glances of all the spectators.

CHAPTER XI

An attendant showed us into a delicious boudoir, and I trembled with emotion at finding myself shut in the discreet retreat, alone with the most entrancing elf of flagellating fairyland.

"You're lucky to be the first," she said.

"Yes, divinity, but I'm afraid you'll be in such a hurry that you won't devote all your talent to the proceedings."

"Don't think so," she rejoined. "I am very conscientious. I do my business with passionate love. I have no intention of spoiling my own pleasure. Strip completely naked, and tell me if you like voluptuous flagellation or cruel discipline."

She selected a small rod, while I hastily tore off all my clothes.

"I have no objection to be treated with some slight degree of severity," I told her.

She immediately threw aside the tiny birch and chose a stronger one.

"If you would also allow me to kiss your lovely little feet, I should be very pleased."

"That's voluptuous flagellation, without a doubt!" she said. "How would you like to lie on the ground and kiss my feet while I birch you?"

"Quite heavenly!" I replied.

"You are a lover of artistic pleasure," she said, taking her small rod again. "You adore womankind. When I noticed you in the front row, I divined your disposition. You never took your eyes off me!"

As soon as I was naked as I had been born, I laid myself down on the carpet, and she thrust out one of her adorable, small feet. The big toe was separated from its companions on the sandal by a ribbon, which was crossed on her instep and tied in a bow above the ankle. I pressed my feverish, eager lips on each of the marvelous creamy, pink digits, with their mother-o'- pearl nails. Lifting her birch, she dealt me sharp, staccato blows. I did not feel the twigs on the skin of my buttocks, but experienced the sensation of entrancing vibration, caused by a shower of what seemed like hot raindrops. Their heat ran through every vein, and I had not enough melting kisses to lavish on the darling little foot, which, to my taste, was made more wonderfully savory than ever under the fascinating caress of the insidious twigs.

The handsome lass, changing her attitude, offered her other foot to my mouth, and then, flogging me slantwise across the rump, I felt a thousand sparks spreading over my posteriors in a sheaf of fire. The ribbons of the sandal were in the way of my lips and hampered the enjoyment I was having at being able to kiss the radian beauty's tiny tootsies. I stood up suddenly, interrupting the rod's action.

"Divine mistress," I supplicated, "permit me to untie your sandals. I am jealous of the ribbons that deprive me of their complete beauty."

"What a baby you are!" said the lovely lass. "All you artists are alike! You always want to tear away every veil! Well then, undo the ribbons! You see how late you're making me. Anyhow, do you think you'll be able to fix the sandals again?"

"That's about the only thing I know how to do, divinity!" I answered. She reclined upon the sofa, and kneeling before her, I unrolled the silk ribbon. Her sweet infantile foot appeared in all its luminous nudity. I lifted it to my caresses. She closed her eyes. So I seized her other small foot and freed it as well. Thus I had them both in my hand. I covered them with mad, moist kisses, and an angelical smile hovered on her lips and remained there.

All at once, she jumped up, and as she seized her rod once more, I humbly offered my submissive stern to her punishing twigs, but without letting her celestial extremities escape from my mouth and tongue. Every pulse in my frame throbbed heavily under her delightful douche of steady cuts.

"We shall never get any good out of this style of thing! I'm letting myself be seduced by your cunning caresses," exclaimed the skillful flogging fairy, discouraged and throwing aside her birch. "I must whip you severely. Come stretch out on the bench, and I'll tie you down!"

She pushed the low settee forward, and I threw myself upon it. With silken cords, she bound me cleverly and securely.

I thought that she would at once start birching me rigorously, but she took a small rod and dealt me a series of tiny taps. She kept on assaulting me thus for a long time. This style of punishment warmed and deadened my flesh. Then she dashed along with much more animation. Her cuts began to sting, growing gradually more violent, until soon she flogged me frenziedly, making me start and writhe under the suddenness of her bitter onslaught.

I was awaiting the delicious moment when the expert flagellating lady would let herself go in the final insensate burst of cruelty. That awful minute came. The fresh rod she chose sprang and rebounded, hissing and flogging terribly, while I shuddered in despair, gasping, and wriggling under the swishing flames. My torturing divinity grew more and more excited, beating me with true furious rage, until she forced my entire being to sink in the abyss where a profound shock of maddening voluptuous ecstasy bore witness to the lascivious influence of her enchanted birch.

"Tie my sandals on again," said the young woman, as soon as she had freed me from my bonds.

She gave me her adorable little feet. I was loath to leave her, and once more clothed them in kisses.

"You're very loving and caressing," she said. "I'd like to pass a night with you. As you're a Frenchman and an artist, I suppose you know all the refined secret delights with which men of your country overwhelm their mistresses. Anyway, tell me – are you satisfied with the way I've whipped you?"

I warmly depicted the extent of my admiration for her and gave her a banknote for a large amount. She was overjoyed at my present, and kissed me effusively as she wished me a most tender farewell.

Returning to the open saloon of the club, it was not displeasing for me to note the expression on the faces of the other members, impatiently waiting their turn to pass under the birch of the two little fairies.

I went into the reading-room, and took from the bookcase a most suggestive French novel.

A charming young girl, seemingly about eighteen, was looking over a pile of photographs representing scenes of flagellation between women. I caught this young lady darting sideway glances at me, until she boldly came and spoke.

"Pardon me for disturbing you while you're reading, sir," she said, rather audaciously, "but I see you're enjoying a French work. Are you a Frenchman?"

"Yes, miss, I have that honor. I am a Parisian too."

"That's splendid!" she replied. "I love French people. A visit to Paris has always been my dream! I'm going there this summer."

"Are you American?" it was now my turn to ask.

"That's so. I'm from Frisco – San Francisco. Poppa and momma have given me my liberty. I travel alone."

"Rather dangerous for a young girl as pretty as you are."

"You're joking. First of all, I'm not pretty. And then why do you reckon a young girl is more exposed to danger when traveling alone than a boy?"

"On account of her sex, I suppose. Most folks would think as I do."

"Not in America, sure! In our country a girl gets around as easily as a lad. I've been right through the States and Canada in all directions and nothing has ever happened to me. Guess I'm not the only female in this position."

"But my dear young lady, a girl of your age, who tumbles into a club like this, is in danger already!"

"Stuff and nonsense!" was her laughing rejoinder. "I've been a fervent flagellant since I was fourteen. Now I'm eighteen. See what sort of a novice you've got in front of you!"

"Allow me to congratulate you, miss!" was all I could answer, as I tried, although astounded, to echo her merriment.

"Is flagellation much practiced in France?" she asked, growing serious again.

"Not so much as in America."

"So I've been told. But you've got a club like this in Paris, haven't you?"

"I don't think so. If there is one, I could not tell you where it is."

"What!" she cried, with a start of surprise. "You don't know? Aren't you a passionate adorer of the birch?"

"If I had not been one already, miss, I should have become so in America."

"Now look here, answer me honestly – without prevarication. In our country we don't beat about the bush. Is it 'yes' or 'no'?"

"It's absolutely 'yes' as I've just told you in plain words."

"Are you active or passive? Do you like voluptuous flagellation? That's the only sort I stand for, as I find it is ideal refinement."

"It's the only way in which I practice the birching religion, miss," I said solemnly. "I'm one of the faithful."

At these words, the charming young girl rose from her chair which she had drawn near mine, and taking my arm made me leave the room with her. "What you tell me is positively charming," she murmured. "I'm so pleased to get to know a Frenchman who is a fervent flagellant. You're a gentleman – a man of honor, I hope. Say, can I confide in you, without fear?"

I reassured the young lady by telling her who I was, and in the lobby leading to the private rooms, she soon found out a secluded nook where she was at her ease to relieve herself of her secret.

"Listen to me," she went on, whispering in my ear. "This will explain all. Look!"

She showed me a small square of pink pasteboard marked No. 29. I recognized one of the checks distributed by the twin sisters. It was good for a dose of private birching.

"You see," said the charming damsel, blushing and dropping her eyes, "I took this number after the Pimlico girls had given their lecture, because I had urgent need of the – the great sensation, you know. I was right behind in the last row, and hesitating too. So I only got the last number but one. These sisters are shockingly slow. Last week it was just the same. They never got through before midnight. I'm suffering terribly, having to wait my turn again for so many hours."

She stopped and covered her face with her hands.

"Therefore – ahem!" she continued slowly, panting with emotion, "as I'm lucky enough to have met you, and as you – you assure me you're a voluptuous flagellant, you might perhaps not mind being so good as to – to curb me under your ruling rod for a minute or two?"

her proposal caused my blood to flow to my brain. Was I dreaming? This spotless dove was offering me the key to heaven.

"I've never yet been whipped by a man," she continued, in a hushed whisper. "If I confess all this to you, it is because I know Frenchmen are tender and caressing with women and incapable of betraying them." With passionate speech I told the delicious girlie what happiness she was offering and with what a wealth of loving care I would do my best to charm her.

CHAPTER XII

I made haste to find a footman who opened a room for me, and it turned out to be the same snuggery where an hour before I had passed such entrancing moments with enchanting Miss Daisy.

All disorders had disappeared, and I was pleased to find several good, thin rods, resembling those that the skilled lady flagellant had selected when she began to birch me.

I went back to my amiable new friend and found the young girl waiting for me in the library. She followed me boldly, overjoyed to be alone with me in the private room.

"I do not hesitate to put my trust in you," said my companion, as soon as I had double locked the door, "because flagellants form a brotherhood seeking refinements and pleasures quite different to the vulgar union of the sexes. I am a virgin. Yet I feel certain you will respect me. You can kiss me all over and cover me with the most exciting caresses, but beforehand I want you to thrill me with the magic twigs."

I promised my radiant child-sweetheart only to go as far as she would permit. I felt myself enchanted by the charming spells her frankness and abandon wove about me.

She disrobed slowly with graceful gestures, like a nymph proceeding to bathe, and bared to my gaze the figure of a divine-sculptured statuette. Her full, round arms were aesthetically perfect; and her miniature, budding breasts stood out like two cups close together. I helped her to take off her little glove-kid shoes and her pearl-grey stockings. Then I saw her baby tootsies with short, rosy toes.

When the last rampart of pudicity had fallen, she drew herself up to her full height and stretched her limbs in nervous lassitude.

"Birch me well," she said. "Pay no attention to my shrieks and entreaties. My governesses were always unmerciful and a good whipping now will calm my nerves. I'm quite overwrought."

Obediently, she stretched herself on the bench, which I had covered with the sofa cushions, so that the contact of the hard, bare wood should not bruise the lassie's delicate frame. She held out her hands for me to tie her wrists, but I preferred to let her arms and legs be free. All I did was to bind her down by passing a long strap round he waist.

What a ravishing picture! The dark material of the pillows contrasted with her dazzling, lily-white, satin skin, and her divine symmetrical body. At the base of her loins was her splendid rotund plump bottom; thighs of sculptural build and slender delicate extremities. I was enraptured at the sight of such beauty in every part. Bending back the adorable creature's legs, and lifting them up with my left arm, I leant her delicious little feet against my cheek, as I took the soft little rod in my right hand. I covered her pretty posteriors with a shower of tapping blows as if celestial dew was falling from the rod. My slight, tender, sweeping strokes made her firm bum quiver and I prolonged my moderate swishing, paving the way for rougher caresses. My graceful birdie put up bravely with my preliminary stinging, arching her light body, as when a filly first feels the whip. I could see that this harmless castigation jarred on her nerves. It was high time to use a strong rod. So, lifting up her legs, I placed my lips to her delicious little feet.

I darted my tongue insinuatingly between her sweet, tiny toes with ardent, profound kisses, while the real, springy rod rebounded from the velvet cheeks of her crupper, which palpitated and was tinged with pink from the force of my attack.

The adorable young girl started wildly and groaned at every cut. Suddenly, she was unable to endure any further suffering, and throwing her tow hands on her hinder cheeks to protect them, I was forced to stop, so as not to strike her tapering small fingers.

Replacing her legs on the bench, and reaching for a rope, I tied my girlie's hands to the bench.

"For this revolt, you will now be flogged more severely, miss," said I, choosing a new rod, much longer and more flexible, with outspreading ends. I returned to my post; that beautiful pair of legs supported by my left arm and the angel's microscopic feet on my lips. I was determined to energetically chastise my girlish rebel whose rounded posteriors I now covered with vigorous blows.

The fresh birch, being much longer that the first, allowed me to stand a little way off, and I was able to get her divine pulsating pedal extremities close to my avid mouth. My delighted tongue slipped between every toe as if gliding into delicate lover-grottoes, but my right arm, actively birching, never failed for an instant.

My amiable maiden writhed in pain, praying for pardon, uttering small sharp shrieks, and her feet stiffened in my mouth. Without ceasing to flog her, I replaced her legs on the bench, as drawing near to it, I applied a few really ruthless cuts that made the courageous lass wriggle and bound, until, at last she stretched out her body and gave a long stifled cry.

Having freed the adorable creature in a twinkling, I carried her in my arms like a baby and with infinite care placed her on the sofa. Maddened with lust, curbed by voluntary respect, I threw myself like a hungry satyr on the divine treasures of her marble body. With a groan of salacious delight my mouth tasted the satin of her blushing bottom, where roses had bloomed among the lilies. My ardent kisses, madly racing, covered this splendid expanse. My moist lips caressed the delicate semi-globes of her swelling bosom; strayed under her perfumed armpits; played up and down her heavenly arms; wandered on her narrow, flat belly; finally resting, fixed in a long and insensate caressing kiss that penetrated her sacred rosebud, making me drunk with its divine nectar. This kiss was so intoxicating that I rolled on the ground swooning with unspeakable enjoyment.

When I regained my senses, the engaging young girl, reclining on the sofa, covered as with a mantle in the golden ripple of her magnificent hair that had rolled down during our love-struggle, drew me to her breast.

"Oh, my adored lover!" she murmured in my ear, clasping me in her arms and giving me a long kiss pulsating with passionate sensuousness, "you have made me taste the greatest joy I have ever know. I am afraid of you and also of myself, for I will not give my heart to any man, and if I do not tear myself away from such supreme witchery, I could never drag myself from your arms; from your influence – nay, I could no longer live without you. What are all my severe governesses and schoolgirl friends compared to a master such as you? My whole body still throbs with the flaming torrent you have set coursing through my veins. Oh! You cannot realize what I felt, when I suffered the martyrdom of your burning birch. While you quenched your thirst with my foot, I fancied I was in a furnace; the flames of hell licking me in every part. Molten lava seemed to swell up in the crater of your mouth and run in an incandescent cascade from my toes, meandering all over my frame. When you took me in your arms to carry me to the sofa, it seemed as if a thousand greedy sucking mouths were devouring me, eating me, drinking me, and penetrating me profoundly simultaneously all over. I shall never forget you – adorable and unique sweetheart!"

I madly kissed her neck while she spoke; her eyes having a faraway delirious look.

"Listen to me, darling," I said. "Would you not like to repeat this feast of love tomorrow?"

"No!" she replied affrighted. "I will not see you again! Besides, tomorrow I must continue my journey." She started to her feet and repulsed me. "I will not see you again!" she repeated. "I should miss you too much! Write to me! I am sure you know how to juggle with golden rhymes and fashion stirring strophes. Your letters will be joy for me and I will reply with pleasure. Perhaps, later, we may see each other once more – in Paris."

She slipped in my hand a small visiting-card, on which read, "Lona Westgate," and an address at San Francisco.

"Dearest, come and dine with me," I said. "We shall then be able to chat about our favorite delights."

"No, I only take tea and toast at night," she replied. "And I am tired. I want to go home and rest. You forget how you've exhausted me. In my own warm bed I will live our beautiful romance over again, and it will often haunt my dreams."

I assisted her to dress, and after having well hidden her pretty face – that of a wayward girlish coquette – under a thick veil, she was gone, like a timid bird taking its first flight from the nest.

CHAPTER XIII

The next day – Friday – I had an appointment with delicious Miss Harriet, who was to have returned from her birching trip to New York. I was vexed at not being able to attend the club lecture with her, as the superb Lady President had invited me to visit her at five o'clock – on the pretext being a cup of tea – and the lecture was set down for four.

The program announced a lesson in flagellation, with a view to reviving virile strength in the man. There were practical demonstrations of the system, and the high-sounding name of the lady-lecturer, Miss Aurelia Dora, fascinated me.

I felt half inclined to give up the idea of taking tea with the President, but it was difficult to find an excuse. I also feared to be caught by her at the club, and thus be taken for a cad. I made up my mind, therefore, to attend the lecture for half-an-hour and go on to Mrs. Islington's afterward.

My first visit was for Miss Harriet, who was expecting me at two o'clock. She lived in a sumptuous flat on the fifth story of a fine house, on a broad avenue. Her maid, extremely neat and polite, showed me into a room with a wide window giving on to a balcony full of flowers.

"Madam is very busy," said the girl, with a knowing smile, as she placed a comfortable rocking-chair for me and handed me the "Boston Police Gazette."

A few minutes later, adorable Harrriet dashed hastily into the room. She looked delicious, in a blue silk wrapper. It was cut very low and afforded glimpses of her most brilliant skin. One of her tiny naked feet, like a lovely rose, peeped out from under the thin material.

Without a word, I rushed to kiss her celestial tootsy, but she repulsed me rather roughly. Her rapid movement caused her peignoir, open from the neck to the ankles, to fly back. I had a snapshot vision of perfect charms. "Do be good!" she said. "I'm whipping a young fellow – quite a boy. I must hurry back to him. You shall do some work for me while you're waiting.

She pointed to a big bundle of birchen twigs, freshly cut; leaves still adhering to the branches.

"You can amuse yourself," she continued, "by stripping off the leaves carefully, and making rods of different sizes. Here is some string. Do it properly and tie them up tightly. There's nothing so annoying as a birch that goes to pieces in the thick of battle!"

She was off again, and I busied myself as requested. Soon, some sturdy rods were arrayed in a row on the table and a heap of leaves littered the carpet.

The fresh branches gave out a peculiar fragrance of their own that tickled my olfactory nerves agreeably, and I was very excited at having handled the supple instruments of birching lust. They rebounded with great elasticity as I tried them one by one. I stroked them with my fingers, and inhaled their odor, while impatiently waiting for the fairy queen who should endow them with potency by means of her divine witchery.

Half-an-hour went by, when Miss Harriet, looking extremely animated, made her appearance once more in the same hurricane style.

"Quick! Give me a fine new birch – rather heavy," she said. "All right! This one will suit me. Only fancy! My boy isn't twenty yet, and he had t be flayed for hours, before he can enjoy the slightest shock of sensuality."

She ran away rapidly, leaving me in a very excited state, brought on by her bold bearing and the whistling of the rod she had tried in my presence with precise gestures and sparkling eyes. To pass the time away, I brandished the birches one after the other, as she had done. I enjoyed the hissing sound they made. I imagined that they possessed life, and thirsted for blood, like the claws of some wild animal seeking to bury themselves in plump flesh.

When the young woman came to me again, my blood was boiling.

"You've worked well," she said. "You're a darling! I've enough rods now to last me a week, but I must the two best just to say 'how d'ye do' to your wicked bottom. Come along, sir!"

She selected a couple of my birches and led me to the bedroom, where her maid was hard at work sweeping up bits of twigs scattered all over the room, and arranging in coils the ropes that had just been used.

The girl being sent away, Miss Harriet gossiped merrily, while helping me to take off my garments. I shuddered delightedly, electrified at the contact of her deft hands and drunk with the heady perfume emanating from her half-naked body.

"You've no idea," she ran on, "what trouble that boy gave me. I'm dead beat. His skin is as soft as a woman's. I'm always afraid of lacerating his rump, for blood starts at any cut that's the least bit severe. It's only by drumming regularly on his bum for a long time that I manage to attain my ends. Nevertheless, with the new rod, I couldn't refrain from cutting him up rather rigorously and that made him leap like a rutting stag."

While talking, she had made me lean over her bed.

"See here, dear," she said, grasping a rod, "this is the way I do it!"

And as she brushed my buttocks with the flat part of her birch, producing an exquisite pricking, enlivening feeling over the whole surface of the part she operated upon.

I was getting used to this tepid shower, when suddenly and without warning, she began to sting me furiously.

I made a great bound and while trying to restrain me, her dressing-gown flew open. As quick as lightning, without knowing how, I found myself in the warm embrace of her naked body.

I clasped her tightly, kissing her with all my might. Like a nymph captured by a satyr, she shuddered at the ardent touch of my greedy mouth, as she rolled on the soft carpet. Mad with desire; murmuring incoherent words of adoration, I threw myself upon her. With a languorous look of love, she gave herself to me. My lips continued to devour her with moist, luscious, burning kisses, full of intense voluptuousness. My mouth wandered all over her supple and perfect frame, touching every part of her brilliant, firm, cool, pink flesh. She submitted unreservedly, writhing in unknowing abandonment, as I did my best to lead her to the goal of supreme tender enjoyment.

I lingered as long as possible in these heavenly intertwinings, and when I found myself again in the street, it was getting late. When I arrived at the club, Miss Aurelia Dora was in the thick of her discourse. The hall was crowded and it was all I could do to find a seat.

The young lady orator was a splendid creature, about thirty. As if to justify her melodious name, her hair was a golden cascade. She was gilt all over, so to say. Her white peplum was edged with broad gold lace; her girdle was a band of the same precious metal, incrusted with precious stones; and even her sandals were fastened with gold braid. Her figure was lissome and majestic, and seeing her so alluring, I regretted being forced to run away again.

"Ladies and gentlemen," she was saying as I entered, "I now come to the practical demonstration of my method, which I shall apply to three persons of different ages. Before beginning my experiment I shall pass round the hall. Anybody feeling inclined to undergo my discipline in public will please step forward. At the same time, I shall distribute numbered checks for the convenience of those who wish me to operate in private."

So saying, the golden idol, gracefully swaying her hips, went down among the spectators. She was immediately surrounded by an admiring crowd, and came near where I was. I felt great admiration for her ravishing beauty. She was a splendid creature, covered with sparkling diamonds and blood-red rubies; a child of the sun, seemingly gleaming with its rays, by reason of her amber-tinted skin and the soft, golden sheen of her luxuriant locks. Smiling and nonchalant, she advanced in her triumphant progress, and I felt irresistibly drawn toward her. I hit upon the expedient of asking her for one of her last numbers, so as to be able to possess her in a cozy boudoir after my visit to the Lady President. Miss Dora's checks were soon exhausted, and as I was at the back of the hall, I was lucky enough to fall on to No. 21. I reckoned that until my turn came, I should be able to get away quietly and have a few hours to the good.

It was just upon five, so I jumped into a cab.

CHAPTER XIV

Mrs. Colonel Islington, President of the Flagellants' Club, lived in a vast flat on the tenth flight of one of those lofty mansions, some of which have as many as twenty-four stories, and are known as "sky-scrapers."

Each apartment was reached by means of an "elevator," and I was sent up at rocket-speed, to the tenth floor, where, between two columns, a gate of forged and gilt iron, like that of a park, gave access to the flat.

A liveried footman showed me into an immense drawing-room. Its wide, plate-glass windows afforded a few of the clouds. I looked down at the busy town stretched at my feet, as if I had been in the car of an anchored balloon. A few minutes passed and then the servant fetched me. I was led into another room, furnished somewhat in the style of an office. Superb sculptured ornamental woodwork covered the walls, where there were many trophies of ancient weapons.

In this fine chamber, I found the President, who looked like a Dresden china statuette that had come to life and wandered into an armory. She was full of youthful charm and captivating beauty. Dressed in a flowing gown of grey satin embroidered with silver; her eyes sparkling; she glided to welcome me with feline grace. I was delighted and astonished to see this adorable fairy and no one else, as I had expected to find her in the midst of a full tea-party.

"I made my appointment with you at an hour when I am generally alone. It's not possible to chat at the Club, where I'm constantly being bothered, and as I'm lucky enough to become acquainted with a most charming French gentleman, I prefer to take refuge here, so as to have him all to myself. Come, my dear friend, to my room. We shall be more comfortable."

She opened a door and I followed her into a bedchamber. I was greatly struck by its sumptuousness. It was upholstered in the purest Louis XVI style, filled with furniture, tapestry, and old paintings of the highest value. I complimented her on her refined taste, so rare in a commercial city like Boston. "Thanks to my authentic eighteenth century bric-a-brac and pictures – all by the best makers and greatest painters of that epoch – I am almost able to evoke a vision of Versailles. Talk to me about Paris."

She dropped languidly into a *bergere*, the ample folds of her silver robe flowing at her feet like the waves of the sea, and she signed me to take a seat on a footstool.

The door opened and I saw arriving, a small wagon on wheels. It was a carriage full of roses and tulips. In the middle was a tray supporting a dazzling silver-gilt tea-service, accompanied by all sorts of sweets and cakes. The motive power of this dainty vehicle was furnished by a young chambermaid, dressed in Louis XVI costume, copied from an old engraving. The girl resembled a fragile figure in colored porcelain.

With great affability and grace, Mrs. Islington made haste to serve me. "I love the French nation," she repeated. "You are poets and artists in all things – especially love."

This sentence was spoken with intentional emphasis and I wondered what her intentions were. She did not leave me in perplexity, for she came and sat quite close to me.

"Tell me everything now," she said in a whisper, clasping my hand coaxingly and blushing. "In France, you don't revel in the pleasures of love brutally, like the Americans. You weave garlands of delicate trifling pastime round your sensuality, as it were, and every sort of excess; all kinds of delirious inventions are allowable in your fair land. Is it not true that previous to the final coupling embrace, you wander and lose yourselves in a maze of mysterious caresses, forming supreme homage paid to the adored one, killing her with pleasurable shame?"

"Divine friend," I replied, "delicious kisses should cover the whole stem of the feminine flower. At the summit of the blossoming but culminates the worship of the lips, which softly sing the glory of the purple petals. The lover's moist mouth, waywardly straying, touches upon every beautiful charm, whether secret or not. He velvet tongue wanders on the warm shoulders – infinitely soft; on the beasts – separated by an ardent valley; on the – covered with amber down, until he is intoxicated with the armpit fragrance. He enjoys the savory taste of all these perfumed delights, until finally, trembling with sensuous longing and servile fervor, he remains fixed in the divine calyx of love and joy, which he treats with a thousand minute refined meretricious teasing tricks."

The adorable young woman leant over me, eagerly drinking in my words; her eyes upturned behind her half-closed lids. Her bosom rose and fell quickly and her hands trembled a little.

"Divine friend," I went on, "have you ever tried one of these delights, so full of attractive intoxication that one would wish to devote one's life to them?"

"Enough!" she exclaimed. "Cannot you see how your words cause flames to burn in my heart?" She sat up stiffly. "I wanted you here with me, because I have seen you straying into the private rooms with our lecturing ladies, and I had a mad longing to flog you, guessing what a fervent lover of the rod you must be! And now you drive me crazy with your criminal proposals! I shall have you birched by my maid."

Starting to her feet she touched an electric knob, and her pretty Louis XVI soubrette, who had pushed in the tea-carriage, re-appeared. She was a charming, arch girlie, about sixteen or seventeen, dark and sprightly. "Jeannette," ordered Mrs. Colonel Islington, "you've got to whip this gentleman. Fetch all that's needful!"

At these commands, the lassie's face lit up. She seemed pleased, and tripped away with lively steps. She was back in a very short time, dragging after her a bench of the same pattern as those at the club; a rod and some rope.

"There's only this one left, madam," said the maid.

"Nonsense!" exclaimed the mistress, "you're joking, I hope? You know very well that I always like to have a good stock of birch ready to my hand. What good is just one rod to me?"

"This one is quite fresh, ma'am," replied the girl.

"Well, send Willie to the club to get some more."

"Willy hasn't come back from his errand, madam."

"Not returned, hasn't he?" said the Lady President indignantly. "Too bad! It was barely noon when I sent him to deliver a letter a few blocks away. The boy's playing in the street, that's sure! Go and see in the kitchen if he hasn't got home yet."

The maid left the room, and Mrs. Islington, her long train thrown over her left arm, walked impatiently up and down.

"Oh, these servants!" she said. "I don't flog them often enough!"

Willy's return was now announced by the little lady's maid who entered followed by a boy between thirteen and fourteen years of age, dressed in a groom's livery.

"Where have you come from, Willy?" exclaimed the Lady President, in a rage. "Been playing marbles on the sidewalk again?"

"No, no, Mrs. Colonel Islington, I – I –" stammered the lad.

"All right! I know! Down with your breeches!" said the President, taking a riding whip.

"No, no, madam," whimpered the youth, "I assure you! There was a funeral."

"What's a funeral got to do with you? You weren't to be buried, were you?"

"No, madam, it wasn't me, but the – the procession was so long that I had to wait till it had gone by to cross the street."

"Do you think I'm fool enough to believe that the funeral took six hours passing? Drop your pants, I tell you!" said his mistress, making the whip whistle closer to his ear, and flourishing it under his nose.

Sobbing and asking for pardon, he unbuttoned his trousers with trembling hands. The young woman seized him, and pressing one hand on the nape of his neck, forced him to bend across an armchair. Then having fully exposed his bare posteriors, she started with a firm hand to apply a number of stinging cuts on the fat buttocks of the guilty youth.

He yelled at the top of his voice, struggling and trying to get away, and at the tenth blow succeeded in escaping. His mistress, now quite furious, threw him out of the room, without giving him time to button up.

This scene made a forcible impression on my feelings. The masterful manner in which the delicious lady handled her whip, revolutionized my sensual being. My beautiful flagellating hostess seemed to turn divine what was passing in my mind, as she turned toward me.

Boston

"Don't worry!" she said, significantly showing me her light switch. "You also shall taste its sting!"

She rang for her maid once more, ordering her to send Willy to the club to fetch a dozen of good new rods.

"When he's gone, Jeannette, come back to me at once," she added, and then I was curtly ordered to strip.

Salacious shudders shook my frame, as I found myself indecently naked, blushing with shame, in front of adorable Mrs. Islington and her engaging maid, who had returned to her mistress's side. Jeannette placed the bench in the middle of the room and drew an easy chair near it for the Lady President. She sat down watching the girl busy tying me to the settee.

"Are you ready, Jeannette?" she said. "Go!"

The charming little maid seized a rod and, under her mistress's vigilant gaze, began to birch me with short, sharp blows. Causing the long ends of the birch to sweep over both my hinder cheeks.

Mrs. Islington drew her chair nearer and lifting her face-a-main, darted impertinent disdainful looks at my poor bum. She evidently took great interest in the effect of the birch on my skin.

"Harder, Jeannette!" she said.

The lively girl attacked me with redoubled ardor, wielding the supple twigs with more energy than I could ever have expected from one so young. I writhed under her assault and clamored for pity. The Lady President appeared delighted at my distress.

"Keep on!" she commanded, without dropping her glasses. "That's good! Don't stop!"

Jeannette worked away, birching my bottom with a will. She put forth all her strength and all her skill. The rod dashed up and down in a furious dance, its ends snapping off, and I groaning and wriggling in great pain. Signing to Jeannette to stop, Mrs. Islington then took up her cruel, light riding-whip, and coming near to me, dealt me a fearful series of formidable cuts. Her terrible, lithe weapon lashed me horribly, and I bounded and leapt in violent voluptuous spasm, whose reaction threw me stiffly down again. Exhausted by the effort, the Lady President, throbbing all over, dropped back into her chair, while Jeannette hurried to deliver me from my bondage. As soon as the girl had left us, I knelt before the young woman, and covered her hands with burning kisses.

"Was it nice?" she asked with a languid look. "Doesn't Jeannette know to birch well?"

"You flog splendidly, divine goddess," I replied. "I've seldom been finished off in such clever, bold style."

She bent over me tenderly, maddening me by the contact of her cheeks and the delicious odor emanating from her bodice. Encouraged by her abandonment, my lips wandered round her pink sea-shell ears, and reached the soft, silky curls on her neck. I quenched my thirst among her tresses and on her perfumed nape, while my hands pressed her waist and hips.

"Let us see how you undress a woman in France," she whispered. Her words set my senses in a whirl. I threw myself on my adorable conquest, and frenziedly dragged off every veil. From the silken and lace trimmed garments that slid to the ground, she emerged as luminous as a rising star, and I drank in her magnetic fluid. Then, lifting her up like a child, I laid her gently on the bed, covering her body with delicate entrancing, soft caresses, lightly touching here and there, as if a timid butterfly was trying to choose the most favorable spot where to linger in never-ending, vibrating intoxication.

She let me do whatever I wished, for she was powerless to resist these cunning voluptuous approaches and lascivious play all quite new to her. It burnt up her being and she murmured unintelligible words, cooing, sighing and palpitating gently. Then her soul melted in an ecstasy of acute enjoyment which engulfed all her faculties, and she inundated me with the heavenly nectar distilled from the delight of her body's secret sexual depths.

CHAPTER XV

When the lovable woman regained consciousness, blushing deeply; a vacant dreamy look in her eyes, as if awaking from a vision, I was standing over her, already dressed, watching her come to her senses. She was greatly ashamed, finding herself naked before me, and she threw herself quickly off the bed, hiding her frame, as if she felt chilly, in a superb *matinee* of silk and lace.

"Whatever have you done to me, you wicked man!" she said with downcast looks, and imitating the voice of a child. "Do you know what I call such lewd ways? Diabolical! Yes, that's the word, for it's only Old Nick himself who could have invented such glorious tricks with which to damn the souls of us poor women. Who gave you permission to dress yourself, naughty boy? I wanted to birch you again, as now that you have unnerved me with your extraordinary caresses, I feel an imperious desire to calm my feelings by lashing a fine pair of fat bottom-cheeks. Come, get every rag off and pass me my riding-whip!"

my stern was still burning from her stinging cuts and although I yearned t suffer at the hands of this sublime creature, I didn't not lose sight of the fact that I had an appointment for that very evening with Miss Aurelia Dora, whose little numbered check was nestling in my ticket-pocket. Therefore, instead of obeying lovely Mrs. Islington, I took her in my arms, and covered her eyes, bosom and neck with hot, humid kisses. She struggled like an affrighted, captured dove.

"Is that how you bare your bum?" said the amiable young woman.

"You're really unkind." Then she added, merrily, "Ah, I've another idea!"

She rang for her maid. The dainty Louis XVI statuette appeared. "Jeannette," said the President, "how was it we had no rods just now?"

"I've got them, madam," she said, beginning to betray anxiety, and crumpling the edge of her apron. "I was going t bring them when I heard the bell."

"That's no answer to my question," rejoined Mrs. Islington, with a wicked glance. "Why were there none in the house?"

"I had forgotten all about them, madam."

"Forgotten indeed! Pass me over that whip and up with your skirts. I'm going to give you a good thrashing, just to prevent you losing your memory another time!"

The obedient chambermaid, trembling in every limb, handed the riding whip to her mistress, who pushed her to a chair, making her lean over it, when she threw the girl's short petticoats as high up as possible. The poor wench wore no drawers, and her firm rotund posteriors were fully exposed.

Mrs. Islington lost no time, but vigorously slashed that pretty bottom which quivered beneath the keen cuts, becoming covered with a multitude of long, thin, red lines. At each stinger, the wretched victim uttered a suppressed moan, but bravely endured the pain caused by the round dozen of strokes that her implacable mistress inflicted with her firm, practiced hand. When allowed to depart at last, Jeannette ran out of the room, I felt certain that if my charming Lady President took it into her shapely head to offer me a fresh disciplinary dose, I should not have the courage to refuse, so excited was I at having seen her handle her whip in such masterful style.

Luckily for me, she tapped her forehead, as if suddenly remembering something.

"Be off at once! I must get dressed," she said. "They're expecting me at the club. I just recollect that I've got to birch a young lady in private. I was nearly forgetting all about it!"

"A young girl?" I asked in surprise.

"Yes. Does that astonish you?" she replied. "She's only fifteen and crazy on being whipped. That's quite a common occurrence. Girls and young women often ask me to flog them."

"A most entrancing picture! Couldn't you let me see you at work?"

"Hold your tongue, you lewd rogue!" she exclaimed, with a jealous pout. "Get out! You make me tired!"

She drove me from her flat, and I went straight off to the club, arriving at seven o'clock. There were still lots of people; the bars and smoking-rooms being full of members, sipping those wonderful iced drinks, so popular in America.

With a repeated cry of "No. 20!" a page-boy was looking everywhere for the holder of that check, but there was no answer.

"No. 21, then!" the boy shouted.

That was my number. I was in the nick of time, and asked to be taken to the private room where the interesting lady orator was busy.

"Are you alone, sir?" interrogated the page, seeming surprised when I replied affirmatively. Without adding another word, he introduced me at once.

Miss Aurelia Dora seemed to me now quite another person. She no longer wore her peplum, but was enveloped in a filmy gauze veil which afforded peeps of her luminous body. The misty, material slowly slid downward to her feet, like a cloud melting at the approach of dawn, and she appeared to me entirely naked, her only drapery being the liquid gold of her hair that covered her as with a magnificent mantle.

She was thus still a vision of the precious metal, reminding me of a bunch of ripe amber grapes lit up by the sun's rays, and the insensate flashed across me that if fair women were crushed in a wine-press, the resulting nectar would be bright and gilt, as was their peculiar beauty.

"Where is your lady?" asked the winning woman.

"I'm alone," I answered.

"I congratulate you!" she replied sarcastically. "So I suppose you're seeking trouble for your backside? It's aching for a rare old hiding, eh? That's what you're up against, I guess!"

Before I could think of defending myself, she had seized me round the waist, throwing me on the sofa, where I rolled on my back, kicking my legs in the air, and quite astounded at this wrestling reception by which the captivating creature gave me a sample of he bodily strength. She began to undress me, with slow, feline movements, turning me round; handling me like a baby. She secured my wrists and ankles with steel chains; fixing their ends to the head and foot of the divan. It was rather long, and my metallic bonds dragged my limbs which were thus tightly stretched.

Miss Aurelia then took hold of a hair-brush with a long handle and rather hard bristles. She began to tap my stern with sharp, short, reiterated blows. This was the first time such a strange instrument had executed this sort of saraband on my body, and I experienced a hitherto unknown sensation. The stiff brush pricked and scratched the surface of my skin, and after a while, this application electrified and inflamed every part of the posteriors it attacked. The whole expanse of my scalded, scarlet bottom soon began to burn as if covered with incandescent embers, producing sharp cutting pain. It seemed that I was being prodded with lancets.

When the beautiful flogging damsel saw how I writhed in agony, and how my sighs had given place to deep groans, she put away her brush and took a fine supple rod. Directly the first blow fell with a hiss and a crash on my excoriated flesh, the feeling was exquisite and grew more delicious as she flogged on.

Hey for the bonny birch! How finely it stung me! Its prickly ends seemed to penetrate to my innermost being, enwrapping my body, as if its hot points were incrusted in my swollen hinder cheeks.

I throbbed and palpitated, every fiber thrilled by electric currents, and the handsome flagellating fairy never ceased flooding me with the heavenly dew of her blows, as she grew more and more excited.

When at last her assault was terminated and she had thrown away her rod, letting the chains that held me fast drop to the ground with a melodious metallic sound, I was seized with an indescribable mad rutting fit of unsurpassed sensuality.

I threw myself on my torturing queen, trying to capture her like a lawful quarry and clasp her to me in the supreme conjunction of the sexes' loving lust, but, lissome and agile as a serpent, she disengaged herself from my straining arms.

"Oh no! Not that!" she said gravely, quickly rolling her clouds of gauze about her, hiding her radiant nudity. "My business is to light the fire, not extinguish it. Why didn't your best girl come along with you? Get your clothes as fast as you can, and fly to her arms. She'll be delighted to find you so audaciously lewd and bold."

THE END

LADY MARGARET

I.

I will now tell you what it was that Lord Thomas saw in the stable-yard yesterday morning.

An hour or so earlier, those who had watched April at her shop work would have seen her summoned from it and led to a waiting vehicle which transported her to the estate on my orders. The young blonde was dressed as usual in the blouse and tight denim of her working costume. At first she thought the grooms were having a romp with her when they set her down in my stable-yard and seized her by the arms. Young April likes a rough and tumble with the boys and has even engaged in such sports with a young shop man before the eyes of the entire world.

On this occasion, however, the grooms tussled with her until they had her standing between the shafts of a little garden carriage with her back to the driver's seat. The vehicle is little more than a toy. It occupies the driver alone and is designed to be pulled by a single two-legged filly. Imagine the fun which might be had if the rump between the shafts belonged to Jane Truman, or Tracey Hope.

To accomplish this, two stout wooden bars have been riveted across the shafts, so that the girl standing with her back to the driver may be made to bend forward over the first bar—which supports her belly—while her wrists and leather collar are attached to rings set in the forward bar! Do you now begin to see what it was that I had in mind for our young blonde—our young pony-girl, as I might call her?

My head groom is the most reliable fellow and he times these matters to perfection. The other two men naturally whispered into April's ears the truth of the ordeal that she was about to suffer. Her lank fair hair flew as she twisted and squirmed in their arms. Those stocky young thighs writhed and her broad young hips surged. Fortunately they were easily able to twist her arms up behind her back, which forced her to bend forward to ease the racking ache.

Two stable-boys ran forward. The first of them slipped a broad harness strap round April's waist—under her blouse and next to the bare skin. With this he fastened her very tightly on the rear bar across the shafts, obliging the stocky young blonde to bend over whether she wanted to or not. The second lad took each of her arms in turn and tightened the leather cuffs of the forward bar round her wrists.

April was now in the posture which drew the attention of so many gentlemen to her as she laid out the polished saddles. Bending over with the curtains of lank flaxen hair hanging down, April in her tightened jeans-denim presented the firm short length of her thighs and a pair of tautly rounded but fattened young buttocks.

I must now confess my deceit, for which I trust your ladyship will forgive me. I had not gone ahead to the plantation but was watching the scene from a window overlooking the yard and opposite to that where Lord Thomas peeped. I could just see his outline behind the glass, a countenance so pale and anxious as he watched April's predicament.

My accomplice in all this was Jewkes the gamekeeper. In his youth he was the hangman's apprentice and deputed for a year to flog naughty young ladies whom the magistrates had sentenced. He, it was, who was to be April's driver. Though the firm features of her fair-skinned face are bold and a little crude, despite the softening of her blond fringe, it was evident that the young stable-lads were very stimulated by her. Even if she is twenty-three-years old and somewhat their elder, one could see that they wanted to do all manner of things inside April's knickers.

The grooms withdrew and left the two boys to prepare her. One of the lads drew the collar-length of April's blond hair into a pony-tail, so that her face could be seen, and fastened it like this with a black velvet bow. At the same time he whispered in her ear, grinning with pleasure at the randy promises of what would be done to her.

The other lad undid her pants at the waist and drew them off with April's knickers inside so that she was now bare from waist to heels as she bent over the two bars. Her underpants were no more than cotton briefs. The lad held up the young blonde's knickers in front of her face and teased her a little.

"A filly must have a proper bridle to complete her harness, April!"

You may imagine how she tried to twist her face away. But they wadded the cotton into her mouth, still warm from its contact with her hips and seat, her loins and cunt. It was secured by the leather bit between her teeth which was fastened firmly by laces tied at her nape.

Still it seemed that April was getting off too lightly. One of the boys knelt behind her as she bent over the bars and eased open her robust pale thighs a little to smile upon the sight of the girl's warm and humid cunt-flesh. The other young spark pressed apart the firmly broadened pallor of April's bottom-cheeks and grinned at what he saw between them. In all this they had a purpose. There is a certain pod which any young lady in the countryside dreads feeling in contact with her bare skin. She knows that the sharp little hairs of its seeds are impregnated with a maddening and virulent sting which will make her want to scratch and squirm without respite for several hours to come. It is the plant known in the tropics as pica-pica but referred to in England by the more homely term of cow-itch!

Brushed against a bare flank or bosom it creates a tormenting itch but applied to more intimate and sensitive areas of the female body its effects are unspeakable! At the sight of a well-filled pod in the hand of one boy, April mewed violently through her wad and tried desperately to twist her hips aside. The boy grinned.

"A good rub with this between your legs, April, to make you frisky!"

Fortunately she had been very firmly strapped down and was unable to struggle much. The other boy held her round the legs to keep her steady. His partner coaxed the warm cunt-flesh back a little and then rubbed it gently with the virulent itch plant. Though April strained and squirmed at once under the torture of the irritation, he took a second pod and rubbed her again between the legs.

"And now some attention to your bottom, April!" he said, teasing her to the point of desperation.

There were two more pods. The first he rubbed thoroughly into the darker valley between April's buttocks. As for the last, he poked its contents up her rear until it disappeared from sight and left her quite frantic. Nor was that all, for they were determined to turn the stocky young blonde into the most proper pony-girl. One of them produced a false ponytail of blond hair which was a match for April's flaxen gold. At one end it was gathered into a thumb-sized leather butt. Ignoring any attempt at lubrication and the young woman's wadded shrillness, the lad inserted the leather butt firmly into April's backside. The twist of hair was drawn tightly up between her rear cheeks, under the leather waist strap in the small of her back, and then rose in a graceful plume of a tail so that its ends swept to and fro across the top of her curved buttocks as she writhed.

Now, my lady, picture the scene when Gamekeeper Jewkes entered the yard to drive his blond filly! April was twisting her hips, squirming her thighs together, dancing and kicking as if she meant to overturn the equipage then and there. It is the kind of disobedience which no driver can permit from a filly, whether she be equine or human!

Jewkes flexed the long slim leather of the switch that he carried in his hands.

"Bend right forward, April, and keep perfectly still!"

He did not know, of course, what the frolicsome lads had done to her. Personally, I was delighted to hear April given a command she could not possibly obey.

"Keep your bottom still, you young slattern!"

April mewed desperately through the wad in her mouth but she could no more control her maddened squirming than she could fly. Her pale broadened hips twisted side to side and the blond ponytail rising from her bumhole brushed to and fro across the bare spread of the young working-girl's backside.

Jewkes's expression did not change. He walked across and stood just behind her, watching the writhing of the girl's stocky thighs and broadened hips. He took the plume of the false ponytail and tucked it under her waist-strap out of the way. Measuring the cold leather switch across her flinching buttocks, he gave the young blonde a long minute to imagine the agony of naked leather-discipline which she was about to feel across her bare rump.

The stones of the yard sang to the smack of the whip across the pale sturdiness of April's bottom-cheeks. A frenzied cry was just audible through the wad in her mouth and the short tail of her own blond hair swept to and fro across the back of her collar. Jewkes thrashed her with the carefully measured strokes of a judicial whipping, impersonal and without pity for the hard-faced young blonde.

April's firm and stocky young thighs squirmed together harder and faster, for all the world as if she sought relief by bringing herself to completion.

"Keep your arse still, April, you young bitch!"

He found the most sensitive areas, high up on the backs of her thighs and low on the softer undercurve of April's full buttocks. With great precision he raised six blueberry weals which interlaced cruelly.

"I'll have obedience from you, April, you young tart!" he said, almost laughing at her. "Keep that backside still!"

He made the leather whip flash down again and again, so that it kissed April's bottom-cheeks with streaks of agony. He even whipped her across the backs of her knees and then gave her a dozen stingers round her thighs.

"Now your bottom, April," he said quietly, "Let's see how much more you can take before you decide to obey me and keep absolutely still!"

What a contest it promised to be. I have no doubt that Jewkes must have seen April at her work, bending lewdly in tight denim, or polishing on all fours with the jeans-seat taut and smooth over her sturdy young buttocks. I daresay most men who paused to admire such a view would have been implacable with her now. And so he was. He whipped and whipped with all the strength of his arm. At last April's knees bent under her, though the straps held her over the bars. Her lank blond hair broke from its ponytail and fell about her face, as her head hung down. In tribute to the power of his discipline, the young window-dresser swooned arse-upwards over the bar. What a price many of her casual admirers would have paid for a keepsake portrait of her as she now appeared!

Lady Margaret

The gamekeeper withdrew and left the stable-lads to prepare her once more. Half a dozen of the boys came out. One of them held the little bottle to her nostrils. Each of the others, in turn, presented his unbuttoned stiffness either in the area of her thighs or her backside.

The young blonde was unmuzzled and revived to the virulence of the pica-pica itch. In the most plaintive accents of her lilting young voice, April begged them for the soothing balm which was in their gift. She whimpered to have each little sausage-like prick in its turn either placed between her legs or bum-cheeks. With the threatened return of the gamekeeper, there was no time to

These vigorous lads soaked her in grand style, though they had a fine reward. April was so frantic to be eased that she gave each boy a splendid time, giving each one more fun than they would even taste on their honeymoon nights. The remaining three lads supplied her elsewhere. This time each young sausage was laid between the cheeks of April's bottom. How the young blonde squirmed and tensed her broadened bum-cheeks upon them. She was even more desperate for them to spend than the lads themselves. April is a hard-faced young bitch and yet she can give a man some fun when she puts her mind to it. I watched her employ every trick in the armory of the most perverse young whore to coax this second triple spending from the boys. In this she succeeded. By the time they left her, April's rear view was amply splattered, from the curves of her arse-cheeks down to the middle of her thighs.

I had been so engaged by this amusing spectacle that I had quite forgotten Lord Thomas at his window. He stood there now, mouth agape and eyes wide in astonishment at what he had seen. If ever a man were turned to stone by the glance of the Gorgon, it was he. Before he could gather his wits, however, the gamekeeper—my own man Jewkes—reappeared.

You may be sure Jewkes smiled to himself when he saw the state in which April now presented herself.

"I'm glad to find you feeling randy, April," he said taunting her. "Does the thought of being harnessed and driven excite you so much that you must even seduce the stable-boys? Such fine stripes across your bottom and legs as well! I daresay some men would be lenient with you, seeing that you must have been whipped already. I view the matter differently. To see such weals across your buttocks is bound to put some very cruel ideas in to my head…"

And so he drove his filly between the shafts of the little carriage, sitting on the driver's perch behind her and watching the young blonde's stumbling and laboring over the bar. The short leather tail of the pony-lash was most convenient and he made her feel it more times than one could count. As the young woman's stocky thighs strained to pull forward the load behind her, her buttocks rounded and contorted in a thrusting and swaying rhythm which fascinated him.

Best of all was the last mile which lay up the steep path of Snow Hill itself. The young blonde's broadened hips and backside shone in a pale gloss of her own sweat. She gasped for breath and writhed over the bar with the most demented energy. Best of all, the steep incline exaggerated her movements. Her thighs squirmed together in an almost masturbating tightness, while her bare hips surged and swayed. April's bottom seemed to thrust back at the driver as if she wished to stick it right into his face with its cheeks pulled hard apart, and her pink cunt peeping back from between her thighs.

It took her almost half an hour to draw the little carriage to the top. Jewkes's whip caught her repeatedly across her buttocks and round her flanks. Soon the weals were adorned by telltale smudges as if red berries had been squashed here and there on April's arse-cheeks. Each time she bent a knee forward, the parting of her legs showed her driver a delicious peep of cunt. Each thrust of her hips drew her buttocks apart and showed him April's arsehole.

The air rang with the smacks of the whip across her smooth bare buttocks. April screamed in her frenzy and her tight little post-horn sounded some extremely vulgar carriage-notes. Indeed, she did things while strapped over the bar which quite disqualified her as a future lady of the manor! The state of April's thighs and backside by the time she stumbled to the top of Horsewhip Hill—as we must surely call it—would require some great painter of sunsets to depict.

Though they had reached the destination, the driver was not quite satisfied with April. He stopped the carriage and applied its brakes. Then, while the young shop girl was still strapped arse-upwards over the bar, he whipped—and whipped—and whipped—the short lash across her bottom. Not until her knees bent and her head drooped as if in tribute to him was he satisfied at last with the state of April's bare backside.

You need have no fears for the consequences, my lady. We shall not, of course, permit April to return to her former way of life. Already her abduction is planned and we are examining her carefully to see if she might not make a gift for our friend in Arabia! It is far and away the most prudent means of ridding ourselves of the young tart.

As for Lord Thomas, you may rest assured that the scenes which he witnessed have done nothing but good. He did not know that I had him "in my sights" all the time. However, I am pleased to tell your ladyship that this was so. Whatever his initial indignation or alarm at seeing April stripped and harnessed, this soon gave way to open-mouthed astonishment. Before long, mat astonishment turned to fascination! With my own eyes, I saw him follow the carriage-outing at a discreet distance. Indeed, he carried a little spy-glass, which he trained eagerly upon April at every propitious moment.

It was afterwards rumored among the servants—with what truth I cannot say—that a certain young lord paid a visit to April in the room where she was later confined. The stable-lads swear it as being overheard by them. Under threat of what he would have done to her, the young gentleman obliged April to kneel before his chair. Her tawny fair hair was once again tied back in its short ponytail so that he might see her face. April was obliged to unbutton him, suck the fine erection lovingly, and consume the ample squirtings of warm gruel which he poured over her tongue.

Who can say? Yet one hopes it is true. A hard-faced young slut like April needs such training in submission. Moreover, it shows hopeful signs of your cousin attaining the age of wisdom. The carriage-outing taught him a lesson for which the world of quality will thank us. In the event of a proposed *mesalliance* between a gentleman and a shop girl, far the best answer is to let him see her with her knickers down being dealt with as befits her kind. However much he may lament what happened to April—though one hopes he secretly enjoyed watching her get it!—he cannot take a wife who has been stripped and whipped by the gamekeeper, and who has squeezed stable-boys' pricks between her thighs and bum-cheeks!

II.

The slim-thighed Scandinavian nymph Marit is being trained to give her man pleasure of every kind. No privacy of any sort is permitted her, for her secret places must be constantly at the disposal of Massoumeh, the Persian beauty who has her under training. I still hold to my opinion that Marit with her calm young beauty and brown tresses will grow up to be a young woman of great loveliness. Yet her life here cannot be what it might have become as a bride of some Norwegian bourgeois.

Each morning the older women take her into the tiled and luxurious-bath-house. They pull Marit's knickers down to her knees and draw the hem of her singlet up, for they choose to give all their attention to these parts of her. She lies on the leather settee and one of the women holds her wrists firmly while another masturbates Miss Aas with skilful fingers in a love lesson which lasts for an hour or more.

In such places a girl of eighteen must expect to be conditioned to the pleasures of such arousal and the release of orgasm repeated several times in a morning. They have done this with such care that Marit will often slink away to her own bed and spend the whole of the following afternoon playing with herself.

When I last saw her, they had taken her into the more perverse realms of a slave-girl's duties. She had been made to lie on her belly over the cushions. An elderly Arab crone had soaped her finger and inserted it to the knuckle between Marit's buttocks. By frequent references to the whip, they obliged Marit to exercise her backside on the intruding finger, tightening herself upon it rhythmically, milking it as she must soon use the guile of her young bottom to draw from the pasha the venom which would otherwise rob him of sleep. In a few weeks, the man's reality will replace a woman's finger!

Sian and Julie are often separated, in order that the young redhead may partner our blond "pony-girl" April as a servant for the Pasha Ahmed's banquets. It will not surprise you to learn that they both act as naked waitresses for the men who assemble in the fine dining hall with its Moorish keyhole arches and the incense rising from the brazier coals. Their sole adornments are tight black straps round waists and thighs, leather cuffs at wrists and ankles, as well as a leather collar. A man who wishes to fasten them in his favorite position has only to give the word. You may be sure that the broad young cheeks of April's bottom collect an ample share of red smack-prints as she passes the chairs of the guests. Sian's trim young buttocks are often smudged by the ash of a fine cheroot. Last night I saw the tendrils of her red-haired mop in disarray and her blue eyes brimming. Alas, some devil had left an angry red streak on Sian's bottom with the glowing tip of his weed!

A guest will often use April or Sian as his mattress or pillow for the night. Sian will lie on her back, her legs splayed. A man has only to lie between them and he may pillow his head on the young redhead's belly, her sensitive little cunt always at his finger's touch. There is one elderly and worthy fellow who loves to sleep like this. At the same time, April with her blond hair in a short pony-tail, must lie on her side with her back to him. She is quite naked, her seat must be at the level of his eyes and curved out to within a few inches of his race. With a rear view of her love-nest between her stocky young thighs, his lips are busy with the young blonde all night. His kisses browse on the broad sturdiness of April's bottom-cheeks, between them, and upon the soft humid folds of her cunt. All this time he enjoys Sian's bare belly as his pillow!

Both Julie and Miss Jones are occupied in teaching younger girls the customs of the harem. They lie on the table before the pupils and have all those things done to them which little girls must learn for the pleasure of their master.

A man as rich as Ahmed Pasha does not confine himself to Arabian beauties alone. Among his collection are two or three dozen English girls but, I fear, some have been brought here much against their will. One night, to entertain us after dinner, he clapped his hands and summoned a harem dancer. It was only when he mentioned that her name was Sarah that I guessed the truth about her. She was indeed an English girl of eighteen or nineteen and it was exquisite to see such a little madam in so amusing a predicament.

Imagine us taking our coffee and sherbet in the fine ornate hall with its pillars and arches, the chessboard marble of its floor and the torches flaming in their iron brackets. There appeared this lithe young creature with a shock of short blond hair, her blue eyes as well as the rest of her features looking painted as a doll's! She was dressed in pale-blue Turkish pantaloons and breast-halter with crimson dancing boots. The Turkish trousers were translucent, not only showing the brief knickers which Sarah wore underneath but also revealing the lithe energy of her movements, her trim thighs and her buttocks which were so taut and agile.

Yet what struck one most about Sarah was her absurdly self-regarding resentment of her situation. Fortunately the vizier with the whip stood by and so we were not denied the pleasure of seeing her dance. He cracked the leather thong once and through the Turkish pants we saw the firm young cheeks of Sarah's pretty bottom tighten together with fear at the sound.

The music of flute and tambourine came from the shadows of the arcading. We saw Sarah's arms twine above her as her feet glided across the marble and her hips began their sinuous and suggestive rhythm. I will be honest with you, my dear friend. Such a self-important little minx with her painted face and flouncing manners can be tortured to the limit by the cruel vizier before I will intercede for her. With the worst possible grace she writhed and twined in her dance, performing immediately in front of her master's chair. The sulky little charmer arched her lithe young belly out towards him and let her head hang back, legs splayed and arms writhing. Straightening up again, she began to turn with sly little wriggling of her trim hips. With his own hands he undid her Turkish trousers and stripped down her panties. She danced with her bum to him. Slowly, at his command, the agile beauty bent over, until he had a splendid view of the trim and pretty cheek of Sarah's nubile bottom. He made her squirm her young arse at him, for all the world like a girl riding a randy saddle. Then the vizier withdrew and gave a signal that the rest of us should follow. It was time for the pasha to be alone with his young dancing-girl.

I confess that curiosity made me linger where one of the doors was open an inch. No suspicion attached to me for I do not suppose they thought an English lady capable of such deceit! I could not see everything, for the trim young blonde bent over in my direction and with her seat and thighs to the pasha. I could tell by the sudden grimaces of pleasure or hating that he found more than one avenue of delight open to him. As is the custom in this part of the world, when a girl exists for her master's pleasure and not for the breeding of children, it seemed that he enjoyed a ride between her legs—which had Sarah groaning and bending tighter to feel more of him— but discharged his seed on the hot infertile soil of her backside, which caused her to bite her lip desperately to check her exclamations of rebellion.

I do not tell this story without purpose. Sarah was prepared to make trouble for him because he used her in a fashion which may be unorthodox in England but is common in Arabia. That night I found a message from her on my pillow. She urged me to inform the world of her unwilling captivity and to aid her escape.

Knowing me as you do, dear friend, you are aware that I have an inflexible morality in social matters. I stop at nothing to uphold moral order. Yet, in the country where I was a guest, that moral order made this young wriggler the slave of Ahmed Pasha. To steal her from him, by the laws of the land, was no better than stealing his finest horse or his most costly silver plate. You will see at once that there was but one course which conscience allowed me to follow. I inquired of the vizier what punishment would be visited upon a girl guilty of such domestic treason. He smiled and spoke of bare-bottom whipping followed by the placing of a certain mark of ownership on the inward slopes of her bottom-cheeks. When Sarah stood upright, it would be concealed. When she was made to bend over, there would be no doubt to whom she belonged.

Delighted to hear that they knew how to deal with her, I at once took the traitorous note to Ahmed Pasha. I confess, however, that my own delight was somewhat exceeded by that of the vizier himself. Can you not guess why? He it was who would have the enjoyable task of commanding the penalties and the thought of doing such things to the young blonde made him hardly able to keep his hands out of his trousers.

As a supporter of justice and the need to punish delinquency however it may arise, I had hoped to be a spectator when Sarah was strapped down astride the bench on all fours. Alas, this was not to be. Such things are done very privately, in order to prevent scandal and tales being told. It is the custom for the vizier to be alone with the girl and to partake of certain preliminary enjoyments as his reward.

I was permitted—as a student of such jurisprudence— to view the scene before the door was closed upon Sarah and her passionate disciplinarian.

To see this lithe and agile girl of eighteen or nineteen strapped down on all fours astride the bench, was a story in itself. The shock of blond hair and the painted young face made such a self-pitying ensemble. She wore her breast-halter, but from the strap round her waist to the strap which pinioned her bare legs just above the knees, she was quite naked. From the back of her waist to the back of her knees, she was at the disposal of the sadistic vizier.

I was not able to witness the sequel, not indeed to hold any conversation of the normal kind with Sarah.

The gag was already in place and so there was wildness in her blue eyes with their mascara'd lashes. Yet there lay upon the floor a trailing whip which would have brought the most disobedient filly to correction after half a dozen strokes. And in the glow of the brazier coals two little marking discs were heating, each the size of a small coin.

I returned Sarah's frenzy with a smile and advised her to learn obedience and gratitude to her master for the tribute of sperm he paid her, when he might have preferred many another harem-girl. With that I nodded to the vizier and urged him to chastise the little whore soundly.

I observe respect for social morality—in whichever society I happen to be. In England we do not permit a man to keep slaves. In Arabia a man may be an outcast who drinks alcohol or eats pork. Ahmed Pasha, as our guest in England, would no more dream of dynamiting a pork butcher's shop or a distillery than I would rob him of a slave-girl in his own land. What would become of the world if each country tried to overthrow the laws of the rest? None would triumph. Chaos and anarchy must overwhelm us all,

He did not deal with her as harshly as he might. He might hang Sarah for her crime, if he chose. It is his right.

III.

Lady Margaret was as good as her word and came straight home upon hearing that her imprudent cousin Lord Thomas had involved himself in yet another dangerous infatuation. She did not at once take action but hung back a little as if hoping that the crisis might pass of its own accord. Even at that time she was much concerned that those who loved Lord A. should lead him towards a true understanding of the duties which he owed to society—and which were not in the least incompatible with the pleasures he sought.

Where pleasure rather than a permanent alliance was intended, her ladyship would never have interfered. Her own brothers had often indulged in such affairs without ever incurring more than her smile. At that moment one of them was riding a pretty blonde of twenty with cropped hair and fringe, a firm suntanned little face and blue eyes. Her lithe and suntanned limbs adorned his couch, the curves of Jane Truman's bottom-cheeks or breasts filled his hands. Lady Margaret was no prude and never dreamt of interfering. It was evident at a glance that her brother would never have married a little wriggler of this sort.

Lady Margaret is among our most respectable and respected younger peeresses. To a lingering affection for her own sex she soon added a fortunate marriage to Lord Rupert N——. He is somewhat her elder and a power in the land. Lady Margaret has always had a strong taste for proper morals. No one could be more zealous in advocating the chastisement of young women who stray from the path of decency or propriety.

Lord Rupert indulges his beloved in this matter of stripping insolent servant girls and promiscuous young wives who must learn their lesson under the whip. Every gaoler and beadle in the county takes his commands from her ladyship. Were you to suggest that the twinkle in Lady Margaret's eye betokens some lewd or perverse pleasure, you would be regarded with incredulity and contempt. Her respectability is armed cap-a-pie against all such reproaches.

Several times her ladyship has been able to save her cousin from the consequences into which his impetuous feelings might have brought him. In this she remembered the example of her friend Mr. Bowler. Alas, even the unmasking of Julie and April had not taught Lord Thomas to behave with more caution.

Scarcely a month after her return from Carda, her ladyship called at a temple of fashion in one of the smartest streets, not a stone's throw from the elegant showroom of her friend the saddler. She observed several gentlemen gazing entranced at the long window where saddles and bridles were set out. With some unease, she observed mat her cousin was one of this group. Lady Margaret moved unobtrusively to see what might be the object of such adoration.

A well-built girl of nineteen was dusting and polishing the floor where the saddles were arranged. Claire was the girl, quite tall and strongly made. Her lank dark hair was worn loose, cut short at the level of her collar and trimmed in a straight fringe. She had firm fair-skinned features, the points of her cheekbones were wide set and there was a most self-assured insolence in her brown eyes.

As was customary in such a place, Claire wore a simple riding costume well-suited to a girl of her type. The close fit of her white singlet followed the lines of a strong and supple young back, the movement of her firm young breasts was seen easily through the cotton. Claire wore a broad leather belt which pulled the faded blue-denim of her riding-jeans smooth and taut over her robust young hips and thighs. Though a strapping young wench, she was well-made rather than plump and it was perhaps this which had made Lord Thomas and the other gentlemen look with such longing upon her.

At that moment, the girl had knelt down and was sitting on her heels with her back to her admirers as she vigorously polished the floor between the rows of saddles. Claire worked with her jaw set resolutely and the collar-length of her lank dark hair falling forward a little round her face as she bowed her head to her task. As she leant forward, the smooth denim of the jeans was tight and smooth as skin over the fuller and broader shape of Claire's bottom-cheeks and thighs. It was understandable that this area of Claire's arse and thighs should draw the most eager attention of the men who watched her.

Yet as Lady Margaret spied upon her cousin, it was clear that another romance of the kind which April had inspired was in the making. That an insolent young scrubber like Claire should be permitted to cause such catastrophe to the social order filled her ladyship with indignation.

Presently, in order to stretch and reach between the saddles with her polishing cloth, Claire had to lift her hips from her heels and go forward on all fours. As she did so, the men drew breath sharply at the provoking rear view which she now offered brazenly to the world. The pale blue-denim was drawn smooth and taut as drum skin over the broadened mounds of Claire's buttocks. In this posture, Claire's backside at nineteen years old was big-cheeked but with little hint of flabbiness. Best of all the stout central seam of the jeans-seat was drawn deep and tight between Claire's bottom-cheeks, parting those rear hemispheres in a most suggestive manner! The stout seam was also strained tightly under her legs where it seemed to part the very lips of her cunt whose soft flesh was molded for the admiration of the men by the clinging denim.

With her head bowed and the dark hair falling forward, Claire backed on all fours towards her admirers, working the cloth hard on the floor. Even Lady Margaret could sense the ardent images of longing which fired their brains as they licked their lips and smiled secretly to themselves. All of them imagined Claire positioned thus but with her denim and knickers removed, harness straps holding her down to prevent reprisals by so sturdy a girl. One might be content with thoughts of his stiffness entering between her legs, of the bamboo and the birch rod across her broadened buttocks. Another, more demanding, must feel the tightness of Claire's anus implacably stretched on his erection—then whipcord and the snakeskin lash across the bare cheeks of Claire's bottom. Another would imagine perversities in the tiled bathroom, Claire secured bottom-upwards over a pedestal. Next to the squirt, the soap-bottle, the china bowl, and rolled paper, would lie the cane and the lash.

So powerful and implacable were the ordeals which they wished to impose upon her in these dreams that they seemed to be communicated to the girl herself! As if sensing the presence of these onlookers for the first time, Claire stopped polishing. Immobile on all fours, she looked back under her shoulder. What she saw of the men caused her to sit back on her heels, two spots of anger glowing at the wide points of her cheekbones. Flicking the lank dark hair clear of her face, she stared round at her admirers. There was defiance in the line of her jaw and mouth, contempt in the slanting glance of her brown eyes. She turned her head away and sat still until the men had moved on.

Lady Margaret could think of nothing but the danger which a strapping young trollop like Claire presented to a well-born gentleman of Thomas's sensibilities. She promised herself that such a temptation must be removed and that Thomas must be cured of his incipient infatuation in the most direct manner.

It was simple enough to suggest to Lord Rupert and to Mr. Bowler, a fellow magistrate, that Claire was guilty of indecent and scandalous conduct in the public view. These two gentlemen had a very clear idea of their duty. They were only too willing to convene a closed session of the justices at Bowler Hall, where they were joined upon the bench by old Mr. Snook who could be counted upon to deal out exemplary punishment to a strapping young trollop of Claire's kind.

Claire was brought before them that evening in her blue-denim skirt and white blouse. Even if they never saw her again, the three gentlemen were very excited at the thought of the fate they had in store for her. Behind thick walls and barred windows her proud young breasts and tautly muscled thighs would be at the disposal of the gaoler and his assistants. The pale sturdiness of Claire's bottom-cheeks would be constantly menaced by the prison cane and the birch.

There was fury in her brown eyes and the points of her broad cheekbones glowed with anger when they assured her that the case would be decided against her. Indeed, when the sentence was pronounced by Mr. Snook—looking up to grin knowingly at Claire from time to time—the warders held her by either arm and her wrists were strapped behind her back as a precaution. They condemned her to eighteen months of penitentiary training, at which she shook her lank dark hair and composed her fair-skinned features into a mask of indifference under her level fringe. Then Claire gave a sudden look of fright as Mr. Snook added, "The girl to be severely whipped by order of the court one month after the beginning of her sentence. Also to receive such further chastisements as may be desirable in the opinion of the gaoler during the remainder of her training."

When Lord Thomas heard of this, he behaved in the most deplorable fashion. Finding out a local attorney, he employed the man to see if the verdict could not be overturned, even at the cost of bringing the matter before the Lord Chancellor himself!

Here was a pretty pickle and no mistake! Fortunately, the attorney was old Silas Grabham, a tenant of Mr. Snook. Though it cost a little, he was soon persuaded to impede his client's case and ensure that no appeal was forwarded for eight more months, by which time it must be invalid.

In the meantime, Lord Thomas himself was appointed a Justice of the Peace. You may be sure that his brother-in-law Lord Rupert and his friend Mr. Bowler took excellent care that he was not chosen to hear such cases as Claire's. However, on Lady Margaret's advice, it was arranged that he and the rest of us should be present to see Claire receive her judicial whipping. Nothing was said to him of what would happen and the young man thought merely that we were to make a tour of inspection round the gaoler's premises.

One Saturday night, which is sacred here to sports of all kinds, was the time appointed for Claire to receive her chastisement: However, it was an hour or more earlier when Mr. Bowler arrived with his valet to exercise his right of examining the culprit.

A door was opened on to the dimly lit room where Claire lay sleeping. She had been positioned face-down on the bed with no sheet or blanket covering her, soft leather cuffs attaching her wrists to the frame of the bed on either side as a measure of precaution. Claire's head was turned aside on the pillow, the light showing her firm young profile, eyes closed and lips parted gently in slumber, while the lank collar-length of her dark hair lay round her white neck and jaw-line.

Lady Margaret

The guardians had undressed her completely, except for her short white singlet. Yet even the singlet hem had been pulled high so that Claire's arse and hips, her thighs and flanks, were completely bare. The turnkeys had wedged two pillows under her loins, to emphasize the spread of her strong young thighs and to give a fuller and broader swell to the firm cheeks of Claire's bottom.

Without waking her, Mr. Bowler sat gently on the edge of the bed at the level of her hips. He bowed his head and examined the area of Claire's anatomy which interested him. The hem of her white singlet had been pulled right up to the small of her back at the rear. In the faint light he was able to admire the pale nudity of Claire's seat and thighs.

So he studied the swelling cheeks of Claire's backside, keenly and closely. The line of his mouth was hard and his eyes unsmiling, as befitted a magistrate. He showed no softening nor affection towards the nineteen-year-old girl. Such sentiments were improper for a disciplinarian moralist. Her body was admirably relaxed as she lay sleeping. Mr. Bowler pondered on the sensitive hollows at the backs of her knees, a blue vein showing here and there. He lingered over the rear of her young thighs, so robust yet trim. All this time Claire lay with her firm young profile on the pillow, the lank dark hair across her face, unaware of the man's intimate prying as she slept.

Her thighs had relaxed in slumber and she had parted them a little so that the folds of her sex were visible from the rear. Mr. Bowler inspected her so closely with his eyes that she might almost have felt his breath on her feminine slit. A healthy and well-built working-girl of nineteen gives rein to her sensual fancies in sleep. In the warmth of the summer night Mr. Bowler was able to enjoy the faint mineral scent of her arousal between Claire's thighs. He spent quite fifteen or twenty minutes musing on the rear view of her open legs and the lightly moistened state between them.

Next he turned to the full and broadened swell of Claire's pale bottom-cheeks, which he had condemned to the lash. His mouth grew tighter still and his eyes more intense with disciplinary severity. His gaze mapped Claire's bare backside. While the girl continued to sleep, unaware of his sadistic contemplation, he brooded on her smooth rear cheeks with tyrannical longing for at least half an hour. His thoughts turned to the objects on the table, designed to subject her behind to certain indignities of the toilet as she lay over the pillows. Such ordeals must often accompany the caning of her bottom by the turnkeys who visited her at night and inflicted summary discipline.

Those who saw the array of objects on the table could guess why Claire was made to lie bottom-upwards over the rubber pillows. They knew quite well what the gaoler would make her do as she lay there. Indeed, a bamboo cane and a loop of whipcord had been placed by the toilet articles to enforce her obedience.

Mr. Bowler inspected more closely the broad curving pallor of Claire's bottom-cheeks. They were slacker in sleep. The pillows packed under her loins also raised and filled out the swell of her seat, causing the two rear mounds to part lightly but suggestively. Thin-lipped and vindictive he gazed from a few inches into the cleavage where Claire's buttocks curved in together. So close did he sigh over her backside that his breath gently warmed the two cool globes of her behind. He settled down to enjoy this view of Claire's sturdy young arse at little more than kissing distance. The night was warm and heavy. It excited him to breathe the humid and intimate girl-scent emanating from between the cheeks of Claire's bottom.

With disciplinary relish his eyes lingered on the dark tight little vortex of Claire's anus. How different was his expression from the meek adoration of Lord Thomas! Mr. Bowler longed to have Claire at his disposal in a harem like that of Ahmed Pasha. The sight of Claire's arsehole and bum-cheeks, her thighs and what lay between them, made him dream of extreme and exemplary punishments for her insolence and defiance. He longed to rid society of her malign influence. As he inspected her robust and vulgar rump, he dreamt of penalties which less resolute moralists call torture. Bowler Pasha imagined himself concluding all this by tightening the sinister leather collar round her throat, slowly and inexorably. He was not dismayed at his desires, for such were the images which Claire inspired in this worthy magistrate.

He stroked her lightly along the inward cleavage of her bum-cheeks. Claire woke with a start and tightened herself instinctively against his intruding fingers. Mr. Bowler smiled.

"Lie still while I inspect you, Claire!" he said sharply. "Don't clench yourself! The bench of justices condemned you to a prison whipping. You'll be getting it tonight! Ah, that makes you tense your buttocks with fright, doesn't it, Claire? The pony-lash across your bare bottom-cheeks will smart like red-hot wire! But first we must make you wait an hour or two for it, just to make sure you're really in the mood!"

He began to examine her robust bare thighs with his hands and, when Claire tried to twist away from him, he pinioned her legs firmly by a strap just above her knees.

"In a while, you'll hear the gaoler cracking the whip to test it," he said teasingly. "It's a sound that will make those strapping young bottom-cheeks tingle with fear, Claire! He badly wants to acquaint himself with your bare backside and teach you a lesson in obedience. You'll get your punishment in the soundproof vault late at night I'm sure you can guess why!"

He coaxed the warm folds of Claire's cunt back through the rear of her legs, his fingers playing with her lightly as she panted and squirmed in a futile resistance.

"I must slide my other hand under your bare belly, Claire. Excellent! I can feel the first flutter of panic there. I promise you that the cheeks of your bottom will itch with fright before you receive the first kiss of the snakeskin lash across them!"

He stroked the soft folds of her cunt, holding it gently in his fingers, as if he might be comforting a nestling bird. Claire bowed her face, allowing the short length of her lank dark hair to fall about her features, as if to hide herself from him and deny him the pleasure of watching her reactions. She gasped through clenched teeth at the indignity of his masturbation of her. The line of her young chin was still firm and resolute in her defiance of him.

"Calm yourself, Claire! It is your bottom that interests me most of all tonight!"

Flicking back her hair, she watched in dismay as he chose the jar of Vaseline. One heard the light sound of a gentleman unbuttoning himself. For some time, Mr. Bowler had secretly wanted to show Claire his prick, to make her stare at it in dismay while he described the manner in which she would get it.

One does not spy upon a gentleman in his private enjoyment of a young bitch like Claire. Yet some most suggestive words and glimpses merit consideration. Mr. Bowler's obsession with the girl's broad-cheeked backside left no doubt that it was where he wished to pay the tribute of his loins. One applauds his moral prudence for there was no danger of giving Claire a baby there. Thus the parish was saved the expense—and the girl avoided the shame—of a swollen belly and a brat to feed.

The marriage of December and May is sometimes frowned upon by ignorant persons. Claire was nineteen. The erection which Mr. Bowler, smiling, showed her rose from the grey-haired bush of a man in his fifties. But his magisterial balls were swollen big and tight with a prodigious load of sperm, thus defeating the objection.

Those unfamiliar with the art of discipline may complain that all the pleasure was to be Mr. Bowler's. Claire must lie there and receive the spending in her arse with no reward or enjoyment.

Yet justice often employs deplorable means for laudable purposes. To cut off a man's head or to disembowel him was prescribed by our law as punishment for treason. To hang a woman or to whip a girl has been a cornerstone of jurisprudence. The Romans made a faithless young wife wear a massive radish up her bottom. How lewd these things would be—how barbaric!—unless sanctioned by law. How trivial, by comparison, was the ordeal which Magistrate Bowler inflicted upon Claire to curb her insolence!

"Another rubber pillow under your belly, Claire, to swell your bare bottom out even fuller! Excellent! Why, you offer your young buttocks parted as shamelessly as any bride on her honeymoon night!"

Held by the straps, Claire was obliged to lie bottom-upwards over the pillows and present her anus to the magistrate. The amount she must receive in her arse would not be determined by what she could take but by what Mr. Bowler needed to spend. The brown eyes under her level fringe slanted fury at him and the points of her broad cheekbones glowed with anger!

The springs of the divan creaked as Mr. Bowler ignored this and sat down level with her waist and racing her feet. He tightened his left arm over her waist to steady her and bowed his gaze. The pale swelling globes of Claire's behind deserved his attention. He settled down for a long browsing and kissing upon them. Leather strained noisily as Claire pulled at her wrist-cuffs and gasped her detestation of what was being done to her. Mr. Bowler paused from time to time and smilingly wagged his stiffness in her face.

"It makes your buttocks tighten to see the size of the knob, Claire! Can this truly be your first time?"

Those whose ears were pressed to the door heard the unscrewing of the Vaseline jar. Claire exclaimed in anger and refusal. One heard a slipperiness being smeared between her rear cheeks. When the springs creaked again, there was a suggestion of Mr. Bowler kneeling astride and much talk of the hammerhead knocking for admission at the tight rear entrance. One caught the whisper of Claire's dark hair threshing from side to side as she squirmed and gasped her refusal.

"No! I won't! I won't! Oh, no-o-o-o-o!"

The shrillness of the last syllable told its own story of the drama. Claire, frantic not to have it, was getting it just the same. Mr. Bowler gasped a tribute to the tightness of the rear dimple which passed so thrillingly over his knob and Claire gave a cry of panic as she felt him press in to the very hilt. Through clenched teeth once more, she panted out her contempt and revulsion for him. But Mr. Bowler was able to enjoy himself at will. For half an hour the springs moved in a steady rhythm. Then they moved faster and with more vigor.

Mr. Bowler breathed hard, like a champion winning a race. His fleshy muzzle became a load in Claire's backside of which the girl desperately needed to ease herself. When his climax came, the tightness of her nineteen-year-old bum on his shaft was exquisite. He shot jet after jet of thick passion into the depths of Claire's bottom, as a sound of repugnance rose from her throat.

Tearing paper from the roll, he mopped a final splash or two of his passion from Claire's bottom-cheeks and wiped the guilty Vaseline smears from between them. Decency forbade that the compromising paper should be found in the folds of Claire's sheets by a female guardian. Making a convenient wad, he therefore thumbed it firmly into Claire's behind. Yet he could not resist leaving the last corner protruding like a little flag. It added a suggestive rudeness to Claire's rear view which would greatly increase the enthusiasm of the magistrates who watched her punished that night.

An hour later the turnkeys came for her. Claire's knickers and riding-jeans were pulled up. Then three of these stalwart fellows escorted her to the vault, where the county magistrates and their ladies were waiting eagerly to see justice done.

A strapping young trollop of Claire's kind is always punished to the limit on these occasions. It is therefore prudent to inflict the discipline at dead of night in one of the soundproof and subterranean vaults. The guests, including Lord Thomas, were assembled there. Gaslight flared on the whitewashed walls of the stone-flagged room. Two hurdles of heavy timber, their top bars padded with leather, were bolted to the floor, parallel to each other and a few feet apart, restraining straps riveted to their structure. An array of whips lay on a nearby table.

It was about half an hour before midnight when a door opened and we glimpsed Claire in her white singlet and working-denim. She was struggling with a wild energy in the grip of the three turnkeys who were propelling her to the place of punishment.

How desperately Claire fought and panted to break free! How violently she braced her strong young legs against the flagstones, contesting every inch of the way! There was still anger in the slant of her brown eyes. Her mouth and chin remained tight with defiance. The collar-length of her lank dark hair fell about her face as she bowed her shoulders and twisted her arms against the grip of the men. The washed jeans-denim strained taut over the sturdy mounds of Claire's bum-cheeks as she squirmed her hips and cursed her captors, lunging with her haunches to drive the men from her.

At nineteen years old, Claire is a strongly built girl but fortunately the three men were more than a match for her. They made her bend forward over the first of the hurdles, both structures being built of solid timbers, heavy and substantial enough to support her easily. Being bolted to the floor and equipped with stout straps, they also held her very securely.

While they bent her over the first hurdle, the men drew her arms out at full stretch in front of her and fastened them down by the wrist-cuffs on the further hurdle. This bar on which her wrists were pinioned could be raised or lowered. By lowering it, the gaoler would be able to make Claire bend over very tightly indeed. It was only to be expected that he would want to do that so that the girl offered a more sexually suggestive target for the whip. It was important that he should feel randy while punishing Claire for that would ensure she was whipped soundly.

The hurdle which supported her belly had a harness strap quite three inches broad. They tightened this round her bare waist to hold her firmly down. Bending over like this, Claire was made to present a most provoking and full-cheeked rear view. The faded washed-out jeans-denim was excitingly tight and smooth over the broadened mounds of her buttocks. The sight which she offered would have made any man a disciplinarian.

She flicked back the dark spilling hair, and the slant of her brown eyes under her level fringe shone with hatred for the three men. One man smiled, standing behind her. His hands began to feel and fondle her rear cheeks through the skin-tight jeans-seat. Claire panted and twisted, trying in vain to evade his stroking. He chuckled as he felt her through the smooth denim.

Lady Margaret

"Did you never have men feeling you like this at your work, Claire? You'll get plenty of it here, I promise you! I must just feel between the back of your legs. Ah, yes! A nice soft swell of pussy-flesh in your pants! Now the cheeks of your strapping young bottom, Claire! You're wearing panties underneath, aren't you, Claire? I can just feel the outline of some tight-fitting briefs. Did you think the justices might let you wear your cotton briefs while you were whipped, Claire? Why, mat would spoil the fun for them! You'll have your panties taken down, never fear. You must feel the snakeskin lash on your bare bottom!"

The men left her with the flutter of panic in her young belly growing to real fright. The gaoler made her wait for half an hour in this torment of suspense. Then he arrived and chose two whips from the table. One was a leather switch about four feet long, slim and wickedly supple. The other was the woven snakeskin of the short pony-lash. Without speaking to her, he undid Claire's riding-jeans at the waist. She twisted her legs, gasping and struggling to prevent him stripping her, but he wrenched the denim down and off. Soon Claire's knickers also lay in an untidy tangle round her ankles.

The gaoler studied the broad-cheeked pallor of Claire's bottom as she bent over the hurdles. He smiled as he glimpsed her sex at the rear of her thighs. Then he spoke to her.

"Later on I'll make you bend over even tighter, Claire. I want you to look as big-bottomed as possible when I whip you. There's no need for pretence here. I shall very much enjoy thrashing you. I'll bend you tighter presently so that you show much more between the backs of your legs. And I'll want your bottom-cheeks stretched hard apart so that I can see everything between them while I whip you, Claire!"

While he was talking to her, two stable-lads slipped into the vault. They hid by the buttresses, having a rear view of Claire, so that the girl saw them every time she twisted her head round. The younger lad was still shy. He stood facing the wall, watching Claire over his shoulder. His hands were clasped in his lap and he seemed to be holding some trinket which he polished vigorously. The older boy unbuttoned proudly and directed Claire's gaze to the fine stiffness which he held in his hand. The insolence in her brown eyes gave way to dismay as he showed it to her so openly. He wanted Claire to know that he was greatly excited by her bare rear view and that he was eagerly looking forward to seeing the shop girl's backside dance to the tune of the whip!

The gaoler flexed the supple length of his leather switch.

"Now get arse-upwards over the hurdle, Claire, you young tart! Get right over it! Properly!

To enforce this, he lowered the forward hurdle bar to which her wrists were strapped, making the nineteen-year-old girl bend over more tightly. This caused the robust pale mounds of Claire's buttocks to be pulled apart a little more. There were smiles of amusement from the onlookers as they glimpsed the little flag of paper peeping out between Claire's bum-cheeks. The two stable-lads pumped their stiffness still harder with excitement at this. These young scamps would greatly have enjoyed making Claire submit to various indignities of the toilet and hoped that they would soon have the chance.

The remarks of the worthy magistrates who watched left Claire in no doubt that we had seen the vulgar sight she offered! Was it anger or humiliation which caused the glow at the points of her broad cheekbones? She sometimes wears her lank dark hair in a collar-length pony-tail and the gaoler now gathered it back in this style and slipped a rubber band round it to hold it. One could now see the slant of resentment in her brown eyes and the defiant resolve in the line of her chin and firm young features.

"The justices must see your face while you're being thrashed, Claire," the gaoler said. "They like to see how you're taking it. All the men and women here approve of a really pitiless whipping given to a young trollop like you with such a strapping young bottom!"

The handle of the four-foot leather switch was thick as his thumb but the whip tapered to a point that was fine as a pencil tip. Smiling, he touched the back of Claire's thigh, high up, with the quivering fine bobble-tip of the whip. We smiled as well to see how she flinched from the cold menace of the leather. For a little while longer he teased the nineteen-year-old wench, stroking the whip gently down each bare flank of her hips. When Claire bends or kneels forward on all fours at her work, her hips have that natural feminine slope which broadens downwards to the top of her legs. As he caressed her with the leather switch one could hear the light sounds of her legs smoothing together in panic and the heavier breathing of her fright.

Then, as if a signal had been given, we knew the punishment was about to begin. All smiles faded and each mouth was tightened in severity. The gaoler's voice was hard and humorless.

"You fat-arsed young tart, Claire! Fifty strokes of the whip across your bare bottom-cheeks to begin with! Bend right over and keep your backside facing the magistrates!"

Without waiting for her response, he raised the quivering switch high behind his shoulder. Light flashed from the polished leather as he brought it down with ear-stunning force across the pale fattened cheeks of Claire's backside. To our delight, Claire's gasp of anguish at the impact rose to a wild cry as the torment swelled to a climax over several seconds. At the moment when the ferocity of the first whip-smack reached its fullest, the gaoler brought the whip down again across the squirming cheeks of Claire's bottom in a still more vicious stroke.

Though she was a strong and broad-hipped girl, the searching intensity of the redoubled smart paralyzed Claire in sound and movement! Her hands were clenched into fists, her leg-muscles tightened as with cramp, and she was up on her toes with the exquisite white fire of the lash.

Far from allowing her a respite, the gaoler touched the switch lightly, aiming across the lower and fatter swell of the young saddle-dresser's buttocks. He knew how sensitive that softer fullness of Claire's backside would be. With savage accuracy he made that pallid fatness jump under the whip's impact. With rapid strokes, he whipped her again—again—and yet again—across that sensitive undercurve. Claire screamed and writhed, her shrillness quickening the excitement of the watching justices. She twisted her face round, her brown eyes wider and her mouth distended in the wildness of her cries.

It was only to be expected that the gaoler should want to make Claire scream as the whip caught her backside. Her shrillness was a tribute to his art. As a disciplinarian he was also bound to enjoy whipping her-cruelly low across her buttocks with the leather switch. Indeed, he now aimed the quivering wand across the light flesh-crease dividing her buttocks and upper thighs. To hear a robust young wench like Claire shriek as she did then is a rare experience. No wonder the gaoler whipped hard again across the rising weal he had just inflicted.

The ladies of fashion smiled privately behind their fans as they watched all this. Each gentleman-magistrate now felt the front of his trousers growing uncomfortably tight and longed to unbutton such stiffness. The stable-lads were more fortunate, watching Claire's short pony-tail of dark hair sweep her collar as she twisted her face round and yelled frantically for a respite. Concealed from their elders but close behind the bending girl, the lads met the frenzy in Claire's brown eyes with open-mouthed delight. Each of them urged her to look at his fine handful which he pumped vigorously.

"Turn your arse towards us properly, Claire! Lets have a good look at those whip-marks on your bum-cheeks! He's given you some real beauties across your fat young arse, Claire! I'd love to change places with him for half an hour! He's cut your bottom twice with the riding-switch, Claire!... Was it old Bowler who poked the paper up into your backside, Claire? I bet it makes the old magistrates randy to see you like that! They enjoy making you look like a rude girl! Open your legs and show us between them... Bend over tightly so that the whip cuts your bottom, Claire! You'll be a pretty sight when they finish with you... I hope they leave you alone with us, Claire!"

The switch smacked peremptorily across Claire's bottom. Her fattened young backside writhed and surged on the bar. One did not blame a gaoler's severity, seeing the sight the girl offered. Claire's buttocks were interlaced by plum-colored weals, which naturally made the gaoler want to be truly sadistic with her. When a well-built and insolent girl of nineteen like Claire shows such brand-marks of the whip across her bare arse, no true moralist takes pity on her. The sight of the whip's weals across her bottom-cheeks show him how badly she needs to be corrected and the sight of Claire's bum-cheeks in such a state would be bound to put certain cruel ideas into his mind. To have Claire's bottom-cheeks smarting so untouchably from the whip and then to have the chance of thrashing her hard in such a responsive state would be an excitement for many men and even some women!

One also excuses the gaoler's severity because Claire, now arse-upwards over the hurdle-bar, was writhing her thrashed bottom in anguish, a twisting and surging which might almost have been an erotic dance. This display she offered would have been seductively lascivious even if performed before her bridegroom on her honeymoon night to entice him to bed. Indeed, though her boyfriend was obliged to express indignation at the sentence of reformatory detention passed upon her, he would secretly have loved to see her arse bucking and squirming under the gaoler's whip. A young tart like Claire is not of the kind to whom a man swears his life. Private information assures me that her boyfriend bribed the stable-boys for details of the whipping. He paid several guineas for photographs of the scene taken after the thrashing had been in progress for more than an hour. Several were of Claire's defiant young face, the brown eyes under the level fringe of her dark hair brimming with tears and her mouth distended in a frantic scream. Others were full-plate camera studies of the bare cheeks of Claire's bottom, covered by welts of the pony-whip and with a dozen wine-red trickles down them from her cuts. So roused was he that he had to use the stable-lads' remedy at once. Later he assured Mr. Bowler that he would make no more objection to the sentence of eighteen months which Claire was to serve. Indeed, he made a private complaint against her so that she might be held for twelve months more!

Such moral resolve is always rewarded here. The young man was apprenticed to a gaoler in another county, for it was thought better to part him from Claire for good.

Meanwhile, the gaoler who dealt with Claire that night was unbearably tantalized by glimpses of her cunt and views between her bottom-cheeks as she writhed. He thrashed the supple riding-switch aslant her buttocks and saw her jam one knee into the back of the other as she tried desperately to contain the agony. The whip smacked her bum-cheeks again and the young whore actually dared to try and kick out at him with her strong bare legs!

'Punish her well for that, Mr. Gaoler!' said Mr. Bowler. 'See that you whip the young slut's legs as well as her backside!'

So the flashing leather of the supple switch smacked savagely across the broad rounding cheeks of Claire's bare bottom again... and again... a slash of the whip high up on the rear of her thighs..-. again... the whip across the backs of her knees... again... and again... the whip high across the rear of her thighs... across the backs of her knees again... and again... her thighs again... and again... a smack of the riding-switch across Claire's bottom... across her thighs... thighs... thighs... bottom... Claire screaming wildly... her dark lank hair breaking from its short pony-tail and flying this way and that... a cruel cut of the whip across the lower fatness of Claire's bottom-cheeks... another across that fetter curve of her buttocks... Claire screaming and kicking madly with her bare legs... a cut with the whip aslant the surging mounds of Claire's arse... another slanting cut... two ruby trickles down Claire's thrashed buttocks and a score of wine-red smudges... Though Claire is a sturdy young wench, it was not surprising that one of the stable-lads had to apply the smelling-salts to her nostrils from time to time. He did this with smiles and randy whispers to her. Though he had to pull up his cotton pants as he came forward, he directed Claire's frantic gaze to the bulge at the front of his briefs, pressing her lips to the hardness and the wet patch on the material itself.

The gaoler discarded the switch and chose the pony-lash with its short tail of woven snakeskin. Such alarm in Claire's eyes as she saw over her shoulder what he was preparing to do to her! But his voice was firm and decided.

"Bend right over, Claire! Better than that! I want to see those strong young thighs filled out a little and those strapping young bottom-cheeks stretched hard for discipline! Show us a big-bottomed view, Claire! Your complete rear view this time!"

She writhed in her straps, protesting and fearful in her anticipation. Fortunately the gaoler could enforce obedience by lowering the front hurdle-bar further. This made Claire bend over until the level fringe of her dark hair almost brushed her knees. To ease the strain on her rear thigh-muscles, she was also obliged to stand astride a little. What a sight she offered! Claire was looking back at an upside-down view of the vault behind her through the narrow arch of her own bare thighs!

The justices and their ladies had an excellent view between her legs. Claire also displayed that lewd little flag of paper which peeped from her bum in such a provocative manner. The gaoler smiled at this and murmured a command which made Claire gasp with shock. He smiled again.

"Very well, Claire. Then the lash must pluck it out."

Claire's sturdy buttocks tightened with instinctive terror at this. For the moment, her insolence and contempt towards him faltered. What followed was certainly not a ladylike display. Yet such things are permitted when dealing with a girl like Claire in the complete privacy of reformatory discipline.

The gaoler laid his hand on the bare pallor of her hip-flank and made Claire turn her broadened young backside more fully towards the onlookers. He pressed a rim of china high against the rear of her thighs. The stable lads' fists went like pistons and the magistrates were visibly excited at the lengths to which the gaoler would go with Claire. The young ladies of fashion watched with exceptional eagerness, eyes sparkling in gleeful expectation. The gaoler stroked Claire through the rear of her legs. He reminded her to show her insolent young face to the magistrates while she obeyed. There was indignation in the slant of her brown eyes but even this young strumpet almost blushed at what she was obliged to do.

We watched her bare bottom intently as Claire bent over tightly before us. She let out a long breath and her young belly tensed with effort. It seemed that Claire swelled her bum-cheeks out more fully. The saucy little tail of paper moved. The tight tear dimple expanded, the little wad appeared. Claire expelled it with great caution so that it emerged slowly and at last fell upon the porcelain. The gaoler placed it on the table, next to Claire's knickers. I could scarcely believe that this trophy was also destined for the collection of senile old Justice Snook who treasures such mementoes of young women under discipline.

The usual rubber wedge between her teeth protected them in the frenzy of the final tanning. At the first crack of the pony-lash across her nineteen-year-old bottom the very stones of the vault sang. The second stroke was aimed short so that the tip of the lash tickled her between her rear cheeks. How Claire shrilled at the searing kiss of skinning leather between her sturdy young bottom-cheeks! The gaoler's eyes shone with anticipation and he caught her between them again with his next stroke. Then he aimed across the cheeks but the smart of the snakeskin was so atrocious that Claire's bum retorted most rudely before she could contain herself. Mr. Snook smiled and caught the gaze of her wild eyes.

That was deliberately done to halt the tanning, Mr. Turnkey! Teach the fat-bottomed trollop a lesson in manners, if you please!'

The front of the gaoler's breeches bulged as if they had suddenly become too small for him. Claire yelled a frantic protest as he let her feel the cool leather dangling between her rear globes while he took his aim. Six times the pony-lash kissed Claire agonizingly between her bottom-cheeks, skinning her finely.

How wise are the new laws which confine the tanning of such girls to private reformatories. Claire was punished in ways best not displayed to untutored eyes. The intensity of her screams thrilled the justices with strange exhilaration. In her frenzy Claire tried to trap the streaking lash by clenching her rear cheeks upon it to detain it! She released it at once with wild soprano shrillness. By clenching her bottom-cheeks on the speeding leather, Claire skinned her arse-crack even more closely than the gaoler would have dared to do deliberately!

The snaking lash smacked across Claire's bottom again... and again... two more wine-red droplets running down her rear cheeks... an ear-stunning impact of the pony-whip across the lower fatness of Claire's bottom-cheeks... Claire gulping and writhing over the hurdle-bar... perfectly positioned for more whip... the lash aimed between her rear cheeks again... across the cheeks... between the cheeks... between the cheeks across the cheeks... the vault ringing with Claire's frenzy a moment's pause... "Get your bottom right over the bar, Claire!" the gaoler said quietly. "I'm not nearly satisfied with the state of your backside yet."

He changed the pony-lash for the slim tapering switch of polished leather. Even during the pause Claire could not control her writhing. Her strapping young bottom smarted too keenly and the panic was swelling in her belly. The gaoler eagerly watched the seductive rounding of her thrashed backside.

A sadistic whip-stroke across the lower fatness of Claire's bare buttocks ended the pause... another lashed the same soft undercurve... Claire kicked and shrieked... the whip aslant her arse to tame her... another slanting cut... the whip across the rear of her thighs... a sizzling smack across the fullest curve of Claire's bum-cheeks... two cuts high up across the rear of her thighs... ruby beads running down to the backs of her knees... the whip low across Claire's bottom... again... red-petal droplets on the flagstones... the state of Claire's bottom stiffening every magistrate... the whip across her thighs... across her bum-cheeks... her backside again... across her thighs... her bottom... her thighs... an ear splitting whip-smack across Claire's bottom... thighs... Claire's bottom... Claire's bottom... Claire's bottom... Even the eyes of the watching ladies sparkled with excitement when they saw that during the torment of the final thrashing Claire's strong young teeth had bitten right through the thick rubber bit in her mouth! When it was over, the strapping young mounds of her bare backside were the color of red fire. The two stable-boys had the enjoyable task of smearing the cheeks of Claire's arse with heavily salted kitchen fat to prolong the scorching smart. Her nineteen-year-old buttocks blazed raw and sleek with grease and—it must be admitted—splashes and blobs of youthful lust trickled down Claire's bottom-cheeks.

In a day or two, Lady Margaret confided to her close friends her great satisfaction at the effect this display of prison discipline had had upon Lord Thomas. He now saw Claire for what she was and at last understood what the proper conduct of society required of him. To adore the broad-cheeked swell of Claire's arse in tight denim as she knelt to her labors, was one thing.

Lady Margaret

But one does not select the future lady of the manor by the width of her hind-quarters!

Lady Margaret guessed—and in this she was right—that the sight of Claire behaving with all her natural vulgarity under the gaoler's lash would cure her cousin's infatuation. He had seen the young strumpet thrashed. He had heard Claire fart under the whip. He had seen the saucy twist of paper protruding in a quite lascivious manner. After that he was safe.

Claire could never be his bride now—the lady of the manor. His lordship knew it. All the magistrates of the county had witnessed Claire farting under the gaoler's whip. Ladies of the manor never fart at all—or at least are never known to. Claire had presented a lewd display between her strapping young bottom-cheeks. It may be allowed that ladies of the manor have bottom-cheeks but they certainly have nothing between them. A true English lady endeavors not to have a bottom of any kind— in short not to exist below the waist.

Worst of all, Claire had been made to show her cunt to the justices of the county. A gentleman cannot take to wife a girl whose cunt-anatomy had been inspected by every person of quality in the county!

In truth, Lord Thomas woke in the nick of time from his trance. He saw that Claire was a fat-arsed young tart a strapping young trollop, a vulgar bitch, an insolent young whore—in short all those things which Lady Margaret had vainly assured him of from the first. How clearly one sees, then, that our nation's system of justice and prison discipline—for all its occasional little faults—is the friend of order and decency in our established society. Claire spent a night screaming under the whip. How small a price to pay for preserving the good name and honest blood of one of our noblest families which she might otherwise have ruined!

Lord Thomas recovered his spirits with great speed and his progress has been heart-warming. He attended a reformatory and watched a cheeky little imp of eighteen, Sally Fenton, caned three times on her bare bottom in one afternoon. He might have intervened on her behalf but he never did. Several foreign girls were brought there for crimes committed in England. Among them was the young Austrian slut, Elke Mahne, with her high-boned face, sly hazel eyes, and short bell-shape of straight brown hair. The soft ripe cheeks of Elke Mahne's eighteen-year-old bottom in tight denim moved Lord Thomas as they should. Before she was tanned, he visited her room. Though

I cannot swear that he ravished Elke, she looked very sorry for herself when the gaoler bent her over the hurdles. The Vaseline on the table by her bed had certainly been used and the red prints of his lordship's cane were visible on the full young cheeks of Elke Mahne's bottom, even before the gaoler dealt with her. So ardently did his lordship wish to reform the girl that he went to her room a good two hours before each of her public disciplines. The prints of his bamboo across Elke Mahne's backside were much admired.

All this was a marked improvement in the young gentleman but it was only a beginning. Next a bride of eighteen was got for him, Lady Nerissa Gray, a charming girl of good family and education. It was not supposed that he would grow cold to the vulgar provocation of such working-girls as Julie or April. Since he could not marry them, he might now enjoy them at will!

The friends of this happy couple did all in their power to aid their life together and were gratified to see that marriage to an estimable young lady had brought Lord Thomas to his senses at last. He lost nothing by doing his duty as society demanded. Lady Nerissa was his companion of bed and board. Her passion conceived quickly. In two years the line of descent in one of England's most noble families was secured by the birth of two vigorous male infants.

Yet his lordship was also able to enjoy the delights of proletarian beauty with greater success and public esteem than when he was a moody neurasthenic boy. He was appointed a justice, a trustee of reformatories for fallen female virtue. Girls whom he once courted in despair were now his to command. In these matters, Mr. Bowler strove to be his example and teacher.

Claire had sex regularly and exclusively from Mr. Bowler. It was fortunate that his thrice-weekly libations of sperm were squirted into Claire's young backside upon hot infertile soil. Otherwise she might have left the reformatory with a squalling brood clutching at her apron-strings!

With his strong and bawdy tastes, Mr. Bowler positively had to attend Claire in a white-tiled toilet-suite. During his residence, she was never permitted such a visit except for the purposes of his pleasure.

Before the door closed upon Mr. Bowler and the girl, it was possible for Lord Thomas to glimpse nineteen-year-old Claire fastened down, bending tightly over the marble table. The firmly broadened cheeks of the young window-dresser's bottom were clad skin-smooth in the washed-out denim of her working-jeans. Beside her on the table stood the china bowl and the Vaseline, the liquid soap and the squirt, the bamboo cane and the rolled paper, the pony-lash and the spanking-strap—all those things necessary to magisterial satisfaction.

Lady Margaret was the first whose influence and moral example served to instruct the young gentleman in his social duties. Not long after the amusing display which Claire had afforded her social superiors, the reformatory at Coombe was the scene of a most edifying spectacle. Two elderly gentle-women, the Misses Edgar and Swann, were in despair over the matter of their eighteen-year-old maid-of-all-work, Michele. By her insolence and disobedience, the girl had quite overturned the proper order of their household so that it was the servant who ruled the mistresses rather than the other way round.

It was most fortunate that Lord Rupert heard something of the predicament in which the elderly spinsters found themselves. By his good offices, pert Michele was enrolled in the fifth-form of the reformatory institution at Coombe.

None of this was known to young Lord Thomas at the time. Yet his cousin Margaret, who now began to have hopes that his neurasthenia was in retreat, took him one afternoon to visit the master of that place. Michele was to be seen skulking with a crony or two in a corner smoking a cigarette on the sly.

What a picture she made! At eighteen she is neither very tall nor large-built, yet her young body has a lithe and quite sturdy look. Then, Michele has the sluttish provoking air of a street girl and it is upon this that she trades! She stood before Lord Thomas, the silken sweep of her brown hair worn in a seductive slant across her forehead and trimmed short at her collar. Michele was not unaware that this style gave her ample opportunity for coquettish tossing of her head and flicking of the sleek veil of hair clear of her face! Her brown eyes appeared narrowed with a knowing mockery and a shifting dishonesty. The long slope of her cheekbones and the provoking tilt of her nose completed the portrait. Like most fifth-form girls, Michele thus had both womanly and childish qualities about her. One remarked how Michele's mouth was a little large and had the vulgar twist of adult whoredom, while her chin had such a youthful softness.

Though Lord Thomas was treated with every courtesy, as became his rank, you may be sure that Lady Margaret and his other friends watched him anxiously m these encounters. It was noticed that his gaze wandered back repeatedly to the face and figure of Michele. Lady Margaret slipped away and had a private word with the warden of that place. A moment later that officer—whose salary is, of course, paid by her ladyship's family—approached the young gentleman. He inquired if Lord Thomas would convey a great honor and assistance upon him by taking Michele under moral correction for a few hours.

With what anxiety did his friends and well-wishers attend the young nobleman's response. It seemed that diffidence wrestled with duty in his heart and was almost the victor. Then he looked a the sly seductive figure of Michele and his tongue ran upon his lips. In short, he accepted the invitation.

A study was at once set aside for him, a mullion-windowed room of buttoned leather and polished mahogany which looked out upon the summer meadow of buttercups and white may. Michele was told to report herself there, which she did with a lewd and impudent grin, a flick back of the sweep of brown hair from her forehead. In her white singlet and the washed blue of tight denim she tapped at the door.

Once he had her in the room, Lord Thomas was able to examine her lithe and agile young figure even before undressing her, for that was his privilege. Standing behind her, his hands curving round her body, he was able to feel the budding swell of Michele's breasts through the warm cotton of the singlet. His words to her, overheard by those who cared for him, told their own story. He exercised his right as moral guardian to draw the singlet up at the front and smooth his hand over her young belly. Then his fingers slid down into the front of her pants, Michele bucking and squirming as his lordship's fingers fondled her pubic fleece and parted the lips of her young puss. Presently, he sat down in a leather chair, obliged her to stand close with her back to him, and observed how the tight jeans-seat molded the lithe round cheeks of Michele's bum.

The sight must have provoked him greatly.

"You lewd little bitch, Michele!" he gasped passionately. "You shall have your knickers off in a moment and learn a lesson or two in discipline before you leave this room!"

Those who eavesdropped upon the encounter were vastly assured by this. At last Lord Thomas was talking in the accents of one of England's moral educators, it seemed certain that he was now safe from the snares which such young sluts of the lower orders are always preparing for innocent young fellows of his sort.

Lady Margaret

He undid the waist of the denim pants himself and drew them down, making eighteen-year-old Michele stand there before him in her underwear for several minutes while he examined her with eyes and hands. He did not hurry himself, knowing that he might prolong the punishment session for as long as he pleased. Presently he was weary of feeling her arse and hips through the white cotton web. He pulled down Michele's fifth-form knickers and gazed eagerly upon the challenge to moral discipline which she now offered.

To punish hastily or in anger is never to be recommended and Lord Thomas used the interval to become better acquainted with the culprit. He obliged Michele to kneel before him at his leather chair while he questioned her about past acts of furtive randiness with lads of her own kind. To confirm the extent to which she had tasted depravity, he commanded her to suck him, saying that he was sure she had done it often enough before for some young ruffian or other.

It is a sad reflection of the prevailing cynicism in England's public life that many malcontents and radicals might accuse our noble young magistrate of making Michele suck upon his stiffened penis and work her tongue about its engorged knob merely for lewd satisfaction. How different is the truth—and how little understood by our moral and social inferiors! Repugnant though it was to him to see Michele suck and lick, the slant of silky brown hair falling like a veil upon the scene, Lord Thomas obliged himself to submit to the ordeal in order to test the extent of her criminality.

The skill with which Michele sucked up and down the shaft of hardened gristle, holding only the base to prevent it going too far into her throat, offered him no consolation. The artful manner in which she worked her agile young tongue under his foreskin and round the vent of his penis moved him only to dismay. One heard this from his gasps.

"You lewd little slut, Michele!… You randy little piece!… Oh, you shall be whipped for this—"

Had he merely been a sensualist, he would have spilt his sperm over her tongue and down her throat. This was far from the case, for he restrained himself admirably and held back the torrent of passion. Obliging her to stand up, he next had Michele lying on the sofa where he examined with great care the state of things between her legs. Here, too, he was most thorough in testing her moral responses to the intrusion of a warm phallus. Indeed, he was more than justified by the result as he worked his stiffness in and out between her spread thighs. Who could doubt the moral response? We heard her, through teeth that clenched and ground with animal excitement, Michele groaning randily, "Fuck... Oh, fuck... Shit... Bollocks... Shit... Fuck... Shit!"

The moral niceness of Lord Thomas may be observed by the fact that he again restrained himself from spending. Indeed, the consequences might have been graver, involving a swollen belly for Michele!

Getting up from the leather sofa, he left Michele lying there and made her wait for what he was going to do to her. He had positioned her on her side, her back to the room, though she soon flicked aside the slant of brown hair and looked over her shoulder with sardonic lasciviousness in her crude young mouth and narrowed eyes. The white singlet ended at her waist, leaving her pale skin bare from that point down to her feet. She lay there looking like the most vulgar child of Venus. Her hind cheeks are trim and resilient as befits her youth, yet they fill to deliciously taut round globes when she touches her toes or thrusts her seat out. A woman's lines are emergent in that part of her figure. One cannot blame Lord Thomas for giving such long and loving attention to the bare rounded pallor of Michele's agile young bottom!

With a truly randy young fifth-form girl there was no need to use threats or reprimand. An aristocratic finger dipped in Vaseline—and he became Michele's teacher! The little vamp was instructed to turn over on her belly a moment and raise her trim young behind towards him. There were gasps and expressions of alarm from Michele at what he was doing to her young backside. But these were surely slanders to compromise him.

To be sure, the sofa creaked in a steady rhythm but that was the girl's restlessness. His lordship gasped with the exertion of instructing the young pupil. He was giving her a lesson in female anatomy, a most worthy endeavor. He remarked that the pussy-flesh between her legs was soft, that Michele's anus was thrillingly tight, and that no amount of sperm would engender an infant in her rear. But these are mere matters of scientific fact. Yet his words would be willfully misconstrued by our country's enemies. The truth is shown by his moral resolve. After a dish of Earl Grey tea he made Michele bend over the study desk. For a moment she tried to argue and resist. The little slut even threatened to tell tales of the past hour's antics if he attempted to thrash her. Lord Thomas met the challenge easily. He informed her that she would be in no position to tell tales anywhere for the next five years. That was the term of reformatory life which he proposed to add to her stay in that place—as its trustee and as a magistrate—

Lady Margaret

for the obvious lewdness and contempt for propriety which he had found in her this afternoon. When she was twenty, she might tell what tales she wished—if she could find anyone who would bother to listen.

He allowed her one choice only. Michele might either bend over the desk of her own accord or be strapped down by two of the servants.

She did as she was told and he drew the singlet hem up above her waist, until Michele's hips and backside were completely bare. He went to the cupboard and chose a prison bamboo which was wickedly long and supple. At the same time he took care to leave the study door ajar, for there was everything to be gained by letting the rest of us see what a severe moralist he could be.

You may be sure that, as she lay forward on the broad desk, Michele had twisted her face round anxiously to watch him, the hair swept aside, the brown eyes and pale complexion a study in fright. One could see her roused little cunt between the rear of her firm young thighs, and the pale cheeks of the girl-pupil's bottom were presented in a womanly posture.

Lord Thomas teased her for five or ten minutes, touching the cane this way and that across her smooth young buttocks, as if taking his aim with great care. At last his jaw hardened and he slashed the cane down with vicious force across the bare cheeks of the schoolgirl bum.

Michele leapt up from the desk with a screech and clapped her hands over her arse. Lord Thomas shook his head and beckoned two servants. These stalwart fellows seized the girl and held her over the desk with the power of their muscular arms.

For the next half hour, Lord Thomas avenged the outrages which Michele had offered to propriety and decency in the brief period of her delinquent career. He measured each stroke of the cane with loving accuracy, made her wait for it, and then gave it with exemplary force. Michele writhed in frantic anticipation even before the bamboo whipped across her young backside. As the agony of the stroke blistered her smooth rear cheeks, she yelled with all the power of her healthy young lungs.

He raised the finest bamboo weals across Michele's bare eighteen-year-old bottom that any of us could recall seeing that summer on any of the sixth-form girls. Twice he broke a cane across her young backside in his enthusiasm and once as he was bambooing the rear of her thighs.

What a rewarding change he produced—from the moral point of view—in this little hussy. The sleek and slanting coiffure of the little vamp was now a disordered spread of brown hair. The hard and narrowed brown eyes brimmed over, the crude young mouth howled and yelled. It is not customary in such places to go beyond thirty-six strokes of the cane given to such a girl, though one does not keep a count. Afterwards it was rumored that Lord Thomas far exceeded this. Who could say? Several of the weals had bestowed a tiny red trickle down one cheek or other of Michele's young arse! However, one accepts such incidents with equanimity in the moral discipline of the reformatory.

The afternoon's events proved that our faith in the young nobleman's potential to fulfill his role in society had been entirely justified. Indeed, he returned a fortnight later and employed the pony-lash upon the bare cheeks of Michele's pretty backside. His reward went far beyond the moral satisfaction felt by a man of noble birth in doing his duty. After these sessions with young Michele, it was observed that he always hurried home to Lady Nerissa. The delightful young couple were apt to retire to bed early and rise late on such occasions. It would be idle to speculate upon the cause. Yet the beautiful Nerissa radiates calm and satisfaction for days after her lord has done his duty on Michele and her kind.

There is need of young blood in the affairs of the county. Mr. Bowler and Lord Rupert are still vigorous, but old Justice Snook is somewhat past his prime. After dinner he retires to his study and his memories. The drawers of his desk are crammed with drawers of a different kind, stripped from the young women whom he has had under discipline these many years. He will study a handful of skimpy and silken translucence, smiling at the images these panties recall, of a harem lash smacking across the agile young cheeks of Sarah Thome's bottom. Or else he chooses a pair of black briefs in cotton web, musing upon this example of young Madam Hollingsworth's knickers. There are the trophies of April and Julie, Claire and the others to awaken smiles on his senile old face.

Leave the old gentleman with the memorabilia of an honored past! Lord Thomas is the new man. His friends declare that he is never more content than when he spends two or three afternoons a week doing his duty of moral reformation. He knows every curve and crease of Michele's fifth-form backside or Elaine's tomboy bottom.

His duty done, he mounts his horse and rides home to the manor house. To see him is to know that all is well. England is in safe hands. With legs and backsides bare, Pauline and Elaine seek sisterly consolation in each other's arms! Their tears still flow a little. Pauline bewails the whip-stripes across her

Lady Margaret

fat young buttocks. As for the younger sister, Elaine's tomboy backside promises a fine panorama of bruises the next day. Is there a splash of male passion on Pauline's thigh? A Vaseline smear between Elaine's sturdy adolescent bum-cheeks? The tone of public life will not be improved by dwelling on such matters.

Lord Thomas rides on. How can one not admire the system which inspires such allegiance? He needs no pair of Sarah Thome's panties to browse upon tonight. The young lord glows with the exhilaration of moral accomplishment. Unlike old Justice Snook, he needs no mementoes in order to recall his days of vigor. Such things are the province of randy boys and old men.

Let us not, however, pretend a sanctimonious ignorance in such matters. Lord Thomas is in fine form after a session in his official study with Pauline and Elaine. He can hardly contain himself until he is close enough to leap upon Lady Nerissa and roger that dear girl as if life itself depended on the release.

And does it not depend upon it? Do not the lives and safety of us all, the hope of the county and the Tory party, depend upon Lord Thomas doing his marital duty with such enthusiasm? The severest whipping on the young buttocks of Michele or Elke would be justified by the effect which the chastisement of adolescent beauty may have upon the young nobleman's amorous energies. Let him hurry home and beget a little Thomas to rule over us all in the future. So long as we remember our allegiance to the young gentleman and his successors, we and our own children shall come to no harm. Neither republicanism nor anarchy shall ever darken this fair land of ours. The descendants of Lord Thomas shall stretch out to the crack of doom.

When the day comes, you may be sure that his lordship's descendants will not begrudge one minute of their duty in reforming the manners of the daughters of the present gang of sluts and trollops who infest our towns and villages. That is our security for the future.

We must not pry upon Lord Thomas and Lady Nerissa in their naked embraces. Yet as his lordship shoves his manhood into her, and thuds home with mighty thrusts of his loins, it would be a churlish fellow who did not charge a glass and wish him success. And if the salvo should hit the mark in her ladyship's womb, shall we not all raise our voices and give him a rousing 'three-times three?

As he is still young and with so many accomplishments yet before him, it would not be surprising if there were to be a sequel to the events of the present summer. Yet for the moment, the editor takes leave of the patient reader and—as manager of his own peepshow—here rings down the curtain upon the little drama of Thomas and his cousin, Lady Margaret.

Magic Carpet Books

Catalog

Victoria A. Brownworth

Victoria A. Brownworth is the author of nine books, including the award-winning *Too Queer: Essays from a Radical Life* and editor of 14, including the award-winning *Night Bites: Vampire Tales of Blood and Lust.* A syndicated columnist, her work has appeared in numerous mainstream, queer and feminist publications, including the *Baltimore Sun*, the *Philadelphia Inquirer*, the *Village Voice*, the *Advocate, OUT* and *Curve*. Her erotic writing has appeared regularly in anthologies and magazines, and she is a former contributing writer to the lesbian sex magazines, *On Our Backs* and *Bad Attitude*. She has published several erotica collections, including most recently, *Bed: New Lesbian Erotica.* She also publishes gay male porn under a psuedonym. She teaches writing and film at the University of the Arts in Philadelphia where she added two new courses to the literary curriculum: Writing Below the Belt and Smut. She has also taught safe-sex education classes as well as classes on S/M and B/D for various lesbian and bisexual venues. She lives in Philadelphia.

JANUARY 2007

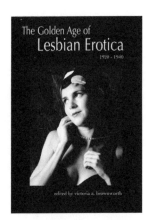

THE GOLDEN AGE OF LESBIAN EROTICA
Edited by Victoria A. Brownworth

Fiction/Erotica • ISBN 0-9774311-4-2
Trade Paperback
5 3/16 x 8 • 320 Pages • $17.95 ($24.95 Canada)

Lesbian erotica of the 1920s through the 1940s had a bold new cast to it. Unlike the tender and affectionate eroticism of the Victorian era with its naughty schoolgirls, convent antics and ladies-in-waiting, these 20th Century tales brought verisimilitude and fantasy together. While Radclyffe Hall was being prosecuted for obscenity for her depiction of "sapphics" and "inverts" in the classic lesbian novel *The Well of Loneliness,* her friend Natalie Barney was riding naked through the streets of Paris on horseback with her lover, the poet Renee Vivienne and Anais Nin were penning lurid and lustful tales of very bad girls while yearning for Henry Miller's sensual wife, June.

THE COLLECTOR'S EDITION OF THE IRONWOOD TRILOGY
by Don Winslow

Fiction/Erotica • ISBN 0-9766510-2-5
Trade Paperback • 5 3/16 x 8 • 480 Pages • $17.95 ($24.95Canada)

The three Ironwood classics revised exclusively for this Magic Carpet Edition

IRONWOOD, IRONWOOD REVISITED, IMAGES OF IRONWOOD

In IRONWOOD, James Carrington's bleak prospects are transformed overnight when the young man finds himself offered a choice position at Ironwood, a unique finishing school where young women are trained to become remiere Ladies of Pleasure. James faces many challenges in taming the spirited beauties in his charge, but no test will prove as great as that of mastering Mrs. Cora Blasingdale, the proud Mistress of Ironwood. In IRONWOOD REVISITED we follow James' rise to power in that garden of erotic delights, that singular institution, where young ladies were rigorously trained in the many arts of love. We come to understand how Ironwood, with its strict standards and iron discipline, has acquired its enviable reputation among the world's most discriminating connoisseurs. In IMAGES OF IRONWOOD, the third volume of the infamous Ironwood chronicles, the reader is once again invited to share in the Ironwood experience, and is presented with select scenes of unrelenting sensuality, of erotic longing, and of those bizarre proclivities which touch the outer fringe of human sexuality.

MASTERPIECES OF VICTORIAN EROTICA
Edited by Major LaCaritilie

Fiction/Erotica • ISBN 0-9774311-6-9
Trade Paperback • 5 3/16 x 8 • 320 Pages • $17.95 ($24.95 Canada)

There is no shortage of great works to compete for the title "masterpiece of Victorian erotica." Indeed, as readers familiar with Dickens or Trollope can attest, the Victorians were nothing if not prolific. Yet to be a masterpiece, a work has to distinguish itself in many ways. It can be without equal in its subgenre or the apotheosis of its tradition. It can offer a deeper insight, a more vivid image, or a more surprising turn. Or it can be unique, truly peerless in its style, plot or execution. Having distinguished themselves in these ways, the works in this volume represent the very best of the Victorian erotic imagination. There's poetry and prose, narrative and instructional guide; there's fetish, queer, s-m, and vanilla; and there's bawdy, tender and daring.   For the newcomer to the Victorian erotic universe, these stories are the place to start. For the connoisseur, this collection offers undiscovered delicacies. For everyone, these stories cannot fail to arouse, stimulate and amaze with their delightful sexiness and bold originality.

however you want me
les bexley

HOWEVER YOU WANT ME
by Les Bexley

Fiction/Erotica • ISBN 0-9774311-5-0
Trade Paperback • 5 3/16 x 8 • 320 Pages
$17.95 ($24.95 Canada)

Pity poor Heritage College. It's hard to be a holier-than-thou Christian girls' school without a dirty little secret or two. And that was before April Cartier even set foot on campus. The banned activities listed in the college's morality code are April's to-do list; the college's dirty little secrets, her major. But it's not just the college that has secrets. Professors Jessica Rowley, Klaus Binder and Alex Gould have made secrets a way of life, and April isn't the type to leave anyone's skeletons in their closets. When this cast of characters finds itself in the perfect storm of desires and taboos, naked appetites and raw emotions, they become more exposed and more intertwined than any of them could have possibly imagined. Sexy and daring, unflinching and humane, *However You Want Me* tells the story of people whose deepest secrets are kept not from others but from themselves.

MY SECRET FANTASIES
Fiction/Erotica • ISBN 0-9755331-2-6
Trade Paperback • 5 3/16 x 8 • 256 Pages • $11.95

Secret fantasies... we all have them, those hot, vivid daydreams that take us away from it all as we wonder, *what if...* In My Secret Fantasies, sixty different women share the secret of how they made their wildest erotic desires come true. Next time you feel like getting your heart rate up and your blood really flowing, curl up with a cup of tea and *My Secret Fantasies*... Beneath the covers of *My Secret Fantasies* you will find 60 tantalizing erotic love stories.

THE COLLECTOR'S EDITION OF VICTORIAN EROTICA
Edited by Major LaCaritilie
Fiction/Erotica • ISBN 0-9755331-0-X • Trade Paperback
5-3/16"x 8" • 608 Pages • $15.95 ($18.95 Canada)

No lone soul can possibly read the thousands of erotic books, pamphlets and broadsides the English reading public were offered in the 19th century. It can only be hoped that this Anthology may stimulate the reader into further adventures in erotica and its manifest reading pleasure. In this anthology, 'erotica' is a comprehensive term for bawdy, obscene, salacious, pornographic and ribald works including, indeed featuring, humour and satire that employ sexual elements. Flagellation and sadomasochism are recurring themes. They are activities whose effect can be shocking, but whose occurrence pervades our selections, most often in the context of love and affection.

THE COLLECTOR'S EDITION OF VICTORIAN LESBIAN EROTICA
Edited By Major LaCaritilie
Fiction/Erotica • ISBN 0-9755331-9-3
Trade Paperback • 5 3/16 x 8 • 608 Pages • $17.95 ($24.95Canada)

The Victorian era offers an untapped wellspring of lesbian erotica. Indeed, Victorian erotica writers treated lesbians and bisexual women with voracious curiosity and tender affection. As far as written treasuries of vice and perversion go, the Victorian era has no equal. These stories delve into the world of the aristocrat and the streetwalker, the seasoned seductress and the innocent naïf. Represented in this anthology are a variety of genres, from romantic fiction to faux journalism and travelogue, as well as styles and tones resembling everything from steamy page-turners to scholarly exposition. What all these works share, however, is the sense of fun, mischief and sexiness that characterized Victorian lesbian erotica. The lesbian erotica of the Victorian era defies stereotype and offers rich portraits of a sexuality driven underground by repressive mores. As Oscar Wilde claimed, the only way to get rid of temptation is to yield to it.

THE COLLECTOR'S EDITION OF THE LOST EROTIC NOVELS
Edited by Major LaCaritilie
Fiction/Erotica • ISBN 0-97553317-7
Trade Paperback • 5-3/16"x 8" • 608 Pages • $16.95 ($20.95 Canada)

MISFORTUNES OF MARY – Anonymous, 1860's: An innocent young woman who still believes in the kindness of strangers unwittingly signs her life away to a gentleman who makes demands upon her she never would have dreamed possible.

WHITE STAINS – Anaïs Nin & Friends, 1940's: Sensual stories penned by Anaïs and some of her friends that were commissioned by a wealthy buyer for $1.00 a page. These classics of pornography are not included in her two famous collections, *Delta of Venus* and *Little Birds*.

INNOCENCE – Harriet Daimler, 1950's: A lovely young bed-ridden woman would appear to be helpless and at the mercy of all around her, and indeed, they all take advantage of her in shocking ways, but who's to say she isn't the one secretly dominating them?

THE INSTRUMENTS OF THE PASSION – Anonymous, 1960's: A beautiful young woman discovers that there is much more to life in a monastery than anyone imagines as she endures increasingly intense rituals of flagellation devotedly visited upon her by the sadistic brothers.

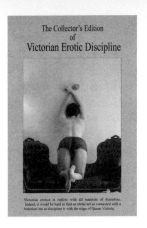

The Collector's Edition
of
Victorian Erotic Discipline

Victorian erotica is replete with all manners of discipline.
Indeed, it would be hard to find an erotic act as connected with a
historical era as discipline is with the reign of Queen Victoria.

THE COLLECTOR'S EDITION OF
VICTORIAN EROTIC DISCIPLINE
Edited by Brooke Stern

Fiction/Erotica • ISBN 0-9766510-9-2
Trade Paperback • 5 3/16 x 8 • 608 Pages • $17.95 ($24.95 Canada)

Lest there be any doubt, this collection is submitted as exhibit A in the case for the legitimacy of theVictorian era's dominion over all discipline erotica. In this collection, all manner of discipline is represented. Men and women are both dominant and submissive. There are school punishments, judicial punishments, punishments between lovers, well-deserved punishments, punishments for a fee, and cross-cultural punishments. These stories are set around the world and at all levels of society. The authority figures in these stories include schoolmasters, gamekeepers, colonial administrators, captains of ships, third-world potentates, tutors, governesses, priests, nuns, judges and policemen.

Victorian erotica is replete with all manner of discipline. Indeed, it would be hard to find an erotic act as connected with a historical era as discipline is with the reign of Queen Victoria. The language of erotic discipline, with its sir's and madam's, its stilted syntax and its ritualized roles, sounds Victorian even when it's used in contemporary pop culture. The essence of Victorian discipline is the shock of the naughty, the righteous indignation of the punisher and the shame of the punished. Today's literature of erotic discipline can only play at Victorian dynamics, and all subsequent writings will only be pretenders to a crown of the era whose reign will never end.

Maria Isabel Pita

Maria Isabel Pita is the author of three BDSM Erotic Romances – *Thorsday Night, Eternal Bondage* and *To Her Master Born*, re-printed as an exclusive hard-cover edition by the Doubleday Venus Book Club. She is the author of three Paranormal Erotic Romances, *Dreams of Anubis, Rituals of Surrender, The Fire in Starlight* and of three Contemporary Erotic Romances *A Brush With Love, Recipe For Romance,* and *The Fabric of Love.* Three of her erotic romances (Dreams of Anubis, Rituals of Surrender, The Fabric of Love) were re-printed under one cover as *Cat's Collar – Three Erotic Romances.* Maria is also the author of the critically acclaimed *Guilty Pleasures* – a book of romantic erotic stories set all through history – and of two non-fiction memoirs – *The Story of M – A Memoir* and *Beauty & Submission,* both of which were featured selections of the Doubleday Venus Book Club. *The Fabric of Love* and *The Story of M – A Memoir* have been translated into German and published in Germany by Heyne/VG Random House GMBH. Maria won second place in the New England Association For Science Fiction & Fantasy for her story *Star Crossed.* She was also a finalist in The Science Fiction Writer's of the Earth Award and the L. Ron Hubbard Award for Science Fiction Fantasy. You can visit her at www.mariaisabelpita.com

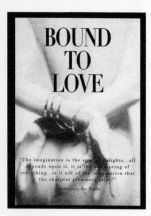

Bound to Love:
A Collection of Romantic BDSM Erotic Stories
Edited by Maria Isabel Pita

Fiction/Erotica • ISBN 0-9766510-4-1
Trade Paperback • 5 3/16 x 8 · 304 Pages
$17.95 ($24.95 Canada)

In *Bound to Love*, Maria Isabel Pita has gathered together nine erotic love stories written by some of today's hottest writers of erotica. In each story the darker side of sexuality is explored through realistic, well-developed characters deeply in love with each other and otherwise leading normal lives together. The men and women in *Bound To Love* are involved in serious, long-term relationships in which their deeper feelings for each other are inseparable from their erotic interaction. The stories in *Bound to Love* are some of the best in their genre precisely because they transcend it.

CAT'S COLLAR - THREE EROTIC ROMANCES
by Maria Isabel Pita

Fiction/Erotica • ISBN 0-9766510-0-9 • Trade Paperback
5 3/16 x 8 • 608 Pages • $16.95 ($ 20.95 Canada)

DREAMS OF ANUBIS: A legal secretary from Boston visiting Egypt explores much more than just tombs and temples in the stimulating arms of Egyptologist Simon Taylor. But at the same time a powerfully erotic priest of Anubis enters her dreams, and then her life one night in the dark heart of Cairo's timeless bazaar. Sir Richard Ashley believes he has lived before and that for centuries he and Mary have longed to find each other again. Mary is torn between two men who both desire to discover the legendary tomb of Imhotep and win the treasure of her heart.

RITUALS OF SURRENDER: All her life Maia Wilson has lived near a group of standing stones in the English countryside, but it isn't until an old oak tree hit by lightning collapses across her car one night that she suddenly finds herself the heart of an erotic web spun by three sexy, enigmatic men - modern Druids intent on using Maia for a dark and ancient rite...

CAT'S COLLAR: Interior designer Mira Rosemond finds herself in one attractive successful man's bedroom after the other, but then one beautiful morning a stranger dressed in black leather takes a short cut through her garden and changes the course of her life forever. Mira has never met anyone quite like Phillip, and the more she learns about his mysterious profession - secretly linked to some of Washington's most powerful women - the more frightened and yet excited she becomes as she finds herself falling helplessly, submissively in love.

GUILTY PLEASURES
by Maria Isabel Pita

Fiction/Erotica • ISBN 0-9755331-5-0
Trade Paperback • 5 3/16 x 8 • 304 Pages • $16.95 ($20.95 Canada)

Guilty Pleasures explores the passionate willingness of women throughout the ages to offer themselves up to the forces of love. Historical facts are seamlessly woven into intensely graphic sexual encounters. Beneath the covers of *Guilty Pleasures* you will find eighteen erotic love stories with a profound feel for the times and places where they occur. An ancient Egyptian princess… a courtesan rising to fame in Athen's Golden Age… a widow in 15th century Florence initiated into a Secret Society… a Transylvanian Count's wicked bride… an innocent nun tempted to sin in 17th century Lisbon… a lovely young woman finding love in the Sultan's harem… and many more are all one eternal woman in *Guilty Pleasures*.

MAGIC CARPET BOOKS

Order Form

Name: _____

Address: _____

City: _____

State:_____ Zip:_____

Title	ISBN	Quantity

Send check or money order to:

Magic Carpet Books
PO Box 473
New Milford, CT 06776

Postage free in the United States add $2.50 for
packages outside the United States

magiccarpetbooks@earthlink.net

Visit our website at:
www.magic-carpet-books.com